KT-422-407

the best a man can get

JOHN O'FARRELL

Doubleday

LONDON · NEW YORK · TORONTO · SYDNEY · AUCKLAND

TRANSWORLD PUBLISHERS
61–63 Uxbridge Road, London W5 5SA
a division of The Random House Group Ltd

RANDOM HOUSE AUSTRALIA (PTY) LTD
20 Alfred Street, Milsons Point, Sydney
New South Wales 2061, Australia

RANDOM HOUSE NEW ZEALAND
18 Poland Road, Glenfield, Auckland 10, New Zealand

RANDOM HOUSE SOUTH AFRICA (PTY) LTD
Endulini, 5a Jubilee Road, Parktown 2193, South Africa

Published 2000 by Doubleday
a division of Transworld Publishers

Copyright © John O'Farrell 2000

The right of John O'Farrell to be identified as the author of this work has been
asserted in accordance with sections 77 and 78 of the Copyright Designs and
. Patents Act 1988.

The slogan 'The Best a Man Can Get' is used with the permission of The Gillette
Company.

All the characters in this book are fictitious, and any resemblance to actual persons,
living or dead, is purely coincidental.

A catalogue record for this book is available from the British Library.
ISBN 0385 600844

All rights reserved. No part of this publication may be reproduced, stored in a
retrieval system, or transmitted in any form or by any means, electronic, mechanical,
photocopying, recording, or otherwise, without the prior permission of the
publishers.

Typeset in 11½/14½ Ehrhardt by Falcon Oast Graphic Art

Printed in Great Britain
by Mackays of Chatham plc. Chatham, Kent

1 3 5 7 9 10 8 6 4 2

£3·50

John O'Farrell is the author of *Things Can Only Get Better; Eighteen Miserable Years in the Life of a Labour Supporter*. His name has flashed past at the end of such productions as *Spitting Image, Have I Got News for You* and, more recently, the film *Chicken Run*. He is a regular guest on Radio 4 for shows such as *The News Quiz* and writes a weekly column for the *Guardian*. He lives in Clapham with his wife and two children, who think that when he is not home he is working.

Also by John O'Farrell

things can only get better

To Jackie, with love

Acknowledgements

With thanks to Georgia Garrett, Bill Scott-Kerr, Mark Burton, Simon Davidson and Charlie Dawson.

chapter one

the best a man can get

I found it hard working really long hours when I was my own boss. The boss kept giving me the afternoon off. Sometimes he gave me the morning off as well. Sometimes he'd say, 'Look, you've worked pretty hard today, why don't you take a well-earned rest tomorrow.' If I overslept he never rang me to ask where I was; if I was late to my desk he always happened to turn up at exactly the same time; whatever excuse I came up with, he always believed it. Being my own boss was great. Being my own employee was a disaster, but I never thought about that side of the equation.

On this particular day I was woken by the sound of children. I knew from experience that this meant it was either just before nine o'clock in the morning, when children started arriving at the school over the road, or around quarter past eleven – mid-morning playtime. I rolled over to look at the clock and the little numbers on my radio alarm informed me that it was 1:24. Lunchtime. I had slept for fourteen solid hours, an all-time record.

I called it my radio alarm, though in reality it served only as a large and cumbersome clock. I had given up using the radio-alarm function long before, after I'd kept waking up with early morning erections to the news that famine was spreading in the Sudan or that Princess Anne had just had her wisdom teeth out. It's amazing how quickly an erection can disappear. Anyway, alarm clocks are for people who have something more important to do than sleeping, and this was a concept that I struggled to grasp. Some days I would wake up, decide that it wasn't worth getting dressed and then just stay in bed until, well, bedtime. But it wasn't apathetic, what's-the-point-of-getting-up lying in bed, it was positive, quality-of-life lying in bed. I had resolved that leisure time should involve genuine leisure. If it had been up to me there would have been nothing at the Balham Leisure Centre except rows of beds with all the Sunday papers scattered at the bottom of the duvet.

My bedroom had evolved so that the need to get out of bed was kept to an absolute minimum. Instead of a bedside table there was a fridge, inside which milk, bread and butter were kept. On top of the fridge was a kettle, which fought for space with a tray of mugs, a box of tea bags, a selection of breakfast cereals, a toaster and an overloaded plug adapter. I clicked on the kettle and popped some bread in the toaster. I reached across for that day's newspaper and was slightly surprised as a set of keys slid off the top and clinked onto the floor. Then I remembered that I hadn't slept for fourteen solid hours after all; there had been a vague but annoying conversation very early that morning. As far as I could remember, it had gone something like this:

'Scuse me, mate?'

'Uh?' I replied from under the duvet.

'Excuse me, mate. It's me. Paper boy,' said the cracking voice of the nervous-sounding teenager.

'What do you want?'

'My mum says I'm not allowed to deliver the paper to the end of your bed any more.'

'Why not?' I groaned, without emerging.

'She says it's weird. I had to stop her ringing Child Line.'

'What time is it?'

'Seven o'clock. I told her you paid me an extra couple of quid a week to bring it up here and everything, but she said it's weird and that I'm only allowed to push it through the letter box, like I do for everyone else. I'll leave your front door keys here.'

If anything had been said after that I didn't remember it. That must have been the moment when I went back to sleep. The clink of the keys brought it back like some half-remembered dream. And as I flicked through the stories of war, violent crime and environmental disaster, I felt a growing sense of depression. Today was the last day I would ever have my newspaper delivered to the end of my bed.

Lightly browned toast popped up and the bubbling kettle clicked itself off. The butter and milk were kept on the top shelf of the fridge so they could be reached without leaving the bed. When I'd first bought the fridge and placed it in my room I had sunk to my knees in mortified disbelief. The fridge door opened the wrong way – I couldn't reach the handle from the bed. I tried putting the fridge upside down, but it looked a bit stupid. I tried putting it on the other side of the bed, but then I had to move my keyboard and mixing desk and all the other bits of musical equipment that were packed into my bedroom-cum-recording studio. After several hours spent dragging furniture into different positions around the room, I finally found a location for the bed that would comfortably allow me to take things from the fridge, make breakfast, reach my phone and watch telly without having to do anything as strenuous as standing up. If Boots had marketed a do-it-yourself catheter kit, I would have been the first customer.

The only thing more self-indulgent than breakfast in bed is having breakfast in bed at lunchtime. There's a decadence to it that makes lightly buttered toast taste like the food of the gods. I sipped my tea and, with one of several remote controls, switched on the telly just in time to see the beginning of one of my favourite films, Billy Wilder's *The Apartment*. I'll just watch the first few minutes, I thought to myself as I fluffed up the pillows. Just the bit where he's working in that huge insurance office with hundreds of other people doing exactly the same monotonous job. Forty minutes later my mobile phone jolted me out of my hypnotized trance. I switched the television to mute and removed the mobile from its charger.

'Hello, Michael, it's Hugo Harrison here – from DD and G. I'm just ringing in case you'd forgotten that you said you'd probably be able to get your piece of music to us by the end of today.'

'Forgotten? Are you joking? I've been working on it all week. I'm in the studio right now.'

'Do you think you'll be able to deliver it when you said?'

'Hugo, have I ever missed a deadline? I'm just doing a remix, so you'll probably get it around four or five o'clock.'

'Right.' Hugo sounded disappointed. 'There's no chance that we might get it before then, because we're sort of hanging around waiting to do the dub.'

'Well, I'll try. To be honest, I was going to go out and get a bite of lunch, but I'll work through if you need it urgently.'

'Thanks, Michael. Bloody brilliant. Speak to you later, then.'

And I turned off my mobile, lay back in bed and then watched *The Apartment* all the way through.

What I hadn't told Hugo from DD&G was that I had in

fact completed my composition four days earlier, but when someone pays you a thousand pounds for a piece of work, you can't give it to them two days after they commission it. They have to feel they're getting their money's worth. They might have imagined that they wanted it as soon as possible, but I knew that they'd appreciate and enjoy it far more if they thought it had taken me all week.

The slogan the agency were going to put over my composition was 'The saloon car that thinks it's a sports car'. So I did a ploddy easy-listening intro which switched into a screeching electric-guitar sound. Saloon car, sports car. Easy-listening for the humdrum lives of all those thirty-something saloon-car drivers and electric guitar for the racy, exciting lives that they are starting to realize have gone for ever. Hugo had thought this was a great idea when I'd put it to him, so much so that fairly quickly he was talking about it as if it was his own.

Generally speaking I did every commission straight away, and would then phone the client at regular intervals and say things like, 'Look, I've got something I'm really pleased with, but it's only thirteen seconds long. Does it really have to be exactly fifteen seconds?' And they'd say, 'Well, if you're really pleased with it, maybe we should have a listen. But is there no way you can make it fifteen? Like, just slow it down a bit or something?'

'Just slow it down a bit! What are you talking about?'

'I don't know. I'm not a composer.'

And then I'd pretend to find a solution and the client would hang up feeling reassured that I was still working on it and pleased that they had helped me get that much closer to completion. And all the time a fifteen-second jingle was already on a DAT in my studio. Whenever I had sent ad agencies work straight away, they were always initially enthusiastic, but then came back to me a few days later saying they wanted it changed. I had learned that it was far better to give it to them at the last minute, when they had no choice but to decide that it was great.

I had persuaded myself that actually I probably did roughly the same amount of work as many men my age, namely around two or three hours a day. But I was determined that I wouldn't waste the rest of my life *pretending* to be working, flicking my computer screen from Solitaire to a spreadsheet, or suddenly changing the tone of personal phone calls when the managing director walked into the office. From what I could gather from my contemporaries, there were a lot of jobs where you arrived in the morning, chatted for an hour or two, did some really useful work between about eleven and lunchtime, came back in the afternoon, sent a stupid e-mail message to Gary in accounts before spending the rest of the afternoon in apparent total concentration while downloading a picture of a naked transsexual from http://www.titsandcocks.com.

The film was interrupted by adverts and I couldn't help but take a professional interest in the music they employed. The jingle for the Gillette commercial claimed that the new twin-blade swivel head with lubrastrip was 'the best a man can get'. I thought that this was a pretty bold claim for a disposable plastic razor. A new Ferrari maybe or a night in bed with Pamela Anderson might arguably have the edge for most men, but not according to this singer, no, give him a good shave any day of the week. Then *The Apartment* came back on and I thought, No, this is the best a man can get: just being tucked up warm and cosy, watching a great film with tea and toast and nothing at all to worry about.

When people asked me what I did I generally mumbled that I was 'in advertising'. I used to say that I was a composer or a musician, but I found this prompted a level of fascination that wasn't fulfilled when they discovered this meant I'd written the music for the Mr Gearbox ad on Capital Radio. I was a freelance jingle writer – although other people in the business were too pretentious to call them jingles – working at the bottom end of the freelance jingle-writing market. If the man who composed 'Gillette! The best a man can get!' was the advertising equivalent of Paul McCartney, that made me the drummer for the band that came fifth in last year's Song for Europe.

People always presume there's lots of money in advertising, but I was beginning to sense that I was never going to make a fortune writing twenty-second radio jingles, even if I took it upon myself to start working an eight-hour day.

There had been a time in my life when I'd really believed I was going to be a millionaire rock star. When I'd left music college I had returned to my home town and formed a group that played in pubs and at university summer balls. Call me immodest, but I think I can honestly say there was a point in the late Eighties when we were the biggest band in Godalming. Then it all fell apart when our drummer left the group because of 'musical differences'. We were musical, he wasn't. Despite being the crappiest drummer I'd ever heard, he had been the most important member of the band because he had been the one with the van. I found you couldn't fit many amplifiers on a moped. After that highpoint I had carried on recording songs and trying to form bands, but now all I had to show for those years was a box of demo tapes and one precious copy of my flexi-disc single.

I got out of bed and played this track again as I got dressed. I was still proud of it, and had never quite forgiven John Peel's producer for saying they didn't play flexi-discs. The journey to my place of work involved walking from one side of my bedroom to the other. Before I started I generally pre-ferred to convert the room from bedroom to studio, which involved transforming my bed back into a sofa and removing any socks or underpants that I had left on top of my keyboard. As well as my Roland XP-60, the recording studio side of my room contained a computer, an eighteen-channel mixing desk, a sampler, a reverb unit, a midi-box, several redundant sound modules, amplifiers and tape decks and, behind it all, seven and a half miles of intertwined electrical cable. If you knew nothing at all about music I suppose all this gear might look quite impressive, but the reality was far more chaotic. The more equipment I acquired, the longer I had to search every time a mystery buzz made it impossible to do any work. Generally I relied upon the keyboard, with its built-in sound module and my multi-talented sampler, which would gamely have a stab at the noise produced by most musical instruments. Although there appeared to be a lot of state-of-the-art technology on display, the stuff was either several years out of date or would be by the time I'd worked out how to use it. Because I'd never got round to reading the manuals I was like the owner of a Ferrari who only drove around in first gear.

I lumbered into the bathroom and stared in the mirror. During the night the grey strands on the side of my head had fought their way to the front and a whole swathe of hair above my ears had acquired a silvery sheen. Those of the wiry grey variety were thicker and stronger than the wispy dark hairs they were gradually replacing. The greys were still in a minority, but I knew that, like the squirrels of the same depressing colour, once a few had got a foothold eventually all the indigenous hair would be pushed to the brink of extinction, with maybe a couple of breeding colonies remaining on either eyebrow and perhaps a few shy black hairs that would occasionally be spotted peeking out of my nostrils. On the side of my nose a large yellow-headed spot had ripened and was deftly milked with the dexterity that came from nearly twenty years' practice. In my teens I think I'd presumed there would be a golden period in my life after my spots cleared up and before my hair started to turn grey. Now I realized that was hopelessly naive of me; in my early thirties I was already past my physical peak. The summer seems to have only just begun when you realize the nights are already drawing in.

At around four o'clock I finally strolled into the living room, where Jim had spent the last couple of years researching his Ph.D. Today this involved playing Tomb Raider with Simon. They both managed to mumble hello to me, though since neither of them managed to look up from the screen I could just as easily have been the creature from the black lagoon wandering in to put the kettle on. Jim and Simon looked like the 'Before' and 'After' drawings in the Charles Atlas body-building adverts. Jim was tall and muscular with the healthy complexion of a boy who'd been skiing every winter since he was five years old, and by contrast, Simon was skinny, pallid and awkward. If they made Tomb Raider any more realistic, Lara Croft would turn round and say out of the TV screen, 'Stop staring at my tits like that, you little creep,' and blast him off the sofa. He had a promising career serving pints of lager in plastic glasses to students of the university from which he had graduated some years ago. He had got the job on the day he'd left and was hoping to earn enough money to one day pay off the debts he had accumulated on the other side of the bar.

At that moment the front door slammed and Paul returned home, dumping a pile of tatty exercise books on the kitchen table with a martyred sigh that was far too obviously intended to elicit concerned enquiries about his day and consequently received none.

'Dear oh dear,' said Paul, but we all still refused to bite. He put a carton of milk back in the fridge and took a couple of old tea bags out of the sink, tutting quietly to himself. His sighs not only announced his irritation that everyone else didn't tidy up as they went along, but also his annoyance that it should be left to him to clear up when he had already done a full day's teaching. It was as if he was implying that Simon's evening job or Jim's Ph.D or my composing at my keyboard were somehow less-demanding work. The fact that this was true was entirely beside the point.

The four of us had shared this place for a couple of years now. None of them had known me when I had first taken the room, and in some ways that was how I preferred to keep things. The flat boasted views across the splendour that is Balham High Road, and was conveniently located above a shop, where we could pop down and buy halal meat at any time of the day or night. But it was not the tatty run-down flat that you would expect four men sharing to wallow in; there was a strict cleaning rota, in which we took turns to leave all the clearing up for Paul.

Paul put what was left of a slab of butter into the butter dish and then folded the foil neatly before throwing it in the bin. Since talking to the entire room failed to get him any attention, he attempted to address someone directly.

'Michael, how was your day?'

'It's been a fucking disaster,' I said.

'Oh no, what happened?' he replied, sounding genuinely concerned.

'Bloody paper boy woke me up at seven o'clock to tell me he's not going to deliver the paper to the end of my bed any more. He said his mother thinks it's weird. I distinctly remember saying to him when we first agreed on the arrangement that it would probably be wise not to mention it to his parents.'

There was a pause.

'No. *I* told his mother,' confessed Paul with the defiant air of a man who had been preparing himself for this confrontation.

'You! What on earth did you do that for?'

'Well, for a start I am not particularly wild about you handing out the front door keys of our flat to a thirteen-year-old delinquent.'

'He's not a delinquent.'

'Yes, he is a delinquent, and do you know how I know that? Because I teach him. Troy is in my class. And the day before yesterday, at seven a.m., I walked out of the bathroom stark bollock naked to see Troy standing there on the landing staring at me.'

At that moment Jim laughed so much he had to spit his tea back into the mug. 'What did you say?'

'Well, I said, "Hello, Troy."'

'What did he say?'

'He said, "Hello, Mr Hitchcock." He looked a little confused, to tell the truth. In fact, it was pretty bad luck on his part as well; he'd been trying to avoid me for a few days because he owed me an essay on the character of Piggy in *Lord of the Flies*. I think for a moment he thought I'd broken into this house at seven in the morning with no clothes on just to ask him for his essay.'

I was still irritated. 'So you bumped into him on the landing. So what? Doesn't mean you have to tell his mother.'

'I am his teacher. It doesn't look too good, does it? BOY VISITS NAKED TEACHER'S FLAT BEFORE LESSONS. Besides, I do not appreciate having to tell my class that the correct pronunciation of my name is Mr Hitchcock, not Mr Titchy-cock.'

Jim's tea had now been spat out so many times it was undrinkable.

'And so, at last night's parents' evening,' Paul continued, 'I told his mother that her son had a key to my flat and that the previous morning he had seen me naked.'

'That probably wasn't the best way to put it.'

'Well, with the benefit of hindsight I realize I might have phrased it differently. She went mad and started hitting me with her shoe. Had to be pulled off by the deputy head.'

Paul looked hurt to be the unwitting subject of such general amusement.

'Don't take it personally, Paul,' I said, 'we're not laughing at *you*.'

'I am,' said Jim.

'Yeah, I am as well actually,' added Simon.

Paul settled down to do his marking, and his pupils got far lower marks than they would have done if we had been nicer to him. He was clearly one of those teachers who are unable to keep control in the classroom. There was just something about him that marked him out as the injured wildebeest limping on the edge of the herd. He always tried to play this down, even when one of the pupils sold his car.

I don't know why they felt they needed to go to such lengths to wind him up when he seemed to get infuriated by the littlest things. He once told us that from now on he would only be removing his own hairs from the gunge that was blocking the plughole, since no-one else ever seemed to do it, and so we found him crouched in an empty bath trying to separate the red hairs from all the others. It wasn't that Paul was petty, it was just that he got annoyed when anyone squeezed the toothpaste from the wrong end of the tube. In fact, all sorts of things about us aggravated him.

We sat around the kitchen table for a bit longer and then Jim announced that he was going to make a brew. Paul always declined Jim's offer of tea because the way Jim made tea was the essence of what Paul found so irritating about him.

Jim's tea-making routine was a triumph of day-dreaming inefficiency. First he would take the mugs from the cupboard and arrange them on a tray. Then he would stop near the sink and look a little lost for a while as he tried to remember what it was that he had been meaning to do. Then it would come back to him: get the milk out of the fridge. After the milk had been poured into each cup he would get the tea bags and put them into the teapot. And then, when he had done all that, when he had got everything ready and realized he'd got out one mug too many and so put it back in the cupboard, and then put the sugar bowl on the tray and decided that there was nothing else he had to do, *then he would put the kettle on*.

For Paul, this sequence alone made Jim virtually impossible to live with. And he didn't just put the kettle on last, he also filled it right to the top so it took far longer than necessary for three cups of tea. And while it was taking an eternity to boil he would just stand there waiting, occasionally moving the mugs about on the tray. And all the while he would be completely unaware that Paul was about to explode with frustration at the impracticality of this order of doing things. Try as he might, Paul could not let Jim do things his way. I knew that within sixty seconds he would ask Jim why he didn't put the kettle on first.

'Jim, why don't you put the kettle on first?' he asked three seconds later.

'Hmmm?'

'I was just saying, it would be a bit quicker if you put the kettle on first. You know, before you put out the mugs and everything.'

Jim gave an indifferent shrug. 'Well, it wouldn't boil any quicker, would it.'

He was as slow to see Paul's logic as he was at making tea.

'No, but it would boil *sooner*, because you would've put it on earlier, and then you could do the tea bags and milk and everything *while* it was boiling.' He had to stop himself screaming the last four words in Jim's face. Jim was bemused by his flatmate's concern.

'They're not in a hurry to go out or anything, are they? You're not in a hurry to go out, are you, Simon?'

Simon looked up from the paper. 'Me? No.'

'No-one's in a hurry, so what does it matter?'

I could see Paul's frustration rising; his face went bright red, which at least had the consolation of making his little ginger beard less prominent. 'It's just a really inefficient way to make a cup of tea.'

'But you're not even having a cup.'

'No, I'm not, because it's so annoying that you always do it wrong.' And with that he stomped out of the room. Jim looked completely perplexed.

'Have I been putting sugar in Paul's tea when he doesn't take it or something?'

Simon mumbled that he didn't think so and Jim shrugged and stood by the sink for a while and after five minutes realized that he hadn't pressed the 'on' button on the side of the kettle.

When the tea was made, the remaining three of us drank it in contemplative silence. Simon was reading the 'Dear Deirdre' column in the *Sun*, in which Deirdre tackled the sexual problems of members of the general public, which I was convinced had been made up by journalists in the next door office.

'"My brother-in-law is my lover,"' he read out. '"Dear Deirdre, I am an attractive blonde and people say I have a good figure. The other night, when my husband was away, his brother came round and one thing led to another and we ended up in bed . . ."' He broke off from reading out the letter. 'They always say that: one thing led to another. How exactly does one thing lead to another, because that must be the bit that I'm getting wrong. I understand the brother coming round, and I understand that they were in bed together. But how did they get from the first stage to the last?'

'It's easy, Simon,' said Jim.

'Well, what? How do you do it?'

'You meet a girl.'

'Yes.'

'She comes back for coffee.'

'Yes, but then what?'

'Well, one thing leads to another.'

After my second cup of tea I felt I'd finally run out of valid excuses for keeping the advertising agency waiting any longer, and so I collected the tape from my room and headed towards Balham tube station. Thirty minutes later I was walking down Berwick Street, where a couple of French students with a disposable camera nearly got run over trying to recreate the cover of *What's the Story Morning Glory?* I loved coming to Soho; it felt exciting and happening, and for a brief moment I liked to pretend I was part of it all. There were people here who earned a thousand pounds a day just for doing one voiceover for an advert, and then they'd blow it all by buying a prawn and avocado on focaccia with a café latte to go.

I glanced across the road and caught sight of Hugo from DD&G, staring at a shop window. That's peculiar, I thought. Why is Hugo staring into the window of a wholesale Asian jewellery shop? Then he glanced up and down the road quickly and disappeared into a tatty open doorway under the glow of a dangerously wired red light. I was shocked. I approached the open doorway and looked in. The words 'New model. Very friendly. First floor' were scrawled onto a piece of card that was stuck by the entrance with thick brown masking tape. I looked up the rickety uncarpeted stairs and wondered what lay beyond. Maybe Hugo was just going in to offer to improve their advertising, to suggest a professional copywriter who could produce a snappier slogan and spell 'friendly' correctly. It seemed unlikely. I was part repulsed, part fascinated and strangely disappointed in Hugo, as if he had let me down personally.

I continued up Berwick Street and finally entered the reception of the grand offices of DD&G, where a certificate boasted that they were runners up for Best Investment and Banking Commercial at last year's Radio Advertising Awards. Apparently, Hugo had just popped out to get his wife a birthday card, so the tape was left with the beautiful waif of a receptionist, who sat in the window framed by lavish arrangements of fresh flowers.

My work for the week was done. It was time to head for North London. In the rush hour I squeezed my way onto the tube with all the people who had spent the day at work. Hundreds of sweaty office workers pressing their bodies together and yet managing to give the impression that they were not the slightest bit aware that there was anyone else in the carriage. Arms bending into impossible angles to read paperbacks bent over at the spine. Necks craning to read someone else's newspaper. Christians re-reading the bible as if they didn't know it all by now.

Suddenly a seat became available and I moved towards it as quickly as is possible without revealing that I was doing anything as undignified as hurrying. As I sat down I breathed out a satisfied sigh, but any relaxation soon flipped over into anxiety. A woman was standing right in front of me, and from under her dress protruded *The Bulge Of Uncertainty*. Was she six months pregnant or was she just a bit, well . . . fat? It was just impossible to say. I looked her up and down. Why can't she give me a sign? I thought. Why couldn't she be carrying a Mothercare bag or wearing one of those naff sweatshirts that say, 'Yes I am!' I looked again. The dress hung loosely everywhere else; it was just on her rounded stomach that the material was stretched and taut. Which was worse, I wondered, denying a seat to a pregnant woman or offering a seat to a woman who wasn't pregnant but just looked as if she was. Maybe this is why men used to give up their seats to *all* women, to escape this embarrassing dilemma. No-one else seemed concerned, but I felt I had to do the decent thing.

'Sorry. Would you like to sit down?' I said, getting up.

'Why would I want to sit down?' she said aggressively.

Shit, I thought. 'Erm . . . Well, you just looked a bit tired . . . um, and I'm getting off at the next stop anyway,' I lied.

On this understanding she took my seat, and I was forced to leave the carriage to maintain the deceit. I fought my way through the throng on the platform and rushed to get back on the train a couple of carriages further up. The not-pregnant woman had given me a very odd look, but it wasn't as strange as the one she gave me when we both went through the barriers at Kentish Town station fifteen minutes later.

As I emerged back into the open air, my mobile phone signalled that I had a message. It was Hugo. He said he was sorry he'd missed me but that he had been in and out all afternoon, which was more detail than I needed. He was pleased with my piece of music and told me that I'd come up with something 'pretty bloody special'. Although I generally found Hugo very insincere and of poor judgement I was prepared to make an exception in this case. I never felt confident that the snippets of music I wrote were any good. Whenever a decent tune came into my head I couldn't believe that I hadn't just subconsciously stolen it from somewhere, so any form of praise was eagerly gobbled up. Sadly, the track was only for a pitch and the agency would probably never use Hugo's production company, so no-one would ever hear it. I had known this when I'd taken the job, but I knew I could do it quickly, it paid the bills and it meant I could afford to spend a couple of stress-free days in the cocoon I had created for myself.

I turned into Bartholomew Close. Tall, monolithic grey wheelie bins lined the street, like Easter Island statues waiting impassively for strangers. I walked up to number 17 and put the key in the lock. As I opened the front door I was hit by the chaos and noise.

'Daddy!' exclaimed my two-year-old daughter Millie with delight as she ran up the hallway and hugged my leg. There was a tape of children's nursery rhymes playing on the stereo and Alfie, my baby boy, was jiggling his limbs delightedly in his mother's arms.

'You're earlier than I expected,' said Catherine with a smile.

I tiptoed over some wooden bricks that were scattered on the carpet, gave her a kiss and then took Alfie from her.

'Yeah, and guess what? I've finished the job and won't have to work at all this weekend.'

'Fantastic,' she said. 'Then it's a double celebration. Because guess who wee'd in her potty today?'

'Did you, Millie?'

Millie nodded with extraordinary pride, which was only surpassed by that of her mother.

'And you didn't get any on the floor, did you, Millie? Which is better than your daddy usually manages and he's thirty-two.'

I gave Catherine an affectionate poke in the ribs. 'Look, it's not my fault the toilet seat always falls down.'

'No, it's that idiot who fitted it,' she concurred, referring to the evening when it had taken me three hours to fit a new wooden toilet seat incorrectly.

Millie had obviously enjoyed the praise that had been heaped upon her, so she quickly found another way to get some more attention. 'I done cat drawing,' she said, presenting me with a scrap of paper, which I took from her and studied carefully. Frankly, Millie's drawing was rubbish. To represent our cat, she had taken the blue crayon and scribbled it up and down on a piece of paper.

'Ooh, Millie, that's a super picture. You are a clever girl.' One day she would turn round and say, 'Don't patronize me, Father, we both know the picture is crap,' but for the time being she seemed to buy it. I loved coming home when I hadn't seen them all for a couple of days; they were always so delighted to see me. It was the return of the prodigal father.

Catherine grabbed the chance to start clearing up the kitchen as I played with the kids for a while. I played hide and seek with Millie, which was made easier by the fact that she hid in the same spot behind the curtains three times in a row. Then I made Alfie giggle by throwing him up in the air until Catherine came back into the room to see why he'd suddenly started crying.

'I don't know,' I said, trying not to look up at the metal chandelier swinging back and forth above her head. She took the crying baby back, and at that moment I thought she looked a little tired, so I said I'd take over tidying up. I slipped upstairs, gathering scattered toys as I went. I ran a big foamy bath, turned off the light and lit a couple of candles. Then I placed the portable CD player in the bathroom and put on Beethoven's *Pastoral Symphony*.

'Catherine, can you just come upstairs a minute,' I shouted. She came up and surveyed the instant sanctuary that I had created.

'I'll take over the kids and load the dishwasher and everything. You get in there and I'll bring you a glass of wine, and you're not allowed out till the end of the final movement, "Shepherds Song; Beneficent Feelings After the Storm".'

She leaned against me. 'Oh, Michael. What have I done to deserve this?'

'Well, you've been looking after the kids on your own for a couple of days and you must need a bit of space.'

'Yes, but you've been working hard, too. Don't you need a rest?'

'I don't work as hard as you,' I said sincerely. After a few half-hearted guilty protestations she clicked on the heated towel rail and turned up the volume loud enough to drown out the indignant shouts of 'Mummy!' that had already started to emanate from the kitchen.

'Michael,' she said as she kissed me on the cheek, 'thanks for being the best husband in the world.'

I smiled a half-smile. When your wife says something like that, it doesn't seem like the right moment to put her straight.

chapter two

live life to the max

We've all done it. We've all kept little secrets from our partners. We've all avoided telling them an awkward detail or subtly skirted over something we'd rather they didn't know. We've all rented a secret room on the other side of the city where we could hide half the week to get away from all that boring, exhausting baby stuff. Oh, that last one is just me apparently.

Different marriages work in different ways. Adolf Hitler and Eva Braun got married, spent one day in a bomb shelter and then committed suicide together. Fine; if that's what they found worked best for them, who are we to pass judgement? Every couple have their own way of doing things – bizarre rituals, idiosyncratic little routines that keep them together. Often these evolve and grow until they completely disappear off the scale of rational behaviour. Catherine's parents, for example, go out into the garden together each evening and find woodlice, which are then ritually crushed in a pestle and mortar before the remains are sprinkled on the roses. They think this is perfectly normal. 'I've got another one, Kenneth.' 'Hang on, dear, you've got a centipede in there as well, we don't want to crush *you* now, do we, little fellah.'

Once Catherine and I went on holiday with another couple, and on the last night we heard them nonchalantly chatting about us through the wall. They were saying they could never be married to anyone as peculiar as Catherine or I. They thought that our relationship was completely weird. Then we heard her muffled voice saying, 'Are you coming to bed or what, because this clingfilm's making my tits sweat.' And then we think he said, 'All right. Hang on, the zip's stuck on my wetsuit.' Every marriage is bizarre if you look under the surface.

There are, of course, plenty of relationships that do not develop tailored survival strategies and these are the ones that don't last. My parents split up when I was five and I remember thinking, Can't you just pretend to be married? Having experienced the grim and twisted diplomacy of Mum and Dad's divorce, I was determined that my children's parents would stay together. It was because I thought our marriage was so important that I kept *resting* it. The strain that small children brought into our lives suddenly seemed to create such tension and petty hostility between us that I was terrified of the damage becoming irreparable. Admittedly, I had developed a personal solution to a joint problem without ever talking it through with Catherine. But I didn't feel I could confess to wanting time away from my children. It's not something that men who are running for president boast about in their election broadcasts. 'You know, sometimes I like to walk alone on the beach because it reminds me of the wonder of God's work and how little time we have in this world to make it a better place. But most of all, it gives me the chance to get away from my bloody kids for a while.' I loved Catherine and I loved Millie and Alfie, but sometimes I felt as if they were driving me mad. Wasn't it better to get away rather than let the pressure just build and build until the whole marriage exploded and the kids had no dad for seven days of the week like I'd had?

So I didn't feel guilty about it. I'm sure I still would have run her a big foamy bath, even if I'd genuinely been working as hard as she imagined I did. I took her the wine bottle and a copy of *Hello!*, which I worried that she was no longer reading ironically. I poured us both a glass and she pulled me down for a loving kiss on the lips, which I engaged in a little awkwardly.

'What are the kids doing?'

'Millie's watching the *Postman Pat* video; the one in which he goes on a shooting spree through Greendale. And Alfie is strapped in his chair watching Millie.'

'Oh well, as long as the telly's on. We wouldn't want to leave them unsupervised.'

'You'll never guess what I saw today: Hugo Harrison disappearing into a prostitute's doorway.'

'Really? Where were you?'

'Well I was just coming down the stairs obviously, doing up my trousers.'

'He's married, isn't he? Remember we met his wife? I wonder if he's going to tell her?'

'Of course he's not going to tell her! "Did you have a nice day at the office, dear?" "Very nice, thank you. I popped out to visit a whore in the afternoon." "That's nice, dear. Supper's nearly ready."'

'Poor woman. Imagine if she found out.'

'I was a bit irritated to be honest. I wanted to know what he thought of the bit of music I'd brought for him and he'd disappeared to have it off with a prostitute.'

'So did you find out if he liked it?'

'Well, you don't like to ask, do you.'

'Your bit of music.'

'Oh yeah, he called me on the mobile. He said it was great.'

'I don't know how you do it. Was it another four o'clock in the morning job?'

'No, not as late as that.'

'I can't see why you don't just work normal hours and tell them they'll have to wait a bit longer.'

'Because they'd get someone else to do it and then we'd have no money and I'd have to look after the children while you worked as a prostitute for the likes of Hugo Harrison.'

'It doesn't bear thinking about – *you* looking after the children.'

We laughed and I kissed her again. I loved it when she hadn't seen me for a couple of days; those were our most perfect times together.

Catherine had smooth pale skin, a pointy little nose and big brown eyes with which I was struggling to keep eye contact as she shifted her body in the steaming bath. She would always contradict me if I told her she was beautiful because she had this ridiculous notion that her fingers were too short. Sometimes I would catch her with her jumper sleeves right over the ends of her hands, and I knew she was doing this because she thought everyone was looking at her and thinking, Look at that woman; she'd look lovely if she didn't have such awful short fingers. Her hair was long and dark, and though it wasn't particularly elaborately styled, for some reason she would travel fifteen miles for a haircut because the man who had always done it had moved shops and she didn't want to risk letting anyone else have a go. I was just glad he hadn't emigrated to Paraguay because we would have struggled to raise the air fare every eight weeks.

What I wanted to do right now was jump into the bath with her and attempt foamy, clumsy sex, but I didn't suggest it because I didn't want to spoil the moment by precipitating rejection. More importantly, I knew there were no condoms in the house and there was no way I was risking a third baby. It wasn't as if I was the perfect father to the first two.

The first time we had ever made love we followed it by sharing a foamy tub like this one. On our first date she said she knew a lovely place for a drink and drove me all the way to a luxurious hotel she had booked in Brighton. On the way down a policeman pulled her over for speeding. She wound down her window as he slowly strode across and then he said to her, 'Are you aware that you were doing fifty-three miles an hour in a forty-mile-an-hour zone?' And with a superior sneer he waited to see how she was going to try and explain herself.

'*Pardonnez-moi; je ne parle pas l'anglais donc je ne comprends pas ce que vous dîtes . . .*'

He looked completely thrown. And considering she'd failed French A level, she almost convinced me. The policeman then decided that the English language might be more comprehensible if it was spoken more loudly and with a number of glaring grammatical errors.

'You break speed limit. You too fast. Driving licence?'

But she just responded with a confused Gallic shrug, saying, '*Pardonnez-moi, mais je ne comprends rien, monsieur.*'

The bewildered officer looked at me and said, 'Do you speak English?' and I felt forced to say, 'Er – non!' in an appalling French accent. I lacked the chutzpah to chat away to the policeman like Catherine; my French was far more limited than hers and I didn't think he would be particularly impressed by my observation that 'on the bridge at Avignon, they dance there, they dance there'. She jumped in before I risked giving myself away, but this time she found a few words of English. 'Mais Gary Lineker – eez very good!'

The officer visibly softened, and with a little bit of patriotic pride restored he felt able to send us on our way with an overenunciated warning to 'Drive – more – slowly'.

'*D'accord*,' she said, and he didn't even notice anything unusual when she added '*Auf Wiedersehen*' as she drove away. We had to pull into a side road a hundred yards later because we were both laughing so much she was in danger of crashing the car.

We had first met when she appeared in an advert for which I had arranged the music. She had just graduated with a drama degree from Manchester University and this commercial was her first professional acting part. She was cast as one of five dancing yoghurt pots. She played fruits of the forest flavour and she was easily the best. It still galls me that orange and passion fruit flavour went on to star in *EastEnders*. After that Catherine got a few walk-on parts in minor soaps and appeared in a health and safety video in which she informed viewers that they should not walk into glass doors but should open them first. I got very excited when she told me she had landed the part of Sarah McIsaac in a major TV drama called *The Strange Case of Sarah McIsaac*. She showed me the script. Page one went like this: a woman is sitting at her desk, working late in a London office. A man walks in and says, 'Are you Sarah McIsaac?' She says, 'Yes,' and then he takes out a gun and shoots her dead. Still, it was the title role and that was definitely a step up.

Then she got a good-size part in a West End play – in the west end of Essex that is – and I drove out to watch her in the glamorous setting of the Kenneth More Theatre, Ilford, every night. At first she said it was very supportive of me, but after a while I think she found it a little distracting to have me sitting in the front row, mouthing all her words as she said them. She was on the stage on her own for quite a lot of the play and was completely mesmerizing, though I didn't like the way all the other men in the audience just stared at her all the time.

But she saved her best performances for when she was winding people up. She could burst into tears if the bus conductor wouldn't let her on the bus without the right change and she was prepared to faint into a chair if the doctor's receptionist tried to prevent her from seeing the doctor. Once, when the bloke in the video shop wouldn't let us take out two films on the one card, she suddenly seemed to recognize him.

'Oh my God, you're Darren Freeman, aren't you?'

'Er, yeah?' he said, looking amazed.

'Do you remember me from school?'

'Er, oh erm, vaguely?'

'God, you were always interested in films and stuff; it's funny that you're working here. Blimey, Darren Freeman. Do you remember that stupid geography teacher? What was he called?'

And then they chatted nostalgically for ten minutes and it turned out that Darren had married Julie Hails, who Catherine said she'd always liked, and he gave us two films on one ticket and, as he handed them over, I noticed he was wearing a badge that said, 'My name is Darren Freeman, how may I help you?'

We shared a casual attitude towards deception. When she asked me to marry her I gave her a cautionary sideways look to see if she was just having me on. I had this vision of myself as a ninety-year-old man at my wife's funeral, with her suddenly sitting up in the coffin going, 'Ha! Ha! Had you fooled!' So to an outsider my double life might seem like some sort of shocking betrayal, but I liked to think it was just part of the fun we had with one another; another round in our on-going game of one-upmanship. Her deceptions always made me laugh. The only trouble with the scam I was pulling was that I wasn't sure what the punchline was going to be.

*

My double life had started to evolve soon after Millie had been born. For years our relationship had been perfect and happy and I never would have imagined that anything could have made me want to run away. But then she fell in love with someone else. Perhaps that was what I had been afraid of. Maybe that was why I had tried to put her off having kids for so long.

I never said I didn't want them, I just said I didn't want them *yet*. Of course I was going to have children *eventually*, just like I was going to die eventually, but I didn't spend a great deal of time planning that, either. Catherine, however, always talked about our future children as if they were imminent. She didn't want a two-door car because it would be such a struggle getting the baby seat in and out of the back. What bloody baby seat is this? I'd felt like asking. Baby clothes would be pointed out in shop windows, and she would insist on calling our spare room 'the nursery'. 'You mean my recording studio,' I would assert every time. Some of her hints were even less subtle. 'It would be nice to have a summer baby, wouldn't it?' she said exactly nine months before the summer. Friends with small babies would be invited round on a Sunday and I would have to pretend to be interested as the mother and father casually chatted about Baby's bowel movements.

I don't know why parents think this is an acceptable way to carry on; it is not a subject we stray onto when we politely enquire about the health of fellow adults.

'Hello, Michael, how are you?'

'I'm fine, thanks. I did quite a big poo this morning, but soon after I did another smaller one that wasn't quite so firm, which is unlike me because I normally only have one poo a day.'

Babies' bodily functions are discussed at length because that's all there is to them. They feed, they puke, they crap, they sleep, they cry and it starts again. And though there is nothing more you can say about the activities of a newborn, their parents still talk about nothing else. If by some miracle our visitors from the Planet Baby did happen to wander from the fascinating topic of the infant digestive system, the conversation only switched to the equally unsavoury subject of the mother's bodily functions. At this point, some of the fathers at least had the good grace to look embarrassed and awkward, while Catherine and the new mum chatted at great length about breast pumps and episiotomies. Those dads were not beyond saving. The fathers I really couldn't tolerate were those who had clearly been turned into gibbering idiots by the trauma of it all. These self-deluding infants' entertainers would maniacally roll around on my carpet, blowing raspberries at their babies and shouting made-up words in the forlorn attempt to engender the slightest response from their new offspring. 'Oooooohhh–bla–bla–bla–bla–bla bum–bum,' they'd squeal. 'Oh, she loves this,' the mother would say with an approving smile, and you could tell the baby loved it because it blinked – possibly – just the once.

After a while the mother would punish me for my obvious indifference by saying, 'Would you like to hold the baby, Michael?'

'Oh, that would be lovely,' I'd dutifully reply and I would take hold of the baby with all the relaxed composure of the Minister for Northern Ireland being handed a mystery parcel during a walkabout of West Belfast. All the while, both mother and father hovered right next to me, keeping their hands under his head, back and legs, just to show how much confidence they had in my ability not to drop an eight-pound baby for the twelve seconds that I held it.

These new parents reminded me of born-again Christians. They had a smugness and a superior air that suggested my life was somehow incomplete because I hadn't heard the

Good News about babies. I would only be a whole person once I had joined their throng of happy clappy parents who went to the church hall every week to sing 'Three Little Men in a Flying Saucer'. They all thought I'd be converted sooner or later. Eventually my soul would be saved and I would take babies into my life. This was Catherine's plan, hence the newborn charm offensive. If she was trying to persuade me that I might like to have a baby then you would have thought that exposing me to a lot of babies was the worst possible tack. But in the end she wore me down. What could I do; the thing that would bring the greatest happiness to the woman I loved was in my gift and I couldn't keep denying her for ever.

I finally agreed that we should start trying for children on one of those let's-be-really-in-love days. These are times of total intimacy and mutual adoration, when all you want to do is agree with everything your partner says. To actually cut across and contradict her by saying, 'No, actually I think "Hotel California" is a dreadful song,' would completely ruin the atmosphere, so you nod and smile and say, 'Mmmm, yeah, that's one of my favourites, too.' It was in one of these moments that I acceded to the idea of being a parent. I agreed to a lifetime of fatherhood so as not to spoil a nice afternoon.

I could never understand those men who complained that it took them and their partners years to conceive. Month after month of constant eager sex! Catherine got pregnant in the first month we started trying. 'You're so clever,' she said to me with a hug, and I was supposed to be proud that we had managed it so quickly. But inside I was thinking, Damn! Is that it, then? Can't we keep doing it every night anyway, just to be sure. She wee'd onto a little stick and we watched it change colour. The instructions said that if it went *light* pink she was not pregnant, but if it went *dark* pink she was pregnant. It went pink. Sort of halfway between light and dark pink, a sort of pinky-pink with just a hint of pink. She went to the doctor's, because that's the only way to be really sure you are pregnant, and the best start an expectant mother can get is to sit for an hour and a half in a hot, stuffy waiting room, inhaling the germs of as many infectious diseases as possible.

Before the baby arrived I was actually more consumed by it all than she was. I read every pregnancy manual I could lay my hands on, researched the best car seats and monitored Catherine's weight gain, which I logged on a wall chart in the kitchen. I was rather hurt when she took it down before a dinner party; I thought it showed just how supportive and interested I was being. This birth was my new project, my new enterprise, an exam that could be passed if I did enough revision. I learned the expectant parents' script off by heart.

'What are you hoping for, a boy or a girl?'

'I don't mind, as long as it's healthy.'

Correct answer.

'What sort of birth are you going for?'

'As natural as possible, but we're not completely ruling out intervention if it's necessary.'

Correct answer.

Maybe I thought mastery of the subject matter might endow me with some sort of control, but as the pregnancy progressed I began to see the warning signs. Women have babies, not men; there is no getting round that fact. 'It's not our show, chaps,' said one of the fathers-to-be at the ante-natal classes. And as much as I dutifully went along to all these gatherings, being supportive and nodding and listening along with all the other silent, embarrassed men, I couldn't help thinking, What is it exactly that I've got to do, then? When the mother is breathing correctly and walking and focusing and contracting and timing her contractions so as not to go into hospital too early, what does the man have to do?

Apparently the answer to this question is 'make sandwiches'. That was the only instruction which I wrote down that was definitely aimed at me. In fact, making sandwiches is the only other thing that men are needed for during the entire nine months. One sperm at the beginning of the pregnancy, two rounds of cheese and pickle at the end of it. But my enthusiasm was resilient – if this was all I had to do, then I wanted to get it right. The teacher went back to describing the first-stage contractions, hardly pausing to give me the slightest guidance on how we might best do our bit, so I put my hand up.

'Just going back to those sandwiches a minute, is there a particular filling that's best for a woman in labour?'

'Well, um, nothing too difficult to digest, but whatever your partner normally likes.'

'It's just that I thought maybe her tastebuds might be affected by hormones or whatever; there might be something that women in labour often develop a violent aversion to.'

'Maybe best to make a selection of fillings, just to be on the safe side. Now, once the cervix has dilated the full ten centimetres—'

'White or brown bread?'

'What?'

'White or brown bread for the sandwiches? You know, I want everything to be perfect for the baby, so I was just wondering which is best. I know brown is normally healthier, but is it easier to digest? I suppose we ought to have brown if we're going for a natural childbirth.'

One of the other men picked up the thread and suggested that we make a selection of fillings inside a choice of white *and* brown bread, which seemed like a sensible suggestion, but at that point a woman with large glasses said that she was sorry if the men weren't used to being in meetings that they couldn't dominate but could we shut the fuck up about the fucking sandwiches because we were getting on her tits. The teacher had spent the last hour discussing intercourse, vaginas and breasts, but still blushed to hear such talk.

Because of minor gynaecological problems during her pregnancy, Catherine had been allocated a specialist consultant at St Thomas's. This was obviously very distressing for her; a North Londoner being told that she would have to travel south of the river. But no problems ever arose, apart from having to drive halfway across London in the rush hour with my wife in labour in the back seat. Once we were in the delivery suite Catherine did everything that she had been told and breathed and pushed and waited and pushed again and produced a perfect little baby girl. I did everything I was supposed to do as well, but the sandwiches never came out of the bag. Of course I dabbed her forehead and said, 'You're doing really well,' and, 'That's really brilliant,' and things like that, but that's not the way I normally talk, so it can't have sounded very convincing. But then nothing about that day was very normal. Having this alien finally pop out of her was quite the most surreal experience of my life. The baby was handed to Catherine and she immediately seemed comfortable and confident with it. Her overjoyment gland had secreted gallons of the overjoyment hormone and she burst into tears. And although I was deeply moved by that moment, I secretly felt guilty that I was clearly not deeply moved in the way that she was. So I managed a wan smile, unsure whether I should try and cheer her up or pretend to cry as well. I think I was probably in a deep state of shock.

Although that was the moment I technically became a father, it didn't really sink in for another couple of hours. Catherine was asleep and I was slumped in the leatherette chair by her bed. A toy coughing noise started to come from the cot and, since I didn't want Catherine to be disturbed, I nervously picked up the baby myself. She seemed so fragile and tiny, and I carried her to my chair as if she were some priceless antique vase.

'Hello, little girl, I'm your dad,' I said. And then for the next hour or so I held her in my arms, just staring at this perfect little model of a person while an enormous sense of responsibility welled up within me. This baby was completely dependent on Catherine and me. We hadn't been made to take any exams or attend any interviews, but here we were, suddenly in charge of a child. It felt moving, thrilling, awe-inspiring, but most of all terrifying. As I sat there looking at her, I thought about all those proud parents who had brought their babies round to our house, and I smiled when I thought how foolish they had all been. They had really thought that theirs were the most beautiful babies of all, when it was obvious to anyone that this little girl in my arms was by far the most beautiful creature the world had yet seen. I was sure that everyone would recognize this fact once they saw her. She was so innocent, so unspoilt, so new. I wanted to protect her from everything in the world and show her all the wonderful things on earth at the same time. When she eventually became restless I walked her across to the window and, while dawn was breaking over London, I looked down over the city from high up in St Thomas's Hospital.

'That's the River Thames down there, little girl,' I told her. 'And that's the Houses of Parliament. That clock there is Big Ben and that big red thing going over the bridge is called a bus. Say, "Bus." '

'Bus,' said a babyish voice to my astonishment. Either I had fathered a genius or Catherine was awake and watching me. The baby had been growing increasingly uncomfortable and Catherine took her from me and placed the baby on her breast where she fed as if they had both been doing it for years.

Catherine and I had agreed on the name Millie for a girl

weeks before the birth. But now that a baby girl had actually come along I felt an urge to name her after my late mother. I shared the idea with Catherine, who said it was a beautiful thought.

'Your mother sounds like a wonderful person, and I wish I had met you earlier so that I could have known her. It would be a lovely thing to name this baby after the grandmother she will never meet; it's a touching and poetic idea. The only trouble, my darling husband, is that your mother's name was Prunella.'

'I know.'

'Don't you think the world is a cruel enough place into which to bring a new human being without lumbering it with the name Prunella?'

We agreed to sleep on the idea and we took Millie home two days later.

Once in the house, we put the baby in the middle of the lounge and I thought, Now what do we do? That was when I realized that I had only revised for everything up to this point. So much of our focus was on the day of the birth itself that I'd only given the slightest thought to what happened after that. Nothing had prepared me for the way she would totally disrupt my life. Not even every parent I knew telling me that the baby would totally disrupt my life prepared me for how much the baby would totally disrupt my life. It was like having your most difficult and demanding relation come to stay with you *for ever*. In fact, it would have been easier to put up with my ninety-year-old great aunt coming into our bed at three in the morning; at least she might have gone back to sleep for an hour or two.

When I first started to feel like a parent that night in the hospital, I was already lagging a couple of hours behind Catherine, and now the gulf between us continued to grow. I felt redundant almost from the outset. Normally when there had been something that Catherine had really wanted, I had been the one who got it out of the box and wired up the speakers. But when we took this baby home, I was the useless one who had no idea what to do. There seemed to be no logic or system to follow. Sometimes Millie slept and sometimes she cried all night. Sometimes she would feed and sometimes she would refuse. There were no rules or routine, no rhythm or narrative to her – for the first time in my life I seemed to be confronted by a problem which had no solution. Life was out of control; I had no idea what was making this baby scream and what course of action should be taken, whereas Catherine just seemed to know. She could tell when Millie was hot, cold, hungry, thirsty, grumpy, tired, sad, whatever. Although the baby didn't seem to cry any less when she applied the appropriate remedy, I never dared question the confidence with which she told me the reason for the baby's distress. Millie was supposed to fill me with joy and fulfilment, but my strongest sensation was an overwhelming anxiety. It was anxiety at first sight. I wasn't in love with the baby, I was 'in worry' with it.

But with Catherine it was like first love all over again. It was an overwhelming, all-consuming, total obsessive love. Her every waking thought was of Millie.

'Mind the red car,' I would say in a panic as she drove along, staring at her baby strapped in the back seat.

'Aah. Millie's got a little hat that colour,' she would say dreamily.

'Ow! I've cut my hand open with the bread knife.'

'Ooh, show Millie; she's never seen blood.'

'Did you read that article about the USA trying to force Europe to import its bananas from American multinationals?'

'Millie likes bananas.'

She put Millie's name on the answerphone. 'Hello. If you

would like to leave a message for Catherine, Michael or Millie, please speak after the tone.' Being a baby who was as yet unable to use the phone or speak English, it was not very surprising that Millie didn't get very many messages of her own.

Everything came back to the baby. I was in a shop buying a new stereo and Catherine said, 'Well, I think you should buy these speakers because they've got a really good bass sound and that's supposed to help relax the baby.' Obviously the most important criterion when buying myself a new stereo is which one is best for relaxing the baby. I already had my heart set on another pair of speakers, but God forbid that I should appear indifferent to the needs of The Baby. 'These are better,' I said. 'The edges are rounder – she won't hurt herself if she falls against these.' And Catherine was delighted with my choice.

Suddenly I never seemed to be doing anything that I actually wanted to be doing. This struck me on our first family holiday together. I realized it wasn't a holiday at all. That having Millie crawling around a rented cottage with extra-steep unguarded stairs and loose electrical sockets and a real log fire spitting out glowing splinters was even less relaxing than sitting at home watching her stuff half-chewed rusks into the video. My first holiday as a parent was when I realized I had become a teenager again, that I was grumpily being dragged along from playground to children's farm and it was all completely stupid and pointless and pathetic. 'Look, Millie, look at the llama eating the hay.' Yup, she definitely glanced at the llama then, so that was worth it. Why couldn't we just have stayed at home in London? I wouldn't have minded taking her out of the front door every now and then and saying, 'Look, Millie, look at the dog crapping on the pavement.' She wouldn't have been any less impressed. But no, we had to drive all the way to Devon and stay in a freezing-cold cottage so the poor disorientated baby could wake up every two hours and then be strapped into the car seat again because there was a children's farm eleven miles away where they had llamas and not enough high chairs and a swing not dissimilar to the one at the bottom of our road. All that effort wasn't for her; it was for us. We had to do too much just to convince ourselves that we were doing enough.

And then, of course, there were the night times. I remembered how Catherine and I used to cuddle up and fall asleep with our bodies still wrapped together. Then Millie came into our bed – quite literally between us. We had tried having her in a cot at the bottom of the bed, but Catherine found that she slept more soundly with Millie at her side, once she no longer felt compelled to sit up in panic at every moan, gurgle or indeed every silence. The baby would drift in and out of sleep feeding at Catherine's breast – the very breasts that I was no longer permitted to touch – and I would lie there awake, resentfully thinking, Honestly! Has that baby no idea who those breasts are for?

I found it hard to sleep through the constant snuffling and kicking of the baby while I perched precariously on the edge of the mattress. On a couple of occasions I actually fell right out and landed face down on the wooden floor. I discovered that it was quite hard to sleep through this as well.

'Shhh, you'll wake Millie,' whispered Catherine as I checked to see if my nose was bleeding. After a few wakeful nights, Catherine suggested I slept downstairs on the sofa. So now she didn't sleep with her husband any more, she slept with her new love, The Baby. She seemed to have become completely immune to the feelings of anyone except The Baby. She was besotted, spellbound, obsessed. It was like when she first fell in love with me. Except this time it wasn't with me.

Millie had pushed me out. She had taken my place in the

bed, my social life and my time with Catherine; she'd even robbed me of my birthday. 'What a perfect birthday present,' everyone said to me when she was born on the day that I turned thirty. That was the last birthday I ever had. A year later, on our 'joint' birthday, Millie got a shape sorter, a ball that bounced in funny directions, a trolley with coloured bricks in, a plastic bath toy, a baby gym, a squeaky book and about thirty cuddly toys. I got a photo album in which to put pictures of Millie. Happy Birthday, Michael! 'Sorry it's not very much, but I didn't have time to go to the shops,' said Catherine as she filled a bin liner with all the packaging from the toys she'd bought Millie from the shops.

I would have liked to go out that night, but Catherine said it felt funny to leave Millie on her first birthday. I pointed out that Millie was not only fast asleep, she was also completely unaware that it was her birthday and, if she woke up, would be perfectly happy to be settled again by Catherine's mother. But Catherine said she wouldn't have enjoyed it and so neither would I, so we stayed in and watched a programme about gardening.

To cap a memorable evening Catherine asked me to pop down to the supermarket for some nappies and, since it was my birthday, I treated myself to two cans of lager and a packet of Cheesey Wotsits. But then, as I returned home, I noticed all the lights were out. I knew immediately what Catherine had done. My wife, God bless her, had secretly organized me a surprise birthday party. The nappy mission had just been a way of getting me out of the house. I checked my hair in the car mirror, let myself in, tiptoed into the lounge and went to switch on the light, ready to appear surprised and delighted as everyone shouted, 'Happy Birthday, Michael!' I braced myself and flicked the light switch. I probably did look really surprised. The room was completely empty. So was the kitchen. I went upstairs and Catherine was fast asleep in bed. I went back downstairs, flopped onto the sofa, drank a can of lager and flicked between the television channels. My Cheesey Wotsits had a free *Star Wars* card inside, so that was some consolation. 'Live life to the max', said the ad on the telly, so I drank my second can of lager before going to bed.

I had thought my youth and freedom would last for ever. When I was eighteen I'd left home and rented a shared flat, thinking that at long last I was free, that now I could do whatever I wanted – for ever. No-one had told me that this emancipation was only temporary, that I'd only enjoy total liberty for a very brief period of my life. I had spent my childhood doing what my parents wanted to do and now my adulthood seemed doomed to be spent doing what my children wanted to do. I was back in the jug again; my home had turned into a prison. I could no longer come and go as I pleased; there were bars on the upstairs windows, security gates on the stairs and monitors and locks and alarms, soon there would even be a stinking potty to be slopped out. This baby that had arrived was part warder and part prison bully. She would not permit me to sleep beyond 6 a.m., after which time I was her gofer, her lackey, fetching and carrying just for her amusement. She would humiliate me by throwing a piece of cutlery to the floor and then demanding that I pick it up, and when I obeyed her she would do it again.

Any prisoner dreams of escape. Mine happened sub-consciously at first. I would lie in the bath and allow my ears to slip under the water so the soundtrack of crying babies and angry shouting would become a dull and distant babble. Once, when Millie was asleep in the buggy, I offered to push her out across Hampstead Heath so Catherine could have a lie-down and relax in an empty house. As I pushed the buggy up and down the only steep hills in London, I realized that the reason I had made this apparently generous offer was just to get some time to myself, because now I needed to escape from Catherine as well. She made me feel as if I always did everything wrong. I headed for the Bull and Last and had two pints sitting in the pub garden, feeling more relaxed and care-free than I could remember. Millie stayed asleep the whole time we were out, and soon all my cares and tensions were washed away on the foamy tide of beer. When I arrived home I felt completely serene and at peace with the world, until Catherine's furious face at the window brought me back down to reality with a disappointing bump. Oh no, what have I done wrong now? I thought to myself. I decided I would try to ignore her obvious displeasure, but as I cheerfully strode up the front path with my hands in my pockets she came to greet me at the door.

'Where's Millie?' she said.

'Millie?'

'Yes, your daughter that you took for a walk on the heath . . .'

I now know that it is possible to run from my house to the Bull and Last pub in four minutes and forty-seven seconds.

I suppose that on that occasion I have to accept some of the blame. Most of the blame. But Catherine seemed to find fault with everything I did with the children. I dried them with the wrong towel, I mixed their baby milk with the wrong water and I put the wrong amount of lotion on their bottoms. I got the impression that Catherine found it quicker and easier to do everything herself. I would dutifully be there at dressing time, feeding time and at bath time, hoping that I might be of some use, but generally I just got in the way. I was offering to be hands-on, but in reality my hands were just hanging down by my sides, not quite sure what to do with themselves. In babyland she was queen; I was Prince Philip, hovering awkwardly in the background making stupid comments.

Was it like this for all fathers? Is this why, for thousands of years, men had made themselves scarce: to be spared the humiliation of being second best at something? Before long, my absence became routine. I would tend to be held up at meetings; I was no longer in a rush to get home in time to be told off for putting plastic teaspoons in the dishwasher. If I was working out of town, I would always seem to end up on the later train back to London, and wouldn't get home until after Catherine was fast asleep.

One day I came home late and crept into the room that I had persisted in clinging to as my recording studio. Then I saw it. A whole wall had been covered with *Wind in the Willows* wallpaper. Where there had previously been a Clash poster of Joe Strummer smashing a guitar, now there were little nursery drawings of Ratty and Mole in tweeds and plus fours. That was my parenting Kristallnacht, the moment I knew I was being driven out.

We had always agreed that when the baby went into 'the nursery' I would have to rent a room away from home for my work, but the move was one of those far-off problems that I preferred to put out of my head. Just because I agreed I would move my stuff out didn't mean that I was actually planning to do anything about it. I pointed out that finding somewhere suitable would be a long and complicated business.

'There's a free room going in Heather's brother's house in Balham; you can rent that in the short term.' Catherine was way ahead of me. The following weekend we packed up all the things that I would need in my new recording studio, and a little bit more. By the end of the morning the hallway was blocked with a large pile of boxes containing my entire youth. CDs, tapes, music magazines, my autographed Elvis Costello baseball cap and all the ironically naff mugs that I had bought before we moved in together. Two birthdays ago I had given her a chrome CD rack in the shape of an electric guitar; that appeared on the pile by the front door as well. I got the feeling there was a side to me that Catherine was looking forward to expunging from the family home.

'Oh, you've got to have your Beatles mirror in your studio. It'll look great there and it doesn't really go in our bedroom,' she said, taking it down off the wall with a little too much relish.

And so I started commuting to a little room in South London. It was only half an hour down the Northern Line, but it felt like a whole world away. If Catherine needed to speak to me she could ring my mobile, except when I was really up against it, when the mobile was switched off. It seems I was often really up against it. Nothing improved our marriage like being apart. The more time I spent at the studio, the more we liked each other. I had always worked unconventional hours and, with a sofa bed that folded out between the amps and keyboards, I continued to do so. As far as Catherine was concerned, the longer I was in my studio, the harder I must have been working, and she was proud to have a husband who could work such long hours and yet still come home and put so much effort into his family.

'Where do you get your energy from?' she asked as she lay on the bed after her bath and watched me swinging Millie round by her arms. 'Well, a change is as good as a rest,' I said modestly, thinking to myself that a change *and* a rest was even better. I gave the kids a quick bath in their mum's perfumed bathwater while she lay on the bed and finished the bottle of wine. She assured me that she wasn't too drunk to tell Millie her bedtime story and proceeded to read perfectly, only ripping two of the tabs on the *Pocahontas* pop-up book. Soon Millie and Alfie were asleep and the house was at peace. Catherine lay on our bed, wrapped in a giant towel, soft and talcum-powdered and still glowing warm from her hour-long soak. She gazed up at me.

'If we're going to have more children, it would be good to have them close together, wouldn't it?'

This particular come-on was somehow left out of the *Erotic Guide to Sexual Seduction*. She looked irresistible, but two children was enough for me.

'Well, Alfie's only nine months; there's no need to hurry,' I said, avoiding a confrontation. But Catherine had always known she was going to have four kids and she had a very persuasive argument in favour of trying for another one right now, namely that she was lying naked on a warm soft bed. We hadn't made love for three weeks and four days, and here she was pressing herself against me and kissing me wet kisses on my lips. I won't pretend that I wasn't very tempted, but I knew I had to be strong. Without any contraception it would simply be too much of a gamble. For a few minutes' pleasure I was not prepared to risk yet more years of sleepless nights and all the marital tension and continued deception on my part that another baby would bring. Any way that you looked at it, it just wasn't worth it. I was not going to have five minutes of ecstatic sexual intercourse with my beautiful wife.

As it turned out, this last bit was true – it was only a minute and a half. I cursed my weakness as I held her close and climaxed. Lots of men apparently shout obscenities at that moment, but I moaned, 'Oh fuck!' Not as in, 'Wow! That was amazing!' But more in the sense of, 'Oh fuck! What have I just done!' Sex was the crime and I'd just blown my parole. I had let this double life develop, thinking it would just be a temporary measure, that soon the kids would reach the age when we could emerge from the war zone of babies and then I could start being a normal husband and father. Fortunately, the chances of Catherine conceiving so quickly were slim. She was still breastfeeding once a day and so I reckoned it was safe.

Two weeks later, Catherine told me she was pregnant.

chapter three

have a break

When Catherine had been expecting our first child, one of the books I had read suggested that, in order to appreciate what my wife was going through, I should fill a balloon up with water and wear it strapped to my stomach for a day. To demonstrate how supportive I was, I actually attempted this exercise. I followed the diagrams and tied the squishy balloon around my waist and then walked around the kitchen with one hand on the base of my back, trying to look radiant. Afterwards, I felt I could look my wife in the eye and say that now, at last, I finally understood how it felt to have a balloon filled with water stuffed under your jumper. I only did it for an hour. My waters burst suddenly while I was pruning the roses.

A good father-to-be is supposed to empathize. In fact, I read that occasionally the most sensitive of men genuinely experience some of the actual *physical* symptoms of their partner's pregnancies, although having an eight-pound baby pop out of their vaginas was obviously not one of them. 'Couvade syndrome', as it's called, happened to me with

Catherine's first pregnancy. In the first six weeks or so, as Catherine started to put on weight, through some deep spiritual sensibility I began to gain weight as well. Amazingly, since we had stopped playing squash together and stayed in ordering takeaway pizzas and tubs of Ben and Jerry's ice cream, my waistline had started to expand at approximately the same rate as hers. Truly, nature is a wonderful thing.

All these concepts and suggestions left me feeling that I was supposed to try and make myself more maternal. That's what they wanted me to be: a back-up mother. I ought to be feeling what she felt; I ought to have the instincts that she had. I almost felt guilty for not blubbing when my milk seemed a bit slow to come in. No wonder I felt that I was no good at it, because it was an aspiration that was impossible to achieve. My wife was always going to be a better woman than I was.

I suppose we were quite a conventional couple in the way we slotted into our gender stereotypes. Catherine had decided she wanted to put her acting career on hold while the children were small. She didn't feel she was getting any-where, despite the fact that after Millie was born she was no longer being cast as 'passer-by' but had progressed to 'passer-by holding baby'. So she resolved to become a full-time mother. 'Ah well, that is the toughest role of all,' said her annoying father a hundred and twelve times. What Catherine found disorientating was how guilty she was made to feel for not being a promotion-hungry career woman. When she told people that she'd given up work, they froze into embarrassed silence. She said she didn't want to go to any more drinks parties unless she could ring a handbell and wear a placard round her neck saying, 'Uninteresting'. Being with the baby was what she wanted and so I was happy to support her decision, even though I had always enjoyed her occasional appearances on television, not to mention the occasional appearance of the cheques that had landed on the doormat.

We had always liked to think of ourselves as artistic and Bohemian, me the musician and her the actress, but in reality we were no different from any of the accountants and insurance brokers who lived in our road. We lived in a small two-bedroom house in Kentish Town which the estate agents had described as a 'cottage'. This meant that you could just about fit the pushchair through the front door, but then getting past it yourself was such a physical impossibility that you had to sleep in the front garden. I can vouch for the fact that there wasn't room to swing a cat in our house because I once caught Millie trying.

Because we aspired to live in a neighbourhood which was quite close to a postal code which was next door to a borough which was quite near a desirable part of London, we had no choice but to live in a tiny house. I remember climbing inside the kiddies' playhouse at Toys "Я" Us and thinking, Blimey, this is roomy! How we were going to fit another baby into our home was quite beyond me, but if the old lady who lived in the shoe had managed, then I suppose we would have to try our best. I never really understood that nursery rhyme until I moved to London. If that had been today, some developer would have bought the old lady's shoe and converted it into flats.

The third baby was not due for another eight months and was no more than half an inch long, but it was still able to make its mother nauseous, tired and tearful. I suppose that's an early warning that there's no relationship between the size of a baby and the scale of disruption it can cause. Of course an embryo disrupts your life in a different way to a small baby, and a small baby disrupts your life in a different way to a toddler. But now we had all three of them wreaking havoc simultaneously. Few of us have any memories of our own lives before we were three years old. This is an evolutionary necessity – if we could recall what bastards we were to our parents we'd never have any children of our own. Millie was two and a half, Alfie was ten months, the embryo was four weeks and I felt about a hundred and five. Nothing could have prepared me for how tired I felt, let alone Catherine. Sleep deprivation is a popular torture device used by the Indonesian secret police and small babies. I suppose at least Alfie couldn't kick me in the testicles every time I eventually dropped off. He left that to his big sister, who generally climbed into our bed at around three in the morning. Even when I slept on my own I still found myself lying there with my hands over my groin in the footballer-in-defensive-wall position.

Catherine was always most exhausted at the beginning of her pregnancies, when they were still secret from everyone else. I had to pretend to friends that she kept fainting and bursting into tears because we'd stayed up very late watching old James Stewart movies, but she always insisted that she was coping all right. 'Tired? No, I'm not tired,' she said as I cleared the dinner plates away, although my suspicions were increased when I came back with the pudding to find her fast asleep with her head on the kitchen table.

Although we had been together five years, I'd not yet learned how to translate the things she said to me. Before her last birthday she had remarked, 'Don't get me anything special this year,' and I had foolishly taken this to mean, 'Don't get me anything special this year.' I had failed to decipher the subtle intonation in her voice, I had listened to the lyrics rather than the notes. In the same way she had a dozen different ways of saying, 'I'm not tired.' Some of them meant exactly that, while others meant, 'I am very tired, please insist that I go to bed right away.'

I knew she was not her usual self that evening when some

Jehovah's Witnesses had come to the door. That's strange behaviour, I had thought, she didn't want to talk to them. Normally she would have invited them in, given them a cup of tea and then asked them if they had thought about taking Satan into their lives. She nearly recruited one of them once when she earnestly described the uplifting spiritual catharsis of naked bouncy-castle night.

But tonight tiredness reduced her to a robotic drone; she had carried out the duties required to get the kids into bed, with no energy or enthusiasm remaining for anything else. Alfie had just given us three terrible nights in a row and we were both completely exhausted and demoralized. I can't say that we had been sleeping badly because I don't actually think we slept at all. The wakeful night-times were totally disorientating and we had lost any sense of time; how Catherine's body clock remembered to make her throw up in the morning was completely beyond me.

When she finally lifted her creased face off the kitchen table, I tried to persuade her to sleep downstairs on the sofa with the door closed, where she would be out of earshot of the baby. I wanted her to delegate some of the sleeplessness to me before I went off to work the next morning. But she found this hard to agree to. She was greedy; she wanted all the misery to herself. But I kept on and on at her, and eventually she didn't have the energy to resist my arguments. So I set her up on the sofa with a duvet and pillows before kissing her good night and heading upstairs to face the night-time on my own.

It was like an approaching storm which I entered into with nervous trepidation. Batten down the hatches; we're going into the night. In the days before children came along I often deliberately chose to stay up until morning. It was a fun and crazy thing to do. We'd climb over the railings of Hyde Park and play on the swings. I went to an all-night sci-fi festival at an independent cinema. I went to parties and took speed or coke and sat at the top of Hampstead Heath watching the sun rise over London. Often, when I had a big piece of work in, I liked to spend an evening with Catherine and then, as she went to bed, I would disappear into the studio, put on the headphones and work at my keyboard until dawn. I would have breakfast with Catherine before she went off to her audition or whatever, and then I'd go to bed until she came back again. I loved working at night when it was all quiet and still and you could really lose yourself in your thoughts. A melody would come into my head and I'd think, Where is this coming from? Somebody else has taken over my body and is giving me this tune for free. Sometimes, if I got stuck, I would go for a walk in the dead of the night and just feel the stillness of the city asleep. The nights were my time to myself. Mr Moonlight she called me. That was Catherine's pet name for her boyfriend who loved to stay up all night. In moments of intimacy and affection she still called me Mr Moonlight, though now that I was secretly moonlighting on our family life, it was no longer a nickname with which I felt particularly comfortable.

I tiptoed into Millie's room and checked that she was asleep. She looked so sweet and trusting and secure. Carefully avoiding the creaky floorboard, I picked up a couple of soft toys that had fallen on the floor and silently placed them behind her pillow. As quietly and gently as I could, I slowly pulled her blanket back over her. With the care and precision of a microsurgeon, I moved the plastic doll from where it was pressing into her face and laid it on the side of the bed. Then, as I straightened up, my head crashed into the stained-glass mobile above her bed, which set it jangling and clinking, and she opened her eyes and looked at me in surprised disbelief.

'Why are you here?' she said in a dreamy voice. It wasn't an easy question to answer on any level. I told her to go back to sleep again, and amazingly she did.

Alfie was asleep in the pram which, for reasons that had once seemed sensible but now eluded me, we carried up to our bedroom every night. He was sleeping soundly, getting his rest in now so that he would have as much energy as possible for the long night ahead. Silently, and on my own, I prepared for bed, wondering how the next few hours might unfold, like a soldier on the eve of battle. The knowledge that I would soon be disturbed made me desperate to get to sleep as quickly as possible, so that I lay down in panicky concentration, thinking, Got to get to sleep. Got to get to sleep, which kept me awake for far longer than usual. Then finally I was gone.

In the first hour or so my mind would race downhill into its deepest, deepest sleep, but it was during this dreamy descent that I was always violently pulled up, jerked awake by the sudden angry scream of the baby. Tonight Alfie was bang on cue, and though I was suddenly conscious of being awake, for a couple of scary seconds I lay there frozen, paralysed while my body struggled to catch up and become operative as well. Then, like some bleary automaton, I threw back the duvet, staggered over to the pram and stuck my little finger in his mouth. The crying stopped as he sucked and sucked, and I sat down on the end of the bed, still only half conscious. Rubbing my aching head I glanced in the mirror and saw the hunched, greying figure of an exhausted man, a ghost of my former self, my thinning hair sticking up and my face creased and lined. When he had been born, one of the cards we had been sent featured a black-and-white photo of a muscular man clutching a naked baby to his rippling chest. That was not how fatherhood felt right now. The clock told me that I had only slept for an hour and forty minutes and that it was far too early to give Alfie a feed. After a while the sucking became less frantic; he slowly calmed down as I gently rocked the pram back and forth for good measure. When I deftly removed the digit, he barely reacted.

My finger was a portable pacifier that had worked for both children. Unsurprisingly, they seemed to find Catherine's long, sharp fingernails rather less comforting, and so my little finger was the only oral comfort they were permitted. Early on I had tentatively suggested that we buy them plastic dummies, but Catherine put up the objections that dummies were unhygienic and that they impaired speech development and that we would only be creating a rod for our own backs and it would be impossible to wean them off them and several other second-hand objections. She never mentioned the real one, which was that she secretly thought dummies looked common and no baby of hers was going to look common. I couldn't offer an argument against a conviction I dared not accuse her of, and so the only pacifier that our children ever had was my upturned little finger. The dummy was me.

To keep little Alfie asleep I knew I had to keep gently rocking the pram, so inch by inch I manoeuvred it to a position beside the bed. Now, at least, I could lie down. I was probably only making it worse for myself. Like an alcoholic going to the pub for a glass of water, I was taunting myself with my proximity to the thing I craved most. But I was just too tired to sit upright, so I lay on the edge of the bed and, with the blood draining from my outstretched arm, I slowly pushed the pram back and forth. As long as this motion was maintained at an enthusiastic enough rate, Alfie would grudgingly lie there in silence and I could pretend to myself that he was going to sleep. But he was made of stronger stuff than I was. The rocking would become increasingly half-hearted; growing slower and weaker until the moment my exhausted arm finally flopped down by the side of the bed. This was his signal to resume crying and then, independently of the rest of my comatose body, my arm would take hold of the pram handle and start pushing it back and forth once again. This pattern was repeated over and over again; for the next hour we took turns to almost drift off. Then eventually I stopped. Silence. Could it be that at last he was finally going to let me doze off and let my weary, demoralized body finally have some rest? All I could think about was sleep.

Oh sleep, I just need to sleep, I would give anything just to have eight hours' solid, uninterrupted sleep. Not this violent bungee jumping in and out of half-consciousness, but real, deep, deep, proper sleep. That's the only drug I need: sleep. Tune in, turn on and drop off. If only I could find a dealer and score some snore; I'd pay good money for it, I wouldn't care if it was illegal or who it had been stolen from; I'd rob my mother's purse to pay for it, I've just got to get a fix of sleep; I'd snort it, smoke it, take a big tab of it, inject it – I'd share a needle if that was all the sleep I could get hold of, and then I'd mainline a massive dose of pure unrefined sleep and just lie back as the hit washed over me, feeling my brain go numb and my body relax, and then I'd just close my eyes and I'd be gone, zonked out, out of this world; there's no drug like it and I've just got to have some sleep or I'm going to die; maybe if I kill myself that'll feel like sleep; please, please, please, I've got to have some sleep; I'll steal the sleep from Catherine; yeah, she doesn't need it; that's it, I'll have her sleep; in the morning I'm going back over the river and I'll tell her I've got to work and I'll get into my room and turn my mobile off, I'll take off all my clothes and I'll fluff up the feather pillows and I'll pull the duvet over my head and I'll feel the heaviness of my limbs on the soft mattress and I'll just feel myself going, going, slipping away, and then I'll have such a massive shot, when I've had that fix I'll feel so great, like an athlete, like the heavyweight champion of the world, like I could run a marathon, but I'm falling asleep now and it feels so good; it's all I want; please let me sleep, baby, let me sleep; I need it now, I can't wait; I've got to sleep now and I'm going, I'm going . . .

Was I dreaming or did I hear a tiny moan from the pram? I held my breath lest even my breathing should disturb him. Sure enough, there followed another barely perceptible half moan and my heart sank. The pattern was always the same. The moans would be weak at first – intermittent, unimpressive attempts to stir, like somebody failing to start a car with a flat battery. But as I closed my eyes and tried to ignore them, eventually the moans would develop into bleats, and then a bleat would break into a coughed-out cry, and then the cries would become more punctuated and insistent, until the engine finally started and roared and revved as the baby screamed with a strength that belied its tiny size.

I lay there awake, listening to the angry crying, unable to summon the enthusiasm to pull my heavy frame upright again. Catherine would normally have leaped up long before now because she didn't want Millie to be woken up by the baby, but I was never particularly convinced of the likelihood of this. It was one of those fussy overprotective worries that Catherine was always coming up with. There was the creak of a floorboard in the doorway.

'Alfie waked me up,' said Millie weepily, standing in the half light, clutching a chewed blanket.

'Oh no.' I sighed. I picked up the baby to stop the crying, prompting Millie to hold her arms out for me to lift her up as well, which I did. And then I just stood there in the lonely nadir of the night-time, balancing two small crying children in my arms, my tired body nearly buckling under the weight, wondering what on earth to do next.

I thought about how there was only one thing worse than children that refused to sleep and that was the self-satisfied parents of babies who did. They believed it was down to them. Whenever Catherine and I were at our most exasperated we would be forced to listen to her stupid hippie sister Judith smugly explaining to us what we were doing wrong. I wanted to pick her up and scream at her, 'It's because you were lucky, that's all. Because you happen to have had a baby that sleeps. It's not because you had a water birth or fed him organic babyfood or *feng shui*-ed the fucking nursery. It's just the luck of the draw.'

Catherine and I had tried everything with Millie and Alfie, and now I was reduced to empty threats. 'Just wait till you're teenagers,' I told them, 'then I'll get my revenge. I'm going to pick you up from your friends' in a purple flowery shirt and I'll do the twist at the school disco and when you bring home your first dates, I'm going to produce those photos of you as babies wriggling in the nude on the carpet.' But my threats meant nothing and now the stakes were raised. I hadn't wanted Catherine to be roused because she desperately needed to sleep. With both her children awake she was more likely to stir, and when she did and saw that I had allowed Alfie to disturb Millie, too, there would be an argument and I wouldn't hear the end of it until Catherine had her head in the toilet bowl the following morning. Millie being awake was a disaster on every front. Apart from anything else the process of feeding and changing a baby in the small hours of the morning was a precise and precarious operation. Generally speaking, having an irritable two-and-a-half-year-old at one's side was a hindrance rather than a help.

'I want to watch *Barney* video,' said Millie.

We were not particularly severe parents, but one regulation that we did agree on was that Millie could not get us up in the middle of the night to watch children's videos. This was fine as an abstract regulation, but it didn't take into account the fact that Millie had the personality of Margaret Thatcher. She was not someone you could negotiate with, meet halfway, bribe or persuade. She would take up a position and you could see in her demonic eyes that she was completely persuaded by the total and absolute rightness of her cause, and at this moment nothing would shift her from her unwavering belief that she was going to watch the *Barney* video.

One of our child-rearing books had said that the clever thing to do is not to confront a toddler head on, but to outwit her by changing the subject or distracting her with the unexpected. Imaginative distraction techniques are for when you are not feeling tired and irritable. I presume that this feeling comes back when the toddlers have grown up and gone to school.

'No! You're not watching the *Barney* video, Millie,' I snapped. On hearing my firm refusal Millie threw herself to the ground with all the agony of a bereaved parent. She repeated her demand one hundred and forty-seven times while I proceeded to try and change Alfie's nappy, but I opted to ignore it. It was fine, I was in control, I was just going to ignore her and not let her get to me.

'FOR GOD'S SAKE *SHUT UP*, MILLIE!' I yelled. Deep down I knew that one way or another she would get to watch the *Barney* video before morning. I was still fighting to put a clean nappy on Alfie, but he wouldn't keep still. The lotion I'd been trying to smear on his red bottom had landed on the front of the nappy, where the sticky tape goes, so the nappy wouldn't hold together. I cast it aside and decided to start again, looking around to see where I had put the pack. It was now that Alfie chose to urinate. A great arc of wee shot up over his head, as if someone had suddenly turned on the garden sprinkler. I attempted to catch the last few drops with the old nappy, but it was a pointless exercise as he had already sprayed most of it in all directions and now his vest and babygro were both soaked.

Millie was now emphasizing her repeated proposal that she

watch the *Barney* video by hitting me on the arm every time she said it. I was unaware that in her other hand she was clutching a bright-red wooden building block, and at that moment her other arm swung round and she hit me full in the face with it. The sharp corner caught me just above the eye. The pain shot through me, and in a flash of temper I picked her up and threw her too roughly onto the bed and she banged the back of her head on the wooden headboard. Now she was really screaming. Frightened by the volume of his sister's cries, or maybe just out of a sense of sibling solidarity, Alfie started screaming at full pitch as well. Almost panicking, I tried covering his mouth with my hand to shut him up, but unsurprisingly this didn't make him more relaxed and he spluttered and wriggled his head and I backed off. And then I felt fear and shame that the boiling sense of anger and frustration within me could have been capable of covering the baby's mouth completely and holding it there until he was completely silent and still.

I left them both to scream and turned and punched my pillow as hard as I could, and then I punched it again and again, and I shouted, 'WHY DON'T YOU FUCKING SHUT UP! WHY DON'T YOU JUST LET ME GO TO FUCKING SLEEP!' And I looked up and saw that Catherine was standing in the doorway surveying the scene.

She had that look on her face that suggested I wasn't coping very well. She picked up Millie and told her that she was taking her straight back to bed, and because of some special code that she must have used, Millie accepted this state of affairs.

'I was just going to do that,' I said unconvincingly. 'Why can't you just let me deal with things *my* way?' She didn't reply. 'You're supposed to be getting some sleep,' I shouted after her as a defiant afterthought, as if she had got up and wandered into a perfectly normal situation.

'Did Alfie's crying wake Millie up?' she asked me directly when she came back in.

'Yeah. I mean, I got straight up and everything, but he was just inconsolable.'

'Oh great, she'll be really ratty tomorrow.' She gave an irritated sigh, and then I noticed that she'd come in with a warmed bottle of milk for the baby. 'Why hasn't Alfie had his bottle?'

'It wasn't time.'

'It's three o'clock.'

'Yes, it's time *now*, but it wasn't time when he started crying. You said not to feed him before it was time. I was only doing what you said.'

Catherine picked up Alfie from where I had changed him and popped the plastic teat of the bottle into his mouth.

'*I'll* feed him,' I protested. 'I said I'd do it tonight. You go to bed and go to sleep.' She handed me the baby and the bottle and, instead of returning to the sofa bed downstairs, climbed into our double bed, where she could spend her break from feeding Alfie in the middle of the night watching me feed Alfie in the middle of the night.

'Don't hold it right up like that or he won't take it,' she heckled from the sidelines. Because of the tone in which she told me this information I felt compelled to ignore her and sure enough the baby wriggled and started to cry.

'What are you doing? Why do you deliberately do it wrong?'

'I wasn't doing it deliberately.'

'Give him to me,' and she got out of bed and took the baby and I sulkily climbed under the covers and sat there, angry and indignant, as she gave the bottle to Alfie. The baby sucked rhythmically and happily, comfortable and relaxed in his mother's arms, and when the sucking began to slow as Alfie fell into a stupefied sleep, Catherine would gently tap the soles of his feet to stir him. It was as if those tiny podgy feet had a little secret button that only Catherine knew about which made the head end start feeding properly. And even though I was lying there feeling injured and resentful, there was a little part of me that thought it was marvellous that she knew how to do that.

She eventually resumed her place in bed beside me and I decided against pressing the point that I could cope perfectly well on my own.

'I've only had an hour and a half's sleep,' I moaned, in the hope of some sympathy.

'That's more than I've had recently,' she parried.

Now the baby was fed, changed and warm. Now, surely he would sleep. We lay together, stiffly and silently, both knowing that the other was listening for the first grating moan to come from the pram. Like patients reclining on a dentist's chair, it was impossible to relax because we were waiting for that moment when the drill hits the tooth – the first fretful cry that told us the baby's pitiful precipitation was beginning again. When it came I said nothing, but I felt Catherine flinch beside me. It was nobody's turn to get up and so, as the moans grew more regular and insistent, neither of us moved from our hopelessly optimistic sleeping positions, like a couple trying to sunbathe in the pouring rain.

'Let's just try leaving him,' I said as the cry broke into full-blown wailing.

'I can't do that when you're working and I'm here on my own.'

'Well, I'm here tonight, so this can be the night that he learns we won't always go running to him.'

'I can't.'

'Just till the clock says three fifty.'

I said that at 3:42. I got up to close the door so that Millie would not be woken up again. Catherine said nothing, but lay there facing the glowing digital display on the radio alarm as the baby bawled its tightly wound, breathless cries.

After what seemed an age – 3:43 – Catherine angrily put the pillow over her head. I think it must have been intended to demonstrate something to me because I noticed her lift it slightly above her ear so that she could still listen to Alfie crying. I had thought the baby's volume needle was already on the red line, that his little lungs and tinny voice box could not produce any more power, but at 3:44 the screaming suddenly went into quadraphonic hypersound, doubling in power, anger and volume. If it had been a *son et lumière* this would have been the moment when the fireworks went off and the chorus all stood up. How could he suddenly find such energy? Where did he get the stamina and strength of purpose from at that time of the night when we, his parents, with twenty times his weight and strength, had been ready to throw in the towel hours ago? Now I understood why mothers used to worry that the big metal nappy pin must have come unclasped and was piercing the flesh of the baby's thigh, because that was the extreme level of pain Alfie was expressing. Even I was worried that he must have a safety pin sticking right through his skin, and we used disposable nappies.

The furious bawling continued throughout 3:45, still at full pitch, but there was a gear change that produced shorter, more erratic noises. They were taut, painful, bewildered cries that screamed, 'Mother, Mother, why hast thou forsaken me?' And though her back was turned to me, I guessed that by now Catherine was probably crying, too. I had tried to make her leave the baby to cry in the first few months when she had still been breastfeeding. As the baby wailed, Catherine had sat up in bed with tears pouring down her cheeks and Pavlovian milk spraying out from her bosoms. At that point I had suggested she go and get the baby. I was

68

worried that one way or another she might dehydrate completely.

If she was crying now I'd feel as if I had caused it. Now I was the torturer; I had brought this poor mother to a darkened room in the middle of the night and forced her to listen to her own baby screaming and writhing in apparent agony. Though the cries maddened and infuriated me, they didn't break my heart as I sensed they did hers. It was clear how much it hurt her to listen to it, but I couldn't feel what she was feeling. I was able to step back from it, to close off the side of my brain that was aware that our baby was unhappy, and now I was forcing Catherine to try and do the same. I was trying to make her be more like a man. Perhaps this was my subconscious revenge. In the daytime she made me feel that I should be more like a woman, that I should instinctively understand all the moods and needs of the baby in the way that she did. The daylight hours were definitely hers. But now, at night, it was my turn. I had made her read the bits of the books that agreed with me; I had shown her written proof of what I kept saying to her: that she shouldn't rush straight to the baby every time it cried, that she had to try and steel herself, to lash herself to the mast and endure her baby's sobbing while it learned to fall asleep on its own. But though she was prepared to entertain the abstract theory of this idea, it was something she could never implement in practice.

Here at last was an aspect of parenting that I was better at than her. Here was something that I could do and she could not. I suppose there's an irony that my particular area of expertise involved leaving the baby to cry in its pram, but I needed something to feel good about and this was it. I was better at lying there and doing nothing than she was. This reversal of power was a subtle one and might even have gone unnoticed if it hadn't been highlighted, so at 3:46 I gently and sympathetically asked her if she was coping all right.

'Yes,' she snapped, irritated at being patronized.

'I know it's hard,' I went on in my most consoling and understanding voice, 'but soon you'll be glad I made you do it.'

She said nothing, so I drove the point home. 'Try and be strong; it's for baby's good as well in the long run.'

Then a grossly unfair thing happened. She agreed with me. 'I know,' she said. 'You're right; we've got to win this.'

'What?' I said, in consternation.

'We can't go on like this every night; the baby making me an exhausted wreck. We have to take control.'

This wasn't what I was expecting at all. I had thought she was about to leap out of bed and run to the baby and say, 'I'm sorry, Michael, I'm just not as strong as you. I can't help it; I'm sorry.'

I tried to cling on to my superior status as tough paternal supervisor. 'I don't mind, if you really feel you have to go to him.'

'No!' she said insistently. 'We've got to be strong.'

'You're very brave, Catherine, but I know you want to go and pick him up.'

'No, I'm not going to. We're going to win this.'

'Do you want me to pick him up for you?'

'Don't you dare! Leave him to cry.'

And I just lay there listening to the baby wailing, and with my last scrap of pride and status taken from me, I felt like joining in.

Alfie did learn to send himself off to sleep, and we felt a sense of triumph and achievement, as if a milestone had been reached. An hour later it seemed that he had forgotten the lesson completely and needed to learn it all over again. We took turns to push the pram up and down the bedroom, we diagnosed colic and wind and every other ailment we'd read about on the tatty noticeboard at the health centre. Then we suddenly panicked that he might be crying so much because he had meningitis, and I ran downstairs and got the torch. If the baby shows an aversion to bright light, that's a definite symptom of meningitis, and sure enough, to our utter dismay, this baby that had been lying in a darkened room all night recoiled from having a 200-watt torch shone in his face. Meningitis is a killer; it's infectious. What if Millie had it as well? We ran into her bedroom and shook her awake in order to shine my super-powered spotlight into her eyes. She recoiled as well. And drowsiness, that's another symptom. Both our children had meningitis! A disorientated Millie was placed in front of the telly while we quickly looked up the other symptoms in the book – headache, temperature, stiffness of the neck. Neither of them seemed to be suffering any of these. And then we realized that if Millie was happy to stare at the light coming out of a television screen then she couldn't have meningitis.

'Come on, Millie. Off to bed.'

'But I'm watching Barney.'

'You know you're not allowed to watch television at night time.'

Her bottom lip stuck out and she started to cry, and we couldn't help but be aware that there was perhaps a slight injustice to shaking a child awake at five o'clock in the morning and putting her in front of the television, only to tell her she wasn't allowed to watch television. So I spent the hour before dawn sitting up with Millie, watching a giant cuddly green and purple dinosaur being hugged by a lot of sickly American children.

Breakfast was tense. It didn't require Catherine's morning sickness to make it tense, but the sound of her throwing up didn't particularly lighten the mood. By this stage we were both so irritably irrational that I was convinced she was just affecting the vomiting to try and demonstrate that she felt worse than I did. These were the times when we needed some space apart, when I needed to go and hide out in my cave. Catherine's father had converted the shed at the bottom of the garden into a little office, which was his private refuge, where he could sit in quiet, peaceful meditation, planning the next massacre of the woodlice. But I had the whole of South London to myself. Having been born and brought up in North London, Catherine would be no more inclined to travel to the depths of Balham than she would consider trekking to Kazakhstan. She had a vague idea of where both of them probably were, but she could not begin to contemplate what sort of visas, maps and local guides you would need to get to such places.

It would have been better if I'd headed across the river there and then; Catherine would be a lot happier once I was out of the way. But there were a few practicalities that had to be sorted out first: I wanted to at least mix the babymilk, then I had to find my phone charger, gather a few things together in my holdall and then we had to have a full-blown marital row. It was approaching with all the depressing inevitability of a Cliff Richard Christmas single.

'Level it off with a knife,' she said as I measured out the milk powder.

'What?'

'You're supposed to level the spoonfuls off with a knife, so you get exactly the right amount.'

'Catherine, what is the worst that could happen if the babymilk is fractionally stronger or weaker? Will Alfie get food poisoning? Will he die of starvation?'

'You only have to follow the instructions,' she said, prickling.

'You mean I only have to follow *your* instructions. Why

72

can't you just trust me to measure out a few poxy spoons of babymilk without watching me like a bloody hawk?'

And then we were off. The fight was nobody's fault, it was just the unavoidable collision of an exhausted couple cooped up together in a poky little house, like battery hens locked up for too long in the same tiny cage. But before long all our anger and frustration was being clumsily knocked back and forth. I hurled obscenities at her and she threw a large paperback at me. It was a book called *The Caring Parent* and it flew straight past me and hit Millie on her leg. Millie looked rather bemused and carried on playing, but I made such a meal of my sympathy for her that she decided perhaps she ought to cry after all, and then I was able to give Catherine a hateful glare and say, 'Look what you've done.' Then, to emphasize who was the caring parent in this marriage, I comforted our distraught toddler by sitting her down to read her a Beatrix Potter book.

'You naughty kittens, you have lost your mittens,' said Mrs Tabitha Twitchet. Then the cuddly pussy cat apparently added, 'You're always so fucking moody, aren't you? You're the only woman who ever managed to be pre-menstrual twenty-eight days a fucking month.' Millie looked as if she didn't remember this bit from the book, but then looked reassured when I continued, 'Just then, three puddle-ducks marched by . . .'

The argument followed its usual symphonic narrative, each movement building on the last. Catherine said that I never told her anything, that I never talked to her about my work or what I was up to. I told her that whatever I did with the children it was always wrong, that she would never permit me the dignity of just doing things my own way. I was shaking now. I couldn't look at her, so I angrily busied myself by washing up some plastic plates, focusing my pent-up anger on domestic work. I suddenly realized that Catherine had already washed them, but I carried on anyway, hoping she wouldn't notice.

'I've already washed those plates,' she said.

Eventually she told me to fuck off back to work, and I made an unconvincing job of saying I'd been planning to hang around a bit longer to help her.

'What's the point?' she said as I put my jacket on. 'I've got to go out anyway, walk to the shops, buy some more babymilk, take Millie to playgroup, blah, blah, blah. It's all so bloody *boring*,' she said.

'But it doesn't have to be boring. I got you that Sony Walkman so that you can listen to Radio 4 when you take the kids to the swings, and you hardly ever use it.'

'It doesn't work like that, Michael. You can't just provide instant answers to my problems like they're a bloody trivia question. I don't want you to try and stop me being bored. I just wish sometimes you could be bored *with* me.'

This was such a strange concept to me that I was completely lost for words. She wanted me to be bored with her. The woman who had the greatest sense of fun of anyone I had ever met. The woman who had told a Dutch hitch-hiker that I was completely deaf and then spent the next hour trying to make me laugh by telling him how useless I was in bed. I wanted that Catherine back; I wanted to rescue her from the body-snatchers and go back to the days when all we had wanted was to spend every second of the day together. Now we were like a couple of magnets, one side drew us together and the other side forced us apart. Alternately attracting and repelling, adoring and then resenting.

It was just as I went to leave that she hit me with another body blow. 'Michael, I don't mind the fact that you're never here, but I do mind the fact that you don't *want* to be here.'

How did she have the time to lie awake and think of lines like that?

Attack was my only possible form of defence. 'That is *so* unfair,' I snapped, raising my voice to give the impression that now she had really overstepped the mark. 'You think I choose to be away from the kids this much? You think I don't rush home to see them as soon as I can? You think I don't go to bed feeling miserable at three in the morning because I'm not going to see them wake up? I can't see them as much as you do because I have to go out to work. I have to work all day and night to pay for a wife and two children and a mortgage we can barely afford. And when you want a dishwasher, the money is magically there, or new clothes or a holiday or a stupid bidet that cost four hundred pounds but is only used as a receptacle for storing plastic bath toys. The money is always there, and it's there because I work so hard for it.'

I was genuinely fired up now, and Catherine seemed at a loss for words.

'It's not easy, you know, going to my studio exhausted, then working thirty-six hours at a stretch to get compositions ready by their deadlines, writing one piece while pitching for another, working non-stop on my own in a cramped studio on the other side of town, crashing out on a lonely bed so that I can get up and carry straight on with it. But I have to do it so that we can afford to have a decent standard of living, so that we can feed and clothe our children, so that we can afford to all keep on living in this house. I have to work this hard because it's the only way we can stay afloat.'

I picked up my holdall and strode angrily towards the front door for a triumphant exit. Lying on the doormat was an envelope the shape and size of which I had come to recognize. I snatched it up and stuffed it in my bag. I didn't need to open it to know what it said. It was another warning letter from our bank. They wanted to know why the mortgage had not been paid for four months.

chapter four

because I'm worth it

One way or another I was always going to be woken up by children. My radio alarm said 3:31 and for a moment I wasn't sure if it was morning or afternoon, but the noise of kids being picked up from over the road convinced me it must be p.m. Your kids would have to be pretty hyperactive for you to leave them at school till half-past three in the morning. Although I had once again broken my own record for sleeping in, I still felt like I needed another twelve hours. When you've been deprived of any proper shut-eye for days, a massive shot of sleep only makes you crave it all the more. All that rest had drained me, now I was tired and groggy, as if emerging from a general anaesthetic. How Sleeping Beauty managed to sit up with such a twinkly smile after a hundred years was a mystery to me. I pulled the duvet over my head and tried to drift off again.

Hedgehogs; they had the right idea, I thought. When they felt the time was right to have a massive kip they just found themselves a huge pile of sticks and leaves and crawled inside. Obviously it was a shame that this generally happened to be around 5 November, but the basic principle was a sound one. Why couldn't humans hibernate, I wondered. We could turn in at the end of October, sleep right through Christmas and the New Year, and finally get up, having set the radio alarm for some time in mid-March. If it was still raining we could press the snooze button and lie in for another couple of weeks, just getting up to catch the end of the football season. Right, I thought, I'm going to try and do that right now. Nope, no good, I was wide awake. I sat up and clicked on the kettle.

I remembered all that spare sleep I'd had when I was sixteen, seventeen, eighteen. I'd spent it so recklessly. If only I could have put it in a sleep bank, saved up for a sleep pension later in life. 'Michael! Get out of bed,' my mother used to shout up the stairs at me. We spend the first few years trying to get our children to stay in bed and then, before we know it, we're trying to get them out again. It's hard to think of a period when we actually get our sleep right. Small children wake up too early, teenagers don't wake up at all, new parents don't get any sleep because of the noise their children make, and then a few years later they can't get to sleep because now there's no noise of their children returning home at night. Then, when we get old, we start waking up as early as we did when we were toddlers, until finally we fall asleep for ever. Sounds quite attractive sometimes, except they'll probably bury me next to some nursery school and I'll be woken from the dead by kids screaming and crying and jumping on top of me at all hours.

I made myself a cup of tea and switched on the television, flicking around, trying to find some commercials to watch. As always there were far too many programmes between the adverts. First up was an inspired interpretation of George Gershwin's 'Summertime' – a Paul Robeson soundalike sang, 'Somerfield . . . and the shopping is easy. Lots of parking, and the prices ain't high.' The next ad was for a shampoo, in which a French footballer told us why he used L'Oréal. 'Because I'm worth it,' he said. That's why I'm still in bed at half-past three in the afternoon, I thought, because I'm worth it. Because I can, and because there's no harm in it. Then there was an advert for a building society which said, 'Remember your home is at risk if you do not keep up repayments' and I quickly switched channels. I'd pay off my overdue mortgage payments soon enough. It would mean a few months of working as hard as Catherine thought I did all the time, but I estimated that I could clear the backlog before the baby was born.

My thoughts had strayed back to our unborn baby as I watched an *Open University* programme on BBC2. It was about some nutty institute in California where pregnant women went to have algebraic formulae and quotes from Shakespeare shouted down a tube pressed against their bumps. Apparently the foetus spends much of its time in the womb asleep, but they're even trying to stop that now. 'It's never too early to start learning things,' said the teacher. Like the fact that your parents are completely mad.

But that must be the soundest sleep of all, I thought, tucked up tight inside that dark, heated waterbed, with the muffled heartbeat hypnotically pattering away, before all the worries of the outside world start to churn over in your subconscious. Everything provided; no need to leave the comfort and security of your fleshy nest. Was that what this was all about? Was my secret refuge in deepest South London an attempt to return to the comforting simplicity I'd enjoyed in the nine months before I was born? I lay down again and curled my naked body into the foetal position, and realized that was how I naturally preferred to fall asleep. My dark, cosy little hideaway had everything my first sleeping place had had. Not literally, obviously; my mother's uterus hadn't had a large poster of the Ramones stuck up with Blu-tack, but practically and spiritually speaking, this little den was an artificial womb of my own. An umbilical cord of tangled electrical leads hung down beside the bed – the electric blanket that brought me warmth, the kettle lead that provided my fluids, the fridge cord for nutrition. The drumbeat from Jim's stereo pulsated rhythmically through the wall and the daylight that seeped through the red patterned curtains gave a veiny pink effect to my window on the outside world. The only way to escape from the tyranny of babies had been to regress into a prenatal state myself.

I told myself I shouldn't feel guilty that I sometimes found my family so oppressive. I reassured myself that what I was doing was no worse than the behaviour of the rest of the men of my generation. Some fathers stayed at work far longer than they really needed to. Some fathers worked all week and then played golf all weekend. Some fathers came home and went straight to their computers for the rest of the evening. These men were not there for their wives and families any more than I was, but at least I wasn't deceiving myself about it. The simple fact was that, for the time being, everyone was better off if I wasn't at home all the time. The problem was that the less I was there, the worse I was at it, and the less I seemed to want to be there.

In all the adverts that I'd arranged the music for, the families always had such fun; they always looked so comfortable with each other. Even though I worked in the industry I still hadn't seen through the lies. Obviously I knew that Lite 'n' lo wasn't really a delicious alternative to butter, but it hadn't occurred to me that they were also lying about the happy smiling kids and parents laughing round the breakfast table together. If that had been my childhood, then the mum would have picked up the butter knife and threatened to stab the dad with it.

The adverts told us we could have it all, we could be great dads and still go off snowboarding and earn lots of money and pop out of the business meeting to tell our children a bedtime story on the mobile phone. But it can't be done. Work, family and self; it's an impossible Rubik's Cube. You can't be a hands-on, sensitive father and a tough, high-earning businessman and a pillar of your local community and a handy do-it-yourself Mr Fixit and a romantic, attentive husband – something has to give. In my case, everything.

But on top of all this, I had another reason for not wanting to spend hours and hours with my children just yet. It was something that no mother or father was brave enough to admit, a guilty secret that I suspected we all shared but dared not mention for fear of being thought bad parents:

Small children are boring.

We all pretend that we find every little nuance of our off-spring wonderful and fascinating, but we're all lying to ourselves. Small children are boring; it's the tedium that dare not speak its name. I want to come out of the closet and stand on top of the tallest climbing frame in the country and pro-claim to the world, 'Small children are boring.' All the other parents would look shocked and offended as they pushed their toddler up and down on the seesaw for the one hundredth time, but secretly they would feel a huge sense of relief that they weren't alone. And all the guilt they had felt because they secretly hated spending the entire mind-numbing day with their little two-year-olds would suddenly be lifted when they realized they weren't bad, unloving parents; there was nothing wrong with them, it was their children. Their children were boring.

Tolerating tedium is not something I'd ever had to do before. If I wasn't enjoying a holiday I would come home. If I was bored by a video I would fast forward it a bit. I wished I could just point the remote control at the kids and fast forward them a couple of years; I knew they would be more interesting by the time they got to four or five. Catherine was more patient than me; she didn't mind waiting a few years to see a return on all that time and love she was investing.

I wandered into the toilet and drowsily went to lift the seat, until I remembered that, in this household, it was always already up. I tried not to think about Catherine. This was supposed to be my time off. My urine had the sulphurous musty smell that reminded me I had eaten asparagus the night before. Catherine had cooked my dinner and she knew I loved asparagus. Even my wee reminded me of her.

I guessed that today, like most days, she would be seeing one of the mothers she had met through Millie's playgroup. Catherine had described all the various species of mums to me. There was the guilty career mother, who was so over-enthusiastic on the one day she was able to come along to playgroup that she completely drowned out everyone else singing, 'The wheels on the bus go round and round.' There was the born-again stay-at-home mother who had previously been a very successful businesswoman, but had then thrown herself into motherhood with exactly the same competitive ambition. Instead of being promoted on a regular basis she just had another baby every year, which she felt allowed her to feel superior to all the women around her. There was the mother of Satan, who was totally unaware that she had given birth to the most evil being in the universe and blithely chatted away to you while her two-year-old kept smacking your child in the face and then casually remarked, 'Aaaah. They seem to be getting on well together.' Then there was the eco-mum, who talked quietly and gently to her child about why he shouldn't talk with his mouth full as the four-year-old sucked away at her breast.

Catherine had befriended all of them. I was constantly impressed by how women made friends with each other so easily. When I was in the playground I found myself engaging in an elaborate paternal dance in which I subtly tried to steer my kids away from the other children being supervised by their dads, lest the two of us should be forced into the embarrassment of actually attempting small talk. Even if communication became unavoidable, we would still not speak to each other directly, but would employ our children as a third party. So if Millie was deliberately blocking the slide, my way of apologizing to the other father would be to say loudly, 'Come down the slide, Millie, and let this little girl have a go.'

The other father would let me know that it was all right by replying, 'Don't push the little girl, Ellie. Let her go down when she's ready.' And no eye contact between the two adult males would ever have to be made. While somewhere over on the other side of the playground, his wife and mine were already discussing how soon they'd had sexual intercourse after giving birth.

Now I found myself socializing with all the new couples we had met through our children. Catherine and the mothers chatted and chatted, our children were the same age and played happily together and the other fathers and I would have nothing in common whatsoever. The previous Sunday I had found myself forced to talk to a man called Piers who relaxed at the weekend by wearing a blazer.

'So, Michael, how do you find the handling on the Astra?'

He'd noticed that Catherine and I had driven to their house in a Vauxhall Astra and evidently thought this would be a good opening subject for a conversation.

'The handling? Well, er, do you know, I've never really understood what that means. What is the handling, exactly? Because for years I thought it was something to do with what sort of handles you had on the doors, but it's not, is it?'

Piers looked at me as if I was mentally retarded and took

another glug from his personalized beer tankard before he took the trouble to illuminate me. 'How does it hold the road?'

So that was what it meant. What a completely bizarre concept. Piers was asking me how our family car 'held the road'. Gravity; that's how it held the road. That can't be the right answer, I thought to myself. So what was it that I had failed to notice about my car? It did everything I asked it to. When I turned the wheel to the left the car went to the left, when I turned the wheel to the right the car went to the right.

'Fine,' I said. 'Pretty good actually. Yeah, the handling on the old Astra's pretty good.'

'What have you got, the SXi or the 1.4 LS or what?'

'Hmm?'

'The Astra. What model is it?'

I wanted to say, Look, I don't know or care what fucking model it is, all right? It's a car. It's got two baby seats in the back and lots of stains from spilt Ribena cartons on the upholstery, and there's a tape of Disney singalong songs permanently stuck in the cassette player.

'Er, well, I don't know that much about the technical side of cars really,' I said pathetically, and Piers regarded me as if I'd just been introduced into Western society from a remote tribe in Papua New Guinea.

'Well, it's pretty straightforward – is it fuel injected or not? That's what the "i" stands for: "injection".'

There was a pause. Every day I had opened the boot of the car, but I couldn't remember which letters I'd seen there. SXi sounded quite possible, but then so did LS. Which one was it? I had to say something.

'Millie, don't snatch!' I blurted out and ran to take a doll from Millie that Piers's daughter had just willingly handed her.

'But she gave it me,' said Millie, looking confused.

'Really, Millie. Try and play nicely. Come on, let's ask little Hermione to show us all the toys in her bedroom.' And I went upstairs with a couple of two-year-old girls, glancing back at the other dad with a mock long-suffering 'kids, eh?' expression and then I hid in the child's bedroom for forty minutes rather than attempt to continue any conversations with the grown-ups downstairs.

'She's really nice, isn't she?' said Catherine as we drove away three hours later. 'I invited them to lunch at our place next weekend.'

She heard my world-weary sigh and said, 'That's what I like about you, Michael. For you there are no strangers, only friends you haven't taken a dislike to yet.'

It was all right for her. The women were always nice; it was just their husbands who were made out of cardboard. She weaved the car in and out of the demonic traffic on Camden Road.

'How do you find the handling on the Astra?' I asked her. 'What?'

'This car, the Astra. How do you find the handling on it?'

'What are you talking about, you boring bastard?'

I felt reassured that I had definitely married the right woman.

I could never see any friendships developing out of the families Catherine met at Millie's playgroup, although I was slightly put out when I learned that Piers and several of the other dads had gone for a drink together one Sunday evening and I hadn't even been offered the chance not to be friends. I chose my mates in the same way as I chose what clothes to wear. In the morning, my jeans and sweatshirt were there on the chair by the bed, so I made do with those. And then, sitting in the chairs in the next room of my flat were Simon, Paul and Jim, and so I spent the rest of my day with them. It wasn't a question of what I liked or what suited me, it was just whatever was most convenient. Male friends seemed to just drift into my life, and then drift out again when the reason for seeing them had passed. I'd often worked with blokes I'd really liked and we had gone to the pub together or whatever. We had probably meant to keep in touch, but you can't just phone someone up two months later and say, 'So, do you fancy just going for a drink?' They might say they couldn't make it that night and then you'd look stupid.

So at the moment my best friends were the other three men in this flat.

'All right?' I muttered as I wandered into the living room.

'All right,' they all mumbled back.

It was great to catch up on all their news. I read an out-of-date tabloid for a while. There was a story about a married couple in France who were both over a hundred years old but were now getting a divorce. They were asked why they were separating after so long. Apparently they'd wanted to wait until all their kids had died.

Since it was the Easter holidays, neither Paul nor Simon had to go into work and so all four of us were left hanging around the flat with nothing to do. It was fascinating to watch the other three wasting time as if they would have the luxury for ever. They were so much better at doing nothing than I was; they didn't work so hard at being lazy. Jim was stretched out on the sofa and had apparently spent the last three hours trying to work out how his palm top could save him time. Paul was pointedly reading a grown-up newspaper, while Simon was sitting at the kitchen table doing nothing at all. He often did this. It was as if he was waiting for something. Waiting to lose his virginity, Jim said.

Simon had learned the secret of eternal adolescence. There were times when he was so awkward and self-conscious that he was unable to talk in normal phrases and sentences. He had developed a whole parallel mode of communication which was expressed purely in trivia questions. Today, instead of saying, 'Hello there, Michael, I haven't seen you around for a few days,' he gave a little excited smile and chirped up with, 'Capital of New York state?'

'Albany,' I dutifully replied, and he gave out a little satisfied grunt to suggest that all was well with the world.

'B-side "Bohemian Rhapsody"?' he continued.

'"I'm in Love With My Car". You won't get me on a piece of music trivia. It happens to be my specialist subject.'

'OK, so which line from "Bohemian Rhapsody" was the title of a song that reached number one in the same year?'

I was thrown into a mild internal panic at hearing a music question I didn't know. 'Get lost. You just made that up.'

'No, it's a well-known fact,' chipped in Jim.

I tried affecting indifference. 'Oh, I don't know, er, "Scaramouche, Scaramouche" by Will Doo and the Fandangos.'

'No.'

'That only got to number two,' said Jim.

Inside, my mind was racing through the lyrics of 'Bohemian Rhapsody', trying to find the title of another 1975 number one. There wasn't one, I was sure of it.

'Do you give up?'

'No, of course I don't give up.' But I decided that instead of wasting any more time I would go into my room and do a bit of work. An hour later I came out and said, 'I give up.'

'The answer is, "Mamma Mia!"' Simon informed me triumphantly.

I was stunned. It wasn't fair. I would have got it if I'd given myself a bit longer. 'You said a line. That's not a line, that's just a phrase. It doesn't count.'

'All hail, the trivia king,' said Simon with his arms held aloft.

An outsider might be impressed by just how much Simon knew. He knew that the Battle of Malplaquet was in 1709 and that the Dodo had lived on the island of Mauritius. However, on the debit side, he did not know the answer to questions like, What are you going to do for a living? He did not know that his parents were rather worried about him or how on earth he was ever going to get a girlfriend. He did not even know that he was a bit smelly. Fortunately, the question, Is Simon a bit smelly? had never come up in the science and nature category in Trivial Pursuit, although, if it had, he would have been far more distressed about getting a trivia question wrong than he would have been to learn that everyone thought he stank like a soggy PE kit that had been left in its bag all through the summer holidays.

Paul had remained aloof from the quiz, but when the final answer was revealed he just said, 'That's right, yes,' and nodded wisely. Perhaps he was unable to take part himself because all his energy was required to pull off the near impossible task of reading a newspaper in an annoying way. When he held up the paper it was not in order to read the articles, it was to declare, 'Look at me, I'm reading a broadsheet.' The silence would be punctuated with affirmative grunts when he wanted us to know that he agreed with the editorial, or slightly too audible tuts when he read some distressing news from the Third World. The cryptic crossword was completed with an almost constant running commentary of satisfied verbal ticks and world-weary sighs.

'Are you doing the crossword, Paul?'

'What? Oh, yeah. Nearly finished it actually,' he replied gratefully, unaware that Jim was gently mocking him.

'Is that the easy or the hard one you're doing?'

'The cryptic crossword. I don't bother with the other one.'

'Wow!' said Jim.

*

The late afternoon eventually turned into early evening and Paul started to become edgy and restless, as he usually did around this time.

'Has anyone given any thought to dinner?' said the person who always ended up cooking dinner. There was mild surprise that anyone should be thinking about food before it was actually time to eat. Jim looked at his watch.

'I'm not really hungry yet . . .'

'Well, no, but you have to buy the food and cook it *before* you are hungry so that it's ready at about the same time as you are.'

Indifferent silence filled the room.

'Well?' said Paul finally, standing by an empty fridge.

'Well, what?' said Jim.

'What shall we have for dinner?'

'Erm, well, it's a bit early for me, thanks.'

'I'm not offering to cook again. I am asking if anyone else has thought about cooking for once?'

The silence was too much for me and I was the first to crack. 'All right, Paul, don't worry, I'll do the dinner. I'll go and get some fish and chips or something.'

'That's not cooking the dinner, that's getting fish and chips. I don't want fish and chips.'

'Indian?' I offered magnanimously, considering that the curry house was another fifty yards' walk.

'Why can't we have proper fresh food cooked freshly here in our kitchen?'

There was another silence while no-one volunteered for such an enormous undertaking. Jim contemplated standing over a cooker for twenty minutes and then said exhaustedly, 'I don't mind fish and chips, Michael.'

'Me neither,' echoed Simon.

'OK, fish and chips for three then,' I confirmed.

'Well, if you're all going to have a takeaway, I'll just

have to cook myself some pasta or something on my own.'

There was a moment's pause in which I could sense Jim's mouth watering at the mention of one of Paul's amazing pasta dishes.

'Oh well, if you're cooking some pasta for yourself, Paul, could you do enough for me, too?'

Paul was trying to find the words to express why that didn't feel fair, but he wasn't given time.

'Yeah, I'll have some of that,' said Simon.

'Oh cheers, Paul,' I said.

Somehow, four men living in a flat together had evolved into a traditional nuclear family. I don't know how it happened, or whether this metamorphosis occurs in every group of people that live together for a while, but we had inadvertently turned ourselves into mum, dad and two kids.

I suppose I was the eldest son, vague, secretive and quiet, who couldn't get up in the mornings on the days when I hadn't stayed out all night. Simon was the youngest child, gauche and unconfident, constantly asking questions to seek attention. Paul was the martyred, long-suffering mum, fussing and worrying for everyone else. And Jim was dad, self-possessed, lazy, mysterious and funny. The confidence that had been purchased at public school gave him a benevolent paternal air which we all looked up to, although sometimes I felt a little uncomfortable having a father figure six years younger than myself.

When I was a child I didn't understand where my dad's money came from, it was just something he always seemed to have, and the same was true of Jim. The only money problem Jim had was spending it all. He bought mini-discs to replace all the CDs that had replaced all his vinyl records. He bought electrical gadgets and designer penknives and new mobile-phone covers. We presumed the money must come from his family, but we were all too polite and English to probe any further when he mumbled evasive answers to comments about his conspicuous wealth.

He had a first-class degree in Italian and Geography, although the only thing he appeared to remember was that Italy was shaped like a boot. He then decided that a Ph.D might be useful, and he was quite right; it saved him any embarrassment when people asked him what he did. Jim was doing a Ph.D, and would be doing it until the day he died. Procrastination would have been his middle name if he could ever have been bothered to get that far. And he would constantly drive Paul mad with his failure to commit to any sort of plan or pre-arrangement. On a Saturday morning Paul might suggest, 'Do you fancy going to the National Film Theatre or something today?'

And in his posh, laid-back way, Jim would shrug in-differently and say, 'Well, let's just see what happens.'

Paul would then go quiet for a while, anxious not to blow his jittery up-tight cover, but when he tried to pitch the idea again, he couldn't help but show the annoyance in his voice.

'Well, nothing will happen unless we get up and do it. Going to the NFT won't just happen to us, we'd have to go down to the South Bank, buy the tickets, go in and sit down. So do you fancy going to the NFT?' asked Paul again, adding, 'or something?' as an affected nonchalant afterthought.

'Well, let's just see how the day shakes down.'

'The day can't shake down! The day is passive! The day is not going to turn up with a taxi and four tickets to see *The Maltese* fucking *Falcon*,' Paul would finally scream. And then Jim would say, All right, keep your hair on, and we'd all tell him to cool it and chill out and we're just hanging out, all right, and he'd storm off and come back an hour later with all the household groceries, including pretzels, olives and fancy Czech lager, which he knew we all really liked.

It really wasn't fair that everyone liked Jim and nobody liked Paul. Paul was a teacher in a tough London school; overworked, underpaid and undervalued. Jim was an idle, privileged Trustafarian, living off inherited money and doing nothing with the huge head start that life had given him. But despite this, I still preferred Jim to Paul, because the rich layabout had a sense of humour and the impoverished public servant did not. Jim made me laugh, and shamefully this was enough to make me forgive him anything. If I had been born in fifteenth-century Wallachia, I probably would have defended Vlad the Impaler on the grounds that he was quite witty on occasion. 'All right, I grant you, he does impale quite a lot of peasants, but you can't help liking the bloke. I mean, getting the carpenter who makes his sharpened stakes to do one extra spike "as a surprise for someone" and then impaling him on it, OK, you could argue it was a bit mean, but hats off, it was a great gag.'

Within the complex dynamics of the household was the added musical alliance between Jim and me. We had quite similar tastes in music, although he had this slightly irritating affectation that he liked jazz. I had no time for jazz. Music is a journey; jazz is getting lost. Jim's laziness hadn't prevented him from becoming a rather accomplished guitar player, and the two of us had combined to form our very own super-group, pooled from the enormous wealth of musical talent that was available to us within the four walls of the top flat, 140 Balham High Road, London SW12.

One day, Jim had said, a new rock pilgrimage would be added to the hallowed destinations of Graceland and the Cavern. Rocks fans will flock to this legendary address and stop in quiet contemplation, for it was here, in those early days, that two musicians struggled against the odds to create what became known the world over as 'the sound of Balham'.

It was, of course, many years since I had truly believed I

was ever going to make it as a pop star. Two things are certain in the world of rock music. One is that image is more important than talent, and the other is that in the year 2525 they will re-release the single 'In the Year 2525'. I was now approaching my mid-thirties and my girth was expanding as fast as my hair was receding. It was hard to imagine anyone who looked less like Kylie Minogue. I knew the pop industry wouldn't be interested in a fat old dad like me, so Jim and I recorded songs together just for the fun of it. There was no sense in which we hoped our tracks would ever be released as singles; they were laid down for our own amusement, just for fun. Although, since I had some reasonable recording equipment, I thought we might as well post them off to the odd record company occasionally just for the hell of it. I mean, I knew they were never going to offer us a contract, but there was nothing to lose by sending them off for a laugh. In fact, only that morning a tape had been returned with a note that it wasn't the sort of thing that particular label was looking for at the moment, and that was fine, that was what we expected. Bastards.

Although my ambition had faded I still had a recurring daydream that I was sitting at my keyboard one day when I suddenly got a phone call from some top A & R man.

'Is that Michael Adams, *the* Michael Adams, composer of the Cheesey Dunkers jingle?' he says.

'Yes?'

'Well, I work for EMI, and I think that riff has all the makings of a number-one hit. If we could just change the lyrics from that Chinaman saying, "Very cheesey if you please-ee," to a young girl singing, "I want to feel your sex in my sex; right now, give me sex," I think we've got an instant smash, no mistake.'

I knew it looked like a long shot, but I wasn't able to completely give up hope, so I wrote the songs and Jim wrote the lyrics and we recorded them in my bedroom and the history of rock and roll remained unchanged. Particularly since the task of getting down to recording our definitive demo tape kept getting put back by more important things, like watching daytime television or changing the screen saver on Jim's laptop. I had managed to team up with someone who was even less motivated than I was. Jim wasn't driven, he was parked.

However, the night before we had agreed that today we would lay down our two new songs, so at the end of the day we finally set about doing a day's work. While Jim tuned his guitar, I did my best to convert my room from a bedroom to a recording studio, picking up socks, turning on amplifiers, folding up the sofa bed, adjusting microphone stands.

'What are you called?' said Simon, hovering by my doorway, hoping he might be allowed to jump on board.

'We haven't really settled on a name yet,' said Jim. 'Have you got any ideas?'

Alarm bells went off in my head. Oh no, I thought, we're heading towards that debate again: the eternal what-shall-we-call-our-band? discussion. It's one of those perilous lobster-pot conversations that you must never, ever get into. For once you have ventured in there is no way out again; the fatal words 'What shall we call our band?' when said in this order actually form an incredible magic spell that can make a whole afternoon disappear.

'Oh come on,' I said, 'let's get this demo recorded. Once we start talking about band names we'll never get any work done.'

There was a general nodding and responsible acceptance of my suggestion, then Jim, who was just writing the label for the DAT, chipped in, 'OK, but what shall I put on the label in the meantime?'

'Well, I still quite like the Extractors.'

'The Extractors? No, it sounds too punky. Like the Vibrators or the Stranglers.'

'Ah ah ah,' I said, laughing. 'No way. We're not getting into this again. Just put our surnames, for the time being. Adams and Oates.'

'Sounds like Hall and Oates,' said Paul, who had wandered in trying to pretend he wasn't fascinated by the process of laying down our first single.

'People will think, Oh, wow! Oates has split up with Hall and got a new partner, and then they'll realize that it's a different Oates and chuck the tape in the bin.'

'All right, our first names then: Michael and Jimmy.'

'Sounds like two of the Osmonds.'

'Stop, stop. We're getting into that conversation again.'

Everyone agreed and I switched on the gear and plugged in Jim's guitar. There was a brief silence while the equipment was firing up and, as an afterthought, I added, 'Just put band untitled for the time being.' The moment I said it I knew it was a mistake. I closed my eyes in weary anticipation.

'Band Untitled. I quite like that,' said Jim. There was a murmur of agreement around the room and I tried to say nothing, but it was impossible.

'No. I meant put "band untitled", meaning our band doesn't have a name yet, not here's a demo from a new group called Band Untitled.'

'Band Untitled. It's got a ring to it, hasn't it?'

'Yeah. It's catchy, isn't it.'

I had to nip this in the bud. 'I'm sorry, but there is no way that we are calling ourselves Band Untitled. It's the worst name I've ever heard.'

Simon had a worse one.

'What about Plus Support?' he said.

There was a groan from Jim and me who, as experienced musos, knew that every band in the world had at one time or another thought that it would be incredibly wacky and original to call themselves Plus Support.

Simon's enthusiasm was undimmed. 'Because, you see, whenever you see a poster for a gig, it already has your name on it. You could turn up and tell the organizers, We're Plus Support. See, our name's on the poster!'

'Yeah, and when you get famous the posters will say Plus Support plus support,' said Paul, 'and you'd have to play twice.' He laughed.

Throughout all this Jim and I were shaking our heads like wise old sages.

'Yeah, but what if you develop any sort of fan base?' Jim butted in. 'They see "Plus Support" on the poster and go along to see you, only to find that not only have you apparently changed all your songs, but also every single member of the band has moved on. Either that or they see your name on the poster and presume it's not Plus Support, but some other band plus support. It's the worst possible name for a band in the history of rock music ever.'

'Apart from Chicory Tip,' I volunteered.

'Oh yeah. Apart from Chicory Tip.'

I think it was then that I realized we were deep into the conversation of no return. I had been unable to prevent it. Like one of the good fairies in *Sleeping Beauty*, I had shouted and forewarned in vain as they walked trancelike towards the spindle.

'Band names are easy,' said Jim, despite all the evidence. 'Just read something out of the paper.'

'Euro-commissioners renew demands for GATT inquiry.'

'Hmm, catchy!'

'Just pick out a phrase.'

'Nordic Biker Feud.'

'I like it.'

'Sounds like some God-awful heavy-metal outfit. Like Viking Blitzkrieg or Titan's Anvil.'

'The Beatles,' announced Simon cheerfully.

'What?' said the rest of the room in disbelief.

'You said just read something out of the paper. There's an article here about the Beatles.'

'Why don't you call yourselves Aardvark, then you'll be the very first entry in the *NME Book of Rock*,' suggested the English teacher.

'Or A1,' said Simon, 'just to be doubly sure.'

'A1? People will keep ringing us to order a cab.'

'What about the Acid Test?'

'Oh God, no,' I said. 'It reminds me of that crappy band the Truth Test who used to support us in Godalming. They've still got my bloody mike stand.'

Then the conversation moved on to the next stage, as it always did – the quick-fire round when hundreds of names were put up and knocked down in record time.

'The Smell of Red.'

'No.'

'Elite Republican Guard.'

'No.'

'Bigger Than Jesus.'

'No.'

'Charlie Don't Surf.'

'No.'

'Come Dancing.'

'No.'

'Buster Hymen and the Penetrations.'

'No, Simon.'

'Dead on Arrival.'

'No.'

'Who's Billy Shears?'

'No.'

'Things Fall Apart.'

'No.'

'Caution: May Contain Nuts.'
'No.'
'Let Fish Swim.'
'No.'
'The Detritus Twins.'
'No.'
'Big Bird.'
'No.'
'The Man Whose Head Expanded.'
'No.'
'Little Fat Belgian Bastards.'
'No.'
'The Sound of Music.'
'No.'
'Semi-detached.'
'No.'
'Mind the Gap.'
'No.'
'The Rest.'
'No.'
'The Carpet Mites.'
'No.'
'Chain Gang.'
'No.'
'Ayatollah and the Shi'ites.'
'No.'
'The Snakepit Strollers.'
'No.'
'Twenty-four Minutes From Tulse Hill.'
'No.'
'Ow!'
'No.'
'No, I mean, Ow! I just got a splinter off this chair.'
After a while your brain becomes numb from continually

searching for an original combination of two or three syllables, and through mental exhaustion you end up just mumbling incomprehensible noises. 'The blub–blub–blah–blahs.'

'What about something sort of royal?'

'They've all been done. There's been *Queen*, *King*, *Prince*, *Princess*; there's only the Duchess of Kent left. You can't name a cutting-edge rock band after some posh bird whose only claim to fame is getting free tickets to Wimbledon.'

'I know,' said Simon excitedly, unjustifiably getting our hopes up, 'what about Hey!'

'Hey?'

'No, not Hey? Not Hey with a question mark. Hey! with an exclamation mark. You know, like Wham! Sort of attention grabbing.'

Nobody ever actually took the trouble to reject this idea; it was too mediocre a suggestion to warrant a response. Instead it was simply ignored to death, and Simon looked rather hurt when he realized that everyone had just carried on suggesting other names without even bothering to acknowledge his. For another hour or so, endless suggestions were released like clay pigeons, and then blown to smithereens by one of us. We rejected, the Scuds, Go to Jail, Rocktober and unsurprisingly St Joan and the Heavy Heavy Dandruff Conspiracy. Until, with a certain gravitas that comes from knowing you finally have the right answer, Jim said, 'Lust for Life.'

'Lust for Life,' I repeated with impressed contemplation.

'It's an Iggy Pop track,' said Paul.

'I know.'

'And a film about Van Gogh.'

'I know.'

Paul pompously put up these objections only to be disappointed to learn they were not objections. We said it a few more times and agreed that Lust for Life it was. Two and a half hours it had taken us, but finally we could do some work. I switched on the mike and adopted the persona of the announcer at the Hollywood Bowl.

'Ladies and gentlemen, tonight playing the first gig of their sell-out US tour; they're number one all over the world, all the way from Balham, England, it's Lust for Life.'

Jim and Simon applauded and whistled, and then Simon held up his cigarette lighter. Paul struck a posture of unimpressed aloofness by just sitting there and reading *Time Out*.

'Anyone fancy going to a gig tomorrow night?' he said rather cryptically.

'Why, who's playing?'

'I was thinking of going to the Half Moon in Putney.' He waved the advert under our noses. 'There's a new band playing called Lust for Life.'

There was a pause.

'Fucking bunch of plagiarists!' spat Jim. 'They've nicked our fucking name!'

No music was recorded that night. At one point I did say, 'Come on, guys, let's work,' but that was rejected as sounding too much like Men at Work. The worst moment had been halfway through the debate when my mobile had rung and I'd answered it to find Catherine on the other end.

'What do you think of the name India?' she'd said.

'There's already a band called India,' I'd replied, confused. And then I'd tried to repeat the sentence, emphasizing the word 'band' as if to say, Well, there's already a *band* called India, but that's not to say you couldn't call a *baby* India. It didn't really matter because I knew the name suggestion was just an excuse to ring and make the first contact after our row.

She made me miss home. My flatmates had been so infuriating all day that now I wanted to go back to Catherine again. With Paul's stupid tantrums about the way Jim made tea or the way I didn't cook dinner, Simon's tedious questions and Jim's impossible procrastination and a whole evening spent discussing bloody band names again, they were driving me mad. And then a terrible realization struck me. It was something I hadn't foreseen when I'd run away from my family to get a bit of sanity: that the surrogate family I'd adopted were just as unbearable as any other. That every time I got to that far-off field I would look back at where I'd just come from and it would suddenly seem far greener than when I'd left it. That wherever I was in my life I would always want to be somewhere else. That I had gone to all this trouble, deceived the woman I loved and got myself into debt, only to find that the things which annoyed and oppressed me followed me around. It wasn't Catherine or the children that were the problem. It wasn't even Jim, Paul and Simon. It was me.

chapter five

it's good to talk

I am fifteen years old and standing outside a theatre close to Piccadilly Circus. Sixty other fifth formers have just slunk off two coaches to see *Hamlet* by William Shakespeare. They look awkward and self-conscious in their jackets and ties. They have all given my English teacher a cheque from their parents, but they haven't had to pay full price because my mother works at the theatre and can get us all discounted tickets. Well, that's what I'd imagined and had carelessly told my English teacher. Actually, my mother only had a part-time job at the theatre, cleaning costumes, and couldn't get us a discount at all. And so no tickets were ever booked.

I'd wanted to be helpful. When he had said the name of the theatre, I'd recognized it, put up my hand and told him about Mum, and he had said, half joking, 'Well, maybe she could get us all discounted tickets, Michael.' And I'd said I was sure she could, and it had just snowballed from there. I don't know why I didn't say anything in the weeks before. I didn't want to disappoint him, I suppose. I really liked Mr Stannard, and he seemed to like me. I didn't tell him when he said, 'Your mother has definitely booked these tickets, hasn't she?' That probably would have been a good time to tell him. I didn't tell him as he was giving out the letters about the school trip for everyone to take home to their parents. And when he was doing a list of who was and wasn't going to see *Hamlet*, I didn't tell him that actually none of us were. I didn't even tell him as everyone clambered onto the coaches.

The two coach drivers took turns to overtake each other on the dual carriageway and all the children cheered. All the kids except me. Only I knew that we were all completely wasting our time and that it was all my fault and that my dreadful secret would soon be exposed. But still I didn't say anything. When all sixty-four of us were standing in the foyer of the theatre and Mr Stannard was arguing with the lady in the ticket office and he turned to me and said, 'Michael, you said your mother had definitely booked sixty-four tickets?' I did tell him then. I adopted the air of someone who had meant to give him a message but had allowed it to completely slip my mind. 'Oh, that's right. Oh, I meant to say . . . um . . . she's not entitled to a discount so I didn't get her to book any.'

My feigned indifference failed to persuade him that this was not a big deal. That night's performance was sold out, the theatre manager explained and Mr Stannard turned to me and completely lost control. They say that the fear of a moment is often worse than the moment itself. Not in this case; my fear was completely justified. I think even the other teachers were embarrassed at the way his face went bright red and his body shook and he spat as he shouted at me. I just stood there, unable to think of anything to say in my defence, shrugging my shoulders silently in response to every question he screamed at me. The veins were standing out on his forehead, and as he yelled two inches from my face, I could smell stale cigarettes. He was so angry with me that he got his words mixed up. As his fury reached a crescendo he shouted, 'And now, now the, the, the entire fifth form aren't going to miss *Hamlet*.'

'Yes they are, sir.'

'What?'

'You said they *aren't* going to miss it.'

'No, I said they aren't going to *see* it.'

'No, you said they aren't going to *miss it*, sir.'

I may have ruined the evening for sixty-four people, but I was definitely right on this point.

'Don't tell me what I did and didn't bloody say. I said *see it*.' His quivering purple face was still just a couple of inches from mine and a bit of his spit landed on my nose, but I thought it better just to leave it there.

One of the other teachers tried to calm him down. 'Actually, you did say *miss it*, Dave.'

And then Mr Stannard turned to Mr Morgan and started shouting at him instead, which all the other kids thought was quite exciting because we'd never seen teachers shouting at each other before.

The stupid thing was that the only reason I hadn't told him was because I hadn't wanted to upset him. As a long-term strategy this had never been very likely to succeed. Eventually we all went out and sat around under the statue of Eros for hours, waiting for the time when the coaches were due to pick us up again, and I sensed that Mr Stannard didn't like me any more and it started to rain.

'Well, if we all die of pneumonia we can thank Michael Adams,' he'd said bitterly, which I thought was a bit unfair because it wasn't my fault it was raining.

'You stupid dingbat, Adams,' said my classmates.

'"Oh! that this too too solid flesh would melt, Thaw, and resolve itself into a dew,"' said Hamlet. I knew how he felt.

*

'Michael, you have a tendency to put off problems until they are no longer problems but have developed into full-scale disasters,' my headteacher announced the following morning as I stood before his desk. And this was pretty much the gist of what my bank manager said to me sixteen years later when we spoke on the phone about my outstanding mortgage payments. He made a date for me to come and see him and sort it all out, and to prove that his analysis of my character was entirely correct, I failed to turn up for the appointment.

I sat down in my bachelor pad and worked out how much I needed to pay to get up to date with the mortgage on my family home. I wrote out how much I owed on all my credit cards and various hire-purchase agreements. In a column next to these I wrote out how much money I had coming in over the next couple of months. I tried bumping the second figure up a little bit by including some unspent record vouchers I'd had since Christmas, but it didn't look any less depressing. I stared long and hard at the two amounts, trying to think of the most sensible and realistic course of action open to me. And then I went out and bought a lottery ticket.

The day when I was going to have to start working like a slave was fast approaching. In the meantime, I resolved to make some economies. I'd try to put less toothpaste on my brush and I'd start buying peanuts instead of cashew nuts. There had been another household expense in my South London flat that had been niggling me for some time, but I hadn't been quite sure of the most tactful way to raise it. The cost of our telephone was split four ways, but closer examination of the bill revealed that well over half the calls were made by Sordid Simon calling up his favourite obscene sites on the Internet. I was subsidizing his ritual self-abuse. It's awkward enough when you feel someone should pay a little bit more towards the bill in a restaurant, but telling a flatmate they owe you a lot of money because they spend half their spare time having sex with their right hand, well it's not the sort of thing that's covered by the *Debrett's* book of social etiquette. But the evidence was there in black and white, the itemized bill showed the same number over and over again, and for how long Simon had been connected to it. On 9 February, for example, he had called it at 10.52 a.m. and it would appear that he had masturbated for seven minutes and twenty-four seconds. That had cost us all thirty-five pence, not including VAT. Later on that day he had called it for twelve minutes and twenty-three seconds, but then I suppose you'd expect it to take a little longer second time around. There were pages and pages of calls, listing the dates, times and duration of his time spent surfing the net. Actually, surfing is too glamorous a word for what Simon did on the Internet. He *lurked* on it, he *prowled* it, he *hung around in the bushes* of the Internet.

I raised this problem with the others and we agreed we would have to confront him about it. We were keen to get the conversation over with as quickly as possible, hoping we could discuss the financial principle without getting into the nitty-gritty of what he was actually watching. We should have known better. Despite what we might have imagined to be embarrassing circumstances, Simon seemed to be delighted to be the centre of attention and positively welcomed the chance to hold forth on the one subject in which he was a real expert.

'It's really very good value,' he explained brightly. 'For the price of a local telephone call you can see people having sex with gorillas.'

'Ah, the wonders of modern technology,' said Jim.

'Or any of the primates for that matter, except orangutans. But they're quite rare, aren't they?'

Simon was completely oblivious to our discomfort and enthusiastically chatted on and on about the fascinating world of hard-core pornography.

'You're a seedy little runt, Simon,' I told him and he seemed quite pleased, as if he had presumed that my opinion of him was far lower. I wasn't so much annoyed by the fact that Simon was obsessed with pornography as I was by the fact that he didn't feel the need to be the slightest bit secretive or embarrassed about it. All men are preoccupied with sex, but at least the rest of us make some attempt to hide it. He chatted about his fixation as if it were a charming little hobby, like amateur dramatics or painting watercolours. 'It's good to talk', said the advert for British Telecom. Or whatever else you did to run up a phone bill.

In the hope that we might share his enthusiasm if only we saw what we had been missing, he showed us some of the pornographic sites he visited. They featured three or four awkwardly contorted people who looked like they were playing Twister in the nude. 'Left hand on red dot; right foot on yellow dot; left breast on black penis.' Except that I remember playing Twister had always been great fun, whereas these people's faces suggested they were in a great deal of pain. I found these photos simultaneously revolting and compelling. Like car crashes and anchovies, you knew they were horrible but you couldn't help double-checking just to make sure they were as sickening as they'd seemed the first time. But my first impressions were generally correct. Most of the images were about as erotic as colour photos of open heart surgery. There was a sequence of photos that told the story of a dinner party turning into an orgy. The transition seemed quite effortless.

'There it is again, you see,' said Simon.

'What?'

'One thing leading to another. Look, picture one, they're being introduced. Picture two, they're chatting a bit. Picture three, she's got his cock in her mouth. I mean, what happened between pictures two and three – that's what I need to know. How does one thing lead to another? If that was me, it would be picture one, "Hello, hello." Picture two, "Chat, chat." Picture three, she'd be slapping me round the face and leaving.'

He called up another Internet site that was stored under 'Favourites' and giggled slightly as the next photo slowly downloaded. The computer gradually revealed the picture from the top downwards, as if it were playing with us, toying with the idea of showing it all, but then holding back and teasing us by disclosing a little more. The woman revealed was undeniably attractive. She had a pretty face, perfectly formed breasts, well-rounded hips and long, smooth legs. The only thing that spoilt it for me – and maybe this is just me being fussy – was that she had a large erect penis. I know that, as a man, we often unreasonably expect women's bodies to fit into some preconceived stereotype, but I think the absence of a penis and testicles is one prerequisite I would probably have to insist upon.

Amid the exaggerated groans, I told Simon that his relationship with this computer wasn't healthy, that it was all one-way sex, with no love or foreplay, and we all agreed that in future he should at least take the computer out to dinner or something before they got down to it.

Eventually a new house rule was proposed: Simon should only be allowed to masturbate in front of his computer during off-peak hours and at weekends. He protested, pointing out that the calls were discounted. Apparently, when he registered with BT Friends and Family, it turned out that his best friend was his Internet server, which seemed tragically appropriate. It wasn't as if this best friend ever called him. But the rule was passed and now we could leave Simon alone again.

'All agreed,' said Jim, 'but could I just see that picture of those blonde twins mud wrestling again . . .'

*

The reason we held Simon in such low esteem is that he naively presented us with so much to find distasteful about him. He didn't keep his dark side to himself. He told people things. It was both a failing and a virtue; he may have been a worm, but he was an honest and unpretentious worm. I felt confident that he wasn't a secret cannibalistic serial killer, because if he had been, he would cheerfully have informed us all about the practical details of cooking human flesh. He was that rare thing, a person with no secrets.

I had lived my life with an instinctive secrecy that had even made me pause before saying, 'Here', when the teacher called the register. Jim, Paul and Simon had no idea that when I wasn't with them I was a husband and father. That was just the way I preferred things to be. Soon after I'd started renting my room, the other tenants had moved on, and there didn't seem any need to illuminate my new flatmates about my unconventional domestic arrangements. I didn't generally lie. I just deceived by omission. Catherine once joked that the reason I never talked about what I'd been doing was to avoid lying about it. How I'd laughed. Obviously, I was compelled to launch an extended defence of my masculine silences. I mumbled, 'Is not.'

My reticence was in her interest as well as mine. I learned early on that if the mother of your children has had a boring day, it isn't particularly tactful to tell them every detail of what a fun and interesting time you've been having. They much prefer it if you've been bored, too. So on the days that I came home to a scene of exhausted ennui, I would do my best to at least play down any enjoyment I'd had while I was out. That Friday I returned to find Millie watching a video while Catherine was on her knees cleaning out the oven, trying to rock Alfie in the baby seat with her foot at the same time.

'How was your day?' she asked.

'Oh, you know, pretty boring.'

'Did you have lunch?'

'Well, I grabbed something.'

'Where?'

'Where? Erm, well I popped into this sort of awards lunch thing.'

'An awards lunch?! Oh, that sounds fun.'

'Well, it was no big deal. You know advertising; there's an awards lunch somewhere most days. Really tiresome, actually.'

'So did you go back to your studio to do some work?'

'Erm, no. I wouldn't have got much work done: I'd had too much champagne. Well, I don't know if it was real champagne; it tasted a bit cheap actually, so I kind of stayed there all afternoon.'

'Oh, that's nice for you.'

'Well, I was obliged really. You know, contacts, networking, all that boring stuff.'

She put her head in the oven again and I double-checked that she was cleaning it, not committing suicide.

'You weren't up for an award were you?' said the echoey voice from inside.

'Er, sort of.'

'Sort of?'

'Erm, well, yes, I was. Best original backing music – for that bank ad I did last autumn?'

'Blimey. You kept that quiet.'

'Well you've got enough on your plate without me boring you about my work,' I said unconvincingly. She paused while she scraped off the last of the crusty grease and I hoped the cross-examination would end there.

'So you didn't win, then?'

'Erm. Well, yes, I did win, actually. Yeah.'

I heard her head bump against the inside of the oven. And then she came out and looked at me in disbelief. 'You went to an awards lunch and won an award?'

'Yeah. A big silver statue thing. I went up on stage to collect it and everyone applauded and it was presented to me by John Peel and he shook my hand and afterwards we chatted for ages.'

'John Peel? I hope you didn't ask him if he remembered your flexi-disc?'

'Catherine, John Peel used to get thousands and thousands of tapes and records every year, I'm not going to expect him to remember one flexi-disc that he didn't play in the late Eighties, am I?'

'So he didn't remember it, then?'

'No, he didn't. No. But he's even nicer than he sounds on the radio and everyone kept coming up and saying congratulations and looking at my award and taking photos.'

And then I realized I'd rather blown my martyred cover, and so I belatedly attempted to claw it back.

'But you know, apart from that it was really tiresome. It's all so phoney. And the award weighed a ton. It was awful walking the length of Park Lane carrying this three-ton award and trying to get a cab.'

'Sounds like hell,' she said, looking up from where she was crouching on the floor. Her face was marked with burned fat from the inside of the oven, which had covered her clothes and clogged up her hair. Alfie started to cry gently in the background because Catherine's foot had stopped rocking the seat.

'Erm, I was maybe thinking I might have a bath,' I ventured. 'But, er, I suppose I could look after the kids for a bit if you wanted to use the bathroom before me.'

'Well, I wouldn't want to put you out. Since you've had such an awful day,' she said pointedly.

As far as I was concerned, telling people things only ever caused problems. It is always presumed that complete and total honesty is the only way to have a happy relationship, but nothing is further from the truth. When a couple have just made love, the last thing they should do is be open and honest with each other. The woman says, 'Mmm, that was lovely.' Not, 'Oh, that was quicker than I would have liked.' And he says, 'Hmmm, it was really nice.' Not, 'Interestingly, I have discovered that I can heighten my climax by pretending I'm making love to your best friend.'

All couples deceive each other to some degree, so what I was doing wasn't particularly unusual. Every father has heard the cry of the baby in the night and then pretended to be asleep as his wife gets out of bed to deal with it. I was more secretive than some men, but far more loyal to my wife than many others. Anyway, I thought to myself, Catherine tells lies. When the Conservatives came looking to canvass me at the general election, she told them that *she* was Michael Adams. She put on this croaky deep voice and asked if you were still allowed to join the Tory Party if you'd had a sex change. The joke rather backfired when the candidate suddenly became very interested in her and we had to hide upstairs every time he came back and rang on the doorbell.

And, of course, she deceived everyone about her pregnancy. She didn't want to tell people for the first three months, so she coerced me into maintaining a front of un-fertilized normality. What was so disconcerting about this was that, although I was the practised liar, when the time came for us to jointly hoodwink everyone else, I realized that she was much better at it than I was. We spent a rare evening out at Catherine's new-age sister's house, listening to Judith's theory that the world was going to end because everyone was leaving on their solar-powered calculators and using up the sun. Judith was a textbook modern hippie. The only time we had been offered meat at her house was years earlier, when we had gone round for a ceremonial meal to celebrate the birth of her child and she had uttered the unforgettable words, 'Red or white wine with placenta?'

'Erm, just a little couscous for me, thank you,' Catherine had replied. 'I had placenta for lunch.'

Now that she was pregnant Catherine wasn't drinking wine, and on this occasion I expected her to refuse, but she was way ahead of me. To say no would have been to draw attention to herself and raise suspicion, so she accepted wine along with everyone else and nobody noticed that she never actually drank any. Once I'd recognized her plan, I thought I would do my bit to help and gallantly stepped in to surreptitiously drink her wine for her. All four glasses. It's the sort of self-sacrifice all fathers-to-be should be prepared to make. Our host kept topping up our glasses and I kept emptying both of them. I gave Catherine a sly wink and a conspiratorial smile to acknowledge that I knew what she was up to and that I was discreetly helping her keep up appearances. And then I fell off my chair.

When the time came for us to leave and I was trying to put my arm down the wrong sleeve of my jacket, our host was adamant that we had both drunk too much to drive home.

'Really, I'm fine to drive. I've hardly drunk a thing,' maintained Catherine, still anxious not to reveal her secret.

'No, I insist. Michael can pick up the car in the morning. I've ordered you a minicab.'

'Yeah. I'll pick up the car in the morning,' I slurred. 'We can't have you doing it, Catherine, not with you being pregnant.'

She was in quite a bad mood when we got home, but then pregnancy can do all sorts of things to a woman's temperament. I suppose the difference between Catherine and me was that she only lied up to a point; she knew when to come clean. If it had been me, I would still have been denying I was pregnant when I was lying in the delivery room with my legs up in stirrups. Apart from her sister and brother-in-law, who had managed to guess after I had let slip that one little clue, Catherine told people that she was pregnant exactly when she had planned to – at the end of the third month. Everyone said congratulations with slightly less excitement and amazement than they had expressed about our second child, which was slightly less than for our first.

'We wanted to have them all quite close together,' she said, using the royal 'we', and I glanced around wondering who else she could be referring to.

'Aaaahhhh,' said all our friends and relations, who patted her tummy as if it were suddenly public property. From now on the little embryo would have to get used to people constantly banging on the walls. I felt quite protective of the miniature baby in there. At twelve weeks the foetus is already the approximate shape of a person. All the major organs are formed. There is a heartbeat, there are lungs that will breathe air, there is a stomach that will digest food, there is a spleen that will, well, do whatever a spleen does . . . get ruptured in accidents.

The embryo has also formed a backbone. I'm glad one of us had. Catherine was still very tired and tearful, so the last thing she wanted was for me to tell her that we were experiencing some temporary financial problems. While she told everyone the happy news, I kept the bad news to myself. To avoid my pregnant wife worrying about threatening letters arriving on the doormat, I decided it was time to act and I finally posted an envelope to the bank. It didn't contain a cheque for all the money I owed them, but it did request that from now on all correspondence should be sent to my South London address, so that was that problem dealt with.

The only person I still hadn't told about the new baby was my father. Dad had retired to live on his own in Bournemouth and I didn't get round to seeing him that often. He had a very carefully worded answerphone message, which was scripted to give as little away as possible. When I listened to it, I could almost see him carefully reading it off a piece of paper. He said, 'The person who you are calling is unable to come to the phone at the moment, although he may well be in.' And he imagined that any burglars calling were going, 'Drat, drat. If only he'd said he was out, then I would have gone round and done the place over.' He had still not seen our little house in Kentish Town, which made me feel guilty every time I thought about it, but he was worried about coming up to London in case there was another poll-tax riot. After he got e-mail we communicated more regularly, because he kept ringing me up to ask why he couldn't get his e-mail to work.

'What about the net, Michael? Do you do the net?'

'You don't "do the net", Dad. It's not some new dance craze, like the twist or the locomotion.'

'Well, I can't seem to do the net, either. I think there must be something jammed in my computer.'

I could have shared the news of his new grandchild over the phone, but I felt I wanted to tell him to his face. Catherine said that by the time I finally got round to this, the baby would probably have been born, grown up and gone off to university, so I rang him back and suggested that we came down and cooked him lunch, and then afterwards I could give him a computer lesson. He was delighted by the idea. 'Ooh, that would be lovely, Michael. Now before you come down, is Microsoft something I ought to buy?'

Dad had spent his life making a respectable living as a drugs dealer. He wasn't the sort that had two rottweilers, lots of gold rings and sold crack behind nightclubs in Manchester; Dad never made as much money as those guys because he dealt in the wrong sort of drugs. He sold Beechams Hot Lemon drink and Settlers Tums. I'd tried to imagine him driving round the country and opening up his briefcase for one of his best customers. The pharmacist ripping open one sachet of Alka Seltzer and dabbing a little on his tongue. 'That's good shit, man. But don't you never try cuttin' in any low-grade Enos, man, or I'll see they have to fish your body outta the East River with no head. You dig?' Dad had been the type of drugs dealer who had a company car and a pension plan.

His job had involved a lot of nights away from home, particularly after he met a dark-haired chemist called Janet from Royal Leamington Spa. He went to extraordinary lengths to persuade her to buy his range of products, even leaving his wife and only child for her. So then it was just Mum and five-year-old me. I grew up in the Home Counties in a semi-detached house with a semi-detached dad. After my parents were legally divorced I had to spend my lonely weekends staying at his funny-smelling bungalow. Just as he himself had been an evacuee in the war, so I was shipped off to a strange town, clutching my suitcase and a few hastily gathered toys, a refugee from the war of my parents' partition.

There was nothing for me to do in his grown-up house miles from all my friends, so I played the piano. All day Saturday and all day Sunday for years and years I practised the piano. There was only one collection of sheet music under the dusty stool, *Traditional Hymns for Pianoforte*, and I played them all over and over again. At first I just tried to pick out the tunes, but over time I became fluent and confident, until finally I imagined that I was Elton John, wearing four-inch platform glitter boots, strutting out at the Hollywood Bowl and launching into my first number one smash hit 'Nearer My God to Thee'.

'Thank you, ladies and gentlemen. And now a song that's been very good to me; everybody get on down to "When I

Survey the Wondrous Cross".' And I'd boogie-woogie my way through all four verses, adlibbing the occasional 'Yow!' or 'Oooh, baby!' after the bit that went 'Did e'er such love and sorrow meet, or thorns compose so rich a crown?' Then I took the tempo down a little with 'We Plough the Fields and Scatter'. I imagined they were holding up their cigarette lighters by now and swaying gently as far back as I could see. Suddenly fireworks exploded all over the stage and I launched into a sequence of my early hits – favourite rock 'n' roll classics like 'Onward Christian Soldiers', 'Jesu – Lover of My Soul' and the title track from my latest album 'I Know That My Redeemer Liveth'. That was my encore and I played it standing up and span around several times as I played the closing bars.

So I could say that, without my parents' divorce, I would probably never have learned to play the piano, studied music at college and gone on to the dizzy heights of having my flexi-disc played three times on Thames Valley FM. Now that I was what Dad called a 'pop-music composer' he was very proud of me, and he sometimes rang up to tell me he'd just seen an advert for which I had written the music being broadcast on the television.

'Yes, well, the agency have bought a hundred spots, Dad, twenty of them in peak time.'

'Well, they must be pleased with your music, then, if they keep showing it over and over again.'

As I carried the kids from the car to his house for Sunday lunch, he came down the path to greet us. It was only ten yards, but he put on his hat for the journey. He had a very good reason for wearing a hat, although he didn't quite feel able to keep it on once he was inside. In the brief couple of years before my dad had split up with Janet the chemist, she had managed to persuade him that he ought to have a hair transplant. Even though his hair hadn't receded very far, he subjected himself to a painstaking and expensive operation in which small clumps of hair were uprooted from the more fertile hair-producing regions and then replanted at the top of his exposed forehead. For a while it seemed the surgeon had pulled off an amazing optical illusion and my father's fringe had returned. But then, behind the fortifications, the original hair continued to recede at the same inexorable rate. Though the tiny tufts of doll's hair heroically stood their ground, all around them the indigenous follicles deserted, leaving the transplanted outpost completely isolated.

Maybe this is what prompted Janet to leave him. His head was by now a classic example of male pattern baldness, a shiny smooth pate stretching from his forehead to his crown, with a straight line of transplanted hair clinging on like clumps of marram grass along the top of a sand dune. It was never ever mentioned.

He hung up his hat and I tried not to let my eyes wander above his. The moment I was in the front door Dad locked on and engaged me. The less I saw him the more anecdotes he stored up to recount, and nothing could deflect him from immediately delivering this month's main items of news.

Top stories on the hour today: Dad's friend Brian has bought a new car in Belgium and made a considerable saving. The queuing system at the bank has been changed and now you have to take a blessed ticket with a number on. And finally, no more printed headed paper, decides Dad, until they sort out the blessed telephone codes once and for all. But first, back to that top story of Brian's new car . . .

Information was fired at me non-stop, oblivious to any preoccupation I might have with child care or preparing the lunch. I had dropped Catherine off at the supermarket to get some bread and vegetables, so I was left looking after the children on my own as I searched through his cupboards and found some gravy powder. Actually, 'powder' is a generous description of what remained when I tore the wrapping away. It was a dark-brown gravy brick which had fossilized some time around the Cretaceous period. Being a war baby, Dad didn't like to waste anything. Stale bread made perfectly good stale toast. The oil from a tin of tuna was saved in a little egg cup and could be used to fry anything that you wanted to taste of tuna. A few years back, when he'd had a new plastic hip-joint fitted, he'd remarked that he didn't like to ask what they'd done with the old hip bone. I could tell he felt it was a bit of a waste just to throw it away. I could have made a nice stock with that, he'd been thinking.

I tried to put on the roast, listen to Dad and deal with the children, but the combination was too demanding for any mortal.

'Brian was going to get the two-litre Mondeo, but opted for the 1.6, what with all the tax they're putting on petrol.'

Millie dropped her beaker, and because I hadn't put the lid on properly, milk started to glug across the kitchen floor. What did Dad say to this? 'Don't worry, I'll get a cloth,' or, 'Let me hold Alfie while you wipe that up'? No. He said, 'The 1.6 still has ABS and power steering, but by buying it from a dealership in Belgium he saved three thousand pounds. How about that!' I didn't know Brian, or how much Mondeos normally cost, but I tried my best to look impressed as I searched in vain for the kitchen towels.

'Well, I told him that I'd been thinking of getting a Ford Focus, but I'm not sure if I want to go all the way to Belgium, especially after the way they caved in during the war.'

His cat had started to drink the milk as it formed a puddle on the lino, and Millie was trying to pull the cat away by tugging its tail, which made the cat liable to spin round at any second and scratch Millie's face.

'Millie, don't pull the cat's tail.'

'She drink my milk.'

'. . . but Brian said that you can get people to bring them over from Belgium for you, as far as Harwich anyway, but I said I can't pay out any money without seeing the car first; they might bring me a left-hand drive or something and then where does that leave me . . .'

'Hang on a minute, Dad, I'll just clear this up. Stop it, Millie.'

But like the creature in *Alien* that locked its tentacles round John Hurt's face, he demanded my full attention and was not going to let go. I tried to nod, as if I was listening, but the potatoes boiled over and the water extinguished the gas ring and then Alfie crawled into the puddle of milk and got his trousers wet and started to cry.

'But they're not just in Belgium, Brian said you can get some very good deals in the Netherlands. I mean, what do you think, Michael? Do you think it would be safe to buy a new car from the continent?'

'It's all right, Alfie. Um, I don't know, Dad. Stop it, Millie.'

The cat finally lashed out at Millie and drew blood from her arm, making her scream in panic which, to his credit, Dad did actually manage to acknowledge.

'Oh dear, the cat's scratched her arm. That'll need a plaster. But Brian says they're all right-hand drive, with air-bag, ABS, central locking and everything as standard. And you should see his, it's very nice, with a proper British number plate and everything.'

Millie could have been sawing her little brother's limbs off with the bread knife but still my dad wouldn't have considered this a valid reason to let up for a second.

'There, there, Millie. Yes, Mummy'll be here in a minute. Don't cry, Alfie, it's only milk. No, I have to wash it, Millie, and then we can put on a *Little Mermaid* plaster . . . Nought per cent finance for three years. Really, Dad?'

My sixty-six-year-old dad was really just another infant in need of attention. He even looked like a baby, with his big bald head and food stains down his front. When you are in your thirties, they both want your attention just as much – your new children and your old parents. They are like selfish siblings competing for your love. 'Daddy! Daddy! Daddy!' went Millie, but I couldn't deal with her because I was still trying to listen to *my* daddy. My only chance of peace was to time everyone's lunch so carefully that Dad had his afternoon sleep at the same hour as the other children. Maybe I should rig up a musical mobile above the sofa to make sure he went off all right.

Catherine and I eventually told him that he was to be a grandfather again and he seemed genuinely delighted and rang his new lady friend, Jocelyn, to tell her, although knowing Dad he would have a different lady friend by the time the baby was born. After lunch he did us a favour by sleeping for an hour and a half. He left a small patch of damp saliva on the cushion beside his mouth. 'That's where you get that habit from,' said Catherine and I was mortified. I always took delight in observing aspects of myself in my children, but I was horrified by the prospect of slowly turning into my dad. My only comfort was that I wasn't the kind of man to have a casual affair and recklessly throw away a marriage in the way Dad had done.

As we drove back to London I wondered why it was that so many men seemed to find it impossible to stay committed to one partner? Jim, for example, had had five or six girlfriends since I'd known him. Where was the happiness in that? I mean, really, how could any young man be attracted to the idea of making love to an endless succession of beautiful women? A voluptuous blonde one month, a svelte brunette the next? It just defied explanation.

Jim had just begun a new relationship with a girl called Monica and the following week, when I was in my studio, he called my mobile to invite me down to the Duke of Devonshire to join them. I had been failing to get my computer to print out some invoices and going to the pub seemed about as likely to get the printer to work as everything else I'd attempted. When I arrived, Monica's best friend Kate was in the pub garden with them and so I found myself chatting to her. Kate was pretty and slim and bubbly and carefree and all the things it is quite easy to be when you're not the pregnant mother of two small children. She had a bob of dark brown hair, which she threw back when she laughed at my jokes, and a white short-sleeved shirt that showed off her tan. This is quite nice, I thought to myself, enjoying the company of attractive young women. Of course, I wasn't going to pursue her, but there was a certain amount of pleasure in chatting and making her laugh. Even if I wasn't going to sleep with another woman ever again, there was a certain excitement to be had in placing myself in a situation where it could at least have been possible. And she warmed to me. She seemed genuinely impressed by the fact that I wrote the music for the Mr Gearbox ad they played on Capital Radio.

Jim had an open-topped sports car, which his parents must have bought him for learning to tie his shoelaces or something, and so, with the hood down and the stereo blaring out Supergrass, we drove up to Chelsea. Jim and his girlfriend in the front and Kate and me in the back. The wheels screeched as Jim overtook a BMW on a roundabout and Kate squealed with laughter and grabbed my arm for a moment. On the stereo they sang about being young and running free and feeling all right, and I thought, Yeah! Look out Wandsworth one-way system! I was enjoying pretending to be cool. So what if it was nearly dark; the sunglasses weren't there for me looking out, they were there for other people looking in.

Suddenly I was as young as the beautiful, posh girl riding beside me.

I felt a tinge of unease as we sped over the river. The Thames ran down the middle of my life; north of the river I was a husband and father, south of the river I was a carefree young man. I once turned down a trip on a riverboat just because I felt I wouldn't know who to go as. Now the young reckless Michael was spreading his wings – all of London was my bachelor playground. We were going to a party, the party of a very rich man for whom Kate and Monica worked in the crazy carefree world of bond yields and corporate leasing. It was the most lavish, glamorous do I'd ever been to. I kept turning my back whenever the photographer appeared in case Catherine spotted me the following week in the pages of *Hello!* The music was supplied by a Japanese man who played Chopin at a grand piano. I'm not sure that anyone else in the room appreciated or even noticed how very, very good he was.

The house was offensively opulent and I felt like I was probably the only guest there who'd had the temerity to turn up without a hyphen in my surname. I attempted to mingle, but none of the circles opened up as I stood on the edges of them, so I stared at the enormous tropical fish tank for a while, but even the guppies seemed to look down their noses at me. All the men were the same – confident, self-possessed rugby captains in their casual gear. Why is it that posh men don't lose their hair, I wondered. Is it in the breeding, or something they put in boarding-school meals? They all had thick, floppy Hugh Grant fringes and bright-red cheeks and loafers and Pringle jumpers and talked about people they knew who were 'bloody great blokes'. I had more chance of striking up a conversation with the Filipino ladies handing round champagne, and they didn't even speak English. So I ended up talking to Kate for most of the evening. She kept asking me what 'song' the pianist was playing, and I told her the name of each new piece and said a little bit about each one. She had just bought a guitar and was having lessons and I told her some good pieces she might try to learn. She was genuinely interested and it was a real pleasure to be able to talk about music to somebody. The fact that she was gorgeous was, of course, an added bonus, but I really wasn't trying to chat her up or make her fancy me. And for someone so beautiful I think she found this quite refreshing. I think it made her fancy me.

A few glasses of wine later, Jim and Monica came over and told us to come down to the basement to see the swimming pool. I thought they were joking, but I followed them into the lift – because you have to have a lift to get to your underground swimming pool – and when the doors opened again I found that we had been transported to an echoey underground paradise. It was like no room I had ever seen. This was the Sistine chapel of swimming pools. This wasn't like the municipal pool I went to with Millie. Nobody had taken the trouble to cultivate green algae between the tiles or leave blood-stained sticking plasters stewing in pools of discoloured water; there were no bad cartoons on the wall telling me what I could and couldn't do. Here I could blow all the smoke rings I wanted, if the mood took me.

Jim informed us that the pool was regularly rented out as a location for films and fashion shoots, and it was obvious why. You just had to walk into the room to feel like an actor; like you were someone else, someone glamorous and sexy. There was nobody down there and the lighting was low and sensitive; the only bright lights were deep at the bottom of the turquoise oasis, which drew you seductively to the water. The surface of the pool was completely still and flat, like the seal on a coffee jar, just waiting to be broken.

'Come on, let's go for a swim,' said Kate infectiously.

'But we haven't got any swimming costumes,' I pointed out, 'though they might have some spare . . . costumes . . . upstairs . . .'

The end of my sentence trailed off. Jim, Monica and Kate had all stripped completely naked.

'Um . . . although there's, er, no sign saying that costumes are compulsory or anything.' The girls were already jumping in and swimming breaststroke with real live breasts.

Deep down I had a sense that cavorting with naked young women was not top of the one hundred ways to remain faithful to your wife, but I couldn't exactly keep my Y-fronts on and just paddle a bit in the shallow end, so I blushingly followed birthday suit. I quickly dived in and the water washed over every part of me. It felt sensuous and liberating. I manfully swam a whole length underwater, partly to demonstrate my athleticism, but mostly to postpone the problem of having to make casual chit-chat with a beautiful, naked twenty-four-year-old. Eventually I surfaced and breathlessly remarked that the water was lovely, which I believe is correct swimming-pool etiquette. We swam a few widths independently and then Jim found a beach ball, which we knocked back and forth in the air. It flashed through my head that there might be some hidden camera somewhere and that Simon was sitting at home watching it all on the Internet. We splashed about trying to be first to the ball and playfully pushing each other out of the way, and then Jim swam underneath Monica and lifted her up on his shoulders. Her skin was brown, except for three white triangles on the parts of her body that were normally covered with a bikini, which seemed to only emphasize the illegality of being allowed to see them. She laughed as Jim struggled to keep his balance.

'Piggy-back fight,' shouted Monica.

'Come on,' said Kate and she looked to me to lift her onto my shoulders and I obligingly did so.

The first time I suspected my wife was interested in me was when she first leaned across and lightly brushed a hair off my jacket. Just that tiny electrical moment of physical contact, that tentative foray into my personal space, had told me that we were more than just acquaintances. Now, as I wrapped my arms round Kate's naked wet thighs and felt her pubic hair bristling against the back of my neck, I thought we had probably crossed that personal space barrier by this juncture. I mustn't let it get too intimate, I thought to myself as she fell forward, pressing her breasts against the top of my head. I had a naked woman literally on top of me, but I was still telling myself I hadn't transgressed the line of actual sexual infidelity. Anyway, it was fun; it was a good laugh. In fact, it was fantastic. I'm playing piggy-back fights with two beautiful, naked women in a luxury swimming pool at midnight; they won't believe me when I'm in my old peo-ple's home. Jim pulled Kate off me and we both plunged underwater and her arm brushed tantalizingly against my groin. I tried to stand up, but I was at the point in the pool where the gradient slipped away dramatically and there was nothing there for me to stand on. I was in deep water. I swam back towards the shallow end, towards Kate as it happened, and then I splashed her and she splashed me back. Then the spray died down and I saw that Jim and Monica were standing in the water kissing, gently at first and then more passionately. And I was standing next to Kate. The pool was warm and the lights were low and this secret grotto felt like the only place in the universe. We looked at the other two, wrapping themselves round each other like a pair of overexcited eels, and Kate smiled at me and I stood there self-consciously for a second and smiled back. Her nipples pointed at me like General Kitchener. I felt a sense of heady recklessness; I'd had sun on my body and wine in my belly, and we were young and tanned and naked. I hadn't meant to fly this close to the flame. The moment was heavy with expectation. I had to do something.

'So tell me,' I said. 'Erm . . . how do you know Monica?'

'Well, we work in the same office, remember?'

'Oh, that's right, you said. Yeah . . . So you, er, so you met her through work.'

'Yes.'

Jim and Monica were writhing a few yards away and had started to moan slightly.

'I think a lot of people, erm, meet other people at work,' I observed.

'Yes, I suppose they do.'

There was another awkward pause.

'I like your erm . . . your . . .' I was trying to remember the word 'pendant', so I pointed at it in the hope she might help me out.

'Breasts?' she said, rather taken aback, looking down at them.

'No, no, no. Good God no. I mean, they're very nice too – not that I was looking particularly – but now you mention it . . . er . . .'

Why is there never a great white shark to drag you underwater and swallow you whole when you want one?

'No, I meant your necklace thingy.'

'Pendant?'

'That's the word. Pendant. I like your pendant.'

'Thank you.'

'Er, I think I'll just do a few more lengths now,' I said, and she smiled a half smile as I rudely left her standing there and took off for the other end of the pool as fast as I could. And as I swam away from her, I wondered what Catherine was doing right now. It was about midnight, so she was probably just feeding Alfie. I hoped Millie hadn't got up as well. I'd meant to tighten the window above her cot to stop it rattling in the wind, in case that was what kept waking her up. Catherine had asked me twice but I hadn't got round to it.

I deliberately didn't look up for the first five lengths, but when I did, I saw that Kate was out of the pool and dressed. I had been so very close to kissing her; I had wanted to press my naked body against hers and kiss her full on the lips; this basement pool had felt like another world, with its own rules and morals. I had travelled deep into the hills of my bachelor Narnia – almost too far to come back.

I couldn't risk getting that close again. I didn't trust myself to be so strong next time, especially if I carried on drinking, so I resolved to leave the party and go back to the flat.

'Yeah, let's,' said Kate when I unilaterally announced I was going.

Oh no, I thought, look I'm trying to be resolute here; don't make it harder for me. But as Jim drove down the King's Road she put her arm around me and I didn't feel able to ask her to remove it, so it stayed there, draped over my rigid shoulders all the way back to Balham. The roles were strangely reversed. I was like the nervous young girl and she was the predatory older boy. I was attracted to her, but I knew I had to fight it. My eye was drawn to the gap at the top of her shirt, where I caught a glimpse of the upper slope of her bosom. Bizarrely, this was still exciting, even though I had just seen them bouncing around naked in the swimming pool. For a second I thought I saw Catherine pushing the buggy under the street lights, but as we drove closer I saw it was in fact a tramp pushing a shopping trolley packed with old bags and that two people could not have looked more dissimilar.

Back at the flat I had to play it carefully. We all stayed up drinking and sharing a joint, but as soon as it was polite I announced that I was off to bed.

'Which one's your room, Michael?' said Kate brightly.

And I instinctively answered, 'Past the bathroom, first door on the left,' as if she were only asking because she was interested in the layout of the house. Then I realized the subtext my directions had given her, so I said a pointed, 'Goodnight, Kate.'

'Goodnight,' she said.

And I thought, Phew!

And then she gave me a naughty wink.

Five minutes later I was nervously lying in bed watching the door handle, waiting for it to turn. I worked out what I would say to her; that she was really lovely and that I found her very attractive, and that I hoped she would understand but I was in love with someone else and that I couldn't betray this other girl. These excuses were mentally rehearsed over and over again until I realized she wasn't coming after all and soon I was fast asleep.

And then I dreamt Kate was next to me in my bed, kissing me on the lips and running her hands through my hair, and it was a nice dream and I wanted it to carry on. I kissed her back and felt her bare buttocks, and this was like a dream that you could navigate because then she clasped mine. I stirred slightly, but the dream didn't end. In fact, it felt even more real. She nibbled my bottom lip and I opened my eyes and Kate smiled at me and kissed me again, and she really was in my bed, all fresh and clean and chlorine-scented, and her body felt different to Catherine, but it still felt good and there were no barriers now. All my defences were blown away and no-one would know, and Kate kissed me long and hard and ran her hands down to between my legs, and I moaned weakly, 'Oh God. You won't tell anyone, will you?'

chapter six

naughty but nice

As Kate and I had sex for the third time that night she discovered that when it came to lovemaking there wasn't much I didn't know. We did every position that I'd seen on Simon's Lover's Guide *video, and then we made love in every position they'd shown in the rip-off sequels. We stood, we lay, we sat, we did it in the shower, on the bed, on the floor and against the wall. Still entwined, I manfully lifted her up and carried her across the room. Since both my hands were clasped to her naked buttocks, she tilted the glass of champagne into my mouth for me. Most of it missed and we laughed decadently as it ran down my chin and fizzed in the space where her bosoms were pressed against my chest. Still carrying her, I pushed her left buttock against the 'play' button on my stereo and it turned on my CD of the* 1812 Overture. *With her right buttock I turned up the volume. Then Tchaikovsky conducted us through our lovemaking. As the Russian national hymn battled symbolically with 'La Marseillaise' we rolled around on the carpet, fighting to go on top, playfully scratching and biting each other throughout the Battle of Borodino. I rose with the string section and she moaned with the brass fanfares. Finally the overture reached its crescendo and we climaxed together on the floor; she screamed, 'Yes! Yes! Yes!' as the cymbals crashed, the artillery guns fired and Napoleon's army was halted at the gates of Moscow. And then we just lay there throughout the coda, panting on the carpet as the peal of bells rang out across all Russia.*

Well, that's how I imagined it would have been if I'd gone through with it. I hadn't been able to do it. I couldn't lie there and betray my wife. I think this became clear to me when I held Kate close and said, 'Oh, Catherine.' I hadn't been able to put her out of my head. Not quite. The compartments in my brain needed slightly thicker walls.

Kate's reaction was not what I expected.

'God. No-one's called me that for years.'

'Sorry?'

'Catherine. You just called me Catherine. How did you know that I was a Catherine not a Kate?'

'Er, well, Kate is short for Catherine, isn't it. I read that in a baby-naming book. Not my baby-naming book; a friend's. The person who was having a baby.'

'I stopped calling myself that when I left boarding school. I hate the name Catherine, don't you?'

'Er, no. No, I don't, actually.'

'Which do you prefer, Kate or Catherine?'

'Er, well, they're both lovely. But I'd have to say I prefer Catherine. Sorry.'

The moment of passion was gone and I quickly pulled myself together. It was better this way. The reality would never have been so erotically perfect. Sexual climax would have been swiftly followed by enormous regret, guilt, self-loathing, fear and depression. Which is quite a high price to pay for five minutes of sweaty groping in the dark. So I invented a memory of what almost was, which I'd be able to keep with me for ever. Kate was very nice about it really. She thought it was rather sweet that I was so faithful to this other girl who I didn't want to talk about. In fact, she was so nice about it that it made me want to kiss her, but I don't think that would have helped clarify where she stood.

'Well, whoever she is,' said Kate, 'she's a very lucky girl.'

'I'm not sure about that,' I replied.

We talked for an hour or two and I felt less guilty when she told me that actually she had a bit of a crush on Jim, but was fighting it because he was going out with her best friend. It was just as well we never went all the way, I thought, because I would have been going, 'Catherine! Catherine!' and she would have been going, 'Jim! Jim!' Eventually I gave her my bed while I slept on the floor with a piece of music by Pyotr Ilyich Tchaikovsky going round in my head as I imagined what might have been . . .

'You're doing it again,' said my Catherine the next day.

'What?'

'Humming the *1812 Overture* to yourself.'

'Was I? Oh sorry.'

We had been sitting in a hospital corridor together. We had been waiting so long that her twelve-week scan felt like it may have to go down as a fourteen-week scan.

'You're very quiet. What are you thinking about?'

'Oh, nothing,' I lied. 'Just wondering how much longer they're going to be.'

'Doesn't matter, does it?' she said, squeezing my arm. 'It's nice just to have some time to ourselves without the kids.'

'Mmm,' I said, unconvincingly. I thought she must be joking. This was her idea of quality time! Sitting for an hour in a sterile-smelling hospital, watching deathly white old people with tubes sticking out of them being wheeled past.

For Catherine, *this* was a treat!

'If you're really good,' I said, 'I'll see if we can get stuck in a two-hour traffic jam on the way home.'

'Ooh, yes please. There'll probably be a play on Radio 4, I can just recline the seat in the car, close my eyes and relax. Sounds like heaven.'

'Well why not?' I said, seizing the moment. 'Why don't we go and sit in the park somewhere and take a book and some wine and spend a couple of hours just doing nothing?'

'Hmm. It would be lovely, wouldn't it?'

'Yes, it would, so why don't we?'

'Just imagine it. Bliss.'

'So let's do it.'

'That would be just paradise.'

She imagined this tiny window of self-indulgence as if it were some impossible dream, a ludicrous fantasy that would never be attainable in her lifetime.

'But it wouldn't be fair on Mum.'

'But she loves looking after the kids.'

'It wouldn't be fair on the kids.'

'They love being looked after by your mum.'

She paused because she'd run out of excuses.

'No. I just can't. Sorry.'

And that was the rub. She wanted to be with the children for every hour of the day and I didn't, which meant I couldn't see her without the children, except on occasions like this when we were waiting to look at a picture of the next one.

Her legs were tightly crossed and she was rocking back and forth in her plastic moulded chair.

'You wouldn't be needing to go to the toilet by any chance, would you?'

'How could you tell,' she squeaked painfully as she swigged another half pint of mineral water from her plastic bottle. She'd had it on good authority that you got a better picture of the embryo if the mother's bladder was full. Judging by the number of gallons she was holding in she must have been hoping for a real David Bailey. 'And can we have the embryo side on, looking round and smiling? That's great. And now put your arm round the placenta and give me a big thumbs up. Fantastic! Now, last one. I want you to point to the birth canal with one hand, and with the other give me a big fingers crossed. Ha ha ha, that's lovely.'

'I can't hold on much longer,' she said. 'The moment he presses that thing against my bladder I'm going to wet my knickers, I know it.'

'Go for a wee now, then.'

'No, I want the first picture of the baby to be a good one.'

'Well try not to think about it. Do your pelvic-floor exercises or something.'

'I'm already doing them.'

I knew she wouldn't wet herself, of course, unless the doctor suddenly announced that he could see twins. It happened to Nick and Debbie, a couple who live near us. They went for the scan and were suddenly told they were expecting two babies. And they thought it was *good* news, bless them. Last time I went past their house I thought I saw the grandparents coming out of the door, but when I looked again I realized that it was Nick and Debbie themselves – six months after the twins were born.

Eventually our turn came and the doctor asked Catherine to lie down. To show that he had every confidence in my wife's personal hygiene, he tore off a huge strip of paper which he placed along the length of the bed before she came into contact with his leatherette mattress. For some reason I wasn't suspected of having any major skin diseases and so was permitted to sit on a chair as I was. He then wheeled across this huge expensive-looking piece of wizardry which he pretended was the ultrasound machine. Of course, foetal scans are all a massive con trick. They don't show you your baby at all. When all the cutbacks were being made in the health service, one of the accountants suddenly realized what a complete waste of money ultrasounds really were. All babies in the womb look completely identical, so what they do these days is just play you a video of a foetus that the consultant made back in the Sixties. That's why it's in black and white. We've all been told to look at the monitor where we've been shown exactly the same footage of the same foetus, and we've all clasped our partner's hand and bitten our lips at the miraculous beauty of our little unborn baby, when really all we are looking at is the gynaecological equivalent of that little girl playing noughts and crosses on the test card. The foetus we are actually looking at was born years ago. He's grown up now; he's a chartered surveyor who lives in Droitwich. He still gets the repeat fees.

Obviously, for appearance's sake, they still have to smear ice-cold Swarfega on your wife's bump, rub a shower attachment around a bit and point to a grey splurge on the screen and say, 'There, that's the head, see?' when it all looks like the bubbles on a bad animated Sixties underground film. But still you go away satisfied with a flimsy little photo which you believe is of your next baby, and no-one is any the wiser when friends say, 'I've got one of Jocasta almost identical to that.'

I approached the scan like a cynical old hand, exuding the blasé air of someone who already had two ultrasound images framed and artistically placed amid the gallery of black-and-white photos of my kids on the wall up the stairs at home. The doctor turned on the screen and I said, 'They're showing the snooker on the other channel,' and Catherine told me I had made the same joke when we'd come in for Millie's and Alfie's scans. So I shut up and squinted at the monitor as the deep-sea probe searched the murky depths for any sign of life. But then, when I saw the shape of our third child suddenly emerge, all my scepticism and facetiousness instantly melted away. It was a miracle. There really was a baby in there. It is simply beyond the bounds of ordinary human comprehension as to how such a thing can possibly have happened. How could our two bodies have combined to create a completely new and separate person? How could Catherine's body know how to grow an umbilical cord and a foetal sac and a placenta and create a little human being exactly the right shape and size? How is it possible that such complex biological information can all be innately pro-grammed somewhere inside her while the conscious Catherine still couldn't understand how to set the bloody video? How could one of my sperm transmit so many million messages when I couldn't even remember to tell Catherine that her mother had rung? Millions and millions of years of evolution to get to this point. Species dying out and others emerging all so that this perfect little baby could be born. It was only *one* baby, thank God. Not like the guilty secrets I could feel kicking inside me; they were quins, sextuplets, octuplets. Thank God there was no machine that could see inside me. Now that would be something. A machine that showed us what was really going on inside. Come to think of it, I would have quite liked to have known. The doctor could have pointed to the various blobs on the screen and said, 'Oh look, there's your anxiety – that's growing worry-ingly large. Does your family have a history of anxiety problems?' Or, 'Hmm, your ego looks like it may have been damaged there. We'll have to get the nurse to massage that for you.'

I looked at Catherine lying there on the bed and thought the two of us couldn't have been more different. Me sitting there quietly, the buttoned-up man with all my secrets inside me, and Catherine, the effusive open-hearted woman with her T-shirt pulled up and her trousers unzipped and the scanner squirming around on her exposed midriff so that even the inside of her body was broadcast on the telly for us all to gawp at.

We watched carefully as the doctor plotted the crown-to-rump length and eventually extrapolated from this measurement that Catherine was twelve weeks pregnant. This seemed a fairly uncontroversial diagnosis considering we had come in for her twelve-week scan. Then he chatted at great length about the stage the pregnancy was at and what Catherine should expect to feel in the coming months, and she listened and nodded as politely as she could, considering that she'd done it twice before and all she wanted to do now the scan was over was run to the toilet and have a wee.

Soon we were driving back home and Catherine sat in the seat beside me just staring at the photo of the three-month-old foetus.

'I think it might be safer if I drove,' I said nervously.

She pulled over at a bus stop and showed the photo to me again. She loved the baby already. I gave her a tentative kiss. I felt so very proud of her, she was so positive and full of optimism. I undid my seat belt so I could lean across and kiss her properly, and then I found myself hugging and kissing her like a rescued child. I had so nearly let myself slip my moorings and I was so glad to be back with her that I just kept on giving her grateful, silent guilty kisses and hugging her slightly too much.

'Are you all right?' she asked.

'I'm so happy this new baby is coming.'

And she was so relieved to hear me say that that she kissed me back passionately. There were no children tugging at our legs or crying in the background; it was just Catherine and me and all the people queuing for the number 31 bus.

Right now we were at the very zenith of our passion cycle. This was the routine emotional loop of our relationship, which came round with all the biological regularity of a menstrual cycle or a biorhythm. It took us from bitter argument to loving, mutual adoration every seven days or so. It fooled me every time. Every week, as we were staring devotedly into each other's eyes, I thought we had finally sorted out all our problems for ever. But then a day or two later Catherine would seem inexplicably irritated with me and I'd become defensive and silent, which in turn made her prickly and oversensitive. The tension would build until we reached the nadir of the cycle, when we would explode into argument, saying hateful, hurtful, stupid things to each other, briefly despising one another as passionately as we had adored each other only days before. Then I would disappear for a while. I was still in orbit around her, still in her gravitational pull, but this was the most distant point between us. Then I would re-emerge, shining brightly in her life for a while, and everything seemed like it was perfect between us again for ever.

If I was ever unsure about what stage we were at in the loop I just had to check the height of the pile of ironing. The crumpled clothes would just be a few items at first and then, during the week, more would be placed on top, until the tower was in danger of toppling over when we finally had a fight and Catherine angrily threw herself into the ironing, smashing the hissing metal onto Barbie and Ken's faces as they smiled up at her from the front of Millie's T-shirts.

We drove the rest of the way home in a blissful haze and Catherine miraculously agreed that we should go out that evening if her mother didn't mind staying on and babysitting the children. Her mum eagerly agreed; she never missed an opportunity to put the kids to bed so that she could send them off to sleep with another thrilling instalment from the neglected copy of *Bible Stories for Children*, which she had given Millie for Christmas.

Catherine's mother was a Church of England fundamentalist, fighting her own holy jihad against anyone who would not take Jesus into their life, or indeed anyone who wouldn't help her with the St Botolph's Christmas fayre and jumble sale.

There was a particular shirt I wanted to wear, but discovered that it needed ironing. It occurred to me that I could, of course, precipitate a row so that I wouldn't have to wait a couple of days, but on balance I decided it was probably unfair and against the natural order of things to try to force an argument before it was organically due, and so I painstakingly ironed the shirt myself. Catherine was amazed and delighted to see me doing the ironing, and then she realized that I was only doing my own shirt and not ironing anything of hers or the children's and a huge row blew up. Before long she was ironing everything, including the very shirt that I had originally made such a hash of myself.

'Jesus, you're a selfish bastard sometimes, Michael,' said Catherine.

'Please do not use the name of our Lord Jesus Christ in that way, dear,' said her mother.

I think that was the only time the passion cycle took a couple of hours instead of the full seven days. We never had that evening out together, instead I found myself heading down the Northern Line to Balham. 'Mind the gap,' said the announcement at Embankment. A few hours later I was back at my flat again, and after I knew she would be asleep I left a brusque message on the answerphone saying that something had come up and I probably wouldn't be able to leave the studio for a couple of days. Lies are like cigarettes – your first one makes you feel sick, but soon you're addicted to them, unaware you are even doing it.

The next day was the hottest day of the summer. The weatherman had predicted that the temperature would be in the mid-eighties, though in London this was probably bumped up another couple of degrees by all the electrical equipment in my studio. It can only have been around half an hour after I had sat down to work that Jim popped his head round the door and asked me if I wanted to come to a barbecue on Clapham Common. The little devil by my right ear said, 'Go on, it's a lovely day, have some fun. All this work can wait.' And the little angel by my left ear said, 'Oh, fuck it, what's the point in even trying?'

The barbecue was already well under way in the semi-wooded hilly area by the Latin American football pitches. There must have been over twenty people at our picnic, all of them about my age – meaning that I was probably seven or eight years older than any of them. Girls with pierced navels laid their heads on the laps of boyfriends in combat trousers, music floated across the grass, a couple of disposable barbecues smoked away and the smell of charcoal mingled with the occasional wafts of cannabis. They were so free they didn't know it. Part of me was nervous about gate-crashing their twenty-something party, as if one of them might suddenly sit up, point at me and say, 'Just a minute, you're not *young*!' Lots of the blokes had little beards, so small they hardly seemed worth the trouble. Not me, though – I was far too old for a beard. I hid behind my sunglasses and sat down in a space amongst the stretched-out legs, some of them sporting flared trousers like the ones I remembered wearing first time round. If anyone asked, I couldn't remember when Elvis died. Elvis who? The Falklands? What was that? Typewriters? Never heard of them. Microsoft Windows '95 – oooh, yes, I think I just about remember that.

The tragic thing was that while I could remember everything from when I was young, I couldn't actually remember anything from the last few years. This lot would all know what song was number one. When was the last time I knew or cared? I could still list all the Christmas chart-toppers of the Seventies and Eighties – I could tell you every track of every album I bought back then – but ask my brain to store any more new information now and it would refuse. Disk full. It ought to be possible to delete some files to make space. For example, thanks to three hours spent racking my brain after having breakfast with Simon, I knew that St John's Wood was the only underground station that doesn't include a letter from the word 'mackerel'. I'd be more than happy to wipe that piece of knowledge from my mind so that I could make room to remember my dad's birthday. But every year I forgot to send him a card, and every time the tube train pulled into St John's Wood I would now think of mackerel.

I accepted a little bottle of French lager, lay back, closed my eyes and let the sun and alcohol carry me away. A few revellers struggled to their feet and youthfully threw a frisbee back and forth. Others busied themselves rolling joints or putting overcooked sausages into bread for everyone. Cannabis was passed one way and hot dogs were passed the other; there's probably some modern youth etiquette to it. There was an efficiency to this picnic that made me realize these kids weren't really the lazy no-hopers they affected to be; their bumming about was far too well organized. Anyone at the advertising agencies would be able to tell me the name of this particular tribe. The pierced navels? The clubbers? The Ibiza posse? I think they were expected to drink Pepsi Max and buy snowboards, or care about the planet, but in the most hedonistic way possible. The girls brushed their shiny long hair away from their faces with the backs of their wrists and they all had the healthy glow of well-bred families. Like Jim, they were hippie posh; they'd dropped out, but had return tickets for when they were older. Their parents would have spent the summer doing Ascot, Henley and Wimbledon, and these kids would have had their own summer season, going to the Fleadh, Reading Festival or Glastonbury.

So if I wasn't one of them, which advertising tribe would I be filed under? When Hugo had asked me to write the musical sting for 'The saloon car that thinks it's a sports car', he had told me they were aiming at the 'Lad Dad'. A shudder had run down my spine as I'd felt instantly categorized in two short syllables. 'Oh, I know the sort,' I had said to him scornfully, simultaneously throwing a glossy men's magazine into the waste-paper bin.

The midday sun felt powerful and I moved into the shade to prevent my tender forehead from burning. It would be hard to explain how I'd become sunburned from sitting at my keyboard all day. Suddenly, from my bag I could hear my mobile phone ringing. I expected to get groans from all the pierced alternative environmentalists, but they all reached for their pockets and bags as well.

'Hi. It's me,' said Catherine.

Her tone was suitably cool considering that we had had a row, but at least she'd made the first contact.

'Are you in your studio?'

I thought I could just about answer that one without lying unnecessarily.

'No.'

'Where are you, then?'

I sensed that she might be angling for me to come home for bathtime. I looked around and decided that it wouldn't be a very good idea to say that I was lying on the grass on Clapham Common. Near by a little boy was wearing a Manchester United top.

'I'm in . . . Manchester.'

Some of the people sitting near by seemed curious, so I smiled at them and mimed a long-suffering tut that the person I was speaking to couldn't grasp this obvious and simple fact.

'Manchester? Really? Whereabouts?'

'Oh. United.'

'What?'

'I mean, um, Piccadilly.' It had been a bad choice. Manchester was where Catherine had been to college.

'Why did you say united?'

'Sorry, I just associate Manchester with United. As opposed to Manchester City, who wear sky-blue shirts, of course.'

'What are you talking about?'

'Sorry. They've just told me to hurry up because this edit suite is costing them five hundred pounds an hour.'

'Oh. So you won't see the kids before bed, then?'

''Fraid not. It's bloody murder up here. I'm having to rewrite something on the spot. Talk about pressure.'

'Oh.' She sounded disappointed. 'Well, we're just off to see Susan and Piers's new house. I'll speak to you tomorrow.'

'Oh, well don't get chatting to Piers about the Astra; you'll never get away.'

She was still too cool towards me to laugh, so I asked her to give the kids a kiss from me and we said our goodbyes and hung up. Neither of us said sorry for the horrible things we had shouted at each other the day before, but the ice had been broken and we would speak more warmly again the next day. It was so much better this way; we wouldn't spend two days slamming doors and ruining each other's weekend. I cracked open another stubby lager bottle and passed an hour lazily trying to make things out of the shapes of clouds. They looked cloud-shaped to me every time.

The mobile rang again and this time it was Hugo Harrison. When I had completed my last job for him I had put the track on the tape three times in a row, knowing that he would need to listen to it over and over again and so saving him the trouble of having to repeatedly cue up the same piece of music.

'Hi, Michael, it's Hugo here. I've had a listen to your tracks.'

'Tracks?' I said, confused that he was using the plural.

'Yeah, now I like the beginning of the first mix, the pace of the second one and the best ending of the three is definitely on the last version.'

What could I say? They are all completely identical, you stupid prat?

'Right, um, interesting,' I stammered.

'Could you have another go at it, incorporating the best bits of all three?'

'Um, well I could try, so let me write that down,' I said as onlookers wondered why I wasn't writing anything down. 'The beginning of one, the pace of two and the ending of three. Right, I'll do my best, but it might take me a day or two.'

'That's OK. Cheers, Michael, gotta dash.'

And I lay back making a mental note to send him a tape with just the one version of exactly the same mix, which I knew he'd be delighted with.

More people turned up to the barbecue as the day progressed, including Kate and Monica. Kate had brought her acoustic guitar, which she placed lovingly down on a rug while she brought out seemingly endless plates of sandwiches that she'd made for everyone. Beside me lay a bloke who called himself Dirk, to whom I had already taken an irrational dislike on the grounds that when he took a puff of his cigarette he held the fag between his thumb and little finger, like he was James Dean or Marlon Brando. I knew there were greater crimes against humanity, but at that moment, holding your cigarette between your thumb and little finger was right up there with the worst of them. In any case, my first impression of him was soon vindicated.

Popping a sandwich in his mouth without acknowledging

Kate's efforts, Dirk then picked up her guitar and started to pluck out a few notes. Kate looked mildly put out at his presumption, but said nothing. He adjusted the tuning slightly and tutted.

'How much did you pay for this?'

'Only fifty pounds,' said Kate proudly. 'I got it second hand.'

'Fifty quid? I'll give you twenty for it.'

Occasionally you meet somebody who is so unlikeable that you can only presume they attend rudeness evening classes.

'Well, I wasn't looking to sell it actually,' said Kate, far too politely.

'Bad luck. It's just gone down to fifteen. You missed your chance.' And he wedged his cigarette under the strings by the keys. 'Fifty quid! For a crappy guitar like this,' he muttered to himself as he began strumming. Kate looked at me in disbelief and part of me wanted to grab her guitar off the bloke and hit him over the head with it. But I didn't because I'm not a violent person, it would have ruined the whole picnic and, apart from anything else, it would have smashed into splinters, because he was right, it was a crappy guitar.

I tried to ignore him, but soon he became the centre of attention as a few other girls started to sing along to his rather loose interpretation of 'Wonderwall'. They sounded more like the Von Trapp children than Liam Gallagher, but they weren't helped by this poser getting half the chords wrong. I could contain myself no longer.

'Um, I think that should be E minor seventh there, actually,' I said tentatively.

That was the first time he noticed me. He took another affected puff of his cigarette and winced, half closing one eye as he inhaled, as if his Silk Cut were mixed with the strongest Jamaican skunk.

'Don't think so, mate,' he replied.

'Yeah, it goes Em7, G, Dsus4, A7sus4.'

Suddenly he could tell I knew what I was talking about, but he couldn't back down in front of all these admiring women. There was a new stag in the herd, butting him with his antlers. He paused. Then, instead of continuing with 'Wonderwall', he started a different song, one that he had obviously practised a few more times over the years.

'Oh no,' said one of the girls, 'not "Stairway to bloody Heaven". What happened to Oasis?'

'I'll have a bash at it, if you like,' I gallantly offered and there was enthusiastic agreement from the assembled audience. He had no choice but to hand over the guitar, and now the whole crowd was watching to see if I was any better.

'Would that be all right, Kate? If I played your guitar?' She nodded and the tension built as I pointedly and slowly adjusted the tuning. A pause. Then I plunged emphatically into the opening chords of 'Wonderwall', strumming with a force and confidence that drew the best possible sound from the nylon strings. The blood drained from Dirk's face as I segued into 'The Passenger', 'Rock 'n' Roll Suicide' and the trickiest bit of Rodrigo's *Guitar Concerto No. 2* for good measure. By the time I finished there were cheers and applause and shouts of, 'Encore!' and the girls looked ready to ask me if I would father their children. 'That's quite a nice guitar you've got there, Kate,' I lied as I passed it back to its owner. It was a great moment. If only all of life could be like that. I noticed that when Dirk lit his next cigarette he held it normally. Mission accomplished, I thought.

I suppose the women were so enamoured of me because I expressed so much emotion with the music. If I had a guitar in my hand or a keyboard under my fingertips I could say, 'I'm so in love' or 'I'm so unhappy' and really convey how those things felt. I could never have just said the words. Right now I had to try quite hard not to show how I was feeling, which was revoltingly self-satisfied. I had just defended the honour of Kate's guitar, it was a beautiful sunny day and the egg-mayonnaise sandwiches even had the crusts cut off. Temporary financial setbacks aside, my double life was a well-oiled machine. I had a wife, but I was independent, I had a job in which I could choose my own hours, I had the perfect amount of time with my beautiful children, but I also had my own space and all the time to myself that I could possibly want.

I eased myself up and went a few yards into the woods and wee'd against a tree. The mixture of sun and lager made me feel dizzy and I swayed slightly as I buttoned up my flies and squinted in the brightness of the sun. And then, coming through a clearing and down a little hill, I saw Millie. My little daughter Millie, not yet three years old, wandering about in the thicket forty feet away. On Clapham Common. On her own.

She appeared to be perfectly happy so I restrained my instinct to call out her name. No matter how hard I looked I couldn't see her mother. With mounting incomprehension I just watched her, pottering along, picking leaves and cheerfully singing a little song to herself. It was as if she were a child I didn't know; she was completely separate from me, as if I were observing her through a one-way mirror or on an old family video recording. I'd never heard her singing that song before. She was just another kid in the park, except she was my daughter. It was the same sensation I'd had when I'd seen our third baby in the scan – I could see my child, but I wasn't able to relate to her. She felt distant and surreal.

Why isn't Catherine with her? I wondered anxiously. I hid behind a bush so I could watch Millie without giving myself away. Part of me wanted to run and give her a big hug, but there was so much at risk. She must be lost. I would just keep an eye on her from a distance, until her mother found her, and then silently slip away. I could not afford to make my presence known, this was the only logical option I could pursue. And yet as she came closer I blurted out her name in spite of myself, not quite sure why.

'Daddy!' she replied.

She wasn't particularly surprised to see me hiding there, which threw me slightly, but mixed in with my panic and incomprehension was elation at seeing my beautiful little daughter so unexpectedly. She ran towards me and I picked her up; she squeezed me tight, which was lovely even though I had no idea what I could possibly do next.

'Where's Mummy?'

'Erm . . . she's, she's, she's, she's . . . Mummy, um, Mummy . . .'

Come on, Millie, spit it out.

'She's . . . she's over there.' And she pointed to the band-stand a good hundred yards away, through the trees. At that moment I heard Catherine calling Millie's name, with terror and panic in her voice. There was no way out of this situation. Catherine had lost Millie; I had found her. Only an hour ago I had told Catherine I was working in Manchester My heart was beating *allegro forte* and I said, 'Oh dear, Millie, what am I going to do?'

'Green bird,' she answered, pointing to the tree. And she was right. Crawling up the tree trunk behind me was a green woodpecker. How about that! In the middle of London! I'd never seen a green woodpecker before.

'Millie! Where are you?' screamed her desperate mother, coming closer. I put her down on the ground and pointed to her mum. 'Look, Millie, there's Mummy. Run to Mummy. Tell her you saw a man that looked like Daddy.'

I let her go and she ran across the open common towards her mother. As she left I heard her shouting, 'Mummy! Daddy said I saw man that look like Daddy.'

I saw the moment that Catherine spotted her. In a split second her face went from terror to enormous relief, but then barely paused as it progressed to anger at the terrible ordeal she had just been put through. She was furious with Millie, although I knew deep down she was angry with herself for losing her. She had Alfie in one arm, but she ran towards Millie with the other outstretched and then grabbed her and burst into tears. She shouted at Millie for running off like that, and any message that Millie attempted to relay was lost in the anger, hugs and tears, so I was safe for the time being.

Still hiding among the trees I watched Catherine get ready to leave the common. What was she doing down here anyway? She was miles from home; she never came south of the river. I knew that getting the kids ready would be a major operation. She tried to strap Alfie into the double buggy, but he wailed and struggled and arched his back, demanding that he be carried. Millie was upset at having been told off and was also crying. Her mother took a bag out of the buggy and put Millie in. As she was hooking the bag over the pushchair handles Millie started to become hysterical, screaming and holding her arms out to be picked up, jealous that her little brother was being carried.

Catherine picked Millie up out of the pushchair, and as she did so the weight of the bag slung over the handles tipped up the buggy and, in a violent surprise see-saw action, the whole thing up-ended. The bag hit the tarmac and I heard the sound of shattering glass. That'll be the bottle of Aqua Libre, I thought to myself. That smelly melon drink she buys with a name that means 'free water' and costs a fortune. The designer drink was seeping out of the bag and onto the ground. Still supporting the weight of both children, I watched as she squatted down and, with her remaining free hand, tried to stop the liquid ruining everything else in the bag. Then I heard her swear as she cut her hand. Her hand bled as she tried to put Millie down but, being just under three, Millie refused to see the situation from Catherine's point of view and would not let go. Catherine angrily pulled Millie off, who then lay on the ground and screamed. At each step I had felt that I could see what was about to happen, but I was powerless to prevent it, like watching a series of cars bumping one another on one of those compilation videos of motorway accidents. I really would have liked to have gone and helped, but how could I? How could I suddenly appear in the middle of Clapham Common an hour after I had said I was up in Manchester?

'Checking out the local nannies?' sneered a voice behind me. It was Dirk, still smarting from being outplayed on a cheap plywood guitar.

'Er, no, I was just watching that woman struggling with those two little kids. She's their mother actually. Er, I'd say.'

'God, who'd have kids, eh?' he said as Millie lay on the floor sobbing and kicking. I found myself half nodding in tacit agreement and then felt guilty for betraying my own children so casually.

'Look at that little brat screaming. I don't think people should be allowed to have kids if they don't know how to control them.'

Suddenly I was fuming. What did he know about it?

'It's not her fault,' I said, bristling. 'It's hard on your own. And most two-years-olds are like that.'

'Look how she's shouting at the poor child. No wonder it's screaming.'

'Well, she's probably at her wit's end. Not sleeping and all that.'

'Yeah, single mother probably,' said Dirk as he headed off back to the barbecue. Catherine was now sitting on the ground crying. She looked utterly defeated by it all. I had never seen her give up like this. Her hand was bleeding and both her children were sobbing, too. And this being London, everyone else rushed past as if she was some drug addict or alcoholic nutter. Wasn't anyone going to step in and help her?

'Are you OK, Catherine?' I said.

She looked up and was so astonished to see me standing there that she immediately stopped weeping.

'How on earth did you get here?'

Since I didn't have an answer to this question I thought the best policy would be to ignore it.

'What have you done to your hand?'

'Oh, I cut it,' she said, holding it up.

'Ah, that would explain all the blood dripping onto the tarmac.' I wrapped my handkerchief around her fingers and she sat there gazing at me as if I were her fairy godmother and a knight in shining armour all rolled into one. 'I can see you cut it, you idiot. What were you doing?'

'Well, I was trying to get all the broken glass out of the bottom of the bag.'

'And you say this broken glass somehow cut your hand? Well talk about a freak accident.'

She smiled and I hoped the moment had passed when she would have asked what I was doing there in the first place.

'Me and Daddy saw a green bird,' said Millie helpfully.

'God, she's still going on about that. We saw a green woodpecker about two months ago.' I tied the handkerchief into a knot. 'Let's go and get a coffee and I'll buy Millie some crisps or something.'

Catherine wiped her smudged eye make-up. 'Oh God, Michael, I'm so pleased to see you. I lost Millie. It was awful; she just wandered away from the bandstand when I was changing Alfie, and I ran round behind the café, but she must have gone in the other direction because I lost her for ages. It was terrifying. And then the buggy tipped up and the bottles smashed and I cut my hand open and the kids were scream-ing and I just couldn't cope . . .'

'OK, forget the coffee, how about a glass of wine?'

'What about the baby?'

'Good point – I'll get one for him, too.'

I hoisted Millie onto my shoulders and we headed towards the Windmill Inn, away from the direction of the picnic. If the empty seat in the double buggy had been slightly bigger I would have strapped Catherine in next to Alfie and pushed her all the way there. We sat outside the pub and Alfie sucked his bottle and I sipped my pint and Catherine knocked back her glass of wine in one. It seemed like everything was all right again, for a moment at least.

'So why did you say you were in Manchester?' she asked suddenly.

I only had one crisp in my mouth, but apparently my mouth was so full it was impossible for me to reply.

'Manchester?' I finally said. 'What are you talking about?'

'You said you were up in Manchester.'

There was a pause in which I tried to regard her as if she must be completely deranged and then I steered my puzzled face into exaggerated realization as a way out suddenly came into my head.

'No, no, no. Manchester *Street*. I said I was in Manchester *Street*. In the West End.'

She looked confused.

'But you said you were in Piccadilly.'

'Piccadilly Circus, yeah?'

She laughed at her foolishness. 'Oh, I'd got it into my head that you'd gone up North for work again.'

We shared a good-natured laugh at this mix-up and I breathed a silent sigh of relief that Catherine had for-gotten, or was unaware, that Manchester Street was a good couple of miles from Piccadilly Circus. Before she had time to think about this I changed the subject.

'So what are you doing this side of the river? Weren't you worried about the border guards stopping you on the bridge?'

'I was supposed to be seeing Susan and Piers's new house in Stockwell, but we got to the front door and there was no-one home, so we thought we'd have a bit of a run about on Clapham Common, didn't we, Millie?'

'Me and Daddy saw a green bird.'

'Yes, all right, Millie. You said,' I interjected. 'Have another packet of crisps.'

'What about you?' Catherine asked me.

'Well, after I'd finished in *Manchester Street*, I got the tube from *Piccadilly Circus* to go to my studio and thought I'd walk across the common when I saw you. Coincidence, eh?'

'Yeah, well let's not tell my sister. She'd probably put it down to ley lines or psychic energy or something.'

'Oh, that's a good idea. I'll tell her I took a diversion across the common because I could sense the negative vibrations you were sending out. We'll never hear the end of it.'

Catherine was laughing again, although there seemed to be a slightly hysterical edge to it. I got her another large glass of wine and Millie her third packet of crisps and Catherine seemed more like the wife I knew; the breakdown by the bandstand far behind her. But then, as the alcohol kicked in, she seemed to become almost too tired to keep laughing. I volunteered to change Millie's nappy and that extracted a brief smile. I laid Millie on the changing mat and set about unbuttoning her baggy pink dungarees.

'Michael?' said Catherine ominously.

'What?'

'I'm not happy.'

'Sorry?'

'I'm not happy.'

'Is it dry enough? I asked for a dry white wine.'

'With my life. I'm not happy.'

'What do you mean, you're not happy; of course you're happy.'

'I'm not. I felt guilty about it so I kept it to myself, but it's just such a strain. It's like there's something missing that I can't put my finger on.'

'It's just the drink talking, Catherine. You're feeling tired and a bit drunk and suddenly you think you're not happy, but believe me, you are one of the happiest people I know. Next you'll be saying you can't cope with the children.'

'I can't cope with the children.'

'Stop it, Catherine, it's not funny. Millie, stop wriggling, will you.'

'I'm not joking.'

'You do cope with the children. You cope brilliantly. Millie, lie still.'

Catherine shrugged and said nothing. I looked up at her from where I was kneeling on the floor, hunched over the changing mat.

'OK, sometimes maybe you feel as if you can't cope with them, but I'm sure that's normal. Generally speaking you like being with the kids on your own.'

'No, I don't.'

'Yes, you do.'

'No, I don't.'

'Well maybe occasionally they feel a bit overwhelming. But, generally speaking, you like having me out of the way.'

'No, I don't.'

'Yes, you do.'

'No, I don't.'

'Yes, you do.'

'No, I don't.'

'Look stop it, you naughty girl.'

'Are you talking to me or Millie?'

Millie was wriggling and making it impossible for me to put the nappy on straight.

'Why do you have to make things bloody difficult?' And then I added, 'Millie!' just to be clear.

'I want Mummy to do it.'

'No, Mummy can't do everything.'

'Yes she can,' said Catherine. 'Clever Mummy can do everything and keep smiling happy smiles all day long, tra-la-la.'

'Catherine, you're pissed.'

'. . . off. I'm pissed off.'

'Look, I understand that you've had a lousy day and that the kids can be wearing, but you have always said how much you love being at home with them.'

'That was for your sake,' she said. 'I thought if you were under all that pressure at work then the last thing you needed was to have me moaning about being at home.'

'You're just saying that.'

'It's true.'

'It's not.'

'It is; it's miserable being on my own half the week. Sometimes I feel like I've already done a day's work, and then I look at the kitchen clock and it's only ten in the morning and I think, Only nine hours till they're in bed.'

'You're just saying that because you feel miserable at the moment. I know you cope really well when I'm not there.'

'I don't.'

'I'm telling you you do. I know you do.'

'How do you know? How do you know better than me how I cope when you're not there?'

'Well, er, because I know you, that's how. You're a very good mother.'

'You used to say I was a very good actress.'

'You still are a very good actress.'

154

'I must be if you believe all that happy-families stuff I turn on when you walk through the front door.'

I didn't have an answer to that, and then Millie tried to wriggle free again and I lost patience with her.

'JUST STOP IT, MILLIE, FOR GOD'S SAKE. YOU'RE A VERY NAUGHTY GIRL! YOU'RE VERY, VERY NAUGHTY AND I'VE HAD ENOUGH OF IT NOW!'

Eventually Catherine decided it was time to go home and she said that I had better get back to my studio to carry on with my work. But this time I didn't take her up on her offer. Something had penetrated my rhino-hide skin and I sensed that she wanted me to change my plans and come home. She needed me to just be there. She needed me to be supportive. And she needed me to drive the car home because she was pissed out of her head.

We headed back over the river, and I told Millie that Albert Bridge was made out of pink icing sugar, and in the late May sunshine it looked as if it might well have been. As we entered Chelsea the people on the street were suddenly very different to those a hundred yards away on the other side of the river. With their Moschino handbags and Ralph Lauren shirts, they were so expensively dressed that they had to wear their labels on the outside. We would have to drive all the way through the richest parts of London before we came out on the other side and were back among the more impoverished middle classes once again.

Forty minutes later we were back in our *bijou* shoebox in Kentish Town. I put some tea in front of Millie, which after three packets of crisps she quite rightly ignored. Why I didn't cook it and then put it straight in the bin to save time, I don't know. Then I sat down beside her and, with Alfie on my lap, we watched *The Lion King* again, right up to the bit where Simba disappears off on his own to grow up and then finally bumps into his long-lost Nala in the forest. Catherine got herself another drink; I was glad that she was no longer breastfeeding because if she had been Alfie would probably have passed out from alcohol poisoning. We didn't talk any more about what she'd said, although I did notice myself making exaggerated aren't-they-sweet? noises every time the kids did anything as much as throw a lump of food on the floor.

I cooked the kids' tea and cleared up, I cooked our dinner and cleared up, I bathed the kids and put them to bed, I tidied away the toys and even put a load of washing on, but it seemed that nothing could extricate any grateful noises of approval from Catherine, who just lay on the sofa, staring at the ceiling. To her credit, she had known when to stop drinking, which was when the wine bottle was empty. Eventually she announced she was going to bed early and she gave me a hug. 'It's not you; it's me,' she said meaningfully, and then she squeezed me so tightly she nearly cracked a couple of ribs.

I stayed downstairs for a while and listened to a few of my favourite bits of music on my own. I listened to 'For No One' by the Beatles three times, which felt like having someone unlock an impossible sequence of secret doors inside my head. When I couldn't think of any more reasons to stay up I got ready to follow Catherine to bed. I mixed Alfie's bottle of babymilk for the night feed, stood it by the microwave and then checked on the kids. Millie had already vacated her bed and taken my place beside Catherine, so I went into the nursery, climbed into her bed and pulled the Barbie duvet up over my head. I kicked a couple of soft toys out of the bottom of the bed and lay there listening to Alfie snuffling in the cot beside me.

An hour passed and I was still awake. I fluffed up the pillow and pulled up the duvet, but it wasn't the bedding that was making me uncomfortable. The picture of her sitting on the ground crying just kept coming back to me. It was so at odds with the image of Catherine that I had kept in my head when we were apart. Unaware that I was watching her, she had just given up and surrendered. And now that her cover was blown she wasn't pretending any more.

'There's something missing that I just can't put my finger on,' she had said. I tried to tell myself it was just some hormonal depression related to the pregnancy, but I knew if it was that simple I wouldn't be lying awake at two o'clock in the morning. An hour later, I listened as Alfie began to stir. Now that he was nearly a year old he generally only woke once in the night, and although the chances of Catherine being stirred from her wine-induced coma were frankly quite slim, I went downstairs and warmed up his babymilk before he started to cry. I took a swig to check the temperature and then spat the disgusting chalky pond water out into the sink, but it left a bad taste in my mouth. The trick now was to give Alfie a good feed without stimulating him so much that he became wide awake. But as we sat together in the half light of the nursery and he sucked eagerly on the bottle, he suddenly opened his eyes as if he had just realized something very important. He stared at me as he fed and I risked a gentle, 'Hello, Alfie Adams,' and he just carried on drinking and staring. He seemed so completely trusting and innocent, so completely dependent on my care that I felt like I had somehow let him down. As I looked into his big blue eyes I imagined for a moment that he knew everything about me, that he understood why his mother felt isolated and abandoned and he was just staring sternly at me as if to say, 'What on earth do you think you are doing, Dad?'

'I'm sorry, Alfie,' I said. 'I'm really sorry.' And I was.

chapter seven

the mark of a man

'It is not possible to maintain your dignity in a ball pit. Once you are lying on your back in the krazy quicksand of brightly coloured plastic balls you must resign yourself to looking like a lumbering, graceless buffoon, a sweaty injured walrus of a grown-up who, just by dint of being there, invites being bombarded by a hail of primary-coloured plastic cannon balls. There is a special fun smile you must wear, even when the little boy with the bullet haircut who you don't know has just got you right in the face with a ball he has squashed to make it hurt more when he throws it. This is just one aspect of the general loss of dignity that is part of the modern paternal contract. You cannot appear aloof and indifferent when your two-year-old is vomiting his chocolate ice cream all over the floor of a designer menswear shop. There is no sophisticated, tasteful way to wipe the shit off your baby's bottom. Don't ever believe those adverts that tell you having kids will make you look cool, because it won't. There is no Action Man double buggy with pull-out baby-changing mat. The mark of a man is no longer splashing on Old Spice and surfing to the chorus of the *Carmina Burana*; it is swallowing your pride and grubbing about on the floor and rolling around in ball pits. It's humiliating, but it's part of the deal.'

The crowd of fathers-to-be listened to me in shocked silence. Despite this pregnancy being Catherine's third, I found myself being dragged back to antenatal classes and, on this particular evening, all the men had been sent into a separate room to discuss the ways in which we expected our lives to change after our babies were born.

'Another thing they don't warn you about,' I continued, like an irate caller on a late-night radio phone-in, 'is what it does to your marriage. Suddenly you niggle at each other and score points and try to make out you've had a much worse time than your partner. Catherine will say to me, "Have you sterilized the bottles," when she can see the dirty bottles piled up in the sink. She knows the answer to the question, but by asking it knows she will force me into a guilty admission of failure. But all that does is make me exaggerate how difficult Alfie was while she was out. No, not exaggerate, lie! I will claim that I haven't had a minute spare, and then Catherine will be forced to pretend she had a far worse time with Millie at the supermarket. It's martyr's poker – I'll see your tantrum-at-the-checkout story and raise it with my account of diarrhoea in mid nappy-change.'

They were as eager to hear about my experiences as I was to recount them. No other man in the room had yet become a parent and they looked to me as the war-scarred veteran, back from battle, full of horrific tales from the front line of fatherhood.

'But the thing that really disappears overnight is your youth. Suddenly your youth is over. I tried to artificially recreate mine,' I said enigmatically, 'but it hasn't really worked. As soon as you become responsible for someone very, very young, it suddenly makes you feel very, very old. For one thing you are exhausted, both physically and emotionally, and if you have any time to still do any of the things you did as a young man, you will find yourself struggling to tackle them with the weary foreboding of an overwhelmed pensioner. By the time the children start to be less physically demanding you've aged ten years in the space of two or three, so it's too late to get it back anyway. You will look in the mirror at the greying hair and sagging face and you will think, Where the bloody hell did *he* come from? But you don't just look old and feel old in your bones, you *think* old. You fuss and you worry about your children, but you don't realize or care that you're walking down the street with odd socks and your hair sticking up. You become fretful and sensible and organized, and if you ever do anything carefree and spontaneous together it's because two weeks ago you set aside an hour to do something carefree and spontaneous together. The day that baby comes out it's over. Your independence, your youth, your pride – everything that made you what you were. You have to start again from scratch.'

The cheery teacher came into the room and clapped her hands together in enthusiastic anticipation.

'Well,' she said, 'how are we all getting on in here?'

And none of the open-mouthed men even looked up from where they were staring silently at the floor.

I found these antenatal classes embarrassing, to tell the truth. It was like I was some backward child being made to do a year at school all over again. At one point our partners had to get on all fours and we had to kneel beside them and rub them on the small of the back, and then the teacher came round to see if we were rubbing our partners correctly. We have classes to help us with the birth of the child; I suppose we should just be grateful we don't have some prim little woman guiding us through the best way to conceive them as well. 'Right, now if the women would all like to lie on the floor, perhaps the men could practise stimulating the clitoris. No, Michael, you're miles out there . . .'

And why are there no classes to help us once the children have come out? That's the bit that the adults get wrong, that's the bit where we need real help. 'Well done, you gave birth, here's your baby. Now the rest is up to you.' I allowed myself a private chuckle at all the naïve enthusiasm of the first-time parents. One of the men even asked what sort of filling he should put in the sandwiches, bless him. They were all completely consumed by their child before it had even been born. I wanted to say to them, don't keep coming to these parenting classes, go to the cinema together instead, go out for dinner, just do things for yourselves while you still can. But they compared bumps and bootees and asked us whether it was best to put the baby straight into a cot or whether they should let it come into the parents' bed, and Catherine shrugged and said she still didn't know.

Catherine and I didn't discuss the things she had said sitting outside the Windmill Inn, but it was clear that she had abandoned the pretence that everything in her life was as perfect as I had always presumed. Her frustration was allayed by redecorating the house; she had come out of the tired stage of pregnancy and flipped over into the manic nesting phase. I tried to assuage my guilt by suggesting that she should be resting and that she should leave it all to me, but she really wanted to do something for this new baby, and so she heroically climbed up and down the stepladder, lovingly painting the nursery walls as the paint splattered down onto her growing bump. Obviously there were some things she couldn't do herself, things that needed the strength and technical expertise of a handyman, which was when she would turn to me and say, 'Michael, pop round to Mrs Conroy's and see if Klaus and Hans can give us a hand.' I could usually just about manage that.

Klaus and Hans were two German students that lodged next door whom Catherine got round on a regular basis to make me feel useless. On this occasion I had failed to assemble a chest of drawers. The instructions were printed in English, German, Italian, Spanish, French and Arabic. It was thoughtful of the manufacturers to print them in English, but it didn't really make any difference; they made the same amount of sense to me in any language. When I read a sentence like 'Attach tab "c" to retaining toggle "g" without releasing pivot joint "f",' a blanket of mist descends on my brain and I am no longer reading instructions, I am just looking at a lot of words. Klaus and Hans put the unit together with the speed and efficiency of a Grand Prix pit-stop team.

'You have a set of Allen keys, Michael, yes?'

'Don't think so.'

'Yes you have. In your toolbox.'

'Allen keys? Are you sure?'

'Yes. They are in the little compartment with the spokeshave.'

'Spokeshave? What's a spokeshave?'

Klaus knew the English for spokeshave. I still don't know what a spokeshave is or how I came to be the owner of one. Klaus and Hans often popped round to borrow my tools, which meant ripping open the packaging in which they'd remained hidden since some long-ago Christmas.

'Is Michael using his power drill at the moment?' Klaus would ask Catherine at the front door. And then I could hear him say, 'I don't understand. What is funny?'

But however charming and helpful Klaus and Hans were, I couldn't help but feel vaguely emasculated by the way Catherine came to depend on them. They mended the lawn-mower, they unblocked the sink, they stopped the radio alarm I had rewired from giving you an electric shock every time you pressed the snooze button. If I ever came home to find one of them putting a new washer on the tap or whatever I'd step in and say, 'Thanks, Klaus, I can take over now.' And then an hour later I'd knock on his door and say, 'So how do I get the tap back on, exactly?'

Catherine always wanted to change things in our house. It was a kind of permanent revolution; as soon as the campaign to have a new carpet in the bedroom was successful, the next campaign to have new kitchen units would begin. I optimistically suggested to her that the nursery wallpaper would be fine for another year or so, but she asserted that it wouldn't be fair if we didn't make it as nice for the next two kids as it had been for our first two.

'The next *two* kids?'

'Yeah, although sooner or later we're going to have to move to a bigger house, aren't we?'

'A BIGGER HOUSE!' and then I realized that my reaction sounded too much like blind panic and so I repeated the phrase with the air of reasoned contemplation. 'A bigger house. Hmm, interesting . . .'

It didn't allay suspicions.

'Why? We're not overdrawn or anything, are we?' asked Catherine, rolling an expensive brand of paint across the ceiling.

I responded with an assertive, 'No!' in the overemphatic, look-straight-ahead-and-broach-no-debate way that I normally reserved for squeegee merchants offering to clean my windscreen at traffic lights. Catherine generally took little interest in the balance of our financial affairs. She did once attempt to pay off an overdraft by writing out a cheque from the same account, but generally her only financial worry was that when the sun was shining you couldn't read the screen on the cash dispenser.

I wanted to tell her about the double life I had been leading and explain how I had got into so much debt, but now she had revealed she wasn't happy I didn't have the heart to make things any worse. She said I seemed very quiet, and with an affectionate smile she asked me if I was all right. I said I was fine, which was the word I always used to deflect any embarrassing emotional probing. I could have said I was OK, but that's two syllables and I didn't want to start gushing on about my feelings and getting all Californian about it. Somehow it never felt like the perfect moment to announce, 'Actually, darling, this decorating we're doing is a complete waste of time because, guess what? I haven't been paying the mortgage!' They say that honesty is the best policy. Well, that's fine when the truth is all nice and lovely, then it's easy to be honest. What if you're the mystery second gunman in the Kennedy assassination? In that case honesty is clearly not the best policy.

'So, Frank, have you ever been to Dallas before?'

'Yes, I came here once to shoot John F. Kennedy from behind the grassy knoll.'

As Catherine had come out of her tired phase so I had entered mine. Suddenly I was working every hour there was in an attempt to make up the mortgage arrears. I wanted to rush home and be with her as much as possible, but financial demands meant that I was trapped in my studio, living the life she thought I'd been living all along. Catherine noticed that I was less patient with the children, that I'd come back to the house and, instead of throwing them up in the air and tickling them, I would flop down on the sofa, exhausted, and then object when they took it in turns to jump on my testicles. What defence could I make for my apparent change in enthusiasm for my kids? 'It was easier before. I'd only been pretending to be at work all day.'

Although I was gradually earning more, the outstanding mortgage payments bred penalty charges and bank expenses and all sorts of other fees to which high-interest charges seemed to be randomly added. I telephoned round the agencies, trying to get extra work, and I was put on hold and made to wait to speak to people whose calls I'd often forgotten to return in the past. Every day I laboured away in my studio, converting favourite tunes I'd been saving for my fantasy first album into jingles to promote low-fat frozen pizzas.

My fatigue from working so hard was compounded by the weight of the secrets I was carrying around with me. The deceit had been tiny when it began; no-one would have noticed it. I could barely remember the moment of conception, the moment I released a tiny seed of dishonesty into our relationship. But somehow it had latched on, and then it just seemed to grow and grow until it became as obvious as the bulge under Catherine's T-shirt. When a baby gets to a certain size, it has to come out; the same is true for a lie. By now its gestation had reached such a stage that I was starting to feel contractions. I knew I couldn't keep it in much longer, but I didn't know who I could possibly tell. If I'd been a Catholic I suppose I would have told the priest in confession. If I'd been an old lady I would have found an excuse to go to the doctors and bore them about it for several hours. To whom did people tell their secrets these days? There was no way I was going on daytime television and breaking down in the studio audience while some cut-price Oprah Winfrey put her hand on my shoulder, barely pausing before she trailed the next item. 'Women who've slept with their daughters' boyfriends – coming right up after the break.'

I had sat alone in my studio, wondering who was my nearest soul mate; with whom was I supposed to share my problems. My mobile rang and it felt good to hear Catherine's reassuring voice.

'Are you OK?' she said, sensing that I sounded preoccupied.

'Fine . . .' And then suddenly it all just spilled out.

'Look, er, Catherine, erm, I've not been straight with you. We're badly in debt and I've been deceiving you about how hard I've been working. Basically I've just been living it up here for the past couple of years while you've been struggling with the babies.'

There was a terrible silence. I waited for her to say something, but she didn't, and so I gabbled to fill the void. 'I know, but I've changed. I'm working really hard now, and I'm going to make it up to you, I promise.'

Still she said nothing. I wished I could have said this to her face, to see how she was reacting; the silence was oppressive. It was so quiet I couldn't even hear the crackle of the phone, which was because there was no crackle of the phone – I'd lost the signal; the mobile had cut off. I didn't know whether she'd hung up in angry disgust or not heard a single word of what I'd said. My mobile suddenly rang again.

'Sorry,' she said brightly. 'Millie pressed the button down on the receiver. So you're all right, are you?'

'Yeah, er, yeah, I'm fine,' I said, breathing an exhausted sigh of relief. 'I'll be back in time to see the kids tonight.'

'Great,' she said. 'You just sounded a bit subdued.'

'Yeah, well, I just wish I was there already.'

At least this wasn't a lie. But today I couldn't go home until I had finished arranging a vital eight-second piece of music that was urgently required to assist in persuading people to visit World of Bathrooms. It was needed first thing the following morning, and I estimated the job would take me a couple of hours, maybe one and a half if it went well. I switched on my computer and loaded up the appropriate program. From the living room came a sudden burst of laughter. My flatmates were obviously enjoying something very funny, but I resolved to ignore it and carry on. The first job I had to complete was the mundane task of importing old PC midi-files into Cubase by manually dragging them across with the cursor. It's even less interesting than it sounds. There was another explosion of giggles, this time even louder. I glanced towards the door, wondering what could possibly be so hilarious. I recognized it as that sort of derisory hyena cackling – amusement that was at someone else's expense – which made it all the more intriguing. There is something magnetic about unexplained laughter; it's not just the simple desire to enjoy a burst of happiness, but the burning curiosity it creates about the cause. When a gunman is holed up in a besieged building, the police always try threats and plea bargaining and appeals from his mother to lure him out. It would be much quicker if, on the count of three, they all fell about in hysterics; the gunman would be out in a flash saying, 'What? What is it?'

I dragged the mouse across the grubby mat; suddenly it seemed heavy and unwieldy. The clock said 16:44, as I was sure it had done for the last three and half minutes. 'Ha ha ha ha ha,' screamed the siren voices of my flatmates again, but they weren't going to stop me working; they weren't going to tempt me away. Although, as it happened, I did just need to get a tiny drop more milk to put in my tea.

'What? What is it?' I said as I walked into the living room.

'We're playing Beat the Intro,' said Jim. This game was a regular household favourite which involved one flatmate playing the opening bars of an old hit or album track and everyone else then going into agonized spasms as they searched for the name of the song. I had spent many an evening in this flat shouting, 'Honky Tonk Women' on hearing the solitary tap of a cow bell, or 'Ballroom Blitz' at the sound of a siren.

It was hard to imagine how Beat the Intro could be causing such hilarity, but Jim explained further.

'Paul is stuck on one particular record. So far he has

guessed that it's "Shaddap You Face" by Joe Dolce or the theme to *Steptoe and Son*.'

'It's obviously a novelty record of some sort,' said Paul.

'See if you recognize it, Michael.' Jim, with a suspicious glint in his eye, played the track and I immediately recognized the best song I had ever written, recorded on flexi-disc and played three times on Thames Valley FM.

'Is it "There's No-one Quite Like Grandma?" said Paul hopefully, and Simon and Jim fell around in further hysterics.

'Not as classy as that,' said Jim.

'It's not the Mini Pops, is it?' he asked.

'No, it is not,' I said indignantly. 'It's "Hot City Metal" by Micky A. and it was played three times on Thames Valley FM. It was quite innovative at the time,' I claimed. Trying not to look too obviously hurt, I put my precious flexi-disc back in its sleeve and went and got myself some milk while Jim continued the game with some more conventional tracks.

As I walked back through the living room towards my studio, Jim was cueing up the next track. There was a few seconds' silence before the music began, and since I was mildly curious as to whether I could identify it, my pace slowed slightly. A gentle guitar strumming started up; the chords were C for one bar and then E minor for one bar, repeating over and over again, and I recognized the song immediately. It was such an obvious and famous intro that anyone would have got it right away. Which was why it was so completely infuriating that I couldn't quite place it for a moment.

'Oh, oh, oh, that's, um. Oh God, that is such a famous track. Um, 1970s, huge hit; it's the Stones or someone, isn't it?'

'Maybe,' said Jim sadistically, 'maybe not.'

'Play it again,' I intoned, standing with one leg outside the doorway, pretending to myself that I really wasn't staying. He pointed the remote control at the stereo, the guitar faded up again and I nodded sagely as the record went through its familiar intro, while the rolodex in my brain was spinning round and round trying to locate the place where I stored the rest of the song. It was just so disorganized in there; I could never find anything.

'Oh, it is so obvious,' said Simon unhelpfully.

'Come on,' said Paul. They had both already got the track; this round was clearly for my benefit only.

C/C/C/C/Em/Em/Em/Em it went yet again, and then, just as the answer was tantalizingly within my grasp, Jim paused the track again. 'I know it, I know it,' I pleaded to my interrogators. 'It's, like, Neil Young or someone, isn't it?' I suggested.

This caused delighted jeering laughter from the other three. Being the master of human psychology that I was, I therefore deduced that it probably wasn't Neil Young, or indeed Crosby, Stills or Nash for that matter.

'Give me a clue.'

They looked at each other, nodded and then Simon volunteered. 'It was the first song ever to get to number one after being re-released.'

This was far too big a clue to do anything but make matters worse. Facts such as this one are kept in a different office to the department where tunes are stored. In fact, it was right over the other side of town; it was two buses away. Now I was further than ever from recognizing the song because I was on a huge diversion trying to remember a separate piece of pop trivia. I had been so close to completing the intro in my head, but now the only lyrics I could put to the tune was the haunting couplet:

> 'This is the first song
> To be re-released and then get to number one.'

It didn't ring any bells.

'Oh God, this is torture. I can't believe it. I know this song so well,' I wailed, now sitting in a chair in the living room with my head in my hands, all thoughts of work forgotten. 'Tum-te-tum-te-tum-te-tum tum tum tum te-tum-te-tum-te-tum,' I repeated to myself over and over again. But no matter how many times I traipsed up that musical staircase, at the same point I suddenly felt as if there was nothing under my feet.

'There was a sequel to the song recorded eleven years after the original which also went to number one,' said Simon.

'Shhh, shhh, shhh. I nearly had it then. It was just coming to me and now it's gone again. Doh!' And then I thought about what Simon had actually said.

'A sequel? To a song? God, what on earth is it?'

'And it was taken from an album of the same name.'

'A début album,' chipped in Paul, and I felt the solution slipping away from me again. Like a salmon that had taken the fly, I was played on the line until exhausted; they had me hooked and were now enjoying the maximum possible sport. When I realized this I resolved to wrench myself free and, summoning all my will power, I stood up and declared, 'Oh, this is ridiculous, I really don't care one way or the other,' and then I stormed off down the hall back to my studio to forget all about it. Three and a half seconds later I came back into the living room.

'OK. Just play it once more,' I said.

'My name is Michael Adams and I am a triviaholic. I am taking one day at a time, but I find that there are certain social situations where I find it really hard to resist the thrill of a quiz question answered correctly.'

In my imaginary self-help group, the other triviaholics are seated around in a circle, nodding and smiling at me sympathetically as I relate my experiences.

'There's no buzz like it; it's like a miniature mental climax, a little cerebral orgasm. But I know that just one will never be enough, and then I'll need another and another, and before I know it all my money will have disappeared on pop-quiz books and I will have lost all my friends after a huge argument about the imprecise wording of one of their trivia questions. I'm trying to give it up, I really am, but it's hard because on every street there's a pub, and I think I'll just pop in for one swift pub quiz and I'm in there all night. So now I have to stay at home and just watch television, but on every channel there's *University Challenge* or *Who Wants to Be a Millionaire?*, and I can't believe that the contestant doesn't know which line on the London Underground map is coloured pink.'

'Hammersmith and City,' blurts out one of the triviaholics, unable to help himself, and his therapy is set back another six months.

The Beat the Intro round ended up turning into a very heavy late-night session. I did finally get the track I'd been searching for, when after trying a thousand different keyholes the music finally unlocked the memory bank where I'd filed the opening line. ' "Space Oddity" by David Bowie,' I declared exhaustedly to the patronizing applause of my flat-mates. But the build-up had been so long and the anticipation so great that now I could feel only a vague sense of empty disappointment. The only possible cure was to get the next song more quickly.

It was hours before I was back in my studio, and in the end I didn't finish my piece of music until about one in the morning. I turned off my computer, looked at my watch and realized that I had missed the last tube home. If I'd had any cash I would have got a minicab, but I'd already been reduced to ripping open the charity envelope by the front door to pay the pizza delivery man. I left a text message on Catherine's mobile, which included a sad little face made up of the appropriate punctuation marks. Then I left another text message, stressing that this was meant to be ironic, that I didn't normally do anything as naff as leave sad or happy faces on people's mobile screens, and by the time I'd done all that I probably could have walked the six miles across London to Kentish Town.

Catherine would have had a night no different to many others, but for me the routine had changed. Now I felt disappointed and stupid, like I'd spent the evening putting coins into a slot machine and had then walked away with empty pockets wondering why I felt so unfulfilled. I got into bed and, with a last glance at the photo of Catherine and the kids that had recently been propped up on my bedside table, I switched off the light. Then I lay there trying to work out how a promise to be home in time to see them turned into an apologetic text message.

My flatmates were like the games on my computer: as long as they were there I would be unable to resist being tempted away from whatever I was supposed to be doing. Because of my new-found determination to stop squandering my working day I had recently deleted Minesweeper, Tetris, Solitaire and all the other distractions from my PC. Now, whenever I got stuck I found myself wasting twice as much time loading the games back on to the hard drive before playing them, and then deleting them all over again until the next time. Why was I so weak? Why could I not resist the temptation of mindless diversions? Why did I always get near to the end of Minesweeper, stop concentrating and then blow myself up?

I felt like a man having an affair, only it wasn't an affair with a younger woman, it was an affair with a younger version of myself. Just as some men get back in contact with old girl-friends after they are married, I'd met up again with the twenty-something Michael Adams. He'd made me feel young again; he'd understood all my problems. And we still had so much in common; we liked to do the same things. It was only when I mentioned my wife and children that he would go all prickly and defensive. He didn't want to know about them; he'd always secretly hoped that he came first in my life, that my future lay with him. Like any affair it had quickly become too complex. Now I was trying to break it off, but I was in too deep. I tried to say to the irresponsible, carefree version of myself, 'I don't want to lose you as a friend,' or 'Can't we just see each other every now and then,' but he wasn't letting go easily. I told him that I had loved the time we'd spent together, that when the younger Michael and I were playing around I was as relaxed and carefree as could be, but I couldn't handle the guilt any more; I couldn't handle the secrecy and the lies; I couldn't keep it bottled up any longer.

I got out of bed and turned on the light. I started to write it all down: how I was deceiving Catherine and had been doing so for years; how I had felt excluded when the babies came along; how I had suddenly felt like a gooseberry, gate-crashing a private love affair between Catherine and her children. At first these notes were just intended for myself, but the more I wrote down, the more I wanted to share them with someone, and eventually my confessional turned into an extended letter to my father. I'd never talked about personal things with Dad; I didn't have that kind of a relationship with him. But I didn't have that sort of relationship with anyone else, either, so perhaps this was an attempt to establish one. At least I could be certain that, whatever else, he would be on my side. When you are having an affair, who better to tell than someone you know who's had one, too.

I thought about when Mum and Dad had split up. Because I had been so young I think much of it had been recreated in my head; the memory was now digitally remastered. But I had a vivid sequence of pictures of Mum and Dad shouting at one another and Dad jumping in the car and scraping the gatepost as he sped off, and I knew that wasn't the normal way to drive away from our house. I had a stronger memory of the years following their divorce, when I was frostily handed over from one parent to another, like a spy being exchanged at an East German border post. For years I had spent the weekdays with my mother and the weekends with my dad, playing music and killing time in a soulless bachelor pad. It occurred to me that this was a double life I'd managed to replicate perfectly as an adult.

Mum had said that all she wanted was for me to be happy, and then she'd burst into tears in front of me, which I can't really say did the job. After a couple of years she had a special friend called Keith who would come and stay. Mum and Keith had an elaborate foreplay which involved them both walking around the garden in the late afternoon while he pretended to be interested in all the flowers she had planted. Then she cooked him a meal and Keith would stay the night. I wondered if he wore that stupid cravat under his pyjamas as well. They would go to bed at the same time and then they would get up about twenty minutes later and go to the toilet a lot. I used to lie in bed listening to them walking across the landing and then flushing the toilet over and over again. I wondered if perhaps Keith's house didn't have a toilet, because whenever he stayed with us, he always seemed to make maximum use of ours.

It was only later that I realized that they'd been having it off, and then the idea of my mother having sex completely horrified me. When it was explained to me that my parents must have had sexual intercourse in order to conceive me, I remember being disgusted and wishing they hadn't. 'But then you wouldn't exist,' my friend had said.

'That's fine. I'd rather take that option.'

174

After a year or so the toilet flushing decreased, but the noise was replaced by the sound of Mum and Keith shouting at each other. I was always packed off to bed early because Mum and Keith couldn't wait to be alone so they could get down to another bit of fighting.

Being only eight years old, I didn't really understand that I was disturbed by yet another round of shouting and tears in my home, but I suppose it wasn't normal behaviour to stand on the end of my bed every night and urinate against the wall. Every night in the same spot. I don't know what possessed me to do it; it's not as if the toilet was constantly engaged any more. Mum had builders, plumbers and plasterers round – none of them could ever work out why the wallpaper was peeling off, the plaster was crumbling and the carpet was rotting. I remember being scared that one of them would guess the cause. As if the head builder would suck the air in through his teeth and shake his head. 'Ooh dear. No, it's not wet rot or a cracked boiler inlet feed. No, that's yer classic subconscious cry for help by an eight-year-old traumatized by his parents' divorce. I could get my chippy to have a look at it for you, but really you want a proper child psychologist, and my one's on another job.'

I decided against putting all this in my letter to Dad because I didn't want him to think I was trying to make him feel guilty for walking out when I was five. Though I bloody well hoped he did feel a little bit guilty for walking out when I was five. There had been a time when I'd hated him for leaving Mum, but now I no longer based my view of people entirely on what my mother had thought. I didn't still think that Liberace had just never found the right girl.

Eventually Keith found someone else's toilet to flush, and for years after she was abandoned the second time, Mum didn't let herself get close to anyone. After that I was her man; I was the one who filled her tank when we pulled into the petrol station. And at the weekends I would obligingly play the role of husband substitute, walking around clothes shops with her, shrugging indifferently as she emerged from the changing room in a variety of equally frumpy dresses. I had to grow up fast; maybe that was partly why I'd contrived a second childhood in my thirties. Finally I left home and went off to college, and Mum suddenly met and married a man from Northern Ireland. I think for the last year of her life she was quite happy. She invited me to the wedding, because she said she thought I might like to meet him, which was thoughtful of her. I can't say I cared for him a great deal; he was all firm handshakes and meaningful eye contact, and he said my name too often when he was talking to me. But that didn't stop Mum from moving back to Belfast with him. I wished I'd made the effort to see her after she moved there, but I never did. And six months later she was walking through the city centre when she got knocked down and killed by a speeding car. And that was it. Now there is a big empty space where she should be. In a shop, sitting in a chair, standing in a bus queue; there's an empty person-shaped gap where she would be now if she hadn't stepped out in front of that car.

Telling people about the death of a loved one is supposed to be a therapeutic part of the grieving process. Not in my case. When I told all my college friends that my mother had been killed in Belfast, they all said, 'By a bomb?'

I would continue to stare solemnly at the ground and explain further. 'No. By a car.'

'Oh, I see.' And then there was a pause. 'A car bomb?'

'No. Just a car. She was run over by a man driving down the street.'

'Blimey. That's awful. She hadn't been informing on the IRA or anything?'

'No, of course she hadn't. It was an accident. He was just driving too fast.'

'Oh. Joyrider, was he?'

'No, it was just an ordinary car accident. It wasn't a car bomb or joyriders or an IRA execution. It was just a common or garden road accident. They do have them in Belfast.'

Every person I had to tell would do the usual embarrassed sympathizing bit, and I'd say thanks a lot and then there was that awkward pause when they felt they had to say something to fill the silence. 'You must have worried about something like this happening when she moved to Northern Ireland . . .'

'No,' I said sharply. Obviously everyone thought that Mum had brought it upon herself, I mean, moving to Belfast, well, that's just asking to be run over by a seventy-five-year-old man, isn't it? At the funeral one of her cousins said loudly, 'I warned her she'd get herself killed if she moved to Belfast.' I finally snapped and shouted, 'For God's sake. She was run over. By an old man in a car. It happens in Belfast; it happens in London; it happens in fucking Reykjavik!' And someone said, 'All right, Michael; there's no need for that.' And another relation put an arm round my mum's cousin and said, 'Well, of course, it's a very dangerous place, Belfast.'

You can always rely on funerals to bring out the worst in a family.

Perhaps if she had still been alive I would have told all my problems to her, because I certainly had little idea how my father would react to this letter when I posted it. I told him about everything that had happened since the children had come along. How I had spent endless days in my room making compilation tapes while Catherine had struggled through the hardest years of being a parent. How Catherine had thought I'd been working sixteen hours a day when really I'd been having naked piggy-back fights with beautiful young girls and boozy barbecues on Clapham Common. How I had tried to have everything – the love of a family and the liberty of a single man, the commitment of children and the carefree wastefulness of youth. There were pages of it by the time I'd finished – frank and emotional outpouring that my father would probably have thought as interesting as I found his news about Brian's discounted Mondeo, but next morning I sent it off to him anyway.

It felt good to have got it all off my chest. As I posted the letter I knew I was definitely doing the right thing. I had no choice but to make myself think that – the postman refused to give me the letter back when he finally arrived to empty the pillar box an hour and a half later. Now that I had shared my secret with someone else I felt as if a huge weight had been lifted from my shoulders. Suddenly everything was crystallized. You cannot break off an affair and carry on seeing your old mistress. Dad had tried that with Janet the chemist and had ended up moving in with her. I had promised Catherine I would be home the previous evening, but I had ended up playing around again. The only way forward was clear to me now: I had decided to move out of the flat: my double life was over. I would set up my studio equipment in the loft or the shed or in our bedroom; it didn't matter, but I couldn't carry on as I was.

As it turned out I never really talked to Dad about the enormous revelation that I had sprung upon him. I suppose the therapeutic act of writing it all down and posting it had been what was important, so in that sense the letter had already done its work. By the time I spoke to Dad again, what he thought of it all no longer seemed very important. Because when Catherine got to read the letter, her reaction rather overshadowed everything else.

chapter eight

just do it

'Michael, how would you like to have your own record in the charts?'

I'd been building a brick tower for Millie when Hugo had rung my mobile. The trill of the phone jolted me out of my trance, and I realized that Millie had actually wandered off some time before and that for the past couple of minutes I'd been playing with little bricks on my own.

'My own record?' I said, standing up.

'Yup. With your name on it and everything. Top of the charts. How does that grab you?'

This was obviously some scam designed to talk me into doing some crappy underpaid job for him, and so a cautious voice at the back of my head told me to say I wasn't particularly interested.

'Well, I'd be very interested,' I said. 'Though, um, in what way would this be my own record?' Hugo proceeded to explain and no amount of phoney excitement on his part could convince me that this project would be my personal *Sergeant Pepper*. Through one of his various Soho contacts,

Hugo was putting together a CD called *Classic Commercials*. Everyone's favourite pieces of classical music – namely the ones they only recognized because they'd heard them on TV ads – now available together on one great album.

'And I immediately thought of you, Michael. You love all that classical stuff, don't you.'

'I'm pretty sure this idea has been done before, Hugo.'

'Not for at least eighteen months,' he said. 'And now there's the technology to recreate the orchestra with all your clever equipment, so we don't have to fork out a fortune to pay a lot of poncey violin players in dinner jackets.'

'Well, when you put it like that, I'm really flattered that you want me on board.'

I attempted to maintain a disdainful air, but Hugo was determined that I was the right man for the job. 'It has to be you, Michael. You're the man that put that tum-te-tum tune into the instant-tea-granules ad.' It was true. I had indeed been the man who had made Verdi's 'March of the Hebrew Slaves' synonymous with 'the cuppa that's easy as one, two, tea'. When Classic FM had its annual vote for their listeners' all-time top one hundred pieces of music I had felt quite chuffed to see Verdi's 'March of the Hebrew Slaves' make its first entry in the charts at number nine. If it hadn't been for instant tea granules I doubt whether it would ever have made the top one hundred.

So this was to be the extent of my recording success as a musician. It wouldn't be my own compositions on the CD, it would be my synthetic arrangements of Beethoven, Brahms and Berlioz listed according to composer, title and brand of panty liners that they had promoted. I couldn't help but feel a slight sense that my dreams had been compromised since I'd left music college.

'Why don't you just do a compilation of all the classic overtures as played by mobile phones?'

'That's not a bad idea. We could do that as a follow-up.'

We talked about which pieces of music they had in mind and I attempted to explain to Hugo that in reality no technology could adequately recreate the sound of an orchestra, but he was unmoved.

'Just stick on a bit of extra reverb or something we'll give you a budget to get in singers or whatever for the ones like when that fat bloke from the opera is so sad he wants just one cornetto.'

' "O Sole Mio" is not from an opera.'

'Whatever.'

'You could do it, but it would sound shit.'

'Yeah, but the sort of people who'll buy it won't be able to tell it sounds shit.'

I told Hugo he was the most cynical person I had ever met and he was genuinely flattered. But by not refusing to do the job I found that somehow I seemed to have agreed to do it. *Commercial Classics* would be a pick-and-mix CD, a collection of cheaply produced orchestral soundbites for people who didn't want to commit to a whole symphony. Although I felt vaguely uncomfortable about the whole idea I sat down to work out which little ditties would make up the list. From the opera *The Tale of Tsar Saltan* there would be Rimsky-Korsakov's famous 'Flight of the Black and Decker Paint Stripper'. There was 'Jupiter' from Holst's *Planets* suite – better known as the theme from the Dulux Weathershield ad. There was the Hovis Ad, sometimes known as the *New World Symphony*. Antonín Dvořák had written this music as a tribute to the United States. I think putting ten seconds of it in a TV ad said more about the American way than his symphony ever could have done. There was the 'Dance of the Little Swans' from *Swan Lake*, for which Tchaikovsky had wrought his emotions in his quest to express the convenience, the delicious flavour and sheer absence of calories that is

Batchelor's Slim A Soup. And there was, of course, *Beethoven's Blue Band Margarine Symphony*.

Within a quarter of an hour I had scribbled a list of about twenty to thirty pieces of music that had been made famous by their repeated exposure on television adverts. Catherine had overheard my phone call and, despite being stretched out on the floor like a beached whale in a futile attempt to be comfortable, she tried to see what it was that I was writing down. I was embarrassed to tell her about the project, but she understood my reservations.

'Don't do it, then, if you find it distasteful.'

'Well I've sort of said that I would now.'

'Well ring him back and tell him you've changed your mind.'

'But you don't know what Hugo's like. I'll come off the phone having just agreed we should make it a double CD.'

Catherine was irritated by my weakness when confronted by people like Hugo. She told me I should stick up for myself and, not having the courage to argue with her, I meekly agreed that I would in future.

'I've got an idea to make some money,' she suddenly announced. 'A compilation novel.' And she started making some notes.

'What?'

'Well, if you can buy all these CDs that bring together the most popular bits of classical music, somebody ought to publish a compilation novel.'

Catherine was more of a literary person than me. Every month she attended a reading group where about half a dozen women got together and spent five minutes talking about *Captain Corelli's Mandolin* and the other three hours slagging off their husbands.

'I don't understand,' I said. 'How can you have a compilation novel?'

She cleared her throat to read out her work in progress. 'The action starts in the Wessex town of Casterbridge when the mayor wakes up one morning and notices that he has turned into a beetle. Now Mrs Bennet decides that he would no longer make a suitable husband for her daughter Molly Bloom so she escapes from the attic where she was imprisoned by Rochester and sets fire to Manderley. "The horror, the horror!" exclaims Heathcliff as the white whale drags Little Nell beneath the waves to a tragic death, and Tom Jones sits alone in the garden of Barchester Towers knowing he had won the victory over himself. He loved Big Brother.'

I chuckled at Catherine's fantastically vulgar idea and pretended to recognize all the references. Inside part of me was thinking, Actually, as someone with absolutely no knowledge of English literature I wouldn't mind reading that.

'Quick, quick!' she said suddenly, placing my hand on her bump. 'There. Did you feel that?'

'No,' I said. 'You're not really pregnant, are you?'

'Ah, you've rumbled me. No, I've just been eating loads and loads of cream cakes.' And we both laughed and then suddenly I said, 'Wow! That was a big one!' Sometimes when Catherine giggled the baby inside her would give approving little kicks to show that it too was enjoying the moment. I watched the baby's heel or elbow or something ripple across under her stretched stomach like Moby Dick just below the surface. Catherine was now over halfway through her pregnancy. A whole new human being was shaping up. In a few months' time I would be a biological parent for the third time, but somehow I didn't really feel like I was a fully formed father yet. The birth of our baby would be a long and painful business; I suppose there was no reason why I should expect my own transition to be any easier.

The baby now made a neat little bump at the front of

Catherine's stomach and the received wisdom was that this made it more likely the baby would be a boy. Folklore and fishwives have provided all sorts of ways to detect the sex of the unborn infant: the shape of the bulge, the nature of the mother's food cravings and, of course, the wedding ring test. This involves lying the mother on her back and dangling her wedding ring on a piece of cotton above her womb. If it sways slightly it's a girl; if it spins it's a boy. Catherine's ring span and swayed and I spent a week worrying that our new baby would grow up to look like the girl on Simon's computer.

A pregnant woman's bulge needs to be a lot larger than Catherine's for her to be absolutely sure of being offered a seat on the underground, but as yet no woman has ever been twenty-two months pregnant. It would be nearly Christmas before Catherine would get really big, and by then men sitting on the tube would have no choice but to do the decent thing and hold their newspapers so close to their face that she couldn't possibly catch their eye. Or so they thought. But Catherine being Catherine would peer over the top of their papers and say, 'Are you comfy enough sitting there or would you like to put your feet up on my bump.' I suspected that it was embarrassment that prevented some men from giving up their seats – the thought of talking to a complete stranger on the tube, a person of the opposite sex who they would specifically be addressing because of that woman's gynaeco-logical condition; it's enough to make the average Englishman shrivel up and die. I put this thesis to Catherine, and she listened carefully and nodded and then proposed her own carefully considered analysis: 'You don't think it might just be because men are all selfish bastards?' Embarrassment was not a concept Catherine really understood, but I suppose that once you've been naked with your legs up in stirrups as a group of medical students look on from the end of the bed, it would take quite a lot to make you blush.

She sat on the floor in front of the telly for another hour or so and I rubbed the base of her back, which had been aching for some weeks. Alfie woke, and though it was too early for his feed I brought him downstairs and gave him his bottle anyway. At every suck Alfie looked surprised, as if he really hadn't been expecting warm milk of all things to follow the previous gulp of warm milk. He started to go to sleep, and I tapped the base of his feet and he started to suck again more fervently; Catherine smiled and said that I had finally learned the knack, and the baby inside her kicked again.

Millie must have woken and seen that her brother's cot was empty and decided she was missing out because she suddenly appeared at the door claiming she had sore hair. Against our better judgement we let her stay with us in the lounge, and the four of us cuddled up on the sofa and watched the opening sequence of *The Lion King* again and when Rafiki held up the newborn baby lion to all the animals and they rejoiced and bowed and cheered, I had to stop myself bursting into tears by turning it into a manic laugh and giving Millie such a tight hug that she said, 'Ow!'

I put the kids back to bed and wound up the mobile which played a tinny version of Brahms' 'Lullaby', the official theme song of every nursery in the land, chosen for its universal popularity, its gentle melody, but mainly for the fact that its copyright expired two centuries ago. I stroked Millie's head as she went to sleep. These were the moments that I had come home for. I thought about all those men at our antenatal classes, so full of enthusiasm and good intentions. How many of them would allow themselves to become alienated from their families? Would seek comfort in the respect they found at work to make up for the lack of status they suddenly felt at home? We had come halfway out of the dark ages and men were now present at the birth of their children, but how many of those men would be there for the *lives* of their children? Now that I was resolved to changing my ways I suddenly felt like a militant family man, like one of those fervent anti-smokers who had recently been on sixty a day. Why was it so many men really cared about how good they were at their jobs or how good they were at sport, but gave less consideration to being better fathers than they did to improving their batting averages?

Millie's eyes eventually closed and the mobile stuttered to an exhausted halt. I knew that it would be hard for me to adjust to spending more time at home, but the alternative just wasn't viable. I had to learn that it wasn't possible to be in the company of my children and have a different agenda to them. I couldn't look after a toddler and a baby and try to restring my acoustic guitar as well. Sitting down, making yourself a sandwich, going to the toilet – these are all luxuries that you have to forgo. You just have to write off the time and throw yourself into whatever they are doing. You have to head into it. You can't take small children swimming and not go in yourself, and that analogy applies to your entire life once children come along. The water might be cold, and you might not feel like it, but you just have to jump in.

'They're asleep,' I said as I came back into the lounge. Catherine said nothing and I realized that she was asleep, too. I'd felt more relaxed with her this evening now that I was no longer mentally vetting every sentence, worrying about what it might reveal. There were just the practicalities of sorting out the flat to be tied up and then my duplicitous days would be behind me. I hadn't told her that I would suddenly be arriving home with a van load of equipment to squeeze into our already cramped home, because if I had she would have successfully dissuaded me. Anyway, a lot of it could go in the loft. The various demo tapes of all my songs could gather dust next to the box of my childhood paintings; they were just more souvenirs acquired on another stage of my journey to adulthood. I would tell Catherine that I was fed up with being away from her and the kids so much and had spontaneously decided to give up my studio and work at home. Which felt quite strange because it was almost true.

Two mornings later I nervously drove a large rented van through the busy London streets and, after a deftly executed twenty-seven point turn, I parked it outside the flat. I would leave the stereo till last so that I could listen to music as I worked. I selected King Crimson's *21st Century Schizoid Man* followed by Verdi's *Force of Destiny*. I hummed along as I folded all my clothes into boxes. It was funny how the ripped jeans and bomber jackets of my bachelor wardrobe contrasted with the cardigans and slippers I wore at home. One thing that I would never have anticipated was how completely differently I had been viewed by the outside world in my two roles. When I was pushing a double buggy along the pavement old ladies would smile at me and I would smile pleasantly back, but when I walked down the street on my own, I'd forget that I was no longer parading my passport to social acceptability and would absent-mindedly grin at some passing lady, who would avert her eyes as if to say, Don't you dare even look at me, you rapist.

There was a huge pile of music papers on top of my wardrobe. I looked back through over twenty years' worth of carefully preserved old editions of the *New Musical Express* and then dumped them into bin liners. I flicked through a few of the interviews with my boyhood heroes – snarling punks spouting nihilistic notions of no future and anarchy, postures I'd once adopted myself. I'd better drop all these newspapers off at the recycling depot, I thought.

I was a dad now and I had kids; they brought enough clutter without me bringing all this worthless history into the home. Although I had attempted to beam myself back to my twenties, I knew now there was no way I could really go back. A few weeks earlier we'd been playing football on the common when a stunning nanny had strolled past with a toddler in her charge. All the men stopped playing and stood staring in her direction.

'She's beautiful,' said Jim.

'I think it's a he,' I'd said, noticing the little boy's Baby Gap jeans.

I just wasn't cut out to be a 'lad' any more. It was as if I was trying to look cool driving around in a Lotus Elan, but with a 'Baby on Board' sticker in the rear window.

I packed away the gear and gadgets which were piled up on the shelves: an out-of-date palm top (without batteries), a prohibitively stiff Swiss army knife, a charger that was only compatible with a games console I had replaced ages ago – all the boys' toys and black plastic detritus I'd accumulated over my years as a thirty-something teenager. It only took another hour to pack all my CDs and books, which left the rest of the afternoon to untangle the seven miles of plastic spaghetti that was spewing out of the back of my keyboard, mixing desk and stereo. Eventually I loaded my musical equipment into the Transit. It reminded me of my days playing in all those bands, and how I had thought that all the humping amps and keyboards into vans would one day lead to a number-one hit record. I consoled myself with the thought that when *Classic Commercials* went platinum I could frame that and put it up above the mantelpiece instead. Or maybe pride of place on the toilet wall would be more appropriate.

Finally everything was locked up in the back of the van, ready to be driven over the river. I finished cleaning my room and put the bucket of cleaning stuff back under the sink as noisily as possible and returned the Hoover to its place under the cupboard with a bang and a clatter, but none of my flat-mates looked up. There was nothing else to do. This was it.

This was the point at which I was saying an overdue farewell to my wilting salad days.

Jim was at the table, failing to work out how to store numbers on his mobile phone, while Paul was almost erupting with frustration, trying to stop himself suggesting that Jim simply read the manual. Simon was slumped in front of the telly watching a non-stop video of goals. Not a video of a great football match, where a goal was a precious and significant thing, but a compilation of lots of different goals, all taken out of context and rendered completely meaningless. It was the sports equivalent of *Classic Commercials*.

'Well, this is it,' I said with a self-conscious mock sense of occasion that was the only way to disguise my feeling of a genuine sense of occasion. Although I knew these people were not my soulmates, I thought they might have made a little more effort when it came to saying goodbye. Men have never been very good at emotional farewells. When Scott's expedition was struggling back across the Antarctic and Captain Oates resolved to lay down his own life rather than be a burden to his comrades, he pretended he was just slipping out of the tent to go to the toilet. He would have said he was going off to die, but he couldn't face the embarrassed, indifferent shrug of his friends, mumbling, 'Yeah, well, see you about then.'

'Yeah, well, see you about, Michael,' said Jim as I prepared to stride out into the icy snowstorm of fully committed married life.

'Yeah, bye,' said Simon and Paul.

I stood there awkwardly for a couple of seconds. When I thought of some of the great times I had had there I felt sad, almost tearful, but the others seemed indifferent and completely unmoved. Of course, they hadn't had kids yet; their emotions were still in the box.

'Oh, one last thing,' said Simon.

'Yes?' I said hopefully.

'Which is the only football club that contains no letters that can be coloured in?'

'Eh?'

'When you're colouring in letters – like filling in the "o"s or the "a"s – in the newspaper. Well, which is the only Englishor Scottish football league club whose name contains no letters that you can colour in?'

'Simon, that is the most pointless question I have ever heard,' and I paused and heard myself say, 'Who is it?'

'Work it out.'

'No, it's stupid, I am not going to waste my time and energy even thinking about it.'

'OK,' he said, 'see you about.' And he went back to watching his video.

'But just for the record, which team is it?'

'I thought you said it didn't matter?'

'No, it doesn't matter; it is a pointless fact. That is so typical of the level of conversation in this household. Hours and hours wasted talking about something of no significance whatsoever. So Simon, pray, do tell us all which team contains only letters that cannot be coloured in?'

'You'll get it eventually.'

'I just thought, having raised it, you might tell me which it is.'

Simon looked up with a matter-of-fact smile.

'No.'

There was a pause. 'Well, I'd better be off,' and I hovered in the doorway.

'Yeah. See you,' they mumbled.

'Ah, I've got it,' I said.

'Well done.'

'Can I just confirm that I'm thinking of the same club as you?'

'Sure. What team were you thinking of?' said Simon, knowing that I didn't have the faintest idea what the answer was.

'Oh come on, which is it?'

'It's not important,' he said without looking up from the television.

'QPR,' I blurted out, without really thinking about it.

'Not bad. Except that you can colour in the Q, the P and the R.'

'Oh yeah.'

I sat down at the kitchen table and started firing out the names of obscure football clubs, only to be told that you could colour in the 'B' in Bury and the 'a' and the 'e' in East Fife. A couple of bottles of lager later Monica came round, and when she heard it was my last night in the flat she made a few calls and the crowd who had been planning to go to a club came to the flat instead with bottles of wine and cans of beer. She spontaneously organized the farewell party that I secretly would have quite liked my flatmates to have surprised me with.

By nine o'clock there were about forty people in the flat, drinking cheap red wine out of coffee mugs and jumping about to songs I ought to have recognized. And when I talked to people it was nice when they said, 'Oh, you're the bloke who's leaving. Well, cheers for the party.' In a way that farewell party was a milestone in my life; it was my paternity bar mitzvah. It was an evening dominated by one over-riding thought. Not Am I doing the right thing or Will this make me happy, but unfortunately, Which is the only English or Scottish league football club that contains no letters that can be coloured in? I couldn't get it out of my mind, I wanted to forget about it but I was ensnared. This was my big night, I was the centre of attention, but it was impossible for me to really enjoy myself because when anyone talked to me I could only pretend to listen while my mind frantically sifted through dozens of lower-division football clubs.

'So whereabouts are you moving to?'

'Fulham,' I said delightedly.

'Fulham, eh?'

'Oh no, not Fulham.'

'Why not?

'Well, you can colour in the letter "a", can't you?'

I danced self-consciously at nine o'clock, and a little less self-consciously two lagers later. Then it came to me; the trick was to think in capital letters. It was a relief to have got it out of the way. I bounded up to Simon, delighted with myself.

'Exeter City,' I announced smugly.

'You can colour in the "e"s.'

'Aha, but not if they're in capitals.'

'True, but if you're in upper case then you can colour in the letter "R".'

I paused and thought about this. 'OK, Exeter City written in upper case, except for the letter "r", which you write in lower case; look, I'm going to get this . . .' and I wandered off, mumbling clubs from the Scottish second division to myself.

The party wore on and Kate arrived with her new boyfriend, which made me inexplicably jealous. Although I knew I could never have a relationship with her, I think subconsciously I hoped she might keep herself single for evermore, just in case I should ever happen to change my mind. And I didn't like the way Jim gave her so much attention. If I wasn't allowed to be unfaithful with her, then no-one else was either. I hardly talked to Simon or Jim all evening. Even then I still hadn't told any of my flatmates that I was married. I had an elaborate story prepared to explain why I was moving out and where I was going, but none of them even bothered to ask.

As the evening drew on, Paul spotted me alone in the corner and came over with two bottles of cold beer, one of which he handed to me. 'So, are you staying tonight?'

'Well, no, the van's all packed up now. I'd better make this my last beer.'

'So you weren't planning to stay and help clear up?'

'Paul, I'm sorry, I hadn't been planning to stay and clear up, but that's often the way when surprise parties are sprung on you.'

'I didn't mean it like that. Sorry.'

I could tell that he'd had quite a lot to drink. He seemed to be gearing himself up for getting something off his chest.

'Michael, I know why you never brought a girl back to the flat.'

Paul didn't know about the night with Kate, but I wasn't about to start boasting about a mythical night of passion when Kate herself was standing only a few yards away.

'Didn't I?' I said, pretending to rack my brain for examples.

'Oh, come on. Three years of living here; all those nights you stayed out, but never a single girl brought back here. I know the reason why.'

I was concerned to find out at this late stage that my secret might have slipped out. I wanted to know more.

'Oh, I see,' I said. 'Did someone tell you or did you just guess?'

'It's obvious.'

'I see. Yes, I suppose there's no escaping the fact that I am just, well, different to you lot.'

'Not that different, Mike. Not to me anyway,' he said enigmatically.

'You don't mean you've been living a double life as well?'

'Yes. Yes, I have.'

He seemed delighted to be able to share this with me.

'Bloody hell! You're a dark horse, Paul.'

'Yeah, but I don't think I can keep it secret much longer.'

'Yeah, I know what you mean.'

'I just thought I'd tell you first because you'd understand. I'm gay, too.'

'What?'

'I'm gay as well. And I think you feel the same way about me as I do about you.'

'No, no, no, Paul. I'm not gay.'

'Don't try and get back in the closet now,' he whispered as the babble of the party carried on all around us. 'If I can share my secret, then so can you.'

'I'm not gay,' I repeated.

'You just agreed that you couldn't keep it a secret much longer.'

'That was about something else.'

'Oh sure. Like what?'

'Well, I'd rather not say, if it's all the same.'

'Michael, it's all right to be gay.'

'I agree. It is all right to be gay. I think it's perfectly all right to be gay.'

'That's good, you're getting there.'

'But it just so happens that I'm not.'

'You're still in denial, Michael.'

'I'm not in denial. I'm just denying I'm gay.'

'I'll come out if you come out.'

'I can't come out because I'm not fucking gay, all right?'

Paul's confident assertion about my apparent homosexuality had rather eclipsed the bigger picture, which was that he had just told me the biggest secret of his life, namely, not only that he was gay, but that he had a crush on *me*. It suddenly all made sense – all the times he had hoped I would be there for meals he'd cooked, all the bizarre sulks he had got himself into. He had behaved like a jilted girlfriend. And having convinced himself that the apparent absence of women in my life was for the same reason as his own, having constructed this fantasy that built deeper meaning around my careless compliments on his baked fish or new trousers, he was not going to accept my shattering of his illusions without a fight. How could anyone allow themselves to become so deluded, I wondered. And then I thought about how happy I'd always presumed Catherine was back at home.

I said I was delighted for him that he'd finally decided to come out, and apologized if the atmosphere in the flat had ever been at all homophobic.

'No. Jim and Simon made the odd joke, but you always corrected them. That's when I first started to realize.'

'Just because I'm *not* homophobic doesn't mean I *am* homosexual, you stupid bugger. No offence.'

'Michael, I love you, and I think you love me, if only you could face up to it.'

'Forget about me. Go and proposition Simon; he's got to have sex with some living creature before he's thirty.' And I pointed to where Simon was failing to make a girl fall in love with him by describing some of his favourite sites on the Internet, hoping against hope that one thing might lead to another. But Paul would not be deterred. 'Look, I do know some other gay men; they've given me the strength to come out. They can help you, too. I've told them all about you.'

This was too much and my patience just snapped.

'WHAT GIVES YOU THE RIGHT TO GO ROUND TELLING PEOPLE THAT I'M GAY?'

The whole room fell quiet at this news and all heads turned to me for an explanation. Mouths were agape that my 'secret' was out. The man who had delivered the pizzas put his beer down and announced that he had better get back to the shop.

'That explains everything,' said Kate loudly.

'I'm not gay, actually, everyone. I just was, er, saying to

Paul here that he shouldn't tell people I was gay. If, erm, the thought should occur to him.'

No-one looked very convinced.

'It's OK, Michael. There's nothing wrong with being gay,' said an encouraging voice from the back of the crowd.

'I know there isn't.'

'Good for you, mate,' shouted someone else.

'Then it's a double celebration,' shouted Monica. 'He's going out into the world *and* coming out of the closet.' Everyone applauded and some joker cued 'YMCA' on the record player, and my lone protestations were drowned out by everyone suddenly singing and dancing along to Village People. They had put the record on especially for me and thought I was really unsporting not to dance, so in the end I did and everyone took that as a final confirmation of my coming out. Space was cleared for me on the dance floor and I was encouraged and applauded as if I'd suddenly had a lifetime of secrecy lifted off my shoulders. I looked across at Paul, standing in the corner mouthing the words of the song but still not liberated enough to dance along to a well-known camp classic. The next time I looked up, I saw Simon looking rather surprised and offended at a proposition that the very drunken Paul was putting to him.

A little later Kate came across to me and said that it had never occurred to her that the 'other person' I had been saving myself for was a man. Now she understood why I hadn't wanted to sleep with her. I think she found this re-assuring. I didn't feel I had the energy to go through my denials again so I just thanked her for being so understanding and smiled. I probably wouldn't see any of these people again, so if they were determined to believe I was homo-sexual, then so what?

After a couple of hours of self-imposed sobriety, my smile began to ache as I watched them all disappear over the drunken horizon. I said goodbye to a few people, but everyone had now forgotten the original reason for the party, so I didn't feel too antisocial for just slipping away. I drove my rented van through the London night and soon I was on Waterloo Bridge, on the old border between my two lives. I looked at the river and the glorious sparkling views of Canary Wharf and the City to the east and parliament and the London Eye to the west. Then I headed up Aldwych, past hunched bodies sleeping in doorways or covered in cardboard. London was just like my life. From a distance it looked great; it's only when you got close you realized how fucked up it was.

Finally I was outside my family home. It was too late to unload now; the van was alarmed and had a couple of padlocks on the back, so I felt safe enough leaving it all till the morning. My home was dark and still as I slipped quietly into the hallway and silently closed the door behind me. Since the children came along, Catherine had become such a light sleeper that I found myself tiptoeing around downstairs, trying not to breathe too noisily.

There was a video tape placed where I would see it on the kitchen table, which meant that Catherine had remembered to record my favourite programme. Though I preferred people not to know, nothing amused me more than home videos of labradors skateboarding into swimming pools and toddlers getting stuck in the toilet bowl. Our own camcorder was set up on the tripod, so Catherine had obviously been inspired to film our own kids. I grabbed a beer from the fridge and settled down in the lounge with the television on extra-considerate, almost-inaudible low volume to have a really good laugh at some other people's misfortunes. The first clip featured some fairly obviously contrived set-ups of people pretending not to be looking where they were going as they walked fully clothed into a river, but their efforts got them five hundred quid, which was enough to pay for their new camcorder, so good luck to them. Then there was a sequence of children being embarrassingly honest – a little boy saying to a very overweight children's entertainer, 'You're a big fat pig.' And then, when he was told off, he pointed to her with a look of gross injustice that this simple truth could be denied and said, 'But she *is* . . .'

Then there was a lavish church wedding. The groom was asked if he would take this woman to be his lawful wedded wife and he said that he would. The bride was asked if she would take this man and she was slightly nervous and struggled to get the words out. She's going to faint, I thought. I can see this one coming a mile off. I was wrong. At that moment, about five rows back, a man in the congregation jumped up wearing a Walkman, and throwing both his arms in the air he shouted, 'GOAL!' I laughed so much I thought I would wake up the whole street, never mind just Catherine. I rewound the tape and watched the clip again. It made me laugh almost as much the second time. Fantastic. I loved this programme. The host liked that one as well, but promised the next clip was even funnier. Well, this should be really good, I thought, and I took another big glug of beer. Then the picture went blank and I thought, Oh no, she's cocked up the recording.

But she hadn't. Catherine's thunderous face suddenly appeared on the screen. 'You wanker!' she shouted at the camcorder. 'You lying, selfish, cowardly, lazy, fucking lying bastard! You want to live away from me and the kids. You want to have your "own space". Well you've got it, shitface. Fuck you!'

I ran upstairs. Our bed was empty. The kids' room was empty. Her side of the wardrobe was bare; some toys and most of the kids' clothes had gone, too. There was a barren hotel-room neatness to our bedroom. I stood staring around the space in bewilderment; my mind was in freefall. Then, from nowhere, it suddenly came into my head. Hull City. The answer to Simon's trivia question was Hull City. And my wife had walked out on me and taken our children with her. My marriage was in ruins. Hull City. Of course.

chapter nine

where do you want to go today

'And this is the children's room,' I said as my father stepped over the unwanted soft toys to look around Millie and Alfie's abandoned bedroom.

'Very nice,' he said. 'I like all those clouds painted on the ceiling. Did you do that?'

'Er, no, that was, erm, Catherine.'

'Oh.'

If I had ever given any thought to how I would feel when I finally showed Dad around my family home, I suppose I would have imagined the scene with my family still in it.

'That's where Millie slept and that's where Alfie slept.'

'I see, yes. And who is this on the eiderdown?'

'On the duvet? Well, that's Barbie,' I said incredulously. I'd lived in a home where Barbie was worshipped as an icon more revered than the Virgin Mary in the Vatican; it was disconcerting to find there were still people who'd never heard of her.

'And, erm, that's Ken, there.'

'Is "Ken" Barbie's husband?'

'Well, I don't think they're married. Ken's just her

boyfriend. Or he might possibly be her fiancé, I'm not sure.'

An awkward silence hung in the air.

'Actually they've been going out for about thirty years now, so if Ken hasn't popped the question yet she ought to start getting worried.' And I gave out a little nervous laugh, but Dad didn't seem aware that I had made a joke. Maybe the area of marriages and commitment wasn't the best subject to josh about at the moment. We stood there for a while as Dad made an effort to look interested in the kids' room.

'I haven't touched anything since Catherine walked out on me,' I said with an air of almost affected self-pity.

Dad thought about this. 'I thought you said she took the car.' No-one can focus on the irrelevant detail quite like an elderly parent.

'OK, since she *drove* out on me, then.'

'So where were you when she drove off?'

'I was loading up all the stuff from my flat to drive back here.'

There was a thoughtful pause. Something was worrying him, but it wasn't the disaster that had befallen his son's marriage.

'So how did she get hold of the car?'

'What?'

'How did she get hold of the car if you were loading up your things?'

I sighed an exhausted sigh to try and make him understand that this really wasn't very important and said through gritted teeth, 'I wasn't using the car. I'd rented a van.'

'I see.' And then he contemplated this for a second. 'Because you knew that she was going to need the car to take the kids and all their things to her mother's?'

'No, of course I didn't know or I would have tried to stop her.'

'So why didn't you use the car to move your things out of

the flat? You can get quite a lot in an Astra, can't you, especially a hatchback.'

'Look, it doesn't matter. There was quite a bit of stuff; it would have needed two journeys.'

He went quiet for a moment and we wandered into the other bedroom. I was slightly embarrassed when I realized how feminine the decor was: the flowery duvet, the frilly edge on the dressing table – it seemed so inappropriate now that I was sleeping there on my own.

'So is it very expensive, hiring your own van?'

'What?'

'Is it expensive, renting a van to move all your things?'

'Oh, I don't know. Yes, it cost a million pounds. Dad, it really doesn't matter about the van.'

'You're not still renting it, are you, to get around in now that Catherine's taken the car?'

'No, I'm not still renting the bloody van!'

Although I wish I had been and then I could have run him over with it.

My irritation was exacerbated by the fact that I couldn't help but blame Dad for my wife's departure. True to form, Dad had recently left his lady friend for a younger woman. Jocelyn was very bitter; it must be hard being chucked when you're fifty-nine, especially when it's because you're not fifty-four any more. And in her fury she had forwarded my extended confessional letter to Catherine to warn her what these fickle Adams men were like.

Perhaps this was why Dad seemed to avoid discussing what had happened. When I telephoned him to invite him up I asked him if he had read the letter.

'Oh yes, of course,' he replied brightly.

'Well, what did you think?'

He didn't hesitate for a second. 'Your handwriting has certainly got a lot better, hasn't it?'

But I needed to know the details of how Jocelyn had found the letter; had she searched through his pockets or opened his drawer or what? I was about to ask him when he said, 'It's a shame you didn't invite me up a few weeks earlier. It would have been nice to see Catherine and the children.'

Yes, what a shame, I thought. What a shame for you that my wife and children have walked out on me. What a shame that is. Poor Dad, poor you.

'Yes, well, it's a shame that Jocelyn read that letter I wrote to you or Catherine and the kids would still be here.'

'Ha. Fair dos!' he said, as if I had just scored a minor point in a school debating club.

'So, did she go through your pockets or what?'

'What do you mean?'

'Jocelyn. How did she get to read my letter?'

There was a pause in which Dad gradually sensed that perhaps he had done something he shouldn't have done.

'No, I, um, I showed it to her.'

'You did what?' I shrieked.

'Was that all right?'

'You showed her an explosive private letter from your son, and then you chucked her?'

He looked perplexed and the withered row of transplanted hair at the top of his head moved slightly as he furrowed his brow.

'What does "chucked" mean?' he said.

'It's what I am, thanks to you. Chucked, jilted, dumped.'

'Well, I think that's a bit unfair. I mean, it was you who was deceiving your wife, not me.'

At this point a whole row of fuses blew inside my head. 'Well at least I didn't fuck off with some pharmacist and walk out on my five-year-old kid.'

'That's not fair, Michael. It was more complicated than that . . .'

'I thought I must have done something really terrible to have suddenly been abandoned by you. I thought it was my fault.'

'Your mother and I were both to blame for the marriage not working.'

'Oh yeah, it's Mum's fault. Of course it is. Blame Mum; it's not as if she's in any position to defend herself, is it?'

'I'm just saying there's a lot you don't know about.'

'Well I do know this, that she'd still be alive if you hadn't walked out on her because she'd never have moved to Belfast with what's-his-face, so it's your fault she was run over.'

'Come on, Michael; it wasn't me driving that car, was it?'

'It might as well have been!' I yelled, and at the back of my brain a little voice was saying, What are you talking about, Michael? That is clearly nonsense, but I was in no mood to retract what I'd just said.

'You left me and Mum for a woman who left you, and so you found another woman and then another and then another. And now what have you got to show for it? One fucked-up son and a ridiculous hair transplant that looks like someone sprinkled a row of mustard seeds across your big, shiny bald head!'

I knew I'd pressed the nuclear button. It was all right to accuse him of being a bad father, of ruining my childhood, even of indirectly causing Mum's death, but no-one ever mentioned the hair transplant. You just knew not to. There was a brief moment of silence while Dad stared impassively into my eyes, and then he got up, picked up his coat, put on his hat and walked out the door.

Twenty minutes later I ate the supermarket pre-prepared shepherd's pie that had been baking in the oven for the two of us. I divided it in half and ate my portion, and then I ate the rest of it as well. Then I remembered why I had finally invited Dad to come up to London in the first place. I had been planning to show him round the house, give him lunch, explain the situation with the mortgage and then ask him if there was any way he could lend me a rather large amount of money. So that had all gone according to plan, then.

I was shocked by the things I had heard myself say to him, and at the level of bitterness that had been bottled up for so long. Why couldn't I have had a father like the ones in the adverts? In the Gillette commercial that I'd sung along to a million times, the father and son go fishing together in America somewhere, and dad helps son reel in a salmon; they're easy and comfortable with each other and he's had a really good shave and someone sings, 'The best a man can get.' That father would never run off with a pharmacist called Janet; they'd never use my dad in the Gillette ad. But then, he did have a beard, I suppose.

Of course my dad had never had a father around when he'd been a child, either. Or a mother most of the time, for that matter. On 1 September 1939 he had been put on a train to Wales, and he didn't see his dad again until the end of the war. I mused that if Dad hadn't been evacuated, then he would have had a father as a role model, which might have made him stay around to be a role model for me, which would have made me a better father and stopped Catherine walking out. So there it was, everything was Adolf Hitler's fault. I don't suppose any of this crossed his mind as he was invading Poland.

That night I just lay on the sofa all evening watching telly, occasionally getting hungry enough to see if the disgusting pizza I'd had delivered was any more palatable when cold. It wasn't, but I ate it anyway. With the television remote control in my hand I flicked through all the cable movie channels, watching three films at once. Trevor Howard kissed Celia

Johnson as she got on the railway carriage and then the entire train crashed into the River Kwai. Then Celia tucked up her children in bed and Jack Nicholson smashed down the door with an axe.

Here I was again, trying to watch several stories and so enjoying none of them. I actually felt a strange empathy with Jack Nicholson in *The Shining*; living in this house, frozen in time, guarding the place till everyone came back, slowly going madder and madder as I tried and failed to work. I don't think I was as bad a husband as he was. I never once tried to kill my wife and kids with an axe, for example, but I don't think Catherine would accept this as a point in my favour.

By now I had spent a couple of weeks living on my own in a child-orientated home. The mobile still span lazily in the breeze and the blue bird pendulum still swung maniacally back and forth under the rainbow clock, but the little isolated pockets of movement only served to emphasize how lifeless and eerily quiet the children's room seemed without them. I didn't want to change anything; it was all ready for them whenever they wanted to come back. I still had to push open the baby gate to get down the stairs, I still had to negotiate the child locks to open the cupboards. The only slight change I had made was to scramble the colourful magnet letters on the side of the fridge where Catherine had spelled out 'wanker' at eye level. I wondered how long she had searched for the letter 'w' before making do with a number 3 turned on its side? I was the lonely caretaker for a family show home – furnished accommodation all ready for my wife and children to move into any day they fancied. It had everything they needed, every safety precaution you could buy to prevent any possible damage being done to our precious little ones, except for the one minor mishap of their parents splitting up, of course. To think that we had dragged our kids round all those shops, buying plug guards, video covers, child locks, baby gates and a barrier to stop Millie rolling out of her bed, but we never saw anything in Mothercare to prevent the divorce for which we were heading. OK, so the kids grow up without a father, and Mum will become lonely, poor and bitter, but at least the little ones never fell down those three steps by the kitchen, and that's the main thing.

I wanted them back. I wanted them back so much I felt hollow and numb and sick. I had been round to her parents' house and pleaded with Catherine to come home, but she'd said she wasn't prepared to talk to me because I was a selfish shitbag, because I had betrayed her trust and because it was half-past three in the morning. So the only punctuation in my long and lonely weeks were my meetings with the children, which Catherine icily granted me. We met once a week at the windy swings in Hyde Park as the last few leaves were blown from the trees. We stood in silence, watching the children play, and because the silence was so oppressive I would occasionally shout things like, 'No! Not on the big slide, Millie,' and Catherine would say, 'It's all right, Millie, you can go on the big slide if you want,' and though she was looking at Millie, she was really talking to me. These few hours a week were supposed to be my quality time with the children, but I never quite managed to see where any quality came into it. I'd have a tense, self-conscious hour with them and then I knew I had to go back to the house on my own again.

And lo and behold, here was my double life all over again. Long days spent on my own, free to do whatever I wanted, and then short periods spent with my wife and family. Catherine was smart enough to say as much. 'This is just what you wanted, isn't it? To see us occasionally and have your own space the rest of the time. You still get to see them and play with them, but you don't have to do any of the boring hard work. All that's different is now you've got a bigger bed to lie in all day.'

'That's not fair,' I said, and then struggled to come up with a reason why it wasn't. From the outside it might have seemed a similar existence, but whereas before I'd believed I had organized myself the perfect life and had revelled in the best of both worlds, now I was utterly miserable. Because now none of it was in my control, now my hours as a father were begrudgingly meted out to me rather than being generously granted by my good self. Catherine had the power. My secret outpost of resistance to the dictatorship of babies had been betrayed by an informer. Now I'd been exiled to parental Siberia, condemned to solitary confinement with two hours' visiting time a week.

Although Catherine initiated these meetings, she was so angry with me that she could hardly bear to make eye contact. On the first occasion I attempted to greet her with a kiss on the cheek, which turned out to be a gross misreading of terms. As I leaned forward she recoiled and turned away; my kiss landed on her ear and I had to carry on as if that were a perfectly normal place to kiss somebody. I had tried to defend myself by claiming it wasn't as bad as having an affair with another woman, but to my disappointment Catherine said she would have preferred that; at least she could have put that down to some insatiable male craving.

She looked tired; apparently she hadn't been able to sleep very well so close to the kids. I was tired, too; I hadn't been able to sleep so far away from them. Her bulge was now comically large. She was either very, very pregnant or she'd already had the baby and was now hiding a space hopper under her jumper. I would have liked to have touched the bump, to feel it and talk to it, but that particular child was even more out of bounds. I wanted to ask about arrangements for the big day, but was too frightened to ask her where she would like me during the birth. She'd probably say Canada. During the previous eight months, while it had grown into a little person and developed eyes and ears and a heart and lungs and blood vessels and nerve endings and all the other incredible things that just happen by themselves, its parents' love had seemingly withered and died. If only babies could burst forth at the moment of passion in which they are conceived and not nine months later when it's all turned to dust.

'Well? Are you going to go and play with them?' she said, since that was what I was there for.

'Right, yes,' and I went off and tried to be as spontaneous and fun a dad as it's possible to be when you are being intensively monitored by their mother who is contemplating divorcing you. Millie was on the climbing frame.

'Shall I chase you round the climbing frame, Millie?'

'No.'

'Would you like me to push you on the swings, then?'

'No.'

'I've got you!' I said as I playfully grabbed her off the frame. My edginess had made me too rough and I grabbed her too hard or made her jump or something because she suddenly started crying.

'What are you doing?' said Catherine angrily, and she came across, took Millie from me and held her daughter close and looked at me with hatred in her eyes. Maybe I would have more success with Alfie, I hoped. He had taken his first steps a few weeks before – an event that I had not been there to witness – and now he was confidently tottering around, only occasionally falling on his nappy-padded bottom. He took up position beside the metal frame of the swing and banged a little pebble against it. I could feel Catherine watching me, and so I squatted down beside him and, with my own stone, banged the metal frame as well. He liked the noise of the stone hitting the metal bar. He didn't get bored of the noise of the stone hitting the metal bar. When after five minutes I wanted to stop, he became distressed, so I continued to bang the little stone against the metal bar. I looked round and did a mock long-suffering smile to Catherine, but she didn't smile back. I was cold to my bones and my squatting position became increasingly uncomfortable, but the spongy playground surface was too wet for me to kneel, so I teetered there as I was, feeling the blood draining from my legs, going tap tap tap with my bit of gravel on the echoey cold steel bar. I'd always wished I could have known which bits of childcare were bonding and which bits were just completely wasting time.

Eventually I sat down beside Catherine on a bench and attempted to find a way to talk about what had happened. She was living with her mad parents, who were even more overbearing than usual as it was no longer the woodlice-crushing season.

'I imagine it must be quite hard, isn't it? Living with your mum and dad, you know, with the kids and everything.'

'Yes.'

'So have you any idea how long you might stay there?'

'No.'

'You could come home, you know.'

'And where would you move to?'

I sensed I wasn't charming her out of her shell.

'Well I'd be there to help with the kids. I've given up the flat.'

'Yeah, you don't need it now, do you? Now you've got us out of the way there's no need for the flat, is there?'

As passively and apologetically as I could, I tried to float the idea that maybe I hadn't been quite ready for fatherhood and was only now adjusting to it. At this point her emotional dam just burst.

'You don't think it was hard for *me* to adjust?' she said in a furious, spitting whisper. 'Giving up work, giving birth and then suddenly being stuck in a house on my own all day with

210

a crying baby? You don't think that was a big shock for *me* to suddenly be ugly, fat, tired and bursting into tears; trying to breastfeed a screaming baby with blood coming out of my cracked nipples and no-one there to tell me it was OK, and that I was doing all right, even when the baby wouldn't feed or sleep or do anything but scream for days on end? I'm sorry it was so fucking hard for you to adjust, Michael.' She was crying now, angry with me and for letting herself break down in front of me. 'But I never fucking adjusted, because it's impossible. I was in a lose-lose situation. I felt guilty when I thought about going back to work and guilty for giving up work, but there's no-one you can talk to about it because the only other women with children at the swings are all eighteen years old and only speak fucking Croatian. So I'm really sorry you found it so hard to be in the same house as your wife when she was going through hell, but it's OK, because you could just leave, you could just fuck off whenever you felt like it and lie around with your mates, having parties and watching videos and leaving your mobile turned off just in case your wife wanted to cry down the phone to you.'

When she put it like that, she did sort of have a point. When I'd been on my own I had spent hours preparing carefully crafted arguments, like North American Indians fashioning beautifully decorated arrows before battle. And now she came along like the US Army, fired her great big cannon and blew me away. I offered up my puny self-justification all the same. I put it to her that the only difference between what I had done and what other fathers did was that I had been aware I was doing it.

'What? And you think it does you credit that you were *consciously* deceiving me? Those men are still part of a team,' she went on. 'They are still operating as a unit with their wives, one at home, one at work. They're still in it *together*.'

'They're at their place of work, sure, just like I was. But

those men don't really have to go on all those trips or have all those meals out in the evening or play golf with clients at the weekend; they do those things because they don't think it's less important than being with their families.'

Everything I said just made her angrier. 'So, let me get this straight, you thought all this through and, instead of resolving not to be that kind of father, you went and behaved ten times worse by being absent *deliberately* as part of a plan.'

'I thought it would help our marriage.'

I could feel most of my excuses dying in my mouth as I said them.

'Well, that worked well, didn't it.'

And then she got up and said she was going back to her mum's, and for some pathetic, desperate reason I said, 'You're lucky to have a mum,' and she looked back at me with contempt. I hated myself for saying it almost as much as she appeared to hate me for saying it. And then as she walked away I thought, Oh well, if we both feel the same way about what a pathetic worm I have become, then that's something we have in common; maybe we could build on that?

After they had gone I sat there in the playground on my own for a while. A young mother with a couple of kids came in and looked at me as if I were some escaped child molester, and when I heard her tell her children not to go near me I stood up and went home.

There was another familiar-shaped envelope on the doormat, though this one had been delivered by hand. I put it, unopened, on the side with all the others. They piled up on the hall table like accumulating evidence against me. Obviously I knew the bank wanted money, but I thought I'd never be able to earn any if I read the threats I feared were contained inside. As long as I was trying to work, then I believed I was doing something about it, and so I just buried my head deeper and deeper into my music. One of the letters came registered post, which seemed a bit of a waste of money. I was quite happy to sign for it; it didn't mean I had any intention of opening or reading it. Sometimes they tried ringing, and when I saw their number flash up on the little screen on our telephone, I'd quickly switch on the answer-phone and then fast forward through their messages. The cross-sounding man wasn't as scary when you speeded him up. He sounded like Donald Duck after inhaling helium.

On some days I would sit at my keyboard for thirteen or fourteen hours but I'd often achieve less than I used to in half a morning. Once upon a time I'd been able to lose myself in music, but that was before I'd been so desperate to do so. It was another couple of months before I was due to put together *Classic Commercials* and so between now and then I had a chance to create my own seminal compositions, which today happened to be a thirteen-second jingle that had to accommodate the line, 'Butterness! Butterness! It tastes like butter but the fat is less!'

Hmm, I thought, I think they're going for a sort of butter theme here. It was a shame the advert would be legally required to feature a large caption that flashed 'NOT BUTTER' along the bottom of the screen, but that wasn't my problem. The woman at the agency had said they wanted it to be just like the Ken Dodd song 'Happiness' without breaching copyright. So it would either sound wrong or be illegal. It had to be completed by six o'clock. I fired up my keyboard.

'Butter. What does that put one in mind of?' I tried out different sounds on the Roland. The oboe setting, the harp-sichord setting, the bassoon setting; none of them reminded me remotely of butter, but then I don't suppose new Butterness would have done, either. I listened to the Ken Dodd track and broke it down into its constituent parts.

Apparently the jingle was going to be sung by a chorus line of pantomime cows, so I had to try and concentrate on that image as I wrote the music. I had never pretended that my job was of vital importance to the future of mankind, but sitting on my swivelling piano stool, trying not to think about the state of my marriage and attempting to concentrate instead on a load of pantomime cows singing about new Butterness, well, it didn't radically improve my feeling of self-worth. It just didn't get the adrenalin going like really important work. The midwife who would deliver our third child, for example, she'd have no choice but to put all her problems out of her head and focus on getting the baby out safely. Damn! There it was; in one short step I was thinking about our next baby and not concentrating on the jingle for a new low-fat margarine containing dairy solids.

'Ah yes, Butterness. Right, concentrate, Michael, concentrate. Butter. I sang the guide track to myself a few times. Had the agency deliberately engineered it so that I would be forced to sing 'Happiness!' over and over to myself when I was feeling at my most miserable? I tried to parody the tune, but I couldn't get the original out of my brain. Concentrate, concentrate. Sometimes, when I had things on my mind, when there was a lot of fluff on the stylus, I could barely hear the tunes inside my head. Today there was so much fluff in there that the needle simply slid right across the vinyl.

It was hard to forget about the children with them all smiling at me from frames on the mantelpiece, so I got up and turned all the frames face down. I went and sat down and decided they looked awful like that, as if I was rejecting their existence or something, so I got up and put all the photos back as they were again.

Hmm. Butter? I thought, Butter. Does Catherine have the legal right to take the kids off like that? I mean, I am their father. How would she have liked it if I'd just whisked the kids away, suddenly announced I wasn't happy with the marriage and left her all alone? I continued to mull this over, and then I looked at the clock and it was quarter past twelve and I hadn't thought about butter or new Butterness for hours, and even if I came up with a suitably similar tune I still had to lay it down and master it, and getting it finished by six o'clock suddenly looked like a very close call. So come on. Butter, butter. Butterness. 'Butterness! Butterness! It tastes like butter but the fat is less!' I said this out loud to myself three times. I tried it again, putting the emphasis on different words. And then I went and made a cup of tea.

The house felt different with only me rattling around in it. I saw it in a different way. This was not unrelated to the fact that I sometimes spent hours just lying on my back on the hall carpet or sitting on the floor underneath the kitchen table. You can do these things when you're on your own. I wandered from room to room with my tea and finally decided to drink it sitting at the top of the stairs.

The cat deigned to vacate its favourite spot amongst Alfie's soft toys and came to lie next to me on the landing carpet. When we had first got the cat, we had told Millie she would be allowed to choose her name. We then spent the rest of the day trying to dissuade Millie from her immediate and un-hesitating choice, but she would not be budged, so we just had to accept it. Cat the cat and I had formed quite a close relationship during my weeks on my own in the family home. I'd buy her treats from the shops and then stand at the front gate shouting, 'Cat! Cat!' as passers-by avoided eye contact and quickened their pace. She would sit on my lap in the evenings and I'd stroke her under the chin and she'd purr ridiculously loudly. I tied a little ball on a piece of string and played with her, and when she wouldn't eat her food I'd give her some fresh fish and she'd always eat that and it was all very comforting. Until Red Collar Day. Cat didn't have a collar. Until Red Collar Day. She walked in through the cat flap, having been out for a few hours, wearing a bright-red new collar. She sniffed her food bowl, didn't fancy it and went out again. I was devastated. All the time I had imagined she was out there keeping other cats out of my garden or trying to catch the odd sparrow to proudly present to her master when really she had been curled up in front of someone else's electric fire, eating someone else's fresh fish, lying in someone else's lap. The collar had a name tag on it which said 'Cleo'. That was her name when she was at her secret other home. Cat had a double life. I felt double-crossed, jilted, rejected. Worst of all, I had been satirized by a bloody cat.

Forty minutes later I was still at the top of the stairs, lying on my back with my legs dangling over the first few steps. Cat the cat had wandered away long before, but the patterns on the landing ceiling were fascinating enough to keep me there for another half an hour. Eventually the clatter of the letter box jolted me out of my trance and I hauled myself to my feet. It was a noise that brightened my day; it made me feel there was hope I hadn't been completely forgotten by the outside world. Obviously I wouldn't read anything from the bank, but it might be a minicab card or a pizza leaflet, and it was always nice to read things from people who'd taken the trouble to keep in touch. On the mat was an estate agents' brochure, full of houses that cost over a million pounds. As I flicked through the glossy pictures of beautiful expensive family homes I became convinced it had been put through the letter box by the cat, who had now gone off to bask in the glory of her sarcastic triumph.

But the punctuation in the long and lonely day was enough to drive me back to work and I sat back on my stool. There were various vital jobs that had to be done before I could really get down to work. I tried to see how much dandruff I could shake out of my hair onto the desktop. I felt a spot halfway down my back and spent ten minutes trying various bizarre yoga-like contortions in order to reach it with both hands to squeeze it. I scraped off some of the greasy greyness that had built up on the keys of the synthesizer. I smelled it, then dabbed it on my tongue. That's when I was reminded of new Butterness. 'Come on, Michael!' I said out loud. 'Butterness! Butterness! It tastes like butter but the fat is less!' I considered ringing the agency to ask them if they were absolutely dead set on this butter tack. Most of the day had somehow disappeared; I had forgotten to have lunch and now I was suddenly so hungry that I had to eat immediately, but there was nothing in the house except some two-day-old bread and the free sample tub of bloody buggering Butterness that I'd been given.

As I threw away the uneaten crust, I faced up to the reality that I was going to let them down, that for the first time in my professional career I was going to miss a deadline, so I tried to ring the producer woman to ask if they could hang on another day. I was held in a queue for ages and then, when I finally got through, it was to an answerphone.

'Hello, this is Sue Paxton on 7946 0003. I'm not at my desk at the moment, though you may be able to reach me on 7946 0007. If you need to speak to me urgently, try my mobile 07700 900004 or my pager, 08081 570980 number 894. You can fax me on 7946 0005 or reach me by e-mail at s dot paxton at Junction5 dot co dot uk. If you want to try me at home my home numbers are 01632 756545 or 01632 758864, or fax me at home on 01632 756533 or e-mail s dot paxton at compuserve dot com. Otherwise just leave a message.'

By the end of all that I'd forgotten what I was ringing about, so I hung up. A few minutes later I armed myself with pen and paper and rang the number again. Then I attempted to reach her by all of the listed means, but each of them just informed me of all the other routes to a reply. By the time I'd tried them all I had wasted another hour. And so I really knuckled down and finally, finally, I managed to get the original tune out of my head and reverse the chords, and suddenly it was going round in my brain; quick get it down, record it before it's gone again, and then the phone went and it was Catherine cancelling the next day's meeting in Hyde Park, and I was furious and powerless and rude and pathetic and I hung up and walked round the house, kicking items of furniture.

Then the phone went again but it wasn't Catherine changing her mind, it was the bank again and I just shouted, 'Fuck off!' at the officious bastard and hung up, and then he rang back half an hour later, with the satisfied air of a Nazi Kommandant who has discovered a tunnel, and said that they had sent a letter to inform me that they had authorized their solicitors to execute a warrant of possession, and I know what this means: that I am close to losing the house, but I reasoned and explained, I tell him that keeping the house is the only chance I have of getting my family back, that I have two small children and a third one on the way and that their mother has left me to live with her parents, but she can't stay there for ever, not with her mother going on about the grandchildren not being christened, and eventually she'll have to come back home, and that's when she'll see that we can work it out, that's when she'll see that I've changed, and then we'll all be together again because that's all that matters, that's the only hope I've got: that they'll all come back home, but that can only happen if I've still got the house, if there's still a home to come back to, so you see, I have to stay here; they can't take the house away from me now. And he listens silently and patiently. And then he tells me they are repossessing the house.

chapter ten

it could be you

'Spare some change, please? Excuse me, could you spare any change, please?'

I had got into the habit of striding past the homeless who did the backing vocals for the music of London's streets. But today it struck me that I had just coldly walked straight past another human being, and so I turned back and put five pounds in his makeshift cardboard money box. Five quid! And he didn't even have a bit of string with a sad-looking dog on the end.

I was briefly irritated that the recipient wasn't ecstatically grateful for my excessive generosity, that five pounds didn't buy me a happier beggar. For a fiver you expect the executive thank-you plus, with a personalized letter to be sent on to you the following week explaining how your money was spent, with a P.S. asking you to convert your gifts into a deed of covenant. But he thought I was just like all the other rich clean people walking past. He thought I had a nice home and a happy wife and everything else he envied.

I had just dropped the keys to my family home off at the

bank. I had walked into our local branch, queued up at the window and given them to the young girl behind the counter.

'Hang on, I'd better get the manager,' she'd said.

'No, it's all right, he's had the paperwork. Can't stay. I've got to find somewhere to sleep tonight.'

'Oh. Is there anything else I need to know?'

'Er, yeah. The downstairs toilet. You have to give it one slow flush and then flush it again very quickly straight away.'

She looked at me blankly, but as I went to leave she remembered the script.

'Thank you for your custom this morning, Mr Adams,' she said. 'Have a nice day.'

'Thank you. You're too kind,' I called behind me as I went out onto the streets of London, unsure as to where I should go now. And then I just walked around for a while; it was quite surreal really. Normally the pavement is for the irrelevant time in between the various parts of your life, now it was all there was. It made me feel that I didn't have a point. The litter bin had a point; it was for putting paper in. The railings had a point; they were for stopping people from stepping out on the road. But what was the point of me? I wasn't doing anything, I wasn't going anywhere, so what was I for?

I stood there for a while and watched a tangle of old cassette tape which was wrapped around the railings – a thin, brown, shiny streamer, discarded and blowing in the wind. There was probably music recorded on that tape, music that had been composed and structured and arranged, and now it was all unravelled and useless. Somewhere along the way the tape had just snapped. Now I had all the leisure time in the world, but the currency had been chronically devalued. Time to myself was no longer stolen away in little treat-size chunks, it was forced upon me like a life sentence. I had with me a holdall that contained a few clothes, a toiletry bag and the *Time Out* guide to London. All my other possessions and all the contents of the family home were crammed into my next-door neighbour's garage.

'Oooh, you are lucky having a fridge with such a big freezer compartment,' said the elderly Mrs Conroy, trying to be positive as I wheeled it up her driveway. Plastic bin liners were packed tight with soft toys, the telly was wrapped in a Pocahontas duvet and placed inside Alfie's cot. Moving everything out had taken me two days, and by the time I'd finished the garage looked like a squashed, post-earthquake version of our family home. Mrs Conroy kindly said I could leave everything there for as long as I wanted. Klaus and Hans were no longer lodging with her and had gone back to Germany, so no-one used the garage any more. She had given me boxes to put things in and sandwiches and cups of tea when I was exhausted from dragging sofas and mattresses up her driveway and my own key to the garage for when I needed to pop over and get anything. She didn't ask how I had got so behind with the mortgage; the only allusion she made to everything that had happened was as I locked up the garage and thanked her again before I left. She looked at me sadly, gave me a brave smile and said, 'You weren't around much, were you?'

Now I walked slowly along Camden High Street, clutching the few belongings that weren't locked up in Mrs Conroy's garage. I found myself taking more interest than I normally would have done in the plastic bric-a-brac in charity shop windows. I passed an arcade of slot machines called Loads o' Fun but judging by the emotionless grey faces inside it looked as if the sign above the entrance was slightly overstating it. Estate agents advertised attractive family homes, building societies offered easy loans. Catherine had learned about the unpaid mortgage from the letter to my father, but this didn't prevent me from bringing the subject up again during the long hours spent shivering by the swings. If I attempted to talk about trivia she would always give me monosyllabic replies, so I tried to use the impending loss of our home as a means of forcing her to talk to me.

'I think the bank are about to repossess our house,' I had announced.

Obviously I didn't expect her to throw her arms around me, but it was the nearest thing I had to a chat-up line. She looked at me and then looked away again.

'Well, we would have had to sell it when we got divorced anyway,' she remarked, as if this were something we had already agreed. It was the first time she had ever mentioned divorce, but hey, at least we were talking now, so I tried to see the positive side.

'Anyway, I could never go back there now,' she continued. 'I was miserable in that house all on my own.'

This was a calculated extra turn of the knife. Though she didn't want to be with me now, I had made her miserable by not being with her then. But I was consoled that she didn't appear mortified by the news about the house. I didn't come away feeling that my achievement in losing the family home had lessened our chances of getting back together. However, this was probably because those chances were currently standing at approximately zero.

As I wandered aimlessly down the main drag, it occurred to me that the fact that I had nowhere to sleep now gave me the perfect excuse to present myself to Catherine as someone she might take pity on. I imagined how she would react. If she'd said, 'Well, if you're ever made homeless you could always come and stay with me,' I'm sure I would have remembered it. 'I've only got a single bed, sweetheart, but hey, that'll make it all the cosier when you cuddle up next to me.' No, it didn't ring any bells.

My father was not an option, either. Apart from the fact that he lived in Bournemouth, a surfeit of masculine pride on both sides meant that we hadn't spoken to each other since he'd walked out of my kitchen. Anyway, if I had turned up at his door to tell him I'd handed my keys in at the bank, his anxiety would never had progressed beyond worrying that I'd made sure the keyring was clearly labelled. Then there was the option of the Balham flat. But all sorts of things had happened there since I'd moved out.

Monica had finished with Jim, who had then waited a decent interval of hours before asking out her best friend, Kate. Within a few weeks he had decamped to her flat in Holland Park, which had all the facilities that Jim required to continue his Ph.D, although Sky Sports 2 was a little fuzzy. Paul had finally come out of the closet and had moved to Brighton to live with his boyfriend, a nightclub bouncer who also worked in the army recruiting office. Simon had then organized three young women to take our places in the house, but when he showed them all his favourite sites on the Internet they had changed all the locks and put all his belongings on the front doorstep.

In the space of a couple of months, all four of us had left the flat. It had been Simon who had told me about all of this when he'd called my mobile phone a few weeks earlier. He was still smarting from his forced eviction and suggested to me that there must have been another reason why the girls didn't like him. He confessed that he had once helped himself to their peanut butter and he thought that this was probably the real explanation.

So my old bachelor pad was not an option, either. In fact, I was struggling to think of anywhere I could go. I thought about all the friends I'd had in my twenties, but I hadn't kept in contact with any of them. On the day your first child is born you might as well go through your address book and whenever you come across any friends who don't already have babies, then just tear out their names there and then. It will save a lot of embarrassment and pointless Christmas cards later on. Of course, Catherine and I had had a wide social circle, but in reality these had just been her friends with husbands attached. Since I'd got married I had lost contact with all my old comrades from college. I certainly didn't blame Catherine for this, she had never discouraged me from seeing the mates I'd had before we moved in together, it was just that I had sat back and lazily allowed her to organize our social diary, and quite reasonably it never occurred to her to make the effort to keep up with my old friends. There was not one couple that I would feel comfortable calling on now. They had made me feel inadequate enough before, with their great big wine glasses and their Italian bread and their wide selection of olive oils lined up on the dresser.

And so, late in a day spent walking aimlessly around, I found myself phoning Hugo Harrison to ask him if I could possibly stay with him for a night or two until I got myself sorted. I didn't really relish having to explain to a work colleague – my main employer really – that I had got myself into dire financial straits, but as it turned out, Hugo was far too insensitive to be the slightest bit interested in any subject of conversation that did not involve the exploits of Hugo Harrison, so he never bothered to ask. He was delighted to be able to invite me up to his flat so that he could have someone to talk at.

His London address was a magnificent penthouse apartment in a high-rise complex near Albert Bridge, with views over the whole of London so that Hugo could look down on everybody. It had once been a block of council flats, but the council had contrived to successfully evict all the local people on the grounds that they had persistently voted Labour. Now the place was highly fortified, with electric gates and security cameras that would immediately spot anyone doing anything suspicious like staying in London for the weekend. Hugo's wife lived in the country with her horses, his children were at boarding school and Hugo spent his weekday evenings in this opulent apartment. As a lifestyle, it wasn't so different to what I'd attempted, except that for some reason this version seemed to have some sort of social legitimacy. But then, Hugo was posh. He might have stood too close to everyone when he was talking to them, but when it came to his own family, he generally liked them as far away as possible.

Although I was receiving charity I was going to have to pay for it by listening to Hugo all evening. And the more he told me, the more I realized why he had this flat. Hugo's hobby was sexual intercourse. I had met golf bores and bridge bores, but this was the first time I had been forced to listen to a sexual-intercourse bore. He told me about his sexual exploits with a presumption that I'd share his attitude that it was all just healthy male behaviour. The fact that my wife had walked out on me made me a martyr to the cause, a heroic victim of the war of the sexes. He plied me with drink and, as dusk fell over the twinkling city below, he tried to cheer me up by telling me what a bastard he had consistently been to his other half. I was interested to know what he actually thought of his wife, and so I probed him a little bit on his marriage.

'Oh, she's a good mum and all that,' he conceded. 'She's always sending things to the kids at boarding school. But she's fat, you see. Big mistake.'

'What? Being fat?'

'No, no, she can't help it,' he generously acknowledged. 'Big mistake on my part. You see, I initially fancied her because she had these enormous knockers,' and in case his choice of words wasn't clear enough, he mimed what enormous knockers were and on what part of the human body one might expect to find them.

'But you should never marry a girl with enormous

225

knockers, Michael. When my eldest son started dating girls I only gave him one piece of advice. I said, "Always remember, son. Big tits at twenty, fat wife at forty." '

'How charming,' I quipped hopelessly. 'I'm sure he'll thank you for that later in life.'

He refilled my glass and talked about his wife's chubbiness as if it were some tragic disability that made it impossible to have any sort of sexual relations with her, thereby justifying him playing the field whenever the fancy took him. And judging by his anecdotes this seemed to be quite often. For example, he was genuinely proud of himself for successfully seducing an actress who was very keen to be in a high-profile and lucrative commercial he was casting. What an incredible achievement, Hugo. Clever old you! He recounted how his wife had been up in London and that he'd been supposed to meet her with tickets for the opera. Instead he'd left her standing outside the Coliseum while he'd taken the young hopeful to a hotel room to have sex. It got worse . . .

'I knew the missus would try and ring me, so I set my mobile phone to vibrate, and I was in the middle of fucking this horny little actress, right – I can't remember her name – when suddenly my mobile started jiggling on the bedside table. I looked at the number on the screen and, sure enough, it was Miranda's mobile.'

'Oh dear. That must have made you feel awful?'

'What? No, I had this really wicked idea, right? This actress was half pissed, a bit giggly, you know, so I picked up the vibrating phone and pressed it against her . . . you know, her little sex button.'

'You did what?'

'Yah. I mean, she thought it was a scream, but she really got off on it, as well. Can you imagine that? So my wife is try-ing to ring me to find out where the fuck I am, but all she can hear is the ringing tone. Totally unaware that the longer she held on, the closer she got to bringing my mistress to a sexual climax!'

'That's obscene, Hugo.'

'Isn't it! My wife gave my lover an orgasm!' And he gave this loud braying laugh, knocked back his drink and slapped me on the back saying, 'Another glass of wine, Michael?' When he came back from the kitchen, I asked him if the girl was good in the commercial, and he looked at me as if I was mad and said, 'Good God, no. I didn't cast her!'

He continued telling me far too many details about the sex he'd had with dozens of nameless women, but the more lovers that he listed, the lonelier he sounded. For all I knew every single story could have been made up; he was just using me as a sounding board for all his private fantasies. The only definite evidence I'd ever had of his incredible powers of seduction was his visit to a seedy prostitute in Soho. Strangely, that particular conquest was never recounted. I felt increasingly uncomfortable sitting there listening to him. He was drawing me in, trying to make me approve. Like him, I had deceived my wife, and Hugo made me feel that entitled me to life membership of his women haters' club. I was resolute that I was not the same as him. I wasn't a prude, I didn't disapprove of sex, but Hugo talked with such contempt about the women he had seduced that it left almost as bad a taste in my mouth as it must have done for them.

'You only live once, Michael,' he said. 'And I can't think of anything more boring than just fucking Miranda once a week for the rest of my life.'

Finally he poured me a glass of wine and asked me if I'd had any more thoughts about *Classic Commercials*, and suddenly I realized something with complete clarity.

'Er, I've decided I'd rather not do it after all.'

'Why on earth not?'

I tried to explain to him. He had said that he wanted a classical album without all the boring bits, so I told him that you have to have boring bits, because what he called the boring bits are what make the memorable bits memorable. 'Life has boring bits,' I declared slightly too loudly. I tried to make him understand that the vocal finale of Beethoven's Ninth Symphony is moving and powerful and wonderful because of what you have listened to during the previous hour, because of the commitment you have put in. The cellos and basses take you through the previous movements, reject each in turn and then tentatively develop the 'Ode to Joy' theme that had been expressed by the woodwind section earlier on. That is why, when it finally bursts forth, the choral climax is one of the greatest moments in the history of music.

Hugo's reaction was, 'OK, we can lose Beethoven's Ninth; we'll stick in that bit of Mozart from the yoghurt ad instead.' So I tried to explain to him all over again that you can't just have the special bits on their own. Art isn't like that, and life isn't like that. I understood that now.

He was bemused by my bizarre principles and soon steered the conversation back to the various ways in which he had betrayed his wife. At this point I got to my feet and announced, 'Actually, Hugo, I'm going to head off now. There's a couple of other people I want to look up, so I'll probably stay with them tonight.' And before I knew it I was looking at myself in the lift mirror, wondering how I had exchanged a warm bed in a luxury penthouse flat for I knew not what.

'Goodnight, sir,' said the uniformed porter who opened the front door for me. It was a very grand entrance for a homeless person to make onto the dark streets of London.

I saw a mock Irish pub and headed for that. Then I sat in the corner and slowly but methodically got myself drunker. There was a self-consciousness to this reckless behaviour; I even bought a small bottle of whisky from the off-licence afterwards, and I've never liked whisky. Catherine had often accused me of having a self-destructive streak, but sitting in that pub with no home to go to, excommunicated from my family and with no friends to turn to, I think I was entitled to feel a little bit sorry for myself. Then, just to compound my private humiliation, a song came on the jukebox which I recognized from years ago.

'What's this music that's playing?' I slurred at the barmaid as she stacked up my collection of empty glasses.

'The Truth Test,' she said in a high-pitched twangy Australian accent that didn't quite chime with the plastic shamrocks on the wall.

'The Truth Test! Oh, not the bloody Truth Test! Are they famous, then?'

'Are you joking? This song's number one.'

'The Truth Test! But they were rubbish! They used to support us in Godalming. I had to lend them my fucking fuzzbox for Christ's sake.'

She attempted a half smile, thought about asking me what a fuzzbox was and then decided better of it. Somebody put the same track on again and I decided that was my cue to leave. Though my wallet was by now empty of banknotes I had found the scrap of paper on which I'd scribbled Simon's new address in Clapham, and so I stuffed it in my pocket and started to walk southwards. It was only a couple of miles as the crow flies, but at least four miles as the drunk weaves, and by the time I got there I had lost my piece of paper. I stood in the darkness of Clapham Common, going through the same pockets a dozen times. Twice I checked that it hadn't fallen into my turn-ups and both times found that I wasn't wearing turn-ups. What was I supposed to do now? Distant headlights circled round the common, the biggest traffic island in London. I sat on a bench. I was drunk, I was tired. Then I finally conceded what had happened to me and shifted my body round so I was lying on the bench. An alarm went off in the distance. I put my holdall under my head, wrapped my coat around myself as tightly as I could and attempted to sleep. In my drunken state I actually allowed myself a flippant little smile at my situation. The last piece of post that I had opened at home was a magazine from my old university, and as always I'd turned straight to the 'Where are They Now?' section. Maybe I could have filled it out, 'Here I am, pissed out of my head, sleeping on a bench on Clapham Common.'

Despite the wind and the occasional mocking laugh from the mallard ducks on the boating pond, I fell asleep quite quickly. I've always dozed off easily when I've had a lot to drink; that's why I was sacked from that summer job driving pensioners to the seaside. But in the middle of the night the drink and the drizzle started to make themselves felt and I came round feeling damp and dehydrated at the same time. As always when you wake up in a strange place, there is a split second while you try to remember where you are. It didn't feel like my bed at home. It didn't feel like the luxury four-poster I had spurned at Hugo's apartment. When I realized that the shivering and aches I felt were due to the fact that I'd been sleeping on a park bench I became so overwhelmingly depressed that I almost felt like throwing myself under the first vehicle that came past, but this turned out to be a milk float, which would only have bruised my leg a bit, and I didn't want another failure to add to the list.

Then in the depressed introspection of the small hours, my mind wallowed into that dangerous quicksand of self-pity. All that I wanted, in fact, all that I had wanted all along, was the love and respect of Catherine. Just to be really sure that the woman I loved, loved me back. In my self-centred universe I had only ever seen her as a planet revolving around me. That misconception was sustainable until the children came along, but then the physics were suddenly exploded. I couldn't accept it; I still tried to force myself back into the centre of her life. If I wasn't the reason she had been pissed off at breakfast, I would make sure I was the reason she was pissed off by lunchtime. I would hijack her irritation, make it relate to me. Maybe this was the way all men thought. Maybe the day after Mrs Thatcher lost her job as prime minister, Denis Thatcher got all prickly and defensive and said, 'I don't know why you're in such a bad mood with me.'

I lay there, cold and hollow, watching the cars speed by. They became more frequent as London began to wake up; now their drivers seemed in an increasing hurry. Under the feeble glow of the street lights I noticed a shape attached to the railings on the other side of the road. A few yards along from the stripped skeleton of a bicycle frame I could just make out a withered bunch of carnations, a small bunch of cheap garage flowers, now brown and lifeless. There is only one reason why people tie flowers to railings: to mark the spot where someone was killed. Another car tore past, oblivious to the significance of the spot, speeding down the road just as the fatal car that precipitated the pathetic, withered memorial must have done. In the summer, ice-cream vans park along here. I wondered if a child had run across to get an ice cream and hadn't stopped to look, like that time Millie had seen a feather in the middle of the road and run across, and I'd shouted at her so much I had made her cry. She'd never seen me be so angry with her, but really I'd been furious with myself for letting go of her hand and imagining what might have happened.

Then my unbridled mind started to gallop down a path too terrible to explore. What if Millie was run over? What if there were some railing where I had to go and tie cheap carnations. *Don't think about it, Michael. Put it out of your head.* But I couldn't help myself, I started deliberately fantasizing about Millie's death, imagining the scene step by step, watching it unfold, constructing a chillingly plausible fatal scenario in my head.

I'm in the front garden watering the window boxes, and I have left the front door slightly ajar because I don't have my door keys in my pocket. I'm half aware of the cat slipping through the gap in the door. I don't see Millie following the cat. The cat is on the pavement now and Millie's holding her tail. The cat doesn't like this game, so it runs off across the road and Millie chases after her, running out between the parked cars. There is a big white builder's van with a copy of the *Sun* on the dashboard; the driver's listening to Capital Gold and they're playing 'Bohemian Rhapsody', and it's the guitar solo, which always makes him drive faster, and suddenly there's a thud and a screech and a loud pop as his tyre goes over Millie, and then the next set of tyres go over her as well, and it all happens so fast, but it's in slow motion, too, and there she is on the road behind the van; she's completely still, just a body, a little broken, useless body; and I put on those shoes that morning and we chose that dress together, and now the driver is standing at the side of the road using every swear word he knows to say that it wasn't his fault, and he's pale and he's shaking, and a BMW coming the other way is tooting his horn because the bloody van is blocking the road, and then the builder throws up on the roadside and his radio's still playing and there's a line about nothing really mattering, and then there's a gong and it's over and that's it – Millie's life only lasted three years.

Another pair of headlights shine on the dried-out brown flowers and I come to. My anti-fantasy is so vivid that I want to see Millie now, I want to pick her up and squeeze her tight and not let her go, but I can't. Not because I lost her to a white van, but because I lost her to another more subtle accident: a marriage break-up. Of course it's not the same, and she'll be all right, and Catherine will bring her up well; but she won't love me like I love her; she won't be bothered about me. And though it's a million times preferable to her being killed by a grubby builder's van, I have lost her; we won't live together; she won't really know me. There has been a terrible accident and I have lost her.

How did this happen? How did this sequence of events unfold? The day that I first deceived Catherine, when I turned off my mobile when I saw my home number on the little screen – that was the cat slipping out of the front door. Then there was the time that Catherine asked me if I'd been working all through the night, and instead of just saying that I'd worked till ten and had been too tired to travel home and then be woken up by the kids all night, I just stared at the ground and nodded, and by failing to put her straight I lied by default – that was like not looking to see where Millie was, not thinking that she might be in danger. Then I lied with increasing nonchalance and lied to myself that Catherine was happy, and I started to deliberately escape from her and the baby – like the cat pulling away as Millie tried to hold on to its tail. And then the cat was over the road and Millie couldn't catch it, and then suddenly, bang, my two lives collide, and Catherine cries and cries and cries and it's all over, it can't be mended. I've lost them, just like Dad lost me. That was another sort of accident, I thought. The affair. My dad had taught me how to cross the road, because he didn't want to lose me; he had told me not to run off the pavement after a football, because he didn't want to lose me; but he didn't see the danger he was putting me in when he went for a drink with that girl he met through work. He just didn't think; like the child running after a cat or a ball, he was excited and he'd run after the pretty girl and then, bang, he had lost his son, his marriage was over and it was all a terrible accident.

The darkest hour before the dawn was lit by the flashing blue light of a speeding police car, though there was no siren to pierce the silence of the winter night. Why didn't they come rushing to marriage break-ups? Why hadn't the police car sped after my dad when he had driven away from our family home and said, 'That's very dangerous, sir, that child could get hurt.' Was it now set to happen all over again?

In my last meeting at the swings with Catherine, I had pleaded with her yet again that I had already given up the flat when she left me, and I think I saw a brief flicker of hesitation, when she was almost tempted to believe me. I had told her how furious I was with my dad for showing his girlfriend the letter.

'Why would he do that?' I had said to her. 'Why would he show Jocelyn a deeply personal private letter that I had written him?'

'Because he was proud,' she said calmly.

In an instant so much suddenly became clear. It was so obvious once Catherine had said it. Dad had shown my extended confession to his girlfriend because he was so proud to have had a letter from me. I'd never sent him so much as a postcard before; I'd hardly ever called him or been to see him in Bournemouth. It didn't matter what I'd put in the letter; if I'd written to tell him I was robbing pensioners to pay for my crack habit he would have waved the letter around to say, 'Look, look, a letter from my son!'

It was my fault that Dad had shown my letter to his girl-friend. It was my fault that Catherine had received it. I'd not been there for the generation above any more than I had been for the one below. So my letter ended up being important not for what it told Dad, or Catherine, but for what it told me. How incredibly betrayed Catherine felt when she learnt the truth about my way of life and how desperate my father was for the slightest attention.

234

Dawn was breaking over the common and I suddenly felt like I had got it. I understood how all this worked; the riddle was solved in my head. You just have to spend time with the people you love. You don't try to change them, you don't get annoyed because they don't behave how you want them to behave, you put up with boredom or tantrums or repetition and you just spend time with them. On their terms, listening to them telling you about cars their friends bought in Belgium, or what they drew at playgroup or whatever. You have to have patience and just be there. Elderly parent or small child; it's all the same. Just pass time with them and then everyone is happy, even you, in the end.

I wanted to see Catherine to share this revelation with her, to tell her that now I knew what I was supposed to do then everything could be all right again. I wanted to join her, be bored with her. In the half light I struggled to sit up, but I felt nauseous and dizzy. Hangovers usually made me clamour for fresh air, but that wasn't a problem on this occasion. I closed my eyes and pressed my fingers against my temples, attempting a gentle circular rubbing movement as if this had the remotest chance of countering the effects of a bottle of wine, several pints of strong lager and a small bottle of blended whisky.

'You look a bit rough there, mate.'

If I looked as rough as I felt I was surprised that anyone would come within a hundred yards of me. Sitting beside me on the park bench was a tramp. A traditional smelly tramp, with a big can of Special Brew in his hand and a huge scab on his chin. The only thing that wasn't traditional about him was that he was Welsh. Scottish drunks, yes, I had seen plenty of those. Irish drunks, yes, they had made Camden tube station their own. But a Welsh homeless alcoholic, that was a new one on me. It was strange how the Scots and Irish seemed to be everywhere – in films, in music, in Celtic dance extravaganzas, even slumped outside tube stations. Here, at last, was a Welshman who was doing his bit to redress the balance.

'Er, yeah, I do feel a bit rough, yeah. I just needed to sit down for a bit.'

'And then you just lay down and spent the night here, ha ha ha ha. This is my bench, see, but you were fast asleep so I let you have it for a night. Drink?' and he offered me a swig from his can of Special Brew which still had a globule of his spittle hanging from the rim.

'No thanks, I never drink warm lager and tramp's gob before breakfast.'

I only thought that; I didn't have the courage to actually say it. It was nice of him to offer to share what little he had with me, even if it was the singularly most unattractive offer I had ever had in my whole life. It concerned me that this tramp was so friendly, that he was talking to me like an equal.

'I've not seen you sleeping around here before,' he said.

'Well, of course you haven't. I'm not homeless.'

'Oh sorry, your majesty,' and he gave an exaggerated grovelling drunken bow from his position on the bench beside me. 'So where do you live then?'

'Er, well, I don't actually live anywhere just at the moment,' I mumbled. 'But as it happens, until very recently I had two homes,' I added, in the hope that this would improve my claim to be a paid-up member of mainstream society.

'So you used to have two homes and now you've got none.' He took a final glug from his can and dropped it on the ground. 'That sounds about fair to me.'

He was right, there was a symmetry in the way things had turned out: the man who had tried to have it all had ended up with nothing. But I resented the way he was trying to bring me down to his level. I wasn't a tramp! OK, I had nowhere to live and I had no money and I'd spent last night on a bench, but however smashed I got on Special Brew I could never have just dropped the empty can on the ground like that.

'I've got a wife and two children, you know, and a third one on the way,' I told him, proudly.

He looked me up and down. He looked at my creased, stubbly face, my sticking-up hair, my crumpled dirty clothes and my pathetic bundle of belongings crammed into a tatty holdall.

'What a lucky girl. I mean, you look like a hell of a catch for any woman.'

'Yeah, well, we had a big bust up, but I'm going to ring her. I'm going to ring her now from that call box over there.'

'Go on, then.'

'And I'm going to make it up with her because I am not some down-and-out.'

'Whatever you say.'

'Because I'm not some homeless beggar.'

'Sure. Go and phone your wife.'

'I would, only . . . Can you spare some change, please?'

With twenty pence scrounged from the Welsh tramp I rang Catherine's parents' number and braced myself for their icy disapproval. But my heart leaped as Millie took it upon herself to answer the phone.

'Hello, Millie, it's Daddy. How are you?'

'All right.'

'Have you had your breakfast?'

There was silence from the other end of the phone, which I realized meant she was nodding.

'Have you been being good children for Gran and Grandad?'

More silence; she might be nodding, she might be shaking her head, it was hard to tell. I had to stop asking questions that didn't require her to speak.

'Do you like my hat?' she asked me.

'It's a lovely hat. Is it Granny's?'

'No!' she said as if I was completely stupid. 'Granny's not a pirate!'

The call box was eating up my units and, lovely as it was to talk to Millie, a discussion about whether or not Granny was a pirate was not going very far towards rebuilding my life. 'Is Mummy there, darling?'

Silence.

'Millie, I can't see you nodding or shaking your head from here. Can you put Mummy on the phone?'

I heard Catherine's voice talking to Millie, telling her to hand over the phone.

'Hello?'

'Hi, it's me. Look, we have to talk, because I know you must hate me and everything, and I can understand that from where you are I can't look like the most wonderful bloke in the world, but I'm not the worst, you know. And the thing is that I love you, and Jesus, men have slept with other women and their wives have forgiven them, but I've never done that. Christ, even when I masturbate I always try and think of you.'

'It's not Catherine, Michael. It's Sheila,' said the frosty voice of her mother. 'Please do not use the Lord's name in that way.'

'Oh, er, sorry, Sheila. God, you sound just like her on the phone.'

'Please do not take God's name in vain.'

'Oh yeah. Fuck, sorry. Can I speak to Catherine, please?'

'No you can't.'

'What? No you won't let me, or no she's not there?'

'No she's not here.'

Sheila was not going out of her way to be more helpful than she needed.

'Er, do you know where she is?'

'Yes.'

'Well, could you tell me where she is, please.'

'I'm not sure I should.'

'Look for Chr— for crikey's sake, Sheila. She is still my wife. She's nine months pregnant with our third child. I think I have a right to know where she is.'

Sheila paused. And then she told me where Catherine was. And then I shouted something and ran out of the telephone box, leaving the receiver swinging back and forth, and the person waiting to use the phone box after me picked it up to hear Sheila saying, 'Please do not use the name of our Lord Jesus Christ in that way.'

I ran up Clapham High Street and through Stockwell and past all the tube stops that I used to whizz through when I commuted between marriage and boyhood, but now I didn't even have a pound to ride on the train and I ran and ran and ran and my body hurt and I felt sick, but I kept on running because I had to get to Catherine. I had to be with her now; I had to be by her side because Catherine had gone into labour. At this moment our third child was being born.

chapter eleven

the real thing

A car tooted and swerved as I ran across the traffic crossing Clapham Road. I had run two miles and felt close to collapsing when I saw the orange beacon of an approaching taxi and maniacally waved my hand.

'Hello.' I panted, leaning on the side of the cab. 'Look I've got no cash on me, but my wife is in labour at St Thomas's, and if you could just give me a lift up there I can post you a cheque for twice the fare.'

'Hop in, I've got two meself, little monkeys. I'll get you there double quick and there's no charge. This one's on me.'

That's what I'd been hoping he might say. I'd seen it in the movies – desperate man with wife in labour meets policeman or cabbie who bends the rules to help him. This taxi driver hadn't seen the same films as me. 'Fuck off,' he snarled, and then drove off, nearly taking my arm with him.

I resumed my marathon dash across South London, occasionally swapping my holdall from one hand to the other, and then eventually dropping it in a litter bin. By the time I reached the river I could only run in short intermittent bursts, in between long stretches of anxious, brisk walking. You can never really appreciate exactly how far away somewhere is until you're desperately trying to race there with a severe hangover in time to witness the birth of your child. Stretches of road that in my head were only fifty yards long seemed to go on and on and on, as if I was trudging the wrong way along the moving walkway at Gatwick Airport. The exertion increased my feeling of nausea; I felt dizzy and sick and could feel the sweat running down my back and soaking through my overcoat.

The Thames stretched out on my left with parliament looming out of the mist on the other side of the river. As I jogged exhaustedly along the embankment path, a stampede of cyclists bore down on me, and for a moment it looked like the only safe option would be to climb up a tree. Finally I arrived at the entrance to St Thomas's Hospital and, gasping for breath, I approached the reception desk.

'Hello, I've come to see Catherine Adams who's giving birth here at this very moment. Can you tell me what floor she's on, please?'

The receptionist did not seem to share my sense of urgency. Still panting, I explained that I was her husband, that I hadn't come in with her because I hadn't been with her when she suddenly went into labour, but that I had to get up there right away and obviously they would want me beside her as soon as possible. And then I threw up in the litter bin.

The hospital receptionist obviously saw people being sick on a fairly regular basis as she was completely unfazed by this. As I rested my head on her desk and moaned, 'Oh God,' quietly to myself, she called the labour ward to confirm my version of events.

'Yes, he's down here at reception,' she said. 'He's just been sick in the litter bin and now I think he may be about to pass out.'

A conversation ensued of which I could only hear one half. 'I see . . . yes . . . yes . . .' but from the tone of her voice I could sense there must be some sort of administrative hold-up.

'Well, what is it? Is there a problem?' I asked impatiently.

'They want to know why you have been sick? Are you ill?'

'No, I'm not ill, I just ran here, that's all.'

'No, he's not ill. He does smell of drink, though,' she added helpfully, and then she gave me a little disappointed shake of the head to suggest that this detail had just failed to swing it in my favour. Finally she informed me that they could not allow me onto the labour ward, that they understood that Catherine and I were separated and that Catherine already had her sister Judith there as her birthing partner. As if childbirth wasn't painful enough.

'OK. That's fine, I understand,' I said calmly. 'I'll, um, call round later, maybe.' And then I walked slowly round the corner and jumped in the lift up to the labour ward. I came out on the seventh floor and the next obstacle was a big scuffed metal door with a security buzzer on the side. I hung around for a while, pretending to study the poster that said, 'How to examine your breasts', and a passing nurse gave me a very strange look. Eventually the ping of the lift announced the arrival of another expectant father, who emerged clutching a large bundle of pre-packed sandwiches which he had bought in the shop downstairs. Excellent, he was heading for the door to the labour ward.

'Ah, the famous sandwiches,' I said, thinking it best to befriend him if I was going to try and follow him into the inner sanctum.

'I didn't know what sort of filling was best for a mother in labour, so I got a selection.'

'Cheese and pickle,' I announced confidently as I moved to stand behind him at the door.

'Oh,' he said, looking crestfallen. 'That's the only one I didn't get. I'll go and change this for cheese and pickle.'

'No, no, egg and cress is even better. In fact, some people think that cheese and pickle increases the chance of a Caesarean.'

'Really? Blimey, thanks for telling me,' and he buzzed and gave his name to the intercom and he was in and so was I.

I adopted the resolute air of someone who definitely knew where he was going, despite the fact that I kept having to slow down in the hope of glancing in any doors that just happened to open. The labour ward's windowless corridor had the atmosphere of a secret prison in some faraway Fascist dictatorship. Screams of agony came from behind various doors as determined-looking men and women marched in and out clutching metallic torture instruments. I saw a door and had a hunch that was the room Catherine would be giving birth in.

'Sorry, wrong room,' I said to the naked lady climbing into the birthing pool. I put my ear to the next delivery room. I could hear a man's authoritative voice. 'No, everyone knows that cheese and pickle increases the chance of having a Caesarean,' he said. At the end of the corridor was the nurse's desk, and I decided there was nothing else for it. I walked confidently past in search of some clue and there on the wall was a large white board with the room numbers and mothers' names scrawled underneath. By Room 8 somebody had scribbled Catherine Addams in blue felt-tip. Adams with two 'd's, as if we were the Addams family. As I caught sight of myself in the mirror, that mistake suddenly seemed quite appropriate. Then I reached Room 8. I tried to flatten down my hair, but I felt it spring straight up again. I knocked gently and walked in.

'Aaarrrrggghhhhhhh!'

'Hello, Catherine.'

'Aaaarrrrggggghhhhh!' she screamed again. I presumed she was having a contraction, unless this was just a natural reaction to seeing me.

'What the fucking hell are you doing here,' she exclaimed.

'I need to talk to you.'

'Oh, that's fine because I'm not doing anything in particular at the moment. Aaaaaaaarrrrrggghhh!'

The only other person in the room was Judith, who had the disappointed look of an understudy who had just seen the lead return in time for curtain-up.

'Shouldn't there be a midwife or a doctor here or something?' I said.

'She's only five centimetres dilated,' said Judith, looking hurt that she didn't even count as an 'or something'. 'They've been popping in and out to see how she's doing. And I've got her sandwiches and everything.'

'She never eats the sandwiches.'

'Oh.' Judith looked even more disappointed.

'Catherine, listen,' I said, 'I've worked it out. I know what I was doing wrong.'

'Oh congratulations, Michael!'

She was sitting up in bed wearing an unflattering hospital gown and she looked almost as hot and dishevelled as me.

'I thought you were always pissed off with me.'

'I am pissed off with you. Completely and utterly disgusted and appalled by you.'

'Yes, obviously you are *now*,' I conceded. 'But before, when you were pissed off with being the mother of small babies, I thought you didn't love me any more, and I think that's why I kept running away.'

'Aaaarrgggghhhh!'

Judith pointedly edged in to give Catherine an annoying

weedy dab on the forehead with a flannel that was even wetter than she was.

'What's that smell?'

'Essential oils,' said Judith with a smug nod. 'They really helped me when I had Barney.'

'They are not essential oils, though, are they, Judith? They are not at all essential. For thousands of years women have given birth without essential oils. Completely fucking superfluous oils would be a better name.'

'Stop it, Michael,' said Catherine, still recovering from her last contraction. 'You lied to me and deserted me and then you think you can just fucking turn up here and everything will be all right again. You're bored with being on your own, so now you'd like another spell of being a dad until you get bored with that again. Well, you can just fuck right off!' She was shouting now.

'Erm, would you like me to massage your feet?' said Judith, looking a little self-conscious.

'No, Judith, I do not want you to massage my feet, thank you very much.'

'Look, Catherine, everything you say is true. But you were the one who wanted kids so soon. I pretended to want them, too, but that was only to keep you happy. Everything I did was because I was trying to make you happy.'

'Oh I see, living it up in your flat was to make *me* happy, was it. There's me thinking this was all about you being a selfish wanker and now I see that I was the one who was getting everything my own way. Well, pardon me for being so selfish.'

'Hang on,' I said suddenly. 'What's that noise?'

'What noise?' said Catherine, irritated at being halted in full flow.

I heard it again. An eerie distant moan was coming from somewhere inside the room. It was like there was a drugged old man groaning from inside the cupboard, only his batteries were running out.

'There it is again. It's awful. What is it?'

Judith looked hurt. 'That's my whale-song tape. It's to help Catherine relax.'

'Aaaaaaaaaargh!' went Catherine.

'Well that's working well, isn't it? A whale-song tape! Oh my God, what a hippie cliché you are. I bet they're not even modern whale songs; I bet they're whale-song classics from the sixties.'

'Gnnnnnnoooooo . . .' went the whale.

'Aaaaaaaaarrrrrggghhhh!' went Catherine again. 'Actually, Judith, could you do me a favour,' she added, shifting uncomfortably.

'Yes?' said Judith brightly.

'Could you turn off the stupid bloody whale-song tape. I feel enough like a big fat whale as it is.'

'Oh, all right.'

'And stop rubbing that stinking oil on my feet before the smell makes me puke up.'

Catherine and I then argued back and forth while she had the distinct disadvantage of being well into the first stages of labour. There were one or two occasions when I thought I had her stumped because she didn't reply, but it always turned out that this was because a huge painful contraction was washing over her. As we shouted at one another I was vaguely aware of Judith flicking through a natural-birth handbook to see if it explained what sort of crystals or herbs might be waved about in this situation. Catherine said I only cared about myself and I said, 'No, I love you, you stupid fuckwit.' She called me a self-centred bastard and I said she was a whinging martyr. I had given up trying to grovel because it was getting me nowhere and thought I'd try going on the offensive instead.

'Well you drove me out so *you* owe *me* an apology.'

'I owe *you* an apology?' she said incredulously.

'Yeah.' I didn't know where this was leading, but I ploughed on anyway.

'I owe you an apology? Do you really want to know what I owe you?'

'Er, yeah, all right?'

And that was her cue to punch me with all her might in the middle of my face. I went down like a felled tree, hitting the back of my head on the metal gas-and-air canisters, which were there for pain relief and which really hurt a lot. Then Catherine started crying and whacking me with a plastic bedpan and I rolled into a ball on the ground, and then Catherine started another contraction and Judith pressed the emergency call button.

For the birth of my first two children I had felt strangely spiritually detached from it all. For the birth of my third I was physically removed by two burly men from hospital security. I helplessly hung around the outside of the hospital for an hour or so while happy visitors to the maternity ward bustled in and out clutching flowers and soft toys. There had been one ray of hope that made me want to stay outside the hospital. Catherine had said 'I love you' over and over again as she struck me round the head with the bedpan. I had thought she hated me, which I suppose she might have done as well. But as the security guards grasped the back of my hair, bent me double and frog-marched me out of the hospital with my arm nearly breaking up my back, I felt a euphoric serenity, as if my feet were off the ground, which they were, in fact, when the two gorillas threw me out onto the pavement.

After a while I approached a group of visitors and persuaded them to convey a message to Room 8 on the labour ward. I handed them a note that I had scribbled on the back of a piece of card I'd found in a telephone box. They were so full of goodwill to the world that it was easy to ask them a favour, although they seemed less sure about helping me when they turned the card over and saw a photo of a large-breasted topless prostitute with the message 'Dominatrix! Let her punish you!' It had been the only bit of card I could find. 'It's a private joke,' I stammered. 'She likes to get her own way at home.' The message told Catherine that I would not be far away and would appreciate a phone call when the baby was born. Catherine would not recognize the number as it was for a telephone box by Westminster Bridge. I then spent the day sitting on a bench beside my chosen public telephone. Occasionally people would move towards it, but then they'd notice a large 'out of order' sticker on the door, and they'd look at me and we'd share a what-is-this-country-coming-to tut.

Every quarter of an hour Big Ben would strike to remind me how slowly the day was going by. Somehow I had con-trived to watch the minutes pass by sitting opposite the largest clock in the world. The London Eye inched slowly round and the tide rose and then started to ebb again. I tucked into my lunch. Before I'd sat down I had approached a shell-shocked couple emerging into the hospital car park with a new baby.

'Congratulations,' I said.

'Thank you,' they both replied, looking proud and bewildered as mother and baby were helped into the back seat.

'Erm, can I ask? Did she eat the sandwiches?'

'I beg your pardon?'

'The sandwiches you made her when she went into labour.'

'No. It's funny you should say that because she didn't touch them.'

'Well, would you mind if I took them for the homeless round here. It's part of a scheme we're running.'

'Of course. What a splendid idea.' And he gave me the sandwiches and fizzy drinks and even a bar of chocolate. And even though she had just given birth and was apparently focusing totally on her newborn baby, a firm voice came from the back seat of the car: '*Not* the chocolate.'

My long vigil beside the phone box went through several stages. At first I was pleased with myself for my powers of organization in the face of such apparent adversity. I had a seat with a view over the Thames. My lunch was in a bag on my left. My private public phone was on my right. It was just a question of waiting. But as hour followed hour and the cold gnawed away at my morale, I began to worry. First I worried that Catherine wasn't going to ring, that she would have just torn up the note and I'd still be sitting there long after she had left the hospital. Then I began to worry that the telephone really was out of order, that I had stuck a sign on it without first making sure the notice was definitely lying. I went into the telephone box and dialled 150.

'Hello, BT customer services, Janice speaking, how may I help you?'

'Thank you, that's all I wanted to know.'

Then I became anxious that the ten seconds it had taken me to make that call had been when Catherine had tried to ring, and she would have got the engaged signal and wouldn't try again. Should I try and scrounge 10p from a passer-by so I could ring the labour ward to find out? But then that might turn out to be the exact moment she chose to ring me. These anxieties span around and around until I had worn them out and then was left with only genuine, serious worries to fret over. What on earth did I think she should want to ring me for? And anyway, what would I do then? Go back to my bench on Clapham Common? Go and sleep in Mrs Conroy's garage? The homeless unemployed have more problems than most people, but worst of all they have hours and hours with nothing to do but dwell on them. At least when General Custer had lots of problems he was busy.

Dusk began to fall. The thousands of people who had walked past me in one direction that morning now walked back the other way. The lights on the riverboats disappeared under Westminster Bridge and the headlights on the bridge slowed to a halt. And with the darkness it grew colder and the need to urinate, which I had hoped might go away if I ignored it, now became my over-riding and all-consuming concern. I walked up and down in front of my bench, I crossed my legs, I jumped up and down, but it became unbearable. I had to remain within earshot of the telephone box, but I desperately needed to go to the toilet. So that's why telephone boxes always smelled of urine. Eventually I had an idea. I furtively took a discarded empty lager can into the telephone box and decided the deed would be done in there. It seemed like a civilized solution at the time, but I had never measured the capacity of my full bladder before. It never occurred to me that it was about four times the volume of an empty 50cl lager tin. The can filled up in about two seconds, by which time the torrent seemed unstoppable. I couldn't bear the idea that I had been reduced to urinating in a public telephone box, and so I squeezed the end of my penis and painfully turned off the tap. Then I awkwardly nudged the door of the box open with my leg and contorted my body so that I could tip the can out onto the muddy patch of grass outside, while with my other hand I continued to grip my poor aching penis, which was swollen to bursting, like a blocked fire hose in a *Tom and Jerry* cartoon. It was then that the telephone rang.

It made me jump and panic all at the same time. 'Hello?' I said into the receiver as urine sprayed like a burst dam all over my trousers. 'Oh no!' Then I realized that I had dropped the can as well and it was glugging out all over my shoes. 'Oh fuck, shit, bollocks!'

'It's me,' said Catherine. 'I thought you wanted me to ring.'

'No, I did. Sorry, it's just you made me drop my can of piss.'

'What?'

'Lager, pissy lager.'

I attempted to affect a casual air of normality as urine sprayed uncontrollably down my trousers.

'So, um, what have you been up to?'

There was a pause.

'Having a baby,' she replied, matter-of-factly.

'Yes, yes, of course, that's right.'

A man was walking past the telephone box and glanced at me through the glass as I struggled to conceal the fact that I was effectively using it as a public toilet.

'So, um, what have you been up to?'

'You just asked me that.'

'Oh yes, sorry. And you said you'd been having a baby. So you see I was listening.'

The steaming Niagara Falls inside the telephone box had finally come to a halt and, still clinging onto the phone, I buttoned up my flies with my other hand.

'Well, I've had it,' she finally said. She sounded strange. Tired, obviously, but cold and remote, which scared me slightly.

'And the baby's OK?' I asked nervously. 'I mean, it's healthy and everything?'

'Yes, completely healthy and beautiful. Seven pounds, three ounces. Born at half-past one this afternoon. It's a boy, by the way, in case you were thinking of asking.'

'A boy! Fantastic! And you're OK, are you?'

'Yes. He came out really easily.'

'Well, that's the wonder of whale song,' I joked, but Catherine wasn't tempted to laugh.

'Look, you'd better come and see us. I have to talk to you. I've persuaded them to let you in now. They've put me in Helen Ward, sixth floor.'

'Great, thanks. I'll be there as quick as I can,' I said and hung up. I could have added, 'I've just got to rinse all this urine out of my trousers', but it didn't seem like quite the right moment. I picked up the half-full lager can and threw it in a nearby litter bin. Out of the corner of my eye I noticed a dosser watch the liquid slosh out of the can as I threw it away, and as I rushed towards the hospital he lumbered up to the litter bin, excitedly anticipating his first taste.

'Good evening,' I said brightly to the porter who came into the hospital toilets. I had decided that if I behaved as if it was perfectly normal to stand there in my underpants, holding my rinsed-out trousers under the electric hand dryer, then he might be temporarily convinced. He wasn't. 'I spilled some coffee on my trousers, so I've just washed it out,' I said, giving him the opportunity to smile and understand. He didn't take it.

Before long I was dressed again. I washed my stubbly face and did my best to flatten down my thinning hair. I looked like an old man, but had the nervous air of a boy on his first date. As I went to pull open the door I noticed my hand was shaking. The elation I felt at the birth of our baby took my private anxiety up another level. One new life had already started today, it was now up to Catherine whether another one could begin for me. It felt like my last chance. I had told her that I would be different, that I'd change. If she didn't feel that we should be together when she had just had our third baby then she never would. I pressed the button for the lift as if I were being summoned to hear the outcome of my appeal. I should have felt excited but instead I felt nervous. She said she loved me, I kept telling myself, but she punched

252

me in the face. These seemed to be conflicting signals. And if she was going to take me back, why had she sounded so cool and loveless on the phone?

The lift doors opened and a joyful young couple came out with a newborn infant; obviously their first, judging by the nervousness with which they were taking it home. I'd forgotten how absolutely tiny newborn babies are, how much they look like something out of a nature documentary. 'He's gorgeous,' I said.

'I know,' said the proud mum, trying to stop the huge blue cotton hat slipping down over the baby's entire face. The event of childbirth is one of the few things that will prompt the British to talk to complete strangers. Newborn babies, puppies and being in major rail disasters.

The lift arrived at the sixth floor and I buzzed my way into Helen Ward. A polished corridor stretched out in front of me. On my right was the first bay, with six beds containing six very different women. Catherine was not one of them. The mothers were all in dressing gowns or nighties, but were too focused on the little packages in their little perspex cribs to worry about the strange man walking past, looking at each of them in turn. The next bay had another batch of new mums, all so completely unlike Catherine that it just confirmed to me that there was no-one else I could ever be interested in. The last bay was next to the television room and the distorted shouting of actors could be heard through the open door.

'Hello, Michael,' said Catherine's voice from behind me. There was a little gap between the tatty green curtains that had been drawn around the first bed and I walked towards it. I stepped through the curtain, where Catherine was sitting up in bed wearing an old Radiohead T-shirt of mine. She didn't look happy to see me. In fact, if anything she looked a little scared. I bent down to kiss her on the cheek and she didn't resist.

'Congratulations,' I said.

She said nothing and looked back blankly.

'Erm, right, well, where's my little boy, then?' I stuttered, trying to affect an air of happy-family normality, made all the more surreal by the jaunty signature tune of a sitcom which echoed through from the TV room.

Then I looked down at the tiny infant asleep in the crib, wrapped in a hospital blanket and with a light-blue plastic name tag around his wrist. He was so perfect and miniature, with every detail lovingly handcrafted, that it made me want to believe in God.

'Oh, he's beautiful,' I said. 'He's so beautiful.'

I looked at how the baby's eyelashes were so expertly curled and placed at tiny but exact intervals, and at how the little circumference of his nostrils formed such perfect circles. And then I heard Catherine's voice say, 'He's not yours, Michael.'

It didn't register at first. Then I took in the meaning of what she had just said to me and glanced up at her, struck dumb with total incomprehension. Tears were welling up in her eyes.

'He not yours,' she repeated, and to answer my puzzled confusion she added, 'You were never there,' and then she started to sob uncontrollably. 'You were never there.'

I just kept looking at her, searching for some logic.

'But how do you know? I mean, who else did you . . .'

'Klaus.'

'*Klaus?!*'

'I was lonely and we shared a bottle of wine and, well, I don't know.'

'What? One thing led to another, I fucking suppose!'

'Don't shout.'

'I am not shouting,' I shouted. 'But you walked out on me for deceiving you, when all the time you were carrying some-one else's baby.'

Her sobs were louder now; graceless animal snorts that contorted her face.

'Anyway, how do you know it's his? We had unprotected sex, remember?'

'I did that because I knew I was pregnant. To cover myself, so you'd never have to know. When I still thought you were a proper father, but it's too late for that now.'

'But he might still be mine,' I pleaded hopelessly, glancing into the crib, hoping to spot some distinctive feature that I shared with this baby. There was none. If it was a question of who the baby looked like, then clearly Catherine had had it off with Sir Winston Churchill.

'The dates make it his. I just know. You can do a DNA test if you aren't convinced, but till then you will just have to take my word for it. This is not your child.'

She fixed me in her gaze; she looked defiant and almost proud to have been the one to put the final nail into this marriage.

'Does he know? I mean, did you tell him before he went back to Munich?'

'No. This child has no father.' And then the weeping started up again, and there was part of me that wanted to say, 'All right, stop crying now; it's not that bad,' but of course it was that bad; it was very bad indeed.

I really didn't know what to do. It seemed like there was no point in me being there at all. I was visiting a woman who had already said she didn't want to be married to me, and now she'd had a baby by another man. So I stepped out through the curtain, walked back down the corridor and floated out of the ward. A passing nurse gave me a beatific smile, which is the normal way to look at someone in a maternity ward, but I don't think I managed to return it. I don't remember walking through the door from the ward, but I must have done.

All those months that I had watched the bump inside her

grow, handing her tissues as she had thrown up in the morning, staring at the little photo of the foetus from the ultrasound machine, going to parenting classes with her, feeling the baby kick inside her, anxiously waiting for news of the birth; all that emotional investment was wiped out in one moment. After she had left me I had dreamed that this baby might be the only thing that could bring us back together. Now it had blown everything completely apart.

I pressed the button for the lift, unsure as to where I might go after I left the hospital, still punch-drunk from the shock. My head was spinning with a hundred confused, angry thoughts. She thought I had done her such a wrong; she had behaved like such an injured party, such a poor victim of my callous deceit, and yet all the time, inside her had been growing this witness to the most fundamental betrayal possible. In my bitter confusion I couldn't help resenting the fact that she'd had sex with our next-door neighbour when she had never seemed to want to have sex with me. It wasn't as if when we'd been together we had made love three times a day and then I'd suddenly disappeared, leaving her insatiable sexual appetite unquenched. Since the children had come along sex had always been something she was too tired for. She told me that when you had the kids pawing at you all day, you didn't want your husband coming home and pawing at you as well. But she hadn't been too tired to have sexual intercourse with the muscular young student from next door. No wonder he'd always been so nice to me. He'd unblocked my sink, reset my fuses, released my stopcock; no job was too much trouble. Get your wife pregnant? Hey, no problem, Mikey. I'll pop round when you're out.'

The lift showed no sign of arriving, so I pressed the button over and over again, even though I knew this never made any difference. Had she thought about Millie and Alfie when she'd cheated on her husband? Had she thought about where that would leave them when I found out about their night of passion? Or maybe it wasn't really just one night, maybe it was lots of nights, maybe this affair had been going on for years. Perhaps he hadn't really gone back to Germany but had set up home somewhere else in London and Catherine and the kids were going to join him with their new child. Yes, when she had found out about my double life it had given her the excuse she'd been waiting for. I mulled over this theory for a while and then decided it had one minor flaw. I had given Klaus a lift to the airport and he had sent me a postcard from Munich to thank me. It seemed like an unnecessarily elaborate cover-up. Anyway, Catherine had told me what had happened; if the truth had been any worse I don't think it would have stopped her relating it.

She'd had sex once with the bloke from next door. Couldn't I forgive her for that? Was that any worse than the extended deception I'd pursued? Hadn't I left her on her own night after lonely night? Hadn't I nearly been sexually unfaithful myself? My resentment was dismantled as quickly as I had built it up. It was as if the lift were deliberately keeping me waiting, forcing me to reflect upon what I was walking away from. I pictured Catherine and me cuddled up with the kids in their pyjamas, watching a video together, and I thought about the trust in Millie and Alfie's faces when they looked at me, and then I just started to cry. What had the kids done to deserve this mess? How had we come to this? 'Oh, Millie, Alfie, I'm sorry.' Everything was in ruins, and my tears gushed forth like a burst water main; all the pressure that had been contained since we split suddenly erupting to the surface. I turned my face to the noticeboard and tried to pull myself together. I looked at the photographs of a reunion of all the babies that had been in intensive care a couple of years beforehand – pictures of tiny premature babies clinging on to life in oxygen tents next to photos of the healthy, thriving toddlers they had now grown into, and that set me off all over again. I was blubbing hopelessly, turning the tap full on, letting it all come out. A couple of lift doors opened and then closed again and, when I'd finally regained my composure, I walked back across and pressed the button once more.

The parting lift doors revealed the skinny frame of an old man in some loose-fitting grubby pyjamas. He looked so close to death that I half expected the Grim Reaper to leap into the lift ahead of me, apologizing for being so late. His shaking body was held upright with the aid of a Zimmer frame, and his blotchy skin was stretched taut around his mouth and cheekbones.

'Well, are you coming or going?' he said to me.

In a few years' time my father would look like this, lonely and close to death. One stupid affair in his thirties and then he spent the rest of his life looking for the love he had once had with my mother.

'Well, are you coming or going?' he repeated, adding, 'Because I haven't got all day,' despite the fact that he clearly did have.

'Sorry!' I said and I turned around and left him there.

I walked up to the closed green curtains around Catherine's bed.

'Yes, he has,' I said to her as I stepped through the gap. She looked up, surprised to see me, her eyes still red.

'What?' she said, looking puzzled.

'You said that this little boy hasn't got a father. But he has. I can be his father.'

She raised her eyebrows at me, which I took as an invitation to continue.

'This is Millie and Alfie's brother, so why can't I be his dad? This is the child of the woman I love. I wasn't there for my own two, so I'll be there for this one. I promise, Catherine. I'll be there for the hard bits as well as the easy stuff. I know how a child feels when it's abandoned by its father. Let me be this little boy's dad; let me show you I can be a proper dad to Alfie and Millie.'

A hospital auxiliary pulled back the curtain to offer a tray of food.

'Excuse me,' I said to him, 'could you just give us a minute,' and I drew the curtain back across again. 'Catherine, I'll be there when you're bored and fed up and you just want someone to moan at, someone who's going to offer you sympathy instead of always suggesting solutions. I'll be there when you're worried about him, and even if I don't think it's anything to worry about, I'll sit and listen until we've talked it through. I'll be there just to play endless games with him, pretending that I really enjoy jiggling little plastic Power Ranger figures about on the carpet. And I'll be there when we're not doing anything at all, just passing the hours together, because I didn't understand before that that's what it's all about – just spending time with your family is the end in itself, and you have to timetable in some wasting time together. Now that I understand what I'm supposed to do, I know that I can do it.'

Catherine didn't say anything, she just looked at me.

'Have you finished now?' said the hospital auxiliary from the other side of the curtain.

'Yes, thank you,' I said, taking the tray from him.

'It's meat curry.'

'Meat curry. How lovely. Her favourite sort.'

Catherine's expression didn't change. I stood there waiting for some sort of clue as to what she was thinking. 'It's not what I want,' she said finally. My insides suddenly felt completely empty.

'But, Catherine, you have to give us another chance.'

259

'No. Meat curry is not what I want. Can you see if they've got a salad or something?'

'In a minute. Can we just sort this out first. Are you going to bring this boy up on your own or are we going to do it together?'

'You can forgive me? Just like that?' she said, slowly.

'Well, I was hoping I might be able to do a deal. Is there any little thing that I've done in the past couple of years that you might want to forgive me for, perhaps even just partially?'

It was the first time I'd seen her smile since we had parted. It was only a bleary half smile, but its return was like the sudden faint bleep on a cardiogram; there was life where I'd thought there had been none.

'But you'll always know that this child isn't yours.'

'So what? You're right, I was never there. But Klaus won't be there for this one and why should you be left alone again?'

I was thinking so clearly now, speaking with a missionary zeal. I knew it was the only way forward. Catherine had to see that it was right.

'You're really prepared to bring up someone else's child as your own?'

'He will never know he's half German. Now what do you think of the name Karl-Heinz Adams? It has a ring to it, doesn't it?'

And she smiled again, properly this time.

'You have to understand, Michael, that if we were to make another go of it, things could never be like they were. I would never totally trust you like I did before – something has gone for ever.'

I nodded, nervous as to which way the coin was about to fall.

'You have been selfish and immature and dishonest and blind and callous and self-indulgent.'

I tried to pick out an adjective that I felt was being unfairly applied to me, but failed. How was it that she had so many words at her disposal? Why did we always have to argue with words? That way she was always going to win. If we could have argued using musical notes, chords and melody lines I might have stood a better chance.

'But,' she continued, 'but if you are prepared to forgive me, then maybe we have something to build upon. Can you promise me that from here on, can you promise that you will always be honest, that you will never again let yourself disappear into some stupid solipsistic fantasy.'

I paused. 'I . . . I don't know.'

Her face fell. It was the wrong answer. 'Well, if you can't be sure, then I don't see how we can have any future together.'

'No, no,' I stammered. 'I just don't know what "solipsistic" means. I was going to pretend and just say yes, but I'm trying to make myself be honest.'

'It means that you have to realize that you are not the only person in the entire bloody universe.'

'Well, I do realize that, yes. I just didn't want to promise not to be solipsistic when it sounded like some sort of eating disorder.'

'You have to realize that from the moment you have children they become more important to you than yourself.'

'They are, Catherine, I promise. All three of them. But you, you're more important still. I love you; I never understood that as clearly as when I'd lost you, and the fact that you ended up in bed with Klaus only confirms to me how abandoned I must have made you feel. Let's start again. Please, Catherine, take me back.'

She paused. 'On approval only.' And then she put out her arms to me and I hugged her long and hard, as if I had just been rescued from drowning.

'Thank you for forgiving me,' she said as she held me to

her. 'I needed to know that you would. If you're really prepared to commit to bringing up Klaus's son as your own then you've got to be worth giving a second chance.' She held me close to her, clutching the back of my head tightly as I winced in silent agony, not wanting to mention the tender bruise where I'd crashed into the gas-and-air cylinders after she'd punched me to the ground. But everything was all right. We were together again. We were a family.

'And I forgive you, even if you still have one major flaw that I will never quite get used to.'

'What do you mean?' I said anxiously, pulling myself away from her.

She looked me in the eye. 'Michael, if you actually believe all that bollocks about me sleeping with Klaus and then having his baby, then you really are an even bigger sucker than I always thought you were.'

And a huge burst of canned laughter came from the TV room.

chapter twelve

the best a man can get

'I now declare you husband and wife,' said the keen young vicar and the congregation burst into spontaneous applause. Older women in bizarre hats exchanged approving smiles and even the vicar joined in the cheers to show that the church didn't have to be all stuffy and serious. I clapped as well as any man could considering I was carrying a nine-month-old baby. The noise excited him and he gave enthusiastic random kicks of his legs and waved his arms about in giggly approval. Catherine held up Alfie to watch as the bride and groom kissed slightly more passionately than would generally be considered appropriate. The vicar had added, 'You may now kiss the bride,' not, 'You may now put your tongue down the bride's throat and squeeze her right tit.'

The invitation to the wedding had been something of a shock; a message on my mobile phone from someone I hadn't seen for months. Jim was marrying Kate. The man I had lived with was marrying the girl I had so nearly slept with. Perhaps I should have explained this to the ushers in the church when they'd asked, 'Bride or groom?' and let them decide. Once I had got used to the idea of this union I was delighted for them both. They were a perfect match: she earned a fortune and worked very hard and he spent a fortune and didn't work at all. There is something so hopelessly romantic about white weddings that you cannot help but think that the couple will be blissfully happy for ever. Even when Henry VIII got married for the sixth time, the congregation must have all thought, Aaah, true love at last, and he's definitely promised not to chop her head off this time. But as I watched Jim and Kate come down the aisle, I couldn't help but think about how little idea they had of the problems that lay ahead.

My own marriage had been slowly nursed back to health over the previous nine months. We had a little boy that we named Henry – for some reason all our children had names that made them sound like orphans from a Victorian costume drama. He had blue eyes and his hair was blond. Neither Catherine nor I were the slightest bit blond, but following her scam in the maternity ward I decided it probably wouldn't be appropriate to challenge her further about the baby's parentage. Events on the day of his birth were now a rather surreal blur. Elation that this really was my son after all was mixed with a suppressed short-term fury that Catherine could have put me through such an emotional mangle. There was even a secret tiny part of me that was briefly disappointed – that she hadn't been as duplicitous as me, that it wasn't a score draw and I was cast back as the only villain. For years I had watched her trick people and defuse seemingly desperate situations with outrageously bold lies, but nothing had prepared me for the test she set me on the day Henry was born. I asked her what she would have done if I'd not come back and forgiven her and committed to be the father of what I thought was Klaus's baby. She said she would have contacted Millie and Alfie's real father and got back together with him. I laughed long and hard and completely unconvincingly.

Now Henry had grown into a happy little baby who laughed for no apparent reason and who woke us up at night with the most abject tears of sorrow which turned quickly into giggles once he had been picked up by the mother and father that he loved so completely. Babies experience their emotions at full volume, with an extreme intensity that doesn't return until they are grown up and have babies of their own. He behaved perfectly throughout the wedding service, indeed some of the noises he made during the singing of 'To Be a Pilgrim' were more in tune than the efforts of the groom's relations standing in front of us. At the wedding reception he fell asleep in the luminous blue nylon backpack that failed to blend in with my rented morning suit. He dribbled on my back, and to all the women at the wedding I became instantly attractive and appealing, and all the other men felt underdressed because they didn't have a baby slobbering on their collars.

We had agreed on the name Henry pretty quickly. It had been my suggestion, and when I told Catherine my reasons she was delighted with the choice. I rang my father and he picked up the phone and said, 'Henry Adams speaking.' I told him that I was calling from the hospital because Catherine and I were back together and she had just had a little boy that I wanted to name after him. He paused for a moment.

'Ooh, that's a good idea because I've got some old Henry Adams name tags somewhere I could let you have for him.'

I wanted to scream, Dad, I've just told you that I have named my son after you. Don't worry about the bloody name tags just yet.

'That'd be great,' I said. 'Thanks a lot.'

Catherine and I actually stayed with my dad for a few weeks until we managed to rent somewhere of our own. She cleared out his larder for him, and claimed that when she shouted, 'The war is over!' several packets of powdered egg emerged from where they had been hiding behind the tinned prunes since 1945. Though we were grateful to my dad, in the end we were desperate to move into a place of our own, where the heating wasn't always too hot and the telly wasn't always too loud and where the children weren't encouraged to go out and play on the A347. I'd never have a mortgage again, but many things about our lives would be very different from now on; we both had a lot of adjusting to do. We finally rented a four-bedroom house in Archway, and I set up a studio in a poky room at the top of the house. On our first night there, we looked at the kids all asleep in their new beds and then I said to her, 'Three children is enough kids for me, Catherine. I know you always wanted four, but I think we should stop at three.'

There was a pause and then she just said, 'OK.'

Then we went downstairs and I made up the bottle for the night feed, and I realized that as I was measuring out the babymilk powder without levelling it off with a knife Catherine was just sitting at the kitchen table, flicking through a magazine. Now, at last, she felt she could leave me to just get on with it. We'd had one argument after she'd been irritated that I was doing something wrong and I had said to her audaciously, 'You can't have it all, Catherine. You can't have a man who does his share at home and yet have everything done the way you want.'

The wedding service ended and we took our three children out of the church and into the sunshine, where I half-heartedly suggested that Millie perhaps shouldn't clamber all over the gravestones as if it were an adventure playground. Before me stood my former flatmates, who hadn't known I was a father throughout the time that we'd lived together. They looked at me in amazement, and I felt extraordinarily proud as we approached them. Then I introduced my three kids to the three kids I used to live with. Millie and Alfie both said a cute and polite 'hello' and I managed to suppress my astonishment and act as if this was completely normal. Everything about that wedding day seemed perfect. The sun shone, the champagne flowed and none of the other women had the same dress as Catherine. She had been genuinely worried about this, which is an anxiety so completely alien to anything that I could ever begin to understand that I suppose it proves how completely and fundamentally different the two sexes really are. The men were all in morning dress, but I didn't burst into tears when I saw that every other man was wearing exactly the same outfit as me.

I introduced my wife to Jim, Paul and Simon. Jim seemed quietly rather impressed that I had kept this little secret to myself. He was charming with Catherine and paid her compliments and made her laugh and, given that he was the groom and therefore already the centre of attention, I was rather concerned at just how much Catherine seemed to be taken by him. Paul was with his boyfriend, who was rather cool towards me, as if I still posed a threat to his new relationship. As for Paul himself, I think he thought that the fact that I had a wife and three children only went to prove the extraordinary lengths to which some repressed gays would go to deny their own sexuality to themselves. But there was something calm about him now; you got the feeling that when the bride cut the wedding cake he was no longer worrying about who was going to wash up the knife. Simon was still single and a virgin. However, in the course of the reception he got chatting to Kate's divorced mother. She had consumed rather a lot of champagne and had a room booked at the hotel and, well, one thing led to another . . .

Kate looked beautiful and, as I approached her to introduce her to my wife, I found myself really hoping that they would like each other. But a terrible thing happened: they got on *too* well. They chatted away for ages and soon Catherine was suggesting dates when they might be free to come over to dinner, while I was trying to catch her eye with subtle shakes of my head. The problem was that I would always fancy Kate. I didn't want to grow into one of those fat old men who kisses his wife's friends goodbye with slightly too much relish at the end of a wine-soaked evening.

'Well, it's been a wonderful wedding,' said Catherine. 'You make a lovely couple.'

'Thank you,' said Kate.

'And it's OK, Michael told me all about swimming-pool night.'

I had made a decision that it was best to be open and honest about everything. 'She's very beautiful,' said Catherine later. 'I'm amazed that you don't think she's particularly attractive.'

Well, honest about virtually everything.

As the reception wore on, I was persuaded to play the beautiful Steinway in the hotel ballroom and I disrespectfully ripped into the polished keyboard and played boogie-woogie piano with careless abandon. The dance floor filled up and Millie and Alfie danced a crazy, excited jitterbug. Each number segued effortlessly into the next and revellers whooped and clapped and cheered, and just when they needed a breather, Millie came and sat on my lap and asked if she could play the tune I had taught her, and the crowd fell still and waited. Then my angelic four-year-old daughter played the opening notes of 'Lucy in the Sky with Diamonds' with such perfection, and a natural musician's ear for the tempo and feeling, that everyone just stared open-mouthed at her talent, and I looked across at Catherine and saw that she was biting her lip, trying to hold back the tears, and she smiled at me with such love and pride that I wanted to float through the ceiling.

The band came back on and I span Millie round and round and then she clasped her hands round my neck as tightly as she could and I wanted to keep her that age for ever, just dancing with her as she clung on to me, trusting and loving me so completely. We stayed the night in the swanky hotel, all five of us in one room, and in the morning I was woken by the sound of children. They jumped into bed with us and we put on the television and they tucked under the duvet between us as we half dozed, trying not to fall out of either side, and then the Gillette ad came on the telly and I heard the man singing, 'The best a man can get,' and I laughed to myself and thought, I've got it now, thanks. I told Catherine about the slogan and how I had once made it my own personal maxim. She said that she had never interpreted the phrase in the same way as me. To her it was not 'the best a man can get' as in get for himself, grab, acquire, have; it was the best he can be, the best he can grow, *the best a man can become*.

Catherine may have been looking at me, but she was keeping one eye on the television in case the commercial she'd been cast in suddenly came on. That was the other consequence of the day Henry was born. The fact that I had been completely convinced by Catherine's bitter self-defence and defiant tears in the maternity ward reminded me of what a brilliant actor she had always been. With some encouragement from me, she contacted her old agent and started going to auditions again, and soon she got a small part in an appalling sitcom that stretched her acting abilities to the limit when the writer asked her whether she thought the script was funny. The amount she was paid was insulting; it was far more than I ever got.

When she was away working I'd take my turn at looking after the kids. She'd be out from early in the morning till late at night, and sometimes the filming even involved overnights.

And so I'd find myself alone with the children for a couple of days at a stretch, being woken up throughout the night and still having to look after them all day. I'd have to put on all their clothes, feed them breakfast, then try to prevent Millie and Alfie from throwing wet Multi-Cheerios at each other while I changed Henry's nappy, get myself dressed while brushing their teeth, then put on their coats and gloves, rush Millie off to nursery for nine o'clock while pushing Alfie and Henry along in the double buggy and always trying to maintain a loving, harmonious atmosphere in the home throughout. Well, nine out of ten's not bad.

Everyone expected me to say that looking after my children all day was the most wonderfully fulfilling thing I'd ever done. Well, it was certainly the hardest thing I'd ever done, but nothing changed my opinion that small children are boring. But now I understood that having kids and raising a family was hard, because anything really worth achieving is hard. It's the difference between one of my jingles and Beethoven's Ninth Symphony.

Catherine's advert never came on, so she consoled herself by disappearing off to use the hotel's sauna and swimming pool while I played with the kids in the hotel grounds. Then she suggested I had some time on my own using the hotel's sports facilities or something, which seemed like a good idea at the time, but I soon discovered you can only play croquet on your own for so long. Now at last we seemed to have established some equilibrium in our marriage, an understanding that we were in this together, for the good of each other as well as for the good of our children. We promised that we would always be straight with one another, that we would always work as a team, and privately I felt rather pleased with myself that after all we'd been through there was now so much honesty and confidence between us.

I paid our hotel bill and the manager said thank you and

then, as an apparent afterthought, he shouted after us, 'See you again soon, Mrs Adams.' As we walked down the steps I asked her why he'd said that. And then Catherine giggled slightly and told me. None of her acting jobs had involved overnights at all. She'd spent all those nights on her own in luxury hotels like this one.

Song of Albion
Book Three

THE ENDLESS
KNOT

Stephen Lawhead

A LION BOOK

Copyright © 1993 Stephen Lawhead

The author asserts the moral right
to be identified as the author of this work

Published by
Lion Publishing
850 North Grove Avenue, Elgin, Illinois 60120, USA
ISBN 0 7459 2240 6
Lion Publishing plc
Sandy Lane West, Oxford, England
ISBN 0 7459 2240 6
Albatross Books Pty Ltd
PO Box 320, Sutherland, NSW 2232, Australia
ISBN 0 7324 0807 5

First edition 1993
First paperback edition 1994

All rights reserved

Library of Congress Cataloging-in-Publication Data
Lawhead, Steve
    The endless knot / Stephen Lawhead
    (Song of Albion : bk 3)
    ISBN 0-7459-2231-7
    I. Title. II. Series: Lawhead, Steve. Song of Albion : bk. 3
    PS3562.A865E5   1993
    813'.54–dc20   92-44645   CIP

A catalogue record for this book is available
from the British Library

Printed and bound in Finland

Song of Albion
Book Three

THE ENDLESS KNOT

For Jan Dennis

Contents

*"Since all the world is but a story,
it were well for thee to buy the
more enduring story, rather than
the story that is less enduring."*

The Judgment of St. Colum Cille
(St. Columba of Scotland)

Hear, O Son of Albion, the prophetic word:

Sorrow and be sad, deep grief is granted Albion in triple measure. The Golden King in his kingdom will strike his foot against the Rock of Contention. The Worm of fiery breath will claim the throne of Prydain; Llogres will be without a lord. But happy shall be Caledon; the Flight of Ravens will flock to her many-shadowed glens, and ravensong shall be her song.

When the Light of the Derwyddi is cut off, and the blood of bards demands justice, then let the Ravens spread their wings over the sacred wood and holy mound. Under Ravens' wings, a throne is established. Upon this throne, a king with a silver hand.

In the Day of Strife, root and branch shall change places, and the newness of the thing shall pass for a wonder. Let the sun be dull as amber, let the moon hide her face: abomination stalks the land. Let the four winds contend with one another in dreadful blast; let the sound be heard among the stars. The Dust of the Ancients will rise on the clouds; the essence of Albion is scattered and torn among contending winds.

The seas will rise up with mighty voices. Nowhere is there safe harbor. Arianrhod sleeps in her sea-girt headland. Though many seek her, she will not be found. Though many cry out to her, she cannot hear their voices. Only the chaste kiss will restore her to her rightful place.

Then shall rage the Giant of Wickedness, and terrify all with the keen edge of his sword. His eyes will flash forth fire; his lips shall drip poison. With his great host he will despoil the island. All who oppose him will be swept away in the flood of wrongdoing that flows from his hand. The Island of the Mighty will become a tomb.

All this by the Brazen Man is come to pass, who likewise mounted on his steed of brass works woe both great and dire. Rise up, Men of Gwir! Fill your hands with weapons and oppose the false men in your midst! The sound of the battleclash will be heard among the stars of heaven and the Great Year will proceed to its final consummation.

Hear, O Son of Albion: Blood is born of blood. Flesh is born of flesh. But the spirit is born of Spirit, and with Spirit evermore remains. Before Albion is One, the Hero Feat must be performed and Silver Hand must reign.

Banfáith of Ynys Sci

Dark Flames

A fire rages in Albion. A strange, hidden fire, dark-flamed, invisible to the eye. Seething and churning, it burns, gathering flames of darkness into its hot black heart. Unseen and unknown, it burns.

These flames of darkness are insatiable; they grow, greedy in their spreading, consuming all, destroying all. Though the flames cannot be seen, the heat scorches and singes, searing flesh and bone alike; it saps the strength, and withers the will. It blisters virtue, corrodes courage; it turns love and honor to hard, dark embers.

The dark fire is an evil and ancient enemy, older than the Earth. It has no face, no body, limbs, or members to be engaged and fought, much less quenched and conquered. Only flames, insidious tongues, and hidden dark sparks that blow and scatter, blow and scatter on every fretful wind.

And nothing can endure the dark fire. Nothing can stand against the relentless, scathing corruption of the unseen flames. It will not be extinguished until all that exists in this worlds-realm is dead cold ash.

The oxhide at the door rippled as Tegid Tathal stepped into the hut. His quick eyes searched the darkness; he could see again. His blindness had been healed, or at least transmuted somehow into vision by the renewing waters of the lake. For he saw me sitting in the straw on the floor, and he asked, "What are you doing?"

"Thinking," I replied, flexing the fingers of my silver hand one by one. That hand! Beauty made tangible in fine, flawless silver. A treasure of value beyond imagining. A gift to me—a warrior's compensation, perhaps—from a deity with a most peculiar sense of humor. Most peculiar.

Tegid assures me that it is the gift of *Dagda Samildanac*, the Swift Sure Hand himself. He says it is the fulfillment of a promise made by the lord of the grove. The Swift Sure Hand, by his messenger, granted Tegid his inner sight, and gave me my silver hand.

Tegid observed me curiously while my thoughts drifted. "And what are you thinking about?" he said at last.

"About this," I raised my metal hand. "And fire," I told him. "Dark fire."

He accepted this without question. "They are waiting for you outside. Your people want to see their king."

"I had to get away for a while. I had to think."

The sound of merrymaking was loud outside; the victory celebration would continue for days. The Great Hound Meldron was defeated and his followers brought to justice, the drought was broken, and the land restored. The happiness of the survivors knew no bounds.

I did not share their happiness, however. For the very thing that secured their safety and gave wings to their joy meant that my sojourn in Albion had come to an end. My task was finished and I must leave—though every nerve and sinew in me cried against leaving.

Tegid moved nearer and, so that he would not be speaking down to me, knelt. "What is wrong?"

Before I could answer, the oxhide lifted once again and Professor Nettleton entered. He acknowledged Tegid gravely, and turned to me. "It is time to go," he said simply.

When I made no reply, he continued, "Llew, we have discussed this. We agreed. It must be done—and the sooner the better. Waiting will only make it worse."

Tegid, regarding the small man closely, said, "He is our king. As *Aird Righ* of Albion it is his right—"

"Please, Tegid." Nettleton shook his head slowly, his mouth pressed into a firm line. He stepped nearer and stared down at me. "It is permitted no man to stay in the Otherworld. You know that. You came to find Simon and take him back, and you have done that. Your work is finished here. It is time to go home."

He was right; I knew it. Still, the thought of leaving cut me to the heart. I could not go. Back there I was nothing; I had no life. A mediocre foreign student, a graduate scholar woefully deficient in almost every human essential, lacking the companionship of men and the love of a woman; a perpetual academic with no purpose in life save to scrounge the next grant and hold off the day of reckoning, to elude life beyond the cocooning walls of Oxford's cloisters.

The only real life I had ever known was here in Albion. To leave would be to die, and I could not face that.

"But I have something more to do here," I countered, almost desperately. "I must have—otherwise, why give me this?" I lifted my silver hand; the cold metal appendage gleamed dully in the darkness of the hut, the intricate tracery of its finely wrought surface glowing gold against the soft white of silver.

"Come," the professor said, reaching down to pull me up. "Do not make it more difficult than it already is. Let us go now, and quietly."

I rose to my feet and followed him out of the hut. Tegid followed, saying nothing. Before us the celebration fire blazed, the flames leaping high in the gathering dusk. All around the fire people rejoiced; snatches of song reached us amid the happy tumult. We had not taken two steps when we were met by Goewyn carrying a jar in one hand and a cup in the other. Behind her a maid carried a plate with bread and meat.

"I thought you might be hungry and thirsty," she explained quickly, and began pouring the ale into the cup. She handed the cup to me, saying, "I am sorry, but this is all I was able to save for you. It is the last."

"Thank you," I said. As I took the cup, I allowed my fingers to linger upon her hand. Goewyn smiled and I knew I could not leave without telling her what was in my heart.

"Goewyn, I must tell you—" I began. But before I could finish, a pack of jubilant warriors swarmed in, clamoring for me to come and join them in the celebration. Goewyn and the maid were pushed aside.

"Llew! Llew!" the warriors cried. "Hail, Silver Hand!" One of them held a haunch of meat which he offered to me and would not desist until I had taken a healthy bite from it. Another saw my cup in my hand and poured ale from his own cup into mine. "*Sláinte*, Silver Hand!" they cried, and we drank.

The warriors seemed intent on carrying me away with them, but Tegid intervened, explaining that I wished to walk among the people to enjoy the festivity. He asked them to guard the king's peace by removing any who would disturb me, beginning with themselves.

As the warriors went their noisy way, Cynan appeared. "Llew!" he cried, clapping a big hand upon my shoulder. "At last! I have been looking for you, brother. Here! Drink with me!" He raised his bowl high. "We drink to your kingship. May your reign be long and glorious!"

With that he poured ale from his bowl into my already full cup.

"And may our cups always overflow!" I added, as mine was spilling over my hand at that moment. Cynan laughed. We drank, and before he could replenish my cup, I passed it quickly to Tegid.

"I thought we had long since run out of ale," I said. "I had no idea we had so much left."

"This is the last," Cynan remarked, peering into his bowl. "And when it is gone, we will have long to wait for fields to be tilled and grain to grow. But this day," he laughed again, "this day, we have everything we need!" Cynan, with his fiery red hair and blue eyes agleam with delight and the contents of his cup, was so full of life— and so happy to be that way after the terrible events of the last days—that I laughed out loud with him. I laughed, even though my heart felt like a stone in my chest.

"Better than that, brother," I told him, "we are free men and alive!"

"So we are!" Cynan cried. He threw his arm around my neck and pulled me to him in a sweaty embrace. We clung to one another, and I breathed a silent, sad farewell to my swordbrother.

Bran and several Ravens came upon us then, saluted me and hailed me king, pledging their undying loyalty. And while they were about it, the two kings, Calbha and Cynfarch, approached. "I give you good greeting," said Calbha. "May your reign ever continue as it has begun."

"May you prosper through all things," Cynfarch added, "and may victory crown your every battle."

I thanked them and, as I excused myself from their presence, I glimpsed Goewyn moving off. Calbha saw my eyes straying after her, and said, "Go to her, Llew. She is waiting for you. Go."

I stepped quickly away. "Tegid, you and Nettles ready a boat. I will join you in a moment."

Professor Nettleton glanced at the darkening sky and said, "Go if you must, but hurry, Llew! The time-between-times will not wait."

I caught Goewyn as she passed between two houses. "Come with me," I said quickly. "I must talk to you."

She made no reply, but put down the jar and extended her hand. I took it and led her between the cluster of huts to the perimeter of the *crannog*. We slipped through the shadows along the timber wall of the fortress, and out through the untended gates.

Goewyn remained silent while I fumbled after the words I wanted to say. Now that I had her attention, I did not know where to begin. She watched me, her eyes large and dark in the fading light, her flaxen hair glimmering like spun silver, her skin pale as ivory. The slender torc shone like a circle of light at her throat. Truly, she was the most beautiful woman I had ever known.

"What is the matter?" she asked after a moment. "If there is anything that makes you unhappy, then change it. You are the king now. It is for you to say what will be."

"It seems to me," I told her sadly, "that there are some things

15

even a king cannot change."

"What is the matter, Llew?" she asked again.

I hesitated. She leaned nearer, waiting for my answer. I looked at her, lovely in the fading light.

"I love you, Goewyn," I said.

She smiled, her eyes sparkling with laughter. "And it is this that makes you so unhappy?" she said lightly, and leaned closer, raising her arms and lacing her fingers behind my head. "I love you, too. There. Now we can be miserable together."

I felt her warm breath on my face. I wanted to take her in my arms and kiss her. I burned with the urge. Instead, I turned my face aside.

"Goewyn, I would ask you to be my queen."

"And if you asked," she said, speaking softly and low, "I would agree—as I have agreed in my heart a thousand times already."

Her voice... I could *live* within that voice. I could exist on it alone, lose myself completely, content to know nothing but the beauty of that voice.

My mouth went dry and I fought to swallow the clot of sand that suddenly clogged my throat. "Goewyn... I—"

"Llew?" She had caught the despair in my tone.

"Goewyn, I cannot... I cannot be king. I cannot ask you to be my queen."

She straightened and pulled away. "What do you mean?"

"I mean that I cannot stay in Albion. I must leave. I must go back to my own world."

"I do not understand."

"I do not belong here," I began—badly, it is true, but once begun, I was afraid to stop. "This is not my world, Goewyn. I am an intruder; I have no right to be here. It is true. I only came here because of Simon. He—"

"Simon?" she asked, the name strange on her tongue.

"Siawn Hy," I explained. "His name in our world is Simon. He came here and I came after him. I came to take him back—and now that is done and I have to leave. Now, tonight. I will not see you any more after—"

Goewyn did not speak; but I could see that she did not understand a word I was saying. I drew a deep breath and blundered on. "All the trouble, everything that has happened here in Albion—all the death and destruction, the slaughter of the bards, the wars, Prydain's desolation... all the terrible things that have happened here—it is all Simon's fault."

"All these things are Siawn Hy's doing?" she wondered, incredulously.

"I am not explaining very well," I admitted. "But it is true. Ask Tegid; he will tell you the same. Siawn Hy brought ideas with him—ideas of such cunning and wickedness that he poisoned all Albion with them. Meldron believed in Siawn's ideas, and look what happened."

"I do not know about that. But I know that Albion was not destroyed. And it was not destroyed," Goewyn pointed out, "because you were here to stop it. But for you, Siawn Hy and Meldron would have reigned over Albion's destruction."

"Then you see why I cannot let it happen again."

"I see," she stated firmly, "that you must stay to prevent it from happening again."

She saw me hesitate and pressed her argument further. "Yes, stay. As king it is your right and duty." She paused and smiled. "Stay here and reign over Albion's healing."

She knew the words I wanted to hear most in all the world, and she said them. Yes, I could stay in Albion, I thought. I *could* be king and reign with Goewyn as my queen. Professor Nettleton was wrong, surely; and Goewyn was right: as king it was my duty to make certain that the healing of Albion continued as it had begun. I could stay!

Goewyn tilted her head to one side. "What say you, my love?"

"Goewyn, I will stay. If there is a way, I will stay for ever. Be my queen. Reign with me."

She came into my arms then in a rush, and her lips were on mine, warm and soft. The fragrance of her hair filled my lungs and made me light-headed. I held her tight and kissed her; I kissed her ivory throat, her silken eyelids, her warm moist lips that tasted of honey and wild flowers. And she kissed me.

I had dreamed of this moment countless times, yearned for it, longed for it. Truly, I wanted nothing more than to make love to Goewyn. I held the yielding warmth of her flesh against me and knew that I would stay—as if there had ever been any doubt.

"Wait for me," I said, breaking off the embrace and stepping quickly away.

"Where are you going?" she called after me.

"Nettles is leaving. He is waiting for me," I answered. "I must bid him farewell."

Three Demands

Darting along the timber wall, I hurried to join Tegid and Professor Nettleton in the boat. I gave the boat a push and jumped in; Tegid manned the oars and rowed out across the lake. The water was smooth as glass in the gathering twilight, reflecting the last light of the deep blue sky above.

We made our landing below Druim Vran, and quickly put our feet to the path leading to Tegid's sacred grove. With every step, I invented a new argument or excuse to justify my decision to stay. In truth, I had never wanted to leave anyway; it felt wrong to me. Goewyn's urging was only the last in a long list of reasons I had to dismiss Professor Nettleton's better judgment. He would just have to accept my decision.

The grove was silent, the light dim, as we stepped within the leafy sanctuary. Tegid wasted not a moment, but began marking out a circle on the ground with the end of his staff. He walked backwards in a sunwise circle, chanting in a voice solemn and low. I did not hear what he said—it was in the Dark Tongue of the *Derwyddi*, the *Taran Tafod*.

Standing next to Nettles, my mind teemed with accusation, guilt, and self-righteous indignation—I was the king! I had built this place! Who had the right to stay here if not me?—I could not make myself say the words. I stood in seething silence and watched Tegid prepare our departure.

Upon completing the simple ceremony, the bard stepped from the circle he had inscribed and turned to us. "All is ready." He looked at me as he spoke. I saw sorrow in his gaze, but he spoke no word of farewell. The parting was too painful for him.

The professor took a step towards the circle, but I remained rooted to my place. When he sensed me lagging behind, Nettleton looked back over his shoulder. Seeing that I had made not the slightest move to join him, he said, "Come, Lewis."

"I am not going with you," I said dully. It was not what I had planned to say, but the words were out of my mouth before I could stop them.

"Lewis!" he challenged, turning on me. "Think what you are doing."

"I cannot leave like this, Nettles. It is too soon."

He took my arm, gripping it tightly. "Lewis, listen to me. Listen very carefully. If you love Albion, then you *must* leave. If you stay, you can only bring about the destruction of all you have saved. You must see that. I have told you: it is permitted no man—"

I cut him off. "I will take that risk, Nettles."

"The risk is not yours to take!" he charged, his voice explosive in the silence of the grove. Exasperated, he blinked his eyes behind his round glasses. "Think what you are doing, Lewis. You have achieved the impossible. Your work here is finished. Do not negate all the good you have done. I beg you, Lewis, to reconsider."

"It is the time-between-times," Tegid said softly.

"I am staying," I muttered bluntly. "If you are going, you had better leave now."

Seeing that he could not move me, he turned away in frustration and stepped quickly into the circle. At once, his body seemed to fade and grow smaller, as if he were entering a long tunnel. "Say your farewells, Lewis," he urged desperately, "and come as soon as you can. I will wait for you."

"Farewell, my friend!" called Tegid.

"Please, for the sake of all you hold dear, do not put it off too long!" Nettleton called, his voice already dwindling away. His image rippled as if he were standing behind a sheet of water. The rims of his glasses glinted as he turned away, and then he vanished, his words hanging in the still air as a quickly-fading warning.

Tegid came to stand beside me. "Well, brother," I said, "it would seem you must endure my presence a little longer."

The bard gazed into the now-empty circle. He seemed to be peering into the emptiness of the nether realm, his features dark and his eyes remote. I thought he would not speak, but then he lifted his staff. "Before Albion is One," he said, his voice hard with certainty, "the Hero Feat must be performed and Silver Hand must reign."

The words were from the *Banfáith*'s prophecy, and, as he reminded me from time to time, they had yet to prove false. Having delivered himself of this pronouncement, he turned to me. "The choice is made."

"What if I made the wrong choice?"

"I can always send you back," he replied, and I could sense his relief. Tegid had not wanted to see me leave any more than I had wanted to go.

"True," I said, my heart lightening a little. Of course, I could return any time I chose to, and I would go—when the work I had begun was completed. I *would* go one day. But not now; not yet.

I forced that prospect from my mind, soothing my squirming conscience with sweet self-justification: after all I had endured, I well deserved my small portion of happiness. Who could deny it? Besides, there was still a great deal to be done. I would stay to see Albion restored.

Yes, and I would marry Goewyn.

Word of our betrothal spread through Dinas Dwr swifter than a shout. Tegid and I arrived at the hall, and walked into the ongoing celebration which, with the coming of darkness, had taken on a fresh, almost giddy, euphoria. The great room seemed filled with light and sound: the hearthfire roared and the timber walls were lined with torches; men and women lined the benches and thronged in noisy clusters around the pillar-posts.

Only the head of the hall, the west end, remained quiet and empty, for here the Chief Bard had established the Singing Stones in their wooden chest supported by a massive iron stand—safe under perpetual guard: three warriors to watch over Albion's chief treasure at all times. The guards were replaced at intervals by other warriors, so that the duty was shared out among the entire warband. But at no time, day or night, were the miraculous stones unprotected.

The din increased as we entered the hall, and I quickly discovered the reason.

"The king! The king is here!" shouted Bran, rallying the Ravens with his call. He held a cup high and cried, "I drink to the king's wedding!"

"To the king's wedding!" Cynan shouted, and the next thing I knew I was surrounded, seized, and lifted bodily from the ground. I was swept back across the threshold and hoisted onto the shoulders of warriors to be borne along the paths of Dinas Dwr, the crowd increasing as we went. They marched along a circuitous route so that the whole *caer* would see what was happening and join us.

In a blaze of torchlight and clamor of laughter, we arrived finally at the hut which Goewyn and her mother had made their home. There the company halted, and Cynan, taking the matter in hand, called out that the king had come to claim his bride.

Scatha emerged to address the crowd. "My daughter is here," she said, indicating Goewyn who stepped from the hut behind her. "Where is the man who claims her?" Scatha made a pretence of scanning the crowd, as if searching for the fool who dared to claim her daughter.

"He is here!" everyone shouted at once. And it suddenly occurred to me, in my place high above the pressing crowds, that this was the preamble to a form of Celtic wedding I had never witnessed before. This in itself was not surprising; the people of Albion know no fewer than nine different types of marriage and I had seen but few.

"Let the man who would take my daughter to wife declare

himself," she said, folding her arms over her breast.

"I am here, Scatha," I answered. At this the warriors lowered me to the ground and the crowd opened a way before me. I saw Goewyn waiting, as if at the end of a guarded path. "It is Llew Silver Hand who stands before you. I have come to claim your daughter for my wife."

Goewyn smiled, but made no move to join me; and as I drew near, Scatha stepped forward and planted herself between us. She presented a fierce, forbidding aspect and examined me head to heel—as if inspecting a length of moth-eaten cloth. The palm of my flesh hand grew damp as I stood under her scrutiny. The surrounding crowd joined in, calling Scatha's attention to various desirable qualities—real or imagined—which I might possess.

In the end, she declared herself satisfied with the suitor, and raised her hand. "I find no fault in you, Llew Silver Hand. But you can hardly expect me to give up such a daughter as Goewyn without a bride price worthy of her."

I knew the correct response. "You must think me a low person indeed to deprive you of so fine a daughter without the offer of suitable compensation. Ask what you will, I will give whatever you deem acceptable."

"And you must think me slow of wit to imagine that I can assess such value on the instant. This is a matter which will require long and careful deliberation," Scatha replied haughtily. And even though I accepted her reply as part of the ritual game we were playing, I found myself growing irritated with her for standing in my way.

"Far be it from me to deny you the thought you require. Take what time you will," I offered. "I will return tomorrow at dawn to hear your demands."

This was considered a proper reply and all acclaimed my answer. Scatha inclined her head and, as if allowing herself to be swayed by the response of the people, nodded slowly. "So be it. Come to this place at dawn and we will determine what kind of man you are."

"Let it be so," I replied.

At this, the people cheered and I was swept away once more on a tideflood of acclaim. We returned to the hall where, amidst much laughter and ribald advice, Tegid instructed me on what to expect in the morning. "Scatha will make her demands, and you must fulfill them with all skill and cunning. Do not think it will be easy," Tegid warned. "Rare treasure is worth great difficulty in the getting."

"But you will be there to help me," I suggested.

He shook his head. "No, Llew; as Chief Bard I cannot take one part over against the other. This is between you and Scatha alone. But, as she has Goewyn to assist her, you may choose one from among your men to aid you."

I looked around me. Bran stood grinning nearby—no doubt he would be a good choice to see me through this ordeal. "Bran?" I asked. "Would you serve me in this?"

But the Raven Chief shook his head. "Lord, if it is a strong hand on the hilt of a sword that you require, I am your man. But this is a matter beyond me. I think Alun Tringad would serve you better than I."

"Drustwn!" cried Alun when he heard this. "He is the man for you, lord." He pointed across the ring of faces gathered around me, and I saw Drustwn ducking out of sight. "Ah, now where has Drustwn gone?"

"Choose Lord Calbha!" someone shouted.

Before I could ask him, someone else replied, "It is a wife for Silver Hand, not a horse!"

Calbha answered, "It is true! I know nothing of brides; but if it is a horse you require, Llew, call on me."

I turned next to Cynan, who stood beside his father, Lord Cynfarch. "Cynan! Will you stand with me, brother?"

Cynan, assuming a grave and important air, inclined his head in assent. "Though all men desert you, Silver Hand, I will yet stand with you. Through all things—fire and sword and the wiles of bards and women—I am your man."

Everyone laughed at this, and even Cynan smiled as he said it. But his blue eyes were earnest, and his voice was firm. He was giving me a pledge greater than I had asked, and every word was from the heart.

I spent a restless, sleepless night in my hut, and rose well before dawn, before anyone else was stirring. I took myself to the lakeside for a swim and a bath; I shaved and washed my moustache, even. It was growing light in the east by the time I returned to the hut, where I spent a long time laying out my clothing. I wanted to look my best for Goewyn.

In the end, I chose a bright red siarc and a pair of yellow-and-green checked breecs. Also, I wore Meldryn Mawr's magnificent belt of gold discs and his gold torc, and carried his gold knife—all of which had been retrieved for me from among Meldron's belongings. "As the rightful successor, they are yours," Tegid had told me. "Meldron had no right to them. Wear them with pride, Llew. For by wearing them you will reclaim their honor."

So I wore them, and tried to forget that the Great Hound Meldron had so recently strutted and preened in them.

Cynan came to me as I was pulling on my buskins. He had also bathed and changed, and his red curls were combed and oiled. "You look a king attired for his wedding day," he said in approval.

"And you make a fine second," I replied. "Goewyn might well choose you instead."

"Are you hungry?" he asked.

"Yes," I replied. "But I do not think I could eat a bite. How do I look?"

He grinned. "I have already told you. And it is not seemly for a king to strain after praise. Come," he put his large hand on my shoulder, "it is dawn."

"Tegid should be close by," I said, "let us go and find him." We left my hut and moved towards the hall. The sun was rising and the sky was clear—not a cloud to be seen. My wedding day would be bright and sunny, as all good wedding days should be. My wedding day! The words seemed so strange: wedding... marriage... wife.

Tegid was awake and waiting. "I was coming to rouse you," he said. "Did you sleep well?"

"No," I replied. "I could not seem to keep my eyes closed."

He nodded. "No doubt you will sleep better tonight."

"What happens now?"

"Eat something if you like," the bard replied. "For although it is a feast day, I doubt you will have much time for eating."

Passing between the pillar-posts we found a place at an empty table and sat down. Bran and the Ravens roused themselves and joined us at the board. Although it was still too early for anything fresh from the ovens, there was some barley bread left over from last night's meal, so the others tucked in. The Ravens broke their loaves hungrily, stuffing their mouths and, between bites, urging me to eat to keep up my strength. "It is a long day that stretches before you," Bran remarked.

"And an even longer night!" quipped Alun.

"It grows no shorter for lingering here," I said, rising at once.

"Are you ready?" asked Tegid.

"Ready? I feel I have waited for this day all my life. Lead on, Wise Bard!"

With a wild, exuberant whoop warriors tumbled from the hall in a rowdy crush. There was no way to keep any sort of order or decorum, nor any quiet. The high spirits of the troop alerted the whole crannog and signalled the beginning of the festivities. We reached Scatha's hut with the entire population of Dinas Dwr crowding in our wake.

"Summon her," Tegid directed, as we came near the door.

"Scatha, Pen-y-Cat of Ynys Sci," I called, "it is Llew Silver Hand. I have come to hear and answer your demands."

A moment later, Scatha emerged from her hut, beautiful to behold in a scarlet mantle with a cream robe over it. Behind her stepped Goewyn, and my heart missed a beat: she was radiant in white and gold. Her long hair had been brushed until it gleamed, then plaited with threads of gold and bound in a long, thick braid. Gold armbands glimmered on her slender arms. Her mantle was white; she wore a white cloak of thin material, gathered loosely at her bare shoulders and held by two large gold brooches. Two wide bands of golden threadwork—elegant swans with long necks and wings fantastically intertwined—graced the borders of her cloak and the hem of her robe. Her girdle was narrow and white with gold laces tied and braided in a shimmering fall from her slim waist. She wore earrings of gold, and rings of red gold on her slender, tapering fingers.

The sight of her stole my breath away. It was like gazing into the brightness of the sun—though my eyes were burned and blinded, I could not look away. I had never seen her so beautiful, never seen any woman so beautiful. Indeed, I had forgotten such beauty could exist.

Scatha greeted me with frank disapproval, however, and said, "Are you ready to hear my demands?"

"I am ready," I said, sobered by her brusqueness.

"Three things I require," she declared curtly. "When I have received all that I ask, you shall have my daughter for your wife."

"Ask what you will, and you shall receive it."

She nodded slowly—was that a smile lurking behind her studied severity? "The first demand is this: give me the sea in full foam with a strand of silver."

The people were silent, waiting for my answer. I put a brave face on it and replied, "That is easily accomplished, though you may think otherwise."

I turned to Cynan. "Well, brother? We are days from the sea, and—"

Cynan shook his head. "No. She does not want the sea. It is something else. This is the impossible task. It is meant to demonstrate your ability to overcome the most formidable obstacle."

"Oh, you mean we have to think symbolically. I see."

"The sea in full foam—" Cynan said, and paused. "What could it be?"

"Scatha laid particular stress on the foam. That may be important. 'The sea in full foam—'" I paused, my brain spinning. "'A strand of silver'... Wait! I have it!"

"Yes?" Cynan leaned over eagerly.

"It is beer in a silver bowl!" I replied. "Beer foams like the sea and the bowl encircles it like a strand."

"Hah!" Cynan struck his fist into his palm. "That will answer!"

I turned to the crowd behind me. "Bran!" I called aloud. The

Raven Chief stepped forward quickly. "Bran, fetch me some fresh beer in a silver bowl. And hurry!"

He darted away at once, and I turned to face Scatha and wait for Bran to return with the bowl of beer. "What if we guessed wrong?" I whispered to Cynan.

He shook his head gravely. "What if he can find no beer? I fear we have drunk it all."

I had not thought of that. But Bran was resourceful; he would not let me down.

We waited. The crowd buzzed happily, talking among themselves. Goewyn stood cool and quiet as a statue; she would not look at me, so I could get no idea of what she was thinking.

Bran returned on the run, and the beer sloshing over the silver rim did look like sea waves foaming on the shore. He delivered the bowl into my hands, saying, "The last of the beer. All I could find— and it is mostly water."

"It will have to do," I said and, with a last hopeful look at Tegid—whose expression gave nothing away—I offered the gift to Scatha.

"You have asked for a boon and I give it: the sea in full foam surrounded by a strand of silver." So saying, I placed the bowl in her outstretched hands.

Scatha took the bowl and raised it for all to see. Then she said, "I accept your gift. But though you have succeeded in the first task, do not think you will easily obtain my second demand. Better men than you have tried and failed."

Knowing this to be part of the rote response, I still began vaguely to resent these other, *better* men. I swallowed my pride and answered, "Nevertheless, I will hear your demand. It may be that I will succeed where others have failed."

Scatha nodded regally. "My second demand is this: give me the one thing which will replace that which you seek to take from me."

I turned at once to Cynan. "This one is going to be tough," I said. "Goewyn means the world to her mother—how do we symbolize that?"

He rubbed his chin and frowned, but I could tell he was relishing his role. "This is most difficult—to replace that which you take from her."

"Maybe," I suggested, "we have only to identify one feature which Scatha will accept as representing her daughter. Like honey for sweetness—something like that."

Cynan cupped an elbow in his hand and rested his chin in his palm. "Sweet as honey... sweet as mead..." he murmured, thinking.

"Sweet and savory..." I suggested, "sweetness and light... sweet as a nut—"

"What did you say?"

"Sweet as a nut. But I do not think—"

"No, before the nut. What did you say before that?"

"Um... sweetness and light, I think."

"Light—yes!" Cynan nodded enthusiastically. "You see it? Goewyn is the light of her life. You are taking the light from her and you must replace it."

"How?" I wondered. "With a lamp?"

"Or a candle," Cynan prompted.

"A candle—a fragrant beeswax candle!"

Cynan grinned happily. "Sweetness and light! That would answer."

"Alun!" I called, turning to the Ravens once more. "Find me a beeswax candle, and bring it at once."

Alun Tringad disappeared, pushing through the close-packed crowd. He must have raided the nearest house, for he returned only a moment later, holding out a new candle, which I took from him and offered to Scatha, saying, "You have asked for a boon, and I give it: this candle will replace the light that I remove when I take your daughter from you. It will banish the shadows and fill the darkness with fragrance and warmth."

Scatha took the candle. "I accept your gift," she said, raising the candle so that all might see it. "But though you have succeeded in the second task, do not think you will easily obtain my third demand.

Better men than you have tried and failed."

I smiled confidently and repeated the expected response. "Nevertheless, I will hear your demand. It may be that I will succeed where others have failed."

"Hear then, if you will, my last demand: give me the thing this house lacks, the gift beyond price."

I turned to Cynan. "What is it this time? The impossible task again?" I wondered. "It sounds impossible to me."

"It could be," he allowed, "but I think not. We have done that one. It is something else."

"But what does her house lack? It could be anything."

"Not anything," Cynan replied slowly. "The one thing: the gift beyond price."

"She seemed to stress that," I agreed lamely. "The gift beyond price... what *is* the gift beyond price? Love? Happiness?"

"A child," suggested Cynan thoughtfully.

"Scatha wants me to give her a child? That cannot be right."

Cynan frowned. "Maybe it is you she wants."

I pounced on the idea at once. "That is it! That is the answer!"

"What?"

"Me!" I cried. "Think about it. The thing this house lacks is a man, a son-in-law. The gift beyond price is life."

Cynan's grin was wide and his blue eyes danced. "Yes, and by joining your life to Goewyn's you create a wealth of life," he winked and added, "especially if you make a few babies into the bargain. It *is* you she is asking for, Llew."

"Let us hope we are right," I said. I took a deep breath and turned to Scatha, who stood watching me, enjoying the way she was making me squirm.

"You have asked for a gift beyond price and a thing which you lack," I said. "It seems to me that your house lacks a man, and no one can place a value on life." So saying, I dropped down on one knee before her. "Therefore, Pen-y-Cat, I give you the gift of myself."

Scatha beamed her good pleasure, placing her hands on my

shoulders, bent and kissed my cheek. Raising me to my feet, she said, "I accept your gift, Llew Silver Hand." She lifted her voice for the benefit of those looking on. "Let it be known that there is no better man than you for my daughter, for you indeed have succeeded where other men have failed."

She turned, summoned Goewyn to her and, taking her daughter's left hand, put it in mine, and then clasped both of ours in her own. "I am satisfied," she declared to Tegid. "Let the marriage take place."

The bard stepped forward at once. He thumped the earth three times with his ashwood staff. "The Chief Bard of Albion speaks," he called loudly. "Hear me! From times past remembering the Derwyddi have joined life to life for the continuance of our race." Regarding us, he said, "Is it your desire to join your lives in marriage?"

"That is our desire," we answered together.

At this, Scatha produced the bowl which I had given her and passed it to Tegid. He raised it and said, "I hold between my hands the sea encircled by a silver strand. The sea is life; the silver is the all-encircling boundary of this worlds-realm. If you would be wed, then you must seize this worlds-realm and share its life between you."

So saying, he placed the silver bowl in our hands. Holding it between us, I offered the bowl to Goewyn and she drank, then offered the bowl to me. I also took a few swallows of very watery beer and raised my head.

"Drink!" Tegid urged. "It is life you are holding between you, my friends. Life! Drink deep and drain it to the last."

It was a very large bowl Bran had brought. I took a deep breath and raised the bowl once more. When I could not hold another drop, I passed the silver bowl to Goewyn, who took it, raised it, and drank— so long and deep and greedily I thought she would never come up for air. When she lowered the vessel once more, her eyes were shining bright. She licked her lips and, handing the bowl to Tegid, cast a sidelong glance at me.

Putting the bowl aside, Tegid said, "Goewyn, do you bring a gift?"

Goewyn said, "Neither gold nor silver do I bring, nor anything which can be bought or sold, lost or stolen. But I bring this day my love and my life, and these I do give you freely."

"Will you accept the gifts that have been offered?" Tegid asked.

"With all my heart, I do accept them. And I will cherish them always as my highest treasure, and I will protect this treasure to the last breath in my body."

Tegid inclined his head. "What token do you offer for your acceptance?"

Token? No one had told me about that; I had no token to offer. Cynan's voice sounded in my ear. "Give her your belt," he suggested helpfully.

I had no better idea, so I removed the belt and draped the heavy gold band across Tegid's outspread hands. "I offer this belt of fine gold," I said and, on a sudden inspiration, added, "Let its excellence and value be but a small token of the high esteem in which I hold my beloved, and let it encircle her fair form in shining splendor like my love which does encompass her for ever—true, without end, and incorruptible."

Tegid nodded sagely and, turning, offered the belt to Goewyn, who lowered her head as it was placed in her hands. She gathered the belt and clutched it to her breast. Were those tears in her eyes?

To Goewyn, Tegid said, "By this token your gift has been accepted. If you will receive the gift you have been given will you also offer a token of acceptance?"

Without a word, Goewyn slipped her arm around my neck and pressed her lips to mine. She kissed me full and free and with such fervor that it brought cheers from the onlookers gathered close about. She released me, breathless, almost gasping. The ardor in her clear brown eyes made me blush.

Tegid, smiling broadly, thumped the earth once more with his staff, three times, sharply. Then he raised the staff and held it horizontally over our heads. "The gifts of love and life have been exchanged and accepted. By this let all men know that Llew Silver Hand and Goewyn are wed."

And that was that. The people acclaimed the wedding loudly and with great enthusiasm. We were instantly caught up in a whirlwind of well-wishing. The wedding was over, let the celebration commence!

The Wedding Feast

Swept away on a floodtide of high exuberance, Goewyn and I were propelled through the crannog. I lost sight of Tegid, Scatha and Cynan; I could not see Bran or Calbha. At the landing we were bundled into a boat and rowed across to the lakeside where Scatha's field was quickly prepared for games.

Feast days and festivals are often accompanied by contests of skill and chance. Wrestling and horse racing are by far the favorites, with mock combat and games of hurley. An earthen mound was raised facing the field, with two chairs placed upon it. One of the chairs was made from stag antler, and adorned with a white oxhide—this was to be mine. And from this vantagepoint, Goewyn and I were to watch the proceedings and dispense prizes.

The sport would come first, the food and drink later—giving the cooks time to see everything properly prepared, and the competitors and spectators opportunity to build an ample appetite. Better to wrestle on an empty stomach, after all, than with a bellyful of roast pork. And after a few bowls of strong wedding mead, who would be able to sit a horse, let alone race one?

When the hastily erected mound was finished, Goewyn and I ascended to our chairs and waited for the company to assemble. Already, many had made their way across the lake from the crannog, and more were arriving. I was happy to wait. I was a happy man—perhaps for the first time in my life, truly happy.

All I had ever known of joy and life, and now love, had been found here, in the Otherworld, in Albion. The thought touched a guilty nerve in my conscience, and I squirmed. But surely, Professor Nettleton was wrong. He *was* wrong, and I would not destroy the thing I loved; he was wrong, and I could stay. I would sooner give up my life than leave Albion now.

I looked at Goewyn, and smothered my guilt with the sight of her gleaming hair. She sensed me watching her, and turned to me. "I love you, my soul," she whispered, smiling. And I felt like a man who, living his entire life in a cave, that instant steps out into the dazzling light of day.

Tegid arrived shortly, attended by his *Mabinogi*, led by the harpbearer, Gwion Bach. Another carried his staff. "I have given Calbha charge of the prizes," Tegid told us. "He is gathering them now."

"Prizes? Ah, yes, for the games."

"I knew you would not think of it," he explained cheerfully.

Calbha carried out his charge in style. He came leading a host of bearers, each carrying an armload of valuable objects—and some in twos lugging heavy wicker baskets between them. They piled their offerings around our chairs. Soon the mound was knee-deep in glittering, gleaming booty: new-made spears with decorated heads and shafts, fine swords inset with gems, shields with rims of silver and bronze, bone-handled knives... Wherever I looked there were cups and bowls—bowls of copper, bronze, silver, and gold; wooden bowls cunningly carved; cups of horn with silver rims, small cups and large cups; cups of stone even. There were fine new cloaks and piles of fluffy white fleeces. Armbands of bronze and silver and gold gleamed like links in a precious chain, and scattered among them were brooches, bracelets and rings. As if this were not enough, there were three good horses which Calbha could not resist adding.

I gaped at the glittering array. "Where did you get all this?"

"It is yours, lord," he replied happily. "But do not worry, I have chosen only the finest for such a celebration as this."

"I thank you, Calbha," I replied, eyeing the treasure trove. "You have served me well. Indeed, I did not know I was so wealthy."

There was so much, and all so lavish, that I wondered aloud to Tegid, "Can I afford this?"

The bard only laughed and indicated the shimmering mound with a sweep of his hand. "The greater the generosity, the greater the king."

"If that is the way of it, then give it all away—and more! Let men say that never in Albion was such a wedding celebration as this. And let all who hear of it in later days sicken with envy that they were not here!"

Cynan, arriving with some of his men just then, looked upon the treasure and declared himself well ready to win his share. Bran and the Ravens came behind him, calling loudly for the games to begin. Alun challenged Cynan then and there to chose whatever game of skill or chance he preferred—and he should be bested at it.

"You are a wonder, Alun Tringad," Cynan crowed. "Can it be you have forgotten the defeat I gave you when last you tried your skill against me?"

"Defeat?" Alun cried. "Am I to believe what I am hearing? The victory was mine, as you well know."

"Man, Alun—I am surprised your teeth keep company with your tongue, such lies you tell. Still, for the sake of this festive day," Cynan declared, "I will not hold your impudence against you."

"It was your voice, Cynan Machae, cried mercy as I recall," Alun replied amiably. "Yet, like you, I am willing to forget what is past for the sake of the day."

They fell to arguing then about the size of the wager—pledging prizes not yet won—and quickly drew a crowd of onlookers eager to back one or the other of the champions and so reap a share of the rewards.

They were still settling the terms when Goewyn leaned close. "If you do not begin the games soon, husband, we will be forced to listen to their boasting all day."

"Very well," I agreed, and rose from my chair to address the crowd. Tegid called for silence and, when the people saw that I would speak, they quieted themselves to listen. "Let us enjoy the day given to us!" I said. "Let us strive with skill and accept with good grace all that chances our way, that when the games are done we may retire to the feasting-hall better friends than when the day began."

"Well said, lord," Tegid declared. "So be it!"

Wrestling was first, followed by various races, including a spectacular horse race which had everyone exhausted by the time the winner—a young man from Calbha's clan—crossed the finish line. I awarded him a horse and, much to the crowd's amusement, he promptly retired from the games lest he lose his prize in a foolish wager.

I tried at first to match each award to its winner, but I soon gave up and I lost track and took whatever came to hand. Indeed, as the games proceeded I called on Goewyn to help, so that sometimes I awarded the prizes and sometimes the winners received their trophies from Goewyn—which I suspected most preferred. I noticed that many who came to the mound to marvel at the prizes, stayed to feast their eyes on Goewyn. Time and again I found myself stealing glances at her—like a beggar who has found a jewel of immense value, and must continually reassure himself that it is not a dream, that it does exist and, yes, that it belongs to him.

One young boy came to the mound and found a copper cup which, once he had picked up the thing, he could not bring himself to put down. "You like that cup," I said, and he blushed, for he did not know he was observed. "Tell me, how would you win it?"

He thought for a moment. "I would wrestle Bran Bresal himself," he answered boldly.

"Bran might be reluctant to risk his great renown by engaging one so young," I answered. "Perhaps you would be persuaded to pit your strength against someone more your own size?"

The boy accepted my suggestion and a match was agreed. It ended well and I was pleased to award him his prize. Thus began a succession of children's games and races, no less hotly contested than the trials of their elders.

The contests progressed and, little by little, the treasure mound was reduced. Tegid disappeared at some point in the proceedings and I was so caught up my role as gift-giver that some long time passed before I missed him. Turning to Goewyn, I said, "I wonder where Tegid has gone. Do you see him anywhere?"

Before she could reply, there came a rush at the mound behind us. I heard the swift approach and saw a confused motion out of the corner of my eye. Even as my head swivelled towards the sound and movement, I saw hands reaching for Goewyn. In the same instant that I leapt to my feet, she was pulled from her chair. "Llew!" she cried, and was borne roughly away.

I hurled myself after her, but there were too many people, too much confusion. I could hardly move. Head down, I drove forward into the mass of bodies. Hands seized me. I was pressed back into my chair. Goewyn cried out again, but her voice was farther away and the cry was cut off.

I kicked free of the chair and made to leap from the mound. Even as I gained my feet, I was hauled down from behind, thrown to the ground, and pinned there. Voices strange and loud gabbled in my ears. I fought against those holding me down. "Let me go!" I shouted. "Release me!" But the hands held firm, and the chaos of voices resolved itself into laughter. They were laughing at me!

Angry now, I struggled all the more. "Tegid!" I bellowed. "Tegid!"

"I am here, Llew," Tegid's voice replied calmly.

I looked around furiously, and saw Tegid's face appear above me. "Release him," the bard instructed.

The weight of hands fell away; the circle of faces drew back. I jumped to my feet. "They've taken Goewyn," I told him. "We were sitting here, and they—"

There were smiles and a spattering of laughter. I halted. Tegid, his fingers laced around his staff, appeared unconcerned. "What is happening?" I demanded. "Did you hear me?"

"I heard you, Llew," the bard replied simply.

His lack of concern appalled me. I opened my mouth to protest, and again heard the laughter. Gazing at those gathered around us, I saw their faces alight with mischief and mirth. It was only then I realized that I was the object of a prank. "Well, Tegid, what is it? What have you done?"

"It is not for me to say, lord," he answered.

It came to me then that this was another of those peculiar Celtic marriage customs. The trick required me to work the thing out for myself. Well, prank or custom, I was not amused. Turning away, I called, "Bran! Cynan! Follow me!"

I strode down from the mound, a path opening before me as I hastened away. "Bran! Cynan!" I called again, and when they did not join me, I turned to see them standing motionless. "Follow me!" I shouted. "I need you."

Cynan, grinning, moved a step forward, then stopped, shaking his head slightly.

"I go alone," I remarked.

"That is the way of it," Bran said.

"So be it!" Exasperation turning to anger, I whirled away across the field in the direction I had last seen Goewyn. It was a stupid jest, and I resented it.

The trail led to the lakeside where I lost it on the stony shore. They might have gone in either direction—one way led along the lake towards Dinas Dwr, the other rose to the heights and the ridge of Druim Vran above. Looking towards the crannog, I saw no sign of flight, so I pivoted the opposite way and strode towards the heights and Tegid's grove.

I reached the path and began the climb. The crowd followed behind, streaming along the lake in a happy hubbub. The trees gradually closed around me, muffling the sound of the following throng. It was cool among the silent trees, and the sun-dappled shadows seemed undisturbed. But I heard the creak of a bough ahead and knew my instincts were true. I quickened my pace, pushing recklessly ahead: ducking low-hanging branches, dodging trunks and shrubs.

Tegid's sacred grove lay directly ahead, and I made straight for it. Putting on a final burst of speed, I ascended the final leg of the trail and gained the grove. I entered with a rush to find a bower of birch branches had been erected in the center of the grove. And before the bower stood seven warriors, armed and ready.

"Put down your weapons," I commanded, but they did not move. I knew these men; they had followed me into battle and stood with me against Meldron. Now they stood against me. Though I knew it to be part of the ritual, the ache of betrayal that knifed momentarily through me was real enough. There was no help for me. I stood alone against them.

Steeling myself, I moved closer. The warriors advanced menacingly towards me. I stopped and they stopped, staring grimly at me. The smiles and laughter were gone. What, I wondered as I stood staring at them, was I supposed to do now?

The first of the onlookers reached the grove. I turned to see Bran, Cynan and Tegid entering behind me and, rank upon rank, my people surrounding the sacred circle. No one spoke, but the eagerness in their eyes urged me on.

If this was a mock abduction, it seemed I would have to undertake a mock battle to win my queen. I had no weapon, but, turning to the task before me, I stepped boldly forth and met the first warrior as he swung the head of the spear level. Moving quickly under the swinging shaft, I caught it with my silver hand and pulled hard.

To my surprise, the warrior released the spear and fell at my feet as if dead. Taking the shaft, I turned to meet the next warrior, who raised his spear to throw. I struck the man's shield with the tip of the spearblade: he dropped his weapon and fell. The third warrior crumpled at the touch of my spear against his shoulder—the fourth and fifth, likewise. The two remaining warriors attacked me together.

The first one struck at me, drawing a wide, lazy arc with his sword. I crouched as the blade passed over my head, and then drove into them, holding my spear sideways. At the lightest contact, the two warriors toppled, fell, and lay still.

Suddenly, the grove shook to a tremendous shout of triumph as I stepped to the bower's entrance. "Come out, Goewyn," I called. "All is well."

There was a movement from within the bower, and Goewyn stepped forward. She was as I had seen her only a few moments before, and yet she was not. She had changed. For, as she stepped from the deep green shadow of the birch-leaf bower, the sunlight struck her hair and gown and she became a creature of light, a bright spirit formed of air and fire: her hair golden flame, her gown shimmering sea-foam white.

The crowd, so noisily jubilant before, gasped and fell silent.

Dazzling, radiant, glowing with beauty, she appeared before me and I could but stand and stare. I heard a movement beside me. "Truly, she is a goddess," Cynan whispered. "Go to her, man! Claim your bride—or I will."

I stepped forward and extended my silver hand to her. As she took my hand, the sunlight caught the metal and flared. And it seemed that a blaze sprang up between us at the union of our hands. Though it was only a game, it was with genuine relief that I clasped her to my heart. "Never leave me, Goewyn," I breathed.

"I never will," she promised.

The sun had begun its westward plunge by the time we returned to the crannog. Tables had been set up outside the hall to accommodate the increased numbers the king would entertain this night. I would have preferred to remain outside—after the brilliant day, the night would be warm and bright—but the interior of the hall had been festooned with rushlights and birch branches to resemble the leafy bower in the grove. With all this preparation specially for us, it would have been unkind not to acknowledge the honor and enjoy it.

Famished with hunger and aflame with thirst, the warriors called loudly for food and drink as soon as they crossed the threshold. The tables inside the hall had been arranged to form a large hollow square so that we could all see one another. As the first were finding their places at the board, the platters appeared—borne on the shoulders of the servers—huge trenchers piled high with choice cuts of roast beef, pork, and mutton; these were followed by enormous platters of cooked cabbages, turnips, leeks and fennel. A fair-sized vat had been set up at the end of each table so that no one would have to go far to refill cup or bowl. Alas, there was no ale left, so tonight the vats had been filled with water flavored with honey and bullace. Along the center of each table were piled small loaves of honey-glazed *banys bara*, or wedding bread—fresh-baked and warm from the ovens.

As the platters were passed, each diner, man or woman, was offered the most succulent portions. Within moments the clamor sank to a muffled din as hungry mouths were filled with good food. The privilege of eating first carried with it the obligation of serving; those who served now would be guests later. Thus, order and right were admirably maintained. The guards watching over the Singing Stones were the only exceptions. They neither served nor ate, but stood aloof from the celebration, as watchful and wary as if they were alone in a hostile land.

Looking out across the crowded hall, my heart swelled with joy to see my people so happy and content. It came to me why it was that the mark of a king was linked to his benevolence: his people lived on it, looking to the king for their sustenance and support; through him they lived, or died. I filled my bowl with the savory morsels served me, and began to eat with a ready appetite.

When everyone had been served, a loud thumping drum resounded through the hall, and into the hollow square advanced eight maidens at a slow and solemn pace. Each maiden gathered her loose-hanging hair and wound it into a knot at the nape of her neck. They then drew up the hems of their mantles so that their legs were bare, and loosened the strings of their bodices. Each maiden then approached a warrior at table and begged the use of his sword.

The warriors—eager accomplices—gave up their swords willingly, and the maidens returned to the center of the square where they formed a circle, each placing her sword on the ground at her feet so that the swordpoints touched. Tegid, harp at his shoulder, appeared and began to play. The harpstrings sang, each note plucked with definite accent; and the maidens began to dance, each step deliberate and slow.

Around the sunburst of swords they danced, treading their way slowly over the hilts and blades, eyes level, fixed on a point in the distance. Around and around, they went, adding an extra step with each pass. By the sixth pass the harpsong began to quicken and the footwork grew more complicated. By the twelfth pass, the harp was humming and the dance had become fantastic. Yet, the maidens danced with the same solemn attitude, eyes fixed, expressions grave.

The music reached a crescendo and the maidens, spinning swiftly, performed an intricate maneuver with their arms. Then, quick as a blink, they stopped, spun around, stooped, and each seized her sword by the hilt and lofted its point to the rooftrees above, shedding the tops of their mantles in the same motion.

The music began again, slowly. Lowering the swords, the maidens began the dance once more, their steps measured and precise. The swords flashed and gleamed, creating dazzling arcs around the twirling lissome shapes. The tempo increased, and those looking on began beating time with their hands on the tables, shouting encouragement to the dancers. The young women's skill at handling the swords was dazzling; handwork and footwork elaborate, cunning, and deft: hands weaving enigmatic patterns, feet tracing complex figures as the keen-edged swords shimmered and shone.

Torchlight and rushlight glimmered on the sweat-glistening flesh of slender arms, rounded shoulders and breasts. The harpsong swelled; the sword-dance whirled to its climax. With a shriek and a shout, the maidens leaped, striking their blades together in simulated battleclash. Once, twice, three times, the weapons sang. They froze for an instant, and then fell back, each maiden clutching the naked blade to her breast. They knelt and lay back until their heads touched the ground and the swords lay flat along their taut chests and stomachs.

Slowly raising the swords by the hilts, they rose to their knees once more, brandishing the blades high. Suddenly, the harp struck a resounding chord. The swords plunged. The maidens collapsed with a cry.

There was a moment's silence as we all sat gazing raptly at the swaying blades standing in the packed earth floor. And then cheers filled the hall, loudly lauding the dancers' feat. The maidens gathered their clothes and retreated from the square.

I looked at Goewyn, and then at the bowl in my hands. All thought of food vanished from my mind—instantly replaced by a hunger of an entirely different, though no less urgent, variety. She sensed me looking at her and smiled. "Is something wrong with the food?" she asked, indicating my half-filled bowl.

I shook my head. "It is just that I think I have discovered something more to my liking."

Goewyn leaned close, put her hand to my face and kissed me. "If you find *that* to your liking," she whispered, "then join me when you have finished." Rising from her chair, she let her fingers drift along my jaw. Her touch sent a delicious shiver along my ribs.

I watched her go. She paused at the door and cast a backward glance at me before disappearing. It seemed to me that the close-crowded hall, so festive only moments before, grew suddenly loud and the crush of people oppressive.

Cynan noticed that I was not eating. "Eat!" he urged. "This night above all others you will need what little strength you possess."

Bran, sitting next to him, said, "Brother, can you not see it is food and drink of a different kind that he craves?"

Others offered their own opinions on how best to maintain strength and vigor in such circumstances. I forced down a few bites and swallowed some ale, but my friends thought my efforts lacked conviction, and redoubled their exhortations. Calbha filled my cup from his own and insisted I drain it in a single draught. I sipped politely and laughed at their jests, though my heart was not in it.

The feasting and dancing would continue through the night, but I could not tolerate another moment. Rising from the table, I tried to make an unobtrusive exit, which proved impossible. I was forced to endure much good-natured, bibulous advice on how to conduct myself on my wedding night.

As I moved past Tegid, he slipped a skin of mead into my hands so that my wedding night should lack neither sweetness or warmth. "In mead is found the flavor of the marriage bed. Twice blessed are lovers who share it on this night."

The more garrulous seemed anxious to accompany me to the hut where Goewyn waited. But Tegid came to my rescue, urging them to sit down and celebrate the new-wedded couple's happiness in song. He took up his harp and made a great show of tuning it. "Away with you," he murmured under his breath, "I will keep order here."

Cradling the mead in the crook of my arm, I hurried across the yard to the nearby hut which had been prepared for us. The house, like the hall, had been transformed into a forest bower with fragrant pine and birch branches adorning walls and ceiling, and rushlights glowing like ruddy stars, creating a dimly pleasant rose-hued light.

Goewyn was waiting, greeted me with a kiss, and drew me inside, taking the meadskin. "I have waited long for this night, my soul," she whispered as she wrapped her arms tightly around me.

Our first embrace ended in a long, passionate kiss. And as the sleeping-place was prepared—fleeces piled deep and spread with cloaks—we tumbled into it. I closed my eyes, filling my lungs with the warm scent of her skin as our caresses grew more urgent, taking fire.

Thus occupied, I do not know whether it was the shout or the smoke that first called me from the bed. I sat up abruptly. Goewyn reached for me, tugging me gently back down. "Llew..."

"Wait—"

"What is it?" she whispered.

The shout came again, quick and urgent. And with it the sharp scent of smoke.

"Fire!" I said, leaping to my feet. "The crannog is on fire!"

4

A Fine Night's Work

"The fire is on the western side," Goewyn said, watching the rusty stain seeping into the night sky. "The wind will send it towards us."

"Not if we hurry," I said. "Go to the hall. Alert Tegid and Bran. I will return as soon I can."

Even as I spoke, I heard another cry of alarm: "Hurry, Llew!" I kissed her cheek and darted away.

The smoke thickened as I raced towards the fire, filling my nostrils with the parched and musty sharpness of scorched grain: the grain stores! Unless the fire was extinguished quickly, it would be a lean, hungry winter.

As I raced through the crannog along the central byway joining the various islets of our floating city, I saw the yellow-tipped flames, like clustered leaves, darting above the rooftops. I heard the fire's angry roar, and I heard voices: men shouting, women calling, children shrieking and crying. And behind me, from the direction of the hall, came the battleblast of the carynx, sounding the alarm.

The flames leapt high and ever higher, red-orange and angry against the black sky. Dinas Dwr, our beautiful city on the lake, was garishly silhouetted in the hideous glow. I felt sick with dread.

Closer, I saw people running here and there, darting through the rolling smoke, faces set, grimly earnest. Some carried leather buckets, others had wooden or metal bowls and cauldrons, but most wielded only their cloaks which they had stripped off, soaked in water, and now used as flails upon the sprouting flames.

I whipped off my own cloak and sped to join them. My heart sank like a stone. The houses, so close together, their dry roof-thatches nearly touching, kindled like tinder at the first lick of flame. I beat out the flames in one place only to have them reappear elsewhere. If help did not come at once, we would lose all.

I heard a shout behind me.

"Tegid! Here!" I cried, turning as the bard reached me. King Calbha, with fifty or more warriors and women came with him, and they all began beating at the flames with their cloaks. "Where are Bran and Cynan?"

"I have sent Cynan and Cynfarch to the south side," Tegid explained. "The Ravens are on the north. I told them I would send you to them."

"Go, Llew," instructed Calbha, wading into battle. "We will see to matters here."

I left them to the fight, and ran to aid the Ravens, passing between huts whose roofs were already smoldering from the sparks raining down upon them. The smoke thickened, acrid and black with soot. I came to a knot of men working furiously. "Bran!" I shouted.

"Here, lord!" came the answer, and a torso materialized out of the smoke. Bran carried a hayfork in one hand and his cloak in the other. Naked to the waist, his skin was black from the smoke; his eyes and teeth showed white, like chips of moonstone. Sweat poured off him, washing pale rivulets through the grime.

"Tegid thought you might need help," I explained. "How is it here?"

"We are trying to keep the fire from spreading further eastward. Fortunately, the wind is with us," he said, then added, "but Cynan and Cynfarch will have the worst of it."

"Then I will go to them," I told him, and hurried away again. I rounded a turn and crossed a bridge, meeting three women, each carrying two or three babes and shepherding a bedraggled flock of young children, all of them frightened and wailing. One of the women stumbled in her haste and trod on a child; she fell to her knees, almost dropping the infants she clutched so tightly. The child sprawled headlong onto the bridge timbers and lay screaming.

I scooped up the child—so quickly that the youngster stopped yowling, fright swallowed by surprise. Goewyn appeared beside me in an instant, bending to raise the woman to her feet and shouldering an infant all in one swift motion. "I will see them safe!" she called to me, already leading them away. "You go ahead."

I raced on. Cynfarch stood as if in the midst of a riot, commanding the effort. I ran to him, shedding my cloak. "I am here, Cynfarch," I said. "What is to be done?"

"We will not save these houses, but—" he broke off to shout orders to a group of men pulling at burning thatch with wooden rakes and long iron hooks. A portion of the roof collapsed inward with a shower of sparks, and the men scurried to the next hut. "These houses are ruined," he continued, "but if the wind holds steady we may keep it from spreading."

"Where is Cynan?"

"He was there," the king glanced over his shoulder. "I do not see him now."

I ran to the place Cynfarch indicated, passing between burning buildings into a valley of fire. Flames leapt all around me. The heat gushed and blasted on the breeze. Everything—the houses to the right and left, the wall ahead, the black sky above—shimmered in the heat-flash.

I heard a horse's wild scream, and directly in front of me a man burst through a bank of smoke holding tight to the reins of a rearing horse. The man had thrown his cloak over the terrified animal's head, and was leading it away from the fire. Immediately behind him came four more men with bucking, neighing, panicky horses, each with their heads bound in the men's cloaks. Only a few horses and kine were kept on the crannog; all the rest ranged the meadow below the ridgewall. But those we stabled in Dinas Dwr we could least afford to lose.

I helped the men lead the horses through the narrow, fire-shattered path between the burning wrecks of houses and sheds. Once on the wider path, I retraced my steps and hurried on. Smoke billowed all around, obscuring sight. Covering my nose and mouth with the lower part of my siarc, I plunged ahead and came all at once into a clear place swarming with people. Fire danced in a hazy shimmer all around. I felt as if I had been thrust into an oven.

Cynan, with a score of warriors and men with axes, chopped furiously at the timber wall. They were trying to cut away a section as a fire-break to keep the flames from destroying the entire palisade. Threescore men with sopping cloaks beat at the wooden surfaces and the ground, keeping the surrounding flames at bay, while more men with buckets doused the smoldering embers of the ruins they had reclaimed. Black curls of soot and grey flakes of ash fell from the sky like filthy snow.

"Cynan!" I called, running to him.

At the sound of my voice he turned, though the axe completed its stroke. "Llew! A fine wedding night for you," he said, shaking his head as he chopped again.

I scanned the ragged, fire-ravaged wall. "Will your fire-break hold?"

"Oh, aye," he said, stepping back from the wall to look at his labor. "It will hold." He raised his voice to shout the order. "Pull it down! Pull it down, men!"

Ropes stretched taut. The wall section wobbled and swayed, but would not fall.

"Pull!" shouted Cynan, leaping to the nearest rope.

I joined him, lending my weight to the effort. We heaved on the ropes and the timbers groaned. "Pull!" Cynan cried. "Everyone! All together! Pull!"

The timbers sighed and then gave way with a shuddering crash. We stood gazing through a clear gap at the lake beyond. "Those houses next!" Cynan ordered, stooping for his axe.

Two heartbeats later, a score of axes shivered the roof-trees of three houses as yet untouched by the relentlessly encroaching flames.

Seizing one of the rakes, I began attacking the smoldering thatch of a nearby roof, throwing the rake as high up the slope as I could reach and pulling, pulling, pulling down with all my might, scattering the bundled thatch, and then beating out the glowing reeds as they lay at my feet.

When I finished one roof, I rushed to another, and then another. My arms ached and my eyes watered. I choked on smoke. Live embers caught in the cloth of my siarc, so I stripped it off and braved the burns of falling thatch. The heat singed my hair; it felt as if my skin was blistering. But I worked on, sometimes with help, more often alone. Everyone was doing whatever could be done.

"Llew!" I heard someone shout my name. I turned just in time to see a pair of long horns swing out of the smoke haze. I dodged to one side as the curved horn cut a swathe through the air where I stood. An ox had broken free from its tether and, frightened out of its dim wits, was intent on returning to its pen. The stupid beast was running among burning huts looking for its shed. Snatching up my siarc, I waved and shouted, turning the animal away. It rumbled off the way it had come, but no one gave chase. We had enough to do trying to stay ahead of the flames.

Everywhere I turned, there was a new emergency. We flew to each fresh crisis swiftly, but with a little less energy than the one before. Strength began to flag—and then to fail. My arms grew heavy and numb. My hand was raw from the rake handle, and from burns. I could not catch my breath; my lungs heaved and the air wheezed in my throat. Still, I doggedly planted one foot in front of the other and labored on.

And when I began to think that we must abandon our work to the flames, Bran and the Ravens appeared with several score men and warriors. With a shout they swooped to the task. Within moments of their arrival, or so it seemed to me, we were working harder than ever before. Raking thatch, beating flames, smothering sparks—raking, beating, smothering, over and over and over again and again.

Time passed as in a dream. Heat licked my skin; smoke stung my nose and my eyes ran. But I toiled on. Gradually, the fire's glare dimmed. I felt cooler air on my scorched skin and I stopped.

A hundred men or more stood around me, clutching tools, vessels, and cloaks in unfeeling hands. We stood, heads bowed, our arms limp at our sides, or kneeling, leaning on our rakes for support. And all around us the quiet hiss of hot embers slowly dying...

"A fine night's work," growled Cynan in a voice ragged as the remains of his burnt tatters of clothing.

I raised my head and turned raw eyes to a sky showing grey in the east. In the pale, spectral light Dinas Dwr appeared as a vast heap of charred timber and smoking ash.

"I want to see what is left," I told Cynan. "We should look for the injured."

"I will look after the men here," Bran said. He swayed on his feet with fatigue, but I knew he would not rest until all the others were settled. So I charged him to do what he deemed best, and left him to it.

In the grim grey dawn, Cynan and I stumbled slowly through the devastation of the caer. The damage was severe and thorough. The western side of the stronghold had been decimated; precious little remained standing, and that little had been ravaged by flame and smoke.

Calbha met us as we pursued our inspection; he had been arranging temporary storage for salvaged food stocks and supplies, and holding-pens for horses and cattle until they could be conveyed to pasturage on the meadows.

"Was anyone hurt here?" I asked him.

Calbha gave a quick shake of his head. "A few with burns and such," he answered, "but no one seriously hurt. We were fortunate."

We left him to his work and continued on, picking our way through smoking rubble. In the center of a small yard formed by the charred remains of three houses, we found Tegid and several women working with the injured. The bard, nearly black with smoke and soot, knelt over a thrashing body, applying unguent from a clay pot. Lying on the ground around him were a dozen more bodies: some gasping and moaning, or struggling to rise; others unnaturally still, and wrapped head to foot in cloaks. Several of these cloak-covered corpses were no bigger than a bundle of kindling.

The full weight of sadness descended upon me then, and I staggered beneath it. Cynan caught my arm and bore me up.

Scatha moved among the living, bearing the marks of one who had walked through flames—as indeed she had. For when the alarm sounded, she had organized a search of each house on the western side. Nearly everyone was at the wedding feast, but a few— especially mothers of small children—had retired to sleep. Scatha had roused them and conducted them through smoke and flames to safety, returning again and again, until the fire grew too hot and she could do no more.

"How many?" She glanced up quickly at the sound of my voice, and then proceeded with her work of bandaging a young man's burned upper arm.

"If there had been time," she replied, "these might have been saved. But the fire spread so swiftly . . . and these young ones were asleep." She lifted a hand to the tiny bundles. "They never woke, and now they never will."

"Tell me, Scatha," I said, my voice husky with fatigue and remorse. "How many?"

"Three fives and three," she replied, then added softly, "Two or three more will join that number before nightfall."

Tegid finished and joined us. "It is a wicked loss," he muttered. "Smoke took them while they slept. It was a merciful death, at least."

"But for the feast," Cynan put in, "it would have been much worse. Almost everyone was in the hall when it started."

"And if almost everyone had not been in the hall, it would never have started in the first place," Scatha suggested.

I was in no mood for riddles. "Are you saying that this was not an accident?" I demanded bluntly.

"It was no accident kindled the flame." Cynan was adamant.

Tegid agreed. "Flames arising in three places at once—the wall, the houses, the ox pens—is not negligence or mishap. That is willful and malicious."

Lord Calbha, coming upon us just then, heard Tegid's

pronouncement. "Someone set the fires on purpose—is that what you are saying?" charged Calbha, unwilling to believe such a thing could happen in Dinas Dwr. "What man among us would do such a thing?"

"Man or men," Cynan replied, his voice raw from smoke and shouting. "There was maybe more than one." He regarded the smoldering ruins narrowly. "Whoever it was knew their work, and did it well. If the wind had changed we would have lost the caer— and many more lives besides."

The sweat on my back turned cold. I turned to those around me, silently scanning their faces. If there was a killer among us, I could not imagine who it might be. A call from one of the women took Tegid away. "Speak of this to no one," I charged the others, "until we have had time to learn more."

Scatha returned to her work, and Cynan, Calbha and I went back to where Bran and the Ravens were sifting the rubble of a storehouse. Closer, I saw that they were slowly, carefully lifting a collapsed roofbeam from a body which was trapped beneath it.

Cynan and I hastened to add our strength to the task. Grasping the blackened timber, we heaved it up, shifting it just enough for the broken body beneath to be withdrawn. The man was pulled free of the debris and carried from the ruin where they laid him gently down and rolled him onto his back.

Bran's head came up slowly, his expression grave. He glanced from me to Cynan. "I am sorry, Cynan..."

"Cynfarch!" exclaimed Cynan. Falling to his knees, he raised his father's body in his arms. The movement brought a faint whimper of a moan. The Galanae king coughed and a thin trickle of blood leaked from the corner of his mouth.

Calbha stifled an oath; I put my hand on the man nearest me. "Fetch Tegid," I ordered. "Hurry, man!"

Tegid came on the run, took one look at the body on the ground, and ordered everyone back. Bending over Cynfarch's side, the bard began to examine the stricken king. He gently probed the body for wounds, and turned the head to the side. Beneath the filthy coating of ash, Cynfarch's flesh was pale and waxy.

Cynan, his broad shoulders hunched, clasped his father's hand in his and stared hard at the slack features, as if willing vigor to reappear. "Will he live?" he asked as Tegid finished his scrutiny.

"He is hurt inside," the bard replied. "I cannot say."

These words were scarcely fallen from his lips when another call claimed our attention. "*Penderwydd*! Llew! Help! Come quickly!"

We turned to see a warrior running towards us. "What is it, Pebin?" I called to him. "What has happened?"

"Lord," Pebin replied, "I went to the hall to take up my watch..." he paused, glancing around quickly. "You had better come at once."

5

Good Counsel

"I will look after my father," Cynan said. "Leave me."

"Take Cynfarch to my hut," the bard ordered. "Sioned will tend him there."

Then Tegid, Pebin and I threaded our way back towards the center of the crannog, passing knots of people hurrying to the site of the fire. The embers were still smoking and ash still hot, but the clean-up was commencing. Those who had taken refuge on the shore were returning to begin the restoration.

Crossing the bridge on the main pathway we came to the cluster of low round houses that sheltered in the shadow of the great hall. Except for the smell of smoke, which permeated everything in the fortress, the houses and hall were untouched by the fire. All appeared safe and secure.

We moved quickly among the huts and across the yard separating them from the hall. "Stay here, Pebin," I instructed the warrior. "Do not let anyone in." Passing between the massive doorposts, I followed Tegid inside. Even in the dim light I could see that the iron stand had been overturned. The wooden chest bearing the Singing Stones was gone. Closer, I saw two figures huddled against the far west wall, and a third sprawled face down on the bare earth floor. They did not stir as we entered.

Approaching the nearest man, I stooped and shook him by the shoulder. When my jostling awoke no response, I rolled the man towards me. His head flopped loosely on his chest, and I knew he was dead.

"One of the warband," I said. I had seen the man before, but did not know his name.

"It is Cradawc," Tegid informed me, leaning near to see the man's face.

I lowered the body gently to the floor, cradling his neck in my hand so that his head would not strike the ground. My hand came away sticky and wet. A sick feeling spread through my gut as I looked at the dark substance on my hand. "The back of his head has been crushed," I murmured.

Tegid moved to the second man, and pressed his fingertips against the man's throat.

"Dead?" I asked.

He answered me with a nod, and turned at once to the third warrior.

"This one as well?"

"No," Tegid answered. "This one still lives."

"Who is it?"

Just then the man groaned and coughed.

"It is Gorew. Help me get him outside."

Carefully, Tegid and I carried the body from the hall and laid it gently on the ground outside. Stretching his long fingers over the fallen warrior, Tegid turned Gorew's head to the side. It was then I saw the hideous blue-black bruise bulging like an egg on the side of his temple above the right eye.

The movement brought another moan. "Gorew," Tegid said loudly, firmly.

At the sound of his name, the warrior's eyes fluttered open. "Ahhh..." The groan was a whisper.

"Rest and be easy," Tegid told him. "We are here to help you."

"They are ... gone," Gorew said, his voice a faint rattle in his throat.

"Who is gone?" Tegid asked, holding Gorew with his voice.

"The stones..." the warrior answered. "Gone... stolen..."

"We know, Gorew," I replied. The injured warrior's eyes fluttered. "Who did this to you?" I asked. "Who attacked you?"

"I, ahh... saw someone... I thought..." Gorew sighed, and closed his eyes.

"The name, Gorew. Give us the name. Who did this?" But it was no use; Gorew had lost consciousness once more.

"We will learn nothing more for the moment," Tegid said. "Let us carry him to my hut."

Pebin, staring down at Gorew, made no move, so I took his arm and directed him to help lift the wounded warrior. We carried Gorew to Tegid's hut where Cynan and Bran were now waiting. Inside, Sioned, a woman much skilled in healing, was watching over the more badly injured. Sioned spread a cloak for him over a mat of straw, and we laid Gorew down beside Cynfarch. "I will tend him now," she said.

"Who would do this?" Pebin asked as we stepped from the hut.

Who indeed, I wondered? Twenty dead so far—with more likely to follow—half the caer ruined, and the Singing Stones stolen. The damage was severe as it was brutal. I determined to lay hands to the thieves before the sun set on this day.

Summoning Bran and Cynan to me, I informed them of the theft. "The thieves set fire to the caer and used the resulting confusion to steal the Singing Stones. Gorew and the other guards were attacked and overpowered."

"The Treasure of Albion stolen?" Bran wondered. "And the guards?"

"Two were killed outright; Gorew still lives. He may yet tell us something."

Cynan's blue eyes narrowed dangerously. "He is a dead man who did this."

"Until we raise the trail, we do not know how many are involved."

"One man or a hundred," Cynan muttered, "it is all the same to me."

"Bran," I said, moving towards the hall, "raise the warband. We will begin the search at once."

The Chief Raven sped away, and Cynan and I began walking back towards the hall. As we came into the yard, the booming battlehorn sounded, and a few moments later the Ravens began flocking to the call: Garanaw, Drustwn, Niall, Emyr, Alun. Scatha arrived too, and a few moments later Bran entered with a score of warriors. All gathered around the cold hearth.

"We have been attacked by enemies," I explained, and told them about the assault during the fire. "So far, twenty are dead, and others are badly injured—Cynfarch and Gorew among them. The Singing Stones are stolen." This revelation brought an instant outcry. "We will catch the men who did this," I pledged, and my vow was echoed by a dozen more. "The search will begin at once."

I turned to Bran Bresal, my battlechief, leader of the Raven Flight. "Make ready to leave. We will ride as soon as horses are saddled."

He hesitated, glancing quickly at Scatha; a look I could not read passed between them.

"Well?" I demanded.

"It will be done as you say, lord," Bran replied, touching the back of his hand to his forehead. Calling the warband to follow him, they hurried from the hall to attend to their various tasks, leaving Cynan and Scatha alone with me.

"I am sorry, Cynan," Scatha said, touching the brawny warrior on the arm.

"The blood debt will be paid, Pen-y-Cat," he replied quietly. "Never doubt it." The pain bled raw in his voice.

Turning to me, Scatha said, "I would serve you in this, lord. Allow me to lead the warband and capture the thieves."

"I thank you, Pen-y-Cat," I declined, "but it is my place. You will serve better here. Tegid will need your help."

"Your place is here as well, Llew," she persisted. "It is time for you to think beyond yourself to those who depend on you. You need rest," Scatha suggested, pressing her point. "Stay here and rule your people."

Her words meant nothing to me. Rage flowed hot and potent through my veins, and I was in no mood for unravelling riddles. I saw but one thing clearly: the men who had practised this outrage on me would be caught and judged. "A bath is all I need," I grumbled. "The cold water will revive me."

Aching in every joint, I dragged myself back to my hut intent on bathing and changing clothes before departing. I reeked of stale sweat and smoke; my hair was singed in a dozen places, and my breecs and buskins looked as if they had been attacked by flaming moths. Inside the hut, I paused only long enough to retrieve a change of clothes, a chunk of the heavy tallow soap, and the strip of linen I used for a washcloth. I had started across the yard when Tegid emerged from his hut. I went to him.

"Gorew may recover," the bard said. "I will know more when he awakes."

"And Cynfarch?" I asked.

"Death is strong, but Cynfarch may yet prove stronger," the bard replied. "The battle will be decided before this day is done."

"Either way, I mean to have the thieves caught and the stones returned before this time tomorrow," I said.

"And are you thinking of going after them yourself?" he asked pointedly.

"Of course! I am the king. It is my duty."

The bard bristled at this, and opened his mouth to object. I did not want to hear it, so I cut him off. "Save your breath, Tegid. I am leading the warband, and that is that."

Turning on my heel, I stalked away across the yard, through the gate, and out to the boat landing. At one end of the landing, the rock base of the crannog formed a shallow area many used as a bathing-place. But there was no one else about.

I stripped off my clothes and slipped into the water; the icy sting on my scorched hide felt like a balm. Sinking gratefully into the water, I floated submerged except for forehead and nose.

The sun rose higher, burning through the thin grey mist while I busied myself with the soap. I washed my hair and scrubbed my skin raw with the cloth. When I lowered myself into the water to rinse, I felt like a snake sloughing off its old dead skin.

I was shaking water from my hair when Goewyn arrived.

"Scatha has told me what has happened," she said. She stood on the landing above me with her arms crossed. Her face was smudged with soot, and her hair was tangled and powdered with ash. Her once-white mantle was leopard-spotted with black and brown burnmarks.

I almost salmon-leaped from the water for, until the moment I saw her again, I had completely forgotten that I was a married man now and had a wife waiting for me.

"Goewyn, I am so sorry, I forgot that—"

"She says you are planning to ride out," she continued coldly. "If you care anything for your people, or what has happened here this night, you will not go."

"But I must go," I insisted. "I am the king; it is my duty."

"If you are a king," she said, flinging each word separately for emphasis, "stay here and act like a king. Rule your people. Rebuild your stronghold."

"What of the Singing Stones? What of the thieves?"

"Send your battlechief and warriors to bring them back. That is what a true king would do."

"It is my place," I replied, moving towards her.

"You are wrong. Your place is here with your people. You should not be seen chasing these—these *cynrhon!*" She used a word seldom used of another in Albion; I had never seen her so angry. "Are you above them?"

"Of course, Goewyn, but I—"

"Then show it!" she snapped. "Are these thieves kings that it takes a king to capture them?"

"No, but—" I began, and was quickly cut off.

"Hear me, Llew Silver Hand: if you allow your enemy to prevent you from ruling, he is more powerful than you—and the whole of Albion will know it."

"Goewyn, please. You do not understand."

"Do I not?" she demanded, and did not wait for my answer. "Will not Bran serve you with the last breath of his body? Will not Cynan move mountains at your word? Will not the Ravens seize the sun and stars to please you?"

"Listen—if I am a king at all, it is because the Singing Stones have made me so."

"You are not just another king. You are the Aird Righ! You *are* Albion. That is why you cannot go."

"Goewyn, please. Be reasonable." I must have presented a forlorn spectacle standing up to my navel in cold water, shivering and dripping, for she softened somewhat.

"Do not behave as a man without rank and power," she said, and I began to see the shape of her logic. "If you are a king, my love, then *be* a king. Demonstrate your authority and might. Demonstrate your wisdom: send Bran and the Raven Flight. Yes. Send Cynan. Send Calbha and Scatha and a hundred warriors. Send everyone! But do not go yourself. Do not become the thing you seek to destroy."

"You sound just like Tegid," I replied, attempting—clumsily—to lighten the mood. It seemed absurd for both of us to be angry.

"Then you should listen to your wise bard," she replied imperiously. "He is giving you good counsel."

Goewyn stood with her arms crossed over her breast, regarding me with implacable eyes, waiting for my reply. I was beaten and I knew it. She was right: a true king would never risk the honor of his sovereignty by chasing criminals across the kingdom.

"Lady, I stand rebuked," I said, spreading my hands. "Also I stand shivering and cold. I will do as you say, only let me come out of the water before I freeze."

"Far be it from me to prevent you," she said, her lips curving ever so slightly at the corners.

"So be it." I took another step towards her, climbing from the water. She stooped and shook out the cloak, holding it out for me to step into.

I turned my back to her and she draped the cloak over my shoulders. Her hands travelled slowly down my back, and then her arms encircled my waist. I turned in her embrace, put my arms around her and held her close. "You will get wet," I told her.

"I need a bath," she replied, then, realizing the truth of what she had said, at once pushed me away and held me at arm's length.

"I have washed," I protested.

"But I have not." She withdrew a quick step.

"Wait—"

"Come home, husband," she called, "but not until you have told Tegid that you are staying in Dinas Dwr, and not until you have sent the Raven Flight to work your will."

"Goewyn, wait, I will go with you—"

"I will be waiting, husband," she called, disappearing through the gate.

I pulled on my breecs, stuffed my arms into the sleeves of the siarc, snatched up my buskins, and hurried back to Tegid's hut to inform him of my change of plan.

Cynan Two-Torcs

I called Tegid from his hut. He emerged looking hunched and old; his dark hair was grey with ash, and his face seemed just as colorless. His eyes were bloodshot from smoke and exhaustion. He must have been dead on his feet. I instantly felt guilty for taking a bath, leaving everyone else to do the work.

"Wise Bard," I said, "I have changed my mind. I am staying in Dinas Dwr. I will send Bran and the Raven Flight to capture the thieves and bring back the Singing Stones."

"A prudent decision, lord," Tegid said, nodding with narrow satisfaction.

"Yes, so I am told."

Emyr Lydaw hailed me just then and came running to say that the warband was ready. "Assemble at the landing," I commanded. "Tegid and I will join you there."

"Come," I told Tegid, taking him by the arm and leading him towards the hall, "we will eat something before we join them. The king and his bard must not be seen to swoon with hunger."

Tegid declared himself well satisfied with this sentiment—it showed I was beginning to think like a king. We stopped long enough for a loaf and a drink of the sweetened water left over from the wedding feast. Thus refreshed, we made our way to the landing.

The Ravens, singed and bedraggled from the night's ordeal, were loading the last of their provisions into the boats. Cynan stood a few paces apart, a spear in each hand, staring at the water. Alun and Drustwn greeted me as we approached. Bran turned from the task to say, "All is ready, lord. We await your command."

"I am needed here—I will not accompany you. And you do not require my help to capture these low criminals," I explained. "I charge you to do this work swiftly and return with all haste."

Bran, somewhat relieved by my change of plan, replied, "I hear and will obey, lord."

Cynan, his jaw hard and his brow set in a lethal scowl, said nothing, but stared away across the lake to the strand where Niall and Garanaw waited with the horses. "Good hunting, brother," I told him.

He nodded curtly and climbed into one of the boats. The others joined him, and the boats pushed away from the landing. We bade them farewell then, and the boats withdrew. The oarsmen had not pulled three strokes, however, when the woman Sioned appeared at the gate.

"Penderwydd!" she called, and came running when she saw him.

"What is it, Sioned?" Tegid turned to meet her, grey eyes quick with concern.

"He is dead," she said hastily. "King Cynfarch has died, Penderwydd. Eleri is with him. He just stopped breathing and—that was all."

Tegid made to hurry away; he took two quick steps, then paused, glancing back over his shoulder towards the departing boats. He opened his mouth to speak, but I spoke first. "Go," I told him. "I will tell Cynan."

While the Chief Bard hastened towards the gate, I called the boats back. "Cynan," I said when he was close enough to hear, "it is your father."

He saw the figures of Tegid and the woman hurrying away, and he guessed the worst. "Is my father dead?"

"Yes, brother. I am sorry."

At my words, Cynan stood upright in the boat, rising so suddenly that he almost tipped it over. As soon as the oarsman brought the vessel near the landing, Cynan leaped from the boat and started towards the gate.

I caught him as he passed. "Cynan, I am sending the Raven Flight without you."

His face darkened and he started to protest, but I held firm. "I know how you feel, brother, but you will be needed here. Your people are without a king now. Your place is with them."

He glanced away, the conflict hot within. "Let them go, Cynan," I urged. "It is for Bran to serve me in this. It is for us to stay."

Cynan's eyes flicked from mine to the boat and back again. Without a word he turned and hurried away.

From the boat Bran called, "Would you have us wait for him, lord?"

"No, Bran," I replied, sending the Raven Chief away. "Cynan will not accompany you now."

I watched as the boats landed on the opposite shore and the pack animals were quickly loaded. The Ravens mounted; Bran lofted a spear and the warriors moved off along the lakeshore. I raised my silver hand in salute to them, and held the salute until they were well away. Then I turned and began walking back to the hall. In truth, I was secretly glad not to be riding with them. Weary to the bone, I longed for nothing more than sleep.

Instead, I returned to Tegid's hut where Cynan had taken up vigil beside his father's body. "There is nothing to be done here," Tegid told me. "You need rest, Llew. Go now while you may; I will summon you if you are needed."

Unwilling to leave, I hesitated, but the bard placed his hand firmly on my shoulder, turned me, and sent me away. I started across the small yard to my hut, and then remembered I had a different home now. I turned aside and went instead to the hut prepared for Goewyn and me. It seemed an age since our wedding night.

Goewyn was waiting for me inside. She had bathed and put on a new white robe. Her hair was hanging down, still wet from washing. She was sitting on the bed, combing out the tangles with a wide-toothed wooden comb. She smiled as I came in, rose, and welcomed me with a kiss. Then, taking my silver hand in both of hers, she led me to the bed, removed my cloak and pushed me gently down onto the deep-piled fleece. She stretched herself beside me. I put my arms around her, and promptly fell asleep.

I came awake with a start. The hut was dark, and the caer was quiet. Pale moonlight showed beneath the oxhide at the door. My movement woke Goewyn, and she put her warm hand on the back of my neck.

"It is night," she whispered. "Lie down and go back to sleep."

"But I am not tired any more," I told her, lowering myself onto my elbow.

"Neither am I," she said. "Are you hungry?"

"Ravenous."

"There is a little wedding bread. And we have mead."

"Wonderful."

She rose and went to the small hearth in the center of the room. I watched her, graceful as a ghost in the pale moonlight, kneeling to her work. In a few moments, a yellow petal of flame licked out and a fire blossomed on the hearth. Instantly, the interior of our bower was bathed in shimmering golden light. Goewyn retrieved the meadskin and cup, and two small loaves of *banys bara*.

She settled herself beside me on the bed once more, broke the bread and fed me the first bite. Whereupon, I broke off a piece and fed her. We finished the first loaf, and the second, then pulled the stopper from the meadskin and lay back to savor its sweetness and warmth, sharing the golden nectar between us in a string of kisses, each more ardent than the last.

I could wait no longer. Laying aside the meadskin, I reached up and gathered her to me. She came into my arms, all softness and warmth, and we abandoned ourselves to the heady delight of our bodies.

Conscious that my metal hand would be cold, I did my best to keep it from touching her—no easy task, for I desired nothing more than to stroke her hair and caress her skin. But Goewyn put me at my ease.

Kneeling beside me, she opened her robe and took my silver hand in both of hers. "It is part of you now," she said, her voice soft and low, "so it shall be no less part of me." Raising my metal hand she pressed it between her exquisite breasts.

The tenderness of this act filled me with awe. I lost myself then in passion. Goewyn was all my universe and she was enough.

Later, we poured mead into a golden cup and drank it in bed. Our wedding night, although untimely interrupted, was all we could have hoped it would be.

"It seems as if I have never lived until now," I told her.

Lips curling deliciously, Goewyn raised the cup to her lips. "Do not think this night is finished yet," she said.

And so we made love again, with passion, to be sure, but without the haste of our previous coupling; we could afford to take our pleasure more slowly this time. Some time towards dawn we fell asleep in one another's arms. But I do not recall the closing of my eyes. I remember only Goewyn, her breath sweet on my skin, and the warmth of her body next to mine.

That night was but a moment's respite from the cares and concerns of the days that followed. Yet, I rose next morning invincible, more than a match for whatever the future held in store. There was work to be done, and I was eager to begin.

I found Tegid and a somber Cynan in the hall, sitting at bread, discussing Cynfarch's funeral. It had been decided that Cynan would return with his people to Dun Cruach for the burial. They must leave at once.

"I would it were otherwise," Cynan told me. His eyes were red and his voice a rasp. "I had wished to stay and help rebuild the caer."

"I know, brother; I know," I answered. "But we have hands enough to serve. I wish I could go with you."

Our talk turned to provisioning his people for the journey. Because of the fire and the long drought before it, our supplies were not what they might have been. Still, I wanted to send him back with enough not only for the journey but for a fair time beyond it.

Lord Calbha, who would be returning to his own lands one day soon, oversaw the loading of the Galanae wagons. After a while, Calbha entered the hall to announce that all was ready; we rose reluctantly, and followed him out. "I will send word when we have caught the thieves," I promised as we stepped out into the yard.

"Until that day," Cynan replied gravely, "I will drink neither ale nor mead, and no fire shall burn in the hearth in the king's hall. Dun Cruach will remain in darkness."

Some of the Galanae warriors standing near heard Cynan's vow and approached. "We would have a king to lead us home," they said. "It is not right that we should enter our realm without a king to go before us."

Tegid, hearing their request, placed a fold of his cloak over his head and said, "Your request is honorable. Have you a man of nobility worthy to be king?"

The Galanae answered, "We have, Penderwydd."

"Name this man, and bring him before me."

"He is standing beside you now, Penderwydd," they said. "It is Cynan Machae and no other."

Tegid turned and placed his hand on Cynan's shoulder. "Is there anything to prevent you from assuming your father's throne?" Tegid asked him.

Cynan ran his hand through his wiry red hair, and thought for a moment. "Nothing that I know," he replied at last.

"Your people have chosen you," Tegid said, "and I do not think a better choice could be made. As Chief Bard of Albion, I will confer the kingship at once if you will accept it."

"I will accept it gladly," he replied.

"It would be well to establish your reign with the proper ceremony," Tegid explained. "But the journey will not wait, therefore we will hold the kingmaking now."

68

Cynan's kingmaking was accomplished with the least possible ceremony. Scatha and Goewyn stood with me, Calbha watching, and the Galanae gathered close about as Tegid said the words. It was simply done and quickly over—the only interruption in the swift affair came when Tegid made to remove Cynan's torc and replace it with the one Cynfarch had worn.

"The gold torc is the symbol of your sovereignty," Tegid told him. "By it all men will know that you are king and deserving of respect and honor."

Cynan agreed, but would not surrender his silver torc. "Give me the gold torc if you will, but I am not giving up the torc my father gave me."

"Wear it always—and this as well." So saying, the bard slipped the gold torc around Cynan's neck and, raising his hands over him, shouted, "King of the Galanae in Caledon, I do proclaim you. Hail, Cynan Two-Torcs!"

Everyone laughed at this—including Cynan, who from that moment wore his new name as proudly as he wore his two torcs.

I embraced him—Scatha and Goewyn likewise—and in the next breath we were bidding him farewell. Cynan was anxious to return to the south to bury his father and begin his reign. We crossed to the plain and accompanied him on horseback as far as Druim Vran, where we waited on the ridgetop as the Galanae passed. When the last wagon had crested the ridge and begun its long, slow way down the other side, Cynan turned to me and said, "Here I am, sorry to be gone and I have not yet left. The burden of a king is weighty indeed." He sighed heavily.

"Yet, I think you will survive."

"It is well for you," he replied, "but I have no beautiful woman to marry me and I must shoulder the weight alone."

"I would marry you, Cynan," Goewyn offered amiably, "but I have already wed Llew. Still, I think you will not long suffer the lack of a bride. Certainly a king with two torcs will be a most desirable husband."

Cynan rolled his eyes. "Och! I am not king so much as a single day and already wily females are scheming to separate me from my treasure."

"Brother," I said, "think yourself fortunate if you find a woman willing to marry you at any price. Ten torcs would be not one torc too many to give for a wife."

"No doubt you are right," Cynan admitted. "But until I find a woman as worthy as the one you have found I will keep my treasure."

Goewyn leaned across and kissed him on the cheek. We then waved him on his way, watching until he reached the valley below and took his place at the head of his people. Goewyn was quiet beside me as we rode back to the lake.

I turned to her and said, "Marry me, Goewyn."

She laughed. "But I have already married you, best beloved."

"I wanted to hear you say it again."

"Then hear me, Llew Silver Hand," she said. She straightened in the saddle, holding her head erect and proud. "I marry you this day, and tomorrow, and each tomorrow until tomorrows cease."

7

The Ravens' Return

Work on the restoration of Dinas Dwr proceeded at once with brisk efficiency. The people seemed especially eager to eliminate all traces of the fire. The people, my people—my patchwork cloak of a clan, made up of various tribes and kin, warriors, farmers, artisans, families, widows, orphans, refugees each and every one—labored tirelessly to repair the damage to the crannog and put everything right once more. As I toiled beside them, I came to understand that Dinas Dwr was more to them than a refuge; it had become home. Former bonds and attachments were either broken or breaking down, and a new kinship was being forged: in the sweat of our striving together, we were becoming a singular people, a clan as distinct as any tribe in Albion.

Life in the crannog, so cruelly assaulted by fire and the Great Hound's desolations, soon began to assume its former rhythm. Tegid summoned his Mabinogi and reinstated their daily lessons in bardic lore. Scatha likewise mustered her pupils and the practice yard rang to the shouts of the young warriors and the clatter of wooden swords on leather shields once more. The farmers returned to their sun-ravaged crops, hopeful of saving some part of the harvest now that the drought had broken. The cowherds and shepherds devoted themselves to replenishing their stocks as the meadows began greening once more.

As I surveyed the work of restoration, it seemed to me that everyone had determined to put the recent horror behind them as quickly as possible and sought release from the hateful memories by striving to make of Dinas Dwr a paradise in the north. But the wounds went deep and, despite the ardent industry of the people, it would be a very long time before Albion was healed. This, I told myself, was why I must stay: to see the land revived and the people redeemed. Yes, the healing had begun; for the first time in years men and women could face the future with something other than deepest dread and despair.

Thus, when the Raven Flight reappeared with their prisoner a scant few days after riding out, we all deemed it a favourable sign. "You see!" men said to one another. "No one can stand against Silver Hand! All his enemies are conquered at last."

We greeted the Ravens' return warmly, and acclaimed the obvious success of their undertaking: riding with them was a sullen, doleful, solitary prisoner—made to sit backwards in the saddle, with hands bound behind his back and his cloak wound over his head and shoulders.

"Hail, Raven Flight, and greetings!" I called as the boat touched shore. A number of us had rowed from the crannog to meet them; we scrambled ashore as the Ravens dismounted. "I see you enjoyed a successful hunt."

"Swift the hunt, great the prize," Bran agreed tersely. "But not without sacrifice, as Niall will soon tell you."

"How so?" I asked and, turning, saw the blood-soaked bandage beneath Niall's cloak.

The injured Raven dismissed my alarm with a wave of his hand—though even that slight movement made him wince. "Zeal made me careless, lord," he replied, speaking through clenched teeth. "It will not happen again, I assure you. Yet, I was fortunate; the swordstroke caught me as I fell. It might have been worse."

"His head might have parted company with his neck," Alun Tringad informed me. "Though whether that be for the worse, or for the better, we cannot decide."

This brought a laugh from the small crowd that had gathered to hail the Ravens' success and learn the identity of the malefactor they had captured.

"A most disagreeable prisoner, this one," Bran affirmed. "He chose death and was determined to have us accompany him."

"We came upon him by surprise," Drustwn offered, "or he would surely have taken two or more of us down with him."

It was then I saw that both Drustwn and Emyr were also wounded: Drustwn held his arm close to his body, and Emyr's leg was wrapped in a thick bandage just above the knee. When I inquired about their injuries, Drustwn assured me that they would heal far faster than the pride of their prisoner, which he reckoned had suffered harm beyond recovery.

"The worse for us, if he had not slipped on the wet grass and fallen on his head," Garanaw added; he made a motion with his hand, indicating how it happened, and everyone laughed again. It was a far from happy sound, however; they laughed out of relief mostly, and also to humiliate the captive further. Not for a moment had anyone forgotten the outrage done to us.

"I am glad none of you were more seriously hurt," I told them. "Your sacrifice will not be overlooked. All of you," I said, raising my silver hand to them, "have earned a fine reward and the increased esteem of your king."

Bran declared himself satisfied with the latter, but Alun avowed that for his part the former would not be unwelcome. The prisoner, who had maintained a seething silence up to then, came to life once more. Twisting in the saddle, the man strained around to yell defiantly: "Loose me, sons of bitches! Then we will see how well you fare in an even fight!"

At these words, a chill touched my heart—not for what he said, but for the voice itself. I knew this man.

"Get him down," I instructed. "And take away the cloak. I want to see his face."

The Ravens hauled the captive roughly from the saddle and

forced him to his knees before me. Bran seized a corner of the cloak, untied it, and pulled the cloak away to reveal a face I recognized and did not care to see again.

Paladyr had not changed much since last I saw him: the night he had put a knife through Meldryn Mawr's heart. True, I had glimpsed him momentarily on the clifftop at Ynys Sci when he had hurled Gwenllian to her death, but I had not had a good look at him then. Seeing him now, I was amazed again at his immense size—every limb enormous, thick-muscled shoulders above a torso that might have been hewn from the trunk of an oak tree. Even men like Bran, Drustwn and Alun Tringad seemed slight next to Prydain's one-time champion.

He had not given up without a fight, however, and the Ravens had not been over-gentle with him. An ugly purple bruise bulged at one temple, his nose was swollen, and his lower lip was split. But his arrogance was as staggering as ever, and his fiery defiance undimmed.

"Bring Tegid," I said to the man nearest me, unwilling to turn my back on Paladyr. "Tell him to come at once."

"The Chief Bard is here, lord," the man replied. "He is coming now."

I turned to see Tegid and Calbha hastening to join us. The sight of Paladyr kneeling before us halted both men in their steps.

Tegid regarded the defiant captive with grim satisfaction. Upon seeing the Chief Bard of Albion, Paladyr clamped his mouth shut, malice burning from his baleful eyes. After a moment, Tegid turned to Bran, "Had he the Singing Stones with him?"

"That he had, Penderwydd," replied Bran. He gestured to Drustwn, who produced a leather bag from behind his saddle, and brought it to us.

"We caught him with them," Garanaw explained. "And we are pleased to restore them to their rightful place in Dinas Dwr." He opened the chest briefly to show that the pale stones were indeed still within; then he passed the chest to Tegid's keeping.

"Was he alone? Did you find anyone with him?" Lord Calbha

asked. I watched Paladyr's expression carefully, but he remained stony-faced, without the slightest flicker of a sign that what I said concerned him.

"No, lord," the Raven Chief answered. "We searched the region, and watched well the trail behind us. We saw no sign of anyone with him."

Turning to some of the men who had gathered with us, I said, "Make ready a storehouse here on the shore to receive our prisoner, for I will not allow him to set foot on the crannog again."

To Lord Calbha, I said, "Send your swiftest rider to Dun Cruach. Tell Cynan we have captured the man responsible for his father's death, and we await his return so that justice can be satisfied."

"It will be done, Silver Hand," the king of the Cruin replied. "He is not so many days away—we may overtake him before reaching Dun Cruach." Calbha then summoned one of his clansmen and the two moved at once.

"What will you do with the Stones of Song?" asked Tegid, holding the bag.

"I have in mind a place for them," I answered, tapping the bag with a finger. "They will not be so easily stolen again."

Leaving our prisoner in the care of a score of warriors, Tegid, Calbha and the Ravens returned with me to the hall where I pointed to the firepit in the center of the great room. "Raise the hearthstone," I said, "and bury the Singing Stones beneath it. No one will be able to take them without alerting the whole crannog."

"Well said, lord," Bran agreed. Tools were brought and, after a great deal of effort, the massive hearthstone in the center of the hall was raised and held in place while a small hole was dug beneath it. The oak chest was put in the hole and the hearthstone lowered into place once more.

"All men bear witness!" declared Tegid, raising his hands in declamation. "Now is Dinas Dwr established on an unshakable foundation."

I dismissed the Ravens to their well-earned rest, and then summoned Scatha and Goewyn to the hall where I informed them that the thief responsible for killing Cynfarch, stealing the stones, and setting fire to the caer had been captured. "It is Paladyr," I said.

Goewyn allowed a small gasp to escape her lips; Scatha's face hardened and her manner grew brittle. "Where is he?"

"He had the Singing Stones with him. There is no doubt he is guilty."

"Where is he?" she asked again, each word a shard of frozen hate.

"We have locked him in a storehouse on the shore," I answered. "He will be guarded day and night until we have decided what is to be done with him."

She turned at once. "Scatha, wait!" I called after her, but she would not be deterred.

When I caught up with her again, Scatha was standing outside the storehouse, railing at the guards to open the door and let her go in. They were relieved to see me approach.

"Come away, Pen-y-Cat," I said. "You can do nothing here."

She turned on me. "He killed my daughters! The blood debt must be paid!" She meant to collect that debt then and there.

"He will not escape again," I soothed. "Let it be this way for now, Pen-y-Cat. I have sent word to Cynan, and we will hold court as soon as he returns."

"I want to see the animal who killed my daughters," she insisted. "I want to see his face."

"You shall see him," I promised. "Soon—wait but a little. Please, Scatha, listen to me. We can do nothing until Cynan returns."

"I will *see* him." The pleading in her voice was more forceful than my own misgivings.

"Very well." I gestured to the guards to open the door. "Bring him out."

Paladyr shambled into the light. His hands were bound and chains had been placed on his feet. He appeared slightly less insolent than before, and gazed at us warily.

Quick as the flick of a cat's tail, Scatha's knife was out and at Paladyr's throat. "Nothing would give me greater pleasure than to gut you like a pig," she said, drawing the knife across the skin of his throat. A tiny red line appeared behind the moving knifepoint.

Paladyr stiffened, but uttered no sound.

"Scatha! No!" I said, pulling her away. "You have seen him, now let it be."

Paladyr's mouth twitched into a faintly mocking smile. Scatha saw the smirk on his face, drew herself up and spat full in his face. Anger flared instantly, and I thought he would strike her, but the one-time champion caught himself. Trembling with rage, he swallowed hard and glared murderously at her.

"Take him away," I ordered the guards and, turning back to Scatha, I watched her walk away, head high, eyes brimming with unshed tears.

Upon Cynan's return a few days later, I convened the first *llys* of my reign; to judge the murderer. Meting out judgment was the main work of a king's llys, and if anyone stood in need of judgment it was Paladyr. The verdict was a forgone conclusion: death.

My chair was established at the head, or west end, of the hall. Wearing Meldryn Mawr's torc and the Great King's oak-leaf crown, I stepped to the chair and sat down: Goewyn and Tegid took their places—my queen standing beside me, her hand resting on my left shoulder, and my Chief Bard at my right hand.

When everyone had assembled, the carynx sounded and the Penderwydd of Albion stepped forward. Placing a fold of his cloak over his head, he raised his staff and held it lengthwise above him. "People of Dinas Dwr," he said boldly, "heed the voice of wisdom! This day your king sits in judgment. His word is law, and his law is justice. Hear me now: there is no other justice but the word of the king."

With three resounding cracks of his staff on the stone at my feet, Tegid returned to his place beside me. "Bring the prisoner!" he called.

The crowd parted and six warriors led Paladyr forward. But if his captivity had cowed him even in the slightest, he did not show it. Prydain's one-time champion appeared as haughty as ever, smiling smugly to himself, his head high and his eye unflinching. Clearly, he had lost none of his insolence in captivity. He stalked to the foot of my throne and stood there with his feet apart, and a smirk on his face.

When Bran saw how brazenly his prisoner regarded me, the Raven Chief forced Paladyr to kneel, dealing him several sharp blows behind the knees with the butt of his spear. Not that this altered the prisoner's demeanor appreciably; he still regarded me with a strange disdainful expression—the condemned man's way of displaying courage, I thought.

The hall was deathly silent. Every man and woman present knew what Paladyr had done, and more than a few burned to see the blood-debt settled. Tegid regarded the prisoner coolly, gripping his staff as a warrior would a spear. "This is the court of Llew Silver Hand, Aird Righ of Albion," he said, his voice a lash of authority. "This day you will receive the justice you have long eluded."

At Tegid's mention of the High Kingship, Paladyr's eyes flicked from Tegid to me. He seemed somewhat taken aback by that, and it produced the first hint of anything approaching fear I had ever seen in Prydain's former champion. Or was it something else?

The Chief Bard, acting as my voice, continued, grave and stern. "Who brings grievance against this man?"

Several women—the mothers of suffocated infants—cried out at once, and others—the wives of the dead warriors—added their voices to the chorus. "Murderer!" they screamed. "I accuse him! He killed my child!" some said, and others, "He killed my husband!"

Tegid allowed the outcry to continue for a time, and then called for silence. "We have heard your accusation," he said. "Who else brings grievance against this man?"

Scatha, cold and sharp as the blade at her side, stepped forward. "For the murder of my daughter, Gwenllian, Banfáith of Ynys Sci, I do accuse him. And for his part in the murder of my daughter, Govan, Gwyddon of Ynys Sci, I do accuse him." These words were spoken with icy clarity and great dignity; I realized she had rehearsed them countless times in anticipation of this day.

Bran Bresal spoke next, taking his place beside Scatha. "For stealing the Treasure of Albion, and killing the men who guarded that treasure, I do accuse him."

Stepping forward, Cynan shouted, "For starting the fire that took my father's life and the lives of innocent men, women, and children, I do accuse him."

His voice cut like a swordstroke through an atmosphere grown dense with pent-up rage, and his words brought another outburst, which Tegid patiently allowed to play itself out. Then he asked for silence again. "We have heard your accusations. For the third and last time, who brings grievance against this man?"

When no one else made bold to answer, I stood. I did not know if it was proper for me to speak in this way, nor did I care. I had a grievance that went back further than any of the others and I wanted it heard. "I also bring grievance against this man," I said, pointing my finger in Paladyr's face. "It is my belief that you, with the help of others now dead, sought out and murdered the Phantarch, thereby bringing about the destruction of Prydain."

This revelation sent a dark murmur coursing through the tight-pressed crowd. "However," I continued, "as I possess no proof of your part in this unthinkable crime, I cannot bring accusation against you." Raising my silver hand, I pointed my finger directly at him. "But with my own eyes I saw you murder Meldryn Mawr, who held the kingship before me. While pretending repentance you took the Great King's life. For this act of treachery and murder, I do accuse you."

I sat down. Tegid raised and lowered his staff three times slowly. "We have heard grievous accusations against you, Paladyr. We have heard how by your hand you murdered your king, Meldryn Mawr. We have heard how by your hand you murdered Gwenllian, Banfáith of Ynys Sci, and violated the ancient *geas* of protection which was the right of all who sheltered in that realm.

"You contrived to steal the Treasure of Albion, using flames to conceal your crime—flames which took the lives of a score of men, women, and infant children. In order to obtain the treasure, you did strike down the warriors pledged to guard it, and by stealth did you remove the treasure from Dinas Dwr."

The Chief Bard continued, slashing like a whip, his voice ringing in the rooftrees. "Ever and again you have betrayed your people and repaid loyalty with treachery; you have practised treason against the

79

one you were sworn to protect with your life. You sought gain through deception in the service of a false king; you sold your honor for promises of wealth and rank, and squandered your strength in evil. By reason of these acts your name has become a curse in the mouths of men."

No one moved; not a sound was heard when he had finished. The people stood as if stunned into silence by the enormity of Paladyr's crimes. For his part, however, the prisoner seemed vaguely contrite but not overly concerned by his predicament. He merely stared with downcast eyes—as if contemplating the patch of floor between him and my throne. I imagine he had long ago come to terms with the risks of his wrongdoing.

"For these crimes, no less than for the crimes you pursued in the service of the Great Hound Meldron, you are condemned," Tegid declared. "Do you have anything to say before you hear the judgment of your king?"

Paladyr remained unmoved, and I thought he would not speak. But he slowly raised his head and looked Tegid square in the eye. Arrogant to the end, he said, "I have heard your words, bard. You condemn me and that is your right. I do not deny it."

His eyes flicked to me then, and I felt my stomach tighten in apprehension. Looking directly at me, Paladyr said, "But now you tell me that I am in the presence of the High King of Albion. If that is so, let us prove the kingship he boasts. Hear me now: I make the claim of *naud*."

The words hung in the silence of the hall for a moment. Tegid's face went white. Everyone else stared at the kneeling Paladyr in mute and somewhat dazed astonishment. Unwilling to believe what we had all heard quite plainly, Tegid said, "You claim naud?"

Emboldened by the effect of his claim, Paladyr rose to his feet. "I stand condemned before the king. Therefore, I do make the claim of naud for my crimes. Grant it if you will."

"No!" someone shouted. I looked and saw Scatha, swaying on her feet as one wounded by the thrust of a spear. She shouted again, and Bran, beside her, put his arms around her—whether to comfort or to keep her from attacking Paladyr, I could not say. "No! It will not be!" she screamed, her face contorted with rage.

"No..." moaned Goewyn softly. Lips trembling, eyes blinking back tears, she turned her face away.

Cynan, fists clenched, fought forward, straining like a bull; Drustwn, Niall and Garanaw threw their arms around him and kept him from the prisoner's neck. Behind them, the crowd surged forward dangerously, calling for Paladyr's death.

Stern and forbidding, Tegid shouted them down. "Silence!" he cried. "There will be silence before the throne!" The Ravens took it in hand to hold back the crowd, and in a moment the crisis passed. Having restored a semblance of order, the Chief Bard turned to me, visibly upset. He bent low in consultation.

"I will refuse him." I said.

"You cannot," he said; though stunned and heartsick, he was thinking more clearly than I.

"I do not care. I will not allow him to walk away from this."

"You must," he said simply. "You have no choice."

"But why?" I blurted in frustration. "I do not understand, Tegid. There must be something we can do."

He shook his head gravely. "There is nothing to be done. Paladyr has made the claim of naud, and you must grant it," he explained, "or the Sovereignty of Albion will belong to a treasonous murderer."

What Tegid said was true, practically speaking. The claim of naud was partly an appeal for clemency—like throwing oneself on the mercy of the court. But there was more to it than that, for it went beyond justice, it transcended right and wrong and went straight to the heart of sovereignty itself.

In making the claim, the guilty man not only invoked the king's mercy, he effectively shifted responsibility for the crime to the king himself. The king had a choice, of course—he could grant it, or he could refuse. If he granted the claim, the crime was expunged: the punishment that justice demanded, justice itself would fulfill. Naturally, only the king could reconcile himself to himself.

If the king refused the claim, however, the guilty man would have to face the punishment justice decreed. A simple enough choice, one would think, but in refusing to grant naud, the king effectively declared himself inferior to the criminal. No king worthy of the name would lower himself in that way, nor allow his kingship to be so disgraced.

Viewed from the proper angle, this backwards logic becomes curiously lucid. In Albion, justice is not an abstract concept dealing with the punishment of crime. To the people of Albion, justice wears a human face. If the king's word is law to all who shelter beneath his protection, then the king himself becomes justice for his people. The king is justice incarnate.

This personal feature of justice means that the guilty man can make a claim on the king which he has no right to make: naud. And once having made the claim it is up to the king, in his role as justice, to demonstrate his integrity. Justice, then, is limited only by the king's character—that is, justice is limited only by the king's personal conception of himself as king.

Thus, the claim of naud swings on this question: how great is the king?

Paladyr had rightly divined the question, and had determined to put it to the test. If I refused his claim, it would be tantamount to admitting that my sovereignty was restricted in its breadth and power. What is more, all men would know the precise limits of my authority.

If, on the other hand, I granted Paladyr his claim of naud, I would show myself greater than his crimes. For if my sovereignty could extend beyond even Paladyr's offences, then I must be a very great king indeed. As Aird Righ, my kingly power and authority would be deemed well-nigh infinite.

Oh, but it was a very hard thing. In essence, I had been asked to absorb the crime into myself. If I did that, a guilty man would walk free.

Tegid was frowning, glaring into my face as if I were the cause of his irritation. "Well, Silver Hand? What is your answer?"

I looked at Paladyr. His crimes screamed for punishment. Certainly, no man ever deserved death more.

"I will grant him naud," I said, feeling as if I had been kicked in the gut. "But," I added quickly, "am I allowed to set conditions?"

"You may establish provisions for the protection of your people," my bard cautioned. "Nothing more."

"Very well, let us send him to some place where he cannot harm anyone again. Is there such a place?"

Tegid's grey eyes narrowed in sly approval. "Tir Aflan," he said.

"The Foul Land? Where is that?" In all my time in Albion, I had rarely heard mention of the place.

"In the east, across the sea," he explained. "To one born in Albion it is a joyless, desolate place." Tegid allowed himself a grim smile. "It may be that Paladyr will wish himself dead."

"So be it. That is my judgment: banish him to Tir Aflan, and may he rot there in misery."

Tegid straightened and turned to address Paladyr. He raised his staff and brought it down with a crack. "Hear the judgment of the king," he intoned. "You have made the claim of naud and your claim is granted."

This declaration caused an instant sensation. Shouts filled the hall; some cried aloud at the decision, others wept silently. Tegid raised his staff and demanded for silence before continuing. "It is the king's judgment that, for the protection of Albion's people, you are banished from all lands under his authority."

Paladyr's expression hardened. Likely, he had not foreseen this development. I could see him working through the implications in his mind. He drew himself up and demanded, "If all lands lie under your authority, Great King," the words were mockery in his mouth, "where am I to go?"

A good question, which showed Paladyr was paying attention. If I was the High King, all of Albion was under my authority. Clearly, there was no place on the Island of the Mighty, or any of its sister isles, where he could go. But Tegid was ready with the answer.

"To Tir Aflan you will go," he replied bluntly. "And wherever you find men to receive you, there you will abide. Know you this:

from the day you set foot in Tir Aflan it is death to you to return to Albion."

Paladyr accepted his fate with icy dignity. He said nothing more, and was escorted from the hall by Bran and the Ravens. Tegid declared the llys concluded. And the people began filing grimly from the hall, shattered, their hearts broken.

8

The Cylchedd

At dawn the next morning, the Ravens and some of the warband left Dinas Dwr to escort Paladyr to the eastern coast where he would be shipped across Mór Glas and set free on the blasted shore of Tir Aflan. Cynan, bitter and angry, left a short while later to return to Dun Cruach. In all, it was a miserable parting.

Over the next days, work on the fire-damaged caer progressed. New timber was cut and hauled from the ridge forest to the lakeshore where it was trimmed and shaped to use for rooftrees and walls. Reeds for thatch were cut in quantity and spread on the rocks to dry. The burnt timber was removed and the ground prepared for new dwellings and storehouses; quantities of ash were transported across the lake and spread on the fields. I would have been happy to see this work to its completion—the sight of the fire-blackened rubble ached in me like a wound, and the sooner Dinas Dwr was restored, the sooner the pain would cease. But Tegid had other ideas.

At supper one night after the Ravens had returned from disposing of Paladyr, Tegid rose and stood before the hearth. Those looking on assumed he meant to sing, and so began calling out the names of songs they would hear. *"The Children of Llyr!"* clamored some. *"Rhydderch's Red Stallion!"* shouted someone else, to general acclaim. *"Gruagach's Revenge!"* another suggested, but was shouted down.

Tegid simply shook his head and announced that he could not sing tonight or any other night.

"Why?" everyone wanted to know. "How is it that you cannot sing?"

The wily bard answered, "How can I think of singing when the Three Fair Realms of Albion stand apart one from another with no king to establish harmony between their separate tribes?"

Leaning close to Goewyn, I said, "I smell a ruse."

Turning to me, Tegid declared that as Aird Righ it must certainly be foremost among my thoughts to ride the circuit of my lands and establish my rule in the kingdom.

"To be sure," I replied lightly, "my thoughts would have arrived there sooner or later." To Goewyn, I whispered, "Here it comes."

"And since you are High King," he announced, brandishing his staff with a flourish, "you will extend the glory of your reign to all who shelter beneath your Silver Hand. Therefore, the *Cylchedd* you contemplate will include all lands in the Three Fair Realms so that Caledon, Prydain and Llogres will be brought under your sovereign authority. For all must own you king, and you must receive the honor and tribute of the Island of the Mighty."

This speech was delivered to a largely unsuspecting throng and so took them by surprise. It took me somewhat unawares as well, but as he spoke I began to see the logic behind Tegid's highflown formality. Such an important undertaking demanded a certain ceremony. And the people of Dinas Dwr promptly understood the significance of Tegid's address.

It was not the first time the Chief Bard had used the title Aird Righ, of course. However, it was one thing to speak the words here in Dinas Dwr among my own people, but quite another actively to proclaim this assertion in the world beyond the protecting ridge of Druim Vran.

Whispers hissed through the crowd: "Aird Righ! Llew Silver Hand is the High King!" they said. "Did you hear? The Chief Bard has proclaimed him Aird Righ!"

There was a solid reason behind Tegid's proclamation: he was anxious to establish the Sovereignty of Albion beyond all doubt. A worthy venture, it seemed to me. All the same, I wished he had warned me. Strictly speaking, I did not share Tegid's enthusiasm for the High Kingship—which is, no doubt, why he chose to announce the Cylchedd the way he did.

Whatever my misgivings, Bran and the Raven Flight, and the rest of the warband, supported Tegid and fairly thundered their endorsement. They banged their cups and slapped the board with their hands; they raised such an uproar that it was some time before Tegid could continue.

The Penderwydd stood there smiling a supremely self-satisfied smile, watching the commotion he had caused. I felt the touch of a cool hand on my neck and glanced up. Goewyn had come to stand beside me. "It is no less than your right," she said, her breath warm in my ear.

When the furore had subsided somewhat, Tegid continued, explaining that the circuit would begin in Dinas Dwr as I held court among my own people. And then, when all the proper preparations had been made, I would ride forth on a lengthy tour of Albion.

Tegid had a lot more to say, and said it well. I listened with half an ear, wondering if, as he claimed, the circuit would actually take a year and a day—an estimate I took to be more a poetic approximation than an actual calculation. Be that as it may, I knew it would not be accomplished quickly or easily, and I found myself working out the details even as Tegid spoke.

"Listen, bard," I said as soon as we were alone together, "I am all for riding the Cylchedd, but you might have told me you were going to announce it."

Tegid drew himself up. "Are you displeased?"

"Oh, sit down, Tegid. I am not angry. I just want to know. Why did you do it?"

He relaxed and sat down. We were together in my hut; since the wedding Goewyn and I preferred the privacy of the one-room hut to the busy bedlam of the hall.

"Your kingship must be declared before the people," he said

simply. "When a new king takes the throne it is customary to make a Cylchedd of his lands. Also, as Aird Righ, it is necessary to obtain the fealty of other kings and their people in addition to that of your own chieftains and clansmen."

"I understand. How soon will we leave Dinas Dwr?"

"As soon as adequate preparation can be made."

"How long will that take? A couple of days? Three or four?"

"Not longer." He paused, regarding me eagerly. "It will be a wonderful thing, brother. We will establish the honor of your name and increase your renown throughout all Albion."

"Has it occurred to you that some of Meldron's mongrel horde may yet ride free? They might disagree with you."

"All the more reason for the Cylchedd to be made at once. Any who still lack proper understanding must be convinced. We shall travel with a warband."

"And will it really take all year? I am newly married, Tegid, and I had hoped to stay close to home for a while."

"But Goewyn will accompany you," he said quickly, "and anyone else you choose. Indeed, the larger the procession, the greater your esteem in the eyes of the people."

I could see that Tegid considered the circuit a great show of pomp and power. "This is going to be a huge undertaking," I mused.

"Indeed!" he declared proudly. "It will be like nothing seen in Albion since the time of Deorthach Varvawc." I saw that this meant more to him than he let on. Well, I thought, let him have his way. After all he had been through with Meldron, he had earned it. Maybe we both had.

"Deorthach Varvawc," I remarked, "now who could forget a name like that?"

The preparations went forward with all haste. Four days later I was looking at a veritable train of wagons, chariots and horses. It appeared that the entire population of Dinas Dwr planned to make the journey with us. Enough would stay behind, I hoped, to look after the fields and proceed with the restoration of the crannog. All well and good to go wandering all over Albion, but there were crops to be gathered and herds to be maintained, and someone had to do it.

In the end, it was agreed that Calbha would remain in Dinas Dwr while we were gone. Meldron had destroyed the Cruin king's stronghold at Blár Cadlys, so gathering enough supplies, tools and provisions to begin rebuilding would occupy Calbha a good while yet. Thus, he became the logical choice to stay behind. Much as he would have liked to accompany us, he agreed that time was best spent looking after the affairs of his people.

And, as there were young warriors to train, Scatha elected to stay behind with her school. Three Ravens would stay with her to aid the training of the young, and enough warriors to protect Dinas Dwr.

The day before we were due to set off, Tegid summoned the people to the hall. When all had gathered, I took the throne and, looking out upon the faces of all those gazing expectantly at me, I felt—not for the first time—the immense weight of duty settling upon me. This would have been daunting if I had not sensed an equally great strength of tradition helping to shoulder the burden. I could bear the weight, because others had borne it before me and their legacy lived on in the spirit of sovereignty itself.

It came to me as I sat there on my antlered throne that I could be a king, even a High King, not because I knew anything about being a king—much less because I was somehow more worthy than anyone else—but because the people *believed* in my kingship. That is to say, the people believed in sovereignty and were willing, for the sake of that belief, to extend their conviction to me.

It might be that the Chief Bard held the power to confer or withhold kingship, but that power derived from the people. "A king is a king," Tegid was fond of saying, "but a bard is the heart and soul of the people; he is their life in song, and the lamp which guides their steps along the paths of destiny. A bard is the essential spirit of the clan; he is the linking ring, the golden cord which unites the manifold ages of the clan, binding all that is past with all that is yet to come."

At last, I began to grasp the fundamental fact of Albion. I understood, too, Simon's deadly design: in attacking sovereignty, he had struck at the very heart of Albion. Had he succeeded in killing kingship at the root, Albion would have ceased to exist.

"Tomorrow," the Chief Bard announced, "Llew Silver Hand will leave Dinas Dwr to make Cylchedd of his lands and receive the homage of his brother kings and the tribes of the Three Fair Realms. Before he gains the esteem of others, however, it is fitting for his own people to pledge faith with him and honor him."

Tegid raised his staff and thumped it on the floor three times. He called for all chieftains—be they kings, noblemen, or warriors—to pay homage to me, and to swear oaths of fealty which he spoke to them. I had only to receive their pledges and grant them protection of my reign. As each chieftain finished reciting the oath, he knelt before me and placed his head against my chest in a gesture of submission and love.

One by one, beginning with Bran Bresal, they came before me: Alun, Garanaw, Emyr, Drustwn, Niall, Calbha, Scatha, Cynan. These were followed by several of those who had come to Dinas Dwr during Meldron's depredations, and lastly by those who had surrendered at Meldron's defeat. To receive the honor of such men touched me deeply. Their oaths bound them to me and, no less securely, bound me to them.

When the ceremony was finished, I was more than ever a king—and more than eager to see Albion once more.

We crossed Druim Vran just as the sun was rising behind the encircling hills. As we started down the ridge trail, I paused to look back along the line to see that the last of the wagons had yet to leave the lakeside.

If, as Tegid suggested, the size of an entourage could increase a king's esteem, then mine was multiplied a hundredfold at least. Altogether there were sixteen wagons with supplies and provisions, including livestock—a larder on the hoof—and extra horses for the hundred or so men and women attending us as cooks, camp hands, warriors, messengers, hunters and stockmen. Leading the cavalcade were my Chief Raven, Bran Bresal, Emyr Lydaw bearing the great battle carynx, and Alun Tringad, astride high-stepping horses. Next came the Penderwydd of Albion attended by his Mabinogi and, behind them, Goewyn, on a pale yellow horse, and myself on a roan. Following us were the warband, and behind them the wagons in a long, long rolling file.

The valley below flooded with light, glowing like an emerald, and my heart soared at the prospect of travelling through this extraordinary land—the more so with Goewyn by my side and the fellowship of amiable companions. I had forgotten how fair Albion could be. Ablaze with color and light: the rich greens of the tree-filled glens and the delicate mottled verdure of the high moors, the dazzling blue of the sunwashed sky, the subtle greys of stone and the deep browns of the earth, the sparkling silver of water, the shimmering gold of sunlight.

I had ranged far through the land on my various forays, and still it held the power to astonish. A glimpse of white birches stark against a background of glossy green holly, or the sight of blue cloudshadow gliding down distant hillsides could leave me gasping with wonder. Marvellous it was—all the more so since Albion had endured the ravages of fire and drought and unending winter. The land had suffered through the desolation of Lord Nudd and his demon horde, and the depredations of the Great Hound Meldron. Yet it appeared reborn.

There must have been some unseen agent toiling away to bring about a continual renewing of the land, for there was no trace of desolation anywhere, no lingering scars, no visible reminders of the tortures so recently endured. Perhaps its splendors were constantly restored, or perhaps Albion was somehow created anew with each dawn. For it seemed that every tree, hill, stream, and stone had just burst into existence from sheer creative exuberance.

After two days of this I was a man enraptured with existence—not only my own, but the entire universe as well. My enchantment extended to the moon and stars and the dark void beyond. Had I been a bard, I would have sung myself dizzy.

As we travelled further, I grew, slowly but surely, more sensitive to the beauty of the land around me. I began to sense a momentous glory radiating from every form that met my eye—every limb and leaf, every blade of grass ablaze with unutterable grandeur and majesty. And it seemed to me that the world I saw before me was merely the outward manifestation of a vastly powerful, deeply fundamental reality that existed just out of sight. I might not discern this veiled reality directly, but I could perceive its effects. Everything it touched it set vibrating like a string on Tegid's harp. I thought that if I listened very hard I might hear the hum of this celestial vibration. Sometimes I imagined that I did hear it—like the echo of a song which lingered just beyond the threshold of hearing. I could not hear the melody, only the echo.

The reason for this delight was, partly, Goewyn. I was so enraptured by her that even Nudd's hostage pit would have seemed like paradise if she were there. As we travelled through the revived splendor of Albion I began to realize that I now viewed the world through different eyes. No longer a sojourner, a trespassing transient merely visiting a world that was not my home, I belonged; Albion *was* my home now. Indeed, I had taken an Otherworld woman for my wife. So far from being a stranger, I was now a king. I was the Aird Righ. Who belonged in Albion if not the High King?

The king and the land were connected in an intimate and mysterious way. Not in some abstract philosophical way, but actually, physically. The relationship of the king to the land was that of man to wife—the people of Albion even spoke of it as a marriage. And now that I was married myself, I was beginning to understand—no, to *feel* it: the concept was still well beyond my comprehension, but I could discern wisdom taking shape in my flesh and bones. I could sense an ancient, primal truth I could not yet put into words.

Thus, the Cylchedd began to take on the quality of a pilgrimage, a journey of immense spiritual significance. I might not apprehend the full meaning of the pilgrimage, less still its more delicate implications; but I could feel, like gravity, its irresistible, inexorable, inescapable power. I did not find this in any way burdensome; all the same, like a soul clothed in flesh, I knew that I would never move without it again.

By day we journeyed through a landscape made sublime by the light of a fulgent sun, imparting an almost luminous splendor to all it touched, creating shimmering horizons and shining vistas on every side. By night we camped under an enormous skybowl bursting with stars, and went to our rest with the blessed sound of harpsong in our ears.

In this way we reached our first destination: Gwynder Gwydd, clan seat of the Ffotlae in Llogres. As it happened, there were Ffotlae with us, and they were eager to discover whether their kinsmen still survived.

We established camp on a meadow near a standing stone called *Carwden*, the Crooked Man, which the Ffotlae used as a meeting place. There was a lively brook running through the meadow which was surrounded by woodlands of young trees. As soon as the tents were erected, Tegid sent the Raven Flight out as messengers into the region and we settled back to wait.

Meanwhile, we had brought my stag-antler chair with us, and Tegid directed that a small mound be raised before the Carwden stone and the chair placed on the mound. The next morning, following Tegid's counsel, Goewyn and I dressed in our best clothing—for Goewyn a white shift with Meldryn Mawr's golden fishscale belt I had given her, and a skyblue cloak; for me, a cloak of red edged with gold over a green siarc, and blue breecs. I wore a belt of huge gold discs, an enormous gold brooch, and my gold torc. Goewyn had to help me with the brooch—I had grown accustomed to managing without a right hand, but I was still unused to my silver hand.

Goewyn fastened the brooch for me, then stepped quickly away again to appraise me with a critical eye. She did not like the way I had folded the cloak, so she deftly adjusted it. "Everything in place?" I asked.

"If I had known you were going to make such a handsome king, I would have married you long ago," she replied, slipping her arms around my neck and kissing me. I felt the warmth of her body and was suddenly hungry for her. I pulled her more tightly to me... and the carynx sounded.

"Tegid's timing is impeccable," I murmured.

"The day is yet young, my love," she whispered, then straightened. "But now your people are arriving. You must prepare to greet them."

We stepped from the tent to see a fair-sized throng advancing across the meadow to the Carwden stone. The people of Gwynder Gwydd and surrounding settlements had gathered—sixty men and women, the remnant of four or five tribes. The Ffotlae among us were overjoyed to see their kinsmen again, and welcomed them with such cheering and crying that it was some time before the llys could begin. Then Tegid commanded Emyr to sound the carynx once more. The bellow of the battlehorn signalled the beginning of the court; Goewyn and I walked to the mound and took our places: myself on the throne, and she beside it where she would be most conspicuous. Tegid wanted them to recognize and honor their queen.

The people of Gwynder Gwydd, eager to cast their eyes on this wonder of a new king—and his ravishing queen—crowded close to the mound for a good view. This gave me a chance to observe them as well. Plainly, they had suffered. Some were maimed, many were scarred from beatings or torture, and despite the renewing of the land all were still gaunt from misery and lack of food. They had come dressed in their best clothes, and these were but well-laundered tatters, for the most part. Meldron had exacted a heavy price for his kingship, and they had been made to pay it.

The Chief Bard opened the proceedings in the usual way, proclaiming to one and all the remarkable thing which had come to pass. A new High King had arisen in Albion, and now was making a Cylchedd of the realm to establish his rule... and so on.

The Ffotlae wore the hopeful, if not entirely convinced, expressions of people who had grown used to being cheated and lied to at every turn. They were respectful, and appeared willing to believe, but the mere sight of me did not altogether reassure. Very well, I would have to win their trust.

So, when Tegid finished, I stood. "My people," I said, "I welcome you." I raised my hands; the sun caught the silver and flashed like white fire. This caused a great sensation and everyone gaped wide-eyed at my silver hand. I held it before them and flexed the fingers; to my surprise, they all fell on their faces and hugged the ground.

"What is this?" I whispered to Tegid, who had joined me on the mound.

"They fear your hand, I think," he replied.

"Well, do something, Tegid. Tell them I bring them peace and goodwill—you know what to say. Make them understand."

"I will tell them," Tegid replied sagely. "But only you can make them understand."

The Chief Bard raised his staff and told the frightened gathering what a fine thing it was rightly to revere the king and pay him heartfelt respect. He told them how pleased I was to receive their gift of homage, and how, now that Meldron had been defeated, they had nothing to fear, for the new king was no rampaging tyrant.

"Give them a cow," I whispered, when he concluded. "Two cows. And a bull."

Tegid raised his eyebrows. "It is for you to receive *their* gifts."

"Their gifts? Look at them, they have nothing."

"It is their place to—"

"Two cows and a bull, Tegid. I mean it."

The bard motioned Alun to him and spoke some words into his ear. Alun nodded and hurried away, and Tegid turned to the people, telling them to rise. The king knew of their hardship in the Day of Strife, he said, and had brought them a gift as a token of his friendship and a symbol of the prosperity they would henceforth enjoy.

Alun approached then with the cattle. "These kine are given from the Aird Righ's own herd for the upbuilding of your stock." Then he asked for their chief to take possession of the cattle on behalf of the tribe.

This provoked some consternation among the Ffotlae; for, as one of the clansmen with us quickly explained, "Our lord was killed, and our chieftain went to serve Meldron."

"I see." I turned back to Tegid. "It seems we must give them a chief as well."

"That is easily done," the bard replied. Raising his staff, he stood before the people and said that it was the High King's good pleasure to give them a new lord to be their chief and to look after them. "Who among you is worthy to become the lord of the Ffotlae?" he asked. There followed a brief deliberation in which various opinions were expressed, but one name eventually won out, apparently to everyone's satisfaction. "Urddas!" they clamored. "Let Urddas be our chief."

Tegid looked to me to approve the choice. "Very well," I said, "have Urddas step forward. Let us have a look at him."

"Urddas," Tegid called. "Come and stand before your king."

At this the crowd parted and a thin, dark-haired woman approached the mound. She regarded us with deep, sardonic eyes, a look of defiance on her lean, expressive face. "Tegid," I said under my breath, "I think Urddas is a woman."

"Possibly," he replied in a whisper.

"I am Urddas," she said, removing any doubt. I glanced at Goewyn, who was obviously enjoying our momentary confusion.

"Hail, Urddas, and welcome," Tegid offered nicely. "Your people have named you chieftain over them. Will you receive the respect of your clan?"

"That I will," the woman replied—three words, but spoken with such authority that I knew the Ffotlae had chosen well. "Nor will it be to me an unaccustomed honor," she added, "for I have been leading my clan since their lord, my husband, was killed by *Mór Cù*. If I am acknowledged in this way, it is no less than my right."

Her speech had an edge—and why not? the clan had been through hell, after all—but it was not rancor or pride that made her speak so. I think she simply wanted us to know how things were with them. No doubt she found blunt precision more suited to her purpose than affable ambiguity. It could not have been easy ruling a clan under Meldron's cruel regime.

"Here, then, is your king," Tegid told her, and asked, "Will you acknowledge his sovereignty, pledge him fealty, and pay him the tribute due him?"

Urddas did not answer at once—I believe I would have been disappointed if she had. But she cast her cool, ironic eyes over me as if she were being asked to estimate my worth. Then, still undecided, she glanced across at the cattle I had bestowed upon the clan.

"I will own him king," the woman replied, turning back. But I noticed she was looking at Goewyn as she answered—as if whatever lack she saw in me was more than made up by my queen. Presumably, if I could woo and win a woman of Goewyn's distinction, then perhaps there was more to me than first met her dubious eye.

Tegid administered the oath of fealty then, and when it was completed, the woman came to me, knelt before me and held her head against my breast. When she rose once more, it was to the acclaim of the Ffotlae. She ordered some of the younger men to take the cows and bull—lest I change my mind.

"Urddas," I said as she made to return to her place. "I would hear from you how you have fared through this ill-favored time. Stay after the llys is completed and we will share a bowl between us—unless something else would please you more."

"A bowl with the Aird Righ would please me well," she replied forthrightly. Only then did I see her smile. The color came back to her face, and her head lifted a little higher.

"That was well done," Goewyn said softly, stroking me lightly on the back of the neck.

"Small comfort for the loss of a husband," I said, "but it is something at least."

There were several lengthy matters to arbitrate—mostly arising from the troubles that had multiplied under Meldron. These were prudently dealt with, whereupon Tegid concluded the llys and, after leading the combined tribes in a simple oath of fealty, declared clan Ffotlae under the protection of the Aird Righ. To inaugurate this new accord, we hosted them at a feast and the next day sent them back to Gwynder Gwydd loudly praising the new king.

This was to become the pattern for the rest of the circuit through Llogres. Sadly, some previously well-populated districts or *cantrefs* were now uninhabited, either abandoned or destroyed. Our messengers rode far and wide, to the caers and strongholds and to the hidden places in the land. And at each place where we found survivors—at Traeth Eur, Cilgwri, Aber Archan, Clyfar Cnûl, Ardudwy, Bryn Aryen, and others, our messengers proclaimed the news: The High King is here! Gather your people, tell everyone, and come to the meeting place where he welcomes all who will own him king.

The years of Meldron's cruelty had wrought a ghastly change in the people. The fair folk of Albion had become pale, thin, haggard wraiths. It tore at my heart to see this noble race degraded so. But I found solace in the fact that we were able to deliver so many from the fear and distress that had held them for so long. Take heart, we told them, a new king reigns in Albion; he has come to establish justice in the land.

As the Cylchedd progressed, we all—each man and woman among us—became zealous bearers of the glad tidings. The news was everywhere greeted with such happiness and gratitude that the entire entourage strove with one another to be allowed to ride with the message—just to share in the joy the tidings brought.

Indeed, it became my chief delight to see the transformation in the listeners' faces when they at last understood that Meldron was dead and his war host defeated. I could almost see happiness descend upon the people like a shining cloud as the truth took hold within them. I saw bent backs straighten, and dead eyes spark to life. I saw hope and courage rekindled from dead, cold ashes.

The Year's Wheel revolved and the seasons changed. The days were already growing shorter when we finished in Llogres and turned towards Caledon. We had arranged to winter at Dun

Cruach, before resuming the Cylchedd. I was for going home, but Tegid said that once begun, I could not return to Dinas Dwr until the round was completed. "The course must not be broken," he insisted. So, Cynan would have the pleasure of our company through Sollen, Season of Snows.

Alban Ardduan

We arrived at Dun Cruach in Caledon just as the weather broke. Rain pelted down and wind whined as we passed through the gates. It had been a good journey, but it was a relief to abandon our tents for the warmth and light of a friendly hall. Cynan and the Galanae threw open the doors and gathered us in.

"Llew! Goewyn!" Cynan cried, throwing his arms around us. "*Mo anam*! But we expected you days ago. Did you get lost?"

"Lost! Goewyn, did you hear that? I will have you know, Cynan Two-Torcs, that I have personally inspected every track, trail, and footpath in Llogres and most of Caledon. Truly, the deer in the glens will lose their way before Llew Silver Hand."

"Ah, Goewyn," Cynan sighed, and I noticed he had not taken his arm from around her. "Why did you ever marry such an ill-tempered man? You should have married me instead. Now look what you must suffer." He shook his head sadly and clucked his tongue.

Goewyn kissed him lightly on the cheek. "Alas, Cynan," she sighed, "if only I had known."

"All this talk of marriage," I remarked. "Are you trying to tell us something?"

The big warrior became suddenly bashful. "Now that you say it, brother, I believe I have found a woman much to my liking."

"That is half the battle, to be sure," I replied. "But, more to the point, will she have you?"

"Well," Cynan allowed with uncommon reticence, "we have talked and she has agreed. It so happens, we will be married while you are here."

"At the solstice perhaps," suggested Tegid; he had overheard everything. "It will be a highly favorable time—the *Alban Ardduan*."

"Welcome, Penderwydd," Cynan said warmly, grasping his arms and embracing Tegid like a wayward brother.

"What is this Alban Ardduan?" I wondered aloud. "I have never heard of it."

"It is," the bard explained slowly, "the one solstice in a thousand coinciding with a full moon."

"And," Goewyn continued, taking up where Tegid had left off, "both setting sun and rising moon stand in the sky at once to regard one another. Thus, on the darkest day, darkness itself is broken."

I remembered with a pang that Goewyn, like her sisters, had once been a Banfáith in a king's house. Govan and Gwenllian were dead, and of the three fair sisters of Ynys Sci, Goewyn alone survived.

"That is why," Tegid resumed, "it is a most auspicious time—a good day to begin any endeavor."

"Yes, do it then," I urged. "If ever a man stood in need of such aid, it is you, brother." My eyes swept the busy hall. "But where is she, Cynan? I would meet the lady who has won your heart."

"And I thought you would never ask!" he cried happily. He turned and motioned to someone standing a little behind him. "Ah! Here she comes with the welcome cup!"

We all turned to see a willowy young woman with milk-white skin and pale, pale blue eyes, advancing towards us with a great steaming bowl of mulled ale between her long, smooth hands. It was easy to see how she had captured Cynan's notice, for her hair was as fiery red as his. She wore it long and it hung about her shoulders in such a mass of curls as a man could get lost in. She stepped briskly, regarding us steadily; there was an air of boldness about her. In all, she looked more than a match for Cynan.

"My friends," said Cynan expansively, "this is Tángwen, the fortunate woman who has agreed to become my wife."

Smiling, she offered the bowl to me, saying, "Greetings, Silver Hand." Her voice was low and smoky. At my expression of surprise she smiled knowingly and said, "No, we have never met. You would remember if we had, I think. But Cynan has told me so much about you that I feel I know you like a brother. And who else wears a hand of silver on his arm?" She gave me the bowl, and as I took it from her, she let her fingertips stroke my silver hand.

I drank the warming liquid and returned the bowl to Tángwen. She passed it to Tegid. "I give you good greeting, Penderwydd," she said. "You, I would know even without the rowan. There is only one Tegid Tathal."

Tegid raised the bowl, drank, and returned it, watching the red-haired charmer all the while. Tángwen, cool under his gaze, turned next to my queen. "Goewyn," she said softly, "I welcome you most eagerly. Since coming to Dun Cruach, I have heard nothing but praise for Llew's queen. We will be good friends, you and I."

"I would like that," Goewyn replied, accepting the bowl. Though she smiled, I noticed that Goewyn's eyes narrowed as if searching for some sign of recognition in the other woman.

Then Tángwen raised the bowl to her own lips, saying, "Greetings and welcome, friends. May you find all you wish to find in your stay among us, and may that stay be long."

All this was accomplished under Cynan's proud gaze. Obviously, he had schooled her well. She knew us all and spoke frankly and directly. Her forthright manner took me aback somewhat, but I could see how it would appeal to Cynan; he was not a man to endure much simpering.

Having served us, Tángwen moved on to welcome Bran and the Ravens who had just entered. We watched her lithe form glide away. Cynan said, "Ah, she is a beauty, is she not? The fairest flower of the glen."

"She is a wonder, Cynan," I agreed. "But who is she, and where did you find her?"

"She is no stranger to a king's hall," Goewyn observed. "I am thinking Tángwen has served the welcome bowl before."

"You cut straight to the heart of it," Cynan replied proudly. "She is the daughter of King Ercoll, who was killed in a battle with Meldron. Her people have been wandering Caledon in search of a steading and came to us here. I saw at once that she was of noble bearing. She will make a fine queen."

Gradually, the hall had filled with people. Food had been prepared in anticipation of our arrival and, when it appeared, Cynan led us to our places at his table. We ate and talked long into the night, enjoying the first of many pleasant meals around the winter hearth.

Thus we passed the winter at Dun Cruach amiably. When the sun shone we rode over the misty hills or walked the soggy moors, slipping over wet rocks and scaring up grouse and partridges. When the sleet rattled on the thatch or snow swirled down in the north wind's frigid wake, we stayed in the hall and played games—*brandub* and *gwyddbwyll* and others—as we had done when wintering on Ynys Sci.

Each night Tegid filled the hall with the enchanting music of his harp. It was joy itself to sit in that company, listening to the stories Albion's kings had heard from time out of mind. I counted every moment blessed.

As the day of Cynan and Tángwen's wedding drew near, Tegid let it be known that he was preparing a special song for the occasion. Though many asked what the tale would be, he would say no more than that it was an ancient and powerful story, and one which would bring great blessing to all who heard it.

Meanwhile, Goewyn and Tángwen attended to the preparations for the celebration. They were often together and appeared to enjoy one another's company. I thought them a strikingly beautiful pair, and thought Cynan and myself the two most fortunate men in all Albion to boast such women as wives.

Cynan was well pleased with his choice, and remarked often on the happy circumstance that brought her to his door. "She might have wandered anywhere," he said, "but she happened to come here, to me."

I saw little more than simple chance in it, but what did that matter? If Cynan wanted to believe that some extraordinary destiny had brought them together, who was I to disagree?

In any event, Tángwen had firmly established herself at the center of Cynan's household. Neither timidity nor humility found much of a patron in her; she was intelligent and capable and saw no reason to affect a meekness or modesty she did not naturally possess. Still, there was something about her—something driven, yet strangely constrained. She often stood apart when Tegid sang, watching from the shadows, her expression almost derisive, scornful—as if she disdained joining us, or spurned the pleasure of the gathering. Other times, she seemed to forget herself and joined in with a will. I felt somehow she was following the dictates of a scheme, rather than the promptings of her heart. And I was not the only one to notice.

"There is a hidden place in her soul," Goewyn said one night when we had retired to our sleeping quarters. "She is confused and unhappy."

"Unhappy? Do you think so? Maybe it is just that she is afraid of being hurt again," I suggested.

Goewyn shook her head slightly. "No, she wants to befriend me, I think; but there is something cold and hard in her that will not let her. Sometimes I wish I could just reach into her heart and pluck it out, and then all would be well with her."

"Perhaps that is her way of covering the pain."

Goewyn looked at me oddly. "Why do you say she has been hurt?"

"Well," I said slowly, thinking aloud, "Cynan said that her father had been killed in a battle against Meldron. I suppose I simply assumed Tángwen, like so many we have met along the way, still carried that grief."

"Perhaps," Goewyn allowed, frowning in thought.

"But you think otherwise?"

"No," she said after a moment. "That must be it. I am certain you are right."

The days dwindled, shrinking down toward Alban Ardduan and

Cynan's wedding. The Galanae warband and the Raven Flight had stocked the cookhouse with wild game of all kinds, and the cooks kept the ovens glowing hot, preparing food for the feast. The brewer and his helpers, foreseeing strong demand for the fruit of their labor, worked tirelessly to fill the vats with mead and ale. On the day before the wedding, the fattened pigs were slaughtered, and next morning we awoke in the dark to the aroma of roast pork.

After breaking fast with a little bread and water, we all dressed ourselves in feast-day clothes and assembled in the hall, eager for the festivities to begin. Torches fluttered from scores of holders, banishing shadows from every dark corner. On this day the torches would burn brightly from dawn to dawn in observance of Alban Ardduan.

Cynan appeared first, resplendent in red-and-orange checked breecs and yellow siarc. He wore a blue-and-white striped cloak and his father's great gold brooch. He had brushed his long red beard and fanned it out across his broad chest, and he had allowed his wiry red hair to be gathered and tied at the back of his head. His gold and burnished silver torcs gleamed like mirrors. He fretted and preened, patting his belt and adjusting his cloak.

"A more regal groom has never been seen in Caledon," I told him. "Stand still, now. Do you want her to think she is marrying a twitch?"

"What can be keeping them?" he asked, glancing nervously around the hall for the third time in as many moments.

"Be at ease," I told him. "You have endured your solitary ways a long time, you can endure yet a little longer."

"What if she has changed her mind?"

"Goewyn is with her," I reassured him. "She will not change her mind."

"What can be keeping them?" He craned his neck around, inspecting the hall yet once more. "Here they come!" he said, darting forward.

"Relax—it is Tegid."

"Oh, it is only Tegid." He began patting himself again, as if he were searching for something he had lost somewhere about his person. "How do I look?"

"Handsome enough for any two men. Now stand still, you are wearing a hole in the floor."

"Only Tegid?" wondered the bard.

"Ignore him," I told Tegid. "Cynan is not himself today."

"My throat is on fire," Cynan complained. "I need a drink."

"Later—after the wedding."

"Just one cup."

"Not a drop. We do not want the king of the Galanae falling down during his own wedding ceremony."

"I tell you I am dying!"

"Then do it quietly."

Tegid broke in, saying, "Here they are." At that instant, a ripple of voices sounded from the far end of the hall. Cynan and I turned to see Goewyn and Tángwen approaching.

Cynan's bride was a vision—a blaze of fiery beauty: two long braids bound in bands of gold swept back from her temples and lost themselves in the luxurious fall of flaming curls that spilled over her shoulders. She wore a crimson cloak and a robe of apricot yellow over a salmon-colored shift. Her feet were bare, and on each ankle was a bracelet of thick gold so that each step glittered. On her breast was a splendid silver brooch set with glowing red gems around the ring; the pin was joined to the ring by a tiny silver chain, and the head shone with a blazing blue jewel. No doubt the eye-catching object was her father's chief treasure.

Cynan could restrain himself no longer. He strode to meet her, gathered her in his arms, and all but carried her to where we stood by the wide, central hearth. "To be surrounded by battle-tried friends in a shining hall," he crowed, "with his arms around a beautiful woman— this is the greatest joy a man can know!" He turned to Tángwen, kissed her, and declared, "This is the happiest day of my life!"

At this, Tángwen put a hand to his ruddy face and turned his lips to hers, kissing him ardently and long. "Come, Tegid," Cynan said, "the bride is here; the hall is filled, and the feast is waiting. Perform the rite and let us begin the celebration!"

With raised staff and a loud voice, Tegid called the assembly to witness the marriage of Cynan and Tángwen. Everyone crowded close and the ceremony began. Cynan's wedding was very like my own. Gifts and tokens were exchanged and, as the bowl was shared, I felt Goewyn's hand slip into mine. She put her lips to my ear and whispered her love to me, nipping my earlobe as she withdrew.

Three sharp raps of the Chief Bard's staff and the wedding was over. Cynan whooped loudly and lifted his bride from her feet. He carried her to the table and set her upon it. "Kinsmen and friends!" he called. "Here is my wife, Tángwen. Hail her everyone, Queen of the Galanae!"

The room resounded with the chorused cries as the Galanae welcomed their queen. Tángwen, her face flushed with happiness, smiling, radiant, stood on the board, receiving the adulation of the people. The expression on her face, at first charmed, took on an aspect of triumph—as if she had won a close-fought campaign.

Cynan reached up to her and Tángwen tumbled into his arms. They embraced to the loud acclaim of everyone. And then Cynan ordered ale to be brought so that we could all drink the health of the happy couple. The brewer and his men brought forth the first vat and placed it beside the hearth. Cups and bowls were plunged deep and brought out frothing. We raised our bowls and our voices. "*Sláinte! Sláinte môr!*" We drank to life and health and happiness. We drank to the prosperity of Cynan's reign.

Outside it began snowing. Cold wind streamed over the hills, lashing the snow which fell from a blanched sky. Inside the hall, the feast began: steaming joints of venison and pork were carried in on their spits; platters of sweet breads of various sorts; huge rounds of pale yellow cheese, and mounds of crisp apples. We ate, and drank, and talked, and ate and drank some more, passing the dark day in the light-filled hall surrounded by fellowship and plenty. And when at last we sat back, stuffed and satisfied, a call went up for a story. Taking up his harp, Tegid came before us, standing at the hearth in the center of the hall, the fire bright around him.

He strummed the harp, waiting for everyone to find a place and for quiet to claim the crowd. Gradually, the hall fell hushed. Lifting his voice, the bard declared, "It is right to celebrate the union of man and woman with weddings and feasts and songs—more so than the victories of warriors and the conquests of kings. It is right to pay heed to the stories of our people, for that is how we learn who we are and what is required of us in this life and the life beyond.

"On this day above all others, when the light of Alban Ardduan burns in the high places, it is right to give ourselves to revelry, it is right to draw near the hearthfire to hear the songs of our race. Gather then and listen, all who would hear a true tale—listen with your ears, Children of Albion, and listen with your hearts."

So saying, he bowed his head and fell silent. Then, fingers stirring on the strings of the harp, he conjured a melody from the air, drew breath, and began to sing.

The Great King's Son

The sweet-sounding notes of the harp spilled like glittering coins from Tegid's fingers; or like bright sparks sprung from the lusty fire, swirling up on rising draughts to the dark-shadowed rooftrees. The Chief Bard's voice rose to join the melody of the harp, and the two twined about one another in matchless harmony as he began to sing the tale he had prepared for Alban Ardduan. And this is what he sang:

"In the first days of men, when the dew of creation still glimmered upon the earth, there arose a great king who ruled many realms and held authority over divers clans. The great king's name was Cadwallon, and he ruled long and wisely, ever increasing the fortunes of those who sheltered beneath his shield. It was his custom in the evening to climb the council-mound beside his stronghold and gaze out upon his lands, to see for himself how matters stood with his people. And this is the way of it...

"One twilight, as Cadwallon sat on his high mound, gazing out upon his lands, it came to him that his holdings had grown vast beyond reckoning. 'I can no longer see from one end of my dominion to the other, nor can I count the number of my people—just to tell out the names of their tribes would take my bard three whole days.

"'What shame,' thought he, 'if trouble were to threaten and I did not hear of it in time to prevent harm befalling my people. This could easily happen, for the kingdom has grown too great for one king to rule. Therefore, I must find someone to help me rule my realm and keep my people safe.'

"As it happened, there was no lack of would-be kings eager to help him rule. Sadly, not all of them cared as much for the welfare of the clans as Cadwallon, and it distressed the great king to think that a self-serving man should gain power at his command. So, he took himself to his *gorsedd* mound to think the thing through, saying, 'I will not come down until I have discovered a way out of this predicament.'

"Through three sunrises and three sunsets, Cadwallon did not stir; and through three more, and yet three more, until at dusk on the ninth day he hit upon a way to determine which of his noblemen was most worthy to aid him. He rose and walked down to his stronghold in confidence.

"The next day messengers rode to the four quarters of the kingdom bearing the message, and it was this: Noblemen all, the great king invites you to attend him for a season and take your ease in his hall where there will be feasting and gaming, and where the circling of mead cups will not cease.

"When the chieftains received this summons, they hastened to their lord. And when they saw the wealth of food and drink which had been prepared for them, they were well pleased and exclaimed that of all lords, Cadwallon must certainly be the most generous and benevolent ever known.

"When they had taken their places at table according to their rank, the feast began. They ate as much as they cared to eat and drank as much as they cared to drink, and after the sharp edge of hunger and thirst had been dulled somewhat, they began to talk, as men will, about the various adventures that had befallen them. One after another spoke, and each told his best tale to delight the others.

"The great king listened to the talk around him and stared unhappily into his cup. When they asked him why he frowned so, the great king replied, 'We have heard some strange tales told among us, but none more strange than the one I shall tell. For of all adventures, mine is the strangest. On my life, I wish someone would tell me what it means.'

" 'Fortunate are you, O king, if that is all that troubles you,' the noblemen replied. 'We are ready to do your bidding. You have but to tell us your story, and we will soon put your heart at ease.'

" 'Listen then,' the king said, 'but do not imagine you will discover the meaning as easily as you think. For I am persuaded that this tale will cause you all no little dismay before the end.'

" 'Know you, Great King, that we fear nothing. Indeed, your words provoke our interest as nothing we have heard before. Speak how you will, you cannot dismay us.'

" 'No doubt you know what is best,' mused the king. So saying, Cadwallon began to relate his adventure.

" 'I was not always the king you see before you,' he told the chieftains. 'In my youth I was very high-spirited and arrogant, supposing that no one could surpass me in any feat of weapons. Thinking I had mastered every feat known in this worlds-realm, I equipped myself and rode to the wild places far from the fields we know. To win glory and renown with my skill was my intent, to hear my name lauded in song was my desire.'

" 'What happened?' they asked. 'What did you find?'

" 'I found the loveliest valley any man has ever seen. Trees of every kind grew in the woods, and a wide river flowed through the valley. I crossed the river and struck a path and rode until I came to a measureless plain blooming with every kind of flower. The path went before me, so I followed. Three days and three nights I rode, and at last came to a shining fortress beside a restless sea of blue.

" 'I approached that fortress and two boys met me—each with hair so dark it made me think of crows' wings—and both dressed in princely garb with fine green cloaks and silver torcs on their necks. Each lad carried a bow of horn with strings of deer sinew, and shafts of walrus ivory with points of gold and eagle feathers. Their belts were silver and their knives were gold. And they were shooting their arrows at a shield covered with white oxhide.

111

" 'A little distance away stood a man with hair so light it made me think of swans' wings. His hair and beard were neatly trimmed, and he wore a torc of gold on his neck. His cloak was blue and his belt and buskins were of fine brown leather.

" 'I rode to meet this man with a ready greeting on my lips, but he was so courteous as to greet me before I could speak. He bade me enter the fortress with him, which I was eager to do for it was a marvel to behold. I saw others inside the fortress, and observed at once that they were a prosperous people, for the least one among them displayed the same wealth as the first man, nor did the greatest one among them display less than three times as much as the least.

" 'Five grooms took my horse and stabled it better than the best grooms I ever saw. And then the man led me to the hall, which had pillars of gold and a roof made of the feathers of speckled birds. Inside were handsome men and beautiful women—and all of them pleasantly conversing, singing, playing games and taking their ease. Twenty maidens were sewing by the window, and the least lovely maiden among them was more beautiful than any maiden in the Island of the Mighty. And as we entered the hall, these maidens rose to greet me and welcomed me most enjoyably.

" 'Five of them drew off my buskins and took my weapons, and five of them took from me my travel-worn clothes and dressed me in clean clothes—siarc and breecs and cloak of finest craft. Five maidens laid the board with good cloth and five maidens brought food on five huge platters. And the five who had taken my buskins and weapons now brought new fleeces for me to sit upon, and the five who had dressed me led me to the table.

" 'I sat beside the man who had brought me, and others of that exalted company sat around us. There was not a single cup or bowl or platter on that table that was not gold or silver or horn. And the food—such food! I have never tasted anything so pleasing to the tongue and satisfying to the stomach as I tasted in that hall surrounded by that bright company.

" 'We ate, but never a word was spoken to me from the first bite to the last. After a time, the man beside me, perceiving that I had finished my meal, turned to me and said, "I see that you would sooner talk than eat."

" "Lord," I said, "it is high time I had someone to talk with. Even the best food is poor fare when it is shared in silence."

" "Well," answered the man, "we did not like to disturb your meal. But if I had known how you felt about it, we would certainly have spoken sooner. But let us talk now if nothing prevents you." And he asked me what sort of man I was and what was the errand that had brought me to them.

" "Lord," said I, "you see before you a man of no small skill in weapon-play. I am roaming the wild places of the world, hoping to find someone who might overcome me. For I tell you the truth, it is no sport to me to overcome men of lesser skill than mine, and it is long since any warrior in my own country could offer me the sport I crave."

" 'The great lord smiled and said, "My friend, I would gladly guide you to your goal if I did not believe some harm would follow."

" 'At his words my face fell in sad disappointment. Seeing this, the lord said, "However, since you desire evil rather than good, I will tell you. Prepare yourself."

" 'To this I replied, "Lord, I am always prepared."

" "Then hear me, for I will say this but once. Spend the night here and rise tomorrow at dawn and take the path that brought you to this fortress until you reach a forest. A short distance into that forest, the path will split in two; take the left turning and follow on until you come to a clearing with a mound in the center. On that mound you will see a huge man. Ask this man where to go and, though he is often uncivil, it is my belief he will show you how to find that which you seek."

" 'That night was endless. All the ages of the world end to end would not last longer than that night lasted. As often as I looked at the sky, morning was no closer than when I last looked. At last, however, I saw the sky greying in the east and knew that night was ending. I rose and put on my clothes and went out and mounted my horse and set off on my way. I found the forest, and found the divided path, followed the left turning, and found the clearing with the mound in the center, the very same which the great lord had described to me.

" 'There was a man sitting on the mound. My host had told me that the man was huge, but he was far bigger than I had imagined—and and far uglier. He had but one eye in the middle of his forehead, and one foot; thick black hair covered his head and grew on his shoulders and arms. He carried an iron spear which would have been a burden for any four warriors, yet this man carried it easily in his hand. And around this man, both upon the mound and all around it, there grazed deer and pigs and sheep and forest animals of every kind—thousands of them!

" 'I greeted this Keeper of the Forest, and received a harsh reply. But it was no less than I expected, so I asked him what power he possessed over the animals gathered so closely about him. Again he made a rude reply. "Little man," he scoffed, "you must be the dullest of your kind not to know this. Nevertheless, I will show you what power I possess."

" 'The huge, hairy man took up his spear and aimed a blow at a nearby stag. He struck the animal with the butt of the spear, causing the stag to bell. And the belling of the stag shook the trees and trembled the very ground beneath my feet. Wild animals of every kind came running to the sound, gathering from the four quarters of the world. By the thousands and tens of thousands the animals came until there was hardly any room for my horse to stand among the wolves and bears and deer and otters and foxes and badgers and squirrels and mice and serpents and ants and all the rest.

" 'The animals gazed upon the huge Keeper as obedient men honor their lord, and he called to them and commanded them to graze, and at once they began to graze. "Well, little man," he said to me, "now you see the power I hold over these animals. But I am thinking you did not come here seeking assurance of my power, undoubtedly great though it is. What do you want?"

" 'I told him then who I was and what I sought, and he replied uncouthly to me. In short, he told me to go away. But I persisted, and he said, "Well, if you are stupid enough to seek such a thing, it is not for me to prevent you." Raising his iron spear, he pointed with it and said, "Follow the path you find at the end of the clearing. After a time you will discover a mountain; climb the slope of the mountain until you reach the summit and from there you will see a great glen the like of which you have never seen before. And in the middle of that glen you will see a yew tree that is both older and taller than any other yew tree in the world. Beneath the branches of that yew tree is a pool, and beside the pool is a stone, and on the stone is a silver bowl with a chain so that the bowl and stone cannot be separated. Take up the bowl, if you dare, and fill it with water and throw the water on the stone. Do not ask me what happens next, for I will not tell you—not even in a thousand years of asking."

" ' "Great Lord," I said, "I am not the sort of man to shrink from anything. I must know what happens next even if I stand here for a thousand and one years."

" ' "Was there ever a more ignorant and foolish man than you?" the Forest Keeper asked. "Nevertheless, I will tell what happens next: the rock will thunder with such force that you will think the heavens and earth must crack with the noise, and then will come a shower of water so fierce and cold that you will probably fail to survive. Hailstones big as loaves will fall! Do not ask me what happens next, for I will not tell you."

" ' "Great Lord," I said, "I believe you have told me enough. The rest I can find out for myself. I thank you for your help."

" 'And it is "Ha!" he says, "what is your thanks to me, little man? As for the help you have had, it will likely be your doom. Though I hope I never meet another as foolish as you, I will bid you farewell."

" 'I followed the path he had shown me, and rode to the mountain summit and spied the great glen and the tall yew tree. The tree was far taller and far older than the Forest Keeper had told me. I rode to the tree and discovered the pool and the stone and the silver bowl and chain—all as I had been told.

" 'Eager to try my skill, I wasted not a moment, but took up the bowl, filled it with water from the pool and dashed the water onto the stone. At once there arose a thunder far louder than the great lord had described, and then a squall of rain with hailstones huge as loaves. My friends, I tell you the truth—if I had not squeezed myself beneath the stone, I would not be here to tell the tale. Even so, my life was on the point of leaving me when the shower and hail stopped. There was not one green spear left on the yew tree, but the weather had cleared and now a flock of birds alighted on the bare branches and began to sing.

"'I am certain that no man before or since has heard music sweeter and more poignant than I heard then. But when the music was most pleasant to me, I heard a most mournful groaning which grew until it filled the great glen. And the groans became words: "Warrior, what do you want of me? What evil did I ever inflict on you that you should do to me and my realm what you have done?"

"' "Who are you, lord?" I demanded. "And what evil have I done to you?"

"'The mournful voice answered, "Do you not know that owing to the shower which you have thoughtlessly provoked neither man nor beast remains alive in my realm? You have destroyed everything."

"'With those words there appeared a warrior on a black horse, dressed all in black; his spear was black and his shield was black, and black the sword on his thigh from hilt to tip. The black horse pawed the ground with a black hoof and without another word the dread warrior charged.

"'Although the appearance was abrupt, I was prepared. Thinking that at last I would achieve everlasting renown, I quickly raised my spear and made my attack. I exulted in the power of the horse beneath me and in the swift advance of the great warrior. But though my charge was far more skillful than the best attack I have ever made, I was quickly swept from my horse and thrown ingloriously down upon the ground. Without so much as a look or word, my dark opponent passed the spearshaft through the bridle rein of my horse and took the animal away, leaving me there alone. He did not think it worth his while to take me hostage or even so much as retrieve my weapons.

" 'Thus I was forced to return by the path I had taken before, and when I reached the clearing the Keeper of the Forest met me, and it is a wonder that I did not melt into a puddle for the shame that sharp-tongued lord heaped upon me. I let him have his say, and he said it with eloquence most rare, and then I sighed and began making my long, slow way back to the shining fortress by the sea.

" 'There I was greeted more joyfully than before, and was made even more welcome and served even better food—if that is possible—than I received the first time. I was able to talk to the men and women in that fair place as much as I liked, and they talked fondly to me. However, no one made mention of my journey to the Black Lord's realm, nor did I speak of it myself. As vast as my former arrogance, so great was now my disgrace.

" 'I spent the night there and, when I rose, I found a splendid bay horse with a mane the color of red lichen. I gathered my weapons and bade the lord of that place farewell, and then returned to my own realm. The horse remains with me to this day, and I am not lying when I say that I would sooner part with my right hand than give up that horse.'

"The king then raised his eyes and looked around his table. 'But it is the truth I tell you when I say that I will give half my kingdom to the man who can explain to me the meaning of my adventure.'

"At this, Cadwallon concluded his peculiar tale. His lords sat stunned by the humility of their king in telling such a story against himself—as much as by the strangeness of the tale itself. Then up spoke a bold warrior lord named Hy Gwyd.

" 'Noblemen all,' he said, 'our lord has told us a tale worth hearing. And, unless I am much mistaken, our most canny king has also set a challenge before us, and it is this: to discover for ourselves the meaning of this strange adventure. Therefore, let us behave as bold men ought; let us go forth to meet the king's challenge and discover the meaning of the tale.'

"And the noblemen began to discuss the matter among themselves. They talked long and earnestly, for not everyone agreed with Hy Gwyd. In the end the noblemen decided that nothing good could come of interfering in such mysteries, thus the matter was better left where it stood. They turned again to their feasting and eating. But Hy Gwyd, ambitious as he was clever, was unwilling to let the matter rest; he continued pressing his argument and in the end won his way with his friend, a warrior named Teleri.

"So, while the others ate and drank at table, the two warriors crept from the hall. They saddled their horses, took up their arms, and rode out from Caer Cadwallon in the grip of the mystery their king had posed for them. They rode far and wide in search of the foreign fields that had been described to them. In good time, the two friends reached the forest and the path, and knew it to be the same forest and the same path Cadwallon had described.

"They followed the path and came to the wonderful valley and crossed the wide, shining river where they found the track leading to the endless plain blooming with every kind of flower. The fragrance of the flowers filled their lungs and the pleasure of that land filled their eyes as they rode along. Through three days and three nights they rode and at last came to the gleaming fortress beside the ever-changing sea of deepest blue.

"Two boys with silver torcs and bows of horn were shooting ivory arrows at a white shield—just as Cadwallon had described. A golden-haired man stood watching the boys, and all three greeted the riders warmly, and welcomed them to come into the fortress to sup with them. The people they saw inside the stronghold were even more fair, and the maidens more lovely than they had imagined. These beautiful women rose up to serve the warriors just as they had served Cadwallon, and the meal they ate in that wondrous hall far surpassed anything they had ever tasted before. When the meal was finished, the lord who had greeted them addressed them and asked them what errand they were on.

"Hy Gwyd answered him and said, 'We are seeking the Black Lord who guards the pool.'

"'I wish you had said anything but that,' the lord replied, 'but if you are determined to seek the truth of this matter for yourselves, I will not prevent you.' And he told them everything, even as he had told Cadwallon.

"At dawn the two rode through that fair realm until they reached the forest clearing where stood the Forest Keeper on his mound. The Keeper of Animals was even more ugly and impressive than they had been led to believe. Following the disagreeable lord's grudging directions, they reached the vale beyond the mountain and the vale where the yew tree grew. There they found the fountain and the silver bowl upon the stone. Teleri was for returning the way they had come, but Hy Gwyd laughed at him and taunted him. 'We have not come this far to turn back now,' he said. 'I feel certain that we will win the renown our king failed to gain. Certainly, we have it in our power to become greater than Cadwallon ever was.' So saying, he took up the bowl, filled it with water from the pool, and dashed the water over the stone.

"There followed both thunder and a hail storm much more severe than Cadwallon had said. They thought they must surely die, and were on the point of doing so when the sky cleared and the birds appeared in the leafless yew. The song of the birds was finer and more pleasing than they could have imagined, but when the singing had filled their hearts with pleasure, the groans began. Indeed, such was the groaning that it seemed as if the whole world was in misery and dying. The two warriors looked and saw a lone rider approaching them: the Black Lord they had been told to expect.

"The Black Lord gazed mournfully upon them and said, 'Brothers, what do you want of me? What evil did I ever inflict on you that you should do to me and my realm what you have done?'

" 'Who are you, lord?' asked the two warriors. 'And what evil have we done to you?'

"The mournful voice answered, 'Do you not know that owing to the shower which you have thoughtlessly provoked neither man nor beast remains alive in my realm? You have destroyed everything.'

"The two warriors turned to one another and bethought themselves what they might do. 'Brother, we are in need of a plan,' Teleri observed. 'For it is as our king has said and we are no nearer the truth of this mystery than when we first began. I say we go back now before something happens we will all regret.'

"'Am I to believe what I hear?' Hy Gwyd hooted in derision. 'We are this close to winning glory and power beyond reckoning. Lash a spear to your spine if you must, but follow me. There is no turning back.'

"With that Hy Gwyd raised his shield and lofted his spear. When the Black Lord saw that they meant to face him, he attacked, unhorsing both warriors with as little effort as if they had been inept children. The dread one made to take their horses; but the two warriors, warned by the example of their king, leapt up at once, grasped the black spear and pulled their foe from his mount. The Black Lord rose to his knees, and his hand found the hilt of his sword. But Hy Gwyd was quicker.

"Up with his sword and down: the Black Lord's head rolled free of his shoulders and his body toppled to the ground like a felled oak. Hy Gwyd leaned on his sword, breathing hard, but well pleased with himself nonetheless. 'We have done it, brother,' he said. 'We have succeeded where our king has failed. Now his renown is ours and we are his betters.'

'Teleri was still searching for his tongue to make reply when there arose a moaning far greater than the groans they had heard previously. The moan grew to a keening wail. Piteous in its misery and mournful in its grief, the sound of this wailing would wring tears from stones. Indeed, if all the misery in the world were suddenly given voice it could not sound more lamentable. The two warriors thought they would not long survive the onslaught of such sorrow.

"They gazed about them to discover the source of this cry, and saw a woman drawing near them, and oh! she was hideous to behold. If all the womanly beauty in the world were turned rancid at a single stroke and bestowed upon the bony back of the most repulsive crone, it still would never match for ugliness the sight which the two warrior friends beheld. Her face was a mass of wrinkles; her teeth black and twisted in her crack-lipped maw. Her sagging flesh was a mass of maggoty sores; lice and worms worked ceaselessly in her hair. The finest of clothes had once been hers, but now the remnants hung on her disgusting body in filthy rags.

"The wails of grief were coming from the throat of this loathsome woman, more mournful with every approaching step. When she arrived at the pool, she looked upon the corpse of the Black Lord and keened even louder than before. Birds dropped dead from the trees at the sorrowful sound.

"'Woe be upon you!' she cried, tears of sadness streaming down her ruined cheeks. 'Look at me! As ugly as I am now, I was once so beautiful. What will happen to me?'

"'Lady, who are you?' asked Teleri. 'Why do you beseech us so?'

"'You have killed my husband!' the loathly lady screeched. 'You have taken my man from me and left me desolate!' She stooped to the corpse before her and lifted the severed head by the hair, and kissed it on the mouth. 'Woe! Woe! My lord is gone. Who is there to care for me now? Who will be my comfort and support?'

"'Calm yourself, if you can,' Teleri said. 'What is it you want from us?'

"'You have slain the Guardian of the Pool,' the appalling woman said. 'He was my husband. Now one of you must take his place. One of you must take me to wife.'

"At this, the hideous crone approached the two warriors. A smell came from her that made their legs go weak and their bowels tremble. Red-eyed from crying, her nose running and spittle flowing from her lips, the crone spread her arms to them; her rags parted, revealing a body so wasted and repugnant that both men shut their eyes lest they retch at the sight.

"'No!' they shouted. 'Do not come any closer or we shall faint.'

"'Well?' the Black Hag asked. 'Which is it to be?' She turned first to Hy Gwyd. 'Will you embrace me?'

"Hy Gwyd turned his face away. 'Get you from me, hag!' he shouted. 'I will never embrace you!'

"She turned to Teleri. 'I see that you are a man of more heart. Will you embrace me?'

"Teleri's stomach squirmed. He felt sweat on the palms of his hands and the soles of his feet. He gulped air to keep from fainting.

'Lady, it is the last thing I will do,' Teleri replied.

"At this the woman began wailing again and so powerful was her keening that the sky darkened and the wind began to blow and the rain began to fall and thunder rolled across the sky. The very ground beneath their feet trembled and the whole world quaked at the sound of trees being uprooted and mountains sliding into the sea.

"The sudden onset of such a storm frightened the two warriors. 'Let us leave this place at once,' shouted Hy Gwyd. 'We have achieved all we came here to do.'

"But, though his heart quailed within him, Teleri was unwilling to leave the woman if he could help put the matter right. 'Lady,' he said, 'although it makes my flesh crawl, I will embrace you.'

"'You are a fool, Teleri!' shouted Hy Gwyd. 'You deserve her.' With that, he leapt onto his horse and rode swiftly away, though the storm crashed all around him.

"Teleri plucked up his courage and stepped toward the hag. His eyes watered—but whether from the sight of her, or the stench of her, he knew not. His arms shook and his strength flowed away like water. He thought his poor heart would burst for the shame and loathing coiling within him.

"Yet he raised his shaking arms and put them around the woman. He felt her hands on him, cold as ice, gripping him, bony fingers digging into his flesh. 'Woman,' he said, 'I have embraced you, and a cheerless embrace it is. Cold death could not be more desolate, nor the grave more grim.'

"'Now you must lie with me,' the hag told him, her breath foul in his face. Close up she was even uglier—if that were possible—and more ghastly and more repulsive than before.

"'Lie with you?' Teleri almost lost his reason. He thought to flee, but the Black Hag had him in her clutches and as there was no escape he resolved to see the thing through. 'I fear it will be a most abhorrent coupling. Yet, if that will satisfy you, I will do it—for your sake alone, the Good God knows I will receive no pleasure from it.'

"So Teleri took the Black Hag in his arms and lay down with her. He put his lips to her stinking mouth and kissed her. They made love, firm flesh to brittle bone, but Teleri could not endure the feat and he fainted.

"When he awoke, he was lying in the arms of the most beautiful maiden he had ever seen. Her long hair was yellow as pollen, and her limbs firm and supple; her breasts were shapely and her legs slender and long. Up he jumped with a startled cry. 'Where am I?' he said, holding his head. 'What happened to the other woman who was here?'

"The maiden sat up and smiled, and it was as if the sun had never shone upon Teleri until that moment. 'How many women must you have to satisfy you?' she asked, and oh! her voice was the melting of sweet honey in the mouth.

" 'Lady,' Teleri said, 'you are all the woman I require. Only promise me you will remain with me!'

" 'I will remain with you through all things, Teleri,' the maiden replied. 'For, if I am not mistaken, I am your wife and you are my husband.'

" 'What is your name?' Teleri asked, feeling foolish that he had a wife but did not know her name.

"But the maiden answered soothingly. 'Beloved, my name is that word which is most pleasing to your ear. You have but to speak it and that is what I shall be called.'

" 'Then I will call you Arianrhod,' he said, 'for that is the name most pleasing to me.'

"Teleri gathered his lovely Arianrhod in his arms and embraced her; her skin was soft and smooth and the touch of her filled him with delight. He kissed her and his soul rose into the heights of ecstasy. His love knew no bounds.

"They dressed themselves then, drawing on the kind of garments with which kings and queens array themselves. Teleri found his horse grazing nearby and mounted. He settled his new wife before him and rode from the pool, returning to his former realm the same way he had come.

"By and by, Teleri and Arianrhod returned to Caer Cadwallon where they were greeted and made welcome. His former friends exclaimed much over Teleri's good fortune at finding a woman so beautiful and wise to be his wife.

"'Welcome home, Teleri,' said King Cadwallon. 'You have returned at last. And here I was thinking that I would have to rule my realm alone, for I could find no one worthy to help me.'

"'What are you saying, lord?' asked Teleri. 'Hy Gwyd left before I did. He it was who killed the Black Lord.'

"'Ah, but it is not Hy Gwyd I see before me,' Cadwallon answered, 'nor is it Hy Gwyd who has entered my presence arrayed in splendor with so fair and queenly a wife.' The great king shook his head slowly. 'The man you speak of has not returned, and I think he never will. Therefore, let no man speak of him more. For I have found the one who is worthy above all others to share my throne, and whom, for this reason, I desire to elevate above all other men in my realm. From this day you are my own son, and as my son you will enjoy the benefit of my power and prosperity.'

"So saying, the Great King removed the torc from his own throat and placed it around Teleri's throat, thereby conferring a kingship no less sovereign than his own, nor yet less honorable. Teleri could not believe his good fortune.

"Cadwallon proclaimed a season of feasting throughout the realm and caused great rejoicing among all who held him sovereign. Then he placed half his kingdom under Teleri's authority, and removed himself to the other side of his realm where he watched with the greatest delight and joy all that Teleri did. For in everything Teleri showed himself an astute and able king, and as Teleri's eminence grew, so did Cadwallon's; and as Teleri's honor increased among the people, so did the great king's prestige increase through that of his adopted son.

"For his part, Teleri was well pleased with his lot and ever looked to increase the great king's honor among men. But of Hy Gwyd he heard nothing more, nor did any man ever lay eyes on him again. It was as if that man had never been born.

"Teleri and Arianrhod ruled long and wisely, ever exulting in their delight. And the love with which they loved one another increased until it filled the whole of the great king's realm with a potent and powerful goodness.

"Here ends the tale of the Great King's Son. Let him hear it who will."

The Boar Hunt

On a high-skied, sunbright day in early spring we left Dun Cruach. Snow still veiled the high ground, but I was eager to return to Dinas Dwr. The necessity of completing the circuit of Albion required a lengthy sojourn in Prydain and Caledon. There were still many clans and settlements to visit in the south, and it would likely be some time yet before we could at last turn our steps once more to Dinas Dwr in the north.

My entourage had swelled in number since setting out. It seemed that we added new members at each place visited. Dun Cruach was no exception—Cynan insisted on escorting us on our journey through southern Caledon, claiming it had been too long since a Galanae king had made the circuit. Now that he was king it was his right; besides, it would increase his renown to be seen in the company of the Aird Righ.

The real reason, I suspect, was that he just wanted to show off his new bride. But I did not mind. It gave us an opportunity to ride together once more, which I enjoyed.

As before, messengers rode before us, summoning the people to the king's llys. We made camp in the holy places—at crossroads, at standing stones and gorsedd mounds. There I received the fealty of the Caledonian tribes, and—as in Prydain and Llogres—placed the people under my authority and protection.

Ever and again, my thoughts turned toward Dinas Dwr, my splendid Water City. I wondered how the people fared, how the herds and crops were growing. I missed the place, missed my motley tribe, and wondered if they missed me. I longed for my hearth and hall. The minimal pleasures of a nomadic life were beginning to pall—the amusement of sleeping in a tent had long since worn off.

"There are only four or five tribes left to visit in the south," Tegid offered by way of consolation. "And as there are still very few people in Prydain at present, it will not be long before we begin making our way north again."

"How long?" I asked.

"Twenty—" the bard replied.

"Twenty days!" I shouted. My impatience got the better of me.

"—or thirty," Tegid added quickly. "Perhaps more. I cannot be certain until we have visited all the gathering places in the south."

"It will be Samhain before we get home again—if ever."

"Not at all. We should be within sight of Druim Vran before Lugnasadh—well before harvest time." He paused, almost beaming with pleasure. "We have done well. The tribes honor your kingship. Your brother kings welcome you. It is all we had hoped."

Truly, the circuit had been a triumph. As Tegid pointed out, people did accept me as Aird Righ, and I could already see a direct benefit. After such a time as we had just been through with Siawn Hy and Meldron, the High Kingship offered a substantial degree of stability—not to mention tranquility. If observing the ancient rite of the Cylchedd had helped bring this about, I would do it all over again. I would do anything to make Albion again what it had been when I came. Absolutely anything.

"Why not go hunting with Bran?" Tegid suggested, stirring me from my thoughts. "We will reach our destination just past midday. Bran and some of the others are planning to explore some of the game runs Cynan has told us about. You could go with them."

"Trying to get rid of me, brother bard?"

"Yes. Go. Please."

Bran was more than happy to include me in his hunting party. It had been a long time since I had ridden the hunt with him, or with anyone else. "It will not do for the High King's spearpoints to rust from neglect," he remarked. I took it as a kindly way of saying he did not want me growing soft now that I sat a throne more often than a charging horse. Fair enough.

Upon reaching our camping place for the night, we gathered our spears and rode to the forest. It was just past midday, as Tegid had said it would be, and the day was warm. We struck the first game run shortly after entering the wood, but decided we would be unlikely to find anything so near to the outer fringes of the forest, and so pressed deeper into the heart of the wood.

There were six of us in our party altogether and, upon reaching a second run, we divided ourselves into three groups and proceeded along the track two abreast. Bran and I rode in the center, three to four spear-lengths between us; and though I could not see the others through the tangled wood, I knew they were within easy hailing distance.

We rode in silence for some time, and at last came upon the spoor of wild pigs. Bran dismounted for a closer look. "How many?" I asked.

Bran, kneeling on the trail, raised his head and said, "A small herd. Four at least—maybe more." He stood and glanced ahead into the shadow-dappled trail. "Let us ride a little further and see what we find."

We proceeded with caution. This is always a tense situation, for until the pigs are sighted there is the very present danger of riding into them or overtaking them unawares. That is when accidents happen. Many is the hunter who has had his horse cut from under him—or worse—by a charging pig he did not see. Wild pigs are fearless fighters and will not hesitate to attack when pressed too close—though, like most animals, given the chance they prefer to flee.

Bran and I proceeded a short distance further down the run, and paused to listen. The air was still in the depths of the forest; only the quick tak-tak, tak-tak of a woodpecker broke the dull silence. Then, a little way ahead, we heard a low, grunting huff—which was followed by the snap of twigs and the shifting of dry leaves. Lowering his spear, Bran pointed into the dense thicket ahead and to the left of us. We waited, motionless, and in a moment a good-sized sow stepped onto the run before us, just beyond a sure throw. Pigs do not see well, though their hearing is acute and their sense of smell is keen. There was no wind, however, and if we kept quiet there was the chance she might wander nearer.

We waited.

Two piglets, small—they had been born only days before— joined their mother on the trail. They were joined by three more, all of them making small mewing sounds and scampering under the sow's belly and between her legs as she moved, snout down, along the run.

Bran shook his head slowly; we would not take the sow and leave the young without a mother. Accordingly, we made to turn off the track to give them a wide berth—a new mother feeling protective of her young would be extremely touchy and we had no wish to upset her. But, just as we turned aside, the thicket gave a shake and out burst a huge old boar.

He seemed more startled than angry, for he halted in the center of the run, turning this way and that—trying to locate the source of his agitation, I suppose—before gathering himself for a foray in our direction. This gave us time to ready ourselves and we were moving forward, spears low, when he charged. He closed the distance between us with surprising speed. We were ready, however, and had decided how to take him; Bran would strike the beast high in the shoulder, and I would go for his ribs.

The boar was a doughty old warrior, wise in his strength. He made his first charge a bluff, breaking off at the last instant so that we were forced to reign up and wheel our mounts to keep him between us. High-backed, his crest bristling over his sharp shoulders, he paused for a moment in the shadows, head down, tusks gleaming, slobbering as he pawed the turf. The sow and her brood had scattered, meanwhile, squealing as they fled down the run.

Bran and I readied ourselves for another charge. My pulse beat in my temples. I felt my blood warming to the challenge of this old boar.

Not waiting for the pig to decide the matter, we urged our horses forward to take him on the run. The beast did not move, but stood his ground and waited. Our spears were almost upon him when he broke sharply to the left, toward me—presenting his massive side as an easy target for my spear. I drew back to throw.

The boar must have sensed the movement, for he swerved and came headlong at me. His legs were a blur, and his tusks a glimmer of white in the gloom as he drove at me, grunting as he came. I braced myself for the impact, having already decide to let him come as near as possible before releasing my spear. Bran raced to join me, hoping to get in a second strike if mine missed.

All at once, there arose a great squeal and two more pigs darted into the run. I saw them only as two dark smudges speeding at an angle towards me. Bran shouted, his cry loud with surprise. I jerked the reins back hard, and my mount's legs all but folded under it as the creature struggled to halt and turn itself in one swift motion.

The first pig darted under the horse's rearing forehooves. The other I managed to ward off with a quick spearthrust as it made to rip into my mount's flank. I got a good look at the beast as it swerved aside to avoid the spear. It was a young tusker, not yet come into its full growth: thin in the hindquarters, and light in the chest. Yet, what it lacked in bulk, the beast more than made up for in speed and determination. For, no sooner had it passed one way than it charged again from another.

I shouted at Bran to warn him, and saw him, out of the corner of my eye, slashing at the second pig with a short, chopping motion of the spear. The pig fell, rolled on its back, legs kicking in the air, and then scrambled away, screaming as it fled.

This gave Bran a brief respite. He raised himself in the saddle and called for help, his voice ringing in the wood. I thought to give voice as well, but was soon too preoccupied to shout. The old boar had passed Bran and was now behind me. I heard a snuffling grunt as he lunged forward. I wheeled my horse and brought the spear down hard and fast. The blade caught the beast on the ridge of tight-muscled flesh atop his hump.

The spear bent and then came a loud, splintering crack as the shaft snapped in two. The next thing I knew I was falling sideways onto the forest floor.

I threw my leg over the saddle as I fell, and landed hard on my side. But at least my leg was not trapped beneath the horse. I scrambled to my feet and dived for another spear—bundled behind the saddle of my floundering mount.

Bran, seeing my predicament, threw his own spear to me. It struck the earth two paces beside me. I dived for it, snatched it up, and then whirled to my horse, seizing the reins and urging it upright. Blood flowed from its hock and I hoped the wound was not serious.

"Llew!" Bran shouted. A spear streaked past my shoulder as I turned. The missile hit the charging boar a glancing blow—only enough to turn it aside. I spun and thrust with my spear as it went past, but missed completely as the wily animal dodged aside, streaming fluid from its nostrils and foam from its tusks.

Just then I heard behind me a crashing sound, and turned to meet Emyr and Alun as they rode to our aid. At the appearance of the newcomers, the pigs turned and began racing away down the trail.

"They're running!" cried Alun, urging his horse to the chase.

Emyr and Bran were next away. I hooked an arm over the neck of my mount and swung myself up into the saddle. An instant later I was bolting after them. The pigs kept to the side of the hunting run, low among the branches, where they were hardest to reach. Our only hope of roast pig was to keep pace with them, and strike when they broke cover and dashed into the open.

We readied our spears and ranged ourselves accordingly. Then, as we drew even with our fleet-footed quarry, the hunting run turned suddenly and we found ourselves in a sunlit, bramble-hedged glade. In the center of the glade stood a dolmen: three upright stones capped by a single huge slab which formed a roof. The dolmen was surrounded by a shallow, grass-grown ditch and ring.

The old boar put his head down and ran straight across the clearing, skirting the dolmen and driving into the thicket on the far side of the glade. His young companion, however, was not so canny. The pig scurried across the ditch and disappeared behind the dolmen with Emyr right behind. Alun and I peeled away, racing for the opposite side to cut off his escape. Bran halted at the entrance to keep the brash porker from retreating back down the run.

The pig cleared the dolmen, saw us, and continued on around for the second time. Emyr picked him up as he passed and gave chase. Then it was Alun's and my chance once more. But the speedy pig darted among the stones and eluded us. Emyr shouted as the pig appeared on his side once more, and then I saw the brown blur as it rounded the ring and sped on for a third circuit.

Alun lofted a spear as the pig appeared once more. The spear struck the soft ground just in front of the young boar's jaw. The pig gave a frightened grunt and lunged for the cover of the dolmen stones.

I saw it scramble into the deep shadow under the capstone—I saw its silhouette sharp against the bright green beyond. And then it disappeared.

The pig simply melted from sight. I saw it go. Rather, I saw it, and then I did not see it any more. The creature had evaporated— tusks, tail, bristles and all—leaving not so much as a squeal behind.

I saw it go and my stomach tightened. My heart sank and I suddenly felt weak. My spear fell from my slack fingers; I made a clumsy grab for it and missed. The spear dropped on the ground.

"Where is it?" shouted Emyr. He looked to Alun, who leaned poised in the saddle with his spear raised, ready to throw. Neither had seen the pig vanish.

"The beast is hiding!" replied Alun, indicating the crevice between stones.

Cautiously, Emyr approached the dolmen and jabbed his spear beneath the capstone, thinking to drive the pig out. With trembling fingers, I gathered the reins and turned my mount, leaving the glade. Bran hailed me as I passed. "Have they made the kill?" he called. "Llew!"

I made no answer. Overcome by the enormity of the crisis, I could not speak. I simply spurred my horse away.

"Llew! What has happened?" Bran called sharply.

I knew what had happened: the web between the worlds had now grown so thin and tenuous that a frightened pig could cross the threshold in broad daylight. The balance between the worlds was skewed; the Endless Knot was unravelling. The Otherworld and the manifest world I had left behind were collapsing inward each upon the other. Chaos loomed.

I could hear the shriek of the void loud in my ears as I passed from the glade. The chill touched my heart—and my hand: my silver hand had grown cold on the end of my arm. The cold spread to my bones. Blackness swarmed the borders of my vision.

"Are you injured, lord?" called the Raven Chief behind me.

Ignoring Bran, I rode on...

I had almost reached the edge of the forest when the others caught me. They were puzzled by my actions, and disappointed at having to abandon the hunt. No one spoke, but I could feel their tacit bewilderment at my behavior. We rode back to camp without explanation and, upon dismounting, I turned to Bran. "Bring Tegid," I said, and ducked into my tent.

Goewyn was not there. No doubt she was away somewhere with Tángwen. I sat down on the red oxhide in the center of the tent, crossed my legs, folded my arms across my chest and bent my head until it almost touched my knees. I waited, feeling a cold tide of desperation rising within me. If I did not think about what I had seen, and what it meant, I could keep the tide from overwhelming me.

"Hurry, Tegid," I murmured, rocking slowly back and forth.

In this way I held the tide at bay and kept it from swallowing me and carrying me away. I do not know how much time passed, but I heard the brushing tread of a step at the doorway and then felt a presence beside me. I opened my eyes and raised my head.

Tegid was bending over me, concern creasing his brow. "I am

here, brother," he said softly. "The hunt went well?"

I shut my eyes again and shook my head. When I did not reply, he said, "What has happened?" He paused. "Llew, tell me. What has happened?"

I raised my silver hand to him. "It is cold, Tegid. Like ice."

He bent down and touched the metal hand thoughtfully. "It feels the same to me," he offered, straightening once more. "Tell me about the hunt."

"Three pigs," I began, haltingly. "They gave us a good hunt. We chased them—deep into the forest. One escaped. We followed two into a clearing. There was a dolmen and ring. We chased one of the pigs around the dolmen and... and then it disappeared."

"The dolmen?"

I cast a quick, disgusted glance at the bard to see if he was baiting me. "The pig. The pig disappeared. I saw it go, and I know where it went."

"Did the others see it?" he asked.

"That is hardly the point—is it?" I spat.

Tegid watched me closely.

"I have seen the pig before," I told him. "Before I came to Albion, I saw that pig. It is just like the aurochs, you see?"

Tegid did not see. How could he? So I explained to him about the aurochs—the aurochs we had hunted on our flight to Findargad, and which had disappeared into a mound the same way the pig had vanished.

"But we killed it," Tegid protested. "We ate its meat and it fed us."

"There were *two*!" I said. "One disappeared and the other we killed. That aurochs is what brought Simon and me to Albion; the one we chased was the one that brought us. And the pig I chased today was the one I saw before I came."

Tegid shook his head slowly. "I hear you, brother, but I still do not understand why this upsets you," he said. "It is unfortunate, but—"

"Unfortunate!"

Tegid stood looking at me for a moment, then sat down facing me. He settled himself, and said, "If you want me to understand, you must tell me what it means." He spoke slowly, but crisply. He was restraining himself, but with obvious effort.

"It means," I said, closing my eyes again, "that Nettles was *wrong*. The balance is not restored. The Knot—the Endless Knot is still unravelling."

The Return of the King

Though Tegid and I talked at length, I was unable to make him grasp the significance of the vanishing pig. Probably I could not explain properly, or at least in a way he could understand. He seemed willing enough, but my explanation lacked some element crucial to persuasion. I could not make him see the danger.

"Tegid," I said at last, "it is late and I am tired. Let us get something to eat."

Tegid agreed that might be best; he rose stiffly, and left the tent. Gloom and doom had so permeated my thoughts that I was amazed to find a stunning sunset in progress—pink, carnelian, copper, wine and fuchsia flung in gorgeous splashes against a radiant hyacinth sky. I blinked my eyes and stood staring at it for a moment. The air was warm still, with just a hint of evening's chill. Soon the stars would come out, and we would be treated to yet another spectacle of almost staggering grandeur.

Through all its travails, Albion still endured. How was that possible? What preserved it? What sustained it in the very teeth of cataclysm and disaster?

"What do you see?" asked Goewyn softly.

"I see a miracle," I replied. "I see it and I wonder how such things can endure."

Upon seeing Tegid emerge from the tent, Goewyn had quickened her step to meet me. She had kept herself away from the tent while Tegid and I talked, but now she was eager to discover the subject of our discussion. "Are you hungry?" she asked, taking my flesh hand in hers. She did not say that she had been waiting long; the curiosity in her dark brown eyes was evident enough.

"I am sorry," I told her. "I did not mean to exclude you. Tegid and I were talking. You should have joined us."

"When a king and his bard hold council, no one must intrude," she replied. There was no irritation in her tone, and I realized that despite her curiosity, which was only natural, she would have fought anyone who tried to disturb us.

"Next time I will send for you, Goewyn," I said. "I am sorry. Forgive me."

"You are troubled, Llew." She reached a cool hand to my forehead and smoothed my hair back. "Walk. Take your ease. I will have food brought to the tent and await you there."

"No, walk with me. I do not want to be alone just now."

So we walked together a while. We did not talk. Goewyn's undemanding presence was a balm to my agitated spirit, and I began to relax somewhat. As the stars began to waken in the sky, we returned to the tent. "Rest now. I will see that food is brought." She moved away, and I watched her go. My heart soared to see her in motion. I loved every curving line.

My melancholy lifted at once. Here was love and life, full and free before me. Here was a soul shining like a beacon flame, shining for me. I wanted to gather her in my arms and hold her for ever.

Never leave me, Goewyn.

Entering the tent once more, I found Tegid and Bran waiting. Tegid had also rousted Cynan from his tent and brought him along. Rushlights had been lit and placed on stands around the perimeter of the tent, casting a rosy glow over the interior. They ceased talking when I appeared.

"This was not necessary, Tegid," I told him.

"You are troubled, brother," the bard replied. "I have failed to console you, so I brought your chieftains to attend you."

I thanked them all for coming, and insisted that it was not necessary to attend me. "I have Goewyn to console me," I explained.

"It is unfortunate that the pig got away," Bran sympathized. "But we can find another one tomorrow."

"The hunting runs are full of them," offered Cynan helpfully.

Shaking my head gently, I tried once more to explain. "It is not the pig. I do not care about the pig. It is what the pig's disappearance represents that worries me. Do you see that?"

I could tell by the way they looked at me they did not see that at all. I tried again.

"There is trouble," I said. "There is a balance between this world and my world, and that balance has been disturbed. I thought defeating Siawn Hy and Meldron would restore the balance—Nettles thought so, too. But he was wrong, and now..."

The blank stares brought my lecture to an abrupt halt. I had lost them again.

"If there is trouble, we will soon know it," Bran suggested. "And we will conquer it."

Spoken like a fighting man. "It is not that kind of trouble," I answered.

"We are more than a match for any enemy," Cynan boasted. "Let it come. There is no enemy we cannot defeat."

"It is not that simple, Cynan." I sighed, shaking my head again. "Believe me, I wish it were."

Tegid, desperate to help, observed, "The Banfáith's prophecy has proven true through all things. All that has happened, and all that is yet to happen, is contained in the prophecy."

"There, you see?" agreed Cynan with satisfaction. "There is nothing to worry about. We have the prophecy to guide us if trouble should come. There is nothing to worry about."

"You do not understand," I said wearily. It was as if a gulf stood between us—a gulf as wide and deep as that which separates the worlds, perhaps. Maybe there was no way for them to cross that gap. If Professor Nettleton were here, he would know what to say to make them understand. Nettles would know what it meant... or would he? He had been wrong about my remaining in Albion; obviously there was still some work for me to finish. Then again, maybe he was right; maybe it was my lingering presence that was causing the trouble.

I almost groaned with the effort of trying to make sense of it. Why, oh why, was this so difficult?

"If it is understanding we lack," the bard exhorted, "then let us look to the prophecy." Pressing the palms of his hands together, he touched his fingertips to his lips and drew a deep breath. Closing his eyes, he began, speaking with quiet intensity, to declaim the prophecy given me by Gwenllian, Banfáith of Ynys Sci.

I needed no help in recalling the prophecy; I remembered the Banfáith's words as if they were engraved on my heart. Still, each time I heard those stern, unforgiving words spoken aloud, I felt the thrill in my gut. This time it was more than a thrill, however; I felt the distinct tug of a power beyond my ken bearing me along—destiny, perhaps? I do not know. But it was as if I was standing on a seastrand with the tide flowing around me; I could feel its irresistible pull. Events like waves had gathered and now were moving, bearing me along. I could resist—I could swim against the tide—but I would be carried along anyway in the end.

Tegid came to the end of the recitation, saying, "Before Albion is One, the Hero Feat must be performed and Silver Hand must reign."

This last seemed to please both Bran and Cynan immensely. Bran nodded sagely, and Cynan folded his arms across his chest as if he had carried the day. "Silver Hand reigns!" he declared proudly. "And when the Cylchedd is complete, Albion will be united once again under the Aird Righ."

"That is surely the way of it," enthused Bran.

I remained unconvinced, but had run out of arguments. Then Goewyn arrived with one of her maidens bringing our supper, and so I decided to let the matter rest for the time being. If anything were seriously wrong, Professor Nettleton would surely return to tell me so, or send a message to me somehow.

"Let us hope that is the way of it," I agreed reluctantly, and then dismissed them to their own tents and to their rest.

"We will remain vigilant, lord," Bran vowed as he left. "That is all we can do."

"True, Bran. Very true."

He and Cynan filed out, followed by Tegid, who, though he appeared anxious to tell me something, merely gazed at Goewyn for a moment, bade her a good night's rest, and went out, leaving us alone to share our meal and my misery.

"Eat something, husband," Goewyn prodded gently. "A man cannot think or fight on an empty stomach."

She lifted a bowl under my nose. The aroma of boiled meat in thick, salty broth made my mouth water. Taking the bowl in my silver hand, I dipped my fingers in and began eating. My mind turned again to the harsh promises of the prophecy, and I ate in silence, ignoring Goewyn as she sat directly before me.

"Here, my love," she said after a time, drawing me from my thoughts. "For you." I looked up to see her break a small loaf of brown bread in her hands. She smiled, extending half the loaf to me.

A small gesture: her hand reaching out to me—as if she would thwart all the unknown hazards of the future with a bit of broken bread—it was so humble and trifling against such overwhelming uncertainty. Yet, in that moment, it was enough.

The next day we resumed the circuit, and all went as it had before. Nothing terrible happened. The earth did not open before our feet and swallow us whole; the sky did not fall; the sun did not deviate from its appointed course. And, when evening came, the moon rose to shed a friendly light upon the land. All was as it should be.

After a few such uneventful days, I began to persuade myself that the wild pig's disappearance was merely a lingering ripple in the disturbance caused by Simon and Meldron; a simple, small, isolated event, it foreshadowed no great catastrophe. Albion was healing itself, yes, but it would be unrealistic to expect everything to return to normal overnight. Undoubtedly, the healing process would go on for a long time. And after all, my reign was, as Cynan and Tegid implied, a major element of that recovery. How could I think otherwise?

Maffar, sweetest of seasons, had run its course full and fair, and Gyd, season of sun, was well begun before we at last turned the wagons north. I was glad to have made the circuit, but more so now that it was finished. I missed Dinas Dwr and all the friends we had left behind. And I wanted to see what had been accomplished in my absence.

The southern leg of our journey completed, Cynan and Tángwen bade us farewell, but not before I extracted a promise to winter with us in Dinas Dwr. "Favor us with the pleasure of your company. Our hall is a cowbyre compared to yours," I declared. "And it is as cold beside the hearth as on the hilltop when the snow drifts deep. But it would be less wretched if you would deign to share our meager fare."

"*Mo anam!*" Cynan cried. "Do you expect me to refuse such a generous offer? See the cups are filled, brother—it is Cynan Machae at your gate when the wind howls in the roof-trees!"

He and Tángwen returned to Dun Cruach, and we proceeded on to Sarn Cathmail. Once we had set our faces towards home, my impatience knew no bounds. We could not move swiftly enough. Each day's distance brought us no nearer, or so it seemed to me, yet with every step my eagerness increased; like thirst burning in a parched throat, I ached with it.

It was not until the land began to lift and I saw the high hills glimmering in the blue heat haze that I began to feel we were at last returning. On the day I saw Môn Dubh, I could contain myself no longer. I rode ahead, with Goewyn at my side, and would likely have left the others far behind if Tegid had not prevented us.

"You cannot return this way," he said when he had caught up with us. "Allow your people to make ready a proper welcome."

"Just seeing Dinas Dwr again is welcome enough for me," I insisted. "We could have been there by now if you had not stopped us. We will go ahead. Let the rest come along in their own good time."

He shook his head firmly. "One more day, then you will enter your city and receive the welcome due a king. I will send Emyr ahead to prepare the way for you." He turned a deaf ear to my protests and insisted, "We have observed the rite without flaw. Let us complete it likewise."

Goewyn sided with him. "Let it be as your wise bard advises," she urged. "It is only one more day, and your people will be grateful for the opportunity of anticipating the return of their king and welcoming you back in a manner worthy of your rank."

So, Emyr Lydaw was sent ahead to announce our arrival. I spent one more night in a tent on the trail. Like a child on the eve of a celebration, I was too excited to sleep. I lay in the tent, tossing this way and that, and finally rose and went out to walk away my restlessness.

It was dark, the moon high overhead and bright. The camp was quiet. I heard a tawny owl calling, and the answering call of its mate a short distance away. I looked up at the sound and saw a ghostly shape flickering through the treetops. The surrounding hills were softly outlined against a sky of silver-flecked jet. All was dark and quiet and as it should be—except for one small detail: a spark-bright glimmer on the crest of a faraway hill.

I watched for a moment before realizing what it was: a beacon. In the same instant, I felt a chill in my silver hand; a sharp cold stab.

I turned to scan the hilltops behind me, but saw no answering flare. I wondered what the signal fire betokened, and thought to fetch Tegid from his bed to show it to him. But the beacon faded and, with its departure, my own certainty of what I had seen. Perhaps it was nothing more than the campfire of hunters; or maybe Scatha had set watchers along the ridge to warn of our approach.

Stalking the perimeter of the camp, I spoke briefly with the guards at the horse picket, but they had seen nothing. I finished my inspection of the camp and returned to my tent. I lay down on the fleece and fell asleep listening to Goewyn's deep, slow breathing.

I awakened early the next morning, dressed quickly, and proceeded to make a general nuisance of myself by urging everyone to hurry. We were but a day's march from Druim Vran, and with all speed we would reach the lake at sunset and dine at Dinas Dwr that night.

By midday I could see the dark line of Raven Ridge, and I thought we would never arrive. Nevertheless, as the sun began sinking low in the west, we entered the broad plain spreading before the ridgewall. The shadow of the gorsedd mound stretched long across the plain and the looming mass of Druim Vran soared above it.

All along the ridge stood the people, my people, waiting to welcome us home. My heart soared at the sight.

"Listen," said Goewyn, tilting her head. "They are singing."

We were too far away to hear the words, but the voices fell like a fine sweet rain splashing down from on high. I halted on the trail, swivelled in the saddle, and called to Tegid, "Do you hear? What are they singing?"

He rode to join me and halted to listen a moment, then smiled. "It is *Arianrhod's Greeting*," he said. "It is the song Arianrhod sings to her lover when she sees him sailing over the waves to rescue her."

"Is it?" I wondered. "I have never heard that story," I said.

"It is a beautiful tale," Tegid said. "I will sing it to you some time."

I turned my face to the heights and listened to the glad sound. I would not have imagined that the sight of my people standing along the ridgewall and singing their welcome to the valley below could touch me so deeply. My eyes grew misty with tears at the sound; truly, I had come home.

13

The Aird Righ's Mill

"Hie! Hie!" cried Goewyn as she galloped past. "I thought you were eager to reach home!" she shouted.

I lashed my mount to speed and raced after her. She gained the ridgewall before me and, without slackening her pace, flew straight up the track. I followed in a hail of dust and pebbles thrown up by the horses' hooves, but could not catch her. She reached the top first and slipped from the saddle, turning to await me.

"Welcome home, O King," she said.

I threw a leg over the neck of my horse and slid to the ground beside her. "Lady, I claim a welcome kiss," I said, pulling her to me. The crowd came running to meet us, and we were soon pressed on every side by eager well-wishers.

What a glad greeting it was! The tumult was heartfelt and loud, the reception dizzying. We were soon engulfed in a heady whirl of welcome. Scatha appeared in the forefront of the press. She seized her daughter in her arms and held her; Pen-y-Cat hugged me next, clasping me tightly to her, and, taking my hand and one of Goewyn's, she gazed at us with shining eyes and declared, "Welcome, my children, I give you good greeting."

She kissed us both, and held us together before her while her eyes drank in the sight. "I have missed you both," she said. Then, fixing each one of us in her gaze, she asked, "It *is* just the two of you?"

"Still just two," my bride told her mother. She squeezed my hand.

"Well," Scatha allowed, "you are no less welcome. I have longed for you every day."

We embraced again, and I glimpsed the crannog in the lake beyond. "I see that Dinas Dwr has survived in our absence."

"Survived?" boomed Calbha, wading towards us through the crowd to stand before us. The Ravens we had left behind followed at his heels. "We have thrived! Welcome back, Silver Hand," he said, gripping my arms. "You have fared well?"

"We have fared exceedingly well, Calbha," I answered. "The circuit of the land is complete. All is well."

"Tonight we will celebrate your return," Scatha announced. "In the hall, the welcome cup awaits."

Thanks to Tegid's foresight, Scatha and Calbha had had time to prepare a feast for our return. Trailing well-wishers, we made our way down to the city on the lake; in the golden light of a setting sun Dinas Dwr seemed to me a gem aglow in a broad, shining band.

At the lakeshore, we climbed into boats and paddled quickly across to the crannog, where we were welcomed by those who had stayed behind to attend to the preparations.

The tang of roasting meat reached us the instant we stepped from the boats. Two whole oxen and six pigs were dripping fat over pits of charcoal; ale vats had been set up outside the hall, and skins of mead poured into bowls. At our approach, a dozen maidens took up gold and silver bowls and ran to meet us.

"Welcome, Great King," said a dimpled, smiling maid, raising the bowl to me. "Too long have you been absent from your hearth, lord. Drink deep and take your ease," she said prettily, and it melted my heart to hear it.

I accepted the bowl, lifted it to my lips, and drank the sweet, golden nectar. It was flavored with anise and warmed my throat as it slid silkily over my tongue. I declared it the finest drink I had ever tasted, and passed the bowl to Goewyn. The king having drunk, the remaining bowls, cups, and jars could be distributed; this was done at once and the feast began.

No one was happier than I to be back home. I looked long on the hall, and on the happy faces of all those I had left behind. They were my people, and I was their king. I truly felt I had come home, that my absence had pained, and that my return was pleasing.

It was not until I stood before my own hall with the taste of herbed mead in my mouth and the shouts of acclaim loud in my ears that I realized Tegid's wisdom in proposing the circuit. In going out like a king, I had become a king indeed. I belonged to the land now; heart and soul, I was part of it. In some ancient, mystical way, the circuit united my spirit with Albion and its people. I felt my soul expand to embrace those around me, and I remembered all those I had met in the course of my circuit of the land. As I loved those around me, I loved them all. They were my people, and I was their king.

I saw Tegid standing a little distance apart with a bowl to his lips, surrounded by his Mabinogi. He sensed me watching him and lowered the bowl, smiling. The crafty bard knew what had happened. He knew full well the effect circuit and homecoming would have on my soul. He smiled at me over the bowl and raised it to me, then drank again. Oh yes, he knew.

Goewyn pressed the bowl into my hands once more and I raised it to Tegid and drank to him. Then Goewyn and I shared a drink. Garanaw, who had stayed behind to help Scatha train the young warriors, came and greeted me like a brother. We drank together then, and I embarked upon a long round of drinking the health of all my long-absent friends.

Food followed, mounds of bread and cakes, and crackling joints of roast meat, great steaming cauldrons full of leeks, marrows, and cabbages. It was a splendid feast: eating by torchlight under the stars, the night dark and warm around us.

After we had eaten, Tegid brought out his harp and we drifted away on wings of song. Under his peerless touch, the skyvault became a vast Seeing Bowl filled with the black oak water of all possibilities, each star a glimmering promise. Dawn was glinting in the east when we finally made our way to bed, but we slept the sleep of deep contentment.

We bade farewell to Calbha a few days later. He was anxious to return to his lands in Llogres and establish himself and his people before Sollen set in. I did not envy him the work he faced. I made certain he took a large portion of seed grain and meal, and the best of the pigs, sheep and cattle to begin new herds. I gave him everything he would need to see him through the first winter, and we parted with vows of everlasting friendship, and promises to visit one another often. He and the remnant of his tribe left with a dozen wagons piled high with provisions, tools and weapons.

As Calbha had said, Dinas Dwr prospered in our absence. The crops and herds had flourished, the people had plenty and were content. The horror loosed by the Great Hound Meldron was fading, and with it the tainting abomination of his reign.

Having completed the Cylchedd of the land, I was not content to sit on my throne and watch the world go by. Indeed, I was more eager than ever to be a good king. As the warm days passed, I found myself wondering what I might do to benefit my people. What could I give them?

My bard suggested I give them wise leadership, but I had in mind something more tangible: an engineering feat like a bridge, or a road. Neither seemed quite right. If a road, where would it go? And if a bridge, what body of water needed spanning?

I ambled around for a couple of days trying to decide what sort of endeavor would serve the people best. And, as luck would have it, one morning I was walking among the sheds and work huts on the lakeshore when I heard the slow, heavy mumble of the grinding wheel. I turned and lifted my eyes from the path to see two women bent over a massive double wheel of stone. One woman turned the upper stone with a staff while the other poured dried grain into the hole in the center. They saw me watching and greeted me.

"Please continue," I said, "I do not wish to interrupt your work."

They resumed their labor and I watched the arduous process. I saw their slender backs bent and their shapely arms straining to turn the heavy stone. It was hard work for meal which would be eaten in a moment, and there would be more grain to grind tomorrow. When they finished, the women collected the flour from around the stone, using a straw whisk to sweep every last fleck into their bag. They bade me farewell then, and left. No sooner was the grindstone idle, however, than two more women appeared and, taking grain from the storehouse, they also began to grind their flour.

This was no new chore in Dinas Dwr. It had been performed in just this way since before anyone could remember, probably since the first harvest had been gathered and dried. But this was the first time I had seen it as the back-breaking labor it was. And so I arrived at the boon I would give my people. I would give them a mill.

A mill! Such a simple thing, rudimentary really. Yet, a wonder if you do not have one. And we did not have one. Neither did anyone else. So far as I knew there had never been a grain mill in Albion. When I thought of how much time and energy would be saved, I wondered I had not thought of it before. And, after the mill, I could see other, perhaps more exalted ventures. The mill was just the beginning, but it was as good a project as any to begin with.

Returning to the crannog, I called my wise bard to me. "Tegid," I said, "I am going to build a mill. And you are going to help me."

Tegid peered at me sceptically and pulled on his lower lip.

"You know," I explained, "a mill—with stones for grinding grain."

He looked slightly puzzled, but agreed that, in principle at least, a mill was a fine thing to build.

"No, I do not mean a pair of grindstones turned by hand. These stones will be much bigger than that."

"How big?" he wondered, eyeing me narrowly.

"Huge. Enormous! Big enough to grind a whole season's supply of grain in a few days. What do you think?"

This appeared to confound Tegid all the more. "A worthy ambition, indeed," he replied. "Yet, I cannot help thinking that grindstones so large would be very difficult to move. Are you suggesting oxen?"

"No," I told him. "I am not suggesting oxen."

"Good," he remarked with some relief. "Oxen must be fed and—"

"I am suggesting water."

"Water?"

"Exactly. It is to be a water mill."

The bewilderment on his face was wonderful. I laughed to see it. He drew breath to protest, but I said, "It is a simple invention from my world. But it will work here. Let me show you what I mean."

I knelt and drew my knife. After scratching a few lines in the dirt, I said, "This is the stream that flows into the lake." I drew a wavy circle. "This is the lake."

Tegid gazed at the squiggles and nodded.

"Now then." I drew a square on the stream. "If we put a dam at this place—"

"If we make a dam at that place, the stream will flood the meadow and the water will not reach the lake."

"True," I agreed. "Unless the water had a way past the dam. You see, we make a weir with a very narrow opening and let the water out slowly—through a revolving wheel. A wheel made of paddles." I drew a crude wheel with flat paddles, and indicated with my hand how the water would push the paddles and turn the wheel. "Like so. See? And this turning wheel is joined to the grindstone." I laced my fingers to suggest cogs meshing and turning.

Tegid nodded shrewdly. "And as the wheel turns, it turns the grindstone."

"That is the way of it."

Tegid frowned, gazing at the lines in the dirt. "I assume you know how this can be accomplished?" he said at last.

"Indeed," I stated confidently. "I mean, I think so."

"This is a marvel I would like to see." Tegid frowned at the dirt drawing and asked, "But will it not make the people lazy?"

"Never fear, brother. The people have more than enough to keep them busy without having to grind every single seed by hand. Trust me."

Tegid straightened. "So be it. How will you proceed?"

"First we will select the place to build the weir." I stood, replacing my knife in my belt. "I could use your advice there."

"When will you begin?"

"At once."

We left the crannog and walked out along the lakeshore to the place where the stream which passed under the ridgewall flowed into the lake. Then we followed the stream towards the ridge. We walked along the stream, pausing now and then to allow Tegid to look around. At a place about halfway to the ridgewall—where the stream emerged from deeply-cleft banks at the edge of the woods which rose up on the slopes of Druim Vran, the bard stopped.

"This," Tegid said, tapping the ground with his staff, "is the place I deem best for your water mill."

The location seemed less than promising to me. "There is no place for a weir," I pointed out. I had envisaged a flat, calm mill pond, with brown trout sporting in dappled shade—not a steep-banked slope on a hill.

"The weir will be easily dug here," Tegid maintained. "There is wood and stone within easy reach, and this is where the water begins its race to the lake."

I studied the waterflow for a moment, looking back along the course of the stream; I considered the wooded slopes and the stony banks. Tegid was right, it would a good place for a mill. Different from what I'd had in mind, but a much better use of gravity to turn the mill wheel and much less difficulty in keeping the water from flooding the meadow. I wondered what the shrewd bard knew about such things as gravity and hydraulics.

"You are right. This is the place for us. Here we will build our mill."

Work began that same day. First, I had the site cleared of brush. While that was being done, I searched for a way to draw some of my ideas, settling for a sharpened pine twig and a slab of yellow beeswax, and I began educating my master-builder, a man named Huel Gadarn, in the ways of water-powered mills. He was quick as he was clever; I had only to scratch a few lines on the beeswax and he grasped not only the form of the thing I was drawing but, often as not, the concept behind it as well. The only aspect of the procedure he found baffling was how the power of the water wheel was transferred to the giant grinding-stones. But this difficulty owed more to my poor skill in sketching a gear than to any failing on Huel's part.

Next we built a small model of the mill out of twigs and bark and clay. When that was finished, I was satisfied that Huel had all the various elements of the operation firmly under his command. I had no fear that, given time and inclination, Huel the master-builder could build the mill himself. We were ready to proceed.

Once the site was cleared, we could begin excavating the weir. But then it rained.

I spent the first day drawing various kinds of gears. On the second day I started pacing. By the fourth day, which dawned just as grey and wet as the three before it, I was pacing *and* cursing the weather. Goewyn endured me as long as she could, but finally grew exasperated and informed me that no grindstone, however huge, was worth the aggravation I was causing. She then sent me away to do my stalking, as she called it, elsewhere.

I spent a wet, restless day in the hall, listening to idle talk and itching to be at the building site. Fortunately, the next day dawned clear and bright, and we were able, at last—and with Goewyn's emphatic blessing—to begin digging the foundations for Albion's new wonder: the Aird Righ's Mill.

14

Intruders

Through Maffar's long days of warmth and bliss the Year's Wheel slowly revolved. Rhyll came on in a shimmering blaze, but the golden days and sharp, cool nights quickly dulled. The high color faded and the land withered beneath windy grey skies and cold, drenching rain.

Our harvest, so bountiful the previous year, yielded less than anticipated due to the rain. Day after day, we watched the skies, hoping for a break in the weather and a few sunny days to dry the grain. Rot set in before we could gather it all. It was no disaster, thanks to the bounty of the last harvest, but still a disappointment.

Progress on the mill slowed, and I grew restive. With Sollen's icy fingers stretching towards us, I was anxious to get as much finished as possible before the snow stopped us. I drove Huel and his workers relentlessly. Sometimes, if the rainfall was not heavy, I made them work through it. As the days grew shorter, I grew more frantic and demanding. I had torches and braziers brought to the site so that we could work after dark.

Tegid finally intervened; he approached me one night when I returned shivering from a windy day in the rain. "You have accomplished a great deal," he affirmed, "but you go too far. Look around you, Silver Hand; the days are short and the light is not good. How much longer do you think the sky will hold back the snow?

Come, it is time to take your rest."

"And just abandon the mill? Abandon all we have done? Tegid, you are talking nonsense."

"Did I tell you to abandon anything?" he sniffed. "You can begin again as soon as Gyd clears the skies once more. Now is the time for rest, and for more pleasurable pursuits indoors."

"Just a few more days, Tegid. It is not going to hurt anyone."

"We neglect the seasons to our peril," he replied stiffly.

"There will be plenty of time for lazing around the hearth, never fear."

Riding out to the building site early the next morning, I regretted those words. We had worked hard, very hard; but the mill had been begun late in the season and now the weather had turned against us. It was absurd of me to expect men to work in the dark, wet, and cold, and I was a fool for demanding it of them.

Worse, I was becoming a tyrant: self-indulgent, insensitive, obsessive and oppressive. My great labor-saving boon had so far produced nothing but plenty of extra work for everyone.

My wise bard was right. The time-honored rhythm of the seasons, of work and play and rest, served the purpose of balance in the sacred pattern of life. I had tipped the scales too far, and it was time for me to put it right.

The day had dawned crisp, the sunlight thin, but bright; the chill east wind tingled the nostrils with the fresh scent of snow. Yes, I thought as I came upon the vacant site, it was time to cease work for the winter. I dismounted, and walked around, inspecting the excavations, waiting for Huel and his builders to arrive.

Despite the incessant delays, we had made good progress on the construction: a shallow weir had been dug and lined with stone; the foundations, both timber and stone, for the mill house had been established. In the spring, we would quarry the huge grindstones, and set them in place—the mill house would be raised around them. The wheel would be built and then the shafts and gears attached. If all went well, I reflected, the mill would be ready to grind its first grain by harvest time next year.

Preoccupied with these plans, I wandered around the diggings and slowly became aware of a peculiar sound, faint and far away, but distinct in the crisp autumn air: a slow, rhythmic thump—like stones falling onto the earth at regular intervals. What is more, I realized with a start that I had been hearing it for some time.

I glanced quickly towards the ridge trail, but saw no one. I held myself completely still and listened. But the sound was gone now. Intrigued, I remounted my horse and rode up the slope of the ridge and into the wood. I paused to listen. There was nothing but the whisper of the wind in bare branches.

Turning away, I thought I heard the soft thudding pat of running steps on the path ahead—just a hint and then the wind stole the sound away again. Raising myself in the saddle, I called out, "Who is it?" I paused. No answer came. I shouted again, more loudly, "Who is there?"

Lifting the reins, I rode forward, slowly, through the close-grown pines and came upon one of the many tracks leading to the top of the ridge. Following the track, I gained the ridgeway and proceeded along the top of the ridge. Almost at once, I came upon a footprint in the damp earth. The print appeared fresh—at least, rain had not degraded it overnight; a swift search revealed a few more leading into the wood.

I turned from the trail, proceeding cautiously towards the edge of the ridge, and immediately came upon an enormous heap of timber: fallen branches and logs fetched from the wood and thrown into a pile at the very edge of the ridge. The place was well chosen, screened from the trail behind by the trees, yet open to the valley beyond. There was no sign of anyone about, so I dismounted and walked to the woodpile.

Scores of footprints tracked the damp earth, and on closer scrutiny I observed the prints of at least three different people. The immense size of the heap astonished me. It was the work of many days—or many hands. Either way, I did not like it. An intruder had raised a beacon on our very threshold.

I whirled from the beacon-heap and vaulted into the saddle. I snapped the reins and urged my mount to speed, skirted the beacon, and galloped along the ridgeway until I reached a place where I could look down on either side of the ridge: on one side, the valley with its brown fields and the long slate-grey lake with the crannog in the center; on the other side, the gravemound beside the river, and the empty plain spreading beyond.

I released my breath through clenched teeth. I had half-expected to see Meldron's massed war host, risen again, streaming into the valley. But all was still and silent.

Even so, I sat in the saddle for a time, looking and listening. The clouds shifted and the light dimmed. A cold, misty rain began drizzling out of the darkening sky. The wind caught it and sent it swirling. I turned away from the ridgeway and started back down the trail to the lake. I had almost reached the lake path when I met the workmen coming up to the mill.

"Go back to your families," I told them. "Sollen has begun; it is time we took our ease."

The workmen were much relieved to hear me say this. So it surprised me to have Huel instantly appeal against the decision. "Lord," said my master-builder, "allow us but one more day to secure the site against the snows to come. It will save much labor when the sun returns and work resumes."

"Very well," I told him. "Do what you think best. But after today there will be no more work until Gyd."

Leaving them to continue on their way, I returned to the crannog. Tegid was standing at the hearth in the hall, and I sent Emyr to fetch Bran. The bard noticed my agitation at once. "What has happened?" he asked.

I thrust my hands towards the fire. My silver hand glowed with the light of the flames, and my flesh hand began to warm. I looked at the gleaming silver, cold and stiff as a chunk of ice on the end of my arm. Why was it so cold?

"Llew?" Tegid placed a hand on my shoulder.

"There is a beacon on the ridge." I turned to regard him. His dark eyes were intense, but he showed no other sign of alarm. "It is on the ridgeway above the mill."

"Did you see anyone?"

"Not a soul. But I heard a sound—wood thrown onto the heap, I think. And I saw footprints: three men at least, maybe more. Someone has gone to a great deal of effort, Tegid."

Bran arrived just then, and I repeated what I had just told Tegid. The bard stared at the flames, stroking his chin. Bran scowled as he listened and, when I had finished, said, "I will take the warband and search the woods and ridge. If the footprints are fresh, the men cannot have travelled far. We will find those who have done this and bring them back to face you."

The Chief Bard continued to gaze into the flames. Bran was waiting for an answer. "Yes," I told him. "Raise the warband at once. We will begin at the beacon—"

Tegid raised his head. "It is not for you to go," he said softly. I started to object, but he gave a slight shake of his head; he did not like to contradict me in front of Bran. Recalling our previous discussion concerning kings chasing criminals, I understood his hesitation and relented.

"Ready the men," I commanded, and told him where to find the beacon. "You can start there." The Chief Raven gave his assent and made to turn away. I caught him by the sleeve. "Find them, Bran. Track them down, and bring them to me. I would know who has done this and why."

A moment later Bran's voice resounded through the hall as he chose the men who were to accompany him. A group numbering twenty or so left the hall at once—to startled speculation all around.

Turning once more to Tegid, I said, "I will ride with them only as far as the beacon." The bard turned his eyes from the fire and regarded me with a sceptical look. "What are you thinking?" I asked.

"You say it is a beacon," he said. "Why?"

"I know a beacon-pile when I see one, brother."

"That I do not doubt," he replied quickly. "But you assumed an enemy had made it."

"You think otherwise?"

"I think you have not told me all." He had not raised his voice, but his gaze grew keen and accusing. "If there is something I should know, tell me now."

"I have told you all I know—just as it happened," I began, but he cut me off with an impatient twitch of his mouth. I stared hard at him. Why was he behaving like this?

"Think!"

"I am thinking, Tegid!" My voice echoed in the hall. I bit back the words and clamped my mouth shut. Why did I assume an enemy? A beacon is a signal made to be seen from a distance; a beacon is . . . I looked at my silver hand almost touching the flames, and felt the chill still tingling there. And I remembered the last time I had felt such a chill . . .

Raising my eyes, I said, "You are right, Tegid. It happened so long ago I had forgotten. I did not think it important."

"Perhaps you are right. Tell me now."

With that, I told him about the beacon-fire I had seen on the night we camped on the plain below Druim Vran. "I am sorry, brother," I told him when I had finished. "I should have told you then. But the next day we were home, and I guess I assumed the beacon had been lit for our return, and I forgot about it—until now."

"That is not the reason you did not tell me," he stated flatly. "You allowed your impatience to obscure your judgment. In your eagerness to see Dinas Dwr you did not want to believe anything could be wrong, so you hid this from yourself, and from me."

My Chief Bard was most astute. "I am sorry. It will not happen again."

He dismissed my apology with an impatient gesture. "It is done and cannot be undone."

"So, you think we have been watched since our return?"

"What do *you* think?"

"I think it likely."

"And I think it certain."

"But why?"

"That we will learn when Bran returns with those who have been watching."

So we settled back to wait, and I found the waiting hard. I wanted to be out on the trail with my men, dealing directly with the threat instead of sitting in the hall doing nothing. One day passed, and then another. I kept my misgivings to myself. As the third day waned—and still no word from the tracking party—I voiced my mounting anxiety to Tegid. "They should have returned by now. It has been three days."

He did not look up from the basket of leaves he was sorting into a bowl. "Did you hear me?"

"I heard you." He stopped sifting the leaves and raised his head. He was bothered by Bran's absence, too; I could tell. "What would you have me say?"

"They have run into trouble. We should go after them."

"They are twenty worthy warriors," the bard pointed out. "Bran is more than a match for any encounter. Leave it to him."

"Three days more," I said. "If we have heard nothing by then, I am going after them."

"If we have heard nothing in three days," he agreed, "then you can go after them. And I will ride with you."

Nevertheless, I rode to Druim Vran the next day, just to learn if there was anything to be seen from the high ridgetop. Though cold, the day was bright, the clouds high and white. Goewyn rode with me and, though we pursued the ridgeway east a fair distance, we saw no sign of any trouble.

Before starting back, we paused to rest the horses. Sitting together on a rock overlooking the valley below, a fresh wind stinging cheeks and chin, I draped my cloak around us both and held her close as we watched the mist flowing down the hillsides to blanket the glen.

"We should be getting back," I said, "or Tegid will send the hounds after us."

We made no move, however, content to sit and watch the valley fill with thick, grey mist. The light began to fail at last and, although luxuriating in Goewyn's nearness and warmth, I nevertheless forced myself to stand. "It will be dark soon," I said. "We should head home."

"Mmmm." Goewyn sighed and drew her feet under her, but did not stand.

Moving to the horses, I pulled the tether pegs and gathered the reins. "Llew?" Goewyn said. Her voice struck a note that made me turn at once.

"What is it?"

"There is something moving down there— along the river... in the mist."

In three strides I was by her side and gazing into the quickly fading glen. "I do not see anything," I said. "Are you certain?"

She stretched her arm to point out the place. "There!" she said, without taking her eyes from the spot.

I looked where she was pointing. The mist parted somewhat and I saw what appeared to be three dark shapes moving along the river bank. Whether afoot or on horseback, I could not say. I saw only three swarthy, shapeless bulks moving along the riverside... and then the mist took them from my sight.

"They are coming this way," I concluded. "They are coming to Druim Vran."

"Is it Bran, do you think?"

"I cannot say. But something tells me it is not Bran— or any of those with him."

"Who then?"

"That I mean to find out." I reached a hand down to Goewyn and pulled her to her feet. "Ride back to Dinas Dwr and alert Tegid and Scatha. Tell them to assemble a warband, and show them where to come."

Goewyn clutched my arms. "You are not going down there."

"Yes, but only to keep an eye on our visitors." I squeezed her hand to reassure her. "Do not worry, I will not challenge them. Go now—and hurry."

She did not like to leave me alone, but she did as I bade her. I returned to the lookout and gazed into the valley. I caught a fleeting glimpse of the invaders making their way along the river, before the mist closed over them once more.

Mounting my horse, I rode back along the ridgetop the way we had come; since the trail was high, it remained light enough to see well ahead, but Goewyn was already out of sight. I rode until I reached the main track leading down into the glen and started down, encountering the swirling mist about halfway to the valley floor.

I continued on—almost blind in the shifting, all-enveloping vapor—until I reached the bottom, whereupon I stopped to listen. Everything was dead still, the foggy murk muffled all sound—and yet, I thought that if there was anything to be heard I would hear it quite plainly.

Absolutely motionless, I sat in the saddle, straining forward to catch any stray sound. After a while, I heard the light jingle of horses' tack and the hollow clop of horses' hooves, moving slowly. I could get no sense of the distance, but the sound did not seem close. I lifted the reins and urged my mount forward, very slowly, very quietly.

No more than ten paces further on, however, the mist swirled away and I saw a horseman directly in front of me. Ice water trickled down my neck and spine.

A distance of a spear's throw separated us. I halted. Perhaps he would not see me.

The rider came on; I saw him raise his eyes from the track in front of him. His face was but a shadow under his cloak which was pulled up over his head. His hands jerked the reins and his dark mount halted. He called something over his shoulder to unseen companions behind him. I heard his shout, sharp and urgent, but could not catch the words.

The fog moved in again on the fitful wind, and the rider was taken from sight. But just as the mist stole him from view, I thought I saw him turn his horse and bolt off the trail.

Drawing my sword from its place under the saddle, I took a deep breath. "Stop!" I shouted as loud as I could.

"Stay where you are!" In reply I heard only the quick scramble of hooves as the horse galloped away.

Gripping the sword—and wishing I had brought a spear and shield with me—I rode forward cautiously and stopped at the place where the rider had appeared. He was not there, of course, and I could see but a few paces ahead in any case. I waited for a while, and when I heard nothing more, decided to return to the ridge track to await Scatha and the others. That way, I could guard the track if the riders tried to reach it by going around me.

Wheeling my horse, I made my way back to the place where the trail began to rise to the ridge, and took up my position. Daylight had gone by now, and a murky twilight had settled over the glen. Soon fog and darkness would make it difficult, if not impossible, to ride at all. No doubt this was what the three intruders were counting on. I took some small comfort from the fact that what was difficult for one, was difficult for all. Anything that would hinder me, would hinder them as well; I was as much protected by the fog as they were.

I waited, watching and listening. I do not know how long I sat there—the fog, like damp wool, curled and shifted, obscuring and confusing all senses—but I gradually began to imagine that I heard the sound of horses once again. Because of the mist, I could not yet tell from which direction the sound reached me.

It might be the warband coming to join me, I thought, but they could not have had time enough to gain the ridgetop, much less descend. More likely, the invaders, having satisfied themselves that I had gone, were proceeding once more.

Listening with every fiber in me, holding my breath, I strained into the darkening murk for any sound that would tell me which way they would come. The sound of horses grew steadily louder as the intruders drew nearer. I turned my head this way and that, alert to any nuance of motion.

Then, swimming out of the fog: dimly glowing orbs of light... torches, two of them, no more than twenty paces away. I tightened my grip on my sword and shouted, "Stop! Go no further!"

At once the invaders stopped. The torches hung motionless in the air; I could not see anyone beneath the hanging lights, but I could hear their horses breathing and blowing, and the creak of leather as they waited.

Not wishing to show myself just yet, I continued speaking from where I sat. "Stand easy, friends," I called, "if peace is your desire, your welcome is assured. But if it is a fight you want, you will receive a warmer welcome elsewhere. Get down from your horses."

There was a moment's silence before the intruder replied. I heard the impatient stamp of a hoof, and a voice: "We are peaceful men. But it is not our way to obey commands from any man we cannot see."

"Nor is it my way to greet travellers with a sword," I replied sternly. "Perhaps we both find ourselves in unaccustomed positions. I advise prudence."

There was a further silence in which I heard the hiss and flutter of the torches. And then the voice said, "Llew?"

15

Child-Wealth

"Cynan?"

I heard a muttered command, and the movement of a rider dismounting... quick footsteps approaching... then Cynan's four-square, solid form looming out of the fog. His hair, moustache, and cloak were pearly with beaded mist, and his eyes were wide.

"*Clanna na cù!*" he muttered, relief washing over his ruddy features. "Llew! Is it you, brother?" He glanced around, looking for others. "*Mo anam*, man! Are you alone out here?"

"Greetings, Cynan!" I said, replacing the sword and swinging down from the saddle. In two steps I was in his embrace. "I am glad to see you."

"A strange welcome this—if welcome it is." He turned to those with him, a party of ten or so, waiting silently on the trail. "Tángwen! Gweir! It is Silver Hand himself come to greet us!" he called to them.

"If I had known it was you," I told him, "I would have ordered a thousand torches to light your way."

"Who did you think it would be?" he asked, concern quickly giving way to bewilderment. "And what do you think you are doing out on the trail alone, challenging travellers at swordpoint?"

I told him of the intruders Goewyn and I had seen in the valley, and I asked if he had seen anyone.

"Have I seen anyone?" he chuckled, gesturing to the all-obscuring fog. "Man, I have not even seen my own face in front of me since entering the valley. Is it worthwhile searching for them, do you think?"

"We would never find them in this stew. Come along," I turned and started towards my horse, "the fire is bright on the hearth, and the welcome cup awaits! Let us warm ourselves and drink to your arrival." I swung up into the saddle. Cynan still stood looking on. "What? Have you forsworn the bowl?"

"Never say it!" he cried, and hastened back to his mount. He shouted a command to those with him, and I turned my horse and led the way up the trail. We had not ridden far, however, when we were met by Scatha, Goewyn, and a warband of thirty, all carrying torches.

We halted and I explained what had happened. After Goewyn and Scatha had greeted Cynan, Tángwen and their retinue, we continued on our way. The fog thinned as we climbed the ridge, and cleared away completely by the time we reached the top—though the sky remained obscured. It would be a dark night, without moon or stars. I spoke briefly with Scatha and we decided to establish a watch of thirty men in threes along the ridgeway, lest the intruders attempt to cross Druim Vran during the night.

Then we proceeded to the crannog and the hall. Tegid awaited us at the hearth. "Hail, Cynan Two-Torcs! Hail, the beautiful Tángwen!" he announced as we trooped in. I called for the bowl to be brought at once. The hall was crowded, and at Cynan's appearance a chorused cry of welcome went up from all those gathered there.

The bard embraced Cynan warmly, and then turned to Tángwen. She inclined her head, offering only her hands to him. "Greetings, Tegid Tathal," she said, smiling; but the smile, like the greeting, lacked any warmth.

I marked the reaction, but the bowl arrived, frothing with new ale; I took it and pressed it into Cynan's eager hands and the moment passed. Cynan drank deeply and, wiping the creamy foam from his moustache on his sleeve, gave the bowl to his wife. She drank, and passed the bowl on to Gweir, Cynan's battlechief. "Thank you," she said in a low voice.

"I have missed you, my friend," said Goewyn throwing off her damp cloak. She gathered Tángwen in her arms and the two women exchanged kisses.

"And it is good to see you," Tángwen replied. "I have been looking toward this day for a long time." She stretched her hands towards the fire, but I noticed that she still held herself as if she were cold. The rigors of the trail, no doubt—the cold and foul weather had put her on edge.

"We would have arrived earlier," Cynan put in, "but the mist slowed us. Still, I did not care to spend another night on the trail."

"Well, you are here now," Goewyn said, taking Tángwen's cloak from her shoulders. "Come, we will find you some dry clothes."

The women withdrew, leaving us to dry ourselves at the hearth. "Ah, this is good," sighed Cynan. "And here was I thinking we would never arrive."

"I had forgotten you were coming," I confessed.

Cynan threw back his head and laughed. "That I could readily see. Here is Silver Hand, guarding the trail with his sword, challenging all comers. Could you not see it was me, man?"

"Obviously, if I had seen it was you, Cynan," I replied, "I would have let you wander lost in the fog."

"The fog! Do not talk to me about the fog!" he said, rolling his eyes.

"It must be fierce indeed, if it daunts the renowned Two-Torcs," observed Tegid.

"Is that not what I am saying? This cursed mist has dogged us for days. I almost turned back because of it. But then I thought of your excellent ale, and so I asked myself, "Cynan Machae, why spend the season of snows in your own draughty hall, alone and lonely, when—"

"When you could be drinking Llew's ale instead!" I finished the thought for him; he regarded me with a deeply wounded look.

"Tch! The thought never entered my head," Cynan scolded. "It is your friendship I crave, brother, not the fellowship of your vat.

Although, now that you say it, your brewmaster is a very man among men." He raised the bowl again and drank deep and long. "Ahh! Nectar!"

"And I have missed you, too," I told him. Seizing the bowl, I raised it to him. "*Sláinte*, Cynan Two-Torcs!" I drained the bowl—there was not much left in it—and called for it to be filled again. One of Tegid's Mabinogi came running with a jar.

"I would hear a good word about your harvest," Tegid said as the bowl was refilled.

"And I would speak a good word if I could," Cynan replied, shaking his head slowly. "Dismal—that is the word. We could not get the grain out of the field for the rain. And then we lost much. But for last year's bounty, we would be looking at a meager planting."

"It is the same with us," I told him. "A good year that ended badly."

Sharing the bowl between us, we fell to talking about all that had happened since we had last seen one another. Goewyn and Tángwen returned to join us; Tángwen was now dressed in clean, dry robes and her hair was combed and dressed. She appeared relaxed; the strained stiffness had left her and she was more herself.

We moved to the table where food had been laid on the board. We began to eat, and I noticed how the two women talked happily to one another all through the meal. The way they talked and laughed together put me in mind of Goewyn with one of her sisters. Raised in the close companionship of Govan and Gwenllian, Goewyn had had no female friend since her sisters were killed.

Scatha entered the hall as we were eating and approached the place where I sat. She bent near to speak a private word. "The watch is established," she reported. "If anyone tries to cross the ridge we will soon know it."

Nothing more was said about this, and indeed I gave it no further thought. The hall was warm and bright—made all the more so by Cynan's arrival—and the conversation lively. I dismissed intruders from my mind.

Nor did I think ill when Goewyn and Tángwen went riding the

next day. The sentries had watched through the night and the ridge remained clear of fog and mist; they had neither seen or heard anyone. And when the mist cleared in the valley there was no trail to be found. So I let the matter go.

Bran and the Raven Flight returned that same day. The watchers on the ridge saw them enter the valley and brought us word of their return. Tegid, Scatha, Cynan and I rode out to meet them; and though they were filthy and tired from their journey they were in good spirits.

"Hail, Bran Bresal!" I called, eager for his news. "I trust you have had good hunting."

"The hunting was excellent," the Raven Chief replied, "but we failed to corner our quarry."

"Most unfortunate," Tegid remarked. "What happened?"

"We found the trail as it left the valley," Bran explained. "Indeed, it was not difficult to follow. But, though we pursued as far and as fast as we could, we never caught sight of those who made it."

"How many were you tracking?" I asked.

"Three men on horseback, lord," a muddy Alun Tringad answered.

"Tell us everything now," suggested Tegid. "Then we will have no need to speak of it within the hall."

"Gladly," replied Bran, "but there is little enough to tell." He went on to explain how they had followed the trail east all the way to the coast before losing it on the rocky strand. They had ranged north and south along the coast for a time without raising the trail again or seeing any sign of an invader, and so at last turned back. "I hoped to bring you better word, lord," Bran told me.

"You have returned safely," I said. "I am well content."

The days dwindled down, growing colder and darker as if Sollen cramped and compacted them with an icy grip. But the hall remained snug and warm and alive with harpsong and fine companionship. We played games and listened to the old tales; we ate, drank, and took our ease, filling the long cold nights with laughter and light.

The lake froze and the children of the crannog played on the ice. It was on one of those rare days, when the sun flared like a fiery gem in a blue-white sky, that we went out to watch the youngsters. A good many had carved strips of bone and tied them to their buskins. The simple skates worked extremely well, and everyone cheered to see the antics of these intrepid skaters.

Cynan, enraptured by the gliding forms, strolled out onto the frozen lake and allowed himself to be cajoled into trying the skates. He cut such a comical figure that others took to the ice, eager to outdo him, if not in skill, then in absurdity. It was not long before there were more skaters than spectators.

We slipped and slid over the ice, falling over ourselves, and improvising silly dances. A gaggle of young girls clustered around Goewyn, beseeching her to try the bone skates, too. She quickly assented and tied the strips to her feet, then, holding out her hand to me, she said, "Take my hand! I want to fly!"

I took her hand and pulled her around the windswept ice—laughing, her lips and cheeks red from the cold, her golden hair and blue-checked cloak flying. The sound of her laughter, and that of all the other skaters, bubbled up as from a fountain, sun-splashed and lavish, a hymn to the day.

Around and around we twirled, stopping only to catch our breath and collapse into one another's arms. The sun shone bright on the silver lake, and set the snow-crusted hilltops glittering like high-heaped diamond hoards. Such beauty, such joy—it made the heart ache to see it, to feel it.

Cynan's frolics, loudly embellished and featuring spectacular falls, carried the day. We laughed so hard the tears flowed down our cheeks. Nevertheless, I could not help but notice that of all those who had come to watch, only Tángwen refused to join in the fun. Instead, she stood on the boat landing with her arms crossed beneath her cloak and a pained look on her face.

"I think someone does not appreciate our sport," I whispered to Goewyn as I lifted her from her latest spill.

Catching my gaze, Goewyn turned to observe her friend standing alone on the landing. "No," she said slowly, "it is something else."

"Do you know?"

She took my hand and pressed it. "Not now. Later," she said, putting her face close to mine. Goewyn slipped her arms around my neck and pulled me close. "Come here."

A directness in her tone aroused my curiosity. "What?" Her eyes sparkled and her lips curved prettily. "What is it?" I asked suspiciously. "What are you hiding?"

"Well, it will not remain hidden for long. The king's wealth is increasing. Soon everyone will know." She released me and pressed a hand to her stomach.

"Wealth? Child-wealth?" She laughed at my surprise. "A baby! We are going to have a baby!" I threw my arms around her and hugged her tight—then remembered myself and released her, lest I crush the tiny life growing within her. "When? How long have you known?"

"Long enough," she said. "I was waiting for the right moment to tell you, but... well, it is such a splendid day I could not wait any longer."

"Oh, Goewyn, I love you." I put my hand behind her head, held her, and kissed her long and hard. "I love you, and I am glad you did not wait. I am going to tell everyone—now!"

"Shh!" she said, laying her fingertips on my lips. "Not yet. Let it be our secret for a few days."

"But I want to tell."

"Please—just a little while."

"At the solstice then," I suggested. "We will have a celebration like the one last year at Cynan's wedding. And in the middle of the feast we will make our announcement. Does anyone else know?"

"No one," she assured me. "You are the first."

"When will it be—the birth, I mean? When will the child be born?"

Goewyn smiled, stepped into my embrace, kissed me and put her cheek against my neck. "You will have your wife a while longer. The child will be born in Maffar—before Lugnasadh, I think."

"A fine time to be born!" I announced. "Goewyn, this is wonderful! I love you so much!"

"Shh!" she cautioned. "Everyone will hear you." She stepped backward, sliding away on the bone-skates. Holding out her hands to me she called, "Come away, best beloved! I will teach you to fly!"

We flew, and the day sped from us. Short, but brilliant in its perfection, it faded quickly: a spark fanned to life in the midst of gathering darkness. It illumined our hearts with its brave radiance and then succumbed to onrushing night.

As the sun sank below the rim of hills, festooning the sky with streamers of rose and scarlet, a few sickly stars were already glowing in a black eastern sky. Night was spreading over Albion. Dazzled by my love for Goewyn, I saw the darkness and knew it not.

That night we left the hall early. Goewyn took my hand and led me to our bed, now piled high with furs and fleeces against the cold. She loosened her belt and unwound it, then drew her mantle over her head and stood before me. Taking up the cup she had placed beside the fire-ring, she drank, watching me all the while. Her eyes never left mine.

Her body, caressed by the rushlight, was a vision of softly-rounded, intimately melding curves, beguiling, bewildering in its smooth subtlety. She stepped toward me, reached out and tugged the end of my belt free, loosened it, and let it fall. She drew me to her; I felt her body warm against me and, taking a handful of her hair, I held her head and kissed her open mouth. I tasted the rich warmth of honeyed mead on her tongue and passion leapt like a flame within me. I abandoned myself to the heat.

We shared the golden mead and made love that night in celebration of the child to be. The next day Goewyn was gone.

16

The Search

I rose early, but Goewyn had already wakened and dressed. She came to the bed-place, leaned over, kissed me, and said, "I did not want to wake you."

"What are you doing?" I asked, taking her hand and pulling her down on me. "Come back to bed—both of you."

"I promised to go with Tángwen," she said.

"Oh," I yawned. "Where are you going?"

"Riding."

"Would you abandon your husband in his cold, lonely bed? Come back and wait until the sun rises at least."

She laughed and kissed me again. "It will be light soon enough. Sleep now, my love, and let me go."

"No." I raised my hand and stroked the side of her neck. "I will never let you go."

She nuzzled the hand and then took it and kissed the palm. "Tángwen is waiting."

"Take care, my love," I said as she left. I lay in our bed for a while, then rose, dressed quickly and went out. The night-black sky was fading to blue-grey and the stars were dim; away over the encircling hills to the east the sky blushed with blood-red streaks like slashes in pale flesh. There was no one in the yard; smoke from the cookhouses rose in a straight white column. I shivered with the cold and hurried across the yard to the hall.

The hall was quiet, but a few people were awake and stirring. The hearthfire had been stoked and I walked to it to warm myself. Neither Goewyn nor Tángwen was to be seen, no doubt intending to break fast when they returned from their ride.

Garanaw wakened and greeted me, and we talked until the oatcakes came out of the oven and were brought steaming into the hall. Seating ourselves at the board, we were quickly joined by Bran and a few early-rising Ravens, and some of Cynan's retinue. Cynan himself arrived a short time later, noisily greeting everyone and settling himself on the bench. The oatcakes were hot and tasty; we washed them down with rich brown ale.

Talk turned to hunting, and it was quickly agreed that a day spent in pursuit of deer or boar would be a day well spent. "We will savor our supper all the more for the chase," Cynan declared; to which Alun quickly added, "And we will relish the chase all the more for a wager."

"Do my ears deceive me?" wondered Cynan loudly. "Is that Alun Tringad offering his gold?"

"If you can bring back a bigger stag than the one I shall find, then you are welcome to the champion's portion of my gold."

"I would be ashamed to take your treasure so easily," quipped Cynan. "And I never would, were it not advisable to teach you a valuable lesson in humility."

"Then put your hand to it," Alun told him, "and let us choose the men to ride with us. The sooner we ride, the sooner I will claim my treasure. Indeed, I can already feel the weight of your gold bracelets on my arm."

"Unless you hope to lull me to sleep with your empty boasting," Cynan said, "you will soon see a hunter worthy of his renown. Therefore, I advise you to look your last upon your treasure."

Alun stood and called to his brother Ravens, "Brothers, I have heard enough of this haughty fellow's idle talk. Let us show him what true hunters can do, and let us decide now how to divide his treasure among us."

Cynan also stood. "Llew, ride with me, brother," he said, and he called others of his retinue by name. "Come, my friends, the chase is before us, and much good gold for our efforts."

They fixed the time for their return: "At sunset we will assemble in the yard," Alun suggested.

Cynan agreed. "And the Penderwydd of Albion will judge between us who has fared the better—although this will not be necessary, for it will be readily apparent to one and all which of us is the best hunter."

"True, true," Alun affirmed casually. "That they will easily discern."

I glanced quickly around, but Tegid had not entered the hall. It did not matter, there would be time to talk to him later, when we returned from the hunt. The hall buzzed with eager voices as side wagers were laid, odds fixed, and amounts agreed. Snatching up the last of the oatcakes, we burst from the hall and hastened across the ice-bound lake to the cattle pens to fetch the horses. We saddled our mounts and, with much friendly banter, rode out along the frozen lakeside.

Cynan and I led the way, following the hoof tracks Tángwen and Goewyn had left in the new snow. Halfway to the wood, the track left the lakeside, leading away to the ridge. We continued around the lake, however, to the game runs on the long slopes. As soon as we entered the wood, we divided our number—those who rode with Alun went one way, and those of Cynan's party the other.

The sun rose above the rim of the hills and the day was good. There was snow on the game runs, but because of the trees it was not deep. We saw the tracks of scores of animals, but as it had not snowed for several days it was impossible to tell which were fresh and which were older.

We spread ourselves across the run and proceeded deeper into the silent sanctuary of the forest, our spears along our thighs as we pushed through the underbrush. The shadows of the trees formed a blue latticework on the crusted snow. The cold air tingled on the skin of my cheeks, nose and chin. I had spread my cloak around me to

173

capture the heat of the horse and help keep me warm. With a bright, white sun, a clear blue sky, and the company of valiant men, it was a fine day to hunt.

I let those most eager take the lead and settled back to enjoy the ride. We followed the long run as it lifted towards the ridge: crossing a small stream we scared a red deer sheltering in a blackthorn thicket. The hounds would have given chase, but Cynan was after bigger game, and forced them back onto the trail. His patience was rewarded a short time later when we came upon the fresh spoor of a small herd of deer.

"It is still warm," announced Cynan's man as I joined them.

"Good," Cynan said. "Be alert, everyone. The prize is near."

We continued at a swifter pace and soon sighted the deer: three hinds and a big stag. The hounds did not wait to be called back a second time, but sounded the hunting cry and sped to the chase. The stag regarded the dogs with a large, inscrutable, dark eye, then lifted his regal head and belled a warning call to his little clan.

The hinds lifted their tails and bounded as one into the thicket. Only when they were away did the stag follow. Rather than try to force a way through the tangle, we let the dogs run and gave ourselves to the chase.

A glorious chase! The old stag proved a cunning opponent and led us a long and elaborate hunt—through deep woods and up along the high ridge and down again into piney forest. We caught him, in the end, with his back to a stony outcrop at the foot of the ridgewall. His clan had escaped, and he was near dead from exhaustion. Still, he turned and fought to the last.

The sun was little more than a day moon, pale and wan on the horizon, when we finished securing the stag to a litter and turned our horses for home. We had travelled far afield in our fevered pursuit. We were tired, and cold where the sweat had soaked our clothes, but well content with our sport, and hopeful of winning the wager. A fine and regal spectacle of a sky washed pale lavender and gold in a brilliant Sollen sunset greeted us as we emerged from the woods and began making our way along the lake.

Alun Tringad's party had returned ahead of us, and they were waiting for us at the cattle pen when we arrived. Their kill—two fine bristle-backed boars—lay on the snow outside the pen. At the sight of our stag, they began exclaiming over our lack of success.

"One lonely deer, is it?" cried Alun, foremost in the gathering. "With all you hardy men on horseback shaking your spears at it, why, I do not doubt this poor sickly thing expired in fright."

"As sickly as it is," Cynan replied, swinging down from the saddle, "our stag will yet serve to separate you from your treasure." He regarded the wild pigs with a sad, disappointed air. "Oh, it is a shameful thing you have done, Alun, my man—taking these two piglets from their mother. Tch! Tch!" He shook his head sadly. "Why not just give the gold to me now and save yourself the disgrace of having your skill revealed in such a pitiful light?"

"Not so fast, Cynan Machae," replied one of Alun's supporters. "It is for the Chief Bard to tell us who has won the wager. We will await his decision."

"Hoo!" said Cynan, puffing out his cheeks, "bring Tegid by all means. I was only trying to save you the fearful humiliation I see coming your way."

At first sight of our party on the lakeside track, Alun had sent a man to fetch Tegid. A call from one of Cynan's men directed our attention to the crannog. "Here he comes now!" shouted Gweir. "The Penderwydd is coming!"

I turned to see a crowd from the crannog hurrying across the ice towards us. I looked for Goewyn, expecting to see her among them, but neither Goewyn nor Tángwen was there. No doubt they had decided to stay in the warm. Nor did I fault them; I had long been wishing myself out of my sodden clothes and holding a warming jar beside the fire.

A genial hubbub arose as the throng arrived. Everyone exclaimed at the sight of the game, extolling the prowess of the hunters and the success of the hunt—as well they might, for we would eat heartily on the proceeds of our effort for many days.

"Penderwydd!" Alun shouted. "The hunt is finished. Here is the result of our labors. As you can see, we have done well. Indeed, we have bested Cynan and his band, which is clear for all to see. It only remains for you to agree and confirm the inevitable decision."

The Chief Bard withdrew a hand from his cloak and raised it. "That I will do, Alun Tringad. What is clear to you may not be so clear to those who lack your zeal for Cynan's gold. Therefore, step aside and allow someone with an eye unclouded by avarice to view the evidence."

Tegid examined first Alun's kill and then Cynan's. He prodded the carcasses with a toe, inspected the pelts, teeth, tusks, eyes, hoofs, tails, and antlers. All the while, the two parties baited one another with quips and catcalls, awaiting the bard's decision. The bard took his time, pausing now and then to muse over this or that point which he pretended to have discovered, or which had been pointed out to him by the extremely partisan crowd.

Then, taking his place midway between the stag and the two boars, and frowning mightily, he rested chin upon fist in earnest contemplation. All this served to heighten the anticipation; wagers were doubled and then tripled as—from the slant of an eyebrow or the lift of a lip—one side or the other imagined opinion swaying in their favor.

At last, the Chief Bard drew himself up and, raising his staff for silence, prepared to deliver his decision. "It is rightly the domain of the king to act as judge for his people," he reminded everyone. "But as the king took part in the hunt, I beg his permission to deliver judgment." He looked to me.

"I grant it gladly," I replied. "Please, continue."

The crowd shouted for the Chief Bard to proclaim the winner, but Tegid would not be hurried. Placing a fold of his cloak over his head, he said, "I have weighed the matter carefully. From the time of Dylwyn Short-Knife," here the spectators groaned with frustration, but Tegid plowed ahead slowly, "and the time of Tryffin the Tall, it has been in the nature of things to hold the life of a stag equal to that of a bear, and that of a bear equal to two boars." The groan turned from impatience to frustration as the crowd guessed what was coming. "It would appear then," Tegid calmly continued, "that a stag is equal to two boars. Thus, the matter cannot be settled according to the quantity of meat, and we must look elsewhere for a resolution."

He paused to allow his gaze to linger around the ring of faces. There were murmurs of approval, and mutters of protest from many. He waited until they were silent once more. "For this reason I have examined the beasts most carefully," Tegid said. "This is my decision." The throng held its breath. Which would it be? "The stag is a worthy rival and a lord of his kind..."

At this, Cynan's party raised a tremendous shout of triumph.

"But," Tegid quickly cautioned, "the boars are no less lordly. And what is more, there are two of them. Were this not so, I would hold for the stag. Yet, since the difficulty of finding and bringing down *two* such noble and magnificent beasts must necessarily try the skills of the hunter the more, I declare that those who hunted the boars have won this day's sport. I, Tegid Tathal, Penderwydd, have spoken."

It took a moment to unravel what the Chief Bard had said, but then all began wrangling over the decision. Cynan appealed to the beauty of his prize and to various other merits, but Tegid would not be moved: Alun Tringad had won the day. There was nothing for it, the losers must pay the winners. Tegid thumped his staff three times on the ground and the matter was ended.

We returned to the warmth and light of the hall, eager for meat and drink to refresh us, and tales of the hunt to cheer us. Upon entering the hall, I quickly scanned the gathering. Goewyn was nowhere to be seen. I turned on my heel and hastened to our hut.

It was dark and empty, the ashes in the fire-ring cold. She had not been there for some time, perhaps not since early morning. I ran back to the hall and made my way to Tegid; he was standing at one end of the hearth, waiting for the ale jar to come his way.

"Where is Goewyn?" I asked him bluntly.

"Greetings, Llew. Goewyn? I have not seen her," he replied. "Why do you ask?"

"I cannot find her. She went riding with Tángwen this morning."

"Perhaps she is—"

"She is not in the hut." My eyes searched the noisy hall. "I do not see Tángwen, either."

Without another word, Tegid turned and beckoned Cynan to join us. "Where is Tángwen?" the bard said.

I looked at Cynan anxiously. "Have you seen her since this morning?"

"Seen her?" he wondered, raising his cup. He drank and then offered the cup to me. "I have been on the trail since daybreak, as you well know."

"Goewyn and Tángwen went riding this morning," I explained, holding my voice level, "and it appears they have not returned."

"Not returned?" Cynan looked towards the door, as if expecting the two women to enter at that moment. "But it is dark now."

"That is the least of our worries," I said, "if something has happened—"

"If they are here, someone will have seen them," Tegid interrupted calmly. The bard stepped away. A moment later he was standing on the table, his staff upraised. "Kinsmen! Hear me! I must speak with Goewyn and Tángwen. Quickly now! Who can tell me where to find them?"

He waited. People looked at one another and shrugged. Some inquired among themselves, but no one offered any information. Clearly, no one could remember seeing either of the women. Tegid asked again, but received no answer. He thanked the people for their attention, and returned to where Cynan and I waited.

"We will search the crannog," he said. Although he spoke quietly, I could tell the bard was worried. This did nothing to soothe my mounting anxiety.

And then one of the serving maids came to where we stood. "If you please, lords," she said, clutching the beer jar tightly, "I have seen Queen Goewyn."

"Where?" I did not mean to be curt with the young woman. "Please, speak freely."

"I saw the queen in the yard," she said.

I started for the door. Tegid caught me by the arm. "When was this?" he said; the maid hesitated. "Speak up," he snapped. "When did you see her?"

"Early this morning," the maid said, her voice quivering. She realized, I think, that this was not at all what we wanted to hear. "They were laughing as they walked—the two of them, the queen and Queen Tángwen. I think they were leaving the crannog to go riding."

"It would have been dark still," Cynan said. "Are you certain?"

"Yes, lord," the maiden said. "I know who I saw."

"And Tángwen was with her?" Cynan pursued.

"Yes, lord."

"Thank you, Ailla," I said, recognizing the young woman at last; she often served as one of Goewyn's handmaids.

Tegid dismissed her then, and said, "Now we will search the crannog."

On our way from the hall, Tegid snared Gwion, his foremost Mabinog, and whispered something in the boy's ear. Gwion nodded once, and darted through the door ahead of us.

We searched, the three of us, each taking a section of the crannog. It did not take long. I ran from house to house, smacking my silver hand on the doorposts to alert those within, then thrusting my head inside. Most of the huts were empty—the people had gathered in the hall—and in those that were occupied, none of the residents had seen either woman. I also looked in the storehouses. As I hurried to rejoin the others at the hall, I knew that Goewyn was not in Dinas Dwr.

Upon returning to the hall, I met Tegid standing at the entrance with Gwion Bach beside him. "It is not good," Tegid told me bluntly. "I sent Gwion to the stables. Their horses have not returned."

My heart sank and my stomach tightened. "Then something has happened."

Cynan approached, and I could tell from the way he walked— head down, shoulders bunched—that he had discovered nothing and was now more than concerned. "The trail will be difficult," he said, wasting no time. "We will need a supply of torches and a change of horses. I will summon my warband."

"The Ravens will ride with us," I said. "Drustwn can follow a trail even in the dark. I will ready the horses. Go now. Bring them. And hurry!"

17

Night Ride

We took up the trail at the place where I had seen it diverge from the lakeshore track. By torchlight the horses' hoofprints showed a staggered black line across the wide expanse of snow.

Across the valley floor we galloped, thirty strong, including Cynan, myself and the Raven Flight. Tegid stayed behind. He would order matters at Dinas Dwr while we were away and uphold us in our search.

I wrapped the reins around my metal hand and clutched the torch with my flesh hand. The torchflame fluttered in the wind above my head, red sparks sailing out behind me as I raced over the undulating snow. The cold air stung my cheeks and eyes; my lips burned. But I did not stop so much as to draw my cloak over my chin. I would not stop until Goewyn was safely beside me once more.

Upon reaching the heights of Druim Vran the trail became thin and difficult to see. The wind had scoured most of the snow from the ridgetop, but some remained in the sheltered places, and we proceeded haltingly from patch to patch where we could find hoofprints.

It appeared they had ridden eastwards along the ridgeway. The day was good. They had moved toward the rising sun. I imagined the two women making their way happily along Druim Vran with the silver-bright dawnlight in their eyes. We, however, followed in Sollen's deep dark, a starless void above; no moon lit our way. The only light we had was that which fluttered in our hands, and that was fitful indeed.

I refused to allow myself to think about what might have happened to them. I pushed all such thoughts from my mind and held one only: Goewyn would be found. My wife, my soul, would be returned unharmed.

Drustwn pushed a relentless pace. He seemed to know where the tracks would lead and found them whenever he paused to look. Thus we followed the Raven's lead along the ridgeway—deep, deep into the dark Sollen depths on our night ride. We rode without speaking, urgent to our task.

Nor did we stop until the trail turned down into the glen. The facing slope was clear of snow, and though we spread ourselves along the brush-covered decline, we could not recover the trail in the dark. In the end, we dismounted to search the long downward slope on foot.

"It may be that we can find the trail again in the morning," Drustwn suggested when we halted at the bottom of the glen to confer. "It is too easily missed on bare ground."

"My wife is gone. I will not wait until morning."

"Lord," Drustwn said, his face drawn in the torchlight, "daylight is not long away."

At these words I raised my head. Drustwn was right, the sky was already paling in the east. Night had passed me in a blur of torchlight on glittering snow.

"What do you advise?" I asked.

"It is no good thrashing around in the dark. We could destroy the trail without knowing it. Let us rest until there is light enough to see."

"Very well," I agreed. "Give the order. I will speak to Cynan."

Drustwn's call rang out behind me as I wheeled my horse and started back up the line. Cynan had been riding to the right of me when I had last seen him. Several of his men passed me, hurrying to

Drustwn's call. I saw Gweir and asked him where Cynan was, and he pointed to two torches glimmering a little distance away. Cynan and Bran were talking together as they rode to where Drustwn waited. I reined in beside them. "Why has he stopped?" Cynan asked. "Have you found something?"

"We have lost the trail," I answered. "There is no point in going further until sunrise."

"Then it is best we halt," Bran replied.

"No," I told him tersely, "finding them would be best. But this is all we can do now."

"It has been a cold night," Cynan fretted. "They were not prepared."

I made no reply, but at Cynan's remark I realized that I had not considered the women having to spend the night on the trail. It had not occurred to me because I did not for an instant believe that they had merely lost their way. It was possible, of course, but the likelihood of intruders on Druim Vran had led me to assume otherwise.

Now Cynan's words offered a slender hope. Perhaps they had merely wandered too far afield and been forced to shelter on the trail for the night, rather than try to find Dinas Dwr in the dark. Perhaps, one of the horses had been injured, or... anything might have happened.

We continued to where Drustwn and most of the other riders were now waiting. They had quickly gathered brush from the slope and had a fire burning. Others were leading horses to a nearby brook for water. I dismounted and gave my horse to one of the warriors to care for and, wrapping myself in my cloak, sat down on a frost-covered stone.

Shivering in the cold while waiting for the sun to rise, I remembered the beacon. I rose at once. "Alun!" I shouted. "Alun Tringad! Come here!"

A moment later, Alun was standing before me. He touched the back of his hand to his forehead. "Lord?"

"Alun," I said, laying my hand to his arm, "do you recall the beacon we found on the ridge?"

"I do, lord."

"Go to it. Now. And return with word of what you find."

He left without another word, riding back up the slope to the ridgeway. I returned to the rock and sat down again. Dawnlight seeped into a grey-white sky. Darker clouds sailed low overhead, shredding themselves on the hilltops as they passed. Away to the north, white-headed mountains showed above the cloudline. The wind rose with the sun, gusting out of the east. Likely, there would be snow before day's end, or sleet.

I grew restless, rose, and remounted my horse. "It is light enough to see," I told Drustwn bluntly.

Bran, standing with him, said, "Lord Llew, allow us to search out the trail and summon you when we have found it."

"We ride together." I snapped the reins and turned to the slope once more.

We were still searching for the trail when Alun returned. Cynan was with me, and Alun seemed reluctant to speak in front of him. "What did you find, man?" I demanded.

"Lord," he said, "the beacon has been lit."

"When?"

"Impossible to tell. The ashes were cold."

Cynan's head whipped toward Alun at the news. "What beacon?"

I told him quickly about the beacon-pile I had found on the ridge. "It has been burnt," I said.

His jaw bulged dangerously. "*Clanna na cù!*" he rasped through clenched teeth. "Beacons on the ridge and strangers in the glen—and we let them go riding alone!"

He did not blame me for my lack of vigilance, but he did not need to; I felt the sting of his unspoken accusation all the same. How could I have let it happen?

"We will find them, brother," I said.

"Aye, that we will," he growled, slapping the reins against the neck of his mount. He rode off alone.

As if in answer to Cynan's gruff affirmation, there came a blast on the carynx. Drustwn had found the trail. We raced to the place and took up the chase again. The sun was well up and the morning speeding as if on wings. The tracks led across the glen. After we had followed a fair way, it became clear that they had made for the far side of the glen. Why? Had they seen something to entice them on?

Across the glen and up into the low hills beyond, the way was straight; they had ridden directly without turning aside or halting. Why? I wondered. Perhaps they had raced.

I pounced on the idea. Yes, they had raced. That would explain the resolute directness of the trail. I expected that upon reaching the hill, we would find where they had stopped to catch their breath before turning back.

Once across the crest of the first hill, however, this certainty began to fade. The tracks did not alter. The double trail led up the hillside and over—without varying, without stopping.

I paused atop the hill to look back briefly. Druim Vran loomed like a wall behind us, blank and unbreachable, with the glen flat as a floor below. The beacon-fire would have been seen from every hilltop in the realm—though not, I reflected, in Dinas Dwr itself. It might have been lit at any time and we would not have seen it. I turned away and pursued Drustwn's lead, grim urgency mounting within me.

It was in the next valley that we found where the women had stopped.

Drustwn halted, stiffened in the saddle and called Cynan and me to him at once. The rest of the search party were still behind us a little distance. The Raven's eyes were mere slits as he scanned the tracks.

"What have you found?" Cynan demanded.

"They stopped here, lord," he said, stretching a hand towards the marks on the ground.

I looked and saw what had upset him. My heart fell. "How many?" I asked, struggling to keep my voice steady. "How many were there?"

"I make it three or four. Five at most. Not more."

"*Saeth du*," Cynan muttered. "Five..."

I stared hard at the trampled snow. The confusion of tracks defied explanation. Clearly, the women had met someone. No one

185

had dismounted; there were no footprints among the hoofmarks.

"They rode on that way," Drustwn said, looking to the east. I could see that he was right. I also saw that a decision was required.

I waited until the others had gathered around us, and showed them what Drustwn had discovered. There was much muttering and mumbling over this, but I cut it short. The day was hastening from us. "Garanaw!" I said, calling on the first man to meet my eye. "You, Niall and Emyr will return to Dinas Dwr. Tell Tegid what we have found here, and then gather provisions and supplies. Cynan and I will ride ahead. Make haste and join us as soon as you can."

Cynan was quick to catch the meaning of my words. He immediately ordered Gweir and four of his band to go with the three Ravens to help carry the provisions. He was evidently thinking, as I was, that we might well be on the trail longer than anyone intended. A depressing thought. Neither of us spoke a word of this to the other, however, and as soon as the riders had departed we pressed on.

The muddled tracks soon reconciled themselves: two horses going side-by-side close together—the two women, I assumed—with a rider on either side a little distance apart; one rider to lead the way and another to follow close behind. That was four strangers accounted for. If there were more, we saw no sign.

The trail led eastward, staying on the low ground, winding through the creases between hills rather than crossing them directly. Clearly, they were in no hurry, seeking instead to stay out of sight.

I had no doubt now that the tracks we followed were already a day old. I knew also that we would not find Goewyn and Tángwen sheltering in the heather somewhere, waiting for us to rescue them. They had been taken. Stolen. Abducted.

I still could not face the implications of that. Indeed, I put the thought from me whenever it surfaced, and concentrated instead on pursuing the trail. I would not speculate on what awaited me at the end.

The sallow sun faded as it passed midday and sank towards dusk on its low Sollen arc. We rode on—a long time, I think, because, when I looked again, clouds had closed over the place and the snow that had held off all day began to fall in icy pellets that bounced where they hit.

I imagined the snow striking Goewyn, becoming caught in her hair and eyelashes. I imagined her lips blue and trembling. I imagined her shoulders shaking as she cast anxious glances behind her, searching the empty trail, hoping to see me riding to her rescue.

We stopped at a brook to rest and water the horses. The snow fell in undulating sheets. I knelt and scooped icy water to my mouth, then went to where Cynan stood staring across the narrow strip of black water.

"The tracks continue on the other side," he said, without taking his eyes from the place. "They did not even stop for water."

"No," I said.

"Then we should not stop, either," he snapped. He was worried about Tángwen and the strain was telling on him.

"They have a fair lead on us, brother," I pointed out. "We do not know how long we must ride until we catch them. We must nurse our strength."

He did not like me saying it, but knew I spoke the truth. "How could this happen?" he demanded.

"The blame is mine. I should never have allowed them to go. I was not thinking."

Cynan turned his face towards me; his blue eyes were almost black. "I do not blame you, brother," he said, though his tone was reproach enough. "The deed is done. That is all. Now it must be undone."

When everyone, men and horses, had drunk their fill, we moved on.

The snow stopped just before sundown and the sky cleared slightly in the west. The setting sun flared with a violent red-orange and then plunged behind the lonely hills. The too-short winter day was ended, but we rode on until it grew too dark to see. We made camp in a narrow valley in the windshadow of a broad hill, huddled close to our fires.

We had nothing to eat, so passed a hungry night. It was midday the next day before those who had returned for provisions reached us. By riding through the night, they managed to catch us before sundown. We paused then to eat and feed the horses, before going on.

The trail we pursued led unerringly east. Long before I heard the far-off crash of the sea against the rocky shore I knew the trail would end at the coast. And when, as another sun set on another cold day, we stood on a wind-battered dune looking at the freezing, foam-blown waves, their ceaseless thunder loud in our ears, I knew beyond all doubt that Goewyn no longer remained in Albion.

In the fast-falling twilight, we fanned out along the strand and found tracks in the sand. Hope kindled bright for a moment, but died when we found one of the women's horses: loose, empty-saddled, trailing its reins along the beach. It was Tángwen's horse, and its discovery plunged Cynan into a frenzy of distress.

"Why one horse only?" he demanded, jerking the reins through his fist. "What does it mean?"

"I do not know," I told him. "Perhaps she tried to escape."

"It makes no sense!" he steamed. "None of this makes sense. Even if she tried to escape and they caught her, why would they leave her horse but take the others?" He glared at me as if I were withholding the answers to his questions.

"Brother, I cannot say what happened here. I wish I could."

Too agitated to stand still, he lashed his mount to speed and galloped away along the shore. I was about to follow him up the coast when Drustwn hailed me. He had discovered two long deep grooves in the sand—grooves made by the keels of boats which had been beached above the tideline.

While two of Cynan's men rode to recall their lord, I dismounted and stood over one of the keel-marks and gazed east across the sea towards Tir Aflan. Somewhere beyond those raw waves, hard and dark as slate, my bride awaited rescue.

I turned from the empty sea, my face burning with rage and frustration. Bran Bresal, who had been standing silently beside me, said, "I think they will not be found in Albion."

"Yet, I tell you they *will be found*," I declared. "Send two men back to the crannog. Bring Tegid; I want him with me. Scatha will want to come, but she is to remain to protect Dinas Dwr."

"At once, lord." The Chief Raven wheeled his horse and clattered away over the pebbled shingle.

"Cynan!" I shouted. "Cynan, here!"

A moment later he joined me. "Send men to bring the boats. We will make camp and await them here."

He hesitated, cocking an eye at the sky, and seemed about to gainsay the plan. Instead, he said, "Done."

Cynan wheeled away, calling for Gweir to join him. I pulled the winter fleece covering from my saddle and spread it on the wet shingle. Then, setting my face to the sea as it gnashed the shore, I sat down to begin the long wait.

18

The Geas of Treán ap Golau

We waited three days for the ships to arrive, and then three more. Each day was slow torture. Just after daybreak on the seventh day, four ships arrived from the winter harborage in the south Caledon estuary where Cynan kept them. He commanded the men to stand ready, and then we returned to our camp on the strand to await Tegid's arrival. The bard appeared just before sunset; Scatha, who would not be left behind, rode with him.

"My daughter has been taken," she said by way of greeting, "I mean to aid in her release."

There was no denying her, so I said, "As you will, Pen-y-Cat. May your presence prove a boon to us."

Tegid explained. "As Scatha meant to join us, I summoned Calbha to watch over Dinas Dwr. That is why we could not come sooner."

I was not pleased with this development. "Let us hope your thoughtless delay has not cost the lives of either Goewyn or Tángwen." I turned away and hastened to ready the ships to sail, calling for torches to be lit and for the provisions to be loaded.

"It will be dark soon, and there will be no moon tonight," Bran pointed out, stirring himself from the fretful silence of the last days. "We should wait until morning."

"We have wasted too much time already," Cynan told him. "We sail at once."

Tegid dismounted and hurried to my side. "There is something else, Llew," he said.

"It can wait until we have raised sail."

"You must hear it now," the bard insisted.

I turned on him. "I will hear it when I choose! I have waited on this freezing shore for seven days. Seven days! At this moment I am interested in just one thing: rescuing Goewyn. If what you have to say will accomplish that the quicker, then say it. If not, I do not want to hear it."

Tegid's face became hard; his eyes flashed quick-kindled fire. "And yet you *will* hear it, O Mighty King," he snapped, fighting to control himself.

I made to turn away from him, but he caught me by the wrist of my silver hand and held me. Anger flared hot within me. "Take your hand off me, bard. Or lose it!"

Several bystanders saw what was happening and stopped to watch—Scatha and Cynan among them. Tegid released me, and raised his hand over his head in the way of a declaiming bard.

"Hear me, Llew Llaw Eraint!" he said, spitting the words. "You are Aird Righ of Albion, and thus you are set about by many geasa."

"Taboos? Save your breath," I growled. "I do not care!" I was doubly angry now. He had disobeyed my commands and put us many days behind, and now had the audacity to hinder us further, talking about some ridiculous taboo or other. "My wife is abducted! Cynan's bride is gone! Whatever it takes, I will have them back. Do you understand that? I will give the entire kingdom to obtain their release!"

"The kingdom is not yours to give," the bard declared flatly. "It belongs to the people who shelter beneath your protection. All you possess is the kingship."

"I will not stand here arguing with you, bard. Stay here if that is what you wish. I am leaving."

Holding me with his voice, he said. "I say you cannot go."

I stared at him—speechless with rage.

"The Aird Righ of Albion cannot leave his realm," he announced. "That is the principal geas of your reign."

Had he lost his mind? "What are you saying? I have left before. I have travelled—"

Tegid shook his head, and I grasped his point. Since becoming king, I had never set foot outside Albion's borders. Apparently, this was forbidden me now for some obscure reason. "Explain," I snapped. "And be quick about it."

Tegid simply replied, "It is forbidden the High King to leave the Island of the Mighty—at any time, for any reason."

"Unless I hear a better explanation than that," I told him, "you will soon find yourself standing here alone. I have ordered the ships to sail, and I mean to be aboard the first one when it departs."

"The ships may depart. Your men may depart," he said softly. "But you, O King, may not so much as set foot beyond this shore."

"My *wife* is out there! And I am going to find her." I made to turn away again.

"I say you will not leave Albion and remain Aird Righ," he insisted, emphasizing each word.

"Then I will no longer be king!" I spat. "So be it! One way or another, I am going to find my wife."

If my kingship would bring her back, I would give it a thousand times over. She was my life, my soul; I would give everything to save her.

Scatha stood looking on impassively. I understood now why she had come, and why Tegid had disobeyed my explicit order. She knew that I would not be able to leave Albion, and she assumed that once I understood the problem I would change my mind. But I was adamant.

I glanced at Cynan, who stood pulling his moustache and gazing thoughtfully at me. I raised my hand and pointed at him. "Give the kingship to Cynan," I said. "Let him be Aird Righ."

But Cynan only grunted. "I am going."

"Then give the sovereignty to Scatha," I said.

Scatha also declined. "I am going to find my daughter," she said. "I will not remain behind."

I turned at once to Bran, only to see him reject the offer as well. "My place is by your side, lord," was all he would say.

"Will no one take the kingship?" I demanded. But no eye met mine, and no one answered. It was rapidly growing dark, and I was quickly losing what little remaining dignity I possessed.

Whirling on Tegid as if on an attacker, I said, "You see how it is."

"I see," replied the bard icily. "Now I want *you* to see how it is." With that, he paused, closed his eyes, and took a deep breath. His first words caught me by surprise.

"Treán ap Golau was a king in Albion," Tegid announced. "Three things he had which were all his renown: the love of beautiful women; invincibility in battle; and the loyalty of good men. One thing he had which was his travail: it was the geas of his people that he must never hunt boar. And this is the way of it..."

I glared at him. A story! He meant to tell me a story. I could not believe it. "I do not have time for this, Tegid," I protested.

His head came up, his eyes flew open, and he fixed me with a baleful stare. "One day," he intoned icily, "when the king is out hunting with his warband, there arises a fearful grunting and growling, like that of a wild beast. So great is the noise that it shakes the trees to their roots and the very hills from top to bottom, cracking the rocks and cleaving the boulders. Once, twice, three times, the mighty grunting sounds, each time louder and more terrible than the last.

"King Treán cries to Cet, his wise bard, 'This sound must be silenced, or every living thing in the land will die! Let us find the beast that is causing this din and kill it at once.'

"To this, Penderwydd Cet replies, 'That is more easily said than done, Mighty King. For this sound is made by none other than the Boar of Badba, an enchanted beast without ears or tail, but with tusks the size of your champion's spears and twice as sharp. What is more, it has already killed and eaten three hundred men today, and it is still hungry. This is why it grunts and growls so as to sunder the world.'

"When Treán ap Golau hears this he says, 'A boar and a bane it may be, but if I do not stop this beast there will be nothing left of my realm.'

"With that, the king rides to meet the monster and finds it tearing at a broken yew tree to sharpen its tusks. Thinking to take it with the first blow, he charges the Boar of Badba. But the giant pig sees him coming and looses such a horrible growl that the king's horse falls to its knees with fright and Treán is thrown to the ground.

"The enchanted boar charges the fallen king. Treán hefts his spear, takes aim, and lets it fly. Closer and closer drives the boar. The spear flies true, striking the pig in the center of its forehead. But the spear does not so much as crease the boar's thick hide, and it bounces away.

"The boar closes on the king. Treán draws his sword, and slash! Slash! But the solid blade flies to pieces in his hand, while the pig remains unharmed. Indeed, not even a single bristle is cut.

"Down goes the boar's head, and up goes the king. He clings for a moment to the pig's back, but the frenzied beast shakes him off with such a fury that the king is thrown high into the air. The king lands squarely on the yew tree: the splintered trunk pierces his body, and he hangs there, impaled on the yew. And the king dies.

"Seeing this, the Boar of Badba begins to devour the king. The beast tears at the dead king's limbs. He devours the king's right arm and the king's right hand, still clutching the hilt of his shattered sword. The broken blade sticks in the beast's throat, and the Boar of Badba chokes on it and dies.

"The king's companions run to aid the king, but Treán ap Golau is dead." Looking directly at me, Tegid said, "Here ends the tale of King Treán, let him hear it who will."

I shook my head slowly. If, by telling me this tale, he had hoped to discourage me, he would be disappointed. My mind was made up.

"I hear your tale, bard," I told him. "And a most portentious tale it is. But if I must break this geas, so be it!"

Strangely, Tegid relented. "I knew that was what you would say." He paused and, as if to allow me a final chance to change my mind, asked, "Is that your choice?"

"It is."

He bent down and laid his staff on the ground before him, then straightened, his face like stone. "So be it. The taboo will be broken."

The Chief Bard paused and regarded the ring of faces huddled around us in the failing light. Speaking slowly, distinctly, so that none would misunderstand, he said, "The king has chosen, now you must choose. If any man wishes to turn back, he must do so now."

Not a muscle twitched. Loyal to a man, their oaths of fealty remained intact and their hearts unmoved.

Tegid nodded and, placing a fold of his cloak over his head, began speaking in the Dark Tongue. "*Datod Teyrn! Gollwng Teyrn. Roi'r datod Teryn-a-Terynas! Gwadu Teryn. Gwrthod Teyrn. Gollwng Teryn.*" He ended, turning to face each direction: "*Gollyngdod ... gollyngdod ... gollyngdod ... gollyngdod.*"

Retrieving his staff, he proceeded to inscribe a circle around the entire company gathered on the beach. He joined the two ends of the circle together and, returning to the center, drew a long vertical line and flanked it either side with an inclining line to form a loose arrowhead shape—the *gogyrven*, he called it: the Three Rays of Truth. Then he raised the staff in his right hand and drove it into the sand and, taking the pouch from his belt, sifted a portion of the obscure mixture of ash he called the *Nawglan* into each of the three lines he had drawn.

He stood and touched my forehead with the tips of his fingers—marking me with the sign of the gogyrven. Raising his hands palm outward—one over his head, one shoulder high—he opened his mouth and began to declaim:

> *In the steep path of our common calling,*
> *Be it easy or uneasy to our flesh,*
> *Be it bright or dark for us to follow,*
> *Be it stony or smooth beneath our feet,*
> *Bestow, O Goodly-Wise, your perfect guidance;*
> *Lest we fall, or into error stray.*

For those who stand within this circle,
  Be to us our portion and our guide;
Aird Righ, by authority of the Twelve:
  The Wind of gusts and gales,
  The Thunder of stormy billows,
  The Ray of bright sunlight,
  The Bear of seven battles,
  The Eagle of the high rock,
  The Boar of the forest,
  The Salmon of the pool,
  The Lake of the glen,
  The Flowering of the heathered hill,
  The Strength of the warrior,
  The Word of the poet,
  The Fire of thought in the wise.

Who upholds the gorsedd, if not You?
Who counts the ages of the world, if not You?
Who commands the Wheel of Heaven, if not You?
Who quickens life in the womb, if not You?
Therefore, God of All Virtue and Power,
Sain us and shield us with your Swift Sure Hand,
Grant us victory over foes and false men,
Lead us in peace to our journey's end.

Through this rite, the bard had sained us—consecrated us and sealed our journey with a blessing. I felt humbled and contrite. "Thank you for that," I said to him.

But Tegid was not finished. He reached into a fold of his belt, withdrew a pale object, and offered it to me. I held out my hand and he gave the object to me. I felt the cool weight in my palm and knew without looking what it was: a Singing Stone. Bless him, he knew I would choose to break the geas in order to save Goewyn, and he meant to do what he could to help me.

"Again, I thank you, brother," I said.

Tegid said nothing, but withdrew two more stones and placed them in my hands. With that, the bard released me to my fate. I tucked the three stones safely into my belt, turned, and ordered the men to board the ships. Everyone raced to be first aboard, and I followed close behind. I had all but reached the water when Tegid shouted. "Llew! Will you leave your bard behind?"

"I would go with a better heart if you went with me," I answered. "But I will think no ill if you stay behind."

A moment later he stood beside me. "We go together, brother."

We waded through the icy surge and were hauled aboard by those waiting on deck. Men took up long poles and pushed into deeper water as the sails flapped, filled, and billowed. Night closed its tight fist around us as the sharp prow divided the waves, throwing salt spray in our faces and spewing sea foam over our clothes.

In the deep dark of a moonless Sollen night I left Albion behind. I did not look back.

The seas were rough, the wind raw and cold. We were battered by rain and sleet, and tossed on every wave as the sea battled our passage. More than once I feared a water grave would claim us, but sailed ahead regardless. There was no turning back.

"What makes you think they have escaped to the Foul Land?" Tegid asked. I stood at the prow, holding to the rail. We had not seen the sun since our departure.

"Paladyr was behind this," I told him, staring at the waves and pounding my fist against the rail.

"Why do you say so?"

"Who else could it be?" I retorted. Nevertheless, his question brought up the doubt I had so far suppressed. I turned my head to meet his gaze. "What do you know?"

His dark brows arched slightly. "I know that no man leaves a trail on the sea."

"The trail leads to Tir Aflan. That is where we banished Paladyr, and that is where he has taken them," I declared, speaking with far more certainty than I felt at the moment. Standing on the shore, there had been no doubt. Now, after two days aboard a heaving ship, I was not so sure. What if they had sailed south, and made landfall at any of a thousand hidden, nameless coves?

Tegid was silent for a time, thinking. Then he said, "Why would Paladyr do this?"

"That much is obvious: revenge."

The bard shook his head. "Revenge? For giving him back his life?"

"For sending him to Tir Aflan," I answered curtly. "Why? What do you think?"

"Through all things Paladyr has looked to himself and his own gain," Tegid countered. "I think he would be content to save himself now. Also, I have never known Paladyr to act alone."

True. Paladyr was a warrior, more inclined to the spear than to subtle machinations. I considered this. "It does not matter," I decided at last. "Whether he acted alone or with a whole host of devious schemers, it makes no difference. I would still go."

"Of course," Tegid agreed, "but it would be good to know who is with him in this. *That* might make a difference." He was silent for a moment, regarding me with his sharp grey eyes. "Bran told me about the beacon."

I frowned into the slate-dark sea.

"Is there anything else you have not told me? If so, tell me now."

"There is something else," I admitted finally.

"What is it?" Tegid asked softly.

"Goewyn is carrying our child. No one else knows. She wanted to wait a little longer before telling anyone."

"Before telling anyone!" Tegid blustered. "The king's child!" Shaking his head in amazement and disbelief, he turned his face to the sea and gazed out across the wave-worried deep. It was a long time before he spoke again. "I wish I had known this before," he said at last. "The child is not yours alone; it is a symbol of the bounty of your reign and belongs to the clan. I should have been told."

"We were not trying to hide it from anyone," I said. "Would it have made a difference?"

"We will never know," he answered bleakly and fell silent.

"Tegid," I said after a while, "Tir Aflan—have you ever been there?"

"Never."

"Do you know anyone who has?"

He gave a mirthless rumble of a laugh. "Only one: Paladyr."

"But you must know something of the place. How did it get its name?"

He pursed his lips. "From time past remembering it has been called Tir Aflan. The name is well deserved, but it was not always so. Among the Learned Brotherhood it is said that once, long ago, it was the most blessed of realms—Tir Gwyn, it was called then."

"The Fair Land," I repeated. "What happened?"

His answer surprised me. "At the height of its glory, Tir Gwyn fell."

"Fell?" I wondered. "How?"

"It is said that the people left the True Path: they wandered in error and selfishness. Evil arose among them and they no longer knew it. Instead of resisting, they embraced it and gave themselves to it. The evil grew; it devoured them—devoured everything good and beautiful in the land."

"Until there was nothing left," I murmured.

"The Dagda removed his Swift Sure Hand from them, and Tir Gwyn became Tir Aflan," he explained. "Now it is inhabited only by beasts and outcasts who prey upon one another in their torment and misery. It is a land lacking all things needful for the comfort of men. Do not seek succor, consolation, or peace. These will not be found. Only pain, sorrow, and turmoil."

"I see."

Frowning, Tegid inspected me out of the corner of his eye. "Yes, you will soon see it for yourself," he said, pointing with the head of his staff to the sea before us. I looked at what appeared to be a dull grey bank of cloud riding low on the horizon: my first glimpse of the Foul Land. "After we have sojourned there awhile, tell me if it deserves its name."

I gazed at the colorless blotch of landscape bobbing in the sea-swell. It seemed dreary, but not more so than many another land mass when approached through mist and drizzle on a sunless day.

Indeed, I wondered after Tegid's description that it did not look more abject and gloomy.

I had come to find Goewyn, and I would go through earthquake, flood, and fire to save her. No land, however hostile, would stand in my way.

But in that I was wildly and woefully naive.

19

Tir Aflan

Easier to carry ships across the sea on our backs than make safe landfall in the Foul Land. The ragged coast was rimmed with broken rocks. The sea heaved and shredded itself on the jagged stumps with a sense-numbing roar. We spent the better part of a day searching along the coast for harborage, and then, as the day sped from us, we happened upon a bay guarded by two rock stack promontories that formed a narrow entrance.

Despite the shelter offered by the headlands, Tegid did not like the bay. He claimed it made him feel uneasy. Nevertheless, after a brief consultation, we concluded that this was the best landfall we had yet seen and the best we were likely to find.

I gave the order, and one by one the ships passed between the towering stacks. Once inside the shelter of the rocks, the water was deathly calm—and deep-hued, darker even than the sea round about. "Listen," Tegid said. "Do you hear?"

I cocked my head to one side. "I hear nothing."

"The gulls have departed."

An entire flock of seagulls had been our constant companions since the voyage began. Now there was not a single bird to be seen.

I stood at the prow as Cynan's vessel passed ours and drew into the center of the bay. Cynan hailed us and pointed out a place where we might land. He was still leaning at the rail, hand extended, when I saw the water in front of his ship begin to boil.

Within the space of three heartbeats it was bubbling furiously. No cauldron ever frothed more fiercely. The water heaved and shuddered; gassy bubbles burst the sea surface, releasing a pale green vapor that curled over the churning water.

The men on board rushed to the rails and peered into the seething water. Exclamations of amazement turned to cries of anguish when out of the troubled water there arose the scaly head of an enormous serpent. Fanged jaws gaping, forked tongue thrusting like a double-headed spear, the creature hissed and the sound was that of ships' sails ripping in a gale.

From behind and a little to one side, I saw the monster with the clarity of fear. Its mucus-slick skin was a mottled green and grey, like the storm-sick sea; its head was flat, its yellow eyes bulged; scales thick and ragged as tree bark formed a ridge along its back, otherwise its bloated body was smooth and slimy as a slug. A steady stream of filmy slime flowed from two huge nostril flaps at the end of its snout and from a row of smaller pits, that began at the base of its throat and ran along the midline of the creature's sinuous length.

If its appearance had been designed to inspire revulsion, the monster could not have been better contrived. My throat tightened and my stomach heaved at the sight. And then the wind-blast of the beast's breath hit us and I retched at the stench.

"Llew!" Tegid appeared beside me at the prow. He pressed a spear into my hand.

"What is that thing?" I demanded, dragging my sleeve across my mouth. "Do you know?"

Without taking his eyes from the creature, he replied in a voice hollow with dread: "It is an *afanc*."

"Can it be killed?"

He turned his face to me, pasty with fright. His mouth opened, but he made no sound. His eyes slid past me to the creature.

"Tegid! Answer me!" I grabbed him by the arm and spun him to face me. "Can it be killed?"

He came to himself somewhat. "I do not know."

I turned to the warriors behind me. "Ready your spears!" I cried. There were five horses in the center of the boat; the sudden appearance of the monster had thrown them into a panic. They bucked and whinnied, trying to break their tethers. "Calm those horses! Cover their eyes!"

A tremendous cracking sound echoed across the water. I turned back to see Cynan's vessel shiver and lurch sideways. Then it began to rise, hoisted aloft on a great, slimy coil. Men screamed as the ship tilted and swayed in the air.

"Closer!" I shouted to the helmsman. "We must help them!"

In the same instant, an eel-like hump surfaced before the prow. The ship struck the afanc and shivered to a halt, throwing men onto their hands and knees. Winding a rope around my metal hand, I leaned over the rail and, taking my spear, drove the blade into the slime-covered skin. Blue-black blood oozed from the wound.

I withdrew the spear and struck again, and then again, sinking the blade deep. On the third stroke I drove the iron down with all my strength. I felt the resistance of hard muscle, and then the flesh gave way and the spear-shaft plunged. The great bloated body twitched with pain, almost yanking my arm from its socket. Black water appeared below me; I released the spear just as Tegid snatched me by the belt and hauled me back into the boat.

Others, quickened by my example, began slashing at the afanc with their weapons. Wounds split the smooth skin in a hundred places. The grey-green seawater soon became greasy with the dark issue of blood. Whether the monster felt the sting of our blades, or whether it merely shifted itself in the water in order to concentrate its attack, I do not know. But the afanc hissed and the wounded hump sank and disappeared. The warriors raised a war cry at their success.

Meanwhile, Cynan and his men, clinging to the rails, loosed a frenzied attack upon the beast's head and throat. I saw Cynan balancing precariously on the tilting prow. He lofted his spear. Took aim. And let fly. He groaned with the effort as the shaft left his hand.

The spear flew up and stuck in the center of the afanc's eye. The immense snaky head began weaving from side to side in an effort to dislodge the spike.

The men cheered.

The praise turned to shouts of dismay, however, as the afanc reared, lifting its odious head high above the water. Its mouth yawned open, revealing row upon row of teeth like sharpened spindles. Warriors scattered as the gaping maw loomed above them. But several men stood fast and let fly their spears into the pale yellow-white throat.

Hissing and spitting, the awful head withdrew, spears protruding like bristles from its neck. The ship, still caught in the afanc's coil, heaved and shook.

We were still too far away to help them. "Closer!" I shouted. "Get us closer!"

Cynan, clinging desperately to the rail, shouted for another spear as the afanc's head rose to strike again.

"Closer!" I cried. "Hurry!" But there was nothing we could do.

The afanc's mouth struck the ship's mast. The crack of timber sounded across the water. The mast splintered and the ship rolled, spilling men and horses into the froth-laced waves.

Amidst the screams of the men, I heard a strange sound, a dreadful bowel-churning sound—thick, rasping, gagging. I looked and saw the top half of the ship's mast lodged sideways in the afanc's throat. The terrible creature was working its mouth, trying to swallow, but the splintered timber had caught in the soft flesh and stuck fast.

Unable to free itself, the afanc lashed its hideous head from side to side, thrashing in the water like a whip. And then, when it seemed the ships would be dashed to bits by the flailing head, the bloated body heaved and, with a last cataclysmic lash of its finless tail, the beast subsided into the deep. The two ships nearest to it were inundated by water and near to foundering, but turned and steered towards the shore. The last ship, swamped in the heavy chop, nearly capsized.

We drove towards Cynan's vessel and aided those we could reach. Even so, three horses drowned and a dozen men had a long, cold swim to shore. We were able to save the damaged ship, but lost the provisions.

When the last man had been dragged ashore, numb with shock and half frozen, we gathered on the shingle, mute, as we gazed out over the now-peaceful bay. We made fast the ships as best we could and then withdrew further up the coast, well away from the afanc's bed, to spend a sleepless night huddled around sputtering fires in a forlorn effort to warm ourselves.

Sleet hissed in the fitful flames and the wet wood sizzled. We got little heat and less comfort for our efforts, and as the sun rose like a wan white ghost in a dismal grey sky, we gave up trying to get warm and began searching the shoreline for signs of Goewyn, Tángwen, and their abductors. Discovering no trace of them, settled for finding our own way inland.

"*Clanna na cù*," grumbled Cynan, mist beaded in his wiry hair and moustache. "This place stinks. Smell the air. It stinks." His nostrils flared and he grimaced with distaste. The air was rank and heavy as a refuse pit.

Tegid stood nearby, leaning on his staff and squinting sourly at the dense tangle of woodland rising sheer from the narrow beach like a grey wall. The strand was sharp with shards of flint. Dead trees lay on the shore like stiffened corpses, shriveled roots dangling in the air. "We should not linger here," he said. "Our coming will be marked."

"All the better," I remarked. "I want Paladyr to know we are here."

"I was not thinking of Paladyr only," the bard told me. "He may be the least of our worries. I sense far worse trouble awaiting us."

"Bring it on," Alun declared. "I am not afraid."

Tegid grunted and turned a baleful eye on him. "The less boasted now, the less you will later regret."

Shortly after, Garanaw returned from his foray up the coast to report that he had found a stream which would serve as a path inland. Cynan proposed a plan to make for the hills we had seen from the ships; from the vantage of height we might discern the lie of the land and espy some sign of the enemy habitation.

The evidence of the hoofprints, beacons, and the grooves of ships' keels left little doubt that Paladyr had the help of others. From the heights we could easily spot the smoke from a campfire or settlement. It was an extremely slender hope resting on the narrowest of chances, but it was all we had. So, we pursued it as if we were sure of success.

Drustwn returned from a survey of the coast to the south. "The land rises to steep cliffs. There is no entry that I could see."

"Right. Then we go north. Lead the way, Garanaw."

We moved off slowly, following Garanaw's lead. Bran and the other Ravens walked with him, Cynan and his warband followed them in ragged ranks, and Tegid, Scatha and I came next, followed by six warriors leading the horses in a long double line. The wood lining the shore was so close-grown and thick there was no point in riding. We would have to go on foot, at least until the trail opened somewhat.

The stream Garanaw had seen turned out to be a reeking seepage of yellow water flowing out of the wood and over the stony beach to slide in an ochre stain into the sea. One sniff and I decided that it was the run-off from a sulphur spring. Nevertheless, the water had carved a path of sorts through the brush and undergrowth: a rough, steep-sided gully.

With a last look at the dead white sky, we turned and headed inland along the ravine. Undermined trees had toppled and lay both in and over the gully, making progress tortuous in the extreme. We soon lost sight of the sky; the ceiling above was a mass of interwoven limbs as close and dense as any thatch. We advanced with aching slowness through a rank twilight, our legs and feet covered in vile-smelling mud. The only sound to reach our ears was the cold wind bawling in the bare treetops and the sniffling trickle of the stream.

The horses refused to go into the wood, and we had barely begun when we were forced to stop while a score or more of the animals were blindfolded. Calmed in this way, the lead animals proceeded and the rest allowed themselves to be led.

We toiled through the day, marking our progress from stump to broken stump of fallen trees. We ended the day exhausted and numb from slipping and sliding against the sides of the gully, and climbed from the defile to make camp. At least there was no shortage of firewood, and soon there were a good many fires ablaze to light that dismal day's end.

Tegid sat a little apart, bowed over his staff. His thoughts were turned inward, and he spoke no word to us. I thought it best not to intrude on his musings, and left him to himself.

After resting, the men began to talk quietly to one another, and those in charge of the provisions stirred to prepare supper. I sat with Scatha, Bran and Cynan, and we talked of the day's progress—or lack of it.

"We will fare better tomorrow," I said, without much conviction. "At least, we can do no worse."

"I will not be sorry to get out of this putrid ditch," Cynan grumbled.

"Indeed, Cynan Machae," Alun said, "the sight of you struggling through the muck is enough to bring tears to my eyes."

Scatha, her long hair bound in tight plaits and tucked under her war cap, scraped mud from her buskins with a stick as she observed, "It is the stench that brings tears to *my* eyes."

Our gloom lightened somewhat at that, and we turned our attention to settling the men and securing the camp for the night. We ate a small meal—with little appetite—and then wrapped ourselves in our cloaks and slept.

The next day dawned wet. A raw wind blew from the north. And though it was cold enough there was no snow—just a miserable damp chill that went straight to the bone and stayed there. The following day was no different, nor was the one after that. We slogged along the bottom of the defile, threading our way over, under, and around the toppled logs and limbs, resting often, but stopping only when we could no longer drag one foot in front of the other.

The ground rose before us in a steady incline, and by the end of the third day we had all begun to wonder why we had not reached our destination.

"I do not understand it," Bran confessed. "We should have gained the top of this loathsome hill long since."

He stood leaning on his spear, mud and sweat on his brow, breecs and cloak sodden and filthy—and the rest of the noble Raven Flight were no better. They looked more like fugitives of the hostage pit than a royal warband.

None of us had shaved in many days, and all of us were covered in reeking mud. I would have given much to find a suitable trickle or pool to wash away some of the muck. But both this and the summit eluded us.

I turned to Tegid and complained. "Why is it, Tegid? We walk a fair distance every day, but have yet to come in sight of the top."

The bard's mouth twisted, as if with pain, as he said, "You know as much as I do in this accursed land."

"What do you mean? What is wrong?"

"I can see nothing here," he muttered bitterly. "I am blind once more."

I stared at him for a moment, and then it came to me what he meant. "Your *awen*, Tegid—I had no idea..."

"It does not matter," he said bitterly, turning away. "It is no great loss."

"What is wrong with him?" asked Cynan. He had seen us me talking, and had joined me just as the bard flung away.

"It is his awen," I explained. "It is no use to him here."

Cynan frowned. "That is bad. If ever we needed the sight of a bard, it is here in Tir Aflan."

"Yes," I agreed. "Still, if wisdom fails, we must rely on wits and strength alone."

Cynan smiled slowly. He liked the sound of that. "You make a passable king," he replied, "but you are still a warrior at heart."

We made camp in the dank wood and rose with the sun to renew our march. The day was a struggle against tedium and monotony but least it was not so cold as previous days. In fact, the higher we climbed, the warmer the air became. We welcomed this unexpected benefit and persevered; we were rewarded in the end by reaching the top of the hill.

Though the sun had long since given up the fight, we dragged ourselves over the rim of the hill to a level, grassy place. A sullen twilight revealed a large, flat clearing. We quickly gathered firewood from the forest below and built the fire high. Bran cautioned against this, thinking that the last thing we needed was a beacon to alert any enemy who happened to be near. But I judged we needed the light as well as the warmth, and did not care if Paladyr and his rogues saw it.

As my wise bard had already warned, however, Paladyr was the least of our troubles—as the shouts of alarm from the pickets soon proved.

20

The Siabur

In the time-between-times, just before dawn, the horses screamed. We had picketed them just beyond the heat-throw of the campfire, so the flames would not disturb them. As we were in unknown lands, Bran had established a tight guard on the animals and around the perimeter of the camp as well.

Yet the only warning we had was the sudden neighing and rearing of the horses—quickly followed by the panicked shouts of the sentry.

I had my spear in my hand and my feet were already moving before my eyes were fully open. Bran was but a step behind me and we reached the place together. The guard, one of Cynan's men, stood with his back to us, his spear lying beside him on the ground.

The man turned towards us with an expression of mystified terror. Sweat stood out on his brow and his eyes showed white. His teeth were clenched tight, and cords stood out on his neck. Though his arms hung slack at his sides, his hands twitched and trembled.

"What has happened?" I asked, seeing no evidence of violence.

By way of reply the warrior extended his hand and pointed to an angular lump nearby. I stepped nearer and saw that what, in the cold light, appeared to be nothing more than a outcrop of rock . . .

Bran pushed forward, and knelt for a closer look. The Raven

Chief drew a long, shaky breath. "I have never seen the like," he said softly.

As he spoke, I became aware of a sweetly rancid smell—like that of spoiled cheese, or an infected wound. The scent was not strong but, like the quivering guard, I was overcome with a sudden upwelling of fear.

Get up! Get out! a voice cried inside my head. *Go! Get away from here while you can.*

I turned to the guard. "What did you see?"

For a moment he merely stared at me as if he did not understand. Then he came to himself and said, "I saw ... a shadow, lord ... only a shadow."

I shivered at the words but, to steady my own trembling hand, bent down, picked up the sentry's fallen spear, and gave it to him. "Bring Tegid at once."

Roused by the commotion, others had gathered around. Some murmured uneasily, but most looked on in silence. Cynan appeared, took one look and cursed under his breath. Turning to me, he said, "Who found it?"

"One of your men. I sent him to fetch Tegid."

Cynan stooped. He reached out his hand, thought better of it and pulled back. "*Mo anam!*" he muttered, "it is an unchancy thing."

Tegid joined us then. Without a word, he stepped to the fore. Scatha followed on his heels.

"What has happened?" asked Scatha, taking her place beside me. "What ..." She took in the sight before her and fell silent.

The bard spent a long moment studying the misshapen heap before him, prodding it with the butt of his staff. Turning away abruptly, he came to where Bran, Cynan and I stood. "Have you counted the horses?" he inquired.

"No," I said. "We did not think to—"

"Count them now," Tegid commanded.

I turned and nodded to two men behind me; they disappeared at once. "What happened? What could ..." I strained for words, "what could do this?"

Before he could answer, someone shouted from the hillside below. We hurried at once to the place and found a second display just like the first: the body of a horse. Though, like the first, it scarcely resembled a horse any more.

The dead animal's hide was wet, as if covered with dew, the hair all bunched and spiky. An oddly colorless eye bulged from its socket, and a pale, puffy tongue protruded through the open mouth. But the remains were those of a creature starved to death whose corpse has collapsed inward upon itself—little more than skin stretched across a jumble of sharp-jutting bone.

The horse's ribs, shoulder blades, and haunches stood out starkly. Every tendon and sinew could be traced with ease. If we had starved the hapless beast and left it exposed on the hilltop all winter the sight would have been no more stark. Yet, as I knelt and placed my hand against the animal's bony throat, the sensation was so uncanny my hand jerked back as if my fingers had been burned.

"The carcass is still warm," I said. "It is freshly killed."

"But I see no blood," Scatha observed, pulling her cloak high around her throat.

"Och, there is not a drop of blood left in the beast," Cynan pointed out.

Appalled by the wizened appearance of the animals, it had not occurred to me to wonder why they looked that way. I considered it now. "It looks as though the blood has been drained from the carcass," I said.

"Not blood only, I think," Bran mused, answering my own thought. So saying, he lifted the point of his spear and sliced into the belly of the dead horse. There was no blood—no bodily fluid of any kind. The organs and muscle tissue were dry, with a stiff, woody appearance.

"*Saeth du,*" Cynan grunted, rubbing his neck. "Dry as dust."

Tegid nodded grimly, and glanced around the long slope of hillside as if he expected to see a mysterious assailant escaping through the trees. There was little to be seen in the thin early morning light; the mist-draped trunks of trees, and a thick hoarfrost covering grass and limbs and branches bled the color from the land until it looked like... like the stiff and bloodless carcass before us.

The horse lay where it had fallen. Aside from a few strange, stick-like tracks around the head of the carcass, I could see no prints in the frosty grass. Nor were there any tracks leading away from the kill.

"Could an eagle do this?" I wondered aloud, knowing the notion absurd as the words left my lips. But nothing else suggested itself to me.

"No natural-born creature," Bran said; he held his chin close to his chest. A good many others were unconsciously protecting their throats.

"Well?" I asked, looking to Tegid for an answer.

"Bran is right," the bard replied slowly. "It was no natural creature."

"What then?" demanded Cynan. "*Mo anam*, man! Will you yet tell us?"

Tegid frowned and lowered his head. "It was a *siabur*." He uttered the word cautiously, as if it might hurt his tongue. I could tell by the way he gripped his staff that he was badly shaken.

The men returned from counting the horses. "Two tens and eight," was their census.

"Thirty-three men," I remarked, adding, "and now we have horses for twenty-eight. Great. Just great."

"This siabur," Scatha wanted to know, "what manner of creature is it?"

Tegid grimaced. "It is one of the *sluagh*," he told us reluctantly. He did not like speaking the name aloud.

Ghost? Demon? I tried to work out the meaning of the word, but could get no further than that.

"The Learned call them siabur. They are an order of spirit beings that derive their sustenance from the lifeblood of the living."

"Blood-sucking spirits?" Cynan blustered, his tone forced and his voice overloud. He was holding fear at bay the best way he knew, and only half succeeding. "What is this you are telling us?"

"I am telling you the truth." Tegid jerked his head around defiantly, as if daring anyone to gainsay him.

"Tell us more, brother," Bran urged. "We will hear you."

"Very well," the bard relented, flicking a cautionary glance in Cynan's direction. "The siabur are predatory spirits—as you have seen with your own eyes. Upon finding their prey, they take to themselves a body with which to make their attack, devouring the very blood as it flows."

I did not blame Cynan for his disbelief; Tegid's description was incredible. But for the two dead horses, sucked dry and cast aside like withered husks, I would have dismissed it as little more than whimsy. Clearly, there was nothing remotely fanciful about it. And Tegid stood before us solemn and severe.

"Nothing like this is known in Albion," said Scatha. "Nothing like this..."

"That is because the Island of the Mighty remains under the protection of the Swift Sure Hand," Tegid said. "It is not so in Tir Aflan."

"What can be done?" I wondered aloud.

"Light is their enemy," the bard explained. "Fire is light——they do not like fire."

"Then tonight we will bring the horses within the circle of the campfire," Cynan suggested.

"Better than that," I replied. "We will build a circle of fire around the entire camp."

Tegid approved. "That will serve. But more must be done. We must burn the carcasses of the horses and the ashes must be scattered in moving water before the sun sets."

"Will that free us from the siabur?"

"Free us?" Tegid shook his head slowly. "It will prevent them from inhabiting the bodies of the dead. But we will not be free until we set foot in Albion once more."

No one was willing to touch the dead horses, and I had not the heart to compel any man to do what I myself abhorred. So we heaped a mound of firewood over the unfortunate beasts and burned them where they lay. The carcasses gave off an excess of thick, oily black smoke with the same rancid cheese smell I had marked earlier.

Tegid made certain that every scrap of hide and bone was burned, and then raked the coals and gathered the ashes in two leather bags. After that we turned our attention to finding a stream or river into which we could strew the ashes.

This proved more difficult than anyone imagined.

Tegid considered the turgid seepage in the ravine unacceptable for our purposes, and we were forced to look elsewhere. Leaving Bran in charge of the camp, Tegid, Scatha, Cynan and I set off in the bright light of a dour, windswept morning in search of a stream or brook. We soon discovered that the hilltop we were camped upon was not a natural hill at all.

Scatha first tumbled to the fact that the plain on which we stood was strikingly flat for a natural plateau, and furthered this observation by remarking the peculiar regularity in the curve of the horizon. We rode a fair portion of the circumference just to make certain, and found as we expected that the rim of the plateau formed a perfect circle.

Despite this evidence, Tegid remained hesitant and withheld judgment, until he had examined the center. It took considerable effort just to *find* it; it was no simple matter to quarter a circle that large. But Tegid lined out a course and we followed it. After a lengthy survey we found what we were looking for: the broken stub of a massive pillar stone.

So immense was the thing, we had failed to recognize the hill for what it was: a gigantic mound, ancient beyond reckoning, raised by human hands. Sheer size obscured its true nature. But the presence of the pillar stone removed all remaining doubt. The mound was the *omphalos*, the symbolic center of Tir Aflan. Judging by the size of the circular plateau, it was something in the order of twenty to thirty times larger than the sacred mound of Albion on Ynys Bàinail.

Tegid was thunderstruck. He knelt in the long grass with his hands resting on his thighs, staring blankly at the bare hump of weather-worn rock protruding from the ground. Cynan used his sword to hack away some of the turf while Scatha and I looked on. The wind gusted fitfully around us and the horses whickered uneasily. I noticed that though the grass was long and green, the horses refused to eat more than a few mouthfuls.

Cynan sliced with the edge of his sword, and rolled away grass and earth in a thick mat. Then he dug with his hands. When he had finished, a portion of grey stone lay exposed to view. The flat, smooth surface of the stone was incised with lines deep-cut and even—the remains of the saining symbols originally carved into the pillar stone.

We all stared at the peculiar marks and struggled to imagine how the great standing stone would have appeared to those who had built the mound and raised it. A relic of the remote past, before the Fair Land declined, the broken stone seemed to defy understanding even as it commanded veneration. It was as if we were confronted by a presence that both overwhelmed and beguiled. No one spoke. We just stood looking on...

Tegid was first to shake off the unnatural fascination. Rising slowly, he staggered and made an arc in the air with his staff. "Enough!" he said, his voice thick and sluggish. "Let us leave this place."

As he spoke, I felt a sudden and virulent resentment at his suggestion. I wanted only to be allowed to remain as I was, quietly contemplating the broken pillar stone. Tegid's voice reached me as a grating annoyance.

"Llew! Cynan! Scatha!" he shouted. "We must flee this place at once."

Into my mind came an image of Tegid lying on the ground bleeding from his nose and mouth; I could feel his staff in my hands. I was seized by an urge to strike the bard down with his own staff. I wanted to punish him for disturbing me. I wanted to make him bleed and die.

"Llew! Come, we must—"

His face swam before me, concern creasing his brow. I felt his hands, grasping, clawing...

"Llew!"

I do not remember moving—nor raising my silver hand at all. I saw a shimmering blaze out of the corner of my eye and felt a jolt in my shoulder. And then Tegid—lurching, falling, hands clutching his head...

Bright red blood on green grass, and Tegid's staff in my hands...

...and then Cynan's arms were around me and I was struggling in his grasp as he lifted my feet off the ground.

"Llew! Let be!" Cynan's voice was loud in my ear. "Peace, brother. Peace!"

"Cynan?" I said, and felt myself returning as if from a great distance, or emerging from a waking dream. "Release me. Put me down."

He still held me above the ground, but I felt his grip loosen somewhat. "It is over, brother," I reassured him earnestly. "Please, put me down."

Cynan released me and together we knelt over Tegid, who was lying dazed on the ground, bleeding from a nasty gash over his temple.

"Tegid?" I said. His eyes rolled in his head and came to rest on me. He moaned. "I am sorry," I told him. "I do not know what happened to me. Can you stand?"

"Ahhh, I think so. Help me." Cynan and I raised him between us, and held him until he was steady on his feet. "That metal hand of yours is harder than it looks—and quicker," he said. "I will be better prepared next time."

"I am sorry, Tegid. I do not know what came over me. It was... uh, I am sorry."

"Come," he replied, shaking off the assault, "we will speak no more of it now. We must leave here at once."

Cynan handed Tegid his staff, and threw me a wary glance. "The horses have strayed. I will bring them," he said, but seemed reluctant to leave.

"Go," I said. "I will not attack Tegid again." Still, he hesitated. "Truly, Cynan. Go."

As Cynan indicated, the horses had strayed. Indeed, they had wandered far across the plain and were now some distance from us. "They must have bolted," I observed, watching Cynan stride away. "But I do not remember it."

Wiping blood from his face with the edge of his cloak, Tegid squinted up at the sky and announced, "We have lingered here longer than we knew."

"What do you mean?" I asked, following his gaze skyward. I tried to gauge the position of the sun, but the bright morning had faded and thick clouds now gathered overhead. How long had we stood there?

"The day has passed us," the bard declared. "It will be dark soon."

"But that cannot be," I objected. "We dismounted only a few moments ago."

He shook his head gravely. "No," he insisted, "the day is spent. We must make haste if we are to reach camp before dark." He called to Scatha and started off after Cynan.

Scatha made no move to join us. Her spear lay on the ground beside her. I retrieved the weapon, and put my hand on her arm. "Scatha?" The skin was cold and hard beneath my touch—more like stone than living flesh. "Tegid!" I shouted.

He was beside me in an instant. "Scatha!" He shouted her name loud in her ear. "Scatha! Hear me!" He shouted her name once and again, but her eyes stared emptily ahead—wide and eerily intent, as if she were transfixed by something that demanded all her attention.

When she did not respond, Tegid groaned deep in his throat and, dropping his staff, seized her by the arms and turned the unresisting Pen-y-Cat bodily away from the stone. He shook her, but she did not respond.

"Let us take her away from here," I suggested. "Maybe—"

The bard's hand flicked out and struck her cheek. The sound of the slap shocked me, but brought no response from Scatha. He slapped her again, and shook her hard. "Scatha! Fight it, Scatha. Resist!"

His open palm connected and her head snapped back. I could

trace the print of his hand on her cheek. He shook her and raised his hand to strike again.

"No!" I said, catching his wrist. "Enough. It is enough. It is not working." On a sudden inspiration, I suggested: "Here, I will carry her."

Without waiting for Tegid's assent, I swept Scatha into my arms and began moving away from the stone. Her body, at first rigid, relaxed as soon as I lifted her feet off the ground and turned my back on the broken stone.

She moaned softly, and closed her eyes. In a moment, tears slipped from under her lashes to slide down the side of her face. I stopped walking and put her down. She leaned heavily against me. "Scatha," I said, "can you hear me?"

"Llew ... oh, Llew," she said, drawing a shaky breath. "What is happening?"

"It is well. We are leaving this place. Can you walk?"

"I feel so—lost," she said. "A pit opened at my feet—I stood at the edge and I felt myself falling. I tried to save myself, but I could not move... I could not scream..." She raised her fingertips to her reddened cheek. "I heard someone calling me..."

"This place is cursed," Tegid said. "We must go from here."

Supporting her between us, we began walking to where Cynan was laboring to catch the horses. They were skittish and he was having difficulty getting close enough to grab the dangling reins. We watched as he stole closer, lunged, grabbed—only to have the horse shy, buck, and run away. Cynan picked himself up off the ground and stamped his foot as the horses galloped further out of reach.

"It is no use," he said, as we drew near. "The stupid beasts are frightened and flee at shadows. I cannot get near them."

"Then we must walk back to camp," Tegid replied, moving off.

"What about the horses?" I asked. "We cannot—"

"Leave them."

"We need our weapons, at least," I maintained. Scatha had kept her spear, but Cynan and I had left ours beneath our saddles when we dismounted.

"Leave them!" the bard shouted, turning to confront us. His voice resounded emptily over the plain. "Believe me when I say that this mound is no safe place for us after dark. Our only protection lies within the circle of the fire."

He turned away again and began striding through the grass with long, swinging steps. Cynan, Scatha and I followed. Tegid was right; the level expanse of the circular plain was unbroken by any feature we could use to advantage. There were no trees, no rocks, no hollows for hiding.

I glanced back at the stump of stone behind us, and saw the eastern sky dark with fast-approaching night. How odd, I thought—I had never known daylight to fade so swiftly.

And with the advance of darkness, there arose a distant, wailing whine, like the howl of the wind in high mountain peaks—but there were no mountain peaks nearby, and it was not the wind I heard.

21

The Sluagh

Darkness overtook us as we hastened from the broken pillar stone. I do not think that even with our horses we could have reached the camp before nightfall. The way back was farther than I remembered it, and the weird twilight came on with unnatural speed. Horses could not have outrun it. Also, with the swiftly-deepening night, the eerie wail increased, as if the source of the uncanny sound were drawing relentlessly nearer.

Tegid kept one eye on the sky as we hurried along. As soon as he saw we could not reach camp before night overtook us, he announced, "We must make for the nearest slope. There we can find fuel for a fire at least."

"That is well," Cynan agreed. "But where is it? I can see nothing in this murk."

Tegid's plan was a good one; the banks of the mound were thickly forested, and firewood abounded. But how could we be certain which way to go when we could not see two steps in front of us?

"We should be near the edge of the plain," Tegid said. The pillar stone marked the center and we have been moving away from it—"

"Aye," allowed Cynan, "*if* we have not been making circles around it instead."

Tegid ignored the remark, and we rushed on. We had not

advanced more than a hundred paces, however, when Scatha halted.

"Listen!"

I stopped, but heard only the weird wailing sound which, apart from growing slightly louder, had not altered in any significant way. "What is it?"

"Dogs," she said. "I thought I heard dogs."

"I hear nothing," said Cynan. "Are you cert—" The bark of a dog—short, quick, unmistakable—cut him off.

"This way! Hurry!" shouted Tegid, darting ahead.

No doubt the bard thought we were right behind him, following in his footsteps. But I turned, and he had already melted into the darkness. "Tegid, wait! Where are you? Cynan?"

A muffled answer reached us. "This way . . . follow me . . ."

"Tegid?" I called, searching the darkness. "Tegid!"

"Where have they gone?" Scatha wondered. "Did you see?"

"No," I confessed. "They just vanished."

The dog barked again—if dog it was.

"It is closer," Scatha said, and the bark was immediately followed by another, a little further off and to the left.

"Yes, and there are more than one." I glanced this way and that, but could see nothing in any direction to guide us. Darkness had penetrated all, obliterated all. "We'd better keep moving."

"Which way should we go?" Scatha wondered aloud.

"Any way will be better than standing here," I replied. I put out my hand and grabbed hold of Scatha's cloak; she took the end of mine. "We will stay together," I told her. "Hold tight, and keep your spear ready."

Clutching one another's cloaks, we proceeded into the formless dark. I did not for a moment entertain any false hopes of eluding the beasts behind us. But I thought we might at least find a place to make a stand if we reached the slope of the mound before the creature on our trail reached us.

We went with as much speed as we dared. It is unnerving running blind. Every step becomes a battle against hesitation, against fear. And the steps do not grow easier with success. Indeed, the fear grows with every step until it becomes a dominating force.

But for Scatha's presence beside me, I would have halted every few steps to work up my courage. But I did not care to appear weak or fainthearted in her eyes, so I braced myself for the inevitable bone-breaking fall—and ran on.

All the while, the barking of the dogs grew louder and more insistent as they drew nearer. Their numbers seemed to have increased as well, for I thought I could make out at least five individual voices—at least, there were more than the two we had heard before.

Whether we would ever have reached camp this way, I will never know. Likely it was as Tegid had said—that darkness held no safety for any creature alone on the mound, and fire offered the only protection. We did, however, reach the rim of the plain and fell sprawling over one another as the ground tilted away beneath us without warning.

I fell, half-tumbling, half-sliding down the unseen slope, and landed on my side, knocking the breath from my lungs. It was a moment before I could speak. "Scatha!"

"Here, Llew," she replied, catching her breath. "Are you all right?"

I paused to take stock. My jaw ached, but that was from clenching my teeth as we ran. "I seem to be in one piece."

From the plain directly above us came the sudden swift rush of feet through the grass—as that of an animal making its final rush on its prey.

"Quick!" I yelled. "Down here!"

Diving, falling, rolling, down and down the slope we slid, until we came to rest in a sharp-thorned thicket. I made to disentangle myself, but Scatha said, "Shh! Be still!"

I stopped thrashing around and listened. I could still hear the dogs, but it sounded as if we had somehow managed to put a little distance between us and our pursuers. I was for moving on while we had a chance, but Scatha advised against it. "Let us stay here a moment," she urged, pushing deeper into the thicket.

Following her example, I wormed my way into the prickly

embrace of the bush and settled down beside Scatha to wait. "Do you still have your spear?" I asked.

"Yes."

"Good," I said, and wished yet again that I had remembered to retrieve my spear when we dismounted. And then I wished for a flint and striker to make a fire—if not that, then at least a single firebrand to light our way. But neither wish appeared likely to be granted.

Yet, as we sat in the inky darkness, waiting for we knew not what, the accursed night loud with the barking of the dogs, I imagined that my silver hand began to shine. The merest gleam at first, the faintest wink of a shimmer. I raised my hand to my face ... the gleam vanished. I lowered my hand and it returned.

I craned my neck to look up and, to my surprise, glimpsed a pale eye peering back at me: the moon. Cloud-wrapped, a cold, wan and waxy blur in the Sollen-black sky, and fitful as a ghost, it gave me heart nonetheless, and I willed the light to stay.

The dogs were right above us on the plain. They were almost upon us. I expected them to be at our throats at any moment ...

Scatha shifted. The glint of her spearblade pricked the gloom as she crouched forward to meet the attack. I felt around me for a stick to use as a club, but found nothing.

Meanwhile, the sound of pursuit had risen to a pitched din. The dogs were all around us, their cry deafening. I drew a last deep breath. *Come on*, I thought, *do what you will*. Amidst the baying I discerned the quick scatter of feet tearing through the undergrowth, and then, as quickly as it had grown, the sound began to dwindle away. Clasping one another's hands, we held ourselves deathly still, hardly daring to believe we had escaped. Only when the sound had diminished to a distant echo did we relax.

The moonlight grew stronger. I could see the glimmer of Scatha's eyes as she gazed steadily up the slope towards the plain. She felt my stare, turned her face towards me and smiled. In that moment, she looked just like Goewyn. My heart clutched within me. She must have sensed my distress, for she said, "Are you hurt?"

"No, I was thinking of Goewyn."

"We will find her, Llew." Her tone offered certainty, warm and confident. If there was any doubt at all in her heart or mind, she kept it buried deep within her, for I heard no trace of it in her voice.

It was now light enough to distinguish broad shapes on the slope. We waited, listening. I became cold sitting still so long. "We should move on," I said at last. "They might come back."

"I will go first," Scatha said, and began slowly disentangling herself from the thorns. She crept from the thicket and I followed, stepping free of the prickly branches to discover that we stood on the edge of an overgrown wood. In the faint moonglow, I could just about make out the rim of the circular plain a short distance above.

"The sky is clearing somewhat. We may be able to see the camp from up there," I said, thinking that if we could not find Tegid, we might at least locate the camp.

Scatha agreed and we climbed slowly back up the slope, gained the rim, and stood gazing across the plain. I had hoped to see the yellow fireglow from the camp—the ruddy smudge of the blaze reflected on the low clouds, at least—but there was nothing. I thought of shouting for Tegid and Cynan, then thought better of it. No sense in alerting the dogs.

"Well," I said, "if we stay close to the edge, we should reach camp eventually."

"We can also retreat to the wood if need be," Scatha pointed out.

Quickly, silently, like two shadows stealing over the dull grey field, we fled. Scatha, spear ready in her hand, led the way, and I maintained a constant lookout behind, scanning the plain for any sign of the camp, or of Tegid—I would have been delighted to find either. We ran a fair distance, and I became aware of a spectral flicker out of the corner of my eye. Thinking I had seen the campfire, I stopped walking and turned... but if I had seen anything it was gone.

Scatha halted when I did. "I thought I saw something," I explained. "It is gone now."

A moment later, it was back.

We had hardly put one foot in front of the other when I saw the strange flittering shimmer once again—just on the edge of sight. And as before, I stopped and turned to look.

"There is something out there," I told Scatha.

"I do not see anything."

"Nor do I. But it was there."

And again, as soon as we began walking, the glimmering image returned. This time, I did not stop, nor did I look directly at it. Rather, I let the subtle shifting glow play on the periphery of my vision while I tried to observe it to learn what it might be.

All I could perceive, however, was a fickle gleam in the air—as if the chill moonlight itself had thickened and congealed into elongated strands and diaphanous filaments that streamed through the night-dark air, rippling and waving like seaweed under water.

Yet, each time I turned my head, thinking to catch a glimpse, the phantoms vanished. There was, I decided, a phenomenon at work similar to the erratic light of certain stars which are clearly discernable when the eye is looking elsewhere, but which disappear completely when an attempt is made to view them directly.

We walked along and I soon observed that the amorphous shapes were not confined to the plain; they swarmed the air above and on every side. Whichever way I turned my head, I glimpsed, as if on the very edge of sight, the floating, curling shapes, merging, blending, wafting all around us.

"Scatha," I said, softly. She halted. "No—keep walking. Do not stop." We resumed, and I said, "It is just that the shapes—the phantoms seem to be gathering. There are more of them now, and they are all around us. Can you see them?"

"No," she said. "I see nothing, Llew." She paused for a moment and then said, "What do they look like?"

Bless you, Pen-y-Cat, I thought, for not thinking me mad. "They look like . . . like shreds of mist, or spider's webs drifting on the breeze."

"Do they move?"

"Constantly. Like smoke, they are always blending and changing shape. I find that if I do not look at them directly, I can see them."

We walked on and after a while I began to discern that the

phantom shapes were coalescing into more substantial forms, thicker, more dense. They still merged and melted into one another, but they seemed to be amassing substance. With this change, I also felt my silver hand begin to tingle with the cold—not the hand itself, but the place where the metal met flesh.

I thought this an effect of the cold night air, then reflected that cold weather had never affected me in that way before. Indeed, my metallic hand had always seemed impervious to either heat or cold. Always, that is, except once: the day I discovered the beacon.

I puzzled over this as we ran along. Could it be that my metallic appendage, whatever other properties it possessed, functioned as some sort of warning device? Given the fantastic nature of the hand itself and how it had come to attach itself to me, that seemed the least implausible of its wonders. Indeed, everything about the silver hand suggested a more than passing affinity with mystery and strange powers.

If my silver hand possessed the ability to alert its owner of impending danger, what, I wondered, did its warning now portend?

So absorbed had I become in these thoughts, that I ceased attending to the shifting shapes on the edge of my vision. When I again observed them, I froze in mid-step. The phantoms had solidified and were now of an almost uniform size, though still without recognizable form; they appeared as huge filmy blobs of congealed mist and air, roughly the size of ale vats. Something else about them had changed, too. And it was this, I think, that stopped me: there was a distinct awareness about them, almost a sentience. Indeed, it was as if the phantom shapes seemed eager, or excited— impatient, perhaps.

For, as I hastened to rejoin Scatha, I sensed an agitation in the eerie shapes—as if my movement somehow frustrated the phantoms and threw them into turmoil. A strange and unsettling feeling overcame me then, for it seemed that the wraiths were aware of my presence and capable of responding to it.

Meanwhile, the frosty tingling in my silver hand had become a definite throbbing chill, striking up into my arm. I quickened my stride and drew even with Scatha. "Keep moving," I told her. "The phantoms know we are here. They seem to be following us."

Following was not the precise word I wanted. The things were all around us—in the air above and on the ground on every side. It was more that we were traversing a dense and hostile wood where every leaf was an enemy, and every branch a foe.

Without slackening her pace, she raised her spear and indicated a patch of darkness to the right. "I see the glow of a fire ahead."

A dull yellow glow winked low on the horizon. "It must be the camp," I said, and an icy realization washed over me. That explains their agitation, I thought. The phantoms do not want us to reach camp. "Hurry! We can make it."

The words were hardly out of my mouth when Scatha threw her arm across my chest to stop me. In the same instant, a sweetly gangrenous stink reached my nostrils—the same as I had smelled coming from the dead horses. The gorge rose in my throat.

Scatha recognized the odor, too. "Siabur," she cursed, all but gagging on the word.

I heard a soft, plopping sound and saw a bulbous shape fall onto the ground a few paces ahead of us. The sickly-sweet stink intensified, bringing tears to my eyes. The round blue-black blob lay quivering for a moment, and then gathered itself like a bead of water on a hot surface. At the same time, it seemed to harden, for it stopped trembling and began to unfold its legs from around a bulging stomach. Its head emerged, beaded with eyes on top and a crude pincer mouth below.

I understood then what I had been seeing. The wraiths were those creatures Tegid called the sluagh. And now, by means of whatever power they possessed, the things had gathered sufficient strength to take on material form as a siabur. The immaterial had solidified, and the form it took was that of a grotesquely bloated spider. But a spider unlike any I had ever seen: green-black as a bruise in the moonlight, with a hairy distended belly and long spindly legs ending with a single claw for a foot, and freakishly large—easily the size and girth of a toddling child.

The immense body glistened with a liquid ooze. The siabur made a slobbering sound as it dragged its repulsive bulk over the grass.

"It is ghastly!" breathed Scatha, and with two quick strides she was over it, her spear poised. Up went her arm, and then down. The spear pierced the creature behind its grotesque head, pinning it neatly to the ground. The siabur squirmed, emitting a bloodless shriek; its legs twitched and its mouth parts clashed.

Scatha twisted the spear; the fragile legs folded and the thing collapsed in a palpitating heap. She raised the spear and drove it into the creature's swelling middle. A noxious gas sputtered out and the loathsome thing seemed to melt, its body losing solid form and liquefying once more into a blob that simply dissolved, leaving a foul-smelling blotch glistening on the grass.

My feet were already moving as the siabur evaporated. I caught Scatha by the arm and pulled her away. I heard the sound of another soft body fall just to the right, and another where we had been standing a moment before. Scatha twisted towards the sound. "Leave it!" I shouted. "Run for the camp."

We ran. All around us the night quivered with the sound of those hideous bloated bodies plopping onto the ground. There were scores, hundreds of the odious things. And still they kept coming, dropping out of the air like the obscene precipitation of a putrid rain.

The stench fouled the air. My breath came in ragged gasps that burned my throat and lungs. Tears flowed down my cheeks. My nose ran freely.

The long grass tugged at our feet as if to hinder us. The plain was alive with crawling siabur heaving their gross shapes over the ground, scrabbling, struggling, straining to get at us. Their thin legs churned and their drooling mouths sucked. They would swarm us the moment we halted or hesitated. And then we would become like the horses we had seen that morning: dry husks with the lifeblood sucked from our bodies.

Our path grew difficult and running became hazardous as we were forced to dodge this way and that to avoid the scuttling spiders. My silver hand burned with the cold.

A siabur appeared directly in my path and I vaulted over it. As my feet left the ground, I felt a cold weight between my shoulder blades—long legs groped for my neck. Its touch was the stiff cold touch of a dead thing. I flailed with my arms, dislodged the creature, and flung it to the ground where it squirmed and shrieked.

Another took its place. The dead cold weight clasped my shoulder, and I felt a sharp, icy bite at the base of my neck. An exquisite chill spread through me from the neck and shoulders down my back and sides and into my thighs and legs. I stopped running. The darkness became close, suffocating. My face grew numb; I could not feel my arms or legs. My eyelids drooped; I longed for sleep... sleep and forgetting... oblivion.... I would sleep—but for a small voice crying out very far away. Soon that voice would be stilled....

Hearing my shout, Scatha whirled around and, with a well-placed kick, detached the siabur from my neck. A quick jab of her spear pierced the spider through its swollen sac. The wicked thing wriggled, then dissolved into jellied slime and melted away.

My vision cleared and my limbs began to shake. I felt Scatha's hands lifting me. I tried to get my feet under me, but could not feel my legs. "Llew, Llew," Scatha crooned softly. "I have you. I will carry you." She helped me stand. I took two wobbly steps and pitched onto my face. The siabur rushed in at once—they could move with startling speed. I kicked out and struck one. It squealed and scurried out of the way, but two more charged me. Their claw-tipped legs snagged the cloth of my breecs as I thrashed on the ground.

Scatha stabbed the first one as it clawed at me and, with a quick backward chop, sliced the second in half. Then, planting her foot, she pivoted to the side and skewered two more as they scuttled nearer. A third tried to evade her, but she pierced the swell-bellied thing, lifted it on the point of her spear and flung it hissing into the air.

Using all her strength, Scatha hauled me upright and drove me forward once more. Tottering like an old man, I stumbled ahead. Moving helped; I regained the use of my limbs and was soon covering ground quickly again. We bolted for the edge of the plain and the wooded slopes below, where I hoped we might more easily elude them. A cluster of siabur tried to cut off our escape, but Scatha's inspired spearwork cleared the way and we reached the slope to a chorus of sharp angry squeals.

We gained the edge and plunged down the slope. The air was clean and I gulped it down greedily. My vision cleared and my nose and lungs stopped burning. Upon reaching the first fringe of the wood, I glanced back to see the siabur boiling over the brim of the plain in a vile, throbbing flood. Although I had expected pursuit, my heart sank when I saw their number: the scores and hundreds had become thousands and tens of thousands.

They flowed down the slope in an enormous pulsating avalanche, shrieking as they came. There was no stopping them, and no escape.

22

Yellow Coat

My heart sank. The hideous cascade of siabur inundated the wooded slope. We could not long evade them; there were just too many.

Scatha appeared at my shoulder. "Take this," she said, thrusting a stout branch into my hand. Ever resourceful, Pen-y-Cat had found me a weapon—suitable for spiders at least.

Taking the branch, I glanced back towards the hillside. The spiders were not coming as fast as before. Their movements were sluggish and they clumped together in an awkward press. "I think they are stopping."

"They are tiring," observed Scatha. "We can outrun them. This way! Hurry!" Scatha began pushing deeper into the brushy tangle.

I took two steps and screamed as pain shot up through my arm, stabbing into my shoulder. "Aghh!"

Scatha's hands were on me. "Are you hurt, Llew?"

"My hand—my silver hand ... ahh, oh, it is so cold." I stretched my hand towards her. "Do you feel it?"

Scatha touched the metal gingerly at first, then grasped it firmly. "It is not cold at all. Indeed, it is warm as any living hand."

"It feels like ice to me. It is freezing."

Turning back to the hillside above us, the siabur had halted their advance and were drawing together into heaving, throbbing piles.

The stench reached our nostrils as a gush of fetid air. Though the moonlight was not strong, I could see their misshapen bodies glistening in lumpen knots as they writhed and wriggled with a sound like the mewing and sucking of kittens at the pap.

And then, rising up out of one writhing heap: the head and forelegs of a hound—a monstrous, flat-headed cur with huge pointed ears and long, tooth-filled jaws. Its coat was a sodden mess of pitch black hair, and its eyes were red. The ugly head thrashed from side to side as if struggling to free itself from the spider mass, which had become an oozy quagmire of quivering bellies and twitching legs.

I watched in sick fascination as the beast clawed its way free, pulling its short back and hindquarters up and out of the stinking, squirming muck. But the hellhound was not escaping, it was being born of the abhorrent couplings of the siabur. Even as this thought took form in my mind, I saw another head emerging and beside it a third and, a short distance away, the snout and ears of a fourth.

"Run!" Scatha shouted.

The first hound had almost freed itself from its odious womb, but I could not tear my eyes from the loathsome birthing.

Scatha yanked on my arm, pulling me away, her voice loud in my ear. "Llew! Now!"

From higher up the slope I heard a slavering growl and the rush of swift feet. Grasping my club and without looking back, I lowered my head and darted after Scatha. She led a difficult race, lunging, bounding, ducking, springing over fallen branches, and swerving around tall standing trunks. I followed, marvelling at the grace and speed with which she moved—flowing through the tangled thickets and trees with the effortless ease of a flame.

The unnerving sound of their weird spectral baying assured me that the first hound had been joined by the other three. They had raised the blood-call—cruelly fierce, baleful, unrelenting—a sound to make the knees weak and courage flow away like water. I risked a fleeting backward glance and saw the swarthy shapes of the beasts gliding through the undergrowth, their eyes like live coals burning in the moonglow. We could not outrun them; and with but one spear between us, neither could we fight them. Our only hope was to keep ahead of them.

We ran for what seemed like an eon. I could hear the demon dogs tearing through the brush behind me. From the noise they were making, I judged that they were gaining ground on us and that there were more of them than before.

Chancing another backward look, I saw that the hellhounds were indeed very much closer now. Three or four more had joined the pack with others, no doubt, on the way. The sound of their baying blood-call cut through me, raising the hair on my scalp.

When I turned back, Scatha had disappeared.

"Scatha!" I cried. What if she had fallen?

I ran to the place where I had last glimpsed her, but she was not there, and nowhere to be seen. I could not stay and look for her, nor could I leave her.

"Scatha! Where are you?"

"Here, Llew!" came the answer—close at hand, but I could not see her.

A howl broke into a snarl as the foremost hellhound closed on me. I turned to meet the beast, putting my back to the nearest tree and holding my makeshift weapon before me, ready to strike. I could reckon to get in at least two good blows before the other hounds arrived. What I would do after that, I did not know.

The creature attacked with breathtaking speed. I braced myself to receive the weight as it sprang...

The butt end of a spear shaft descended directly before my face. "Take hold!" a voice cried from above.

I dropped the club, seized the spear with my flesh hand and jumped, swinging my legs up towards the boughs above. Hooking a branch with one knee, I caught another with my metal hand. A hair's breadth beneath me the hound's jaws closed with the force of a sprung trap. Clutching for dear life to the shaft of the spear, I felt myself lifted higher. "Let go the spear, Llew," my savior told me. "There is a branch beside you."

But I could not release my grip on the spear—the instant I did so, I would plummet to the ground. Another hound had joined the first and both were leaping at me, jaws snapping, teeth cracking.

"Let go, Llew."

I looked to the right and left. If I released the spear I would fall and be torn apart by the hounds.

"Llew! I cannot help you if you do not let go."

I hesitated, dangling dangerously close to the snarling creatures below. A third hound bounded over the backs of the other two and snagged my cloak in its teeth, almost tearing my grip from the spear, and dragging me down with its weight.

"I cannot hold you!"

Clinging to my cloak, the hellhound tugged furiously, trying to pull me from my precarious roost. The fabric of my cloak began to give way. A second hound caught a corner of the cloak and began to yank, its forelegs lifted off the ground. My grip on the spear began to slip as I was dragged down yet further. More hounds had reached the tree and were leaping at me, trying to snag a piece of my dangling cloak.

"Llew! Let go!"

Grip failing, slipping backward bit by bit, cloak pulled tight against my neck to choke me, there was nothing for it but to let go of the spear and try for a more secure handhold on the unseen branch.

"I cannot hold you!"

I released the spear and flung my hand out. The weight of the hounds jerked me down. But my hand closed securely on a branch and I quickly wrapped my arm around its sturdy length and held fast.

Scatha was there beside me, trembling with the effort of supporting my weight on the end of her spear. "I might have dropped you," she said.

"I could not see the branch," I replied through clenched teeth.

Kneeling on the branch beside me, Scatha leaned low and thrust down with the spear. A rabid snarl became a squalling yelp and the weight on my cloak decreased by half. Another quick thrust of the spear brought another bawl of pain and I was free. I fumbled with the brooch pin and somehow managed to unfasten the brooch and let the cloak fall free.

I pulled myself upright and climbed higher into the tree. Below were no fewer than eight hellhounds—some leaping frantically in the air, others running insanely around the tree, and at least two trying to scale the trunk by their claws. One of these managed to reach a fair height but, gripping the branch with one hand, Scatha leaned down and stabbed the creature in the throat. It fell yelping to the ground, landed on its spine and thrashed around, furiously biting itself as the black blood gushed from its wounded throat.

The beast died and, like the spiders, simply dissolved into a shapeless mass that quickly evaporated leaving nothing but a glutinous residue behind. But there were a dozen or more dogs running beneath the tree now. They sprang at us, clashing their teeth and snarling. Often one would try to climb the tree, whereupon Scatha would spear it, and it would fall back either wounded or dead. The dead quickly dissolved and disappeared, but were just as swiftly replaced by others.

We were trapped, clearly, and I began to think that by sheer strength of numbers the hounds would bring down the tree. Just watching the swirling, vicious chaos of their frenzy made me fearful and weary. Scatha, too, felt the futility of fighting them; for, although she still gave good account of herself with her spear when opportunity presented, I noticed that she seemed to be losing heart. Gradually, her features lost all expression, and her head drooped.

I tried to encourage her. "We are safe here," I told her. "The camp is near. The warriors will hear the hounds and come in force to rescue us."

"If they are not themselves under attack," she replied bleakly.

"They will find us," I said, doubt undercutting my words. "They will rescue us."

"We cannot escape," she murmured.

"They will find us," I insisted. "Just hold on."

Nevertheless, it soon began to look as if Scatha was right. The monstrous hounds did not tire, and their numbers, so far as I could tell, continued to increase. Scatha eventually ceased striking at them with her spear. Instead, we edged higher into the tree and sat staring hollow-eyed at the frenzy, growing gradually numb from the cold and the continual shock of the baying, snarling, howling cacophony below.

Watching the moonglint on teeth and claws, and the dizzy tracery of red-glowing eyes, my mind began to drift. The gyrating black bodies seemed to merge into one savage torrent like a raging cataract, fearful in its wrath. And I wondered what it would be like to join that swirling maelstrom, to become part of that horrific turbulence. No intent but chaos, no desire but destruction. What defiance, what strength, what abandon—to give myself over to such fury.

What would happen to me? Would I die? Or would I simply become one of them, primal and free? Knowing no limits, no restraint, a creature of naked appetites, feral, possessed of a savage and terrible beauty—what would it be like to act and not think, to simply *be*—beyond thought, beyond reason, beyond emotion, alive to sensation only...

I was startled from my dire reverie by the sudden shaking of the branch beside me. Scatha, eyes fastened on the tumult raging around the trunk of the tree, was standing on the limb, teetering back and forth, her arms outflung to keep her balance. She had dropped her spear.

"Scatha," I called. "Do not look at them, Scatha! Take your eyes off them."

I continued speaking as I cautiously crept closer along the branch until I was sitting beside her. Standing slowly, I put my arm around her shoulders to steady her. "Let us sit down again, Pen-y-Cat," I said. She yielded to this suggestion, and allowed herself to be guided to a sitting position on the branch. "That is better," I told her. "You had me worried, Scatha. You might have fallen."

She turned blank, unseeing eyes on me and said, "I wanted to fall."

"Scatha, hear me now: what you feel is the sluagh—they are doing this to us. I feel it, too. But we must resist. Someone will find us."

But Scatha had turned her gaze once more towards the howling, boiling mass beneath us. Desperate for some way to distract her, I fought the urge to return to my own contemplation of the turmoil below, and scanned the surrounding wood for some hopeful sign.

To my astonishment, I saw the faint glow of a torch moving down the slope.

"Look! Someone is coming. Scatha, see—help is on the way!"

I said this mostly to divert Scatha's attention, but I took heart myself. There was no logical reason to believe that rescue had come, but a multitude of reasons to assume that some fresh horror had found us instead.

Indeed, my hopes were all but extinguished when Scatha said, "I see nothing. There is no torch."

It was true—the glow was not a torch. What I had seen, burnished by hope into bright-gleaming flame, appeared now to be nothing more than a dull moonstruck yellow glow. It moved steadily through the wood towards us, however, and I gradually became aware that it moved to a sound of its own—difficult to hear above the snarling, growling, hellhound yowl, but distinct from it all the same.

"Listen . . . can you hear it?"

Scatha listened for a moment, turning her eyes away from the maelstrom below. "I . . . um, I hear . . . barking," she concluded uncertainly.

"That is it," I assured her. "Barking, exactly—the same as we heard before the siabur appeared."

Scatha regarded me sceptically, as well she might, considering how we had fled in terror of the sound upon hearing it. Odd to find comfort in it now. And yet, I did take comfort in it. I peered intently through the close-grown wood as the strange yellow glow wafted through the trees. The barking sound grew as the glow drifted, and there could be no doubt that it was the same that we had heard earlier.

My silver hand, which had long since become a chunk of ice on the end of my arm, began to tingle. A moment later, I glimpsed several smooth white shapes racing through the underbrush towards us.

"Something is coming!" I gasped.

The warming tingle quivered up into my arm as three sleek

white dogs broke through the undergrowth and drove straight into the impossible turmoil of hounds beneath our tree. White as new snow from snout to tail—except for their ears which were bright, blood red—the dogs were smaller and leaner than the black hellhounds, but swifter of foot and just as fierce.

I expected them to be torn apart in an instant, but to my amazement the hellhounds reacted as if they were being scalded alive. They reared on hind legs, leapt in the air, and scrambled over one another in a desperate struggle to escape the onslaught of the newcomers. And, as soon became apparent, with good reason.

The red-eared dogs charged in a frenzy of bared teeth, each seizing a hound by the throat, ripping furiously, and then lunging to another kill. The stricken hounds whined and crumpled, decaying into shapeless jelly and vanishing within moments.

Like lightning shattering the stormcloud, the three white dogs routed our assailants, killing with keen efficiency and striking again. Within moments of their arrival, dozens of their opponents were dead and hellhounds were fleeing for cover, clawing one another to get away. Soon the wood rang to the sound of the dogs' triumphant howls as they pursued the retreating hounds into the wood.

"They are gone," Scatha said, releasing her breath in a rush.

I opened my mouth to agree, and then I saw him: standing almost directly below us and looking in the direction the dogs had gone. He was wearing a long yellow coat with sleeves and a belt. It was this coat I had seen moving through the trees like a will-o'-the-wisp.

He stood for a moment without moving, and then he raised his face to look into the branches where Scatha and I were hiding. I almost fell from my perch. Peering up at me was easily the ugliest man I had ever seen: big-faced, gross in every feature, his long nose ending in a fleshy hook, and his mouth the wide thick-lipped cleft of a frog. Ears like jug handles protruded from under a thick pelt of wild black hair, and large wide-spaced eyes bulged balefully from beneath a single heavy ridge of black brow.

He held my gaze for the briefest instant, but long enough for me to know that he saw me. Indeed, he lifted his hand in farewell just before he stepped from beneath the branch and disappeared into the wood once more.

Only after he had gone could I speak. "I have seen that face before," I murmured. Once, long ago . . . in another world.

I felt a hesitant touch on my arm. "Llew?"

"It is over," I told her. "The dogs belonged to him."

"Who?"

"The man in the yellow coat. He was just there. I saw him; he—" I broke off. It was no good insisting. Clearly, Scatha had not seen him. Somehow that did not surprise me.

"We can go now," I told her, and began easing my weight from the branch.

I lowered myself to the lowest branch and prepared to drop to the ground. Just as I released my hold, Scatha called from above, "Wait! Listen!"

But her warning came too late. I landed awkwardly and fell rolling on my back. As I did so, I heard something big and heavy crashing through the wood. I jumped to my feet, searching wildly for Scatha's fallen spear, wishing I had saved the club.

"Llew!" Scatha called. "There—behind you!" The spear lay a few steps behind me. I ran to it, picked it up, and whirled to meet . . . Bran and Alun Tringad, swords drawn, along with twenty or more torch-bearing warriors.

"Over here!" I cried. "Scatha! It is Bran! We are saved!"

Bran and Alun advanced warily, as if I might be an apparition.

"Here I am!" I shouted again, lowering the spear and hurrying to meet them. "Scatha is with me."

"Llew?" the Chief Raven wondered, lowering his sword slowly. He glanced at Alun, who said, "I told you we would find them."

"We were returning to camp and lost our way," I explained quickly. I hurried back to the tree and called to Scatha. "You can come down now. It is safe."

Scatha dropped from the branch and landed catlike on her feet.

"Are Cynan and Tegid with you, too?" Alun asked, peering up into the branches.

"We became separated," I replied. "I do not know where they went."

"They did not return to camp last night," Bran said.

"How did you know where to find us?"

"We heard the dogs," Bran explained. "They circled the camp, and Alun saw someone—"

"Three times they circled the camp," Alun put in eagerly. "The fellow with them beckoned us to follow."

"I did not see anyone," stated Bran firmly. "I saw only the dogs."

"This fellow," I asked Alun, "what was he wearing?"

"A long mantle with a broad belt," Alun replied readily.

"And the mantle—what color?"

"Why, dun colored it was. Or yellow." Alun allowed. "Difficult to tell in the dark, and he carried no torch."

"And the dogs?"

"White dogs—" said Bran.

"With red ears," added Alun Tringad. "Three of them. They led us here."

"You heard nothing else?"

"Nothing else, lord," Alun answered.

"The baying of hounds perhaps?" I prodded. "Here in this very place?"

Bran shook his head. "We heard only the dogs," he declared. "And there were but three of them."

"And the man," Alun maintained.

"Yes, there was a man—the man in the yellow coat," I confirmed. "Scatha did not see him, but I did."

"I saw only the dogs," Scatha said with relief. "But that was enough." I noticed she said nothing about the hellhounds or the spiders. But then, neither did I.

23

Crom Cruach

Tegid and Cynan had in fact returned to camp before us and were waiting for our arrival. The sun broke above a grey horizon as we entered the still-smoldering circle of the protective fire. Upon stepping across this threshold of ashes, I was overcome with exhaustion. My legs became leaden and my back ached. I stumbled and almost fell.

Tegid grabbed my arm and steered me to a place at the campfire. "Sit," he commanded, and called to a nearby warrior. "Bring a cup!"

I stood swaying on my feet, unable to make the necessary movement. The ground seemed very far away.

Cynan, none the worse for lack of a night's sleep, hastened to Scatha's side, put his arm around her shoulders, and brought her to where I stood.

"Sit, brother," the bard urged. "You are dead on your feet."

I bent my knees and promptly collapsed. Scatha, dull-eyed and pale from our all-night ordeal, crumpled beside me.

The cup arrived. Tegid pressed it into my hands and helped me raise it to my lips. "What happened to you?" he asked as I drank.

The ale was cold and good, and I all but drained the cup before recalling that Scatha was thirsty too. I passed the cup to her as I replied, "We lost you in the dark. We called for you—we could not have been more than ten paces apart. Why did you leave us?"

242

"But we heard nothing," Cynan declared, mystified. "Not a sound."

"No?" It did not surprise me in the least. "Well, when we could not find you, we made for the edge of the mound."

"We were chased by hounds," Scatha said, shivering at the all-too-fresh memory.

"Then the dogs came and drove the hounds away," I told them simply. "Bran and Alun arrived a few moments after that and brought us back."

"Tell me about the dogs," Tegid said, kneeling before us.

"There were three of them—long-legged and lean, with white coats. They came through the wood and drove the others away."

Scatha supplied the details I had neglected. "The hounds had red ears and there was a man with them. I did not see him, but Llew did."

"Is this so?" the bard asked, raising his eyebrows.

Before I could reply, Alun answered, "It is so. I saw him, too. He was wearing a yellow mantle and running with the dogs."

Bran confirmed Alun's report. "I saw the dogs; they circled the camp three times and then led us to the very place where Llew and Scatha were hiding."

Tegid shook his head slightly. "What of the hounds?" he said.

I did not want to speak of them. I saw no point in planting yet more fear in the warriors' hearts—there was enough already.

"Well," I said slowly, "there is not much to tell. They were big, ugly beasts. Fierce. If Bran and Alun had not come when they did we would not be here now."

"The man with the dogs, you mean. He saved you. We came after." said Alun, dragging the facts before us once more.

"The point is," I said, "we could not have survived much longer."

"The hounds," Tegid persisted, "tell me about them."

"They were just hounds," I replied.

"They were sluagh," Scatha informed him.

Tegid's eyes narrowed. He did not ask how we knew this, but accepted it without comment. For this, I was grateful.

"The same as attacked our horses?" Cynan demanded.

"The same," Tegid replied. "The sluagh change bodies to suit their prey."

"Changelings!" Cynan shook his head and whistled softly between his teeth. "*Clanna na cù*. It is a fortunate man you are, Llew Silver Hand, to be drawing breath in the land of the living this morning."

Tegid said nothing, his expression inscrutable. I could not guess what he was thinking.

But Cynan was eager to talk. "After you and Scatha wandered away in the dark," he volunteered, "we found a grassy hollow and settled there to wait until sunrise. Oh, but the night was black! I could have seen no less if I had been struck blind. By and by the sky began to pale and the sun came up. We came on to the camp then. Indeed, we were no great distance away—but did we ever see the fire? No, we never did."

Tegid rose abruptly. "This mound is cursed. We cannot stay another night here."

"I agree. Send out scouts—two parties of four each, one to ride east and the other west around the perimeter of the mound. If they see any sign of an encampment two are to keep a lookout, and two are to return here at once."

"But they must not be long about it," Tegid added. "We will leave at midday."

"It shall be done," the Raven Chief said, rising to leave.

"I will send Gweir to lead one of the parties," Cynan offered, "and they will return the swifter."

Bran and Cynan moved off to begin organizing the scouts. I lay down to rest until the scouting party returned. But I did not bear the waiting easily, for I fell into an anxious reverie over Goewyn. Where was she? What was she doing at this moment? Did she know I was searching for her?

I entertained the idea of building a tremendous signal fire to let her captors know that we were here. In the end, I decided against the notion, however. If they did not know, we might yet surprise them; and if Paladyr and his thugs knew already, it would be better to keep them guessing our intentions.

Near midday, Tegid came with some food for me. He placed the bowl beside my head and squatted at my side. "You should eat something."

"I am not hungry."

"It is not easy to fight demons on an empty stomach," he told me. "Since you are not sleeping, you might as well eat."

I raised myself on one elbow, and pulled the bowl toward me. It was a thick porridge of oats flavored with turnip and salted meat. I lifted the bowl and sucked down some of the mush. Tegid watched me closely.

"Well, what is on your mind, bard?"

"How are you feeling?"

"Tired," I replied. "But I cannot rest. I keep thinking of Goewyn."

"Goewyn will not be harmed."

"How can you be so certain?"

"Because it is you they want, not her. She is the bait in the trap."

Tegid spoke frankly. His calm manner allowed me to speak my deepest fear: "If that is true, they might have killed her already." My heart skipped a beat at the thought, but it was spoken and I felt the better for it. "We would not know it until we walked into the trap and by then, of course, it would be too late."

Tegid considered this for a moment, then shook his head slowly. "No." His tone was direct and certain. "I do not think that is the way of it." He paused, looking at me, studying me—as if I were an old acquaintance newly returned and he was trying to determine how I had changed.

"What is it, bard?" I said. "You have been inspecting me since I walked into camp this morning."

The corner of his mouth twitched into an awkward smile. "It is true. I want to hear more about this man with the white dogs—the man with the yellow mantle."

"I have told you all I know."

"Not all." He leaned towards me. "You know him, I think."

"I do not know him," I stated flatly. Tegid's look of reproof was quick and sharp. "I have seen him before," I confessed, "but I do not know him. It is not the same thing."

"Where did you see him?"

Anger spurted up like bile into my mouth. "It is nothing to do with any of this. Leave it."

But the bard did not desist. "Tell me."

Tegid's probing was making me remember my life in the other world and I resented it. I glowered at him, but complied. "It was not in this worlds-realm," I mumbled. "It was before, when I was with Simon—Siawn Hy—in the other place; he had gone into the cairn, and I was waiting for him to come out. I saw the man nearby."

"Describe this cairn," said Tegid. And when I had done so, he asked, "Did you also see the white dogs?"

"Yes, I saw the dogs—white with red ears. But they were with someone else—a farmer, I think—oh, it was all so long ago, I cannot remember. They were all there, I think."

The bard was silent for a long moment; at length he mused, "He was the same."

"Who was the same?"

"With the dogs or without them, it makes no difference," Tegid announced cryptically. When I asked for explanation, he said: "Yellow Coat is usually seen with the dogs, it is true. But you saw the dogs and you saw him—together or apart, it makes no difference."

"Bard, make plain your meaning."

"*Crom Cruach, Tuedd Tyrru, Crysmel Hen*—he goes by many names and in many forms," he said, his voice falling a note. "But in all he remains who he is: Lord of the Mound."

Tegid spoke the name and I felt a clammy hand at my throat. "I do not remember any mound," I said.

"When a warrior sees the Washer at the Ford," Tegid said, "he knows that death is at hand."

I had heard stories of this sort before. Typically, a warrior going into battle arrives at a river ford and sees a woman—sometimes sometimes wonderfully fair, sometimes brute ugly—washing bloodstained clothes in the water. If he asks whose clothes she is washing, the Morrigan will tell him that they are his own. By this the warrior knows his doom is near. I considered this, then asked, "Is it the same with Yellow Coat?"

"Only those whose affairs concern Crom Cruach may see him," Tegid replied with typical bardic ambiguity.

"Does it mean death?" I demanded bluntly.

He hesitated. "Not always."

"What does it mean then?"

"It means that Crom Cruach has acknowledged you."

This explanation fell somewhat short of full elucidation, and Tegid appeared reluctant to expand further. "Is this connected with me breaking my geas?" I asked.

"Rest now," Tegid said, rising. "We will talk later."

I finished my meal and tried to sleep. But Tegid's dark insinuations and the bustle of the camp kept me awake. After a time I gave up and joined the waiting men. We talked idly, avoiding any mention of the disturbing events of the previous night. Cynan tried to interest the warriors in a wrestling match, but the first grappling was so half-hearted that the game was abandoned.

The morning passed. The sun, almost warm, climbed through its low southern arc, trailing grey clouds like mouldered grave-clothes. Just before midday, the first scouting party returned to camp to report that they had discovered no sign of the enemy. The four who had ridden east, however, did not return.

We waited as long as we dared, and longer than was wise. Tegid kept one wary eye on the sun, and muttered under his breath while he stumped around impatiently. Finally, he said, "We cannot stay here longer."

"We cannot desert them," Cynan said. "Gweir was leading. I will not leave my battlechief and warriors behind."

The bard frowned and fumed a moment, then said, "Very well, we will go in search of them."

"What if it is a trap?" put in Bran. "Perhaps that is exactly what Paladyr expects us to do."

"Then we will spring his trap and be done with it," Tegid snapped. "Better to face Paladyr and his warband than spend another night on this accursed mound."

"True," agreed Bran.

"Then we ride east," I said.

We rode across the plain following the trail of the missing scouts through the coarse grass—granting the stubbed pillar stone a wide leeway—and reached the eastern rim as daylight dwindled. We stood looking out across the treetops at the land beyond: all brown and mist-faded grey, what we could see of it below the low-hanging clouds.

"This is where the trail ends," Bran said, his voice low.

"Ends?" I turned to look at him. His dark aspect was made darker still by the thick black beard he was growing; he seemed to be slowly changing into a raven.

He pointed to a trodden place in the grass; the snow was well trampled with hoofprints, but there was no sign of a skirmish of any kind. "The scouts stopped here, and here the trail also stops. They might have gone down into the wood," he said doubtfully.

"But you told them not to do that."

"Yes. I told them."

We started down the long wooded slope. The dense wood made our going difficult. We had not ridden far, however, when we were forced to dismount and blindfold the horses. As before, the animals stubbornly refused to be ridden into the wood, and we had to lead them on foot in order to continue. Even so, this did not slow our progress much, the undergrowth was so thick and the tangle so impenetrable.

Bran led, ranging the Ravens on either side of him in the hope that we might raise the trail of the missing scouts. But by dusk we had not seen a single footprint, much less any sign of a trail. We moved with maddening slowness, hacking a halting path through the underbrush with our swords. And despite this exertion, I noticed that the further down the slope we went, the colder it got—so that by the time we began looking for a likely place to camp, we were all wrapped chin to heel in our cloaks, and our breath hung in frosty clouds above our heads.

We made camp under a great gnarled oak beneath whose twisted limbs we found a reasonable clearing. Brushwood was gleaned from round about and heaped into three sizeable piles from which we would feed three good fires. Tegid lit each fire himself, saying, "With three, if one goes out there are always two with which to rekindle it."

"Are you thinking the fires will fail?" I wondered.

"I am thinking that it is dangerous to be without a fire at night," was his reply. Accordingly, we appointed men to tend the fires through the night just to make certain they did not falter.

The night passed cold, but uneventful, and we awakened to nothing more sinister than a dull dogged rain. The next day brought no change, nor did those that followed. We pushed through an endless succession of barbed thickets dense as hedge, hauling ourselves over fallen trunks, wading through mud and mire, scrambling over and around great rocks. By day we shambled after one another in a sodden procession; by night we did our best to dry out. With every step the air grew colder so that by the fifth day the rain changed to snow. This did nothing to improve our progress, but the change was welcome nonetheless.

We walked in silence. Scatha, grim-faced and morose, spoke to no one; nor did Tegid have much to say. Cynan and Bran addressed their men in terse, blunt words, and only when necessary. I could find nothing to say to anyone, and slogged along as mute and miserable as the rest.

The slope flattened so gradually that we did not realize we had finally left the mound until we came to a slow-moving stream fringed with tall pines and slender birches. "It will be easier going from now on," Bran observed.

Although we had not been attacked by the sluagh again, I felt a rush of relief wash over me once the mound was left behind. I sensed we had also left behind its preying spirits. We rested under the pines and followed the stream all the next day. The trees were old and the branches high; the undergrowth thinned considerably, which made the going easier. Gradually, the stream widened to become a small, turgid river which wound between mud-slick banks among the exposed roots of the pines. From time to time, we glimpsed a desultory sun through breaks in the close-grown branches overhead.

As daylight faded in a dull ochre haze, we reached the end of the wood at last and looked out upon a wide valley between two long rock-topped bluffs. Snow covered the valley floor, but the snow was not deep. The river took on new life as it flowed out from the wood over a rocky bed. There were few trees to be seen, so we decided to stay the night at the edge of the wood where we would be assured of fuel for the fires. We spent all the next morning amassing firewood and loading the horses with as much as they could carry. Still, despite a late start, we made fair progress and by day's end had travelled further than we had any day since coming to Tir Aflan.

The sun remained hidden behind a solid mass of low, swart cloud for the next few days as we traced a course along the river, stopping only to water the horses and to eat and sleep. The weather continued cold, but the snow fell infrequently, and never for long. We saw neither bird nor beast at any time; neither did we see any track save our own in the thin snow cover.

For all we knew, we were the only people ever to penetrate so far into the Foul Land. This impression lasted for a long while—until we began seeing the ruins.

At first it seemed that the bluff-top on the left-hand side of the valley had simply become more ragged with impromptu heaps of stone and jagged, toothy outcrops. But, as we pushed further down the length of the valley, the bluffs sank lower and closer to the valley floor to reveal the shattered remnants of a wall.

We looked on the ruined wall with the same mixture of dread and fascination we had experienced on encountering the mound. Day succeeded day, and with every step the wall grew higher and more ominous: snaking darkly along the undulating ridgetop above us, gapped where the stone had collapsed and slid down the sheer bluffsides into broken heaps below. On the sixth day we came in sight of the bridge and tower.

The tower sat on a bare hump of rock at a place where the valley narrowed. The remains of a double row of demolished columns stumbled across the valley floor and river to the facing bluff opposite. We proceeded to the huge round segments lying half-buried in the ground—like the sawn trunks of megalithic trees—sinking into the land under their own bulk and an enormous weight of years. Here we halted.

At some time in the ancient past, the river must have been a roaring torrent spanned by a great bridge—a feat for giants. And guarding the bridge at one end, a bleak, brooding tower. The same questions were on every man's mind: who had raised the tower? What lay beyond the wall? What did they keep out? Curiosity grew too much to resist. We halted and made camp among the half-sunken columns. And then Cynan, Tegid, the Ravens and I scaled the bluffside.

The tower was stone, comprised of three sections raised in stepped ranks. There were odd round windows, like empty eye sockets staring out across to the other side. At ground level was a single entrance with a gate and door unlike any I had ever seen: round, like the windows; and the door was a great wheel made of stone, not wood, banded with iron around its rim and set into a wide groove. The surface of the gate and door were covered with carved symbols which were now too weathered to comprehend. The remains of a stone-flagged road issued from the gate and ended where the bridge had once joined the bluff. Judging from the width of the road, the bridge would have been wide enough for horsemen riding four abreast.

The wall joined the tower level with its first rank, easily three times a man's height. There was no way in, except through the round gate, and there was apparently no way to budge the great stone door. But Alun and Garanaw grew inquisitive and began examining the gate. It was not long before they put their shoulders to it, and between the two of them got it to move.

"It will roll," cried Alun. "Help us clear the groove."

The track in which the stone rolled was choked with rock debris. In no time, with the help of Emyr, Drustwn, and Niall, they succeeded in removing the grit and stone. And then they turned their attention to the door itself. The five Ravens gave a mighty heave and pushed.

To everyone's amazement the stone rumbled easily aside, revealing a darkened chamber beyond.

After warily poking their heads inside, they reported that they could see nothing. "We need torches," Tegid advised, and at a nod from their chief, Emyr and Niall scrambled back down the cliff to fetch a bundle each. We waited impatiently while Tegid set about lighting them. But soon the torches were kindled and distributed and, with pulses pounding, we passed through the imposing gate and into the strange tower.

24

The High Tower

Cautiously, shoulders hunched, walking on the balls of our feet, prowling like thieves desperate not to wake the sleeping occupants, we entered the dark tower.

The air was damp and smelled of earth and wet stone like that inside a cave. And even with the torches, it was dark as a cave. Gradually, however, as our eyes became adjusted to the fluttering light, we began to pick out individual features in the darkness.

We stood in a single large chamber, two or three times larger, for all I could tell, than any king's great hall. There was a single row of stone pillars through the center of the room supporting the floor above. Huge iron rings were fixed in the pillars at various heights.

"Here!" called Drustwn from a little way ahead. "Look here!"

In a jumbled heap, as if tossed aside in a moment's wrath, were a score of bronze chariots, their wheels warped and poles bent or broken, the metal green with age. The high, circular sides of the chariots appeared to be wicker, but were in fact triangular strips of bronze woven together, immensely strong for their weight.

Lying a little apart from the chariots was a small pyramid of large discs, stacked one atop another. And beside this, a pile of oversized axeheads—unusual in that they consisted of a short stout blade on one side balanced by a blunt spike on the other. There must have been several hundred of these and as many discs which, on closer inspection, turned out to be bronze shields.

Bran pulled one of the shields from the stack, causing a dusty avalanche. He lifted the round device by the rim and held it before him; it was huge, much larger than any the men of Albion used, and plain. Its only markings appeared on the center boss: a few curious symbols worked in raised bronze around the simple image of a peculiar thick-bodied serpent.

"Whoever carried this was a stronger man than me," Bran remarked, replacing the shield, and retrieving his torch.

We continued our examination but, aside from a neat row of short, heavy bronze thrusting spears, we found nothing else in the lower chamber, and took our search up a flight of stone steps to the next level.

The round windows in the center of each of the four walls allowed some light to enter the large, square room, the floor of which was littered with helmets and war caps—high crowned and rising to a slight point at the top, all of bronze, and all with a bronze serpent coiled around the rim with its flat head raised upon the brow. Alun picked one up and set it on his head, but it was made for a man twice his size. There were perhaps two hundred or more of these serpent-crested helmets scattered on the floor, but nothing else in the room.

On the floor above we discovered a great stone table set with huge bowls of silver and bronze, with one gold vessel among them. The silver was black and the bronze green, but the gold was good as the day it was made; it gleamed dully in the light of our torches. Also on the table were three piles of coins in the rotted remains of leather bags. The coins were silver and gold. The silver coins were little more than black lumps, but the gold shone bright. We took up some of these and looked at them.

"Here is their king," said Tegid, holding a coin before his eyes. "I cannot read his name."

The coin showed the image of a man as if etched by a precocious child. The man clasped a short spear in one hand and a spiked axe in the other. He was bareheaded and his hair was long, curling down to his shoulders; he wore beard and moustache almost as long. His chest was bare—he bore no torc or other ornament—but he wore what appeared to be striped breecs or leggings, and tall boots on his feet. Words in strange letters clustered like wasps around his head, but they were impossible to read.

We each took a handful of the coins to show the others, and Cynan took the gold bowl. "For Tángwen, when I see her," he said.

Beside the table stood a large iron tripod bearing a huge bronze cauldron. Beneath the cauldron was a ring of fire-blackened stones, and inside it the baked, brick-hard shards of the last meal. But the outside of the cauldron was what caught my eye. The surface was alive with activity: warriors in chariots charged around the bottom of the cauldron lofting spears, long hair trailing in the wind; on the next tier above, narrow-eyed men on horses galloped, brandishing swords and spears; above these were ranks of warriors on foot, shoulder to shoulder, bearing round shields and helmets such as we had seen in the lower chamber; on the highest tier a number of winged men were running, or perhaps flying, and each bore a serpent in his right hand and a leafy branch in his left. The rim of the cauldron was a scaly serpent with its tail in its mouth.

"The Men of the Serpent," Tegid said, indicating the warriors.

"Do you know of them?"

"Their tale is remembered among the Derwyddi but, like the song of Tir Aflan, we do not sing it." I thought he would not say more but, gazing at the cauldron, he continued, "It is said that the Serpent awoke and with a mighty war host subdued the land. When there were no more enemies to conquer the Serpent Men fell into disputes and warring among themselves. They destroyed all they had built, and when the last of them died, the Serpent crawled back into the underworld to sleep until awakened again."

"What awakens it?" I asked.

"Very great evil," was his only reply.

Strewn about the room were objects of everyday use: more cups and bowls; many short, bone-handled swords fused to their scabbards; a few round shields; a collection of small pots, flasks, and boxes carved of a soft reddish stone—all of them empty; several long, curved spoon-shaped ladles and long-handled forks for getting meat and broth from the cauldron; numerous axeheads; knives of various sizes; a mask of bronze showing the glowering face of a bearded warrior with a great flowing moustache, elaborately curled hair, and a serpent helmet on his head, his mouth open in full cry; four very tall lampstands, one in each corner, bearing stone-carved oil lamps.

Underneath one of the shields, Emyr found a curious object—a circlet of small shield-like discs linked together around a protruding conical horn. Turning it this way and that, he announced, "I think it is a crown." Like most of the other objects we had seen, it was made of bronze and, when he put it on his head, it was shown to have been made for a much larger head.

"*Mo anam*," muttered Cynan, trying the crown himself, "but these serpent men were giants."

"Look at this!" called Garanaw, holding his torch to the far wall.

We crossed to where he stood and saw a painting on the wall. It was well done, and no doubt brightly colored at one time. And though the colors had faded to an almost uniform grey-brown, leering out at us was the face of a serpent man, fleshy lips curved in a mocking smile, pale reptilian eyes staring with frozen mirth, his mouth open and forked tongue extended. A mass of coiled curls wreathed the face, and below the chin it was still possible to make out the winged torso and a raised hand grasping a black serpent which coiled around the arm.

We turned from the painting and Niall called our attention to an iron ladder set in a recess of one wall. The ladder rose through the stone ceiling to the roof above. He climbed it and then called down for us to follow. There was nothing on the roof, but the view was breathtaking. Looking to the south, far below us in the riverbed among the fallen columns, lay our camp, men and horses gathered near the grey thread of moving water.

To the west rose the gigantic hump of the mound, its top lost in the low-hanging cloud, and to the east only the river flowing on between its rock-bound bluffs. To the north, behind the high stone wall stretching away to the east and west, lay an endless series of low, snow-covered hills, rising and falling like white sea waves in a frozen ocean.

The size and emptiness of the landscape, like that of the dark tower and its objects, made us feel small and weak, and foolish for trespassing where we did not belong. I scanned the rolling hillscape for any sign of habitation, but saw neither smoke nor any trail by which we might go. "What do you think, bard?" I asked Tegid, who stood beside me.

"I think we should leave this place to its dire memories," he answered.

"I am all for it, but where do we go from here?"

"East," he replied without hesitation.

"Why east? Why not south or west?"

"Because east is where we will find Goewyn."

This intrigued me. "How do you know?"

"Do you remember when Meldron cast us adrift?"

"Mutilated and left to die in an open boat—could I ever forget it?"

"In exchange for my eyes, I was given a vision." He made it sound as if he had merely traded one pair of breecs for another.

"I remember. You sang it in a song."

"Do you remember the vision?"

"Vaguely," I said.

"I remember it." He closed his eyes as if he would see it anew. He began to sing, and I listened, recalling the terrible night that vision had been given.

Softly, so that only I would hear, Tegid sang of a steep-sided glen, and a fortress on a shining lake. He sang of an antler throne adorned with white oxhide and established high on a grass-covered mound. He sang of a burnished shield with the black raven perched on its rim, wings outspread, raising its raucous song to heaven. He sang of a beacon-fire flaming the night sky, its signal answered from hilltop to hilltop. He sang of a shadowy rider on a pale yellow horse, riding out of the mist which bound them; the horses' hooves striking sparks from the rocks. He sang of a great warband bathing in a mountain lake, the water blushing red from their wounds. He sang of a golden-haired woman in a sunlit bower, and a hidden Hero Mound.

Some things I recognized: Druim Vran, Dinas Dwr, my antler throne; the golden-haired woman in the bower was Goewyn on our wedding day. But other things I did not know at all.

When he had finished, his eyes flicked open again and he said, "This land has a part in my vision. I did not know it before coming here to this tower."

"You mentioned no tower in your vision—was there a tower?"

"No," he confessed, "but this is the land. I know it by the feel and taste and smell." His dark eyes scanned the far hills, rising and falling one behind another to the edge of sight and beyond. "In this worlds-realm a mighty work waits to be accomplished."

"The only mighty work I care about is rescuing Goewyn before—" I broke off abruptly. The others were not listening, but they were close by.

"Before the child is born," Tegid finished the thought for me.

"Before anything happens to *either* of them."

"We will journey in hope, and trust the Swift Sure Hand to guide us."

"A little guidance would not go amiss right now," I confessed, gazing out at the trackless waste of hills and empty sky.

"Llew," he said, "we have ever been led."

We left the roof, retreating back through the tower to the gate. Tegid advised us to close the door, so we rolled the stone back to its place. Then we climbed down the bluff to rejoin our waiting warband. We showed them the coins we had found and they wanted to go back up and get the rest, but Tegid would not allow it. He said further disturbance would not be welcome.

They let it go at that. The tower had a dolorous air, and even those who had not been inside felt the oppressive sadness of the place. Besides, it was already getting dark and no one wanted to risk being caught outside the fire-ring after nightfall.

That night we listened to the plaintive cry of the wind tearing itself on the broken stones of the wall on the bluffs high above. I slept ill, my dreams filled with winged serpents and bronze-clad men.

Twice I wakened and rose to look at the tower—a brooding black bulk against a blacker sky. It seemed to be watching us, perched on its high rock like a preying bird, waiting to unfold its wings of darkness and swoop upon us. I was not the only one bothered by bad dreams; the horses jigged and jittered all night long, and once one of the men cried out in his sleep.

We continued on our way the next day, listening to the wind hiss and moan through the valley. The snow fell steadily and drifted around our feet; we pulled our cloaks over our heads, bundled our saddle fleeces around our shoulders for warmth, and slogged through the weary day. The scenery altered slightly, but never really changed—always when I lifted my head there were the sheer bluffs and the wall looming ragged and dark above.

For five days it was the same—cold and snow and deep starless nights filled with wailing wind and morbid dreams. We struggled through each day, riding and walking by turns, shuddering with cold, and huddling as close as possible to the fires at night. And then, as the sixth day neared its end, we saw that the bluffs had begun to sink lower and the river to spread as the valley opened. Two days later we came to a place where the bluff ended and the wall turned to continue its solitary journey north over the endless hills. Rising before us was the dark bristling line of a forest.

Seeing it, like a massive battlehost arrayed on the horizon, my spirit quailed within me. Tir Aflan was a wasteland vast beyond reckoning. Where was Goewyn? How would we ever find her in this wilderness?

"Listen, bard, are you sure this is the way?" I demanded of Tegid when we stopped to water the horses. We had left the wall behind and were drawing near the leading edge of the forest, but there was still no clear sign that we were going in the right direction.

Tegid did not reply at once, and did not look at me when he did. "The forest you see before us is older than Albion," he said, his dark eyes scanning the treeline as he rolled his ashwood staff between his palms.

"Did you hear me?" I demanded. "Is this the way we are to go?"

"Before men walked on Albion's fair shores, this forest was already ancient. Among the Learned it is said that all the world's forests are but seedlings to these trees."

"Fascinating. But what I want to know is, do you have even the haziest notion of where we are going?"

"We are going into the forest," he answered. "In the forest of the night, we all find what we seek—or it finds us."

Bards!

25

The Forest of the Night

Taking the river as our only guide, we passed into the forest. The snow, which had drifted deep in the exposed valley, was but scant under the trees. And such trees!

There were trees of every kind: along the river were stands of silver birch, willows of various types, thickets of elder, blackthorn, hawthorn, hazel and holly; and on the broad meads stood great groves of oak, chestnut, hornbeam, lime, elm, sycamore, plane, walnut, ash, larch, and others; on the high ground there were evergreens: fir and pine and spruce in abundance, as well as cedar and yew. Lichen and moss flourished, making every trunk and branch look as if someone had slathered it in thick, grey-green plaster.

I could well believe that the forest was ancient. The moss-bound branches were bent and the trunks bowed by ages of years beyond counting, eons of accumulated leafmould cushioned the forest floor, dry grass like wisps of unkempt hair clustered in elderly hanks around massive curving roots. The trees were old.

And big! The river, wide and deep as it entered the forest, seemed to dwindle to the size of a mere brook beneath those massive boles. Some of the larger limbs stretched from one bank clear across to the other, arching over the river like huge arboreal snakes.

We moved in a world of outsize proportions. And the further into the forest we penetrated, the smaller and more vulnerable we felt—shrinking in our own eyes. In the shadows of those ancient trees we were not men at all, but insects: insignificant, powerless, futile.

Dismaying though it was to be a mere insect, more unsettling by far was the silence.

As we entered the forest, the sound of the world beyond faded, and it diminished further with every step until we could hear nothing at all—not even the wind. No alien birdcall reached our ears, no tick of leafless branch, or creak of sagging limb. Our own footfalls were muffled in the spongy leafmould, and the river flowed mute in its slime-slick bed.

I was speculating whether the cold had stolen my hearing, when Cynan called out, "*Mo anam*, brothers! But this quiet is not natural among men of noble clans. What do we fear that we dare not raise a pleasant tune when and where we please?"

When no one answered him, the red-haired hero began to sing, roaring out the words as if he were bending horseshoes with them. Full-throated, his head thrown back, he sang:

> *Hie, up! Rise up, brave and dauntless friends!*
> *The sun is red on gorsey hill,*
> *and my black hound is straining to the trail.*
> *Hie, up! Rise up, bold and doughty men!*
> *The deer do run on heathered brae,*
> *and my brown horse is tending to the trace.*
> *Hie, up! Rise up, raven-haired lady fair!*
> *A kiss before I join the chase,*
> *A kiss before I fly ... Hie!*

It was a valiant effort, and I admired him for it. He even succeeded in rousing some of the men for a time, but no one had the heart to sustain it. This angered Cynan, who sang on alone for a time out of sheer stubbornness. But eventually even Cynan's brash spirit was stifled by the vast, all-absorbing silence of the forest.

Thereafter we pursued our way with hushed steps, dull in sense and dispirited. The forest seemed to prey upon our minds and hearts, stirring our fears, bringing doubt and dread to the surface where they could wear away at us with their corrosive power. I suspected that we were being watched, that in the forest around us, hidden from sight, the enemy waited.

In the lattice-work of limbs high over us, in the shadow-choked darkness beyond the river trail, behind every trunk and bole, cold eyes watched and cold hands waited. I imagined a multitude of winged serpent-men clutching their short bronze thrusting spears, eyeing us with icy reptilian malice. I imagined that they moved as we moved, matching us stride for stride, gliding with the silence of snakes in the silence of the forest.

I told myself that my fears were mere inventions of my mind, but I watched the shadows all the same.

Night stole secretly over the forest, and it marked little change. In this place, ever dark and preternaturally still, daylight was a weak and alien presence. *Coed Nos*, Forest of the Night, is what Tegid had called it, and he was right. The sun might boldly pursue its diurnal course, might rise and set in blinding flames that caught the outside world alight; but we had entered Night's own realm and the sun had no power in that place.

We made camp by the deep-flowing river and banked the fires high. If I hoped fire would offer us some comfort, I was deceived. The forest seemed to suck the warmth and light, the very life, from the flames, making them appear pale and wan and impotent. We sat with faces close to the tepid blaze and felt the stealthy silence hard at our backs.

I could not rest. I could not eat or speak to anyone, but every few moments I must turn my head and peer over my shoulder. The feeling was strong—I was certain of it—we were being stalked. Others felt it too, I think; there was no talk, no genial exchange around the fire as there usually is when men gather after a long day's journey. It seemed that if we could not overcome the all-subduing silence, we preferred to sink into it, to let it cover us and hide us from the things that stalked the shadows.

We made a miserable night of it. No one slept; we all lay awake, gazing into the crowded tangle of limbs and branches faintly illumined by our feeble fire. That does not mean, however, that we did not dream. We did. And I think each man among us was visited by queer, disturbing nightmares.

Sitting hunched over my knees, staring hollow-eyed into the limb-twisted darkness, I saw a faintly glimmering shape that resolved itself into a human form as it approached: a woman, slender, clad in white. Goewyn?

I jumped to my feet.

Goewyn!

I ran to her. She was shivering, her arms were bare and cold, and it was clear that she had been wandering in the forest for many days. She must have escaped from her captors and fled into the forest.

"Goewyn! Oh, Goewyn, you are safe," I said, and reached out to take her hand, forgetting that my metal hand would be cold against her skin. I touched her with it and she cried out.

"I am cold, Llew," she whimpered.

"Here, take my cloak," I said, drawing it from my shoulders. "Put it around you. Come to the fire. I will warm you," I said, and thrust my silver hand into the flames of the campfire.

In a moment, the metal warmed and I turned and took Goewyn's hand in mine. The metal was too hot and it seared into her flesh. Acrid smoke flared up, stinging my eyes. Goewyn screamed and pulled away, but the skin stuck to the metal and came off as she jerked her hand from my grasp. And not the skin only—the burned muscle stuck too.

Screaming in agony, she raised her hand before her face, but only bones were left. Without the muscles or ligaments to hold them together they separated and fell to the ground and were lost in the snow. Goewyn clutched her stub of arm and screamed.

I stood in a panic of indecision, wanting to comfort her, but not daring to touch her for fear that my touch would maim. Tegid ran to us. He took Goewyn by the shoulders and began shaking her violently. "Be quiet!" he shouted. "Be quiet! They will hear you!"

But she could not control herself. Tears flowed from her eyes and she sobbed, holding her arm. Tegid kept shouting at her to be quiet, that she would alert the enemy.

Bran came running with his sword. Without a word to anyone, he struck Goewyn. She turned toward him and he thrust the blade into her heart. He pulled it out again and a scarlet stain flowed down her white mantle. She turned and cried out. "Llew! Save me!"

But I could not move. I could do nothing to save my beloved. She fell, scattering drops of blood from her wound. She lay on her back and raised her arm toward me. "Llew..." she gasped, her voice already fading. My name was the last word on her lips.

Her warm blood seeped from the wound, melting deep into the white-drifted snow. And the snow began to melt—and went on melting. Soon I could see green showing through the snow; grass was growing, growing up where the blood melted the snow.

I raised my eyes to look around. I was not in the forest any more. Tegid and Bran had departed and left me standing alone on a hilltop above a stream; across the stream stood a grove of slender silver birches. I watched as the snow melted from the sides of the hill and hundreds of yellow flowers appeared. The clouds parted, revealing a bright blue sky and a warming sun.

When I turned back, Goewyn was gone, but there was a slight mound in the place where she lay—little more than a grassy hump of earth. Upon this mound a cluster of white flowers grew: a yarrow plant had sprouted where Goewyn lay.

With tears in my eyes, I turned away and stumbled down the hill to the stream where I knelt and bathed my face in the clear cold water. While I was washing there, I heard a voice coming from the birch grove—a melody falling light as birdsong. I rose and splashed across the stream and entered the grove.

I stepped softly through dappled green shadows and passed among the slender white birch trees, following the song. I came to a clearing and paused. In the center of the clearing in a pool of golden sunlight stood a bower made of birch branches; the song was coming from the bower.

My senses quickened. I moved cautiously from the cover of the trees and entered the meadow. At my approach the singing stopped. I saw a movement from within the green-shadowed interior, and I, too, halted.

A woman clothed in green and yellow emerged. Her hair was softly golden in the sunlight, falling around her face and, with her head bent, I could not see who it was. She stepped gracefully from the arbor and cupped her hands to the sun as if she would gather in sunbeams like water. And then, though I had not moved or even breathed, she turned to me and said, "Llew, there you are. I have been waiting for you. Why do you tarry so?"

At this she pulled back the hair from her face. I gaped in disbelief. She laughed at my distraction and said, "Well, where is my welcome kiss?" And oh, her voice was sweet music to my ear.

"Goewyn?"

She held out her arms to me. "I am waiting, best beloved."

"Goewyn, you are dead. I saw you die."

"Dead?" She said the word as gently as a butterfly lighting on a petal. Still smiling—her lips formed a delicious curve that swept into the fold of her soft cheek—she lifted her chin in mock defiance. "I am done with dying," she said. "Now, where is my kiss?"

I stepped willingly into her embrace and felt her warm lips on mine and a taste like honey on my tongue. I crushed her to me, kissing her mouth and cheek and neck, holding her tight lest she slip like bright sunlight through my fingers.

"I thought I had lost you," I told her, tears of joy welling in my eyes. I breathed in the warm living scent of her as if I could breath her in with it, make her part of me. "Never leave me, Goewyn."

She laughed softly. "Leave you? How could I ever leave you? You are part of me now, as I am part of you."

"Tell me, again. Please, tell me you will never leave me."

"I will never leave you, my soul," she whispered. "I love you for ever ... for ever ..."

"Llew? What are you doing?"

The voice was Tegid's. I turned on him with some exasperation.

"Can you not see what I am doing? You are not wanted here. Go away."

"Llew, come back to the fire. You have been dreaming."

"What?"

Tegid's face grew dim, as if a cloud had passed overhead, blotting out the sun.

"Come back to camp with me," he said. "You have been walking in your sleep."

With these words, the sun-favored clearing vanished. I looked around and saw that I was back in the forest and it was night. The leafy bower was gone, and Goewyn was nowhere to be seen.

I spoke to no one for two whole days after that. Heartsick, discouraged and embarrassed, I avoided all my companions. If any command was required, Cynan or Bran saw to it and gave the order.

We pushed deeper into the forest. The trees grew larger, their great entwined limbs and interlaced branches imprisoning the light, making our passage dim and, if that were possible, even more silent. If we had been sewn in leather sacks it could not have been closer or more stifling than Coed Nos had become.

An air of malignant weariness emanated from the twisting roots and boles around us; languor seeped like an ooze from the soft leafmould under our feet. Lethargy, like the grey lichen that covered everything, clung to our limbs, bleeding strength with every step.

We rode single file, heads down, shoulders bent. Those on foot went ahead so that no one should be left behind. Tegid feared that if anyone fell back, we would never see them again. Cynan and Bran took it in turn to lead, changing every time we stopped to rest and water the horses. They did their best to keep a steady pace and keep the men moving despite the torpor.

Even so, we seemed not so much to journey as to view a slowly-revolving trail. We moved, but did not advance; we proceeded, but never arrived. We staggered steadily forward toward a perpetually receding destination. Day passed day, and we gradually lost track of the days. We slept little, talked less, and drove ourselves relentlessly on.

Food became scarce. We had hoped to hunt in the forest—at least to encounter game we might take along the way. If there was game in the forest, we never saw it, nor crossed any animal trail. Our dried meat gave out, and we subsisted on old bread and ale, soaking the crusts in our cups to soften them. When the ale ran out, we used water from the river. The bread became moldy and unfit to eat, but we ate it anyway. There was nothing else. And when the bread was gone, we boiled the precious little grain we had left with roots and bark that Tegid found to make a thin gruel. The horses ate the grey lichen which we harvested from the trunks with knives and swords, and bound into bales for them. It was food ill-suited for such noble beasts, but at least there was an unending supply of the stuff and they ate it readily enough.

We grew long-bearded, and sallow-skinned from lack of sunlight. But we bathed regularly in the river—until the men began to encounter leeches whenever they entered the slow-flowing water. Thereafter, we left off bathing altogether and contented ourselves with washing only.

Cynan grew restive. As the days progressed, he urged us to greater speed and complained with increasing regularity that we were not making enough effort to get clear of the forest.

"Be easy, brother," Bran advised. "Nothing will be gained by pushing too hard."

"It is taking too long," Cynan grumped. "We should have come through this forest long ago."

"Do not lose heart," I told him. "We will come to the end soon."

Cynan turned on me. "My wife is taken, too! Or have you forgotten? I tell you she is no less a queen than your precious Goewyn!"

"I know, brother," I soothed. "Please, be—"

"You think I do not care for my wife?" he challenged. "You think, because I say nothing, that I do not speak her name in my heart with every step?"

"I am sure you do, Cynan. Calm yourself. We will find them both." I put my hand on his arm. He knocked it away, glared at me, and then stormed off.

Some time later—two days or ten, I no longer knew—we stepped from the forest into a clearing bounded by the high rock bluffs of the river. And in the center of the clearing on the left bank stood a city, ruined and deserted, carved into the red stone bank. I call it a city, though closer scrutiny soon revealed that it was a single structure: an enormous palace with hundreds upon hundreds of dwelling places, halls, walls, columns, courts, and shrines, all heaped together in a haphazard jumble of red stone.

We came upon it suddenly and stood blinking in the light of a faded day. It was the first we had seen of the sky for days uncounted, and all we could do was to stand and stare, our hands shielding our sore eyes. And then, quivering with the shock of the sun and sky and easy air, we crept cautiously forward—as if the strange red palace were a mirage that might vanish if we glanced away.

But the structure was solid stone from the countless pinnacles of its high-peaked rooftops to its many-chambered foundations. Most of the columns were broken and the roofs collapsed; the round eye-socket windows stood empty and unlit. However, by far the greater part of the palace remained intact. Carved figures of animals and birds were placed in the pediments, but we saw no human figures represented. The edifice had been constructed to front the river. Indeed, a single round entrance like that of the high tower, but larger by far, opened onto a terrace which ended in a wide sweep of steps descending directly to the black water. The stone-carved walls flowed in curves, bending into one another like limbs, merging without joints or straight lines. This gave the place a disturbingly organic quality which Cynan identified at once. "Aye, see it lying there—like a great red lizard asprawl on the riverbank."

"Indeed," agreed Alun Tringad. "It is a sleeping lizard. Let it lie."

Nothing moved; no sound could be heard among the rubble. The red palace was as lifeless and deserted as the tower we had seen before, and just as old. And yet, whatever power preserved the structure had not entirely abandoned it. For clearly the palace still exerted dominion over the forest, or else the red stone would have been overgrown long ago. Something yet lingered which prevented the vegetation from invading and reclaiming the clearing and its deserted edifice, root and branch.

At the far end of the terrace, the broken remains of what appeared to be a wide, stone-paved road led from the city at an angle away from the river. Tegid observed the red palace for a long time, and then counselled us to move on, saying, "It is an evil place. We will find nothing but misery here."

Alas! We should have heeded his wise counsel.

26

Yr Gyrem Rua

Even in the short time we had been contemplating the ruin, daylight began to dwindle; it would be dusk soon, and night followed swiftly. We would have to find a place to make camp, and I was determined not to spend another night in the forest. So we decided to pass by the palace to the road beyond and see where it might lead.

In two tight lines, we moved out onto the terrace. Strange to feel solid rock under foot, stranger still to hear the hollow echo of hoofs after the smothering silence of the forest. We crept slowly across the wide terrace, every step ringing in our ears, reverberating from a hundred angled walls.

Bran, leading the procession, reached the center of the terrace—midway between the river steps and the gaping entrance to the palace. I saw him look to this door, turn, and stop. He raised his hand for those behind him to halt. "I saw something move in there," he explained as Cynan and I joined him.

I looked to the entrance—round as a wheel, and five times the height of a man, it was also dark as a pit; I could not imagine how he saw anything inside.

"Let us move on," I said, and was still looking at the empty doorway when we heard the cry: plaintive, pitiable, the wail of a lost and frightened child.

"Mo anam," muttered Cynan, "there is a babe in there."

We stared at one another for a moment, wondering what to do. "We cannot pass by and leave the poor thing," Cynan said. "It is not right."

Loath as I was to agree with him, I conceded to a quick investigation. "It must be swift indeed," Tegid warned. "It will be dark soon. We dare not linger."

Leaving Scatha and the rest to guard the horses, Bran, Emyr, Garanaw, Tegid, Cynan and I prepared torches and crept toward the red palace, watching the vacant entrance as we drew nearer. We saw nothing and the cry did not come again.

At the threshold, we paused to light the torches and entered an enormous, empty hall. Surprisingly, the room was many times larger on the inside than it appeared from the outside. The reason for this, Tegid immediately discovered. "It is all one," he pointed out. "There is but a single chamber."

All the hundreds of windows which, on the outside, appeared to open onto separate rooms, served to shed light on this single gigantic chamber. Even so, there was precious little illumination, just enough to see that we stood on a ledge with wide, shallow steps leading down to a floor somewhere below. Neither the floor below nor the roof above could be seen from where we stood, and the light of our torches did little to challenge the darkness of the place.

The air inside the hall was dank and cold—colder than outside. We stood and listened, our breath hanging in clouds around us. Hearing nothing, we started down the steps, shoulder to shoulder, torches held high. Each step stirred an echo that flitted like a bat into the darkness.

"A cheerless house, this," muttered Bran, his voice ringing in the vast emptiness.

"Even with a blaze the hearth would be cold," added Emyr.

"Still, I would welcome a fire now," Garanaw said. "The darkness here is dark indeed."

Six steps down, we came onto a wide landing, and then six more to another landing, and a final six to the floor, which was covered with six-sided glazed black tiles. The tiles glistened with moisture and made a slick surface for our feet as we moved slowly to the center of the hall where the firepit would be.

"Your hopes for a welcome fire are in vain, Garanaw," remarked Tegid. "There is no hearth."

No hearthstone, no fire-ring, nor even a brazier such as we had seen in the tower. The room, as far as we could tell, was devoid of any furniture whatsoever. Instead, where the hearth would have been, there was a mosaic picked out in small red, white and black tesserae depicting the same winged serpent emblem we had seen in the tower. The serpent here, however, was less stylized and somewhat more lifelike: sinuous red coils shimmering in the torchlight, red eyes glaring, reptilian wings spread behind its flat head. And there was a word spelled out in red tiles beneath it, which I took to be the creature's name.

I looked at the image traced upon the floor and my silver hand sent a warning tingle up my arm.

My eyes were better adjusted to the dark now, and I saw that the great room was oval-shaped, its many-peaked roof supported by rows of tapering columns whose tops were lost to the blackness above. Directly opposite the entrance door across the expanse of floor, a second round doorway, nearly as large as the first, opened into the smooth rockface of the bank.

We proceeded warily across the room to this second doorway, which proved to be the opening of a cave—elaborately dressed with fine finished stone without, but nothing more than a ragged rock tunnel inside. It came to me that the whole palace was but a façade built to conceal or, more likely, to enshrine this single cave entrance.

"Well," said Cynan, eyeing the tunnel doubtfully, "we have come this far. Will we turn back without seeing what lies beyond?"

Up spoke Tegid. "Do you yet wonder what lies beyond?"

"Enlighten us, bard," Cynan said. "I cannot guess."

"Can you not? Very well then, I will tell you. It is the creature whose image we have seen since coming to the Foul Land."

"The beast set in the floor back there?" wondered Cynan,

gesturing to the empty hall behind us.

"The same," said Tegid. "It is in my mind that this hole leads to the lair of the beast. *Yr Gyrem Rua* is its name."

"The Red Serpent?" murmured Cynan. The warriors glanced around warily. "Do you know this beast?"

"Unless I am much mistaken," the bard replied, "the creature within is that which the Learned call the Red Serpent of Oeth." He hesitated. "Some call it Wyrm."

"Wyrm..." Bran muttered, glancing over his shoulder.

Sick dread broke like a wave over me; I understood now why the palace consisted of just one room, and why the bronze men of the high tower revered the image of the serpent: it was their god; they sacrificed to it. And this was Yr Gyrem Rua's shrine and sanctuary.

"Let us leave this place while we may," urged Bran.

With that, we turned from the door, retreating back across the floor but three paces when the cry sounded again—the thin, tremorous whimper of a forlorn and miserable infant.

"The child has wandered in there," gasped Cynan, hurrying back to the cave entrance. Peering inside, he put his hands to his mouth and called to the child, waited, and when he received no reply, started into the tunnel.

I snatched him by the cloak and pulled him back. "You cannot go in there alone."

"Then come with me, brother."

I turned back to the others. "Stay here," I said. "We will take a quick look inside."

Trembling in every limb, Cynan and I started down the tunnel, the light of our torches flickering on the damp red stone. We moved cautiously on, but encountered little more than a strong smell: musty and somewhat sweet, but with a ripe gamey taint, like rancid oil or fat.

Fifty paces more and I saw a glistening mass lying on the floor of the passage. My metal hand went suddenly cold and I stopped in my tracks.

"What is that?" breathed Cynan, gesturing with his torch.

I stepped closer and held my torch nearer. My stomach tightened and my mouth filled with bile. I gagged and choked.

Lying in a pool of vomitus on the floor before us was the undigested head of one of our missing scouts. The flesh was badly corrupted, the face horribly marred; even so, I recognized the man.

Cynan made to brush past me, but I swung towards him and put my hand in the center of his chest. "Brother, no ... It is Gweir."

He strained forward, anger, sorrow and disbelief battling across his features. He glanced over my shoulder. "*Saeth du!*" he cursed and turned away.

There was nothing to be done for Gweir, so we moved on, the odor growing more potent with every step. In a little while the passage turned and widened out somewhat, forming a low grotto. The stench hit me full force as I stepped into this inner chamber; it rocked me back on my heels, but I choked back the bile and staggered ahead. Cynan entered quickly after me.

In the center of the grotto was a hole in the rock floor. The rough edges of the hole were smoothed to an almost polished luster. It was not difficult to guess how the rough stone had gained its glassy sheen.

Scattered on the floor of this hateful chamber were various body parts of our missing warriors and their mounts: a foot still in its buskin, a mangled horse's head and several hooves, jawbones, human and animal teeth, the stripped rib cage and spine of a horse. There were other, older bones, too, skulls and broken shanks scoured clean and brown with age—sacrificial victims of a distant age.

I could not bear the sight and turned away. The eerie child-like whine sounded again, rising from the depths below, and I realized it was the Wyrm itself, not a child, that made the cry. Tightening my grip on the torch, I stepped towards the hole. A blade of ice stabbed up into my arm.

Cynan caught me by the shoulder. "Stay back," he barked in a harsh whisper, pulling me roughly away. "We can do nothing here."

We retraced our steps to the great hall. Tegid saw the grim set of our faces and asked, "Well? Did you find the child?"

Cynan shook his head, "There was no child," he answered, his voice a low growl in his throat. "But we have found the serpent . . . and our missing scouts as well."

Tegid swallowed hard and bowed his head as we described what we had seen. "The evil which has slept untold ages has awakened," the bard said when we had finished. "We must leave this place at once."

The sky outside had lost all color and light. Bran wasted no time moving the men along. We hurried towards the road beyond the palace. The first warriors reached the far end of the terrace, and paused to allow the rest of the party to assemble before moving on. It was then the Wyrm struck.

The attack came so swiftly and silently, that the first we knew of it was the choked-off scream of the man it seized and carried away. Hearing the man's dying shriek, I spun around in time to see a sinuous shape gliding into the dusky shadows.

A heartbeat later, we were all racing back across the terrace to where the others had halted. "Did you see?" they shouted. "The Wyrm! It took Selyf!"

I shouted above the clamor. "Did anyone see where it went?"

The Wyrm had attacked and vanished once more into the shadows without a trace. "We cannot go that way," Bran concluded, staring in the direction of the road. "We will have to go around."

I peered around doubtfully. On one hand, the river, itself as silent and deadly as a serpent; on the other, the red palace and its evil occupant. Behind loomed the forest, rising like a massive, impenetrable curtain. Turning towards the forest with great reluctance, I said, "This way; we will try to find another path."

"What about Selyf?" Cynan demanded. "We cannot leave him behind."

"He is gone," Bran said. "There is nothing to be done for him."

Cynan refused to move. "He was a good man."

"And will it help Selyf if we all join him in the pit?" Bran asked. "How many more good men must we lose to the Wyrm?"

My sympathies lay with Cynan, but Bran was right—fleeing made the best sense. "Listen to him, brother," I said. "What benefit to Tángwen if you are not there to rescue her? The serpent could return at any moment. Let us go from here while we have the chance."

Leaving the terrace, we entered the forest, pausing only long enough to light torches, before moving on. Bran led, with myself and Cynan behind, keeping the river to our backs. We worked our way into the undergrowth in an effort to skirt the palace. The further we moved from the river, the more tangled and close-grown the wood became. We slashed and hacked with our swords, and forced our way, step by step, until we reached a rock wall rising sheer from the forest floor.

"It is the same bank from which the palace is carved," said Bran, scratching away the moss with his blade to reveal red stone beneath.

Raising our torches, we tried to gauge the height of the bank, but the top was lost in the darkness and we could not see it. "Even if we could climb it," Cynan pointed out, "the horses could not."

Keeping the rock bank to our right, we continued on, moving away, always away, from the palace. When one torch burned out, we snatched up another brand from the snarl of branches all around us. Time and again, we stopped to examine the bank and, finding neither breach nor foothold, we moved on. A late-rising moon eventually appeared and poured a dismal glow over us. Now and then, I glimpsed its pale face flickering in the wickerwork of branches overhead.

"I see a clearing ahead," called Bran from a few paces on.

"At last!" It seemed as if we had walked half the night and had yet to discover any way we might cross the stone bank. I signalled for the rest of the men to stop while Bran and I went ahead to investigate the clearing. Shoulder to shoulder, we crept slowly forward, pressing ourselves against the rock bank. We entered the clearing to see the red palace directly before us and, a little distance to the right, the darkly glimmering river.

"We have come full circle," I remarked. Indeed, we were standing just a few paces from where we had started.

"How is it possible?" wondered Bran.

"We must have become confused in the dark. We will go the other way."

Retracing our steps, we informed the others of the mistake, and struck off once more. Again, we kept the rock bank hard at the right hand so that we would not go astray. The moon reached the peak of its arc and began descending. We pressed relentlessly on, arriving after another long march at yet another clearing. Bran and I stepped together from the shielding edge of the wood into the open: the palace stood directly before us, and off to the right, the dark river.

I took one look and called for Tegid. "See this, bard," I said, flinging out my hand, "it makes no difference which way we go, we return to this place in the end. What are we to do?"

Tegid cocked an eye to the night sky and said, "Dawn is not far off. Let us rest now, and try again when it is light."

We gathered at the edge of the clearing near the river and set about making a rough camp. We lit fires, established a watch, and settled down to wait for sunrise. Cynan wrapped himself in his cloak and lay down. I had just spread a saddle fleece on the ground and sat down crosslegged, a spear across my knees, when Tegid leapt to his feet.

He froze. Listening.

A faint, rippling sound reached me. It sounded like a boat moving against the riverflow. "It is coming from the water," I whispered. "But what—"

"Shh!" Tegid hissed. "Listen!"

Faintly, as in the far-off distance, I heard the nervous whicker of a horse; it was quickly joined by another. Cynan rolled to his feet, shouting, "The horses!"

We flew through the camp towards the horse picket. I felt a sharp icy stab of pain in my silver hand and in the same instant saw, outlined against the shimmering water, a monstrous serpent, its upper body raised high off the ground and great angular head weaving slowly from side to side. The enormous body glistened in the faint moonlight; the head, armored with horned plates, swung above three tremendous coils, each coil the full girth of a horse, and a stiff forked tail protruded from between the first and second coil.

Two long, thick, back-swept ridges ran down along either side of its body from just below the ghastly swaying head.

A trail of water led up from the river. Obviously, the creature had more than one entrance to its den. It had come up from the river close to the horses, no doubt intent on gorging its fearsome appetite on horseflesh. The horses, terrified, bucked and reared, jerking on their picket lines and tethers. Several had broken free and men were trying to catch them.

The Wyrm seemed keenly fascinated by the commotion, its plated head swerving in the air, eyes gleaming in the firelight. I saw the plunging horses and the campfires...

"Help me, Cynan!" I shouted. Dashing forward, I speared one of the lichen bales with which we fed the horses, and ran with it to the nearest fire. I thrust the bale into the flames and lofted the spear. Then, with the courage of fear and rage, I ran to the serpent and heaved the flaming spear into its face.

The missile struck the bony plate below the monster's eye. The Wyrm flinched, jerking away from the fire.

I whirled away, shouting to those nearby. "Light more bales!" I cried. "Hurry! We can drive it away."

Cynan and two other warriors bolted to the stack of fodder, skewered three bales and set them ablaze. Cynan lunged to meet the Wyrm, raising a battle cry as he ran.

"*Bás Draig!*" he bellowed. The two warriors at his side took up the cry. "*Bás Draig!*"

Returning for another spear and bale, I saw Scatha running towards me. "Rally the warband!" I shouted. "Help Cynan drive the serpent away from the horses." Turning to Tegid, I ordered, "Stay here and light more bales as we need them."

Bran and Alun, having seen my feat, appeared with bales ablaze. I quickly armed myself again and joined them; together we charged the Wyrm. Scatha and the warband had taken up a position on the near side, midway between the serpent and the river—dangerously close to the creature, it seemed to me. They were already strenuously engaged in trying to attract the beast's attention and draw it away from the camp.

I made for a place opposite them, thinking that if the serpent turned towards them, we three would be well placed for a blind-side attack. Upon seeing our approach, the Ravens, flying to meet us with weapons alight, sent up a shrill war cry, distracting the serpent. Scatha and her band saw their chance and rushed forward, weapons low and shields raised high. They struck at the huge coils, driving their blades into the softer skin of the belly between the scales. The huge snaky head swung towards them.

"Now!" I shouted, sprinting forward. My silver hand burned with a freezing fire.

Scatha's band stood fearless to the task, jabbing their spears into the Wyrm's side. The annoyed beast lowered its head and loosed a menacing hiss. As the awful mouth cracked open, I heaved the shaft with all my might. The unbalanced missile fell short, striking the creature on the underside of its mouth with a great flurry of sparks, but no hurt to the creature at all. As my first missile fell harmlessly away, I was already running for another.

Alun had no better luck with his throw. But Bran, seeing how we had fared, managed to compensate for the top-heavy spear with a well-judged, magnificent throw. The serpent, aware of our presence due to our first clumsy attempts, swung towards Bran, hissing wickedly.

As soon as the great wide mouth opened, Bran's spear was up and in. The Ravens cheered for their chieftain. But the serpent gave a quick shake of its head and dislodged the barb and fire bale.

I thought that Bran, like Cynan and me, would return to Tegid for another fire bale. Instead, he simply bounded forward and took up the shaft I had thrown. He impaled the fiery bale and prepared for another throw.

Perhaps the beast anticipated Bran's move. More likely, Yr Gyrem Rua, enraged by our attack, struck blindly at the closest moving shape. I glanced around just in time to see the huge horny head swing down and forward with breathstealing speed just as Bran's arm drew back to aim his throw.

The serpent's strike took the Raven Chief at the shoulder. He fell and rolled, somehow holding on to his weapon. He gained his knees as the Wyrm struck again, raising the spear in both hands as the head descended so that he took the blow on the shaft instead. The spear with its flaming head fell one way and Bran was sent sprawling the other. The serpent drew back and tensed for another strike.

The Ravens leapt forward as one man to save their chieftain. Alun, reached him first and, taking up the fallen weapon, flung it into the serpent's face while the others dragged Bran to safety.

"Alun! Get out of there, man!" Cynan cried.

Diving sideways, Alun hit the ground, rolled, and came up running. But instead of retreating to the campfire with the others, he stooped to retrieve the spear Bran had thrown.

I saw him do it and shouted. "No! Alun!"

27

Battle Awen

The Wyrm struck. Alun whirled, throwing the flaming bale at the same time. The throw grazed the serpent's jaw and bounced away as the head descended, knocking Alun off his feet and throwing him onto his back.

I seized a spear Tegid had readied and ran to Alun's defence. Garanaw and Niall heard my shout, turned, and ran to his aid. Scatha's warriors redoubled their attack. They drove in close, stabbing fearlessly. Scatha, by dint of sheer determination, succeeded in forcing a spear into a soft place between two scales on the serpent's side. With a mighty lunge, she drove the blade in. I saw the shaft sink deep into the beast's flesh, and I heard her triumphant cry: "*Bás Draig!*"

Spitting with fury, the red serpent hissed and the long neck stiffened; the two ridges on the side of its body bulged, then flattened into an immense hood, revealing two long slits on either side and two vestigial legs with clawed feet. The legs unfolded, claws snatching, and suddenly two great membranous wings emerged from the side slits behind the legs. These huge bat wings shook and trembled, unfurling like crumpled leather, slowly spreading behind the Wyrm in a massive canopy.

Scatha gave the embedded spear another violent shove. The

serpent hissed again and swivelled its head to strike, but Scatha and her warrior band were already retreating into the darkness.

Meanwhile, Garanaw and Niall pulled Alun away. And I took advantage of the momentary lapse to position myself for another throw. Cynan, flaming spear streaking the night, ran to my side. As its evil head turned, the Wyrm's mouth came open with an angry, rasping, seething hiss.

"Ready? ... Now!" I cried, and twin trails of fire streaked up into the monster's maw. Cynan's spear struck the roof of the serpent's mouth and fell away causing little hurt; mine hit on one of the long fangs and glanced away. I ran back to the campfire. "Give me another spear," I demanded. "Hurry!"

"It is not working," Tegid began. "We must find another way to—"

"Hurry!" I shouted, grabbing the firebrand from his hand and setting it to the nearest bundle. I took up a spear and plunged it into the bale. "Cynan! Follow me!"

Scatha had seen us return for more bales and understood that we meant to try again. As we flew once more to our positions, she launched another attack on the Wyrm's side. This time both she and one of the warriors with her succeeded in forcing spears between the thick scales. Two other warriors broke off their attack and leaped to Scatha's side, adding their strength to help drive the shaft deep into the serpent's flesh.

Scatha's success inspired the Ravens, who raced to repeat the feat on the opposite side. Drustwn and Garanaw charged in close, working their weapons into a crack between scales. They, too, succeeded in wounding the beast.

Yr Gyrem Rua screamed and flapped its enormous wings; its forked tail thrashed from side to side like a whip.

Cynan and I took up our positions. Placing the butt of the spear in the palm of my metal hand, I stretched my other hand along the shaft as far as I could reach. As the Wyrm's head veered towards me once more, I crouched low, my heart racing. The flames flared; sparks fell on my upturned face and singed my hair.

"Come on, you bloated snake," I growled, "open that ugly mouth!"

The massive neck arched. The hideous head tensed high above me. I saw the fireglint in a hard black glittering eye.

With a shout of "Die, dragon!" Cynan took his place slightly behind and to the left of me. The serpent shrieked, and the sound was deafening; its awful wings arched and quivered, and clawed feet raked the air. My stomach tightened. I clenched my teeth to keep from biting my tongue.

"Strike!" I taunted. "Strike, Wyrm!"

The enormous mouth opened—a vast white pit lined with innumerable spiked teeth in a triple row. Two slender fangs emerged from pockets in the upper mouth. The blue-black ribbon of a tongue arched and curled to a frightful screech.

And then the awful head swooped down.

I saw the fangs slashing towards me. My body tensed.

"Now!" cried Cynan. His spear flashed up over my shoulder and into the descending mouth. "Llew!"

I hesitated a rapid heartbeat longer, and then heaved my flaming missile with every ounce of strength I possessed. My metal hand whipped up, driving the missile into a high, tight arc.

Cynan's spear pierced the puffy white flesh and stuck fast. My spear flashed up between the two fangs, over the teeth, and into the throat.

The red serpent recoiled. Its mouth closed on the shaft of Cynan's spear, driving the spearhead even deeper into the soft skin and forcing the mouth to remain open. The creature could not close its mouth to swallow, which would have allowed it to quench the flames now searing its throat.

The Wyrm began thrashing violently from side to side. With great, slow strokes, the terrible wings beat the air. Burning lichen rained down on our heads. The lethal tail slashed like forked lightning, striking the ground with killing clouts.

"Run!" Cynan shouted, pulling me away.

We fled to the fire where the Ravens now stood shouting and

cheering. Bran lay on the ground bleeding from a wound on the side of his head. Alun sat slumped beside him, white-faced, a foolish, dazed expression on his face.

Blood oozed from Bran's head, and Alun's eyelids fluttered as he fought to remain conscious. Rage seized me and spun me around. I saw the winged serpent slam down its head as if to bite the earth. The force of the blow splintered the spear holding open its mouth. The huge jaws closed, the throat convulsed, and up came my spear with the smoldering bale still attached.

Wings beating a fearful rhythm, the serpent slowly lifted its flat head and upper body, loosed its coils and began half-flying, half-slithering away. Our campfire guttered in the gale of its retreat.

"It is fleeing!" shouted Drustwn, lofting his spear in triumph.

"Hie-e-ya!" crowed Emyr with a jubilant whoop. "Yr Gyrem Rua is defeated!"

"The Wyrm is conquered!" Cynan shouted. He grabbed me and clasped me to his chest. I saw his mouth move, but his voice had become the irritating buzz of an insect. His face creased with concern; sweat gleamed on his skin in the firelight. The glint of each bead became a needle of stabbing light, a naked star in the frozen universe of night. The ground beneath my feet trembled, and the earth lost all solidity.

And I felt my spirit expand within me; I was seized and taken up, as if I were no more than a leaf released from a branch and set sailing on a sudden gust of wind. My ears pounded with the bloodrush; my vision hardened to a sharp, narrow field; I saw only the winged serpent—scales gleaming blood red in the shivered light of our fire, grotesque wings stiffly beating, lifting that huge body to the freedom of the night sky. I saw the Red Serpent of Oeth escaping; all else around me dimmed, receded, vanished.

A hand grasped my shoulder, and then two more laid hold to my arms. But Ollathir's battle awen burned within me and I would not be held back. Power surged up in a mighty torrent. Like a feather in a flood, lightly riding the currents, upheld by them, I became part of the force flowing through me. The strength of the earth and sky was mine. I was pure force and impulse. My limbs trembled with pent energy demanding release. I opened my mouth and a sound like the bellow of the battlehorn issued from my throat.

And then I ran: swift as the airstream in the wind-scoured heights, sure as the loosed arrow streaking to its mark. I ran, but my feet did not touch the earth. I ran, and my silver hand began to glow with a cold and deadly light, the etchwork of its cunning designs shining like white gold in the Swift Sure Hand's refining fire. My fist shone like a beam of light, keen and bright.

A gabble of voices clamored behind me, small and confused. But I could not be bound or deflected. Can the spear return to the hand that has thrown it?

I was a ray of light. I was a wave upon the sea. I was a river beneath a mountain. I was hot blood flowing in the heart. I was the word already spoken. The Penderwydd's awen was upon me and I could not be contained.

The serpent's bulk rose like a curving crimson wall before me, and I saw Scatha's spear buried mid-shaft in the creature's side. Grasping the shaft with my silver hand, I pulled myself up. My flesh fingers found a crack between scales and my foot found the spearshaft. One quick scramble and I reached the serpent's back.

Solid beneath me, but fluid, like a molten road undulating slowly over the land, the red beast fled, fell wings stroking the air. Moving with the quickness of a shadow and the deftness of a stalking cat, I skittered over the sinuous backbone, over scales large as paving stones. A notched ridge down the center of the creature's back made good footing as the earth dropped away below. The foul beast had gained the air, but I heeded it not.

With the uncanny skill of a bard's inspiration I climbed towards the vile creature's head, and passed between the buffeting wings. Keen-eyed in the night, I glimpsed a fold of skin at the base of the serpent's skull and, above it, a slight depression where the spine met the skull; thin skin stretched tight over soft tissue.

The Wyrm's body stiffened beneath me as it rose higher. Mounting to the bulging mound of muscle between the two wings, I planted myself there and, raising my silver hand high, I smashed it down hard.

The metal broke the skin and slipped under the ridge of bone at the base of the serpent's skull. I stabbed deep, my metal hand a thrusting blade—cold silver sliding as in a sheath of flesh, plunging, piercing, penetrating the red serpent's cold brain.

A blast like the windscream of a Sollen gale rent the night. The wingbeats faltered as the immense leathery wings struggled to the sprung rhythm of a suddenly broken cadence.

"Die!" I shouted, my voice the loud carynx of battle. "Die!"

I slammed my fist deeper, metal fingers grasping. My arm sank past the elbow and my fingers tightened on a thick, sinewy cord. Seizing this cord, I ripped up hard and my fist came out in a bloody gush. The left wing faltered and froze. The Wyrm slewed sideways, plunging deadweight from air. I clung to the bony rim of scales and held on as the earth rushed towards me.

My feet struck the ground with an abrupt bone-rattling jolt. I rolled free and stood unshaken. The Wyrm convulsed, recoiling, rolling over and over, wrapping itself in itself, pale belly exposed in twisted loops.

The Red Serpent began striking its underbelly. The poisoned fangs slashed again and again, sinking into the exposed flesh. I laughed to see it, and heard my voice echo in the empty depths of the nearby shrine.

Once more I felt the hands of men on me. I was encircled in strong arms and lifted off my feet. Laughing, I was hauled from the path of the writhing serpent. I glimpsed men's faces in the darkness, eyes wide with awe, mouths agape in fright and wonder as they carried me away from the writhing Wyrm and out of danger.

The death throes of Yr Gyrem Rua were harrowing to behold. The serpent screamed—curling, twisting, spinning, crushing itself in its own killing coils, clawed feet raking the soft belly, battered wings rent and broken. The forked tail lashed and stung, striking the earth in a violent frenzy.

The Wyrm's paroxysms carried it to the portal of the palace

shrine. The tail smashed into the stone, loosened the ancient pillars and knocked them from their bases. Chunks of stonework began falling from the time-worn façade. The serpent spun in a knot of convoluted wrath, shattering the forecourt of the obnoxious temple, which began to crumble inward like an age-brittle skull. The dying serpent squirmed, beating against the hard shell of its cavern sanctuary. Red stone crashed and red dust rose like a blood mist in the moonlight. The frenzy gradually began to ease as the life-force ebbed. The movements became languid and sluggish; the sibilant shrieks dwindled to a pathetic strangled whine, its last cry a monstrous parody of a child in distress.

Slowly, slowly, the potency of its own poison began to work its deadly effect. Even so, the red Wyrm was some time dying. Long after the thrashing had stopped, the forked tail twitched and a broken wing stump stirred.

As I stood watching, my eyesight dimmed and my limbs began to twitch. The trembling increased. I fastened my teeth onto my lower lip and bit hard to keep from crying out. I wrapped my arms around my chest and hugged myself tight to keep my limbs from shuddering.

"Llew! Llew!" a sharp voice assaulted me.

Pain exploded in my head. I felt hands on me. The taste of blood filled my mouth; words bubbled from my bleeding tongue and I prated in a language unknown to those around me. Faces clustered tight over me, but I did not know them—faces without identity, familiar strangers who stared in anguish. My head throbbed, pounding with a fierce and steady ache, and my vision diffused, dwindling to vague patterns of light and dark, shapes with no clear features.

And then I tumbled over the edge into senselessness. I felt waves of warm darkness lapping over my consciousness and I succumbed to oblivion.

I awoke with a start as they laid me on the ground beside the fire. The awen had left me—like a gale that has passed, leaving the rain-soaked grass flattened in its wake. I struggled to sit up.

"Lie still," advised Tegid. Placing his hands on my chest, he pressed me down on the oxhide.

"Help me stand," I said; my words slurred slightly as my wooden tongue mumbled in my mouth.

"All is well," the bard insisted. "Rest now."

I had no strength to resist. I lay back. "How is Bran?"

"Bran is well. His head hurts, but he is awake and moving. Alun is unharmed—a scratch; it will heal."

"Good."

"Rest now. It will be daylight soon and we will leave this place."

I closed my eyes and slept. When I woke again the sun was peeping cautiously above the trees. The men had struck camp and were ready to go. They were waiting for me to rise, which I did at once. My arms and shoulders were stiff, and my back felt like a timber plank. But I was in one piece.

Tegid and Scatha hovered nearby. I joined them and they greeted me with good news. "We have scouted the high road beyond the shrine," Scatha reported, "and it has been used recently."

A spark of hope quickened my heart. "How recently?"

"It is difficult to know for certain," the bard answered.

"How recently?" I demanded again.

"I cannot say."

"Show me."

"Gladly." Scatha, haggard and near exhaustion, smiled and her features relaxed. "All is ready. You have but to give the command."

"Then let us go from here," I said. "It is a hateful place and I never want to see it again."

We passed the ruined temple to reach the road. Little of the shrine remained intact. Scarcely one stone stood upon another; it was all a jumble of red rubble. In a twisted mess amidst the debris, lay the wrecked body of Yr Gyrem Rua. A single broken wing fluttered in the wind like a tattered flag. The venom of its bite was quick about its grisly work of dissolving the muscled flesh; decay was already far advanced. The stink of the decomposing Wyrm brought tears to our eyes as we rode quickly past.

While it stood, the temple had hidden much of the road which could now be seen stretching out straight and wide, leading on through the forest and away from the river. It was, as Scatha had said, a proper high road: paved with flat stone, fitted together so closely and with such cunning that no grass grew between the joins.

"Show me the evidence of its use," I said as Tegid reined in beside me.

"You will see it just ahead," he replied. We continued on a short distance and stopped. Tegid dismounted and led me to the side of the road. There, nestled like round brown eggs in the long grass, I saw the droppings of perhaps three or four horses. A little way beyond, the grass was trampled and matted where a camp had been established. There was no evidence of a fire, so we could not tell how long ago the travellers had sojourned there. Nevertheless, I reckoned it could not have been more than a few days.

We returned to our horses, remounted, and moved out upon the high road with a better heart than at any time since entering the Foul Land.

28

On the High Road

Once on the high road, we journeyed with something approaching speed—a mixed blessing, as it soon exposed the loss of our horses. Those on foot could not keep pace, and we were constantly having to halt the mounted column to allow the stragglers to catch up. Thus we were obliged to rotate the men, foot-to-saddle, with increasing frequency as the swifter pace began to tell.

At the end of the day, we had travelled a fair distance. Since we planned to camp right on the road itself, we pushed on until it became too dark to see more than a few hundred paces ahead. There were stars shining in the sky and, though still cold, the air seemed not so sharp as on other nights. This served clear notice that time was passing. The weather was changing; Sollen was receding and Gyd would soon arrive.

I begrudged the time—every passing day was a day without Goewyn and empty for the lack. I felt an urgency in my spirit that nothing, save the light in Goewyn's eye, could appease. I was restless and craved the sight of my beloved. The infant was growing now within her, and I wondered if it had begun to show. I repeated her name with every step.

As Cynan and I walked together, taking our turn on foot, I asked, "Do you miss Tángwen greatly?"

His head was bent low. "My heart is sore for yearning, I miss her so much."

"You never say anything," I prodded gently.

"It is my heartache. I keep it to myself."

"Why? We share this pain together, brother."

Cynan swung his spear shaft forward, rapping the butt sharply on the stone, but kept his eyes fixed on the road. "I keep it to myself," he said again, "for I would not grieve you with my complaint. Bad enough that Goewyn is stolen; you do not need my troubles added to your own."

He would say no more about it, so I let the matter rest. His forbearance humbled me. That Cynan could forswear the very mention of his own hurt lest it increase mine, shamed me; doubly so, since I had scarcely given *his* suffering a second thought. How could I be worthy of such loyalty?

That night we came to the end of the little grain that remained, and it was a sorry meal.

"The sooner we leave this accursed forest, the better," grumbled Bran Bresal. We sat at council around the fire while the men ate, wondering what to do. "It cannot go on for ever."

"Nor can we," I pointed out. "Without meat and meal, we will soon grow too weak to travel."

"We have meat on the hoof," Scatha suggested delicately. "Though every horse we take means that another warrior must walk."

"I have never eaten horsemeat," Cynan muttered. "I do not intend to start now."

"I have eaten horse," said Tegid. "And I was glad to. It warmed the belly and strengthened the hand to the fight."

I remembered the time Tegid meant: the flight to Findargad in the mountains of northern Prydain. Then, as now, it was winter. We were pursued by the Coranyid, Lord Nudd's demon host, while making our way to Meldryn Mawr's high stronghold. Freezing, starving, we fought our way step by faltering step to the safety of the fortress. We were not freezing this time; but the starving had begun.

"Nothing good can come of eating a horse," rumbled Cynan, pressing his chin to his chest. "It is a low endeavor."

"Perhaps," agreed Scatha, "but there are worse."

I stirred at the sound of footsteps, and Emyr appeared, anxious and uneasy. He spoke directly to Tegid. "Penderwydd, it is Alun. I think you should come and see him."

Rising without a word, Tegid hurried away.

"What has happened to him?" asked Cynan, jumping to his feet. Bran had risen at Emyr's approach and was already following.

We fell into step with Emyr. "Garanaw found him sitting back there," the Raven said, indicating the road we had that day travelled. "He took his turn walking, but he did not join us when we stopped to make camp. Garanaw rode back to look for him."

Alun sat slumped by the campfire. The other Ravens hovered near, quietly apprehensive. They did not speak when we joined them, but gathered close as Tegid stooped before their stricken swordbrother.

"Alun," began the bard, "what is this I hear about you taking your ease by the road?"

Alun's head came up with a smile, but there was pain behind his eyes, and his skin glowed with a mist of perspiration. "Well," he replied in a brave tone, glancing around the circle of faces above him, "I have not been sleeping as well as I might—what with one thing and another."

Scatha knelt beside him. "Where is the hurt, Alun?" she asked, and put her hand on his shoulder. The touch, though gentle, brought a gasp from the Raven. The color drained from his face.

Gently, she reached to unfasten the brooch that held his cloak. Alun put his hand over hers and shook his head slightly. "Please."

"Let us help you, brother," Tegid said softly.

He hesitated, then closed his eyes and nodded. Scatha deftly unpinned the cloak and loosened the siarc. Alun made no further move to hinder her, and soon the shoulder was exposed. A ragged welt curved over the top of the shoulder towards the shoulder blade.

"Bring a torch," the bard commanded, and a moment later Niall handed a firebrand forward. Tegid took the torch and, stepping behind the seated Alun, held the light near.

"Oh, Alun!" sighed Scatha. Several of the Ravens muttered, and Bran looked away.

"Fine brave warriors you are!" complained Alun. "Has no one seen a scratch before?"

There was a small rip in the siarc, and little blood; indeed, the scratch itself had already scabbed over. But the flesh beneath was red and swollen, with a ghastly green-black tinge.

Tegid studied the shoulder carefully, holding the torch near and probing gently with his fingertips. Then he placed his hand flat against the swollen shoulder. "The wound is hot to the touch," he said. "It is fevered."

Scatha reached a hand to Alun's head and pressed her palm to his brow. She withdrew it almost at once. "You are roasting, Alun."

"Perhaps I have been sitting too near the fire," he laughed weakly. "And here I thought I was cold."

"I will not lie to you, brother," Tegid said, handing me the torch and squatting before Alun once more. "It is not good. The wound has sickened. I must open it again and clean it properly."

Alun rolled his eyes, but his exasperation was half-hearted and mingled with relief. "All this fuss over a scratch?"

"Man, Alun, if that is a scratch only," said Cynan, who could contain himself no longer, "then my spear is a pot sticker."

"Bring fresh water—and clean cloths, if you can find any," Tegid ordered impatiently. Cynan left at once, taking Niall with him. "I need a knife," the bard continued, "and I need it sharp."

"Mine will serve," said Bran, pushing forward. He drew the blade from its place at his belt, and handed it to Tegid.

The bard tested the edge with his thumb and gave it back, saying, "Strop it again. I want it new-edged and keen."

"And hold the blade to the firecoals when you have finished," I instructed. Bran raised his eyebrows at this, but I insisted.

"Do it," said the Raven Chief, handing the knife to Drustwn, who hastened to the task. Tegid turned to the remaining Ravens. "Gather moss, and spread oxhides and fleeces; prepare a bed."

"I will not need a bed, certainly," Alun grumbled.

"When I am through," Tegid replied, "*one* of us will be glad of a place to lay his head. I will use it if you will not." He nodded to Garanaw and Emyr, who turned and disappeared at once.

Scatha and I retreated a little apart. "I mislike the look of this," Scatha confided. "I fear the serpent's poison is in him."

"If the poison was in him, he would have been well and truly dead by now," I pointed out. "Help Tegid, and come to me afterwards."

Thus, I set about keeping myself and the rest of the men busy until Tegid and Scatha had finished. The horses were picketed and the fires banked high; Cynan and I positioned the guards and saw the men settled to sleep before returning to the fire to wait.

I dozed, and after a while Cynan nudged me awake. "Here now! He is coming."

I yawned and sat up. "Well, bard?"

Tegid sat down heavily. Fatigue sat like a burden on his shoulders. Cynan poured a cup of water and offered it to him. "If I had a draught of ale," Cynan said, "I would give it to you. As soon as I get another, it is yours."

"And I will drain that cup," Tegid replied, gazing at the fire. He drank and, setting the cup aside, pressed his eyes shut.

"What of Alun?" I asked again.

Ignoring me, Tegid said, his voice cracking, "The wound was but a scratch—as Alun said. But it has sickened, and the sickness has spread into the shoulder and arm. I cut into the wound and pressed much poison out of the flesh. I bathed the cut with water and wrapped it with a poultice to keep the poison draining."

"Yet he will recover," Cynan declared flatly, willing it to be so.

"He is sleeping now. Scatha will sit with him through the night. She will rouse us if there is any change."

"Why did he let it go untended?" I asked. "He should have said something."

Tegid rubbed his face with his hands. "Alun is a brave man. He thought the hurt but small, and he did not wish to slow us.

Until he collapsed on the road, I do not believe he knew himself how ill he had become."

I asked the question uppermost in my mind. "Will he be able to travel tomorrow?"

"I will examine the wound again in the morning; I may see more by daylight. A night's sleep can do much." He rubbed his face again. "I mean to see what it can achieve myself."

With that, he rolled himself in his cloak and went to sleep.

We did move on the next day. Alun seemed to be stronger and professed himself much improved. I made certain that he did not walk, and Tegid gave him healing draughts which he made with the contents of the pouch at his belt. In all, Alun looked and acted like a man on the mend.

So we journeyed on—growing more footsore and hungry by the day, it is true, but more determined also. Two days later, we noticed that the forest was thinning somewhat. And two days after that we came to the end of the forest. Despite the lack of food, our spirits soared. Just to see blue sky overhead was a blessing.

And though the land beyond the forest rose to bald hills of rocky and barren peat moor—as wide and empty as the forest had been dense and close—the warriors began to sing as we stepped from the shadow of the last tree. Tegid and I were riding at the head of the column and we stopped to listen.

"They have found their voices at last," I remarked. "I wonder how long it has been since such a sound was heard in Tir Aflan?"

Tegid cocked his head and favored me with one of his prickly sidelong glances.

"What have I said now?"

He straightened, drew a deep breath, and turned to look at the road ahead—stretching into the hill-crowded distance. "All this by the Brazen Man is come to pass," he intoned, "who likewise mounted on his steed of brass works woe both great and dire."

It was the Banfáith's prophecy, and I recognized it. With the recognition came an arrow-pang of regret for Gwenllian's death. I saw again the dusky shimmer of her hair and her bewitching emerald eyes; I saw her graceful neck and shoulders bent to the curve of a harp, her fingers stroking the strings, as if coaxing beauty from thin air.

"Rise up, Men of Gwir!" I said, continuing the quote just to show Tegid that I remembered. "Fill your hands with weapons and oppose the false men in your midst!"

Tegid supplied the final section: "The sound of the battleclash will be heard among the stars of heaven and the Great Year will proceed to its final consummation."

To which, I replied: "Bring it on. I am ready."

"Are you?" the bard asked.

Before I could reply, we heard a shout. "Tegid! Llew! Here!"

I swivelled in the saddle and saw Emyr running towards us along the side of the road. I snapped the reins and urged my mount forward to meet him. "Come quickly!" he said. "It is Alun."

We raced back along the high road to where two riderless horses waited. A cluster of men stood at the roadside, the Ravens among them. We pushed through the press and found Alun lying on the ground. Bran and Scatha bent over him, and Cynan was saying, "Lie still, Alun. You are ailing, man. It is no shame to tumble from the saddle."

"I fell asleep," Alun protested. "That is all. I fell asleep and slipped off. It is nothing. Let me up."

"Alun," said Tegid, hunkering down beside him, "I want to look at your shoulder."

"But I am well, I tell you." Alun's insistence fell somewhat short of absolute conviction.

I motioned to Cynan, who leant his head towards me. "Move the men along. We will join you as soon as we have finished here."

"Right!" said Cynan loudly. He rose and began turning men around. "It is for us to move on. We can do nothing for Alun— standing over him like trees taken root. The road grows no shorter for stopping."

Reluctantly, the warriors moved along, leaving us to examine Alun's wound. Tegid deftly unfastened the brooch and drew aside the cloak. The siarc beneath was caked with dried blood.

"You have been bleeding, Alun," observed Tegid, his voice dry and even.

"Have I?" wondered Alun. "I did not notice."

Tegid proceeded to draw aside the siarc, pulling it carefully away from the skin. A sweet smell emanated from the wound as the cloth came free. The whole shoulder and upper back were inflamed and discolored now, the flesh an ugly purple with a grotesque green-black cast. The scratch Tegid had opened was raw and running with a thin yellow matter.

"Well?" said Alun, twisting his head around to see his injury.

"I will not lie to you, Alun," Tegid's tone was solemn. "I do not like this." The bard pressed his fingers to the swollen flesh. "Does that hurt?"

"No." Alun shook his head. "I feel nothing."

"You should," replied Tegid. He turned to Bran. "Take Garanaw and Emyr, and ride back to the forest. Cut some long poles and bring them to me. We will make a *cadarn* for him."

Alun twisted free and struggled up. "I will not be dragged behind a horse on an infant's bed," he growled. "I will ride or walk."

The bard frowned. "Very well," he agreed at last, "we will spare you that. But you will endure my medicine before I let you take the saddle again."

Alun smiled. "You are a hard man, Tegid Tathal. Hard as the flint beneath your feet."

"Leave us the horses," Tegid instructed. "We will join you when I have finished."

Bran and I left Tegid and Scatha there, and returned to the column. "Tegid is worried," Bran observed. "He does not want us to know how bad it is." He paused. "But I know."

"Well," I replied lightly, doing my best to soothe the Chief Raven, "Tegid has his reasons. No doubt it is for the best."

We took our places at the head of the line with Cynan. And though the men continued to sing, the good feeling had gone out of it for me.

The day ended in a dull, miserable drizzle. A cold wind whined across the rocky wastes and made us glad of the firewood we had collected to bring with us upon leaving the forest. The wind, mournful and cold though it was, made a welcome change from the stifling close silence and dead air of the forest. So we did not begrudge the chill and damp.

We ate thin gruel, mostly water, boiled with handfuls of a sort of coarse, spiky grass which we pulled from side of the road. The grass lent a stimulating aromatic quality to the brew, and served to flavor it somewhat, although it added little bulk. The water, collected from small rock pools, was far better than that which we got from the river. Some of the warriors scouted the nearest braes for mushrooms, but found none.

Tegid and Scatha watched over Alun through the night. At dawn I went to them to see how the patient had fared. The bard met me before I came near Alun. "I do not think he should travel today."

"Then we will camp here," I said. "We could all use the rest, and the horses have grass enough to graze. How is he?"

Tegid frowned; his dark eyes flicked away from me, and then back. "It is not well with him."

"But he will recover," I asserted quickly.

"He is strong. And he is not afraid of a fight. Scatha and I will do all that can be done to heal him." He paused. "Meat would help as much as rest."

"Say no more. I will see to it."

I chose one of the smaller horses, though not the youngest whose meat might have been more tender. But I was not choosing for culinary value; I wanted to keep the more experienced war horses as long as possible. Bran approved the choice, and Garanaw helped me slaughter the poor beast.

Cynan insisted he would have nothing to do with either killing or eating horses. He kept muttering, "It is not fitting for a king of Caledon to devour his good mount, his helpmate in battle."

"Fine. Then just hold your tongue when the stew starts bubbling and the smell of roasting meat tempts your nostrils."

Despite the cold, Garanaw and I put off our cloaks, siarcs, breecs and buskins. We led the animal a little apart and made the swordthrust as quick and painless as possible. The horse fell without a cry, rolled onto its side and died. We skinned it quickly and spread the hide on a nearby rock. Then we began the grisly task of hacking the carcass into suitable joints. We were covered in blood when we had finished, but we had a fair amount of good meat stacked on the hide.

Niall, Emyr and Drustwn, meanwhile, busied themselves preparing spits on which to roast the meat. Garanaw and I distributed the meat to the men, saving the choice pieces for Tegid's use. Shivering with cold by the time we had finished, we knelt beside a peaty pool and washed away the blood, dressed again, and hurried to warm ourselves while the meat cooked.

Soon the wind carried the smoky-sweet aroma throughout the camp, dispersing any lingering qualms about our meal. When the meat was done, it did not look or smell much different from beef; and the men consumed it happily—not to say greedily. I could see Cynan's resolve wavering, but I knew if I asked him again, he would say no again out of stubborn pride.

Scatha came to his rescue. She collected a double portion and sat down crosslegged beside him. "I always told my Mabinogi," she began, chewing thoughtfully, "that a warrior's chief task is to stay alive and remain fit for battle. Any warrior who fails to do all he can to achieve this aim is no help at all to his kinsmen."

Cynan frowned and thrust out his chin. "I remember."

"I taught you to find birds' eggs and seaweed and—" she paused to lick the juice from her long fingers, "and all such that might make a meal for a hungry warrior away from his lord's hearth."

The broad shoulders bunched in a tight shrug, but the frown remained firmly fixed.

"That is why I make certain to serve horsemeat to all my brood," Scatha continued casually.

The red head turned slowly. "You served us horsemeat?"

"Yes. I find that one taste and it—"

Some of those sitting near overheard this conversation and grinned. No one dared laugh aloud. Cynan's chagrin was genuine, but wonderfully short-lived.

Scatha raised a portion of roast meat and offered it to him. Cynan took it between his hands and stared at it as if he expected it to reproach him. "Never let it be said that Cynan Machae spurned the learning of his youth."

So saying, he lifted the meat to his mouth and bit into it. He chewed grimly and swallowed, and the subject was never mentioned again. We slept well content that night, our stomachs full for the first time in many days. But my sleep was cut short. Tegid came to me and jostled me awake. The wind had risen during the night and was blowing cold from the north.

"Shh!" he cautioned. "Come quickly and quietly."

He led me to where he and Scatha had made a place for Alun between two small fires, one at his head and the other at his feet. Bran stood beside her, leaning on his spear, his head lowered. Scatha had a rag in her hand, and a bowl of water in her lap; she was bathing Alun's face. His eyes were closed and he was lying very still.

Tegid bent over the ailing warrior. "Alun," he said softly, "Llew is here. I have brought him as you asked."

At this, Alun's eyes flickered open and he turned his head. The vile purple stain of the rotten wound had reached the base of his throat. "Llew," Alun said, his voice little more than a whispered breath, "I wanted to say that I am sorry."

"Sorry? Alun, you have nothing to be sorry about," I replied quickly. "It is not—"

"I wanted to help you rescue Goewyn."

"You will, Alun. You will recover. I am counting on you."

He smiled a dry, fevered smile. His dark eyes were glassy and hard. "No, lord, I will not recover. I am sorry to leave you one blade less." He paused and licked his lips. "I would have liked to see the look on Paladyr's face when you appeared. That is one fight I will be sorry to miss."

"Do not speak so, Alun," I said, swallowing hard. My throat

ached and my stomach knotted.

"It is well with me," the Raven said, reaching towards me with his hand. I took it and felt the heat burning in him. "But I wanted to tell you that I have never served a better lord, nor known a king I have loved more. It is my greatest regret that I do not have another life, for I would gladly give you that as well." He swallowed and I saw how much it hurt him. "I was ever keen for the fight, but never raised a blade in malice. If men speak of me in aftertimes, I would have that remembered."

My vision blurred suddenly. "Rest now," I told him, my voice cracking.

"Soon . . . I will rest soon," he said; his dry tongue licked dry lips. Scatha raised his head and tilted a little water into his mouth.

He gripped my hand almost desperately. "And remember me to Goewyn. Tell her it would have been the chief pleasure of my life to have fought Paladyr for her freedom. She is a treasure of Albion, Llew, and if you had not seen that at last, I would have married her myself."

"I will tell her, Alun," I said, almost choking on the words. "When next I see her."

He swallowed and a spasm of pain wracked him. When he opened his eyes again, some of the hardness had gone—he was losing the fight. But he smiled. "Ahh, it is enough. It is sufficient." He looked from me to Bran. "I am ready now to see my swordbrothers."

Bran raised his head, nodded, and hastened away at once. Alun, still gripping my hand, though less tightly now, held me. "Lord Silver Hand," he said, "I would make but one last request."

"Anything," I said, tears brimming in my eyes. "Anything, Alun; speak the word and it is yours."

"Lord, do not bury me in this land," he said softly. "Tir Aflan is no honorable place for a warrior."

"I will do as you ask," I assured him.

But he clutched desperately at my hand. "Do not leave me here alone. Please!" he implored; and then added more gently, "please." He swallowed and his features clenched with pain. "When you are finished here, take me back with you. Let me lie on Druim Vran."

That such a noble warrior should have to beg so broke my heart. Tears began rolling down my cheeks and I smeared them away with my sleeve. "It will be done, brother."

This cheered him. "My heart belongs in Albion," he whispered. "If I may not see that fair land again, I will go easier knowing that my bones return."

"It will be done, Alun. I vow it."

His hand relaxed and fell back. Scatha gave him another drink. Bran returned just then, bringing the rest of the Raven Flight with him: Garanaw, Emyr, Drustwn and Niall. One by one, they knelt at the side of their swordbrother and made their farewells. Bran roused Cynan, too, who made his way to Alun's side. All the while, Tegid stood looking on, head bent low, watching with mournful eyes, but saying nothing.

Bran was the last, speaking earnestly and low; he placed his hand on Alun's forehead, then touched his own in salute. When he rose, he announced, "This Raven has flown."

29

Fly, Raven!

Somber in his brown cloak, Tegid scanned with dark eyes the far hillscape. Dun-colored, but for the bleached white rocks, endlessly austere and desperately empty—nothing but sparse heather and peat bogs surrounding outcropped stones rising like bone-bare islands in a rusty sea—the moorland stretched vacant and forlorn as far as the eye could see. Humps of barren hills, hunched like shoulders, jostled one another to the horizon in all directions.

He did not look at me as I came to stand beside him. "You should not have promised Alun to take him home."

"I made a vow, bard. I mean to keep it."

His lips pressed into a thin, disapproving line. "We cannot travel with his body, and there is no way to return him to Albion. We must bury him here."

Regarding the dismal moorland waste, I replied, "Alun deserves better, and he will have it."

"Then I suggest you think of a way."

"What about burning the body? I know it is not the most honorable way, but it could be done with dignity and respect."

Tegid turned his frown on me, thinking. I understood Tegid's reluctance: burning a corpse was reserved only for enemies, outcasts, and criminals. "It is not unknown in Albion," he admitted finally.

"There have been times when such a thing was necessary."

"Might this be one of those times?" I queried lightly. "Our need is on us."

"Yes," the bard relented, "our need is on us and we are bound by a king's vow. This is such a time. But, the fire must be tended properly so that the bones are not burned. For they must be gathered and preserved. I will see to it."

"And when we return to Albion," I added, "they will be buried on Druim Vran."

"So be it."

"Good. We will gather wood to make the pyre."

I sent eight men with extra horses back to the forest to collect the required timber. They rode under Bran's command because, once I had explained what I intended doing, the Chief Raven insisted on leading the party himself. "It is not necessary, Bran. Another can serve in this."

"If Alun's body is to be burned," he replied stiffly, "then I will choose the wood myself. Alun saved me from the Red Wyrm, it is the least I can do for him."

Since he would have it no other way, I gave him leave to go. The forest was no great distance behind us, and the horses were fed and rested; the party would, I reckoned, return by dusk the next day. The day was young yet, and they left as soon as the horses were saddled. We saw them away—sending them with the small amount of horsemeat we had left over.

I watched them out of sight, and then turned reluctantly to the task of choosing another horse for the slaughter.

The wood-gatherers returned early the next morning out of a sodden mist. The moorland squelched to a soggy drizzle brought by a fresh easterly breeze which had replaced the cold northern wind in the night. The damp moors appeared decidedly bleak and miserable in the leaden grey light.

We greeted them, and sent them to warm themselves by the fire. I ordered men to unburden the horses and release them to graze, and then joined Bran at the fire. The Raven Chief gave a terse report.

"The land is dead," he said, shaking out his cloak. "All was as we saw it before. Nothing has changed."

I called for some of the stew we had prepared the previous day, and left them to their meal. Meanwhile, Tegid and I set to work preparing the pyre for Alun's cremation. The wood had been dumped in a heap beside the road, and the bard was busy sorting it according to length when I joined him. When the ordering was finished, we carried armloads of selected timber to a large flat rock nearby and began stacking the wood carefully.

I fell in with the task and we worked together without speaking, carrying and stacking, erecting a sturdy wooden scaffold limb on limb. It was good work—the two of us moving in rhythm—and it put me in mind of the day Tegid and I had begun building Dinas Dwr. I held that memory and basked in its warm glow as we labored side by side. When we finished, the pyre stood on its lonely rock like a small timber fortress. Some of the men had gathered as we worked and now stood looking dolefully at the finished pyre.

Tegid observed them standing there and said, "When the sun sets we will light the fire."

The mist cleared as the day sped from us and the sky lightened in the west, allowing us a dazzling glimpse of golden light before dusk closed in once again. I turned from the setting sun to see the warriors coming in twos and threes across the moor to the rock where Tegid and I waited.

When all had gathered, Alun's body, which had been covered and sewn into an oxhide after his death, was brought by the Ravens and laid carefully upon the pyre. Tegid kindled a fire nearby and prepared torches, giving one to each of the remaining four Ravens and Bran.

The bard mounted the rock and took his place at the head of the pyre. He raised his hands in declamation. "Kinsmen and friends," he called loudly, "Alun Tringad is dead; his body lies cold upon the pyre. It is time to release the soul of our swordbrother to begin its journey through the High Realms. His body will be burned, but his ashes will not abide in Tir Aflan. When the fire has done its work, I will gather the bones and they will return with us to Albion for burial on Druim Vran."

Then, placing a fold of his cloak over his head, the Chief Bard raised his staff and closed his eyes. After a moment, he began to chant gently, tunelessly, a death dirge:

> *When the mouth shall be closed,*
> *When the eyes shall be shut,*
> *When the breath shall cease to rattle,*
> *When the heart shall cease to throb,*
> *When heart and breath shall cease;*
>
> *May the Swift Sure Hand uphold you,*
> *And shield you from evil of every kind.*
> *May the Swift Sure Hand uphold you,*
> *And guide your foot along the way,*
> *May the Swift Sure Hand uphold you,*
> *And lead you across the sword-bridge,*
> *May the Swift Sure Hand shield, lead, and guide you*
>   *Across the narrow way*
> *By which you leave this world;*
>
> *And guard you from all distress and danger,*
> *And place the pure light of joy before you,*
> *And lead you into Courts of Peace,*
> *And the service of a True King*
>   *In Courts of Peace,*
> *Where Glory and Honor and Majesty*
>   *Delight the Noble Kin for ever.*
>
> *May the eye of the Great God*
> *Be a pilot star before you,*
> *May the breath of the Good God*
> *Be a smooth way before you,*
> *May the heart of the Kingly God*
> *Be a boon of rich blessing to you.*
>
> *May the flames of this burning*
> *Light your way . . .*
> *May the flames of this burning*
> *Light your way . . .*
> *May the flames of this burning*
> *Light your way to the world beyond.*

So saying, the Chief Bard summoned the Ravens. One by one they stepped forward—Garanaw, Emyr, Niall and Drustwn—each bearing a torch which he thrust into the kindling at the base of the pyre. Bran came last and added his torch to the others. The fire ruffled in the wind, caught, and began climbing towards Alun's body lying so still on his rough wooden bed.

Like those around me, I watched the yellow flames licking up through the latticework of wood to caress the cold flesh of my friend. Grief I felt for myself: I would never again hear his voice lifted in song, nor see him swagger into the hall. I would miss his preposterous bragging, his bold and foolish challenges—like the time he challenged Cynan to a day's labor plowing land and felling and hauling timber, nearly ruining himself with the exertion, and all for a golden trinket.

I felt the tears welling in my eyes, and I let them fall. It was good to remember, and to weep for what was lost and could not be again.

Farewell, Alun Tringad, I said to myself as the fire hissed and cracked, mounting higher. *May it go well with you on your journey hence*.

A voice, hoarse with grief, rent the silence: "Fly, Raven! Try your wings over new fields and forests; let your loud voice be heard in lands unknown." Bran, his noble face shining with tears in the firelight, drew back his arm and lofted his spear skywards. I saw the tip glint in the cold starlight and then it disappeared into the darkness—a fitting image of release for the spirit of a warrior.

The flames grew hot; I felt the heat-sheen on my face and my cloak steamed. The flame-crack grew to a roar; the light danced, flinging shadows back into the teeth of the ever-encroaching darkness. In a little while, the pyre collapsed inward, drawing the hide-covered corpse into the fierce golden heart of the funeral fire, there to be consumed. We watched long—until only embers remained, a glowing red heap upon the rock.

"It is done," Tegid declared. "Alun Tringad has gone." Whereupon we turned and made our way back to camp, leaving Tegid to perform the tasks necessary for reclaiming the bones from the fire.

I found myself walking beside Bran. I thought his farewell apt and told him so. "It was a fitting farewell to a Raven who has gone."

Bran cocked his head to one side and regarded me as if I had suggested that I thought the moon might sleep in the sea. "But Alun has not gone," Bran observed matter-of-factly, "he has only gone on ahead."

We walked a little further, and Bran explained: "We have made a vow, we Ravens, to rejoin one another in the world beyond. That way, if any of us should fall in battle, there is a swordbrother waiting to welcome us in the world beyond. Whether in this world or the next, we will still be the Ravens."

His faith in this arrangement was simple and marvellous. And it was absolute. No shadow of doubt intruded, no qualm shadowed the bright certainty of his confidence. I, who had no such assurance, could only marvel at his trust.

We departed the next morning at dawn. Mist gathered thick, making our world blurred and dull. The sky, dense as wool to every horizon, drooped like a sodden sheepskin over our heads. As the unseen sun rose towards midday, the wind stiffened, rolling the mist in clouds across the darkening moor.

We moved in a ragged double column, shivering beneath our wet cloaks. The horses walked with their heads down, noses almost touching the ground, hooves clopping hollow on the stone-paved high road.

Wet to the skin, my hair plastered to my scalp, I stumped along on numb feet and longed for nothing more than to sit before the fire and bake the creeping cold from my bones. So Tegid's abrupt revelation, when it came, caught me off guard.

"I saw a beacon last night."

My head whipped around and I stared up at him, incredulous that he had not bothered to mention it before. He did not look at me, but rode hunch-shouldered in the saddle, squinting into the drizzle: soggy, but unconcerned.

Bards!

"When the embers had cooled," he continued placidly, "I gathered Alun's bones." My eyes flicked to the tidy bundle behind his saddle wrapped in Alun's cloak. "I saw the beacon-flare when I returned to camp."

"I see. Any particular reason why you bring this to my attention now?"

"I thought you might like to hear a good word." At this, my wise bard turned his head to look down on me. I glared up at him, water running down my hair and into my eyes. "You are angry," he observed. "Why?"

Frozen to the marrow, having eaten nothing but horsemeat for days, and heartsick at Alun's death, the last thing I expected or wanted was my Chief Bard withholding important information from me. "It is nothing," I told him, heaving my anger aside with an effort. "What do you think it means?"

"It means," he replied with an air that suggested the meaning was obvious, "we are nearing our journey's end."

His words filled me with a strange elation. The final confrontation would come soon. Anticipation pricked my senses alert; my spirit quickened. The dreariness of the day evaporated as expectation ignited within. The end is near: let Paladyr beware!

We pressed our way deeper into the barren hills. The peat moors gave way to heather and gorse. Day followed day, and the road remained straight and high; we travelled from dim grey dawn to dead grey dusk, stopping only to water the horses and ourselves. We ate only at night around the campfire when we could cook the flesh of yet another horse. We ate, bitterly regretting the loss with every bite; but it was meat, and it warmed an empty belly. No one complained.

Gradually, the land began to lift. The hills grew higher and the valleys deeper, the descents more severe as the hill-country rose towards the mountains. One day we crested a long slope to see the faint shimmer of snow-topped heights in the distance. Then cloud and mist closed in again and we lost the sight for several more days. When we saw them again, the mountains were closer; we could make out individual peaks, sharp and ragged above darkly streaming clouds.

The air grew clearer; and though mists still held us bound and blind by day, nights were often crisp and clear, the stars sharp and bright as spearpoints in a heaven black as pitch. It was on such a night that Tegid came to me while I slept beside a low-burning fire.

"Llew..."

I came awake at the touch of his hand on my shoulder.

"Come with me."

"Why?"

He made no answer, but bade me follow him a little way from camp. A late moon had risen above the horizon, casting a thin light over the land. We climbed to the top of a high hill, and Tegid pointed away to the east. I looked and saw a light burning on a near-distant ridge and, some way beyond it, another. Even as we watched, a third light flickered into existence further off still.

Standing side by side in the night, straining into the darkness, my bard and I waited. The wind prowled over the bare rock of the hilltop, like a hunting animal making low restless noises. In a little while, a fourth fire winked into life like a star alighting on a faraway hill.

I watched the beacons shining in the night, and knew that my enemy was near.

"I have seen this in my vision," Tegid said softly, and I heard again the echo of his voice lifted in song as the storm-frenzied waves hurled our frail boat onto the killing rocks.

The wind growled low, filling the darkness with a dangerous sound. "Alun," Tegid said deliberately and slow, choosing his words carefully, "was the only one among the Ravens to see Crom Cruach."

At first I did not catch his implication. "And now Alun is dead," I replied, supplying the answer to the bard's unspoken question.

"Yes."

"Then I am next. Is that what you mean?"

"That is my fear."

"Then your fear is unfounded," I told him flatly. "Your own vision should tell you as much. Alun and I—we both saw Yellow

311

Coat. And we both fought the serpent. Alun died, yes. But I am alive. That is the end of it."

Indicating the string of beacons blazing along the eastern horizon, he said, "The end is out there."

"Let it come. I welcome it."

The sky was showing pearly grey when we turned to walk back down the hill to the camp. Bran was awake and waiting for us. We told him about the beacons and he received the news calmly. "We must advance more warily from now on," he said. "I advise we send scouts to ride before us."

"Very well," I concurred. "See to it."

Bran touched the back of his hand to his forehead and stepped away. A little while later, Emyr and Niall rode out from the camp. I noticed that they did not ride on the hard surface of the road, but in the long grass beside it. They would go less swiftly, but more silently.

So it begins at last, I thought.

I followed them a short distance from camp and watched the riders disappearing into the pale dawn. "The Swift Sure Hand go with you, brothers!" I called after them; my voice echoed in the barren hills and died away in the heather. The land seemed unsettled by the sound. "The Swift Sure Hand shield us all," I added, and hastened back to camp to face the day's demands.

30

Dead Voices

The hills grudgingly gave way to an endless expanse of rock waste—all sharp-angled, toppling, sliding, bare but for tough thickets of thorny gorse. The land tilted precariously all around, yet the road held firm and good. Rain and wind battered us; mist blinded us for days without end. But the road held good.

And with each day's march the cloud-shrouded mountains drew nearer. We watched the wind-carved peaks rise until they crowded the horizon on every side—range upon range, summit upon summit fading into the misty distance. Brooding, fierce, and unwholesome, they were no kindly heights, but loomed stark and threatening over us: white, like splinters of shattered bone or teeth broken in a fight.

Enough grass grew along the roadside to keep the horses fed, and the horses fed us. This meant losing another mount every few days, but the meat kept us going. We drank from mountain runnels and pools, numbing the ache of hunger with cold water.

Gyd, Season of Thaws, drew ever nearer, bringing wet gales to assail us. The snow on the lower slopes began melting and filling the gorges, gullies and rock canyons with the icy run-off. Day and night, we were battered by the sound of water gushing and smashing, gurgling and splashing, as it rushed to the lowlands now far behind us. Mists rose from deep defiles where waterfalls boomed; clouds hung low over crevices where fast-flowing cataracts clattered and echoed like the clash of battle-crazed warbands.

The bleak monotony of naked rock and the harshness of the wind and crashing water bore constant reminder—if any was needed—that we journeyed through a hostile land. The higher we climbed among the shattered peaks, the greater grew our trepidation. It was not the wind that screamed among the ragged crowns and smashed summits; it was fear, raw and wild. We lay shivering in our cloaks at night and listened to the wind-voices wail. Dawn found us ill-rested and edgy to face the renewed assault.

Twice during each day's trek, we met with the scouts—once at midday, and then again when they returned at dusk. The Ravens took it in turn to carry out the scouting duty, two at a time, rotating the task among their number so that each day saw a fresh pair ride out. One day, Garanaw and Emyr returned as we were making camp for the night beneath a high overhanging cliff.

"There is a better place just beyond the next turn," Emyr informed us. "It is not far, and it would prove a much better shelter should the wind and rain come up in the night."

As we had not yet unsaddled the horses or lit the fires, we agreed to move on to the place they suggested. Garanaw led the way and, when we arrived, said, "This is as good a shelter as these bare bones provide."

Cynan heard this and replied, "Broken bones, you mean. I have seen nothing for days that was not fractured to splinters."

Thus, the mountains became *Tor Esgyrnau*, the Broken Bones. And what Cynan said was true; through naming them, they became less threatening, less frightening—however slightly. At least, we began looking on them with less apprehension than previously.

"That is the way of things," Tegid offered when I remarked on this a few days later. "Among the Derwyddi it is taught that to confer a name is to conquer."

"Then get busy, bard. Find a name with which to conquer Paladyr. And I will shout it from the crown of the highest peak."

Later, as darkness claimed the heights, I found him standing, peering into the gloom already creeping over the lowlands behind. I stared with him into the distance for a moment, and then asked. "What do you see?"

"I thought I saw something moving on the road down there," he replied, still scanning the twisted ribbon.

"Where?" I looked hard, but could make out nothing in the murk. "I will send someone back to see."

Tegid declined, saying, "There is no need. It is gone now—if anything *was* there. It might have been a shadow."

He walked away, but I stayed, staring into the dull twilight, searching the darkness for any sign of movement. We had climbed a fair distance into the mountains and, though the days were slightly warmer now, the nights were still cold, with biting winds sweeping down from the snow-laden peaks above. Often we woke to frost on our cloaks, and the day's melt frozen during the night to make the road treacherous until the sun warmed the stone once more.

For warmth we burned the hard-twisted knots of gorse trunks we hacked from their stony beds with our swords. They burned with a foul smell and gave off an acrid, oily smoke, but the embers remained hot long after the fire had gone.

We reached a high mountain pass and crossed the first threshold of the mountains. I looked back to see the land dull and shapeless behind us; a bleak, treeless, mist-obscured moor, colorless, sodden and drear. It was good to leave it behind at last. I stood long, looking at the road as it stretched into the distance. Ever since Tegid's suggestion that we might be followed, I had spent a fair amount of time looking back, and this time even managed to convince myself that, yes, there was something, or someone, back there—very faint and far in the distance. Or was it only the fleeting shift of mist or cloud shadow?

Up among the barren peaks, the wind whined and howled, swooping down to tear at our flesh with talons of ice. The gale was unrelenting, save for the chance protection afforded by a rock or wall as the road twisted and wound its tortured way along—sometimes no more than a footpath clawed from the mountainside, little wider than a scar. Everyone walked, for we dared not risk a fall on such a treacherous trail.

Since we could no longer ride, we loaded all the horses with as much hard-scrabble gorse as they could carry. Each animal looked like a walking furze hillock bouncing along. We went more slowly than I would have liked. Still, but for the road, we could not have made the climb at all.

On and on we went, dragging ourselves blue-lipped and shivering from one march to the next, cringing, tears streaming from our eyes as the wind and cold pared us to the bone. We grew hard as leather and sharp as knives. We grew hungry, too, with a fierce and gnawing desire no feast could satisfy. It was a longing to be healed as much as filled, a yearning to return to Albion, and allow the sight of its fair hills and glens to salve our ravaged hearts. It was *taithchwant*, the profound hunger for home.

But I could not go home. I would sooner abandon my life than my beloved. My enemy's head would adorn my belt before I turned my steps towards Druim Vran; my wife would stand once more beside me, before I turned my face towards Dinas Dwr. My queen would return with me to Albion, or I would not return at all.

At dusk, the first night after crossing the mountain threshold, we sensed a change in the mood of the land. But it was not until two nights later, when we had penetrated deep into the mountain fortress, that the change began to make itself felt. Where the lowland moors had been bleak and broody, the mountains were threatening; where the forest had been forbidding, the mountains were menacing. And it was not merely the threat of plunging from the narrow road to die broken on the rocks below. There was a wary malevolence aprowl among the peaks, a dark power that deemed our presence an invasion and reacted accordingly.

On the third night we finally understood the nature of our adversary. The day's march had gone well; we had made good progress and had found a suitable refuge for the night in a deep divide between two peaks. Solid rock walls rose sheer from the roadside, the surface raked jagged as if the road had been hacked through the mountain with a dagger; the peaktops were lost in cloud above us. Here the wind could not reach us so easily, thus the place provided a welcome respite and made as good shelter as could be found in those bare crags.

We huddled close to the fires, as always, but that night as the gale rose to its customary shriek, we heard in the wind-wail a new and chilling note. Tegid, ever alert to the subtle shifts and shades of light and sound, was first to perceive it. "Listen!" he hissed.

The talk, low and quiet around the fire, ceased. We listened, but heard nothing—save the icy blast tearing itself on the naked peaks of Tor Esgyrnau.

I leaned close. "What did you hear?"

"Did and do," Tegid said, cocking his head to one side. "There—again!"

"I hear the wind," Bran volunteered, "but nothing more."

"Nor will you if you keep drowning it with your own voice."

We waited a long while. When the sound did not come again, I asked, "What did it sound like?"

"A voice," he said, hunching his shoulders more tightly. "I thought I heard a voice. That is all."

The way he said it—curt and dismissive—made me curious. "Whose voice?"

He poked a loose ember back into the campfire with the tip of his staff, but made no reply.

"Whose voice, Tegid?"

Cynan and Bran, and several others sitting near, looked on with increasing interest. Tegid glanced around, and then back to the fire quickly. "The storm is rising," he said.

"Answer me, bard. Whose voice did you hear?"

He drew a breath, and said the name I least expected to hear. "Ollathir's," he replied softly. "I thought I heard Ollathir."

"Ollathir? He has been dead for years. He is—"

"Well I know it!"

"But—"

"You asked me whose voice I heard," he replied, speaking angrily and low. "And I am telling you the truth. I thought I heard Ollathir, Chief Bard of Albion, long dead in his grave."

The words were still hanging in the air when Bran leapt to his feet. "I heard it!" He stood over us, his face in shadow. "There! Do you hear?" He paused. "And again! But it is not your Ollathir—it is Alun Tringad!"

Cynan turned a baleful eye towards me. "There is something uncanny here, I feel." His voice was a wary whisper, as if he feared being overheard.

The fire creaked and ticked, and the wind cried. Then Cynan himself rose slowly to his feet, placing a finger to his lips. "No... no..." he said, his voice little more than a sigh, "it is not Alun I hear, it is..."—amazement transformed his features in the firelight— "Cynfarch... my father!"

Soon the whole camp was in turmoil, as everyone succumbed to the eerie voice of a dead friend or kinsman. Everyone, that is, except me. I heard only the wild wind-wail, but that was unnerving enough. For as night wore on the gale raked more fiercely at the unseen peaks and fell shrieking from the heights. We could only cower closer to the fires and hold our hands over our ears.

And then even the fires were taken from us. The wind screamed down between the walls like a rushing waterfall. The campfires flattened, guttered, and went out. Plunged into a chill darkness churning with the gale and the cries of dead friends and loved ones, the men began scrambling for their weapons.

"Tegid!" I shouted, trying to make myself heard above the wind-roar. "Someone is going to get hurt if we do not act."

"I fear you are right," agreed Cynan. "It is most unchancy in the dark."

"What do you suggest?" replied Tegid. "I cannot stop the wind!"

"No, but we can stop the men from running amok."

At that, he jumped up onto a nearby rock and raised his staff. "*Aros! Aros llawr!*" he shouted in the bullroar voice of command. "Stay! Stand your ground. It is not the voices of the dead!" he cried. "Some treachery is upon us. But do not be deceived. Take courage!"

"They are calling us!" someone shouted. "The dead have found us! We are doomed!"

"No!" I told them. "Listen to our Wise Bard: we have all lost friends and loved ones. Our thoughts are with them, and so you imagine you hear their voices. It is a trick of the wind and storm. Nothing more."

"Do you not hear them yourself?" another frightened voice demanded.

"No, I do not. I hear only the wind," I told them sternly. "It is raw and wild, but it is only the wind. Sit down, all of you, and we will wait it out together."

This seemed to calm the men. They drew together, some with weapons at the ready, and crouched shoulder to shoulder to wait. And, gradually, the gale died down and the eerie assault ceased.

We rekindled the fires and slowly relaxed and settled down to sleep, thinking the trouble was ended. Wishful thinking, as it turned out: the ordeal was just beginning.

31

Bwgan Bwlch

We had just settled to our rest when the eerie sounds began again, but not voices alone. This time, the dead also appeared.

As the wind dropped, fog descended from the icy altitudes—a strange, ropy mist that ebbed and flowed in rippling tidewaves. Grey as death and cold, the elusive vapor stole along the bare rockface of the wall and slid over and around the rubble at the roadside, groping and curling like tendrils. The sentries were the first to see it and raised a tentative alarm. They were concerned but uncertain, as there was no clear danger.

"No, no," I told Niall who apologized for waking me, "this night was never meant for sleeping. What is happening?"

His face, deep-shadowed in the fitful light, screwed into a squint as he peered beyond me into the darkness. "A fog has come up," he said, paused, and glanced back to me. "It has an evil feel, lord. I do not like it."

I rose and looked around. The fog had crept thick, forming a solid cover on the ground beyond the ring of light thrown out by our campfires. If it had been a living creature, I would have said it seemed reluctant to come into the light. Probably it was just the heat of the flames, creating a margin of space around us. Yet, it seemed almost sentient, the way it snaked and coiled as it thickened.

"It is watching us," Niall whispered.

He was not the only one to feel that way. Very soon the unnatural vapor had formed a weird landscape almost man-height around us. Queer shapes bulged up from the mass only to melt back into it again. Men began to see things in the grey billows: floating limbs, heads, torsos, ethereal faces with empty eyes.

The horses did not like the fog; they raised such a commotion with their jerking and jigging and whinnying that I ordered them to be blindfolded and brought within the fire-ring. They liked that scarcely better, but allowed themselves to be pacified.

Our fears, however, could not be so easily allayed. I ordered the men to arm themselves and to stand shoulder to shoulder and shield to shield. We took what comfort we could in the heft of our weapons and the nearness of our swordbrothers, watching helpless as the spectral display continued.

Disembodied heads mouthed silent words; detached arms gesticulated, legs twitched, and other body parts melded and separated in monstrous couplings. Grasping hands reached out from the mass and beckoned to us, melted and reformed as toothless sucking mouths. I saw a huge lidless eye split into smiling lips, and then dissolve into a puckered fistula.

"*Clanna na cù!*" Cynan growled under his breath.

Tegid, hovering near, whispered, "Something is stirring here that has slept for ages. The ancient evil of this land has awakened, and its minions stalk the land once more."

Cynan turned his face, sweating despite the cold. "What could do that?"

"Could it be Paladyr?" I wondered. "Could he have done something to rouse this—this evil power, whatever it is?"

"Perhaps," Tegid allowed. "But I think it is a thing more powerful than Paladyr alone—a presence, maybe. I do not know. I feel it here." He pressed his fist to his chest. "It is a sensation of deep wickedness. I do not think Paladyr capable of such hatred and malice." He paused, thinking, and added, "This is more like..."

The ghostly shapes formed and congealed, altering in subtly

suggestive ways. Watching this silent, shifting dance of the macabre put me in mind of Lord Nudd's Demon Host at the Battle of Dun na Porth at Findargad. "Lord Nudd," I said aloud. "Prince of Uffern and Annwn."

"From the tale of Ludd and Nudd?" wondered Cynan.

"The same."

At mention of the name, I began to feel an almost hypnotic effect. Whatever hostile power animated the fog, it was beginning to exert a fell authority over us. I was drawn to it, coaxed, beckoned. Fascinated, my spirit yearned towards the billowing panoply of mutating forms.

Come to me, the fog seemed to say. *Embrace me, and let me comfort you. Your struggle can be over; your striving can end. Sweet release. Oh, your release is near.*

The sly seduction of this insinuation proved potent indeed to a band of bruised and exhausted warriors. Long on the trail in a harsh and hostile land, there were those among us who had begun to weaken. One young warrior across the circle from me threw down his shield and staggered forth. I called to his companions who hauled him back.

He was no sooner returned to the fold than another warrior, a man named Cadell, gave a cry, dropped his weapons, and made to dash into the fog. Thinking quickly, those on either side of him grabbed him by the arms and restrained him.

Cadell resisted. He dug in his feet and shook off those holding him. Turning, he made to run into the fog. A nearby warrior tripped him with the butt of a spear. His kinsmen were on him in a moment, dragging him back to the line. As if overcome by a gigantic strength, kicking and flailing with his arms, Cadell sent his holders flying. Screaming terribly, he staggered to his feet, turned, and lumbered towards the fog once more.

Calling for Bran's aid, I darted after him. He had reached the fog, which seemed to surge towards him in an embrace, curling around his wrists and ankles. I felt a cold exhalation emanating from the undulating fog as I put my hand on the warrior's shoulder—it was like touching a damp rock.

Cadell twisted around me, flinging out his arm. His flying elbow caught me on the point of the chin and I was lifted off my feet and thrown back; I thought my head had come off. I rolled onto my knees, black stars spinning in dark circles before my eyes.

I shook my head fiercely. My assailant was once again staggering into the fog. I stood on unsteady legs and launched myself at him. I did not try to turn him again, nor did I try to restrain him; it was too late for that. I simply sprang, raising my silver hand and bringing it sharply down on the nape of his neck.

The warrior stiffened and threw out his arms. He raised his head and screamed, then toppled backwards like a felled tree. He hit the ground and lay still.

Fearing I had killed him, I stooped over Cadell and pressed my fingertips against his throat. The instant I touched the body it began jerking and trembling—all over, head to foot, all at once—as if he were dancing in his sleep. His eyelids snapped open and his mouth gaped wide; his clawed fingers clutched at me, grasping for my throat.

I swung my silver hand hard against the side of his head. He convulsed and I heard a gurgle low in his throat. The breath rushed out of his lungs and with it something else: a transparent, formless shape like a flying shadow. It brushed me as it fled and I felt a sick, slimy chill and an aching, piercing emptiness—as if all the loneliness and misery in all the world were gathered into a swiftly fleeing distillate of woe. In that fleeting touch, I felt the creature's mindless anguish, and knew what it was to be a tortured animal, able to feel pain, but unable to fathom its cause or reason. My heart felt as if it would burst with the utter desolation of that sensation.

And then hands seized me, pulling me to my feet. The despair passed as swiftly as it had come. "I am myself," I told them, and looked down at the body before me. To my surprise, the man opened his eyes and sat up. The warriors hastened us both back to the safety of the circle.

I had no sooner returned to my place beside Tegid and Cynan when the eerie spirit voice beckoned once more:

Come to me. Oh, come and cast away your care. Let me hold you and comfort you. Let me free you from your pain. Come to me ... come to me ...

"Hold, men! Stand your ground!" I shouted. "Do not listen!"

"It is gaining strength." Tegid said, glancing all around. "Our fear is feeding it, and we are losing the will to resist." He spun away, tugging me with him. "There might be a way ... Help me!"

"Cynan, you and Bran take over," I ordered as I hastened to follow. "Whatever happens, stand firm."

The squat twisted stems of the gorse bushes we burned for warmth were not large enough to serve, but our spear shafts were made of ashwood. Working quickly, we cut the blades from three shafts and Tegid had me hold them while he dipped into the pouch at his belt for the Nawglan, the Sacred Nine, as he called it.

Taking the specially-blended ashes, he sprinkled a portion into the palm of his right hand and then rubbed it the length of the bladeless shafts, each in turn.

"There," he said when he finished. "Now let us see if they will stand."

It was not possible to drive the wooden shafts into the stone-paved road, of course. But we tried wedging the ends between cracks in the stones. "This would have been easier with the blades still attached," I complained.

"There can be no metal in this rite," the bard replied. "Not even gold."

We persevered, however, and eventually succeeded in wedging the three spear shafts into cracks: one standing upright, two on either side inclined at a slight angle to form a loose arrowhead shape—a gogyrven. Gathering live coals on the inner rim of a shield, we placed a small pile of embers around each standing shaft. Taking up the hem of his cloak, Tegid quickly fanned the embers into a flame that licked slowly up the slender poles.

Holding his staff in both hands over his head, the bard began walking rapidly around the blaze in a sunwise direction. I could hear him muttering something under his breath in the Taran Tafod; I was not supposed to hear or know what he said.

"Hurry, Tegid!" I urged.

At the completion of the third circuit, the bard stopped, faced the blazing gogyrven and said, *"Dólasair! Dódair! Bladhm dó!!"*

The words of the Dark Tongue resounded in the pass, echoing up the sheer rock divide. Extending the staff vertically, Tegid began to speak the words of a saining rite.

Gifting Giver!
You whose name is very life to them that hear it, hear me now!
Tegid Tathal ap Talaryant, Chief Bard of Albion, I am.
See me established in the sunwise circle;
hear my entreaty.

Earth and sky, rock and wind, bear witness!
By the power of the Swift Sure Hand, I claim this ground
and sain it with a name: Bwgan Bwlch!

> *Power of fire I have over it,*
> *Power of wind I have over it,*
> *Power of thunder I have over it,*
> *Power of wrath I have over it,*
> *Power of heavens I have over it,*
> *Power of earth I have over it,*
> *Power of worlds I have over it!*

> *As tramples the swan upon the lake,*
> *As tramples the horse upon the plain,*
> *As tramples the ox upon the meadow,*
> *As tramples the boar upon the track,*
> *As trample the forest host of hart and hind,*
> *As trample all quick things upon the earth,*
> *I do trample and subdue it,*
> *And drive all evil from it!*

> *In the name of the Secret One,*
> *In the name of the Living One,*
> *In the name of the All-Encircling One,*
> *In the name of the One True Word, it is Bwgan Bwlch,*
> *Let it so remain as long as men survive*
> *To breathe the name.*

So saying, the Chief Bard brought his staff down with a loud crack upon the rocks. He turned to me. "It is done. Let us hope it is enough."

The writhing mist shuddered and drew inward upon itself, as if contracting under a hail of blows; or as if it were a creature cowed by fire, but reluctant to allow its prey to escape. The mutations rippled through the churning mass with ever-increasing frequency.

Returning to my place in the front rank, I lofted my spear and called aloud:

"In the name of the Secret One, In the name of the Living One, In the name of the All-Encircling One, In the name of the One True Word, this place is Bwgan Bwlch!"

Bran, standing next to me, took up the words, calling out in a clear, strong voice. Soon others were shouting them, too, raising a chant against the malignant spirit bubbling like a foul froth all around us. We chanted and the fog churned with ghastly half-formed shapes whose origins could scarcely be guessed.

I saw an eyeless face with a swine's snout and goat's ears; a grasping hand became a five-headed cat before dissolving into the form of a gross, grinning mouth that opened to reveal a huge, bloated toad for a tongue. A pair of emaciated bovine haunches mutated into a coiled snake before disintegrating into a scattering of scuttling cockroaches.

I saw a horse's head on the body of an infant; the infant torso stretched into a pair of thin scabby stork shanks with the long skeletal feet of a rodent. An immense belly swelled and split, spilling out blind lizards before dissipating into a clutch of palpitating reptile eggs which merged to become two slack-jawed haglike heads...

"Louder!" I shouted, taking heart that our chanting seemed to be producing some effect. "Sain the ground! Claim it!"

The men redoubled their efforts. The voices of the warriors, so long pent by Tir Aflan's dismal hush, swelled to fill the troubled pass; their voices raced up the sheer rock walls to strike the icy heights. Indeed, it seemed as if by the vigor of shouting alone we might drive the wicked *bwgan* spirit from its roost.

With blinding swiftness, the ghastly metamorphoses became instantaneous. Bizarre shapes blurred together in a fantastic stream of mutating forms—changing too fast now to be recognized as anything but hazy images of vaguely human and animal shapes.

I heard Tegid's powerful voice lifted above the rest. On his lips a song, the words of the saining rite. Man by man, we added our voices to Tegid's and the song soared up strong and loud, and the bwgan shrank before the sound. We sang:

> *Power of fire I have over it,*
> *Power of wind I have over it,*
> *Power of thunder I have over it,*
> *Power of wrath I have over it,*
> *Power of heavens I have over it,*
> *Power of earth I have over it,*
> *Power of worlds I have over it!*

The bard's saining song drove into the vile spirit like the thrust of a flaming spear, a gogyrven of song. The fog began to fade and dissipate, vanishing as we watched.

> *As tramples the swan upon the lake,*
> *As tramples the horse upon the plain,*
> *As tramples the ox upon the meadow,*
> *As tramples the boar upon the track,*
> *As trample the forest host of hart and hind,*
> *As trample all quick things upon the earth,*
> *I do trample and subdue it,*
> *And drive all evil from it!*

At the precise moment of its fading, the bwgan revealed itself as a huge hulking thing, a beast with the immense hairy body of a she-bear, its hind legs those of an ox, and its front legs those of an eagle. Its tail was the long, naked, hairless cauda of a rat, but its head and face were disturbingly human—flat-featured, big-lipped, with huge, pendulous ears, round, staring eyes and a thick protruding tongue.

In the name of the Secret One,
In the name of the Living One,
In the name of the All-Encircling One,
In the name of the One True Word, it is Bwgan Bwlch,
Let it so remain as long as men survive
To breath the name.

And then, growing transparent as the mist dissipated, the bwgan vanished.

The mountain pass echoed with the resounding cheers of the warriors, who sent their song spinning up into a night sky suddenly splashed with bright burning stars.

"We have done it!" cried Cynan, happily slapping every back he happened upon. "We have beaten the bwgan beast!"

"Well done, men!" shouted Bran. "Well done!"

We were all so busy praising one another that we did not at first hear the thin wail coming from the peaks above. But Tegid heard it. "Silence!" he called. "Silence!"

"Silence!" Cynan shouted, trying to quiet the men. "Our bard is speaking!"

"Listen!" Tegid said, lifting a hand towards the darksome peaks.

As the jubilation of the men died away, I heard a bloodless and mournful shriek—like that of a great predatory bird—far away, and receding swiftly, as the unclean spirit passed out of the world of men.

I looked to Tegid. "Bard?"

"That is the bwgan," Tegid explained with satisfaction. "It is searching for a new home among these broken peaks. If it finds no home before sunrise, it will die." Throwing high his hands, he cried, "Behold! A new day is dawning in Tir Aflan."

Turning as one, we saw the sun was rising in the east. We watched it rise—hungry for it, like men too long away from the light. Soon a shaft of clear light touched the narrow pass and filled it, expelling any lingering shadows with the force of its radiance. The rocks blushed red-gold; the peaks glowed, every one a gem.

"That evil spirit will not return here," the bard continued. "This ground is sained now, reclaimed for humankind."

"We have conquered indeed!" Bran Bresal shouted.

It was a happy moment, a blessed relief to look upon that new day. Yet even in the midst of such celebration I could feel the deep melancholy despair of the land reasserting itself once more. We might have recovered one mountain pass among a myriad others but, as the inexorable tide of grief flowed back, I understood that no mere saining rite could banish the long ages of torment and misery. It would, I reflected, take something more than a song to redeem Tir Aflan.

We struck camp and journeyed on. It was not long before dark clouds gathered to obscure the sun. The day, so brightly begun, sank into gloom once more—a gloom made all the more palpable for the glory of the dawn we had witnessed. I felt it—we all did—as a wound in the chest, a hole through which the soul leaked away like blood.

Five days, two horses and three mountain passes later, we stood together, wind-wracked and wrapped in our tattered cloaks, staring dully at a peculiar dark pall of cloud hanging over the wide bowl of a valley far below us.

"A very odd-looking cloud," I observed.

"It is smoke," replied Tegid. "Smoke and dust and fear."

32

Strangers

I gazed into the valley. The road showed as a narrow scar winding down the mountainside to lose itself in the pall of smoke and dust. My whole body leaned towards the sign in anticipation: direct evidence of human habitation. The end of our journey was near. I felt no fear.

"Why do you say fear?" Cynan asked Tegid.

"See it rising on clouds of smoke and dust," the bard replied, extending his hands and spreading his fingers, "see it casting a shadow over this unhappy land. Great distress lies before us, and great fear." Tegid lowered his hand and his voice. "Our search has ended."

"Goewyn is there?"

"And Tángwen?" Cynan asked with eager impatience. "*Mo anam*, brothers! Why do we delay? Let us hasten to free them at once." He looked quickly from one to the other of us. "Is there anything to prevent us?"

Had it been left to Cynan we would have raised the battle call of the carynx then and there, and stormed the valley by force. But Bran's cooler head prevailed. "Paladyr is surely awaiting us," he said, harking back to the beacons we had seen. "It is likely he knows our strength, but we do not know his. It would be well to discover our enemy's might before beginning battle."

"Then come," I told him. "You and I will spy out the land."

"I will go with you," Cynan offered quickly, starting away at once.

I placed my silver hand in the middle of his chest. "Stay, brother. Bran and I will go. Ready the warband and await our return."

"My wife is taken also," he growled. "Or have you forgotten?"

"I have not forgotten. But I need you to prepare the men," I replied, adding, "and to lead them if anything should happen and we do not return." Cynan scowled, but I could see him weakening. "We will not be gone long, and we will hasten back as soon as we have learned what we need to know."

Cynan, still glowering, relented. "Go, then. You will find us ready when you return."

Bran quickly readied two horses and as we mounted Tegid took hold of the reins and stopped me. "You asked me what could rouse the ancient evil of the Foul Land," he said.

"Do you know the answer now?"

"No," he confessed, "but this I know: the answer will be found down there." The bard indicated the smoke-dark valley.

"Then I will go and put an end to this mystery," I told him.

Bran and I started down into the broad valley. The road was lined with enormous boulders all the way. We thought to ride to the level of the smoke haze, then leave the horses where we could reach them at need. We would continue on foot to get as near as we could.

We made our way silently, every sense alert. Bran carried his spear, and I my swordblade naked against my thigh. But we heard nothing save the hollow clop of our horses' hooves on the road, and saw only the smoke gently undulating like a filthy sea swell. Down and down we went, following the sharp switchback of the road as it uncoiled into the valley. I watched the smoke sea surge as we descended to meet it.

In a little while we dismounted and led the horses off the road to tether them behind a rock. A little grass growing at the base of the boulder would keep the animals occupied until we returned. We then proceeded on foot, all but blind in the haze. The acrid smoke burned our eyes, but we remained watchful and proceeded with all caution, pausing every few paces to listen. Having come this far, we could not allow a moment's carelessness to ruin our cause.

We flitted from rock to rock, scanning the road below before moving on. After a while, I began to hear a drumming sound, deep and low, like an earth heart beating underground. The rhythmic rumble vibrated in the pit of my stomach and up through the soles of my feet.

Bran heard it, too. "What is that?" he asked when we stopped again.

"It is coming from the valley." The smoke pall was thinning as we descended, and I saw that we would soon drop below it. "Down there." I pointed to a large, angular boulder jutting up beside the road. "We should be able to see better from there."

We made for the boulder, pursuing the sinuous path as it slid down and down. The humming, drumming sound grew louder. In a little while we reached the rock and paused to rest and survey the land below.

The smoke cloud formed a ceiling above us, thick and dark. And, spreading below us, a vista of devastation: the entire bowl of the wide valley was a vast, denuded pit; rust-red mounds of crushed rock formed precarious mountains teetering over tier upon tier of ragged trenches and holes gouged into a rutile land, deep, angry red, like violent gashes in bruised flesh.

Plumes of foul smoke rose from scores of vents and holes, and from open fires burning on the slopes of slag heaps. And rising with the smoke, the stink of human excrement mingled with that of rotting meat and putrid water. The smell made our throats ache.

Crawling over this hellish landscape, swarming the slag heaps and plying the trenches, were thousands of men and women—thronging like termites, delving like ants, toiling away like tireless worker bees—more insect than human. Half-naked and covered in dust and mud and smoke, the wretches struggled under the enormous burdens upon their backs; scaling rickety ladders and clinging to ropes, they toiled with dull but single-minded purpose, hoisting leather bags and wicker baskets filled with earth, and then bearing them away. Squalid beyond belief, the valley squirmed with this teeming, palpitating tumult.

Gazing out over the desolate valley, straining to comprehend the methodical, meticulous thoroughness of its devastation, we could only gawk in dismay. I felt sick, disgusted by the horrific extent of the destruction.

"Maggots," muttered Bran under his breath, "feeding on a rotten corpse."

A fresh-running stream had once passed through the center of the vale. But the stream had been dammed at the further end of the valley and the waters backed to make a narrow lake, now choked with scum and rust-hued mud. Beyond the dam a column of orange-brown smoke issued from an enormous chimney in puffing gusts to the rhythm of the deep pounding earthbeat. The smoke rolled slowly, relentlessly from the stack to add to the heavy canopy of filth hanging over the whole vale.

It took me some moments to work out that I was looking at a crude strip mine. The earthmovers and loaders working this mine were human: bemired, befouled and bedraggled men, women and children.

"It is a mine," I lamented.

Bran nodded woodenly. "They are digging for iron, do you think?"

"Probably. But I want a closer look."

We crept from our hiding place and continued picking our way down. The road curved away from the valley, rimming an inner bend in the mountains. At one place the rock wall climbed steeply on the left-hand side of the road and fell sharply on the right. Water from above seeped down the cliff, gathered in a shallow pool and flowed across the road to splash away below. This small stream had washed loose silt and mud from the cliff above to form a bed. As we crossed this stream, I caught sight of something in the mud that stopped me in midstep.

I halted, putting out my hand to Bran. He froze, spear at the ready, looking quickly around for danger. Seeing nothing, he turned to me. I pointed to the muddy track at my feet. The Raven Chief looked long at it, then bent for a closer inspection.

"Do you know what made this?" he asked.

"I do," I told him. Blood throbbed in my temples, I felt dizzy and sick. "It is a . . ." I paused, searching for words he would understand. "It is a wheel track," I said at last.

Kneeling, Bran pressed his fingertips into the intricate lacework in the mud. "It is no wheel track that I have ever seen."

"It was made by a—" Before I could say another word, I heard an oddly familiar rumble. "Hurry! We must get off the road."

Bran heard the sound, but made no move. He frowned, cocking his head to one side as he listened, unaware of the danger. Snatching the Raven Chief by the arm, I yanked him to his feet. "Hurry! We must not be seen!"

We sprinted across the road and flung ourselves down the slope. An instant later, I saw a streak of yellow and the dull glint of dark glass as the vehicle passed directly over our heads with a rush. It slowed as it came to the stream; there came the sound of gears grinding as it downshifted, the engine roared—a gut-clutching, alien sound—and the vehicle cruised on.

We pressed our faces flat to the dirt and held ourselves deathly still. The vehicle drove on. When it had gone, Bran raised his head, a stricken expression on his face.

"It was a kind of wagon," I explained. "It comes from my world. That is what made the tracks."

"An evil thing, certainly," he said.

"It has no place here," I replied, rising. "Come on. We must hurry before it returns."

We climbed back onto the road and hurried on. Bran kept looking back to see if any more of these strange wagons were coming at him. But the road remained empty, and I could see nothing moving on it down below.

The appearance of the vehicle shocked and disturbed me more than I could say. But I had no time to consider the implications. It was more crucial than ever now to learn the enemy's strength and position. I ran headlong down the road, dodging behind rocks, pausing to catch my breath and lurching on. Bran ran behind me and we entered the valley, staying well out of sight behind the slag heaps and rock piles.

A tainted rain began to fall. It left black-rimmed spots where it splashed onto my skin. The laborers took no notice. The red dust slowly turned to red mud, transforming the valley into a vast oozy quagmire. Yet the workers toiled on.

Bran and I crept under an overhanging boulder and settled down to watch. The first thing that struck me, after the shock of the desolation and the presence of *Dyn Dythri*, the outworld strangers, was the relentless labor of the miners. They worked as driven slaves, yet I could not see anyone compelling them. There were, as far as I could see, no overseers, no taskmasters. There was no one directing the frenzied toil. Slaves under an invisible lash, then, the mudmen struggled and strove, sinking under their burdens, floundering in a thick stew of ordure and sludge and soot.

The poor, ignorant brutes, I thought, and wondered who, or what, had so enslaved them.

There was a track made of cut logs thrown across the mire on the far side of the valley. I watched as men fought their way up from the pits and trenches to stumble along this track towards the dam. The track crossed the dam and descended out of sight behind it in the direction of the smokestack. This seemed to be the workers' destination.

I considered whether the impetus for the wretches' toil might derive from the object of that labor, rather than any external force or threat. Perhaps they were enslaved by some deep passion within themselves. Maybe they *wanted* to work like beasts of burden. Lacking any other explanation, I decided they must be prisoners of their own rapacity.

"I want to see what is behind the dam," I told Bran. Slowly, carefully, we began making our way around the slag heap. We had not crept more than a dozen paces when we came face to face with two mudmen digging into the mire with crude wooden shovels. They looked at us with dull eyes, and I thought they would raise a cry at seeing intruders. But they merely bent their backs and proceeded with their work without so much as a backward glance as we pushed past and continued on our way.

This was the way of it elsewhere, too. There were so many slaves about that it was impossible not to be seen by some of them; but when we were seen, our presence went unremarked. On the whole they took no notice of us, or if they did, they appeared not to care. If they showed no fear, neither did they show any interest. Their labor was, apparently, all-absorbing; they gave themselves to it completely.

"Strange," concluded Bran, shaking his head slowly. "If they were beasts I would not work them so."

Upon reaching the dam, we skirted the track and kept to an upper path so that we could observe the ground below from a distance. The chimney we had seen was part of an untidy complex of structures. Attached to the largest of these buildings was the spewing smokestack, and from this came the ceaseless dull rumble of heavy machinery. Into this main building trudged an endless succession of miners lugging their burdens in one portal and emerging with empty bags and baskets from another.

My spirits, already low, sank even further. For, if there had been any uncertainty before, every last particle of doubt crumbled away before the belching smoke and rumble of heavy machinery. There was no sign of Paladyr or any warriors; nor of any place large or secure enough to hold hostages—except the factory, and I doubted we would find them there.

"Goewyn and Tángwyn are not here," I told Bran. "Let us return to camp." I saw the question on his face, so before he could ask, I added, "The Dyn Dythri have come in force to plunder Tir Aflan. We will tell the others what we have seen and make our battle plan."

Bran and I turned away to begin making our long way back to where the warband waited. We had almost gained the cover of the smoke layer when I heard the hateful rumble of the vehicle returning.

My mind raced ahead. "That rock!" Whirling, I pointed to a place in the road behind us. A large rock marked the bend: there Bran and I could hide. Upon reaching the place, we flattened ourselves behind the rock and waited for the thing to pass.

I heard the motor race as the driver downshifted into the bend. The vehicle's tires squelched on the wet stone a few short paces from where we hid. The sound ground away, dropping rapidly as it receded into the valley. We waited until we could no longer hear it, and then crept back onto the road. We retrieved the horses and stopped to catch our breath. The valley spread far behind and below us, dull red in the sullen rain like a wound oozing blood.

Bran got to his feet and mounted his horse. "Let us leave this, this *cwm gwaed*," the Raven Chief said bleakly. "It sickens me."

"Cwm Gwaed," I muttered, Vale of Blood. "The name is fitting. So be it." Bran made no reply, but turned his horse onto the road and his back to the valley.

Upon reaching our encampment, we were met by two anxious warriors, Owyn and Rhodri, who ran to greet us with the news, "Strangers are coming!"

Rhodri added, "Cynan and Garanaw have gone down to meet them."

I slid from the saddle, scanning the camp. "Where is Tegid?"

"The Penderwydd is watching from the road," Owyn said. "He said to bring you when you returned. I will show you."

Rhodri took the horses, and Owyn led us a short distance away from camp to a lookout where we could gaze down upon the road rising to meet the pass where we had made our camp. Tegid was there, and Scatha with him, watching, as the warriors had said, a group of horsemen approaching in the distance.

The bard turned his head as we took our places beside him. "Who is it?" I asked. "Do you know?"

"Watch," was all he said.

In a moment, I was able to pick out individual riders, two of whom were smaller and slighter than the others. One of these wore a white hat or headpiece. Closer, the white hat proved to be hair. The man raised his face towards the place where we stood and the sun flared as it caught the lenses at his eyes.

"Nettles!" I shouted. My feet were already running to meet him.

33

Return of the Wanderer

Professor Nettleton urged his horse to speed when he saw me running down the slope to meet him. Gaunt and haggard from his journey, his broad smile measured his relief. I reached up and swept him from the saddle in a fierce embrace. "Nettles! Nettles!" I cried. "What are you doing here? How did you know how to find us?"

The old man grinned, patting my arm and chuckling. "King Calbha sent three stout warriors with me, and Gwion led the way."

At this I glanced at the others, observing them for the first time. Flanked by Cynan and Garanaw were three warriors, looking none the worse for their journey, each leading a packhorse loaded with provisions and, on a fourth, Tegid's young Mabinog, Gwion Bach.

"How did you find us?" I asked, shaking my head in amazement. "I cannot believe you are here."

"Finding you was simplicity itself," the professor replied. "We had but to sail east. Once ashore, we simply followed your trail." He lifted a hand in the young Mabinog's direction. "Gwion has a special gift in that regard," he explained. "We would have been lost many times over without his guidance."

I turned as the others gathered around us. "Is this true, Gwion? You followed our trail?"

"It is so, Lord Llew," the boy replied.

"Well," I told them, "however you have fared, your journey is at an end. You have found us. But you will be tired. Come, rest, and tell us what news you bring. We are all eager to hear how you have fared and what brought you here."

We returned together, talking eagerly to one another about the rigors of the journey. "See here!" I called as we came into camp. "The wanderer has returned."

Scatha and Tegid hailed the travellers, greeting them with astonished admiration. All the warriors gathered around to acclaim their feat, not least because they had seen the provision-laden packhorses and could almost smell the food awaiting them.

"Gwion tracked us," I told Tegid, clapping a hand to the boy's shoulder.

The Mabinog drew himself up and answered with an air of immense satisfaction. "Where you have walked," he replied, "there is a trail of light. Day or night, we merely followed the *Aryant Ol*. The Radiant Way led us to you."

"Well done, lad," said Tegid proudly. "I will hear more of this later." Looking to the others, he said, "You have all faced great hardship and danger. The need must be great to have brought you here. Why have you come?"

Gwion and the warriors looked to Nettles, who answered, "It was at my insistence, Penderwydd. Lord Calbha warned me about Tir Aflan. With every step I feared we would arrive too late."

He paused, turning his bespectacled eyes to me. "It is Weston and his men," he said, licking his lips. He had travelled far with this news burning in him. "They have succeeded in creating a veritable gateway from our world to this. They have learned how to move machinery through the breach and they have devised systems for exploiting the land—diamonds, or something equally valuable."

"Not diamonds," I corrected. "Some kind of precious metal, I think." I explained quickly about the chimney and the machinery, which indicated a smelting process. Then I related to Tegid and the others what Bran and I had discovered in the valley.

Nettleton listened, a pained expression on his face. When I had finished, he said, "It is even worse than I thought. I had no idea ..." He fell silent, considering the enormity of the crisis.

"Come," I said, thinking to make it easier for him. "Sit down. Rest yourself, and we will talk."

But he resisted, putting his hand on my arm as if to hold me back. "There is something else, Llew. Siawn Hy is alive."

I stared. "What did you say?"

"Simon is alive, Lewis," he said, using my former name to help drive the point home. "He and Weston are working together. They have been from the beginning."

As he spoke the words, I felt the certainty fall like a dead weight upon me. It was Siawn Hy, not Paladyr, who sought revenge through Goewyn's abduction. Paladyr might have had a hand in the deed, but Siawn Hy was behind it. Siawn's poisonous treachery was at work once more in this worlds-realm.

"Llew?" the professor asked, studying me carefully. "Did you hear me?"

"I heard you," I replied dully. "Siawn Hy alive—that explains much."

"Afer their initial contact," the professor continued, "Weston furnished Simon with information in exchange for funding arranged through Simon's father. It was Simon's ambition to set himself up as king—he even boasted about it. But you thwarted him in that. Indeed, you succeeded where he failed," Nettles stressed. "I do not think he will forgive you that."

"No," I mused. "I do not think he will."

I stepped away from him and, raising my voice, I addressed the warriors. "Unload the provisions and prepare a feast of welcome. Then look to your weapons. Today we ready ourselves and take our ease. Tomorrow we meet the enemy." As the warriors dispersed to their various tasks, I summoned Cynan, Bran and Scatha, saying, "We will hold council now and lay our battle plans."

Darkness had long claimed the camp by the time we finished; the stars shone down hard flecks of light in the black skybowl of night. We had spent the remainder of the day in deliberation, pausing only to share a most welcome meal of bread, salt beef and ale, prepared from the provisions brought for us. That night, while the warband slept, I walked the perimeter of the camp, my thoughts returning time and again to the meaning of the professor's revelation.

Simon, badly wounded by Bran's spear, had fallen across the threshold to be rescued by some of Weston's men. They had rushed him to hospital, where he had spent a lengthy convalescence. "Immediately upon his release," Nettles explained when we had a moment together, "Simon disappeared. And shortly after that the activity began in earnest."

"How did you find out?"

"I have been keeping an eye on the entire operation. Also, I had help." He leaned forward. "Do you remember Susannah?"

At his mention of the name, a face flickered in my memory: a keen-eyed firebrand of a young woman with brains and pluck for any challenge. Yes, I remembered her.

"Susannah has been a godsend," Nettles informed me soberly. "I have told her everything. I do not know how I could have managed otherwise."

He grew grave. After a moment, he said, "It was after Simon disappeared again that I began noticing the signs. I knew something had to be done. The damage is fearful."

"Damage?"

"The damage to the manifest world. There are," he hesitated, searching for the right word, "there are *anomalies* breaking through. Aberrations appear almost daily. The Knot, the Endless Knot, is unravelling, you see. And the manifest world is diminishing; the effect is..."

His eyes were intense behind his round spectacles, imploring, entreating, willing me to understand. "That is when you decided to come back," I suggested.

"Yes, and when Calbha told me that Goewyn had been abducted

and taken to the Foul Land, I feared I had returned too late." Professor Nettleton's voice grew stern and insistent. "They must be stopped, Llew. They are manipulating forces they do not understand. If their violation continues, they will destroy literally *everything*. You cannot imagine..."

With this warning reverberating through my mind, tolling like a bell of doom, I stalked the silent camp through the night's cold. The end was near, I could feel it approaching with the speed of the dawn. Tomorrow, I would meet my enemy and, with the aid of the Swift Sure Hand, I would defeat him. Or die.

The valley appeared as Bran and I had left it, a red gash in the belly of the land. The smoke hung like a sooty ceiling over all, shutting out what little light might have come from the pale and powerless sun. I imagined, for a moment, that sunlight penetrating the fog and burning away all the filth and corruption. Oh, but it would take something stronger than sunlight to reverse the devastation that met our sight.

The scum-filled lake, lethally still beneath the shroud of smoke, lay like a tarnished mirror. The stench of the lake and from the wounded land hurt our lungs and stung our eyes. The men must accustom themselves to this before going nearer.

"The Dyn Dythri are there," I told them, pointing with my speartip to the dam and chimney. Cynan, Bran, Scatha, Tegid and Nettles stood with me; the warband was assembled behind us. "I do not know how many strangers have come, but it may be that they know we are here and will be ready for us."

"Good," grunted Cynan. "Then men will not say we defeated a sleeping foe."

Scatha observed the valley, studying it in detail, green eyes narrowed to attentive slits. "You described it well. But it will be difficult to walk that slope. I think we should use the path," she said, indicating the track on the left-hand side of the lake which the mudmen used to trundle their burdens to the compound behind the dam.

"The slaves will not hinder us," I said. "There is no need to avoid them. They will not fight."

"I do not see any of the strangers, nor their *olwynog tuthógi*," Bran said, and some of the men laughed. But it was nervous laughter; there was no real mirth in it.

I turned to address them, using the words I had pondered during my long, sleepless night. "Kinsmen and friends, we have journeyed far and endured much that would have daunted lesser men." There was a general murmur of approval at this.

"Today," I continued, "we will face a most deceptive and cunning enemy. Deceptive, for his weapons are those of cowardice and guile. Cunning, for he is shrewd in malice and devious in hostility. He will appear to you a weak and unworthy foe, unlike any you have met in battle. His weapons will appear low and inferior, but do not be deceived. For they can kill at a distance, without warning. You must be wary at all times—for when the foeman stands far off, then is he most dangerous."

The men looked at one another in bewilderment, but I went on. "You must understand," I told them. "Heed me well. The enemy we face today will not stand against you. They will run and they will flee. They will fight from hiding." This brought sneers of contempt.

"Hear me now!" I continued. "You must not be deceived. Do not expect skill, neither expect honor. Instead, expect confusion and cowardice—for these are sturdy shields for a foe who understands neither valor nor courage."

The warriors acclaimed this outright, raising their voices in hoots of derision.

"Their strength is not in numbers, but in rapacity and lust for destruction. The enemy will destroy swiftly, without thought or remorse. Pity will not restrain him, nor will mercy stay his hand. He feels no shame."

There were calls and shouts of scorn for such a worthless foe, but I raised my silver hand for silence. "Listen to me! We do not fight today for honor; there is no glory to be won. We fight only for survival. We are few, but we stand between this foe and the ruin of our world. If we fail, Albion will fall beneath the shadow of evil and desolation that has overcome Tir Aflan.

"We fight today for the freedom of those held captive to the foe: for Goewyn and Tángwen, yes, but no less for those who do not yet know their danger.

"Therefore, let us advance with shrewdness and cunning. We must use stealth where we would take the battleground openly, if by stealth and concealment, even flight, we may save ourselves to fight again."

The warband did not like this. They grumbled against such cowardly tactics, but I held firm. "Cling to pride and we will perish. Cherish dignity and we will die."

"We *will* fight today," I told them, "but we must survive the fight. For, if we fail, Albion will fall. And once Albion has fallen, all the pride and dignity in this worlds-realm will not restore it."

There were no shouts or grumbles now. My words had found the mark and taken hold.

I paused before concluding. "Listen, brothers. If I have learned anything in my time among you, it is this: true honor lives not in the skill of weapons or the strength of arms, but in virtue. Skill fades and strength fails; virtue alone remains. Therefore, let us put off all that is false. Let us prefer instead the valor of virtue, and the glory of right."

I had spoken my heart, but could they understand? It appeared I had misjudged the moment. The warriors did not understand; I had lost them, and perhaps the battle as well.

Yet even as doubt began to grow, I heard a small clicking sound. I turned my head towards the sound and saw Bran, eyes level and hard, tapping the shaft of his spear on the rim of his shield. Click, click, click . . .

The Raven Flight quickly joined him; Scatha and Cynan soon followed. Click! Click! Click! And, by twos and threes, the rest of the warband joined in. Click! Click! Click! The sound became a rattle, and grew to an ominous thunder as the ashwood shafts struck the metal rims. CRACK! CRACK! CRACK!

It mounted to a crashing climax and then stopped so abruptly I could hear the final report echoing away across the valley. And then we turned and descended into Cwm Gwaed, the Vale of Blood.

34

The Trap

Sinuous as a snake, the road twisted down into the valley. Though I had entered it before, I felt the shock afresh—like a fist in the throat. It was still early morning, but the mudmen were already teeming like maggots over the slag heaps and swarming the trenches. The high chimney spewed its noxious emissions into the air beyond the dam to the dull thunder of hidden machinery.

Those with me gazed glass-eyed and dumbstruck at the enmired misery around them. Unable to comprehend the mindless ardor of the toiling wretches, the warriors simply stared and moved on.

We had divided the warband into three divisions each under the command of a battlechief; Scatha, Cynan and I each led a band on foot. The Raven Flight alone was mounted, leaving Bran to range the battleground at will wherever need was greatest. As for the rest, I judged horses would not help us; without them we could make better use of the cover provided by the holes and heaps of crushed rock. Tegid, Gwion and Nettles had stayed behind to look after the other horses. As in the battle against Meldron, the Chief Bard meant to oversee the fight and uphold us in the bardic way.

Cynan's warband descended to the valley floor and worked its way towards the dam along the shore of the polluted lake; I led those with me on the upper road; Scatha and her warriors approached by way of the path on the far side of the lake, doing their best to blend into the pocked and mottled landscape. Bran advanced behind us, out of sight; when I paused to look back I could not see the Raven Flight anywhere.

The first shot came without warning. I heard the whine of a bullet and the dry ricochet on the hillside below us. A moment later the report echoed from below like the crack of a splitting tree trunk. I motioned to the men to lie down on the road. Several more shots dug into the hillside. Over-anxious, undisciplined, our foe could not wait for us to come into range and had opened fire prematurely. This gave us a prime opportunity to fix the enemy's position and assess their numbers without risk to ourselves.

Wisps of white smoke from their guns betrayed the enemy's placement along the top of the dam. I scanned the valley and the far side of the lake to see that Scatha and Cynan had halted and were marking the place as well. The enemy had seen us on the road, as I intended, but had not thought to look elsewhere.

"Such stupidity should be rewarded," I muttered to the man nearest me.

"Then let us be generous, lord," the warrior replied dryly.

The bullets chunked harmlessly into the rock waste below us for a time, and then the shooting tapered off. I signalled to the men to keep low, and we advanced once more, slowly, listening for the bullet's whine and watching for the tell-tale white puff that revealed an enemy gunman. I took heart from the fact that, as yet, the gunmen still concentrated all their attention on us; they had so far failed to notice Scatha and Cynan working their way ever closer below them.

If I could keep the enemy occupied but a little longer, it would allow the others a more protected approach.

Raising my hand, I halted my warriors. We were by now nearly within range of the guns. "Keep down!" I told those with me. "And wait for my command."

Then I stood and, lofting my spear and shield, I began to yell. "Cowards!" I shouted. "Leave your hiding places and let us fight like men!"

I knew the enemy would not understand me. It was to encourage my own warband that I cried my challenge in Albion's tongue. "Why do you crouch like vermin in your holes?" I taunted. "Come out! Let us do battle together!"

My simple ruse worked. The enemy opened fire. The bullets dug into the slag-covered hillside below me, throwing up dust and splinters—but falling well short of the target. They were using small arms—handguns and light rifles. Larger caliber weapons would have carried further, and with far greater accuracy.

"Where is your battlechief?" I called loudly, my voice echoing back from the blank face of the dam. "Where is your war leader? Let him come and meet me face to face!"

This brought a further heated and wasteful volley from the dam. The warriors with me laughed to see it. I summoned them to rise, now that I knew it was safe to do so. And taking my lead, they too challenged the enemy to come out and fight like true warriors. The gunfire beat like a staccato tattoo, and the white smoke drifted up from behind the dam.

"How many did you count?" I asked the nearest warrior.

"Three fives," he replied.

His tally matched my own. I would have thought that fifteen men with guns could have defeated three score with spears—and we were far fewer than that. But without more battle-cunning than these fifteen had so far demonstrated, their weapons would not win the day.

Scatha, sharp as the blade in her hand, was not slow to turn our diversion to advantage. In two rapid, ground-eating advances, she and her warband reached the dam, crossed it and descended the other side. Cynan followed her lead, disappearing behind the dam while we jeered and danced like madmen, drawing the enemy's fire.

All through this commotion, the mud-covered slaves toiled away, scarcely pausing to raise their dull heads as the bullets streaked above them. Were they so far gone that they no longer knew or cared what was happening around them?

The gunfire eventually ceased. But by then the trap was set.

"Now we must find a way to draw them out of hiding so that Scatha and Cynan can strike," I said, thinking aloud.

"The battlelust is on them," said the warrior next to me. "They are greedy for the kill."

"Then let us see if their greed will make them foolish. We will form the shield line." I gave the order and the warriors took their places beside me. We formed a line, shoulder-to-shoulder, and began slowly to advance along the road.

"Raise shields!" I called, and we put our shields before us, rims overlapping. We continued walking.

The enemy gunmen held their fire. We had advanced as far as we dared, and still they did not shoot.

"Halt!" I raised my silver hand. The bluff had not worked; we had not drawn the enemy into the open. Any nearer and a well-aimed shot might easily penetrate our oak-and-iron shields.

"Cowards!" I called down to the dam. We were close enough now to see the shallow holes the men had dug along the top of the dam. "False men! Hear me now! We are the *Gwr Gwir*! Leave your hiding holes and we will show you what true warriors can do!"

At this, the warriors began striking their shields and taunting the hidden foe. The clash of spear upon shield became a rattling roar. The gunmen could not resist such obvious targets: they began firing again. The bullets struck the stone flagging at our feet. I ordered the line to move two paces back.

The temptation proved too strong—they were drawn from cover at last—all fifteen of them, shouting as they came.

The initial volley tore into the stones a few paces ahead of us. One warrior turned away a glancing shot off the pavement; a slug struck the bottom of my shield. I felt the wood shiver as it ripped through. It was time to retreat.

"Back!" I cried. "Three more paces."

The line fell back and halted; the jeering catcalls continued. Seeing that we would come no closer, the enemy gunmen attacked.

They had no sooner abandoned their hiding holes than Scatha and Cynan materialized out of the drifting smoke behind them. The gunmen were neatly trapped.

They whirled in sudden panic, shooting wildly. Two of their number went down—victims of their own incompetence. One of Cynan's men took a shot through his shield and fell. The gunman paid for his last act as a streaking spear sank to its shaft in his belly. The man fell to the ground writhing and screaming.

At this single casualty the fight went quickly out of the rest and they began crying surrender and throwing down their weapons.

"It is over!" I shouted. "Let us join our swordbrothers!"

We hastened down the road to the top of the dam. I cast a quick backward glance for the Ravens, but they were still nowhere to be seen. What could be keeping them?

"Splendid, Pen-y-Cat! Well done, Cynan!" I called. Scanning the throng of warriors, I was surprised to see the man who had been shot standing in the forerank once more. His shield had a chunk bitten out of the upper left quadrant, he was pale and bleeding just below the shoulder, but he was clear-eyed and undaunted.

The wounded gunman was not so fortunate. The spear had done its work. The man lay silent now, and quite still.

I detailed my warband to dispose of the enemy guns. "Gather their weapons," I told the warriors. "Cast them into the lake."

Scatha and Cynan had lined up the twelve remaining gunmen in a row. "Where is Weston?" I demanded, using their own speech.

No one made bold to answer. I nodded to Cynan. He stepped swiftly forward, striking the nearest man in the center of the chest with the butt of his spear. The man dropped like a stone, and lay rolling on the ground, eyes bulging with pain, mouth agape, unable to breathe.

"I ask you again: where is the man called Weston?"

The prisoners glanced anxiously at one another, but made no reply. Cynan moved along the line. He stopped and raised his spear again. The man cringed. "Wait! Wait!" he screamed, waving his hands.

Cynan paused, his spear still hovering.

"Well?" I demanded. "Speak."

"Weston is at the mill," the man sputtered, gesturing wildly in the direction of the smokestack behind him. "They are guarding the mill."

"How many are with him?" I asked.

"Three or four, I think," the man replied. "That's all."

"Is there anyone else?"

The man grew reticent. Cynan aimed the butt of his spear once more.

"No!" he replied quickly. "No one else. I swear it!"

I looked towards the cluster of buildings below the dam. Weston with three or four gunmen holed up in the mill. Rooting them out could prove a difficult and costly undertaking. I raised my silver hand, summoning four warriors to take the gunmen away. "Bind them fast," I ordered. "Guard them well. See that they do not escape."

I summoned Scatha and Cynan to join me, and related what I had learned. "What do you suggest?" I asked.

Cynan spoke first. "The lives of these strangers are not worth the risk of noble warriors," he said with arch disdain.

"Even so, we have taken the men: we cannot allow their leader to go free." I turned to Scatha. "What say you, Pen-y-Cat?"

Scatha was gazing thoughtfully at the smoking chimney. "Smoke will cure fish. It may also cure these foemen."

It was a simple matter to scale the chimney and stuff down a few cloaks to block the flue. Before long, smoke was pouring from every crack in the crudely constructed building.

We advanced, crossing the compound warily. As we neared, I heard a door slam and a motor sputter to life, and a moment later a van broke from hiding behind the building and flew past us. The startled warriors stared aghast as the yellow vehicle, wheels churning up dust and gravel, sped away. Some of the closer warriors heaved stones as it passed, breaking two side windows, but the van gained the road, turned, and raced away, climbing from the valley by another route.

"We will never catch them on foot," I observed, watching the vehicle disappear into the hills. Turning to Cynan, I ordered, "Send men to bring the horses." To Scatha, I said, "We will follow them. If Nettles is right, they will lead us to Siawn Hy and Paladyr."

We hurried on, following the vehicle's trail. It soon became apparent that it was a well-used track. Wary of ambush, I sent scouts ahead on either side of the advancing warband. We hastened along the ascending track, which soon turned away from Cwm Gwaed and began climbing into the mountains once more.

I called a halt at the crest of a hill near a small stream. "We will rest here and wait for the horses," I told them.

As we made to leave the valley, I turned and looked back one last time. "Where is Bran?" I wondered aloud. "What can have happened to him?"

"You need have no worry for Bran," Scatha said. "He will be where he is most needed."

"You are right, Pen-y-Cat," I agreed. "But I would that my War Leader rode with me."

The words were scarcely out of my mouth when we heard the sound of gunfire coming from the other side of the hill. Flying to the hilltop, we looked down to see the yellow van trapped in a narrow defile and stranded halfway across a shallow rock-filled stream. Circling the stalled vehicle were Bran and the Ravens on horseback, shouting and flourishing their spears. Two men were firing indiscriminately from the broken windows of the vehicle.

We hastened to their aid, calling on the Ravens to retreat. The four in the van would be easy to deal with, and I did not want any of my warriors hit by a stray shot. Leaving the vehicle, they came to where we had taken up position, just outside the rifle's lethal range.

The gunfire continued for a few moments and then stopped.

"I did not see you ride from the valley," I told Bran. "I wondered what had become of you."

"Paladyr attacked the camp as soon as we left," the Raven Chief informed me. "We rode to Tegid's aid and drove the enemy away. We pursued, but lost them in these hills. When we saw the *tuthóg-ar-rhodau* fleeing I thought to prevent their escape."

The van's engine whined, there came the sheering whir of

grinding gears and the vehicle jounced across the stream, wheels spinning, and fled the valley.

"Follow," I told Bran, "and keep them in sight, but do not try to stop them and do not go too near. Their trail is clear; they cannot escape. I have sent men for the horses; we will join you as soon as they arrive."

The Raven Flight flew off in pursuit, and as we made our way back up the hill to await the arrival of our horses, we were greeted by the dull drumming of hoofbeats coming from the other side of the hill. "Tegid is here with the horses," I told Cynan, and a moment later the first rider appeared over the crest of the hill directly above us.

But it was not Tegid who appeared, lofting a spear as he crested the hill; and the warriors mounted on horses behind him were strangers.

We had blundered into a trap.

35

Tref-gan-Haint

"Paladyr!" I shouted, halting in mid-step.

The enemy hesitated, hovering on the crest of the hill. There came the clear call of the battlehorn, loud and strong. And then they plummeted down the hillside in an avalanche of pounding hooves and whirring blades. We had only an instant to raise our weapons and they were on us. Scatha took measure of the situation at once. "We cannot fight them here!" she cried, whirling away. She dashed towards the stream: "Follow me!"

Cynan, spear lofted high, bellowed at his warriors to join him as he followed Scatha's lead. I did the same, and we ran for high ground on the other side of the stream, the battlehorn blaring loud in our ears and the dull thunder of hooves shaking the ground beneath our feet. Two of our warriors were ridden down from behind, and we lost another to an enemy spear. But our feinting flight had not been anticipated and we succeeded in gaining the high ground before Paladyr, over-eager for an easy victory, could stop us.

Though we were on foot against a larger force of mounted warriors, we now held a superior position: the horsemen would have to fight uphill on steep and treacherous terrain. Scatha's unfailing battle sense had not only saved us, but given us a slight advantage.

"They are hungry for it!" shouted Cynan, watching the horses struggle up the loose scree of the mountainside. "Come, brother, let us feed our impetuous guests!"

Ducking under his upraised shield, he darted forward, slashing a wide swath before him with the blade of his spear, cutting the legs from under the nearest horse. The beast screamed, plunged, and spilled its hapless rider on the ground. Cynan struck down swiftly with his spear before the foeman could roll free of his thrashing mount.

Cynan threw back his head and loosed a wild war whoop of terrible delight. Two more enemy riders fell to his swift spear before they could turn aside. I dispatched another using Cynan's trick, and when I looked around I saw that Scatha had succeeded in unseating three of the foemen in as many swift forays.

The first clash lasted but a few heartbeats. Gaining no clear benefit for his efforts, Paladyr soon signalled his men to break off the attack. They withdrew to the far side of the stream to regroup.

"This Paladyr is no fool," observed Cynan. "He knows when to retreat, at least."

Looking across the stream, I saw Paladyr, naked to the waist, face and chest daubed with blue warpaint, the muscles of his back and arms gleaming with sweat. He clutched a bronze spear and shield, and was shouting at his men, upbraiding them for their carelessness and incompetence. There was no sign of Siawn Hy among them, but this did not surprise me.

"He is not a fool," I agreed, "but he is impulsive. That may prove his undoing."

"Who is with him?" wondered Cynan.

I studied Paladyr's warband. They were a raw-looking crowd, armed with ancient bronze weapons like those we had seen in the ruined tower. Their shields were small and heavy, their spears short, with blunt heads. Some wore helmets, but most did not. And only a few carried swords as well as spears. They moved awkwardly—as if they were unused to riding and uncertain of themselves. No doubt they had expected to overwhelm us in the first rush; and now they faced a more determined adversary than anticipated.

It came to me that this was not so much a trained warband as a gang of ill-disciplined cutthroats. They were mercenaries, chosen perhaps from among the laborers slogging through the mud in the valley beyond. Though they had horses, it was obvious that they were not accustomed to fighting on horseback: their first disastrous sally proved as much.

"Llew!" shouted Scatha, hastening towards me. "Did you see him?"

"No," I replied. "Siawn Hy was not with them. But what do you make of the rest?"

"It seems to me that Paladyr has tried to stitch himself a warband from very poor cloth," she replied.

"That is just what I was thinking," I told her. "And it will soon unravel in his hands."

"A boast? From Llew?" crowed Cynan, scrambling back up the hillside. "Brother, are you feeling well?"

"Never better," I told him.

The blare of the carynx signalled a second attack and the enemy clattered across the stream once more. This time Paladyr ranged his men along a line and they advanced together, hoping to spread our thin defence and separate us.

Scatha had other ideas. She called the warbands together and formed them into a narrow-pointed wedge. Unable to climb the steep mountainside and strike at us from the flank, the horsemen had no choice but to meet the point of the wedge head on.

They rode at us yelling and screaming, trying their best to frighten and scatter us. But we stood firm and hewed them from their saddles as quickly as they came within striking distance. Eight enemy riders went down before they could even wheel their horses to retreat. And Paladyr was forced to break off the attack once more.

As the enemy turned tail and fled back across the stream, I summoned the battlechiefs to me. "It seems they lack the will to press the attack."

"*Clanna na cù*, what a poor foray," Cynan sneered, thrusting out

357

his chin. "I would be shamed to lead such ill-suited warriors."

"Yes, and Paladyr is a better war leader than this—or once was. I do not understand it."

"Their inexperience is against them," I observed. "They dare not challenge us, so they seek to harry us and wear us down."

"Then they will be disappointed," Scatha said, quickly scanning the hillside. "If they offer no better assault than we have seen, we can stand against them all day."

"We would not have to stand here at all if we had our horses," Cynan said.

"Then let us take theirs," Scatha suggested. "We would make better use of them than they do."

Swiftly we devised a plan to liberate as many of the foemen's horses as possible in the next clash. And it might have worked. But, just as Paladyr's warband crossed the stream and started up the hillside to engage us once more, the Ravens arrived. One fleeting glimpse of the Raven Flight swooping in full cry down the mountainside, and the cowardly enemy scattered. They splashed across the stream to disappear around the far side of the slope. Bran would have offered pursuit, but I called him back.

"I would rather you stayed with us," I told him. "What did you find ahead?"

A strange expression flitted across the Chief Raven's face. "There is a settlement, lord," he said. "But unlike any I have seen before."

"Is it safe?" wondered Cynan. "It could be another trap."

"Perhaps," the Raven Chief allowed. "But I think not."

"Why do you say that?" asked Scatha.

By way of reply Bran said, "I will show you. It is not far."

Calling to Drustwn and Garanaw, I commanded, "Tegid and the horses should have been here by now. Ride to meet them, and bring the horses to us at the settlement. We will await you there." To Bran, I said, "Show us this place you have found."

"It is this way," Bran said, wheeling his horse, and began to lead us up the mountainside and along a ridgeway. The remaining Ravens took up a position well behind, guarding the rear, lest

Paladyr and his band return and try to take us unawares. But the enemy did not return.

A short distance along the ridge, the trail turned and began descending towards a steep-sided valley. A muddy river wound its slow way along the floor of the valley, and at the nearer end, hard against the ridge, a crude holding had been erected. The few larger, more substantial structures were made from rough timber: the rest appeared cobbled together, a patchwork of bits and pieces. A small distance beyond the settlement, a narrow lake gleamed dully in the foul light.

We descended into the valley and entered the town on the single street of hard-packed earth, passing between the patched-together, tumbledown shanties jammed one on top of the other and leaning at all angles. At a wide place before one of the larger dwellings, we halted. A row of rickety stalls had been thrown up along the side of the street facing the building, and a mud-caked stone well stood between them. We stopped here to wait for Tegid and the horses.

We had seen no one since our arrival and, but for the garbage and dung scattered around, I would have thought the place long abandoned. But as soon as it became clear that we meant to stay, the hidden population began to creep forth. Like vermin crawling from the cracks and crevices they emerged, hesitantly at first, but with increasing boldness. Hobbling, scuttling, dragging battered and deformed limbs, they scrambled into the square. In no time at all we were besieged by a tattered rabble of beggars.

They swarmed us with outstretched hands and open mouths, mewing like sick animals for food and cast-offs—though we had none to give. Like the mudmen working the mines, they were dull-looking with dead eyes and slack expressions. More brute than human, they stood splay-legged and slump-shouldered, abject in their misery. Beggars are unknown in Albion, so the warriors did not understand at first what the grasping mob wanted of them. They shrank from the outstretched hands, or pushed them away, which only increased the clamor.

Cynan and Bran watched the press warily and with increasing unease, but said nothing. "We should move on," Scatha said, "or there may be trouble."

"When they see we have nothing to give them," I replied, "they will leave us alone."

But I was wrong. The beggars became more insistent and demanding. They grew belligerent. Some of the women swaggered up to the warriors and rubbed themselves against the men. The warriors reacted with predictable revulsion and chagrin. But the whores were persistent as they were blatant. They wheedled in shrill voices, and clutched at the warriors.

"Llew," Scatha pleaded, "let us leave this... this *Tref-gan-Haint* at once."

"You are right," I relented. "We will go on to the lake and await the horses there."

The beggars began wailing at our departure, shrieking terribly. The women, spurned and roundly rejected, followed, shouting abuse and scorn. One of them, little more than a girl, saw my silver hand and ran to me. She fell on her knees before me, seized my hand, and began caressing it.

I gently tried to disengage my hand from her grasp, but she clung to me, pulling on my arm, dragging me down. She moaned and pouted, and rubbed her lips over my metal hand.

"I have nothing for you," I told her firmly. "Please, stand up. Do not shame yourself this way."

But she made no move to release me. Taking her by the wrist, I peeled her hand from mine and made to step over her. When she saw I meant to leave her, she leapt at me with a raking swipe of her fingernails. I jerked my head away and she fell in the dirt where she lay writhing and pleading. I stepped over her and moved on. She kicked and cursed me, her sharp voice gradually dissolving into the general uproar around us.

I moved through the crowd, leading the warband away. Hands clutched at my arms and legs. Voices whined and cried. I pushed ahead, eyes level, looking neither right nor left. What could I give them? What did they want from me?

We entered the cramped, stinking street once more, and continued to the end where the refuse heaps of the shanty town smoldered and burned with a noisome smoke. There were beggars here, too, pawing through the garbage and filth for any overlooked morsels.

Scrawny, long-legged dogs nosed in the filth. One man, naked, his skin black from the smoke, lay half-covered in garbage; he struggled onto an elbow and hailed us obscenely as we passed. His legs were a mangled mess of open sores. The odious dogs hovered around him, dashing in now and then to lick at the man's oozing wounds. Turning away from this ghastly sight, I was met by another. I saw two dogs fighting over a carcass—little more than a shred of putrid flesh clinging to a rotting skeleton. With a sudden sick shock, I realized the remains were human. The gorge rose in my throat and I turned my face away.

Tref-gan-Haint, Scatha had called it, city of pestilence, place of defilement. Diseased and dying, it was a cankerous sight and filled the air with the stench of a rotting wound. This, I reflected, was the fate awaiting the slaves when their usefulness was over. They ended their days as beggars fighting over scraps of garbage. The thought grieved me, but what could I do? Swallowing hard, I walked on.

Beyond the settlement a small distance, we came to the shallow lake from which the stream issued, and found it slightly more tolerable. Although the strand was sharp shards of flint, the water was clean enough. No one followed us from the town so we had the lake to ourselves and hunkered down on the hard shore to wait.

I dozed, and fell into a light sleep in which I dreamed that Goewyn had found us and now stood over me. I awoke to find Bran sitting beside me, and no sign yet of the horses. I rose, and Bran and I walked back along the flinty shore together. A dirty yellow sun was lowering in the western peaks, and stretched our shadows long on the rocky strand.

"Where is Tegid?" I wondered aloud, gazing towards the blighted town and the ridge beyond. "Do you think he ran into Paladyr?"

"It is possible. But Drustwn and Garanaw know where to find us," Bran pointed out. "If there was any trouble, they would have summoned us."

"Still, I do not like this," I told him. "They should have reached us by now."

"I will go and find out what has happened," Bran offered.

"Take Emyr and Niall with you. Send one of them back with word as soon as you find out anything."

Bran hastened to his horse, mounted, summoned the remaining Ravens, and the three rode away at once. I watched them out of sight, and then called Scatha and Cynan to me. "I have sent Bran to see what has become of Tegid and the others."

"It is growing late," Scatha said. "Perhaps we should try to find better shelter elsewhere."

"Darkness will be our only shelter tonight, I fear." Looking to the ridge, I scanned the heights, but saw no sign of anyone returning. What could have happened to Tegid and Nettles?

The sun sank in an ugly brown haze, and a turgid twilight gathered. As the sun departed, the thin warmth vanished; I felt the mountain chill seeping out of the air and creeping up out of the ground. Mist rose from the lake and night vapors began threading down the mountainsides in snaking rivulets.

The men had foraged for wood on the stony slopes around the lake, and the little they found was kindled and set alight as night fell, making small campfires that sputtered fitfully and gave little light. We were hungry, having had nothing to eat since early morning; we eased the pangs with lake water. It tasted flat and metallic, but it was cold, and it quenched our thirst.

Dusk deepened in the valley. The sky held a faint glimmer of dying light, and the mist off the lake and slopes thickened to a fog. I walked restlessly along the flinty strand, alert to any sound of our returning horses. Apart from the liquid lap and lick of the water and the occasional bark of a dog in the distance, I heard nothing.

I stood for a long time, waiting, listening. A red moon floated low over the mountains, peering like an eye down through the fog and mist, casting a dismal pall of ruddy light over the lake and slopes.

At length, I turned and walked back to the campfires glowing soft in the fog-haze. I passed the first fire and heard the men talking quietly, their voices a gentle mumble in the mist. But I heard something else as well. I stopped and held my breath...

A thumping sound, low and rhythmic as a heartbeat, sounded in the darkness—thump... thump... thump. Because of the fog and mist, the sound seemed to come from everywhere at once. Cynan heard it as well and joined me. "What can it be?" he asked softly.

"Shhh!"

We stood motionless. The sound grew gradually louder, gaining definition. Thump-lump... thump-lump... thump-lump... To resolve itself into the slow, loping gallop of a horse, coursing along the flinty strand.

"We have a visitor," I told Cynan.

The pace quickened as the horse drew near, approaching from the far end of the glen away from Tref-gan-Haint. My pulse quickened with the speed of the horse and my silver hand sent an icy tingle up my arm.

"I will bring a torch," Cynan said, darting away at once.

I walked a few paces further along the shore towards the sound. My metal hand burned with an icy cold. The rider was nearer than I knew. All at once, I saw him: a rider on a horse pale as the fog itself, charging out of the swirling mist, the horse's iron-shod hooves striking sparks from the flint as they came.

The rider was armored head to heel in bronze; it gleamed dully in the ruddy moonlight. His helmet was plumed and high-crested; a strange battlemask covered his face. He carried a long bronze spear; a small round bronze shield lay on his thigh. His feet were shod in bronze war shoes, and on his hands were gauntlets covered with bronze fish-scales. The high-cantled saddle was ornamented with round bronze bosses. The horse was armored, too; a bronze warcap with long, curving horns was on its head. Bronze breastplates and greaves graced both horse and rider.

Although I had never seen the rider before, I would have recognized him. The Banfáith had warned me long ago, and even in the dead of a foggy night I knew him: it was the Brazen Man.

36

Clash By Night

The Brazen Man drove straight at me. I dodged to the side at the last instant, and he pulled back hard on the reins. The horse reared, its legs fighting the air. The man raised his hand and I made ready to deflect a blow. Instead of a sword, however, I saw he held a knotted sack. He turned his bronze-clad face towards me, blank and staring; and though I could not see his eyes behind the burnished mask, I felt the force of his hatred as a heatblast on my flesh. My silver hand burned with frozen fire.

The mysterious rider swung the sack once around his head and loosed it. The bag struck the ground and rolled to my feet. Then, with a wild, triumphant cry, the rider wheeled his horse and galloped back the way he came.

Cynan ran to me with a burning brand he had pulled from the fire. "Was it Paladyr?"

I shook my head slowly. "No," I told him. "I do not think it was Paladyr..."

"Who then?"

I looked at the knotted sack lying on the strand. Cynan stooped and picked it up. I took it from him. There was something round and bulky but not too heavy in the bottom. I loosened the knot, opened the sack, and peered in, but could not see the contents clearly.

"Here," I said, lowering the bag to the ground and spreading the opening wide. Cynan held his torch closer. I looked again and instantly wished I had not.

Professor Nettleton's pale, bloodless face stared up at me. His glasses were gone and his white hair was matted with clotted blood. I closed my eyes and shoved the sack away. Cynan took it from me.

Scatha, holding a sword in one hand and a firebrand in the other, hastened to us. "Is it...?" Her question faltered.

"It is the white-haired one," Cynan told her. "Llew's friend."

"I am sorry, Llew," she said after a moment. Her voice was grave, but I could tell she was relieved that it was not her daughter.

"What do you wish me to do with it?" asked Cynan.

"Put it with Alun's ashes for now," I told him, sick at heart. "I will not bury it in this place."

"Alun's... the ashes are with Tegid," Scatha reminded me.

I heard her, but made no reply. My mind boiled with questions. Why had this been done? A challenge? A warning? Who would do such a thing? How had he been taken? What did it mean? I stared into the swirling fog willing the answers, like the bronze-clad rider, to appear.

The Brazen Man! The words whizzed like arrows straight to my heart. I heard again the Banfáith's voice speaking out the dire prophecy:

All this by the Brazen Man is come to pass, who likewise mounted on his steed of brass works woe both great and dire. Rise up, Men of Gwir! Fill your hands with weapons and oppose the false men in your midst! The sound of the battleclash will be heard among the stars of heaven and the Great Year will proceed to its final consummation.

"Llew?" Cynan said, touching me gently on the arm. "What is it, brother?"

I turned to him. "Rouse the men. Hurry!"

Scatha stood looking at me, her forehead creased with concern. In the fluttering firelight she looked just like Goewyn. "Arm yourself, Scatha," I told her. "Tonight we fight for our lives."

Cynan alerted the men with a shout and Emyr blew a long,

withering blast on the carynx. Within two heartbeats the camp was a chaos of men running and shouting, arming themselves to meet the foe already swarming onto the strand. Like phantoms they appeared out of the fog—rank on rank, scores of them, an enemy war host arrayed in bronze battlegear.

A spear was thrust into my hand. I could not find a shield, so grabbed a brand from the fire and ran to take my place in the front rank of warriors, Scatha on my right hand, Cynan on my left. We stood with our backs to the lake and leaned into the battle.

They fell upon us in a rush, as if they would drive us into the lake with one great push. But our warriors were battle-hardened men, skilled in close fighting; all had faced the Great Hound Meldron. After the shock of surprise had passed, they fell to with a fierce delight. To a man, they were sick of Tir Aflan, sick of the deprivation and hardship, and eager to lash out at the enemy who had caused them so much misery.

As before, the enemy, though well-armored, were ill-matched to fight real warriors. But there were more of them now than we had faced earlier in the day, a good many more.

Absorbing the initial onslaught, the warriors of Albion leapt like a quick-kindled flame, striking swift and hot, searing into the onrushing foe. The resulting clash threw the attacking enemy back on their heels. Heartened by this early success, Emyr loosed a shattering blast on the battlehorn, and the warriors of Albion answered the call with rousing shout. The battlecry of Albion's warriors echoed along the flint shore, driving into the enemy like a fist.

Scatha, hair streaming, cloak flying, whirled into the enemy line; sword in one hand, firebrand in the other—a Morrigan of battle!—she struck, throwing off sparks and killing with every stroke. The enemy fled before her as before a flaming whirlwind.

Cynan called the cream of Caledon's warriors to him and began hewing a swathe wide enough to drive a chariot through from the water's edge to the top of the strand.

I threw myself into the confused mass between the two battlechiefs, striking with my spear, slashing, stabbing. The spearhead blushed red in the torchlight, and I scanned the churning floodtide of the enemy for the brazen rider. But my silver hand had lost its uncanny chill, and by this I knew he was not near.

Two bronze-clad foemen sprang into my path, brandishing swords above their heads. Their eyes glinted under their horned helmets, and their teeth flashed above the rims of their shields as they shouted a jeering battlecry. Ignoring their blades, I sliced the air in front of their noses with the blade of my spear, and they halted. Spinning the shaft of my spear, I struck aside first one sword, then the other. Then... Crack! Crack! Two sharp raps of the spear butt and both helmets flew off as heads snapped backwards, and the foemen toppled like statues.

Step by step, we hacked our way up the shingle away from the lake, advancing over the bodies of the slain enemy. We fought well. We fought like champions. And the battle settled into a grim and desperate rhythm.

We battled through the night. Sometimes we gained the top of the shingle and made a stand. Sometimes the enemy rallied and we were forced back. Once, we stood in water to our knees, hacking with battle-blunted blades at our armored enemy. But Scatha, moving through the chaos with the grace and poise of a dancer, pierced deep into the heart of the enemy line with a small force of warriors. Rather than face her fearful wrath, the foemen fell back and the advance collapsed.

As the night drew on, the enemy grew disheartened. Fatigue set in. They moved in their heavy bronze armor with a curious lumbering gait. Their shields and weapons wavered in shaky arms; unable to lift their feet, they stumbled back and forth over the flinty strand. Desperate, they lurched at us. We struck. They fell before our skill. The bodies of the wounded and slain began to stack like felled timber around us, yet they would not retreat.

"Whatever it is that drives them," Cynan observed, drawing a bloody hand across his sweaty face, "they fear it more than they fear us."

We had stopped to catch our breath, and leaned on our spears, shoulders heaving with the effort of drawing air into our lungs. "They fear their lord," I told him.

"Who is that?"

"The Brazen Man."

"Brazen coward if you ask me," Cynan snarled with contempt. "I have not had a glimpse of him since the fight began."

"True. He has not yet taken the field."

"Yet? Yet? His war host is being slaughtered. If he thinks to wear us down, he has waited for nothing."

It was true; the weary foe was everywhere falling to the skill and experience of our vastly superior warriors. Darkness and surprise had done their worst, and we had conquered; now we were conquering their numbers as well, slowly, relentlessly paring them down and down.

It came to me that they had no need of a war leader, because the enemy's only plan had been to overwhelm us. They strove to surround us, engulf and smother us; or, failing that, to drive us into the lake by sheer irresistible press of numbers. We fought against a foe lacking any subtlety or craft, an enemy whose only hope lay in dragging us down by brute force alone.

The Brazen Man did not care how many of his men fell to us, because he did not care about his men at all. They were simply fodder to our scything blades. He sent them into battle in wave after heedless wave, trusting to the grim attrition of battle to wear us down. When finally we were too few to resist, he would swoop down from his hidden perch and claim the victory.

Watching the hapless foemen struggling to raise their weapons, my heart softened towards them. They were blind, ignorant and confused; they were stumbling in the dark, bleeding and dying. And, most cruelly of all, they did not know, would never know, why.

These men were not our true enemies; they were puppets only, pawns in the hands of a pitiless master. Their deaths were meaningless. The slaughter had to be stopped. I lowered my spear, straightened and looked around.

The sky was showing grey in the east; red streaks hinted at a raw sunrise. We had fought the whole night to no purpose or advantage. It was insane, and it was time to stop. Turning once more to the battleline, I saw the bronze warriors standing flat-footed, their heads bowed under the weight of the helmets, unable to lift their arms. With long bold strides, I advanced towards them. The blunt spears in their hands struggled up as they stumbled backwards.

"Llew!" shouted Cynan, running after me.

I reached out and seized the nearest spear, and yanked it from the foeman's numb fingers. I threw the spear down on the ground and grabbed another. The third enemy made a clumsy stab at me with a sword. I caught the blade with my silver hand and twisted it easily out of his hand. It was like disarming children.

"Enough!" I shouted. "It is over!"

All along the lakeside, men stopped and turned to gawk at me. I disarmed two more warriors, snatching weapons from limp hands. I brandished my spear and lifted my voice. "Men of Tir Aflan!" I called, my voice carrying along the strand. "Throw down your weapons, and you will not be harmed."

I gazed along the battleline. The fighting had shuddered to a halt and men were gaping stupidly at me. Scores of exhausted foemen swayed on their feet, unable to lift their weapons any more.

"Listen to me! The battle is over. You cannot win. Throw down your weapons and surrender. Stop your fighting—there is nothing to fear."

The enemy stared stupidly at me. "I do not think they understand," said Cynan coming up behind me.

"Perhaps they will understand this," I replied. Raising my own spear, I threw it down on the rocky strand. I motioned for Cynan to drop his weapon as well. He hesitated. "Do it," I urged. "They are watching."

Cynan tossed his spear on top of mine and we stood together unarmed, surrounded by bewildered warriors. I raised my silver hand and said, "Listen to me! You have fought and suffered and many have died. But you cannot win and now the fighting must stop. Throw down your weapons, so that the suffering and dying can end." My voice resounded over the strand. They watched, but no one answered.

"You fight for your lives," I continued. "Men of Tir Aflan! Surrender! Throw down your weapons, and I will give you your lives. You can walk away free men."

This caused a stir. They gaped in wonder, and murmured their amazement to one another. "Is it true?" they asked. "Can it be?"

Extending my hand towards a nearby warrior, I beckoned him. "Come," I told him. "I give you your life."

The man glanced around awkwardly, hesitated, then stumbled forward. He took two steps, but his legs would no longer hold him and he fell forward to lie at my feet. Reaching down, I caught him under the arm and raised him. I took his sword from his hand and tossed it aside. "You are safe," I told him. "No one will harm you now."

I heard a clatter on the rocks as a shield slipped from the grasp of one who could not hold it any longer. The man sank to his knees. I strode to him, raised him and said, "You are safe. Stand there beside your kinsman."

The man took his place beside the first and the two stood trembling in the dim dawn light, not quite believing their good fortune.

The onlookers may have expected me to kill the defectors. But seeing I had not harmed the first two, a third decided to risk trusting me. I welcomed him, and two more stepped forward, laying their weapons at my feet. I welcomed them also and told them to stand with the others. Another defector stepped forward, and then three more.

"Cynan! Scatha!" I turned and beckoned them to help me. "Get ready! The flood is upon us!"

Weapons and armor clattered to the stony shingle all along the lake; the battle-weary foemen could not shed it fast enough. After their initial hesitancy, they gave themselves up freely and with great relief. Some were so overcome, they wept at their unimaginable good fortune. Their long nightmare was over; they were rescued and released.

When we had disarmed the last adversary, I turned to my own warriors standing silent behind me. I looked at their once-fine cloaks, now journey-worn and dirty; I looked at their once-handsome faces, now gaunt and grim, ravaged by want and war. They had given up health and happiness, given up wives, children, kinsmen and friends, given up all comfort and pleasure.

Staunch to the end, they had supported me through all things, and stood ready still to serve, to give their lives if I asked. Battered and bleeding, they stood as one, weapons at the ready, waiting to be summoned once more. Truly, they were the Gwr Gwir, the True Men of Albion.

Raising my silver hand, I touched the back of my hand to my forehead in silent salute. The warriors responded with a shout of triumph that sent echoes rippling across the lake and up into the surrounding hills.

I released them to their rest, whereupon they turned to the lake to drink and to bathe. I stood for a moment watching my ragged warriors lower their exhausted bodies into the water. "Look at them," I said, pride singing through me like a song of exultation. "With such men to support him, any man might be king."

Cynan, leaning on his spear, thrust out his chin, "They would not support just *any* man. Nor would I," he said, and touched the back of his hand to his forehead.

The lake proved a blessing. We waded into the chill, mist-covered water and bathed our aching limbs. The water revived and refreshed us, washing away the blood and grime of battle. I felt the cold thrill of the water on my flesh and remembered another time when, after my first battle, I had bathed like this and felt reborn.

The good feeling proved short-lived, however. Bran and the Ravens had still not appeared by the time the sun had risen well above the surrounding hills.

"I do not like this at all," I told Cynan and Scatha plainly. "Something has happened to them or they would have returned long ago."

"I fear you are right," Scatha agreed.

"We are finished here," Cynan said. "We can go back to Cwm Gwaed to look for them."

I surveyed the armored men sitting splay-legged on the strand. "We will talk to some of these." I indicated the huddled men. "Perhaps they can tell us something."

"That I doubt," Cynan replied. "But I will do it if you think best."

I turned to Scatha who, having washed the soot and blood away, now appeared less like the Morrigan and more like Modron, the Comforter. She had plaited her hair and brushed her cloak, and, from the way the surrendered warriors followed her with their eyes, I thought she might more easily succeed than we in loosening reluctant tongues.

"I will entrust this task to you, Pen-y-Cat," I told her. "I am certain they would rather confide in you than in Cynan Two-Torcs here."

So we watched as she moved among the former enemy warriors, stopping now and then, bending near one or kneeling beside another, speaking earnestly, looking into their eyes as they answered. I noticed she put her hand on their shoulders in the way of a wife or mother, addressing them with her touch as much as with her voice.

In a little while, Scatha returned. "There is a caer near here. Some of them have been there. They say that the Brazen Man keeps captives there."

"Are Tángwen and Goewyn there?" asked Cynan eagerly.

Scatha turned to him, her expression grim. "They do not know. But it is known that the Dyn Dythri often go there, and the *rhuodimi* come from there."

"Roaring things?" wondered Cynan.

The vehicles and machines, I thought. "Then that is where Siawn Hy is waiting, and that is where we will find Goewyn and Tángwen. And," I quickly added, "unless I am far wrong, that is where Tegid and the Ravens are now captive as well."

Scatha agreed. "But there is something else: they say the caer is protected by a powerful enchantment. They are terrified of the place."

We turned our backs to the lake and marched east, following the directions we had been given. A gap, unseen from the shore, opened in the hills; we passed through to find ourselves on a broad plateau. The sea lay before us, green and restless under a mottled grey sky. And on the cracked summit of a rocky headland jutting out into the wave-worried sea stood a crumbling stone fortress. Much like the high tower we had seen before, the caer stood lonely and forsaken on its bare rock, a relic of a forgotten age.

"The Brazen Man has taken that for his stronghold," Scatha said. We had paused to survey the land beyond the pass and, aside from the ruined fortress and a scattering of stone huts in which the warriors had been housed, the land was empty. The defectors had described the place well.

Nevertheless, we approached the fortress slowly, watching for any sign from the ragged walls. I walked first, with Scatha and Cynan leading the Gwr Gwir; unwilling to be left behind, the defeated foe followed at a distance. As we passed onto the promontory, I saw the tracks of heavy vehicles pressed into the soft turf. Many rhuodimi had passed this way. The entrance to the special gate Professor Nettleton spoke of must lie somewhere near by, but I could not see it.

The sea heaved and sighed around the roots of the headland; the wind moaned over the ruins. Great chunks of fallen stone were sunk deep into the thick green moss below once-soaring battlements. We stood gazing at the toppled walls, searching for any sign of life.

"Arianrhod sleeps in her sea-girt headland," I said, thinking aloud, as I looked at the broken gate, black with age and hanging half off its hinges.

To which Scatha replied, "Only the chaste kiss will restore her to her rightful place."

Cynan cast a sidelong glance at us. "Well?" he demanded impatiently. "Are we to stand here waiting all day?"

"No, but first we must see if there is another entrance to this place," I said.

"It will be done." Cynan gestured to Owyn and three other warriors, who disappeared around the near corner of the stone curtain on the run.

They reappeared on the far side a short while later. "There is no other entrance," Owyn said.

"Did you see anyone?" Scatha asked.

"No one," the Galanae warrior answered.

"Then we will go in." I raised my spear in silent signal and the warband, ranged behind me, moved towards the gate.

As we passed under the shadow of the wall, a voice called out. "Stop! Come no closer!"

My head swivelled to the broken battlement. The Brazen Man stood above and to the left, leering bronze mask in place and spear in hand, gazing down upon us.

"Your war host is defeated!" I shouted. "Throw down your weapons and release your captives. Do this at once or you will certainly die."

The bronze warrior tilted back his head and laughed, an ugly, hateful sound. I had heard it before.

The laughter stopped abruptly. "You do not rule here!" he shouted angrily. Then, softening in almost the same breath, he said, "If you want your bride, come and get her. But come alone."

He vanished from the wall before I could answer.

"I mislike this," Cynan grumbled.

"I do not see that we have any other choice," I pointed out. "I will go alone."

Scatha objected. "It is a foolish risk."

"I know," I told her. "But it is a risk we must take for Goewyn's sake."

She nodded, put her hand beneath her cloak and withdrew a slender knife. She stepped close, reached behind me and tucked it into my belt. "I armed you once, and I do so again, son of mine. Save my daughter."

"That I will do, Pen-y-Cat," I replied. She embraced and kissed me, then turned away quickly, taking her place at the head of the warband.

I took two steps towards the gate.

"Wait!" Cynan came to stand beside me. "You will not go alone while Two-Torcs draws breath," he said firmly. "My wife is captive, too, and I am going with you."

He took a step towards the door. "We can dispute the matter, or we can rescue our wives."

There would be no dissuading him, so I agreed, and we advanced together through the gate and into the courtyard beyond.

Dry weeds poked up through the cracks of the paved yard; they shifted in the wind like long white whiskers. Fallen stone lay all around. Arched doorways opened off the courtyard, revealing black, empty passages beyond. At the far end of the yard, opposite the gate, stood a steep-peaked building; the roof was collapsed and curved rooftiles littered the yard like dragon scales. A short flight of stone steps led up to a narrow wooden door. The door, twice the height of a man, stood open.

A chill shivered up through my silver hand. "He is near," I whispered to Cynan.

We moved steadily, stealthily, up the steps, paused, then pushed the door open wide. Instantly we were assailed by the stench of rotting meat mingled with urine and excrement. The outside door opened into a dark vestibule thick with filth. The severed heads of two unfortunates were nailed to the lintel above a low inner door. The doorposts were smeared with blood.

Stepping cautiously through the low door, we passed into the hall beyond. "I have been waiting," a voice said. "We have all been waiting."

37

The Hero Feat

Torches illumined the single great room, casting a thin, sullen light that did little to efface the deep-shadowed darkness. In the center of the room stood the Brazen Man. The torchlight flickering over the facets of his bronze mask made it seem as if his features were continually melting and reforming.

Behind him were two doors barred and bound with iron. As I looked, Goewyn's face appeared at the small window of one door, and Tángwen's at the other. Neither woman cried out, but both stood gripping the bars of their prisons and watching us with the astonished yet fearful expressions of captives who have long ago abandoned hope of release, only to learn that hope has not abandoned them.

My first thought was to run to Goewyn and pull that prison apart with my bare hands. I wanted to take her in my arms and carry her away from that stinking hellhole. I stepped towards the Brazen Man. "Let them go," I said.

"You did not come alone," the man said ominously.

"My wife is captive, too," Cynan spat. "If you have harmed her, I will kill you. Let her go."

"*Your* wife?" the bronze-clad warrior queried. "She might have shared your bed, but Tángwen was never wife to you, Cynan Machae."

"Who are you?" Cynan demanded, pushing past me into the room. The sword in his hand trembled in his clenched fist, he gripped it so hard.

"You want them freed?" the Brazen Man shouted suddenly, taking a swift sidestep. "Free them yourselves." He put out his hand and extended a bronze-mailed finger, pointing to a spot on the floor surrounded by torches. "Do what you will."

I looked where he pointed and saw two keys in an iron ring lying on the stone-flagged floor. Glancing quickly at the cell doors, I saw that they had been recently fitted with new brass locks.

With a nod to Cynan, we moved forward cautiously. My silver hand began to throb with cold, sending sharp pains up my arm. I gritted my teeth and stepped closer, spear ready. The keys had been placed in the center of a knotwork design, the figure outlined on the floor in lines of fine black ash and bits of bone—the ash of burnt sacrifice, I supposed. The braziers burned with a bitter smoke.

"What is it?" Cynan wondered. "Do you know?"

The sign was a crude parody of the *Môr Cylch*, the Life Maze, but it was backwards and broken, the lines haphazard, erratic. All the elegance and beauty of the original had been willfully marred.

"It is a charm of some sort," I told Cynan.

"I am not afraid of a mark on the floor," he sneered.

Before I could stop him, Cynan pushed past me and stooped to grab the keys. Upon entering the circle, however, he was gripped by an instant paralysis, caught and unable to move. "Llew!" he cried, through quick-clenched teeth in a frozen jaw. "Help me!"

I glanced at the bronze-clad man. His eyes glittered hard and black behind the brazen mask. "Oh, help him, yes." The brazen snake almost hissed. "By all means, do help him." Then he laughed.

I knew the laugh. I had heard it too many times before not to recognize it now. He laughed again, and removed every last crumb of doubt, confirmed every suspicion.

"Enough, Simon!" I shouted. "Let him go."

Lifting a bronze gauntlet to his chin, the man lifted the metal mask and took off the helmet. The face was pale, deathly pale, and thin, wasted. The flesh seemed almost transparent; blue veins snaked beneath his eyelids and the skin of his throat. He looked like a ghost, a wraith, but there was no mistaking the set of his chin, nor the hatred smoldering in his eyes.

"Siawn Hy," he corrected, and stepped closer. My silver hand throbbed; icy spikes stabbed into my flesh.

"I made that for you," Siawn said, indicating the circle on the floor. "But I like it better this way. Just you and me. Face to face."

He stood before me and drew the bronze-mailed glove from his left hand, then slowly raised it to his forehead, palm outward. It was a bardic gesture—I had seen Tegid do it many times—but as he turned his hand I saw on the palm, carved into the very flesh, the image of an eye.

Siawn loosed a string of words in a tongue I did not know. I could not take my eyes from the symbol carved into the flesh of his palm. The skin was thickly scarred, but the cuts were fresh and a little blood oozed from the wound.

He spoke again, and the muscles in my arms and legs stiffened. My back and shoulders felt like blocks of wood. Locked in this strange seizure, I could not move. The spear fell from my fingers and clattered on the floor; my limbs grew instantly rigid. More words poured from Siawn's mouth, a dizzying torrent to drown all resistance, a dark chant of wicked power. My breath flowed from my mouth and lungs. Cynan, immobile beside me, made a strangled, whimpering noise.

Someone screamed my name—Goewyn, I think. But I could not see her. I could not close my eyes or look away. The evil eye drew all thought and volition to itself; it seemed to burn itself into my mind as Siawn Hy's words swirled around me, now buzzing like insects, now rasping like crows. My breath became labored, halting; but my vision grew keen.

The ancient evil of Tir Aflan... this was how Siawn Hy had awakened it, and he now wielded it as a weapon. But there existed a power far more potent than he would ever know.

Goodly-Wise is the Many-Gifted, I thought, *who upholds all that call upon him. Uphold me now!*

In the same moment, I felt the Penderwydd's sacred awen quicken within me. Like the unfurling of a sail, my spirit slipped its constricting bonds. A word, a name formed on my tongue and I spoke it out: "Dagda ... Samildanac ..."

Up from my throat it came, leaping from my tongue in a shout. "Dagda Samildanac!"

Searing bolts of icy fire streaked from my silver hand, up my arm and into my shoulder. Whatever the source of the power Siawn possessed, it could not quench the cold fire aflame in my silver hand: the smooth silver surface glowed white; the intricate-patterned mazework of the Dance of Life shone with a fiery golden light.

Siawn's voice boomed in my ears as he moved closer, barking the words. I saw the hideous eye carved into the flesh of Siawn's palm as he reached to touch me with it, to mark me with that hideous symbol.

"By the power of the Swift Sure Hand, I resist you," I said, and raised my silver hand, pressing my palm flat against his.

He screamed, jerking his palm away from mine. Threads of smoke rose from the wound on his hand. Air flowed back into my lungs, and with it the smell of burning flesh. Siawn Hy staggered backwards moaning, cradling his injured hand. The red wound on his palm had been obliterated, the obscene stigmata cauterized; in place of the evil eye was the branded imprint of the Môr Cylch, the Life Maze.

Suddenly free, I leapt to Cynan's aid, knelt beside him, drew a deep breath and blew the black ash away, breaking the power of the charm. Cynan fell forward onto his arms and sprang quickly to his feet. "Brother, that was well done!"

I grabbed the keys. "Watch him!" I commanded Cynan.

"Gladly!" Cynan raised his sword and advanced on the stricken Siawn, pressing the blade into the base of his throat.

I ran to the iron-bound doors, thrust a key into the first lock and turned. The lock gave grudgingly and I pulled with all my might; the hinges complained, but the door swung open. Goewyn burst from her prison and caught me in a crushing embrace. I kissed her face and lips and neck, and felt her lips flitting over my face. She kept repeating my name over and over as she kissed me.

"You are free, my love," I told her. "It is over. You are safe now. You are free."

I held her to me again, and she gave a little cry and pulled away. Her hands went to her stomach, now swelling noticeably beneath her stained and filthy mantle. I put my hand to the softly rounded mound to feel the life within.

"Are you well? Did he hurt you?" I had refused the thought of her suffering for so long that belated concern now overwhelmed me.

Goewyn smiled; her face was pale and drawn, but her eyes were clear and glowing with love and happiness. "No," she said, cupping her hand to my face. "He told me things—terrible things." Tears welled up suddenly in her eyes and splashed down her cheeks. "But he did not hurt me. I think Tángwen is safe, too."

Cynan, holding Siawn Hy at the point of his sword, turned at the mention of his wife's name. The swordpoint wavered as his eyes shifted to the door of her cell. Wrapped in Goewyn's embrace, glancing over her shoulder, I saw the door swing open. Cynan's first response was elation. And then the full significance of the unlocked cell hit him.

The joy on his face turned sickly and died. His eyes grew wide with horror.

"Treachery!" he cried.

The door to Tángwen's cell banged open and armed men charged out of its dark depths and into the room. Cynan was already moving towards them, sword raised. Siawn reacted with blinding speed: his foot snaked out and Cynan pitched forward. He hit the stone floor with a crack; his blade flew from his grasp and skittered across the floor.

A heartbeat later, four men were on his back and four more, with Paladyr chief among them, came for me. I thrust Goewyn behind me, shielding her with my body and drawing the knife Scatha had given me. But I was too late. They were on me. Paladyr's blade pricked the skin of my throat.

Two more foemen caught Goewyn and held her by the arms. Just then, Tángwen, smug with victory, emerged from her cell. "One should always be careful who one marries," Siawn said, as Tángwen came to stand beside him.

"What I did, I did for my father and for my brothers," Tángwen exulted. "They rode with Meldron and you cut them down. The blood debt will be satisfied."

Siawn, still cradling his branded hand, stalked forward, laughing. He came to stand before me, his face the terrible, twisted leer of a demon. He spat a command to one of his minions and the man disappeared into the shadows somewhere behind me. "So, you begin to see at last."

"Let the others go, Siawn," I said. "It is me you want. Take me and let the others go."

"I have you, friend," he jeered. "I have you all."

Just then there arose a commotion from the far corner of the room. A door opened behind me—I could not see it, but I heard the hinges grind—and in shuffled Tegid, Gwion, Bran, and the Ravens, handbound all of them, with chains on their feet and a guard for each one. Tegid's face was bruised and his clothing torn in several places; Bran and Drustwn could not stand upright, and Garanaw's arm dangled uselessly at his side. My proud Raven Flight appeared to have been battered into bloody submission. Behind them came Weston and four other strangers, looking frightened and very confused.

Upon seeing me, Bran cried out and struggled forward; the other Ravens shouted and turned on their captors, but all were clubbed with the butts of spears and dragged back into line.

"You see?" Siawn Hy gloated. "You never fully appreciated me, did you? Well, you have underestimated me for the last time, *friend*." The word was a curse in his mouth.

"Listen to me very carefully," I said, speaking loudly and fighting to keep my voice calm. "My warband is waiting at the gate. They are invincible. If anything happens to any of us, you will die. That is a fact."

If Siawn Hy cared, he did not show it; my words moved several of his warriors, however. Paladyr's sword relaxed.

"It is true, lord," he said. "We cannot hope to defeat them."

Siawn waved aside the remark. "But I am not interested in defeating them," he replied casually. "I am only interested in defeating Silver Hand."

"Then let the others go," I said again. "Once they are free, I will command the warband to allow you safe passage. Without my word, none of you leave this place alive."

"Listen to him, lord," Paladyr said; an note of uncertainty had come into his voice.

"What is he saying?" demanded Weston, his voice an almost incoherent babble in my ears. He started forward. "I demand to know what is going on! You said there wouldn't be any trouble. You said it was all under control."

"Get back!" Siawn snarled in the stranger's tongue. "I gave you what you wanted. Now it is *my* turn. That was the agreement."

"Some of my men have been killed," Weston whined. "What am I supposed to do ab—"

"Shut up!" Siawn growled, cutting him off with a chop of his hand. He turned to me once more. "If I let the others walk free, you will give us all safe conduct to leave—is that right?"

"I give you my word," I vowed. "But they go free first."

"No, Llew," Goewyn pleaded softly. "I will not leave you."

Siawn chuckled. "Oh, I am enjoying this."

"The warband is waiting," I told him. "They will not wait for ever."

"Do you think I care about any of that?" he mocked. "I will not be ordered about by my own prisoner." He brought his face close to mine, breathing hard. The veins stood out on his neck and forehead. "Your word is nothing to me! *You* are nothing to me. I have had nothing but grief from you ever since you came here. But that is about to end, old friend."

He backed away from me. "Do it!" he yelled.

"What do you want us to do, lord?" Paladyr asked.

"Kill him!" Siawn cried.

Paladyr hesitated.

"Do it!" Siawn shouted again.

Paladyr's head whipped around; he glared at Siawn. "No." He lowered the blade and stepped aside. "Let the others go free, or they will kill us."

"Paladyr!" The voice was Tegid's; the bard had waited for precisely this moment to speak. "Hear me now! You claimed naud and Llew gave it," he said, reminding Paladyr that he owed his life to me. "He did not lie to you then; he is not lying now. Release us all and you will not be harmed."

"Silence him!" screamed Siawn Hy. I heard a crack and Tegid slumped to the floor.

"I gave you your life, Paladyr," I said.

"He is lying!" insisted Siawn. "Kill him!"

Paladyr shook his head slowly. "No. He is telling the truth."

"Siawn Hy!" I said. "Take me, and let the others go." To show I meant what I said, I turned the knife in my hand, took the blade and offered him the handle.

"Oh, very well," snarled Siawn Hy. He snatched the knife and half-turned away. Then, with a quick, cat-like movement, he lunged into me. The blade came up sharp and caught me in the center of the chest just below the ribs. I did not even feel it go in.

Goewyn screamed and fought free. She ran two steps towards me, but Paladyr turned and caught her by the arm, and held her fast.

I looked down to see the sharp blade biting into my flesh. With a cry of delight, Siawn thrust the knife deeper. I felt a burning sensation under my ribs and then my lung collapsed. Air and blood sputtered from the wound. Siawn forced the blade deeper still and then released it. The three men holding me stepped away.

My legs grew suddenly weak and spongy. I lifted my foot to take a step and the floor crashed up against my knees. My hands found the knife hilt, grasped it and pulled. It felt as if a beacon-fire had been lit in my chest and was now burning outwards. I flung the knife from me.

Blood, hot and dark, welled from the wound, spilling over my hands. A dark mist gathered at the periphery of my vision, but I was conscious of everything around me: Siawn staring at me with wicked glee; Cynan fighting with all his might, still pinned to the ground by Siawn's men; Paladyr grim and silent, clutching Goewyn's arm.

My throat tickled and I opened my mouth to cough, but could not. My breath rasped in my throat. My mouth was dry—as if the fire in my chest was devouring me from within. I gasped, but could get no air. A strange, sucking sound came from my throat.

I put out my hand to support myself, but my elbow buckled and I rolled onto my side. Goewyn jerked her arm from Paladyr's grasp and ran to me. She gathered me in her arms. "Llew! Oh, Llew!" she wept, her warm tears falling onto my face. "Llew, my soul..."

I gazed up at her face. It was all I could see now. Though she wept, she was beautiful. A flood of memory washed over me. It seemed as if all I had endured in her pursuit was nothing—less than nothing—beside her. I loved her so much, I ached to tell it, but could not. The burning stopped, and I felt instead a chill numbness in my chest. I tried to sit up, but my legs would not move. Instead, I raised my hand to Goewyn's face and stroked her cheek with trembling fingertips.

"Goewyn, best beloved," I said; my voice came out as a dry whisper. "I love you ... farewell ..."

Goewyn, tears streaming from her eyes, lowered her face to mine. Her lips, warm and alive, imparting a final sweet caress, was the last sensation I knew.

Darkness descended over me. Though my eyes continued to stare, I could see nothing for the black mist that billowed over and around me, swallowing me down and down. It seemed that I was floating and falling at the same time. I heard Goewyn weeping, saying my name, and then I heard a roaring crash like that of the sea rolling in upon a far-off shore.

The sound grew until I could hear nothing else. It grew so great that I thought my head would burst with the pressure of the noise. For one terrible instant I feared the sound would consume me, obliterate me. I resisted, though how I resisted, I do not know. I could not move, could not speak or see.

But when I thought I could not bear it any more, the sound stopped abruptly and the dark mist cleared. I could see and hear again, more clearly than I ever had before. I could see, but now saw everything from slightly above and outside my normal view. I saw Goewyn bent over me, cradling my still body in her lap, her shoulders heaving as she wept. I saw Siawn and Tángwen looking on, their faces flushed with a hideous gloating pride. I saw Paladyr standing a little apart, subdued, his arms hanging limp at his sides. I saw the Ravens and Tegid, stunned and staggered at the atrocity they were powerless to prevent.

I saw Cynan lying on the floor, enemies kneeling on his back as he raged against my death. I felt sorry for him. His wife had betrayed us all to Siawn, had deceived us from the beginning; he would bear the burden of that shame for the rest of his life, a fate he did not deserve. Through all things he was my good friend; I would have liked to bid him farewell. Peace, brother, I said, but he did not hear me.

Siawn turned and ordered his men to bind Cynan. Then he turned to Paladyr. "Pick up the body and carry it outside," he commanded.

Paladyr stepped forward, but Goewyn clutched me tighter and screamed, "No! No! Do not touch him!"

"I am sorry," he mumbled as he bent over her.

"Take her!" shouted Siawn. Two of his minions scurried forward, grabbed Goewyn and tore her from me. Shouting, crying, she fought them, but they held her tight and pulled her away.

Paladyr knelt and gathered my corpse into his arms. Straining, he lifted my limp body and held it.

"Follow me!" Siawn Hy barked. He turned on his heel and started from the room, taking a torch from a nearby sconce as he passed.

At the vestibule, Siawn paused and let Paladyr pass. "They are waiting for their king," he smirked. "They shall have him."

Paladyr carried me out of the hall, across the empty courtyard, and out of the gate to the warband gathered beyond. Behind him came Siawn and Tángwen, followed by Cynan and Goewyn, both with a guard on either arm, though the fight had gone out of Cynan, and the guards had to support Goewyn to keep her upright. Tegid and the Ravens marched boldly forth, quickly recovering something of their dignity and mettle. Lastly came Weston and his hirelings, edging their way with fearful and uncertain steps.

The emerging procession provoked a quick outcry among the waiting warriors, but the sight of my lifeless body shocked them to silence. Scatha made to run to her daughter, but Siawn shouted, "Stop! No one move!"

Then Siawn ordered Paladyr to lay my body on the ground. Brandishing his torch, he stood over me. "Here is your king!" he crowed, his voice raking at the shattered warband.

"Siawn Hy!" Scatha shouted. "You will die for this! You and all your men."

But Siawn only laughed. "Do you want him? I give him to you. Come! Take him away!"

Scatha and two warriors stepped forward slowly. Siawn allowed them to approach and, as they neared, he pulled a flask from behind his bronze breastplate and quickly doused me with the contents. And then, as they stooped, their hands reaching for me, Siawn lowered the torch and touched it to the liquid glimmering on my skin.

A ball of bright yellow flame erupted with a whoosh. The heat was instant and intense. The fire spread swiftly wherever the liquid had penetrated. My clothing burned first and then my flesh.

Goewyn screamed, and fought free of her captors. She would have thrown herself upon the flames, but they caught her again and hauled her back.

Siawn looked on my burning corpse with an expression of immense satisfaction. He had been planning his revenge for a long time, and he savored the moment to the full. Cynan, mute, immobile, did not look at the flames, but at his treacherous bride standing haughtily beside Siawn.

The layers of cloth burned away from my body. The skin of my face and neck began to shrivel and smoke as the flames licked over them. The fire crackled and fizzed as the fat from my flesh ignited. My hair burned away, and my siarc and breecs. My belt, because it was wound around my waist in several layers, was slower to burn. But as the first two layers of my belt were consumed, there appeared three round lumps.

Siawn, glancing down, saw the lumps and stared more closely. A strange light came into his eyes as he recognized the stones Tegid had given me to carry into Tir Aflan. Singing Stones, three of them, glowing white as miniature moons in the fire. Three Singing Stones within easy reach.

38

Bright Fire

Siawn Hy could not resist them. Despite the flames, he edged close and, quick as a striking snake, snatched up one of the song-bearing stones. He raised it with a wild shout of triumph. "With this stone, I conquer!"

The stone was hot and as he held it high, his cry still ringing in the air, the milk-white rock turned translucent as ice and melted in his hand. Siawn stared as the liquid rock ran through his fingers and down his upraised arm like water.

He bent to retrieve another stone, braving the flames once more. His fingers flicked out and closed on another of the precious stones; but as he made to withdraw it, the liquid rock ignited. Flames engulfed his hand and raced up his arm along the molten trail of the previous stone.

Siawn jerked back, still clenching the second stone. He held the flaming hand before his face. With a blast of pure white light the stone in his fist burst into a thousand pieces, scattering flaming fragments far and wide in a rain of shimmering white fire.

Each fragment melted and began to burn with a wonderful incandescence.

The third stone, still resting on my stomach, melted and the liquid stone began flowing like silver honey, like shining water. It covered my burning corpse, and quickly seeped out onto the ground around me. Like a fountain it flowed, increasing outwards of itself, pouring up from my body, spreading and spreading in bright-shimmering waves. And where the melted stone touched one of the flaming fragments, it burned with flames of shining white.

Men drew back from the fire, and many ran. But there was no escape. The flames were swift as they were bright. They raced before the wind of their burning, gathering greater speed as the fire kindled other fires and mounted, leaping towards the sky. The grass burned and the earth and rocks. The air itself seemed to ignite like touchpaper. Nothing was spared, nothing escaped the all-devouring white fire.

Everyone, friend and enemy alike, fell before the all-engulfing flames. Siawn, standing nearest, was the first to succumb; he crumpled into a writhing heap. Tángwen rushed to him, and was caught as the flames raced towards her, igniting her cloak and mantle; her hair became a fiery curtain. Seeing this, the guards dropped their weapons and ran, but the fire was swifter than their feet.

Cynan and Goewyn fell to the flames. Cynan alight from heel to head, staggered towards Goewyn to protect her, but she slumped to the ground before he could reach her, and after a few steps he expired.

Bran and the Ravens were caught, along with Tegid and Gwion. Their feet chained, they could not run, so turned to face the flames unafraid. Not so the enemy warriors guarding them. They stumbled over one another in their haste to flee. But the fire streaked like lightning along the ground and ignited them. At first they wailed in fear and agony, but their voices were quickly drowned in the roar of the onrushing blaze.

On and on it sped, inundating all of Tir Aflan in a rolling flood of bright silver-white fire, that consumed all it touched with a keen and brilliant flame. The grass and rocks blazed. And as the conflagration spiralled higher and higher, leaping skyward in dazzling plumes, igniting the very air, there came a sound like a crystal chime. It was the voice of the inferno, belling clear and clean. And it rang with a song, the matchless Song of Albion:

Glory of sun! Star-blaze in jeweled heavens!
Light of light, a High and Holy land,
Shining bright and blessed of the Many-Gifted;
A gift for ever to the Race of Albion!

Lifted high on the wings of the wind, the cleansing fire streaked through the sky, kindling the clouds and gloom-laden vapors, scouring the heavens. Grey and black turned to glowing blue and then to white. The airy firmament glowed with a light more brilliant than starlight, brighter and more radiant than the sun. The Song rang through the heights and raced on:

Rich with many waters! Blue-welled the deep,
White-waved the strand, hallowed the firmament,
Mighty in the power of the One,
Gentle in the peace of great blessing;
A wealth of wonders for the Kinsmen of Albion!

Reaching the shore, the fire sped out across the sea. From wave-top to wave-top, leaping in liquid tongues, spreading over the sea-well. The sea began to boil, and then flashed from turgid green to jade and then the color of white gold in the crucible. The waters became molten flame and the great, glowing sea resounded like a bell to the Song, blending its deep-voiced toll to the high tone of the heavens. And the Song raced on:

Dazzling the matchless purity of green!
Fine as the emerald's excellent fire,
Glowing in deep-clefted glens,
Gleaming on smooth-tilled fields;
A Gemstone of great value for the Sons of Albion!

Down the broad headland the bright fire flew, a towering wall of blistering, shimmering flame, raking the wasted valleys of Tir Aflan, flashing across the wasted expanse of moorland. The filth-crusted settlement exploded at the first touch of flame; the mudmen in the mines saw the flames streaking towards them and threw themselves into their pits. But the cunning flame-fingers searched out the dark, small places and set them ablaze, streaking across the mud, scorching the earth, turning every boulder in Cwm Gwaed into a pillar of fire. And the Song raced on:

> *Abounding in white-crowned peaks, vast beyond measure,*
> *the fastness of bold mountains!*
> *Exalted heights—dark-wooded and*
> *Red with running deer—*
> *Proclaim afar the high-vaunted splendor of Albion!*

The mountaintops round about sprouted crowns of silver-white flame, blazing like titanic beacons. Each mountain became a fiery volcano; rock and snow, moss and ice fed the ravenous fire. Heatwaves flowed out in every direction. The mountains' stone skin turned glassy and their stony hearts glowed white. Sheets of flame danced among the stars. And the Song raced on:

> *Swift horses in wide meadows!*
> *Graceful herds on the gold-flowered water-meads,*
> *Strong hooves drumming,*
> *a thunder of praise to the Goodly-Wise,*
> *A boon of joy in the heart of Albion!*

> *Golden the grain-hoards of the Great Giver,*
> *Generous the bounty of fair fields:*
> *Redgold of bright apples,*
> *Sweetness of shining honeycomb,*
> *A miracle of plenty for the tribes of Albion!*

> *Silver the net-tribute, teeming the treasure*
> *of happy waters; Dappled brown the hillsides,*
> *Sleek herds serving*
> *the Lord of the Feast;*
> *A marvel of abundance for the tables of Albion!*

Following the rivers and streams, setting the myriad waterways alight, stretching across the Foul Lands with fingers of fire, the bright flames flew, striking deep into the heartland of Tir Aflan, kindling the fields and meadows. Marshlands steamed and then smoldered, then became lakes of fire. Reeds and grasses, gorse thickets and gnarled trunks, whole forests burst into flowering flame. By blade and twig the hungry fire devoured the wasted heartland. And the Song raced on:

> *Wise men, Bards of Truth, boldly declaring from*
> *Hearts aflame with the Living Word;*
> *Keen of knowledge,*
> *Clear of vision,*
> *A glory of verity for the True Men of Albion!*

> *Bright-kindled from heavenly flames, framed*
> *of Love's all-consuming fire,*
> *Ignited of purest passion,*
> *Burning in the Creator King's heart,*
> *A splendor of bliss to illuminate Albion!*

Silver-white columns of fire danced and leapt—high, high, burning with the intensity of ten-thousand suns, scourging both the land below and the heavenly places above, filling the black void of night with blazing light. And the Song raced on:

> *Noble lords kneeling in rightwise worship,*
> *Undying vows pledged to everlasting,*
> *Embrace the breast of mercy,*
> *Eternal homage to the Chief of chiefs;*
> *Life beyond death granted the Children of Albion!*

> *Kingship wrought of Infinite Virtue,*
> *Quick-forged by the Swift Sure Hand;*
> *Bold in Righteousness,*
> *Valiant in Justice,*
> *A sword of honor to defend the Clans of Albion!*

> *Formed of the Nine Sacred Elements,*
> *Framed by the Lord of Love and Light;*
> *Grace of Grace, Truth of Truth,*
> *Summoned in the Day of Strife,*
> *An Aird Righ to reign for ever in Albion!*

No one could stand before the ferocity of the fire. The frail human frame vaporized in the heat, flesh and bone dissolved, spilling their molecules into the fiery atmosphere. The All-Encompassing Song raced on and on in ever-widening rings of purifying fire.

And everything touched by the holy fire was scoured, consumed, melted, reduced to the very core elements, and then further reduced to atoms. The released atoms ruptured, fused, and recombined in new elements of being. Deep in the white-hot heart of the fire, I saw the Swift Sure Hand moving, gathering unformed matter and molding it into pure new forms.

I alone saw this, and I saw it with the eye of the True Aird Righ, the sacred, eternally self-sacrificing king. I saw it with the unblinking eye of the Everliving One, whose touch quickens the insensate soul, who swallows death in life. Out of the molten heat, I saw the foul land of Tir Aflan recast, reshaped, and in fire reborn.

Nothing escaped the refining fire of his irresistible will: all imperfection, all ugliness, all weakness and deformity, all frailty, infirmity, disease, deficiency and defect, every fault and failing, every blight and every blemish, every flaw effaced, purged, and purified. And when the last scar had been removed, the cleansing flames diminished and faded away. All this might have taken eons; it might have happened in the blink of an eye; I cannot say. But when the fire at last subsided, Tir Aflan had been consumed and its elements transmuted in a finer, more noble conception: recreated with a grandeur as far surpassing its former degradation as if an old garment had been stripped away and not merely restored, but replaced with raiment of unrivalled splendor. It was not a change, but a transformation; not a conversion, but a transfiguration.

The mudmen, whores, slaves and prisoners—all the Foul Land's wretched—were gone, and in their places stood men and women of stature and grace. The empty fields and forests were empty no longer; animals of every kind—deer and sheep, wild pigs, bears, foxes, otters, badgers, rabbits, squirrels, and mice, as well as kine, oxen, and horses—filled the meadows and glens and browsed the forest trails and ran among the hills and watermeads; trout and salmon, pike and perch, sported in the lakes and streams; the shining blue skies were full of birds and the treetops delighted in birdsong; the forlorn mountainsides, moors, and blasted heathlands wore a fresh glory all their own in the form of wildflowers of every shade and hue; the rivers ran clean and uncorrupted, the water crystalline and pure.

Tir Aflan was no more, Tir Gwyn stood in its place.

Tegid Tathal was the first to revive. He opened his eyes, stood up, and looked around. Scatha lay nearby, dressed now in a mantle of holly green with a belt of cornflower blue and a crimson cloak edged in green and gold. Gwion lay at Tegid's feet, and Bran beside him, and around Bran the Raven Flight as Tegid remembered them—but now the Ravens' cloaks were midnight blue and each wore a torc of thick-braided silver. Cynan lay a little distance away, his hand stretching towards Goewyn.

And all of them, Tegid himself included, reclothed in the finest apparel—of such material and craft, such color and quality as had never been known. Tegid, Scatha, the Ravens, every member of the Gwr Gwir and their prisoners—all arrayed in clothes of the most splendid color and craftsmanship.

The warriors' weapons had changed, too. The luminous luster of gold and bright-gleaming silver shone in the light of a dawn as clear and fresh as the first day of creation. The spears, both shaft and head, were gold, and golden too every swordblade and hilt. Shield rims, bosses and rings shone with silvery brightness.

Tegid turned his wondering eyes from the warriors and their weapons. He gazed skyward and saw the radiant heaven, alive with a living light. He saw the Foul Land made fair beyond words, and he began to understand what had happened.

Shaking, trembling in every part, he knelt beside Bran Bresal and touched him gently. The Raven Chief awoke and Tegid helped him to stand. He woke Scatha next, and then Cynan; Bran awakened the Ravens who, with Cynan and Tegid, began to wake the Gwr Gwir.

Scatha, her heart beating fast, ran to her daughter and knelt down beside her. Goewyn's hair was brushed bright and plaited with tiny white and yellow flowers. She wore a gown of hyacinth blue with a mantle of pearly white over it, and a henna-colored cloak sewn with plum purple figures. Cupping a hand to Goewyn's cheek, Scatha gently turned her daughter's head. Goewyn drew a deep breath and awoke.

"Llew?" she asked. Then memory rushed in upon her. "Llew!"

She jumped to her feet and ran to me. My body lay where Paladyr had left it. Arrayed like a king in siarc, belt and breecs of deep-hued scarlet, with scarlet buskins on my feet, I lay wrapped in a scarlet cloak; woven into the cloak in silver thread was the Môr Cylch, the Life Dance.

Goewyn lifted a cool hand to my forehead, then touched my face. Tears welled in her eyes as she felt my cold, lifeless flesh. Scatha came to stand beside her, and Cynan; Bran and the Raven Flight gathered around. As Tegid joined them, Goewyn raised tearful eyes. "Oh, Tegid, I thought..." She began to weep.

"He is dead, Goewyn," Tegid said softly, kneeling beside her. The bard placed his hand upon my still chest. "He will not come back."

"Look," said Bran, "his silver hand is gone."

They raised my right arm and saw that my silver hand was indeed gone, the metal replaced by a hand of flesh. Goewyn took the hand and clasped it to her. She pressed the unfeeling flesh to her warm lips and kissed it, then laid it over my heart.

"Where is Siawn Hy?" asked Cynan suddenly. "Where are Tángwen and Paladyr?"

Until that moment, no one had thought to look for them, nor, now that they did make a search, could they find them. The wicked ones had vanished, but not completely.

"Here!" shouted Cynan, closely scanning the place where Siawn was last seen. "I have found something."

The others joined him as he examined a curious spot on the ground. "What is it?" he asked, pointing at a small pile of powdery residue.

Tegid bent down and examined it. "All that remains of Siawn Hy," the bard announced at length.

It was the same with Paladyr and Weston, and all those who had willingly followed Siawn. The refining fire had burned away the dross and, when it had finished its purifying work, there was nothing left. Nothing, that is, save a handful of ashes soft and white as snowflakes.

Cynan wanted to gather the ash and throw it in the sea, but Tegid counselled otherwise. "Leave it," he advised. "Let the wind take it. There shall be no resting-place for these."

"What has happened?" asked Bran, trying to comprehend the changes that had been wrought in them and in the world around them. He spoke for many—especially the defectors who, in surrendering to me, had escaped the fate of their lord. Remade men, they simply stared in mute wonder at their transformed bodies and the world re-created around them, unable to comprehend it or their own good fortune.

Tegid lifted the rod of gold that now replaced his rowan staff. Raising his other hand over his head, he addressed the bewildered gathering: "The sound of the battleclash will be heard among the stars of heaven and the Great Year will proceed to its final consummation.

"Hear, O Sons of Albion: Blood is born of blood. Flesh is born of flesh. But the spirit is born of Spirit, and with Spirit evermore remains. Before Albion is One, the Hero Feat must be performed and Silver Hand must reign."

Lowering the rod, he stretched it over my body. "So it was spoken, so it is accomplished," Tegid said. "The Great Year is ended, the old world has passed away and a new creation is established." Indicating my crimson-clothed body, he said, "The Aird Righ of Albion is dead. The Hero Feat for which he was chosen has been performed. Behold! He has reclaimed Tir Aflan and brought it under his sovereign rule. Thus, all lands are united under one king: from this day, Albion is One. This is the Reign of Silver Hand. The prophecy is fulfilled."

Back through the mountains, now remade: glistening, silver-crowned giants bearing the wide, empty skybowl on their handsome shoulders. Pure white clouds graced the slopes like regal robes and raiments; sparkling streams sent rippled laughter ringing through the valleys, and mist-shrouded falls filled the heights with rainbows. The road was no longer; instead, a grassy path curved up through the high places and joined them with the lowlands beyond...

Back through the moors, transformed into meadows of vast aspect, dotted with trees and brimming with sparkling spring-fed pools. Herds of deer and wild sheep grazed the grassy expanse; birds passed overhead in chattering flocks, or trilled their songs to a sky so fair and blue it made the heart ache to see it...

Back through the hills and valleys, now made new: gently sculpted mounds rounding to grand crests and descending to shade-sheltered glens of solitude. The greens of the hills and glens were as verdant and various as the shifting hues of golden light that played on the cloud-dappled knolls...

Back through the forest now remade: towering columns of magnificent trunks rising to a vaulted archway of a myriad spreading branches beneath a fine leafy canopy: nature's own sanctuary, illumined by a softly-diffused light. By day the grassy path was lit by an endless succession of falling shafts of sunlight; by night the moon and stars poured silver upon rounded boles and slender branches, favoring every leaf and limb with a delicate tracery...

Back along the river, now a noble watercourse, handsome in its generous sweep and broad-bending curves, deep-voiced in the sonorous music of its stately passage. Swans and geese and other waterfowl nested in its reed-fringed banks; fish aplenty lazed in its cool shallows, and leaped in the sun-warmed currents of clean, clear water...

Back through a world reborn: more fair than a loving heart's fondest dream of beauty, more elegant than delight, more graceful than hope. Back through Tir Gwyn they carried my body, back to the place where three swift sleek-hulled ships waited on the strand. And then back across a white-waved sea of startling color and clarity.

Back across this luminous, ever-changing firmament of liquid light they bore me to Albion. And though it took many days, my corpse showed not the slightest sign of decay or corruption. It was as if I slept; yet no breath stirred in my chest, and my heart was still and cold.

My corpse lay on a bier made from the silver shields of the Gwr Gwir bound to golden spearshafts. My scarlet cloak covered me and Goewyn rode, or walked, or stood ever by me. She would not leave my side for a moment. When the company stopped at night, she even slept beside the bier.

They reached Albion and in procession carried my body through a land familiar, yet transmuted into a higher vision of itself. Albion had been transformed into a wonder that swelled the soul with joy and made the breath catch in the throat, as if its former beauty had been but a reflection compared to the reality. For Albion now wore a splendor purer and finer than harpsong and more exquisite than music, and it made their hearts sing to see it.

The procession bore my body to Caledon, over the hills and across the plain, up Druim Vran to Dinas Dwr, where Lord Calbha and my people waited. Upon learning of my death, the people mourned with a deep, surpassing grief. The bones of Alun Tringad were interred in the dolmen atop the Hero Mound at the foot of Druim Vran. Professor Nettleton's head was buried there, too. My body, however, was placed in the king's hall to await burial, for Tegid had determined that I should be buried in a special tomb that he would build. Meanwhile, I lay on my golden catafalque in the king's hall, and Goewyn, inconsolable, stayed beside me day and night while they prepared the gorsedd.

One evening, Tegid came to the hall and knelt beside Goewyn. She was spending the night, like every other night, sitting in the antler chair beside my lifeless body. "It is time to release him, Goewyn," the bard told her.

"Release him? I never will," she replied, her voice softened by grief to a whisper.

"I do not mean you should forget him," Tegid soothed. "But it is time—and past time—for Llew to begin his journey hence. You hold him here with you."

"I hold him here?" Goewyn wondered. "Then," she said, reaching out to take my cold hand in hers, "I shall always hold him and he shall always remain here with me."

"No," Tegid told her gently. "Let him go. It is wrong to imprison him so."

Taking her by the shoulders, he held her at arm's length, staring into her eyes, willing her to look at him. "Goewyn, listen to me. All is as it should be. Llew was sent to us for a purpose, and that purpose has been accomplished. It is time to release him to continue his journey."

"I cannot," Goewyn wailed, grief overwhelming her afresh. "I shall be alone!"

"Unless you release him, your love will sicken in you: it will steal your life and the life of the child you carry," Tegid replied firmly.

Tears came to her eyes. She put her face in her hands and began to weep. "Oh, Tegid, it hurts," she cried, the tears streaming down her face. "I hurt so much!"

"I know," he said softly. "It is a hurt not soon healed."

"I do not know what to do," she cried, the tears falling freely.

"I will tell you what you must do," the wise bard answered, putting his arms around her. "You will give birth to the child that he has given you, and you will love the child and raise it in his memory." He took her hands in his. "Come with me, Goewyn."

She rose and, after a last loving look, went out with Tegid. Scatha and the Raven Flight were waiting at the hall's entrance. As soon as Goewyn and Tegid emerged, the Ravens entered the hall and came to the bier. They lifted the shield-and-spear litter to their shoulders and carried it outside; they then processed slowly through the crannog to a boat, and rowed the boat across the lake to where Cynan waited on the shore with horses and a wagon. Three horses—a red and a white, with a spirited black to lead them—drew the wagon; the horses' hooves and the wagon's wheels were wrapped in black cloth. Beside Cynan, holding a shield and spear likewise shrouded, stood Lord

Calbha, and behind them, unlit torches in their hands, thronged the people of Dinas Dwr.

The corpse was placed on the wagon, and the procession slowly made its way along the lakeside to the place where Tegid had erected the Hero Mound inside the sacred grove he had established for his Mabinogi. Mounting the long slope to the grove, the company passed by the mill, completed in my absence by Lord Calbha and Huel, the master-builder. As we passed, I blessed the mill to its good work.

The cortège entered the shadowed grove, dark under a sky of brilliant twilight blue. The gorsedd had been raised in the center of the grove—a hollow stone chamber, mounded with earth and covered over with turf, and surrounded by a ring of slender silver birches. Someone had left a shield beside the cairn, and upon entering the grove, I heard the croak of a raven. A swift shadow passed overhead and a great, black glossy-feathered bird swooped down and settled on the rim of the shield. Alun, I think, had sent a messenger to say farewell.

The golden bier was laid at the foot of the gravemound before the silent throng. The Chief Bard, standing over the corpse, placed a fold of his cloak over his head.

Raising his golden rod over me, he said, "Tonight we bury our king. Tonight we bid farewell to our brother and friend—a friend who did for us what we could not do for ourselves. He sojourned among us for a while but, like Meldryn Mawr, who held sovereignty before him, Llew served the Song of Albion. His life was the life of the Song, and the Song claimed the life it briefly granted.

"The king is dead, cut down in a most vile and hateful manner. He went willingly to his death to gain the life of his bride, and those of his friends whose release he sought and won. Let it never be said that he grasped after glory; let all men remember that he humbled himself, breaking his geas so that he might lead the raid on Tir Aflan.

"And because he did not cling to his high rank, great good has come to this worlds-realm. For in Llew's death, the Song of Albion has been restored. Hear, O Albion! The Great Year is ended, a new cycle is begun. No longer will the Song be hidden; no longer will it rest with the Phantarchs and kings to preserve it, for now the Song is carried in the heart and soul of every woman and every man, and all men and all women will be its protectors."

Tegid Tathal, Penderwydd of Albion, lowered his hand then, saying, "It is time now to release our brother and send him on his way."

He kindled a small fire and lit a torch. The fire was passed from brand to brand until all the torches glowed like stars in the night-dark grove. Then he directed the Ravens to lift the bier once more. Drustwn, Emyr, Niall and Garanaw, with Bran at my head, began, at Tegid's direction, to carry my body around the gorsedd mound slowly in a sunwise direction. The people, led by Tegid, with Goewyn walking directly behind him, Scatha on at her right hand and Cynan at the left, followed the body—and they all began to sing.

I was there with them in the grove. I saw the torchlight glowing on their faces and glinting in their tears; I heard their voices singing, softly at first, but more strongly as they released their grief and let it flow from them. They sang the *Queen's Lament* and it pierced my heart to hear it. Goewyn sang, too, head held high, eyes streaming with tears which threaded down her cheeks and throat.

I could feel the weight of sorrow bearing down her spirit, and I drew near to her. *Goewyn, best beloved, you will live for ever in my soul*, I whispered in her ear; *truest of hearts, your grief will ease.*

Tegid led the funeral procession once around the mound... and then a second circuit... and a third. At the completion of the third circuit, the people formed a long double line, holding their torches high. They formed the Aryant Ol, the Radiant Way by which a king's body is conducted to its rest. And, in the time-between-times, I was carried to my tomb.

The Ravens, tall and grim, shouldered the bier and, with slow, measured steps, began moving towards the gravemound along the Radiant Way. Tegid, with Goewyn and Cynan behind him, lofted his torch and the three followed the Ravens up the Aryant Ol and into the cairn. They placed the bier on a low stone pallet in the center of the chamber and, one by one, made their farewells, each kneeling by the body and touching the back of the hand to his forehead in a final salute.

Finally, only Cynan, Goewyn, and Tegid were left. Cynan, tears clinging to his eyelashes, raised his hands to his throat and removed his gold torc. He placed the ornament on my chest and said, "Farewell, my brother. May you find all that you seek—and nothing you do not seek—in the place where you are going." With that, his voice cracked and he turned away, rubbing his eyes with the heels of his hands.

Goewyn, eyes bright with tears in the flickering torchlight, stooped and kissed me on the forehead. "Farewell, best beloved," she said bravely, her voice quivery and low, "you go, and my heart goes with you."

Tegid handed his torch to Cynan and reached into the leather pouch at his belt. He withdrew a pinch of the Nawglan, the Sacred Nine, which he deposited in the palm of his left hand. Then, taking some of the Nawglan on the tip of his second finger, he drew a vertical line in the center of my forehead. Pressing his fingertip to the Nawglan again, he drew a second and then a third line, one on either side of the first—both inclining towards the center. He drew the gogyrven, the Three Rays of Truth, in the ash of the Sacred Nine on my cold forehead.

"Farewell, Llew Silver Hand. May it go well with you on your journey hence," the bard said. Then, quickly planting his torch at the head of the bier, he turned away to lead Goewyn and Cynan from the tomb.

The Ravens, waiting outside, began to close up the entrance with stones. I watched the cairn opening grow smaller, stone by stone, and I was on the inside, looking out. I saw the faces of those I had loved: Scatha, Pen-y-Cat, regal, brave and beautiful; Bran Bresal, Chief Raven, dauntless lord of battle; the Raven Flight: Drustwn, Emyr Laidaw, Garanaw Long Arm, and Niall, stalwart companions, men to be trusted through all things; Lord Calbha, generous ally; Cynan, steadfast swordbrother and friend of the heart; Goewyn, fairest of the fair, wife and lover, forever part of me; and Tegid, wise Penderwydd, Chief Bard of Albion, truest friend—whose love reached out beyond death to smooth my passage.

I saw the people, my people, passing the stones hand to hand up the Aryant Ol to seal my tomb. And then I heard Tegid's voice, clear and strong, lifted in a song which I recognized as a saining song. Cradling his harp, his fingers playing over the sweet-sounding strings, he sang:

> *In the steep path of our common calling,*
> *Be it easy or uneasy to our flesh,*
> *Be it bright or dark for us to follow,*
> *Be it stony or smooth beneath our feet,*
> *Bestow, O Goodly-Wise, your perfect guidance*
> *Upon our kingly friend,*
> *Lest he fall, or into error stray.*
>
> *In the shelter of this grove,*
> *Be to him his portion and his guide;*
> *Aird Righ, by authority of the Twelve:*
> *The Wind of gusts and gales,*
> *The Thunder of stormy billows,*
> *The Ray of bright sunlight,*
> *The Bear of seven battles,*
> *The Eagle of the high rock,*
> *The Boar of the forest,*
> *The Salmon of the pool,*
> *The Lake of the glen,*
> *The Flowering of the heathered hill,*
> *The Craft of the artisan,*
> *The Word of the poet,*
> *The Fire of thought in the wise.*
>
> *Who upholds the gorsedd, if not You?*
> *Who counts the ages of the world, if not You?*
> *Who commands the Wheel of Heaven, if not You?*
> *Who quickens life in the womb, if not You?*
> *Therefore, God of All Virtue and Power,*
> *Sain him and shield him with your Swift Sure Hand,*
> *Lead him in peace to his journey's end.*

The opening in the cairn was little more than a chink in the stone now. And then that small hole was filled and I was alone. Tegid's voice as he stood before the sealed gravemound was the last thing I heard. "To die in one world is to be born into another," he called to the people of Dinas Dwr. "Let all hear and remember."

The fire-flutter of the torch filled the tomb, but that faded gradually as the torch burned down. At last the flame died, leaving a red glow which lingered a little while before it went out. And darkness claimed me.

How long I stood in the rich, silent darkness, I do not know. But I heard a sound like the wind in bare branches, clicking, creaking, whispering. I turned and saw behind me, as if through a shadowed doorway, the dim outline of a white hillscape, violet in a blue-grey dawn. Instinctively, I moved towards it, thinking only to get a better look.

The moment I stepped forward, I heard a rushing sound and it seemed as if I were striding rapidly down a long, narrow passage. And I felt a surge of air, an immense upswelling billow like an ocean of air flowing over me. In the same instant, the pale violet hillside before me faded and then vanished altogether.

Trusting my feet to the dark path before me, I stepped forward. The churning air swelled over and around me with an empty ocean's roar. Emptiness on every side, and below me the abyss, I stretched my foot along the swordbridge and stepped out onto that narrowest of spans. In the windroar I heard the restless echo of unknown powers shifting and colliding in the dark, endless depths. All was darkness—deepest, most profound darkness—and searing silence.

And then arose the most horrendous gale of wind, shrieking out of nowhere, striking me full force, head on. It felt as if my skin were being slowly peeled away, and my flesh shredded and pared to the bone. My head began to throb with pain and I found that I could not breathe. My empty lungs ached and my head pounded with a phantom heartbeat.

Ignoring the pain, I lifted my foot and took another step. My foot struck the void and I fell. I threw my hands before me to break the blind fall; my palms struck a smooth, solid surface, and I landed on all fours in the snow outside the cairn in the thin grey dawn.

"Llew . . .?" It was Goewyn's voice.

39

The Endless Knot

I raised my head and looked around to find her. The effort released something inside me and cold air gushed into my lungs. The air was raw and sharp; it burned like fire, but I could not stop inhaling it. I gulped it down greedily, as if the next breath would be my last. My eyes watered and my arms and legs began to tremble. My heart pounded in my chest, and my head vibrated with the rhythm. I squeezed my eyes shut and willed my heart to slow.

"Lew..." came the voice again, concerned, caring. I felt a light touch on my shoulder, and she was beside me.

"Goewyn?" I lifted my eyes and glimpsed a trailing wisp of reddish hair—not Goewyn, but her sister, the Banfáith of Albion. "Gwenllian!"

"Lew...Lewis?"

My eyes focused slowly and her face came into view. "Gwenllian, I..."

"It's Susannah, Lewis. Are you all right?"

From somewhere in my mind a dim memory surfaced.

"Susannah?"

"Here, let me help you." She put her arms around me and helped me stand. "You're freezing," she said. "What happened to your clothes?"

I looked down to see myself naked, standing in about an inch of light, powdery snow. The wind sighed in the bare branches of trees, and I stood outside the narrow entrance to a hive-shaped cairn, reeling with confusion, despair breaking over me in waves, dragging me under, drowning me.

"Put this on," Susannah was saying, "or you'll catch your death." She draped her long coat across my shoulders. "I've got a car—it's on the road up the hill. We'll have to walk, I'm afraid. Nettles didn't tell me to bring any clothes, but I've got some blankets. Can you make it?"

I opened my mouth, but the words would not come. Very likely, there *were* no words for what I felt. So I simply nodded instead. Susannah, one arm around my shoulders, put my arm around her neck and began leading me away from the cairn. We walked through long grass up a snow-frosted hill to a gate, which was open. A small green automobile waited on the road, its windows steamed over.

Susannah led me to the passenger side of the car and opened the door. "Just stay there," she said. "Let me get a blanket." I stood staring at the world I had come to, trying to work out what had happened to me, grief powerful as pain aching in my hollow heart.

Spreading one blanket over the seat, she swathed another over me, taking back her coat as she did so. Then Susannah helped me into the car and shut the door. She slid into the driver's seat and started the car. The engine complained, but caught and started purring. Susannah put on the heater and defroster fan full blast. "It'll warm up in a minute," she said.

I nodded, and looked out through the foggy windshield. It took all the concentration I could muster, but I asked, "Where are we?" The words were clumsy and awkward in my mouth, my tongue a lump of wood.

"God knows," she replied above the whir of the fan. "In Scotland somewhere. Not far from Peebles."

The defroster soon cleared a patch of windshield which Susannah enlarged with the side of her hand. She shifted the car into gear and pulled out onto the road. "Don't worry," she said. "Just sit back and relax. If you're hungry, I've got sandwiches, and there's coffee in the flask. We're lucky it's a holiday and traffic will be light."

We drove through the day, stopping only a couple of times for fuel. I watched the countryside rush by the windows and said nothing. Susannah kept clearing her throat and glancing at me as if she was afraid I might suddenly disappear—but she held her tongue and did not press me. For that, I was profoundly grateful.

It was late when we reached Oxford, and I was exhausted from the drive. I sat in my blankets and stared numbly at the lights of the city from the ring road and felt utterly devastated. How could this have happened to me? What did it mean?

I did not know where I would go. But Susannah had it all worked out. She eased the car through virtually empty streets and stopped at last somewhere in the rabbit warren of Oxford city center. She helped me from the car and I saw that we stood outside a low door. A brass plaque next to the door read D. M. Campbell, Tutor. Susannah pulled a set of keys from her pocket, put a key in the lock and turned it.

The door swung open and she went before me, snapping on lights. I stepped into the room and recognized it. How many lifetimes had passed since I last stood in this room?

"Professor Nettleton told me to give these to you," Susannah said. She pressed the keys into my hands. "He isn't here—" she began, faltered, and added, "but I suppose you know that."

"Yes," I told her. Nettles, I suspected, would never return. But why had I come back? Why me? Why here?

"Anyway," she said, her keen dark eyes searching my face for the slightest flicker of interest, "there's food in the larder and milk in the fridge. I didn't know who or how many to stock up for, so there's a bit of everything. But if you need anything else, I've left my number by the phone, and—"

"Thanks," I said, cutting her off. "I'm sure it's ..." Words escaped me. "It's fine."

She gazed at me intently, the questions burning on her tongue. But she turned towards the door instead. "Sure. Umm... well." She put her hand on the doorknob and pulled the door open. She hesitated, waiting for me to stop her. "I'll look in on you tomorrow."

"Please, you needn't bother," I said, my mouth resisting the familiar language.

"It's no bother," Susannah replied quickly. "Bye." She was out of the door and gone before I could discourage her further.

How long I stood, wrapped like a cigar-store Indian in my blanket, I could not say. I spent a long time just listening to the sounds of Oxford, a crashing din which the heavy wooden door and thick stone walls of the professor's house did little to shut out. I felt numb inside, empty, scooped hollow. I kept thinking: *I am dead and this is hell*.

At some point I must have collapsed in one of Nettles' overstuffed wing chairs, because I heard a scratch at the door and opened my eyes to see Susannah bustling into the room, her arms laden with parcels and bags. She was trying to be quiet, thinking me asleep in bed. But she saw me sitting in the chair as she turned to pile the packages on the table.

"Oh! Good morning," she said. Her smile was quick and cheerful. Her cheeks were red from the cold, and she rubbed her hands to warm them. "Tell me you *didn't* sleep in that chair all night."

"I guess I did," I replied slowly. It was difficult to think of the words, and my tongue still would not move properly.

"I've been up since dawn," she announced proudly. "I bought you some clothes."

"Susannah," I said, "you didn't have to do that. Really, I—"

"No trouble." She breezed past me on the way to the kitchen. "I'll get some breakfast started and then I'll show you what I bought. You can thank me later."

I sat in the chair without the strength of will to get up. Susannah reappeared a few moments later and began shifting parcels around the table. "Okay," she said, pulling a dark blue something out of a bag, "close your eyes."

I stared at her. Why was she doing this? Why didn't she just leave me alone? Couldn't she see I was in pain?

"What's the matter, Lewis?" she asked.

"I can't."

"Can't what?"

"I can't do this, Susannah!" I snapped. "Don't you understand?"

Of course she didn't understand. How could she? How could anyone ever understand even the smallest, most minute part of all I had experienced? I had been a king in Albion! I had fought battles and slain enemies, and had, in turn, been killed. Only, instead of going on to another world, I had been returned to the one I had left. Nothing had changed. It was as if nothing had happened at all. All I had done, all I had experienced meant nothing.

"I'm sorry," Susannah said, with genuine sympathy. "I was only trying to help." She bit her lip.

"It's not your fault," I told her. "It's nothing to do with you."

She came to me and knelt beside the chair. "I want to understand, Lewis. Honestly. I know it must be difficult."

When I did not answer, she said, "Nettles told me a lot about what was happening. I didn't believe him at first. I'm still not sure I believe it. But he told me to look for some things—Signs of the Times, he called them—and if I saw them, I was to go to that place—he even gave me a map—and wait there for someone to show up." She paused, thoughtfully. "I didn't know it would be you."

The silence grew between us. She was waiting for me to say something. "Listen," I said at last, "I appreciate what you've done. But I need..." I was almost sweating with the effort, "I just need some time to work things out."

She gave me a wounded look and stood up. "I can understand that. But I want to help." She paused, and looked away. When she looked back, it was with a somewhat forlorn smile. She was trying. "I'll leave you alone now. But call me later, okay? Promise?"

I nodded, sinking back into the all-enfolding chair, back into my grief and pain. She left.

But she was back early the next morning. Susannah took one look at me and one look at the room and, like a rocket blasting off, she lit up. "Get up, Lewis. You're coming with me."

411

I had no will of my own any more, and hers seemed powerful enough for any two people, so I obeyed. She rummaged through the untouched packages on the table. "Here," she said, thrusting a pair of boxer shorts into my hand. "Put these on, for starters."

I stood, the blanket still hanging from my shoulders like a cloak. "What are you doing?"

"You've got to get out of here," Susannah replied tartly. "It's Sunday. I'm taking you to church."

"I don't want to go."

She shrugged and shook out a new shirt, cocking her head to one side as she held it up to me. "Put this on," she ordered.

She dressed me with ruthless efficiency: trousers, socks, shoes, and belt—and then professed herself pleased with the result. "You could shave," she said, frowning. "But we'll let that go for now. Ready?"

"I'm not going with you, Susannah."

She smiled with sweet insincerity and took my arm in hers. Her hands were warm. "But you are! I'm not leaving you here to languish all day like a dying vulture. After church I'll let you take me out to lunch."

"I know what you're trying to do, Susannah. But I don't want to go."

The church was absolutely packed. In all the time I'd lived in Oxford, I'd never seen so many people at a church service. There were a thousand at least. People were crammed into pews, and lined up in the wide windowsills all around the sanctuary. Extra chairs were crowded into the back in every available space. The kneeling-benches had been pulled out and placed in the aisle to accommodate the overflow. When that did not suffice, they opened the doors so the people standing outside could hear.

"What's going on?" I asked, bewildered by the noise and hubbub. "What's all this?"

"Just church," Susannah said, puzzled by my question.

The service went by me in a fog. I could not concentrate for more than a second or two at a time. My mind—my heart, my soul, my life!—was in Albion, and I was dead to that world. I was cut off and could never go back.

Susannah nudged me. I looked around. Everyone was kneeling, and the minister—or priest, or whatever—was holding a loaf of bread and saying, "... This is my body, broken for you..."

I heard the words—I'd heard them before, many times; I'd grown up hearing them, and had never given them a thought beyond the church sanctuary.

This is my body, broken for you...

Ancient words, words from beyond the creation of the world. Words to explain all that had happened to me. Like a star exploding in the frigid void of space, understanding detonated in my brain. I knew, *knew*, what it meant!

I felt weak and dizzy; my head swam. I was seized and taken up by a rapture of joy so strong I feared I might faint. I looked at the faces of those around me: eager in genuine devotion. Yes! Yes! They were *not* the same; they had changed. Of course they had. How could they not change?

Albion had been transformed—and this world was no longer the same, either. Though not as obviously manifest, the great change had already taken place. And I would find it hidden in a million places: subtle as yeast, working away quietly, unseen and unknown, yet gently, powerfully, altering everything radically. I knew, as I knew the meaning of the Eucharistic words of Holy Kingship, that the rebirth of Albion and the renewal of this world were one. The Hero Feat had been performed.

The rest of the service passed in a blur. My mind raced ahead; I could not wait to get outside and bolted from the church as soon as the benediction was pronounced. Susannah caught me by the arm and spun me around. "You worm! You could at least have pretended to pay attention."

"Sorry, it's just that I—"

"I've never been so embarrassed in all my life. Really, Lewis, you—"

"Susannah!"

That stopped her. I took her by the shoulders and turned her to face me squarely. "Listen, Susannah. I have to talk to you. Now. It's important." Having begun, the words came rolling out of my mouth in a giddy rush. "I didn't understand before. But I do now. It's incredible! I know what happened. I know what it's all about. It's—"

"What *what* is all about?" she asked, clutching my arm and eyeing me carefully.

"I was a king in Albion!" I shouted. "Do you know what that means, Susannah? Do you have any idea?"

A few nearby heads swivelled in our direction. Susannah regarded me with faint alarm, biting her lower lip.

"Look," I said, trying a different approach, "would you mind if we didn't go out? We could go back to Nettles' place and talk. I have to tell somebody. Would you mind?"

Overcome with relief, she smiled and looped her arm through mine. "I'd love to. I'll fix lunch for us there, and you can tell me everything."

We talked all the way home, and all during lunch. I put food in my mouth, but I did not taste a single bite. I burned with the certainty of the truth I had glimpsed. I had swallowed the sun and now it was leaking out through every pore and follicle. I talked like a crazy man, filling hour after hour with words and words and more words, yet never coming near to describing the merest fragment of what I had experienced.

Susannah listened to it all, and after lunch even suggested that we walk by the river so that she could stay awake and hear some more. We walked until the sun began to sink into a crisp spring twilight. The sky glowed a bright burnished blue, red-gold clouds drifted over emerald hills and fields of glowing green. Couples and families ambled peacefully along the path, and swans plied the river like feathered galleons. Everywhere I looked, I saw tranquility made visible—a true Sabbath rest.

"You were right," she said when I at last ran out of breath. "It *is* incredible." There was more, much more to say, but my jaw ached and my throat was dry. "Simply incredible." She snuggled close and put her head on my shoulder as we turned our steps towards home.

"Yes, it is. But you're the only one who will ever know."

She stopped and turned to me. "But you've got to tell people, Lewis. It's important." I opened my mouth to object and she saw it coming. "I mean it, Lewis," she insisted. "You can't keep something like this to yourself. You must let people know—it's your duty."

Just thinking of the newspapers made me cringe. Reporters thrusting microphones and clicking cameras in my face, television, radio—an endless progression of sceptics, cranks, and hectoring unbelievers... Never.

"Who would believe me?" I asked hopelessly. "If I told this to anyone else, it would be a one-way ticket to the loony bin for yours truly."

Maybe," she allowed, "but you wouldn't actually have to *tell* them."

"No?"

"You could write it down. You know your way around a keyboard," Susannah pointed out, warming to her own idea. "You could live in Nettles' flat and I could help. We could do it together." Her eyebrows arched in challenge and her lips curled with mischief. "C'mon, what do you say?"

Which is how I came to be sitting at Nettles' desk in front of a testy old typewriter with a ream of fresh white paper, with Susannah clattering around in the kitchen making tea and sandwiches. I slipped a sheet of paper under the bail, and stretched my fingers over the keys.

Nothing came. Where does one begin to tell such a tale?

Glancing across the desktop, my eye caught a corner of a scrap of paper with a bit of colored ink on it. I picked up the scrap. It was a Celtic knotwork pattern—the one Professor Nettleton had shown me. I stared at the dizzy, eye-bending design: two lines interwoven, all elements balanced, spinning for ever in perfect harmony. The Endless Knot.

Instantly, the words began to flow and I began to type:

It all began with the aurochs...

Also by Stephen Lawhead:

THE PARADISE WAR 'C' format	£7.99 ☐
THE PARADISE WAR 'A' format	£4.99 ☐
THE SILVER HAND 'C' format	£7.99 ☐
THE SILVER HAND 'A' format	£4.99 ☐
TALIESIN	£4.99 ☐
MERLIN	£4.99 ☐
ARTHUR	£4.99 ☐
IN THE HALL OF THE DRAGON KING	£4.99 ☐
THE WARLORDS OF NIN	£4.99 ☐
THE SWORD AND THE FLAME	£4.99 ☐
EMPYRION	£5.99 ☐

Also from Lion Publishing:

OLD PHOTOGRAPHS Elizabeth Gibson	£5.99 ☐
PARALLEL LIVES Elizabeth Gibson	£5.99 ☐
RABSHAKEH J. Francis Hudson	£5.99 ☐
ZOHELETH J. Francis Hudson	£5.99 ☐

All Lion paperbacks are available from your local bookshop or newsagent, or can be ordered direct from the address below. Just tick the titles you want and fill in the form.

Name (Block letters) _____

Address _____

_____

Write to Lion Publishing, Cash Sales Department, PO Box 11, Falmouth, Cornwall TR10 9EN, England.

Please enclose a cheque or postal order to the value of the cover price plus:

UK INCLUDING BFPO: £1.00 for the first book, 50p for the second book and 30p for each additional book ordered to a maximum charge of £3.00.

OVERSEAS INCLUDING EIRE: £2.00 for the first book, £1.00 for the second book and 50p for each additional book.

Lion Publishing reserves the right to show on covers and charge new retail prices which may differ from those previously advertised in the text or elsewhere, and to increase postal rates in accordance with the Post Office.